MW01407388

DISCARD

Lilian Jackson Braun
THREE COMPLETE NOVELS

Also by Lilian Jackson Braun

THE CAT WHO COULD READ BACKWARDS
THE CAT WHO ATE DANISH MODERN
THE CAT WHO TURNED ON AND OFF
THE CAT WHO SAW RED
THE CAT WHO PLAYED BRAHMS
THE CAT WHO PLAYED POST OFFICE
THE CAT WHO KNEW SHAKESPEARE
THE CAT WHO SNIFFED GLUE
THE CAT WHO WENT UNDERGROUND
THE CAT WHO TALKED TO GHOSTS
THE CAT WHO LIVED HIGH
THE CAT WHO KNEW A CARDINAL
THE CAT WHO MOVED A MOUNTAIN
THE CAT WHO WASN'T THERE
THE CAT WHO WENT INTO THE CLOSET
THE CAT WHO CAME TO BREAKFAST
THE CAT WHO BLEW THE WHISTLE
THE CAT WHO SAID CHEESE
THE CAT WHO TAILED A THIEF

THE CAT WHO HAD 14 TALES (SHORT STORY COLLECTION)

Lilian Jackson Braun
THREE COMPLETE NOVELS

The Cat Who Talked to Ghosts

The Cat Who Lived High

The Cat Who Knew a Cardinal

G. P. PUTNAM'S SONS
NEW YORK

G. P. Putnam's Sons
Publishers Since 1838
200 Madison Avenue
New York, NY 10016

Copyright © 1990, 1990, 1991 by Lilian Jackson Braun
All rights reserved. This book, or parts thereof, may not
be reproduced in any form without permission.
Published simultaneously in Canada

Library of Congress Cataloging-in-Publication Data
Braun, Lilian Jackson.
[Novels. Selections]
Three complete novels / Lilian Jackson Braun.
p.   cm.
Contents: The cat who talked to ghosts—The cat who lived high—
The cat who knew a cardinal.
ISBN 0-399-14258-4
1. Qwilleran, Jim (Fictitious character)—Fiction. 2. Detective
and mystery stories, American. 3. Journalists—United States—Fiction.
4. Cats—Fiction. I. Title.
PS3552.R354A6 1997   96-38001 CIP
813'.54—dc21

Printed in the United States of America
1 3 5 7 9 10 8 6 4 2

Book design by Patrice Sheridan

*Dedicated to
Earl Bettinger, the Husband Who . . .*

Contents

THE CAT WHO TALKED TO GHOSTS   1
THE CAT WHO LIVED HIGH   203
THE CAT WHO KNEW A CARDINAL   405

The Cat Who Talked to Ghosts

Chapter 1

Jim Qwilleran is a very rich man—the richest individual in Moose County, to be exact. Moose County, as everyone knows, claims to be 400 miles north of everywhere, a remote rockbound outpost comfortably distant from the crime, traffic, and pollution of densely populated urban areas to the south. The natives have a chauvinistic scorn for what they call Down Below.

Before Qwilleran inherited his enormous wealth he had been a journalist Down Below, covering the crime beat on major newspapers for twenty-five years. His name (spelled with the unconventional Qw) and his photograph (distinguished by a luxuriant moustache) were known to millions. Then, at the uneasy age of fifty, he became heir to the Klingenschoen fortune and retired to Moose County.

Currently he lives quite simply in Pickax City, the county seat (population: 3,000), sharing a modest bachelor apartment with two Siamese cats, writing a column for the local newspaper, driving an energy-efficient car, dating a librarian, and ignoring the fact that he owns half of Moose County and a substantial chunk of New Jersey. The tall husky man with a prominent moustache is frequently seen riding a bicycle in Pickax, dining in restaurants, and going into the secondhand bookstore. He reads much, and although his mournful eyes and drooping moustache give his countenance an aspect of sadness, he has found contentment.

Not surprisingly Qwilleran has retained his interest in crime, possessing a natural curiosity and a journalist's cynicism that can scent misdoing like a cat sniffing a mouse. Recently he was haunted by private suspicions following an incident that others accepted as a whim of fate. The initial circumstances are best related in his own words. He recorded the following on tape shortly after his midnight ride to North Middle Hummock:

I knew the telephone was about to ring. I knew it a full ten seconds before it interrupted the first act of *Otello*. It was a Sunday night in early October, and I was in my pajamas, taking it easy, listening to an opera cassette that Polly Duncan had brought me from England. The Siamese also were taking it easy, although not necessarily listening. Koko was on the coffee table, sitting tall and swaying slightly, with a glazed expression in his slanted blue eyes. Opera puts him in a trance. Yum Yum was curled up on my lap with her paws covering her ears—a feline commentary on Verdi, no doubt. I'm not a great opera-lover myself, but Polly is trying to convert me, and I admit that Verdi's *Otello* is powerful stuff.

Suddenly, during the tense build-up to the drunken brawl scene, Yum Yum's body stiffened and her toes contracted. At the same instant Koko's eyes opened wide and his ears pointed toward the telephone. Ten seconds later . . . it rang.

I consulted my watch. In Pickax not many persons venture to call after midnight.

"Yes?" I answered brusquely, expecting to hear a befuddled voice asking for Nadine or Doreen or Chlorine against an obbligato of late-night bar hubbub. Or the caller might say abruptly, "Whoozis?" In that case I would say grandly, "*Whom* are you calling, sir?" And he would hang up immediately without even an expletive. Of all the four-letter words I know, the speediest turn-off in such circumstances is *whom*.

It was no barfly on the line, however. It sounded like Iris Cobb, although her voice—usually so cheerful—had a distinct tremor that worried me. "Sorry to call so late, Mr. Q, but I'm . . . terribly upset."

"What's the trouble?" I asked quickly.

"I'm hearing . . . strange noises in the house," she said with a whimper.

Mrs. Cobb lived alone in an old farmhouse rather far out in the country, where noise is an uncommon factor and any slight sound is magnified at night. The thumps and clicks from a furnace or electric pump, for example, can be unnerving, and a loose shutter banging against the house can drive one up the wall.

"Does it sound," I asked, "like a mechanical problem or something loose on the outside of the house?"

"No . . . no . . . not like that," she said in a distracted way as if listening. "There! I just heard it again!"

"What kind of noise, Mrs. Cobb?" My curiosity was aroused at that point.

She hesitated before replying timidly, "It's frightening! Sort of . . . unearthly!"

How should I react? Mrs. Cobb had always thought it amusing to have a resident ghost in an old house, but tonight her voice expressed abject terror. "Could you describe the sounds specifically?"

"It's like knocking in the walls . . . rattling . . . moaning . . . and sometimes a scream."

I ran a questioning hand over my moustache, which always perks up at moments like this. It was October, and Moose County likes to celebrate Halloween for the entire month. Already there were pumpkins on every front porch and ghostly white sheets hanging from trees. The pranksters might be getting an early start—perhaps some kids from the nearby town of Chipmunk, which is noted for its rowdies. "You should call the police," I advised her calmly. "Tell them you suspect prowlers."

"I called them the night before last," she said, "and everything was quiet when the sheriff got here. It was embarrassing."

"How long has this been going on? I mean, when did you first hear mysterious sounds?"

"About two weeks ago. At first it was just knocking—now and then—not very loud."

Her voice was more controlled now, and I thought the best course was to keep her on the line. She might talk herself out of her fears. "Have you mentioned the situation to anyone around there?" I asked.

"Well . . . yes. I told the people who live at the end of the lane, but they didn't take it seriously."

"How about reporting it to Larry or Mr. Tibbitt?"

"Somehow I didn't want to do that."

"Why not?"

"Well . . . in the daylight, Mr. Q, when the sun is shining and everything, I feel foolish talking about it. I don't want them to think I'm cracking up."

That was understandable. "I suppose you keep the floodlights turned on in the yard after dark."

"Oh, yes, always! And I keep peeking outside, but there's nothing there. It seems to be coming from inside the house."

"I agree it's a puzzling situation, Mrs. Cobb," I said, trying to appear interested and helpful but not apprehensive. "Why don't you jump in your car and drive over to Indian Village and spend the night with Susan? Then we'll investigate in the morning. There's sure to be some logical explanation."

"Oh, I couldn't!" she said with a faltering cry. "My car's in the barn, and I'm afraid to go out there. Oh, Mr. Q, I don't know what to do! . . . Oh, my God! There it goes again!" Her words ended with a shriek that made my flesh creep. *"There's something outside the window!"*

"Get hold of yourself, Mrs. Cobb," I said firmly. "I'll pick you up and take you to Indian Village. Call Susan and tell her you'll be there. Pack a bag. I'll see you in twenty minutes. And drink some warm milk, Mrs. Cobb."

I pulled on pants and a sweater over my pajamas, grabbed the car keys and a jacket, and bolted out of the apartment, half stumbling over a cat who happened to be in the way. Mrs. Cobb had a health problem, and the noises might very well be imaginary, the result of taking medication, but that made them no less terrifying.

The farmhouse in North Middle Hummock was thirty minutes away, but I made it in twenty. Fortunately there was no traffic. This was late Sunday night, and all of Moose County was at home, asleep in front of the TV.

The old paving stones of Main Street, wet from a recent shower, glistened like a night scene in a suspense movie, and I barreled through the three blocks of downtown Pickax at sixty-five and ran the town's one-and-only red light. At the city limits the streetlights ended. There was no moon, and it was hellishly dark on the country roads. This had been a mining region in the nineteenth century. Now the highway is bordered with abandoned mineshafts, rotting shafthouses, and red Danger signs, but on this moonless night they were obliterated by the darkness.

I drove with my country-brights, following the yellow line and watching for the Dimsdale Diner, a lonely landmark that stays open all night. Its lights glimmered faintly through dirty windows, identifying the intersection where I had to turn onto Ittibittiwassee Road. There the highway was straight and smooth. I pushed up to eighty-five.

Beyond the Old Plank Bridge the route became winding and hilly, and I slowed to a cautious sixty-five, thinking about this woman who was depending on me tonight. Poor Mrs. Cobb had survived more than her share of tragedies. A few years ago, when I lived Down Below and wrote for the *Daily Fluxion*, she was my landlady. I rented a furnished room over her antique shop in a blighted part of the city. After the murder of her husband she sold the shop and moved to Pickax, where she applied her expertise to museum work. Now she was resident manager of the Goodwinter Farmhouse Museum, living in one wing of the historic building.

It was not surprising that she phoned me in her desperation. We were good friends, although in a formal sort of way, always addressing each other as "Mrs. Cobb" and "Mr. Q." I suspected that she would like a closer relationship, but she was not my type. I admired her as a businesswoman and an expert on antiques, but she played the clinging vine where men were concerned, and it could be cloying. She also played the witch in the kitchen. I'll admit to being a pushover for her pot roast and coconut cake, and the Siamese would commit murder for her meatloaf.

So here I was, speeding out to North Middle Hummock in my pajamas to rescue a helpless female in distress. For a brief moment it crossed my mind that her agonized phone call might be a ploy to get me out there in the middle of the night. Ever since inheriting all that damned Klingenschoen money I've been wary of friendly females. And ever since Mrs. Cobb arrived in Pickax with her vanload of cookbooks and her worshipful attitude, I've been on my guard. I enjoy a good meal and have always considered her a great cook, but she wore too much pink and too many ruffles—not to mention those eyeglasses with rhinestone-studded frames. Besides, I was involved with Polly Duncan, who was intelligent, cultivated, stimulating, loving . . . and jealous.

Hunting for North Middle Hummock in the dark was literally going-it-blind. It had been a thriving community in the old days when the mines were operating, but economic disaster after World War I had reduced it to a ghost town, a pile of rubble overgrown with weeds and totally invisible on a moonless night. With no streetlights and no visible landmarks, all trees and bushes looked alike. Finally my headlights picked out the white rail fence of the Fugtree farm, and I gave three cheers for white paint. After another dark stretch there was a white-painted cottage with a flickering light in the window; someone was watching TV. The cottage marked the entrance to Black Creek Lane, and the lane dead-ended at the Goodwinter place. I felt a flood of relief.

Mrs. Cobb had inherited the historic Goodwinter farmhouse from Herb Hackpole, her third husband, after a shockingly brief marriage. She immediately sold it to the Historical Society for use as a museum—sold it for one dollar! She was that kind of person, good-hearted and incredibly generous.

As I drove down the gravel lane I noticed that the Goodwinter farmyard, which should have been floodlighted, was in darkness. So was the house. Power failures are common in Moose County . . . and yet, I remembered seeing lights in the Fugtree farmhouse, and someone was watching TV in the cottage up at the corner. I felt a tingling sensation on my upper lip.

Driving around to the west side of the sprawling farmhouse, I parked with the headlights beamed on the entrance to the manager's apartment and took a flashlight from the glove compartment. First I banged the brass knocker, and when there was no answer I tried the door and was not surprised to find it unlocked. That's customary in Moose County. Flashing my light around the entrance hall I found a wall switch and flipped it experimentally, still thinking the power might be cut off. Unexpectedly the hall fixture responded—and on went four electric candles in an iron chandelier.

"Mrs. Cobb!" I called. "It's Qwilleran!"

There was no answer, nor was there any knocking or rattling or moaning. Certainly no screaming. In fact, the rooms were disturbingly silent. An archway at the left led to the parlor, and its antique furnishings were illuminated as soon as I found the wall switch. Why, I asked myself, had this frightened woman turned out all the lights? The roots of my moustache were sending me anxiety signals: Sometimes I wish it were less sensitive.

Across the hall the bedroom door was standing open, and there was an overnight case on the bed, partly packed. The bathroom door was closed. "Mrs. Cobb!" I called again. Somewhat reluctantly I opened the bathroom door and steeled myself to look in the stall shower.

Still calling her name, I continued down the hall to the old-fashioned kitchen with its fireplace and big dining table and pine cabinets. I flipped on the lights, and in that instant my instincts told me what I would find. There was a milk carton on the kitchen counter, and on the floor was a sprawled figure in a pink skirt and pink sweater, the eyes staring, the round face painfully contorted. There were no signs of life.

CHAPTER 2

When Qwilleran discovered Mrs. Cobb's lifeless body he reacted with more sorrow than shock. He had sensed the worst as soon as he turned down Black Creek Lane and found the premises in darkness. Now, looking down at the pink-clad figure—pink to the very end!—he pounded his moustache with his fist, pounded it in sadness mixed with anger. It was unthinkable that this good woman should slip away in the prime of life, at the apex of her career, at the height of her joy. She had won the admiration of the community; her last husband had left her well-off; and at the age of fifty-five she was a grandmother for the first time. But then, he reminded himself, Fate had never been known for its good timing.

Finding the kitchen telephone, he punched the police emergency number and reported the incident without emotion, stating all the necessary details. The phone stood on a relic from an old schoolhouse: a cast-iron base supporting a wooden seat and a boxlike desk with lift-up top. The writing surface was grooved for pens and pencils and inkwell, and it was carved with generations of initials. Also on the desk was an alphabetized notebook containing phone numbers; it was open to *E*. Qwilleran called Susan Exbridge in Indian Village, and she answered on the first ring.

"Susan, this is Qwill," he said somberly. "Did Iris call you a short time ago?"

"Yes, the poor thing was frightened out of her wits for some reason or other. She was almost incoherent, but I gathered that you're bringing her over here to spend the night. I've just put pink sheets on the guestbed."

"That was the plan. I'm at the farmhouse now. She won't be able to make it."

"Why? What happened, Qwill?"

"I found her on the kitchen floor. Not breathing. No pulse. I've called the police."

Susan wailed into the phone. "How terrible! How perfectly awful! What will we do without her? I'm devastated!" She had a tendency to be dramatic and a personal reason to feel bereft. The two women were partners in a new enterprise in downtown Pickax, and the gold lettering had just been painted on the shop window: Exbridge & Cobb, Fine Antiques. The formal opening was scheduled for Saturday.

Qwilleran said, "We'll talk tomorrow, Susan. The sheriff will be here momentarily."

"Is there anything I can do?"

"Get some rest and prepare for a busy day tomorrow. I'm calling Larry, and I'm sure he'll need your help with arrangements."

Larry Lanspeak was president of the Historical Society and chairperson of the Goodwinter Farmhouse Museum as well as owner of the local department store. As merchant, civic leader, and talented actor in the Pickax Theatre Club he brought boundless energy to everything he undertook. Qwilleran put in a call to the Lanspeak country house in fashionable West Middle Hummock, and, although it was almost two o'clock, Larry answered the phone as briskly as he would in midday.

"Larry, this is Qwill. Sorry to disturb you. We have trouble. I'm calling from the museum. Iris called me in hysterics not long ago, and I rushed out here. You know about her heart condition, don't you? I was too late. I found her dead on the kitchen floor. I've called the police."

There was a prolonged silence at the other end of the line.

"Larry . . . ?"

In a hollow voice Larry said, "It can't be! We need her! And she was too young to go!"

"She was our age." Qwilleran's tone was understandably morose.

"I'll throw on some clothes and get there as soon as possible. God! This is terrible news. Carol will be floored!"

Qwilleran turned on the yardlights and turned off his headlights just as the sheriff's car came down the lane.

A young officer in a wide-brimmed hat stepped out. "Somebody report a dead body?"

"It's Mrs. Cobb, manager of the museum. She called me in a panic, and I came out to see if I could help. I'm Jim Qwilleran from Pickax."

The deputy nodded. Everyone knew the outsize moustache that belonged to the richest man in the county.

They went indoors, and Qwilleran pointed the way to the kitchen.

"Emergency's on the way," said the deputy. "They'll take the body to Pickax Hospital. The medical examiner will have to sign the death certificate."

"He might want to check with Doctor Halifax. She was being treated for a heart condition."

The deputy nodded, writing up his report.

Qwilleran explained, "Mrs. Cobb called me because she was hearing strange noises and was afraid to stay here."

"She put in a call a couple of nights ago. I checked it out, but I couldn't find anything irregular. No evidence of prowlers on the grounds. Are you next of kin?"

"No. She has a son in St. Louis. He'll have to decide where we go from here. I'd better call him and break the news."

At that moment the emergency vehicle arrived, and silent attendants removed the pink-clad remains of one who had captivated the community with her generosity, her cheerful personality, and her encyclopedic knowledge of antiques. And her baking, Qwilleran thought. Whenever there was a charity bazaar or civic reception, Mrs. Cobb stayed up all night baking cookies—not just chocolate chip but an array of lemon-coconut squares, butterscotch pecan meringues, apricot-almond crescents, and more. Ironically, there were Moose County citizens who would remember Iris Cobb chiefly for her cookies.

Qwilleran leafed through the notebook on the school desk in search of her son's phone number. Unfortunately he was unable to remember the young man's name. He had a vague recollection that it was Dennis. The last name was not Cobb but something like Gough, pronounced Goff . . . or Lough, pronounced Luff . . . or Keough, pronounced Kyow. Under *H* he found a listing with a St. Louis area code, and he punched the number. A man's sleepy voice answered.

Many a time Qwilleran had been enlisted to notify a victim's next of kin, and he did it with sensitivity. His voice had a richness of timbre and a sympathetic gentleness that gave the impression of genuine feeling.

"Dennis?" he said in a sober monotone. "Sorry to wake you at this hour. I'm Jim Qwilleran, a friend of your mother, calling from North Middle Hummock."

The young man was immediately alarmed. "What's wrong?" he demanded. His gulp was audible.

"I received a phone call from Iris after midnight. She was afraid to stay at the farm alone, so I offered to drive her to a friend's house . . ."

"What's happened? *Tell me what's happened!*"

"I found her on the kitchen floor. No doubt she'd had a heart attack. It pains me to bring you this news, Dennis."

Her son groaned. "Oh, God! I was flying up there to see her tomorrow—I mean, today. Her doctor suggested it."

"Her going is a great loss. She made many friends here and won over the entire community."

"I know. She told me in her letters how happy she was. For the first time in her life she felt as if she really belonged."

"That brings up the matter of funeral arrangements, Dennis. What should we do! It's your decision, although the Klingenschoen Memorial Fund would consider it a privilege to cover all expenses. Had Iris ever expressed her wishes?"

"Gosh, no," said her son. "She was too busy living! I don't

know what to say. This is so totally unexpected. I've got to think about it—talk it over with Cheryl."

"Call me back, here at the farmhouse, soon as possible. The hospital is waiting for instructions."

Returning the receiver to the cradle Qwilleran noticed the shelf of paperback cookbooks on the wall—a sad substitute for the three-dozen hardbound cookbooks she had lost in a disastrous fire. Other shelves displayed antique pewter plates, porringers, and tankards; the overhead beams were hung with copper pots and baskets; around the fireplace were wrought-iron utensils used in the days of open-hearth cooking. It was a warm and friendly place. Mrs. Cobb loved her kitchen.

Absently he browsed through her phone book, where the listings were written with bold-tip pen in large block letters, a sign of her failing eyesight. The book contained the numbers of museum volunteers for the most part . . . also someone named Kristi . . . and Vince and Verona, whoever they were . . . and Dr. Halifax. Both his home and office numbers were listed. In Pickax one could call the doctor at home in the middle of the night. HB&B obviously was the law firm of Hasselrich, Bennett and Barter. No doubt they had handled her inheritance and drawn up her will. Mrs. Cobb had realized a sizable estate from her third husband, although she chose not to use his name.

As he waited Qwilleran wandered about the apartment, looking for clues to the final minutes of her life. In the open luggage on her bed were a pink robe and pink slippers. The milk carton was still on the kitchen counter, and he put it in the refrigerator. There was a mug of milk in the microwave; the oven had been turned off, but the milk was warm. He poured it down the drain and rinsed the mug. The door leading from the kitchen into the main part of the museum was unlocked, and he was browsing through the exhibit rooms when the phone rang. He was pleased that Dennis would call back so soon. The voice he heard, however, was that of a woman.

"This is Kristi at the Fugtree farm," she said. "Is Iris all right? I saw a police car and ambulance going down the lane."

"I regret to say," he announced solemnly, "that Mrs. Cobb has had a fatal attack."

"Oh, no! I'm so sorry. I knew she was seeing Doctor Hal, but I didn't know it was so serious. Is this Mr. Lanspeak?"

"No, just a friend from Pickax."

"How did it happen?" She sounded young and breathless.

"The details will be in tomorrow's paper, I believe."

"Oh . . . Well, I'm very sorry. I really am! I was sitting up with my sick kids and I saw the flashing lights, so I just had to call."

"That's all right."

"Well, thank you. What's your name?"

"Jim Qwilleran," he mumbled.

Most women would have reacted with an excited "Ooooooh!" as they realized they were talking to an eligible and very wealthy bachelor, but this young woman merely said, "My name is Kristi Waffle."

"It was good of you to call. Good night."

He heard a car pulling into the farmyard and went to meet Larry Lanspeak. Despite the man's elevated standing in the community he was unprepossessing. Ordinary height, ordinary coloring, and ordinary features gave him an anonymity that enabled him to slip into many different roles for the Theatre Club.

"What a tragedy!" he said, shaking his head and speaking in the well-modulated tones of an actor. He walked into the apartment with the deliberate and elongated stride of a man who wishes he were taller. "No one will ever appreciate how much that woman has done for our community! And she wouldn't take a penny for it! We'll never find a manager to equal—"

He was interrupted by the telephone bell.

"This will be her son calling from St. Louis," Qwilleran said as he picked up the receiver, but he winced at the first words he heard.

"Say! This is Vince Boswell!" It was a loud piercing voice with a nasal twang. "I called to see about Iris. Something happen to her? The wife and me, we were sort of watching a video, and we saw the ambulance lights."

Qwilleran replied coolly, "I regret to say that Mrs. Cobb has had a fatal attack."

"No kidding! That's a damn shame!" said the ear-shattering voice, adding with muffled volume as he turned away from the mouthpiece, "Some guy says Iris had a fatal attack, honey!" Then he shouted into the phone, "We liked Iris a helluva lot, my wife and me. Anything we can do?"

Qwilleran was holding the receiver six inches from his ear. "I don't believe so, but thanks for calling."

"We're right close by if you need any help at the museum, understand? Glad to pitch in at a time like this."

"That's kind of you. Good night, Mr. Bosworth."

"Boswell," the man corrected him. "We're staying in the cottage up at the corner, the wife and me. Larry Lanspeak is a friend of ours."

"I see. Well, good night, Mr. Boswell. We appreciate your concern."

Qwilleran hung up and said to Larry, "Who's Boswell?"

"Haven't you met Vince and Verona? She's one of our volunteers, and Vince is cataloguing the antique printing presses in the barn. He's writing a book on the history of printing."

Qwilleran thought, Does the world need another book on the history of printing? "Where did you find this guy, Larry?"

"He came up here from Pittsburgh."

Must have been a coach for the Steelers, Qwilleran thought.

Larry went on, "Vince offered to do the job gratis, so we let him live in the hired man's cottage rent-free. Now that Iris is gone we should have someone living on the premises for security reasons. I'm thinking the Boswells might fill in temporarily."

"I'll be willing to move in until you locate a permanent resident," Qwilleran said.

"That's a kind offer, Qwill, but it would be an imposition."

"Not at all. I've been wanting to spend some time at the museum—especially in the document collection—digging up material for my column."

"If you're serious, Qwill, it would solve our problem, and you wouldn't have to be involved with the museum operation. It's a separate telephone line, and the volunteers come and go with their own key. No one would bother you."

"I'd have the cats with me, of course," Qwilleran pointed out.

"Koko is a self-appointed security officer, and Yum Yum once distinguished herself by catching a museum mouse. Iris used to invite them over here once in a while, and they never did any damage."

"I'm not worried about that," Larry said. "I know they're well-behaved, and they could have a ball, socializing with the barncats and stuffing themselves with fieldmice."

"They're indoor cats," Qwilleran quickly corrected him. "I'm very careful not to let them out."

The telephone rang again, and this time it was Dennis. "We've talked it over, Mr. Qwilleran, and Cheryl and I think the funeral and burial should be up there, where Mother had so many friends. I'll fly up today as I originally planned, and in the meantime you can make whatever decisions have to be made. She always wrote about you in her letters. You were very good to her."

"I'm glad you're coming up, Dennis. I'll meet your plane at the airport and make a reservation for you at the Pickax Hotel, but I don't have your last name."

"It's H-o-u-g-h, pronounced Huff."

"Are you catching the five o'clock shuttle out of Minneapolis?"

"That's right . . . and Mr. Qwilleran, there's something I want to tell you when I arrive, something that was happening to my mother in the last week or so. It had to do with the museum. She was greatly disturbed."

Qwilleran touched his moustache tentatively. "I certainly want to hear about it."

"Thanks for everything, Mr. Q. Isn't that what Mother always called you?"

"Most people call me Qwill. You do the same, Dennis."

As he slowly hung up the phone, questions about Iris Cobb's mental state raced through his mind. It had to be the medication!

"What's the decision?" Larry asked.

"The arrangements are all up to us. Funeral and burial here. Her son will arrive this evening. I'll have the Klingenschoen Fund cover expenses, and I want everything done right."

"I agree. We'll use the Dingleberry funeral home and have the service at the Old Stone Church."

"Would you be good enough to make a couple of phone calls while I rustle up some instant coffee?" Qwilleran asked. "We should line up Dingleberry and inform the hospital. If they need to know the next of kin, it's Dennis H-o-u-g-h, pronounced Huff. Then I'll call WPKX and the night desk at the paper. They can run a bulletin on page one, and I'll write an obituary for Tuesday."

Larry said, "Tell them the museum will be closed for the entire week."

They sat at the dining table in the kitchen, pushing aside the pink candles in milk-glass holders and swigging coffee from majolica mugs as they worked out the details: friends invited to call at Dingleberry's Tuesday evening, final rites to be held at the church on Park Circle Wednesday morning, the Pickax Funeral Band to lead the procession of cars to the cemetery. As past president of the chamber of commerce Larry was sure that all places of business would close on the morning of the funeral. As current president of the board of education he would ask that schools also close for half a day.

"Grades K to twelve have all made field trips to the museum," he said, "and Iris always had cookies and lemonade for the kids."

For a century or more, funerals had been events of moment in Pickax. The townspeople always turned out en masse to pay their respects and count the number of vehicles in the procession. These statistics became a matter of record, to be memorized and quoted: ninety-three cars for Senior Goodwinter's funeral the year before; seventy-five when Captain Fugtree was buried. Most spectacular of all was Ephraim Goodwinter's funeral in 1904; fifty-two buggies, thirty-seven carriages, more than a hundred mourners on foot, and seventeen on bicycles. "Everything but camels and elephants," one irreverent bystander was heard to remark on that occasion. Ephraim, owner of the Goodwinter Mine, was intensely disliked, and his funeral procession resembled a march of triumph, but that was a long story, veiled in hearsay and prejudice—one that Qwilleran hoped eventually to research.

Next came the question of flowers or no flowers. "I'm sure Iris would like flowers," he said. "There's a certain sentimentality in floral tributes, and our friend was a sentimental soul."

"And how about eulogies? Iris was modest to a fault."

"Yes, but she craved approval. When she first came to Pickax I introduced her at a city council meeting, and the audience applauded as a matter of courtesy. Iris was so touched by the applause that she went home and cried. So I vote for eulogies."

"Good! We'll line up the mayor and the president of the county commissioners. Or should we have a woman give one of the eulogies? Susan, perhaps. Or Carol."

"Knowing Iris, I'd say the eulogies should be given by men."

"Maybe you're right. We'll ask Susan to pick out the casket and something for Iris to wear." Larry leaned back in his chair. "Well, I believe that's all we can do tonight. I have Columbus Day specials at the store tomorrow—I mean, today—and if I rush home now I can snatch about three hours of sleep."

Qwilleran said, "I'd like to mention one thing: Iris complained of hearing peculiar noises after dark. Did you ever hear anything unusual?"

"Can't say that I did. I've been here many times at a late hour when we were setting up exhibits, and all I ever heard was crickets and frogs and maybe a loon."

"When I arrived tonight, Larry, the whole place was in darkness. I thought it was a power failure, but when I tried the wall switches, everything worked. How do you explain that?"

"I don't know," said Larry, obviously tired and impatient to leave. "When we found out her eyesight was getting bad, we told Iris not to try to conserve electricity, but she had thrifty habits. I'll get you some keys from the office." He went through the doorway to the museum and soon returned, holding up two keys. "This one is for the front door of the apartment, and this one is for the barn. You might want to put your car in the barn in bad weather. There's a good supply of wood for the fireplaces, too."

"Which barn?"

"The new steel barn. The old barn is full of printing presses."

"How about this door to the museum? Does it lock?"

"No, we've never bothered to install a lock, and Iris always left it open except when she was cooking."

"I'll keep it closed," Qwilleran said, "because of the cats. I don't want them prowling around the museum."

"Do whatever you wish, Qwill. I don't know how to thank you for coming to our rescue. I hope you'll be comfortable. Let me know how it works out."

The two men walked to their cars and drove up Black Creek Lane, Larry in the long station wagon that signified a moneyed country estate, and Qwilleran in his economy-model compact. He drove back to Pickax at a normal speed, thinking:

Someone turned off the lights—switch by switch, room by room, indoors and out.

Someone turned off the microwave oven.

Someone closed the door between the kitchen and the museum.

Chapter 3

It was almost dawn when Qwilleran arrived at his apartment in Pickax. The city was eerily silent. Soon alarm clocks would jolt the populace awake, and the seven o'clock siren on the roof of the city hall would rout late sleepers out of bed. They would turn on their radios and hear about the death of Iris Cobb, whereupon the Pickax grapevine would go into operation, relaying the shocking news via telephone lines, across back fences, and over coffee cups at Lois's Luncheonette near the courthouse.

Qwilleran labored wearily up the steep narrow stairs to his rooms over the Klingenschoen garage. Waiting for him at the top of the flight were two disgruntled Siamese—Yum Yum giving him her reproachful look and Koko giving him a piece of his mind. With glaring eyes, switching tail and stiff-legged stance he delivered a single high-intensity syllable, "YOW!" that said it all: *Where have you been? The lights were on all night! Nobody fed us! You left the window open!*

"Quiet!" Qwilleran protested. "You sound like Vince Boswell. And don't weary me with petty complaints. I have news that will turn your ears inside out. We've lost Mrs. Cobb! No more homemade meatloaf for you two reprobates!"

He shooed them into their own apartment—a room with soft carpet, cushions, baskets, and TV—and then fell into bed. He slept through the seven o'clock wailing of the siren, and he slept through the first blast of the pneumatic drill on Main Street, where the city was digging up the pavement again.

At eight o'clock he was jerked back to consciousness by a phone call from Arch Riker, his lifelong friend, now publisher of the local newspaper.

Without greeting or apology Riker blurted, "Did you hear the newscast, Qwill? Iris Cobb was found dead at her apartment last night!"

"I know," Qwilleran replied, grumpy and hoarse. "I was the one who found the body, called the police, notified next of kin, planned the funeral, phoned the news to the radio station and your news desk, and got home at five o'clock this morning. Got any more hot breaking news?"

"Go back to sleep, you old grouch," said Riker.

At eight-thirty Polly Duncan called. "Qwill, are you up? Did you hear the distressing news about Iris Cobb?"

Qwilleran controlled his umbrage and gave her a gentler version of his tirade to Arch Riker. Then in the next half hour he was called by Fran Brodie, his former interior designer; Mr. O'Dell, his janitor; and Eddington Smith, who sold secondhand books, all of them taking seriously their commitment to the Pickax grapevine.

In exasperation he rolled out of bed, pressed the button on his computerized coffeemaker, and opened a can of red salmon for the Siamese. As he gulped the first welcome swallows of the hot beverage he watched them eat—bodies close to the floor, tails horizontal, heads snapping sideways. After that, they performed a primitive ritual with wide-open jaws and long pink tongues, followed by a laving of mask and ears with moistened paws, all painstakingly choreographed. And this mundane chore was done with elegance and grace by a pair of fawn-furred, brown-pointed, blue-eyed objects of living art. Qwilleran had discovered that watching the Siamese was therapeutic, relieving fatigue, frustration, irritability, and restlessness—a prescriptionless drug with no adverse side effects.

"Okay, you guys," he said, "I have more news for you. We're moving to the Goodwinter Farmhouse Museum." It was his policy to communicate with them in straightforward terms. As if they understood what he said, they both scooted from the room; they abhorred a change of address.

Qwilleran loaded his car with writing materials, an unabridged dictionary, two suitcases of clothing for the nippy weather ahead, his portable stereo, a few cassettes including *Otello*, and the turkey roaster that served as the cats' commode. Then he produced the wicker hamper in which they were accustomed to travel.

"Let's go!" he called out. "Where are you rascals?" Eighteen pounds of solid cat-flesh had suddenly evaporated. "Come on! Let's not play games!" Eventually, crawling on hands and knees, he found Yum Yum under the bed and Koko in the farthest corner of the clothes closet, hiding behind a pair of running shoes.

Limp and silent they allowed him to drop them into the hamper, but they were hatching a countertactic. As soon as he headed the car for North Middle Hummock they began their program of organized squabbling and hissing. Their lunges at each other rocked the hamper, and their snarls suggested bloody mayhem.

"If you heathens will shut up," Qwilleran yelled, "I'll give you a running commentary on this trip. We are now headed north on Pickax Road and approaching the defunct Goodwinter Mine. As you may recall, it was the scene of a disastrous explosion in 1904."

There was a momentary lull in the backseat racket. The cats liked the sound of his voice. It had a resonance that soothed the savage breasts under that pale silky fur.

He continued in the style of a tour director. "Coming up on the right is the Dimsdale Diner, famous for bad food and worse coffee. Windows haven't been cleaned since the Hoover administration. Here is where we turn onto Ittibittiwassee Road."

His passengers were quietly contented now. The sun was shining; the sky was an October blue with billowing white clouds tinged with silver; the woods were aflame with autumn color. The journey was far different from the game of blind-man's buff that Qwilleran had played the night before.

"Hold on to your teeth," he said. "We are about to cross the Old Plank Bridge. Next we'll be rounding some sharp curves. On the left is the infamous Hanging Tree."

After that came the ghost town that had once been North Middle Hummock . . . then the white rail fence of the Fugtree farm . . . and finally the sign carved on barnwood:

GOODWINTER FARMHOUSE MUSEUM
1869
Open Friday through Sunday
1 to 4 P.M. or by appointment

Black Creek Lane was lined with trees in a riot of gold, wine red, salmon pink, and orange—living reminders of the ancient hardwood forests that had covered Moose County before the lumbermen came. At the end of the vista was the venerable farmhouse.

"We're here!" Qwilleran announced. He carried the hamper into the west wing of the rambling building. "You'll have two fireplaces and wide windowsills with a view of assorted wildlife. That's something you don't get in downtown Pickax."

The Siamese emerged from the hamper cautiously, and then made straight for the kitchen, Yum Yum to the place where she had caught a mouse four months before and Koko to the exact spot where Mrs. Cobb had collapsed. He arched his back, bushed his tail, and pranced in a macabre dance.

Qwilleran shooed them out of the kitchen, and they proceeded to explore methodically, sniffing the rugs, leaping to tabletops with the lightness of feathers, testing the seats of chairs for softness and congenial contour, checking the view from the windowsills, and examining the bathroom, where their commode had been placed. In the parlor Koko recognized a large pine wardrobe—a Pennsylvania German *Schrank*—that had come from the Klingenschoen mansion. It was seven feet high, and he could sail to the top of it in a single calculated leap. On the bookshelves he found only a few paperbacks, most of the space devoted to displaying antique bric-a-brac. Chairs were covered in dark velvet, the better to show cat hairs, and the polished wood floors were scattered with antique Orientals, good for pouncing and skidding.

While the Siamese inspected the premises, Qwilleran brought in the luggage. The writing materials he piled on the dining table in the kitchen. The stereo equipment he placed on an Austrian dower chest in the parlor. His clothing was a problem, however, since the bedroom was filled with Mrs. Cobb's personal belongings. Worse still, in his opinion, was the bedroom furniture: chests and tables with cold marble tops, a platform rocker too dainty in scale, and an enormous headboard of dark wood, intricately designed and reaching almost to the ceiling. It looked as if it might weigh a ton, and he had visions of the thing toppling on him as he lay in bed.

"Tonight will be the test," he said to the prowling Siamese. "Either this old house emits weird noises after dark, or they were all in the poor woman's head. But I doubt whether we'll ever solve the mystery of the darkened house and yard. How many lights were on before she collapsed? There would be light in the kitchen where she was warming milk, perhaps in the bedroom where she was packing a bag, certainly in the yard because she was expecting me. And obviously the microwave had been in use."

Koko said "ik ik ik" and scratched his ear.

Qwilleran locked both cats out of the kitchen while he sat at the dining table and typed Mrs. Cobb's obituary on her own typewriter. He needed no notes. He was well aware of her credentials as an antique dealer and licensed appraiser, of her accomplishments in cataloguing the vast Klingenschoen collection, of her generous gift to the Historical Society and her tireless efforts in restoring it as a living museum, wheedling cash donations and treasured heirlooms from tight-fisted Moose County families. She had staged programs for schoolchildren, infecting them with a germ of interest in their heritage. And Qwilleran could not end his paean without lauding the cornucopia of cookie delights that poured from her kitchen.

He omitted the fact that all three of her husbands had died unnatural deaths: Hough from food poisoning, Cobb from a murderous accident, and Hackpole . . . Qwilleran preferred not to think about Hackpole.

The obituary finished, he telephoned it to the copydesk of the *Moose County Something* for Tuesday's edition. Admittedly this was an unusual name for a newspaper, but Moose County took pride in being different.

The work had given Qwilleran an appetite, and he foraged in the freezer, putting together a lunch of beef-barley soup and homemade cheese bread.

Before he could finish his repast, the banging of the brass knocker summoned him to the front door. The caller proved to be a scrawny man of middle age, sharp-eyed and sharp-nosed.

"I saw your car in the yard," said a loud twangy voice. "Is there anything I can do for you? I'm Vince Boswell. I've been working on the printing presses in the barn."

It was the voice he had heard on the telephone, the kind that punctures the eardrums like a knife. Qwilleran winced. He said coolly, "How do you do. I've just moved in and I'll be living here for a few weeks."

"That's just fine! Then I don't need to worry about the place. I sort of kept an eye on the museum when Iris was away. You must be Jim Qwilleran that writes for the *Something*. I see your picture in the paper all the time. Will you be spending much time here?"

"I'll be coming and going."

"Then I'll watch the place when you're away. I'm a writer, too—technical stuff, you know. I'm writing a book on the history of the printing press and cataloguing the antique equipment in the barn. Big job!" Boswell looked past Qwilleran and down at the floor. "I see you've got a kitty."

"I have two," Qwilleran said.

"My little girl loves kitties. Maybe my wife could bring Baby over to meet them some day."

Qwilleran cleared his throat. "These are not your usual cats, Mr. Boswell. They're Siamese watch-cats, highly temperamental, and not accustomed to children. I wouldn't want . . . your child to be accidentally scratched." He was aware that Moose County courtesy required him to invite the caller in for a beer or a cup of coffee, but Boswell's clarion voice annoyed him. He said, "I'd ask you in for a cup of coffee, but I'm leaving for the airport. Someone is coming into town for the funeral."

Boswell shook his head sadly. "My wife and me, we felt bad about that. Iris was a nice lady. When is the funeral? Will there be a visitation at the mortuary?"

"I believe the information will be in tomorrow's paper." Qwilleran glanced at his watch. "I'm sorry, but you'll have to excuse me, Mr. Boswell. I want to be there when the plane lands."

"Call me Vince. And let me know if there's anything I can do, you hear?" He left with a wave of the hand that included the cat. "Goodbye, kitty. Nice to meet you, Mr. Qwilleran."

Qwilleran closed the door and turned to Koko. "How did you react to that noisy oaf?"

Koko laid his ears back. Qwilleran thought, No one has ever called him "kitty." A more appropriate form of address would be "Your Excellency" or "Your Eminence."

Before leaving for the airport he telephoned Susan Exbridge at her apartment in Indian Village. He said, "Just want you to know I've moved into Iris's quarters, in case you need me for anything. How's it going?"

The vice president of the Historical Society had energy and enthusiasm to match that of the president. She said, "I'm beat! I rushed out to the museum early this morning and selected some clothes for Iris to be buried in. I decided on that pink suede suit she wore for her wedding last year. Then I chose the casket at Dingleberry's. Iris would love it! It has a pink shirred lining, very feminine. Then I discussed the music with the church organist and lined up hosts for tomorrow night at the funeral home and hired the marching band. I also talked the florists into flying in special pink flowers from Minneapolis. Moose County goes in for rust and gold mums, which would be ghastly with the pink casket lining, don't you think?"

"That sounds like a full day's work, Susan."

"It was! And all so emotional! I haven't had time to cry yet, but now I'm going to drink two martinis and have a good wet weep for poor Iris . . . What did you do today, Qwill?"

"I wrote her obit and phoned it in, and now I'm leaving for the airport to pick up her son," Qwilleran said. "I'll take him to dinner and drop him off at the hotel. His name is Dennis H-o-u-g-h, pronounced Huff. Will you and Larry do the honors tomorrow?"

"What did you have in mind?"

"You might see that he's taken to lunch and dinner and escorted to Dingleberry's at the proper time."

"Is he attractive?" asked Susan without missing a beat. Recently divorced, she was constantly alert to possibilities.

"It depends upon your taste," Qwilleran said. "He's five feet tall, weighs three hundred pounds, and he has a glass eye and dandruff."

"Just my type," she said airily.

Qwilleran changed his clothes, found cold roast beef in the refrigerator, which he warmed for the Siamese, and then drove to the airport.

Two years before, the Moose County airport had been little more than a cow pasture and a shack with a windsock, but a grant from the Klingenschoen Fund had upgraded the airstrip and terminal, built hangars and paved a parking lot, while the local garden clubs had landscaped the entrance and planted rust and gold mums.

In the terminal, copies of the Monday *Something* displayed this news on the front page, within a black border:

BULLETIN

Iris Cobb Hackpole was found dead at her apartment in North Middle Hummock early this morning, following an apparent heart attack. She was resident manager of the Goodwinter Farmhouse Museum and partner in a new antique shop opening in Pickax. She had been in ill health. Funeral arrangements to be announced.

As the two-engine turboprop landed and taxied toward the terminal, Qwilleran wondered if he would recognize Dennis from their previous meeting Down Below. He remembered him as a clean-cut, lean-jawed young man just out of college, who worked for an architectural firm. Since then Dennis had married, fathered a child, and started his own business as a building contractor—developments that had brought joy to his mother's heart.

The young man who now walked toward the terminal showed the evidence of a few added years and responsibilities, and his gaunt face showed the evidence of grief and weariness.

Qwilleran gave him a sincere handshake. "It's good to see you again, Dennis. Sorry it has to be under these circumstances."

The son said, "That's the hell of it! My mother kept inviting Cheryl and me up here for a visit, but we were always too busy. I could kick myself now. She never even saw her grandson."

As they started the drive to Pickax Qwilleran asked him, "Did Iris tell you anything about Moose County? About the abandoned mines and all that?"

"Yes, she was a good letter writer. I've saved most of her letters. Our son can read them some day."

Qwilleran glanced at his passenger and compared his lean and melancholy face with Mrs. Cobb's plump and cheery countenance. "You don't resemble your mother."

"I guess I resemble my father, although I never knew him or even saw his picture," Dennis said. "He died when I was three years old—from food poisoning. All I know is that he had a lousy disposition and was cruel to my mother, and when he died there was a snotty rumor that she poisoned him. You know how it is in small towns; they don't have anything else to do but peddle dirt. So we moved to the city, and she brought me up alone."

"I have profound sympathy for single parents," Qwilleran said. "My mother faced the same challenge, and I'll be the first to admit it wasn't easy for her. How did Iris get into the antique business?"

"She worked as a cook in private homes, and one family had a lot of antiques. Right away she was hooked. We used to study together at the kitchen table—me doing my math and her studying about drawer construction in eighteenth-century highboys or whatever. Then she met C. C. Cobb, and they opened the Junkery on Zwinger Street where you lived. I guess you know the rest."

"Cobb was a rough character."

"So was Hackpole, from what I hear."

"The less said about that zero, the better," said Qwilleran with a frown. "Are you hungry? We could stop at a restaurant. Pickax has a couple of good ones."

"I had some chili in Minneapolis while I was waiting for the shuttle, but I could stand a burger and a beer."

They went to the Old Stone Mill, a century-old grist mill converted into a restaurant, with the waterwheel still turning and creaking. Dennis had his beer, and Qwilleran ordered Squunk water with a twist.

"It's better than it sounds," he explained. "It's a local mineral water that comes from a flowing well at Squunk Corners." Then he said, "I'm sorry Iris didn't live to see the opening of Exbridge and Cobb. It's a far cry from the Junkery on Zwinger Street. Her apartment at the museum is also filled with important antiques. You'll probably inherit them."

"I don't think so," said Dennis. "She knew I didn't go in for old furniture and stuff. Cheryl and I like glass and steel and that molded plastic from Italy. But I want to see the museum. I used to work for a firm that restored historic buildings."

"The Goodwinter farmhouse is a remarkable example, and its

restoration was all her brainwork. It's about thirty miles out of Pickax, and I questioned the advisability of her living there alone."

"So did I. I wanted her to get a Doberman or a German shepherd, but she vetoed that idea in a hurry. She wouldn't like a dog unless it had Chippendale legs."

"Did you two keep in touch regularly?"

"Yes, we had a good relationship. I phoned every Sunday, and she wrote once or twice a week. Do you know her handwriting? It's impossible!"

"Only a cryptographer could read it."

"So I gave her a typewriter. She loved that machine! She loved the museum. She loved Pickax. She was a very happy woman . . . and then the wings fell off."

"What do you mean?"

"She went to the doctor for indigestion and found out she'd had a silent coronary. Her cholesterol was sky-high; her blood sugar was iffy; and she was about fifty pounds overweight. Psychologically she crashed!"

"But she always looked healthy."

"That's why it was such a bummer. She got depressed, and then she began to turn off about the museum . . . Do you believe in ghosts?"

"I'm afraid not."

"Neither do I, but Mom was always interested in spirits—friendly ones, that is."

"I know all about that," Qwilleran said. "On Zwinger Street she claimed there was a playful apparition in the house, but I happen to know that C. C. Cobb was playing tricks. Every night he got out of bed without disturbing her and put a saltshaker in her bedroom slippers or hung her underpants from the chandelier. He must have worked hard to think up a new prank every night."

"That's what I call devotion," Dennis said.

"Frankly, I think she knew, but she didn't want C. C. to know that she knew. That's *real* devotion!"

The hamburgers were served, and the two men ate in silence for a few minutes. Then Qwilleran said, "You mentioned that

Iris began to be disillusioned about the museum. I was not aware of that."

Dennis nodded soberly. "She began to think the place was haunted. At first she was amused, but then she got frightened. Cheryl and I tried to get her down to St. Louis for a visit. We thought a change of scene would do her some good, but she wouldn't leave until after the formal opening of the shop. Maybe it was her medication—I don't know—but she kept hearing noises she couldn't explain. That can happen in an old house, you know—creaking timbers, mice, drafts in the chimney . . ."

"Did she give you any particulars?"

"I brought some of her letters," Dennis said. "They're in my luggage. I thought you could read them and see if anything clicks. It doesn't make sense to me. I want to ask her doctor about it when I see him."

"Doctor Halifax is a wonderful, humane being, willing to listen and explain. You'll like him."

They drove to the New Pickax Hotel, as it was called, Qwilleran warning Dennis not to expect state-of-the-art accommodations. "The hotel was 'new' in the 1930s, but it's convenient, being right downtown and handy to the funeral home. Larry Lanspeak will be in touch with you tomorrow—or even tonight. He's president of the Historical Society and a great guy."

"Yeah, Mom raved about the Lanspeaks."

They parked in front of the hotel, and Qwilleran accompanied Dennis to the front desk, where the presence of the famous moustache assured deluxe service from the hotel staff. The night desk clerk was one of the big good-looking blond men who were in plentiful supply in Moose County.

Qwilleran said to him, "Mitch, I made a reservation for Dennis Hough, spelled H-o-u-g-h. He's here for Mrs. Cobb's funeral. See that he gets the best . . . Dennis, this is Mitch Ogilvie, a member of the Historical Society. He knew your mother."

"I was sorry to hear the bad news, Mr. Hough," said the clerk. "She was a terrific person, and she loved the museum."

Dennis mumbled his thanks and signed the register.

"Good night, Dennis," Qwilleran said. "I'll see you at the funeral home tomorrow evening."

"Thanks for everything, Qwill . . . Hold it!" He took an envelope from his carry-on duffel and handed it over. "These are photocopies. You don't need to return them. They're some of her recent letters. The last one arrived Saturday. Maybe you can figure out what was going on at the museum . . . or whether it was . . ." He tapped his forehead.

CHAPTER 4

After dropping Dennis Hough at the hotel Qwilleran drove to North Middle Hummock through a cloud of spectral blue vapor—moonlight mixed with wisps of fog settling in the valleys of the Hummocks. When he arrived home and turned off his headlights, the farmyard and the farmhouse were bathed in a mystic blueness.

He let himself in and turned on the four-candle ceiling fixture. Only three candles lighted. At the same time two shadowy forms came slinking from the dark parlor and blinked at him.

"What happened to the lights?" he asked them. "Last night all four were operating."

The Siamese yawned and stretched.

"Have you anything to report? Did you hear any unusual sounds?"

Koko groomed his breast with a long pink tongue, and Yum Yum rubbed against Qwilleran's ankles, suggesting a little something to eat. This was the first time they had been left alone here, and Qwilleran looked for tilted pictures, books on the floor, dislodged lampshades, and shredded bathroom tissue. One could never guess how they might react to abandonment in a new environment. Happily, only a few cat hairs on a blue velvet wing chair and some dried weeds on the parlor floor testified to their feline presence; they had chosen Mrs. Cobb's favorite chair as their own, and one or both of them had leaped to the top of the seven-foot *Schrank* to examine the dried arrangement that filled a Shaker basket.

Qwilleran made a cup of coffee before sitting down to read Iris Cobb's last letters, thankful that Dennis had given her the typewriter. The first letter was dated September 22 and began with grandmotherly questions about Dennis Junior, comments on the fine weather, raves about the new antique shop scheduled to open October 17, and a lengthy recipe for a new high-calorie dessert she had invented, after which she wrote:

> *I'm having so much fun at the museum. The other day I thought it would be nice if we displayed a long-handled bedwarmer in one of our exhibit bedrooms, and I remembered that someone had donated a bedwarmer in poor condition. I looked it up on the computer. (The Klingenschoen Fund paid to have our catalogue computerized. Isn't that nice?) Sure enough, it said the brass pan was dented and the handle was loose but it was worthy of restoration. So I went downstairs to look for it.*
>
> *The basement is a catchall for damaged stuff, and I was poking around, looking for the bedwarmer, when I heard a mysterious (did I spell that right?) knocking sound in the wall. I said to myself—Oh, goody! We've got a ghost! I listened and decided which wall it was coming from, and then I picked up an old wooden potato masher that was lying around and went rat-tat-tat on the wall myself. After that there was no more knocking. If it was a ghost, I guess I frightened it away.*
>
> *I wish you could come for the shop's grand opening. It's going to be very gala. Susan's arranging for champagne punch and flowers and everything.*
>
> *Love from Mother*

Qwilleran thought, Gold and rust mums, no doubt. He turned to the next letter, dated September 30, and discovered a drastic change of mood. Mrs. Cobb wrote:

> *Dear Dennis and Cheryl,*
> *I'm terribly upset. I just got my report from Dr. Hal and everything is wrong!! Heart, blood, cholesterol, everything! I've been crying too*

hard to talk, or I would have phoned. If I don't go on a strict diet and do certain exercises and take medication, I'll need surgery!! It was a horrible shock. Never thought this would happen to me. I felt so good! Now I feel positively suicidal. Did I spell it right? Forgive me for unloading my troubles on you. Can't write any more tonight.

Mother

Poor Iris, Qwilleran thought. His mother had experienced the same panic when her doctor handed her a sentence of death. He picked up the next letter, pleased to find her in a better frame of mind. It was written five days later.

Dear Kids,
Your phone call cheered me up no end. I should have gone down there when you first invited me, but now I have to stay here for the grand opening. In the daytime I feel okay, but at night I get very nervous and depressed, mostly because of the wierd (did I spell that right?) noises. I told you about the knocking in the basement. Now I hear it all the time—moaning and rattling too. Sometimes I think it's all in my head, and then I get really worried and that awful tightness in my chest.

I've always said an old house reflects the people who've lived in it, like something gets into the wood and plaster. It sounds crazy, I know, but bad things have always happened to the Goodwinters—suicide, fatal accidents, murder. I can feel it in the atmosphere of the house, and it's making me very uncomfortable. Is it my imagination? Or is it evil spirits?

I've been so concerned about my own troubles that I forgot to ask about little Denny. Did you find out what caused his rash?

Love from Mom and Grandmom

The last letter was not dated, but Dennis had received it on Saturday, the day before his mother died.

Dear Dennis,
I don't know how much longer I can stand it—the noises, I mean. The volunteers don't hear anything. I'm the only one that hears it. I told Dr. Hal, and he took me off medication for a few days, but it doesn't make any difference. I still hear the noises, but only when I'm alone. I hate to tell Larry. He'll think I'm crazy. The museum's open Friday,

Saturday, and Sunday, and there'll be people around. I'm going to wait until Monday, and if it isn't any better, I'm going to resign.

Mother

P.S. Now I don't hear it any more.

Dennis, receiving the letter on Saturday, called Dr. Halifax and bought a plane ticket for Monday. On Sunday night she died, her face contorted with pain—or what? She was frightened to death, Qwilleran decided. By what? Or by whom?

After reading the last letter he was in no hurry to go to bed with that monstrous headboard towering over him. He considered sleeping on the sofa, but first he had to conduct an experiment. It was his intention to sit up until midnight with lamps and chandeliers alight in every room and with the stereo blasting at full volume. Then, precisely at midnight, he would turn everything off and sit in the dark, listening.

For Phase One of this strategy he marched through the apartment, flipping on light switches and activating lamps. In the entrance hall only two candles responded. The night before, it had been four. An hour ago it was three. He huffed into his moustache, having little patience with electrical equipment that failed to do its duty, and he was in no mood to go hunting for spare lightbulbs.

Comfortable in his Mackintosh bathrobe and moosehide slippers, he treated the cats to a sardine and prepared another cup of coffee for himself. Then he inserted the *Otello* cassette into the stereo and settled into the blue velvet wing chair in front of the fireplace. He refrained from building a fire; the crackling logs would spoil the pure tones on the cassette.

This time he hoped to hear the recording from start to finish without interruption. To his consternation, just as Othello and Desdemona approached their love duet in Act One, the telephone rang. He turned down the volume and went to the phone in the bedroom.

"Qwill, this is Larry," said the energetic voice. "I've just talked to Dennis Hough on the phone. Thanks for getting him installed at the hotel. He says his accommodations are very good."

"I hope they didn't give him the bridal suite with the round bed and satin sheets," Qwilleran said moodily, resenting the interruption.

"He's in the presidential suite—the only one with a telephone and color TV. Everything's set for tomorrow. Susan will take him to lunch; Carol and I will take both of them to dinner. Is everything okay at the museum? Are you comfortable there?"

"I expect to have nightmares from sleeping in that monster of a bed."

In a tone of mock rebuke Larry said, "That monster, Qwill, is a priceless General Grant bed that was made a century ago for a World's Fair! Look at the quality of the rosewood! Look at the workmanship! Look at the patina!"

"Be that as it may, Larry, the headboard looks like the door to a mausoleum, and I'm not ready to be interred. Otherwise, all is well."

"I'll say good night, then. It's been a hectic day, and neither of us had much sleep last night, did we? I finally lined up the other pallbearers, so now I'm going to have a much deserved nightcap and turn in."

"One question, Larry. Did you see Iris during museum visiting hours this past week?"

"I didn't, but Carol did. She said Iris looked tired and worried—the result of her medical report, no doubt, and maybe the stress of opening the new shop. Carol told her to go and lie down."

Qwilleran went back to his opera, but he had missed the love duet. He turned off the machine peevishly, checked the cats' whereabouts, doused the lights, and sprawled in the blue wing chair with his feet on the footstool. Then he waited in the dark—waiting and listening for the knocking, moaning, rattling, and screaming.

Four hours later he opened his eyes suddenly. He had a kink in his neck and two Siamese on his lap, their combined weight having caused one foot to be totally numb. Asleep they weighed twice what they weighed on the veterinarian's scale. Qwilleran limped about the room, grumbling and stamping his deadened foot. If there had been noises in the walls, he had slept through them in a blissful stupor. Larry's phone call was the last thing he remembered.

In retrospect there was something about the call that bothered him. Larry had mentioned pallbearers. He said he had lined up "the other pallbearers." What, Qwilleran wondered, did he mean by "other"?

He waited fretfully for seven o'clock, at which time he telephoned the Lanspeak country house. Without preamble he said, "Larry, may I ask a question?"

"Sure, what's on your mind?"

"Who are the pallbearers?"

"The three male members of the museum board and Mitch Ogilvie—in addition to you and me. Why do you ask?"

"Just for the record," Qwilleran said, "no one up to this minute has even hinted that I might be a pallbearer—not that I have any objection, you understand—but I'm glad I happened to find out."

"Didn't Susan talk to you?"

"She talked to me at considerable length about a pink suede suit and a casket with pink lining and pink flowers being flown in from Minneapolis, but not a word about pallbearing."

"I'm sorry, Qwill. Does it create a problem?"

"No. No problem. I merely wanted to be sure."

The truth was that it created a definite problem. It called for a dark suit—something Qwilleran had not owned for twenty-five years. Neither in his lean years nor in his newly acquired affluence had he found an extensive wardrobe important to his lifestyle. In Moose County he could get by with sweaters, windbreakers, a tweed sports coat with leather patches, and a navy blue blazer. At the moment he owned one suit, a light gray, purchased when he was best man at Iris Cobb's marriage to Hackpole. It had not been off the hanger since that memorable occasion.

At nine o'clock sharp he telephoned Scottie's Men's Shop in downtown Pickax, saying, "I need a dark suit in a hurry, Scottie."

"How darrrk, laddie, and in how much of a hurrry," said the proprietor. He liked to burr his *r*'s for Qwilleran, who always made it known that his mother's maiden name was Mackintosh.

"Very dark. I'm going to be a pallbearer, and the funeral's at ten-thirty tomorrow morning. Do you have a tailor on tap?"

"Aye, but canna say for how long. He were goin' to the doctor. Get over here in five minutes and he can fit you."

"I'm not in Pickax, Scottie. I'm living at the Goodwinter farmhouse. Can you keep him there for half an hour? Bribe the guy!"

"Weel, he's a stubborrrrn Scot, but I'll do my best."

Qwilleran made a dash for his razor, slapped on the lather, and cut himself. Just as he was stanching the blood and muttering under his breath, the brass door knocker clanged.

"Damn that Boswell!" he said aloud. He was sure it was the bothersome Boswell; who else would call at such an hour?

In his short shavecoat and with half a faceful of lather, he strode to the entrance hall and yanked open the door. There on the doorstep stood a startled woman holding a plate of biscuits. She covered her face with one hand in embarrassment. "Oh, you're shavin'! Pardon me, Mr. Qwilleran," she said in a soft southern drawl. Each lilting statement ended with emphasis on the last word and an implied question mark. "I'm your neighbor, Verona *Boswell*? I brought you some fresh biscuits . . . for your *breakfast*?" It was a refreshing sound in Moose County, 400 miles north of North, but Qwilleran had no time for refreshment.

"Thank you. Thank you very much," he said briskly, accepting the plate.

"I just wanted to say . . . *welcome*?"

"That's kind of you." He tried not to be curt. On the other hand, the lather was drying on his face and Scottie's tailor was pacing the floor.

"Let us know if there's anythin' we can . . . *do for you*?"

"I appreciate your thoughtfulness."

"I hope we can get better acquainted after the . . . *funeral*?"

"Indeed, Mrs. Boswell." He had stepped back and was beginning to close the door.

"Oh, please call me . . . *Verona*? You'll see us around a lot."

"I'm sure I shall, but I must ask you to excuse me now. I'm leaving for Pickax on urgent business."

"Then I won't hold you up. We'll probably see you tonight at the ... *visitation*?" Reluctantly she backed away, saying, "My little girl would love to meet your kitties."

Qwilleran finished dressing with clenched jaw. He had always lived in cities, where one could ignore neighbors and be completely ignored in return. The smothering neighborliness of the Boswells, he feared, might be a problem—not to mention "Baby" who wanted to meet the "kitties." Was that really her name? Baby Boswell! Qwilleran disliked the child even before setting eyes on her. He was sure she would be one of those insufferable tots—cute, vain, and precocious. Like W. C. Fields he had never developed a liking for small children.

As for Verona Boswell, she was not unattractive, and her gentle voice was a welcome contrast to her husband's shrillness. Verona was somewhat younger than Vince, but she had lost her freshness—probably, Qwilleran decided, from listening to his whining harangue. Whatever their neighborly virtues, he determined to see as little as possible of the Boswells.

Driving to Pickax in a huff he was stopped for speeding, but the state trooper looked at his driver's license and the distinctive moustache and merely issued a warning. At the men's store Scottie was waiting with a selection of dark blue suits, while a tailor with a tape measure around his neck stood nervously in the background.

"I don't want to pay too much," Qwilleran said, scanning the pricetags.

"Spoken like a true Mackintosh," said the storekeeper, nodding his shaggy gray head. "That clan always had deep pockets and shorrrt arrrms. Perhaps you'd like to rent a suit if it's only for a funeral."

Qwilleran scowled at him.

"On the other hand, mon, a darrrk suit is handy to have in the closet in case you suddenly want to get married."

Qwilleran made a selection reluctantly, considering all the suits overpriced.

As the tailor checked the fit, hoisting here and tugging there, Scottie said, "So you're stayin' at the Goodwinter farmhouse, are you? Have you seen a dead man sittin' on a keg of gold coins?"

"So far I've been denied that pleasure," Qwilleran replied. "Is he supposed to be a regular visitor?"

"Old Ephraim Goodwinter was a miser, you know, and they say he still comes back to count his money. How do you want to pay for this suit? Cash? Credit card? Ten dollars a week?"

From the men's store Qwilleran drove to the Pickax industrial park, where the *Moose County Something* occupied a new building. Designed to house editorial and business offices as well as a modern printing plant, the building was a costly project made possible by an interest-free loan from the Klingenschoen Fund. The daily masthead on page four listed the following:

ARCH RIKER, *editor and publisher*
JUNIOR GOODWINTER, *managing editor*
WILLIAM ALLEN, *general manager*

Qwilleran first walked into the managing editor's office, which was dominated by a large, old-fashioned rolltop desk that dwarfed the young man sitting in front of it. The desk had belonged to his great-grandfather, the miserly Ephraim.

Junior Goodwinter had a boyish face and a boyish build and was growing a beard in an attempt to look older than fifteen. "Hey! Pull up a chair! Put your feet up!" he greeted Qwilleran. "That was a swell piece you wrote about Iris Cobb. I hear you're house-sitting at my old homestead."

"For a while, until they find a new manager. I hope to do some research while I'm there. How's the ancestral desk working out?"

"Not so swift. All those pigeonholes and small drawers look like a good idea, but you file something away and never find it again. I like the idea of the rolltop, though. I can stuff my unfinished work in there, roll the top down, and go home with a clear conscience."

"Have you discovered any secret compartments? I imagine Ephraim had a few secrets he wanted to hide."

"Golly, I wouldn't know where to start looking for secret compartments. Why don't you bring Koko down here and let him sniff around. He's good at that."

"He's been doing a lot of sniffing since we moved into the farmhouse. He remembers Iris and wonders why she's not there. By the way, just before she died she talked about hearing unearthly noises. Did you ever have any supernatural adventures when you lived there?"

"No," said Junior. "I was too busy riding horses and scrapping with my six-foot-four brother."

"You never told me you were an equestrian, Junior."

"Oh, sure. Didn't you know that? I wanted to be a jockey, but my parents objected. The alternatives were a bell-hop or a hundred-ten-pound journalist."

"How's the new baby?" Qwilleran asked, never able to remember the name or sex of his young friends' offspring.

"Incredible kid! This morning he grabbed my finger so hard I couldn't pull away. And only four weeks old! Four weeks and three days!"

Tight-fisted like his great-great-grandfather, Qwilleran thought. Then he pointed toward the door. "Who's that? Is that William Allen?" A large white cat had walked into the office with a managerial swagger.

"That's him in person—not a reincarnation," Junior said. "He escaped from the fire in the old building, miraculously. Probably incurred a little smoke damage, but he cleaned it up without making an insurance claim. We found him a month ago, ten months after the fire. Guess where he was! Sitting in front of the State Unemployment Office!"

Next Qwilleran visited the office of the publisher. Arch Riker was sitting in a high-backed executive chair in front of a curved walnut slab supported by two marble monoliths.

"How do you like working in this spiffy environment?" Qwilleran asked. "I detect the fine hand of Amanda's Design Studio."

"It cramps my style. I'm afraid to put my feet on my desk," said Riker, who claimed to do his best thinking with his feet elevated.

"Those underpinnings look like used tombstones."

"I wouldn't be surprised if they were. Amanda has all the

instincts of a grave robber ... Say, that was a decent obit you wrote for Iris Cobb. I hope you write one that's half that good when it's my turn to go. What's the story behind the story?"

"Meaning what?"

"Don't play dumb, Qwill. You know you always suspect that a car accident is a suicide, and a suicide is a murder. What really happened Sunday night? You look preoccupied."

Qwilleran touched his moustache in a guilty gesture but said glibly, "If I look preoccupied, Arch, it's because I've bought a dark suit for the funeral—I'm one of the pallbearers—and it's a question whether Scottie will have it ready on time. Are you going to Dingleberry's tonight?"

"That's my intention. I'm taking the lovely Amanda to dinner, and we'll stop at the funeral home afterward, if she can still stand up and walk straight."

"Tell the bartender to water her bourbon," Qwilleran suggested. "We don't want your inamorata to disgrace herself at Dingleberry's."

As lifelong comrades the two men had sniggered about their boyhood crushes, gloated over their youthful affairs, confided about their marriage problems, and shared the pain of the subsequent divorces. Currently they indulged in private banter about Riker's cranky, outspoken, bibulous friend Amanda. There were many complimentary adjectives that could apply to this successful businesswoman and aggressive member of the city council, but "lovely" was not one of them.

Riker asked, "Will you and Polly be there?"

"She has a dinner meeting with the library board, but she'll drop in later."

"Perhaps we could go somewhere afterward—the four of us," Riker proposed. "I always need some liquid regalement after paying my respects to the deceased."

Qwilleran stood up to leave. "Sounds good. See you at Dingleberry's."

"Not so fast! How long are you going to be downtown? Can you hang around until lunchtime?"

"Not today. I have to go home and unpack my clothes, and

find out where they store the spare lightbulbs, and take inventory of the freezer. Iris always cooked as if she expected forty unexpected guests for dinner."

"Home! You've been there half a day, and you call it home. You have a faculty for quick adjustment."

"I'm a gypsy at heart," Qwilleran said. "Home is where I hang my toothbrush and where the cats have their commode. See you tonight."

Driving to North Middle Hummock he noticed that the wind had risen and the leaves were beginning to fall. On Fugtree Road the pavement was carpeted with yellow leaves from the aspens. It would be a pleasant day to take a walk, he thought. His bicycle was in Pickax, and he missed his daily exercise. He was feeling relaxed and in a good humor; a little banter with his colleagues at the *Something* always put him in an amiable mood. A moment later, his equanimity was shattered.

As he turned the corner into Black Creek Lane he jammed on the brakes. A small child was standing in the middle of the lane, holding a toy of some kind.

At the urgent sound of tires crunching on gravel Mrs. Boswell ran out of the house, crying helplessly, "Baby! I told you to stay in the yard!" She picked up the tiny tot under one arm and took the toy away from her. "This is Daddy's. You're not supposed to touch it."

Qwilleran rolled down the car window. "That was a narrow escape," he said. "Better put her on a leash."

"I'm so . . . *sorry,* Mr. Qwilleran?"

He continued slowly down the lane, experiencing a delayed chill at the recollection of the near-accident, then thinking about Verona's ingratiating drawl, then realizing that the "toy" was a walkie-talkie. As he parked in the farmyard the Boswell van was pulling away from the old barn; the driver leaned out of the window.

"What time is the funeral tomorrow?" trumpeted the irritating voice, resounding across the landscape.

"Ten-thirty."

"Do you know who they got for pallbearers? I thought they

might call on me, being a neighbor and all that. I would've been glad to do it, although I'm plenty busy in the barn. Any time you want to see the printing presses, let me know. I'll take time out and explain everything. It's very interesting."

"I'm sure it is," said Qwilleran, stony-faced.

"We're thinking of going to the visitation tonight, the wife and me. If you want to hitch a ride with us, you're welcome. Plenty of room in the van!"

"That's kind of you, but I'm meeting friends in Pickax."

"That's okay, but don't forget, we're here to help, any time you need us." Boswell waved a friendly farewell and drove up the lane to the hired man's cottage.

Plucking irritably at his moustache Qwilleran let himself into the apartment and searched for the cats—always his first concern upon returning home. They were in the kitchen. They looked surprised that he had returned so soon. They seemed embarrassed, as if he had interrupted some private catly rite that he was not supposed to witness.

"What have you two rapscallions been doing?" he asked.

Koko said "ik ik ik" and Yum Yum nonchalantly groomed a spot on her snowy underside.

"I'm going for a walk, so you can return to whatever shady pastime has been giving you that guilty look."

Leisurely, after changing into a warm-up suit, he walked up the lane, enjoying the glorious October foliage and the vibrant blue of the sky and the yellow blanket of leaves underfoot. When he reached the hired man's cottage he hurried past, lest the Boswells should rush out and engage him in neighborly conversation. At the corner he turned east to explore a stretch of Fugtree Road he had never traveled. It was paved but there were no farmhouses—only rocky pastureland, patches of woodland, and squirrels busy in the oak trees. He walked for about a mile, seeing nothing of interest except a bridge over a narrow stream, evidently Black Creek. Then he retraced his steps, hurrying past the Boswell cottage and slowing down in front of the Fugtree farm.

The Fugtree name was famous in Moose County. The farmhouse had been built by a lumber baron in the nineteenth century, and it was a perfect example of Affluent Victorian—three stories high, with a tower and a wealth of architectural detail. The complex of barns, sheds, and coops indicated it had also been a working farm for a country gentleman with plenty of money. Now the outbuildings were shabby, the house needed a coat of paint, and the grounds were overgrown with weeds. The present occupants were not taking care of the Fugtree property in the manner to which it had been accustomed.

As Qwilleran speculated on its faded grandeur, someone in the side yard looked in his direction with hands on hips. He turned away and walked briskly back to Black Creek Lane. Passing the hired man's cottage he was careful to keep his gaze straight ahead. Even so he was aware of the tot running across the front lawn.

"Hi!" she called out.

He ignored the salutation and walked faster.

"Hi!" she said again as he came abreast of her. He kept on walking. As a youngster in Chicago he had been cautioned never to speak to strange adults, and as an adult in a changing society he considered it prudent never to speak to strange children.

"Hi!" she called after him as he marched resolutely down the lane, scattering leaves underfoot. She was probably a lonely child, he guessed, but he banished the thought and finished his walk at a jog-trot.

Arriving at the apartment he flipped the hall light switch out of sheer curiosity. Three candles responded. First it had been four, then three, then two. Now it was three again. Growling under his breath he strode to the kitchen, where Koko was sitting on the windowsill gazing intently at the barnyard. Yum Yum was watching Koko.

Qwilleran said in a louder voice than usual, "Since you two loafers spend so much time in the kitchen staring into space, perhaps you can tell me where to find the spare lightbulbs. Come on, Koko. Let's have a little input."

With seeming difficulty Koko wrenched his attention away from the outdoor scene and executed a broad jump from the windowsill to the large freezer chest that Mrs. Cobb had left well stocked with food.

"I said lightbulbs, not meatballs," said Qwilleran. He opened and closed the pine cabinets until he found what he needed—a flame-shaped lightbulb intended for use in candle-style fixtures. He carried this and a kitchen chair to the front hall, the Siamese romping alongside to watch the show. Any action out of the ordinary attracted their attention, and a man climbing on a kitchen chair rated as a spectacle.

After Qwilleran had climbed on the chair, he forgot which light needed replacing. He stepped down and flicked the switch. All four candles responded.

"Spooks!" he muttered as he returned the chair to the kitchen and put the lightbulb back into the broom closet.

CHAPTER 5

The Dingleberry funeral home occupied an old stone mansion on Goodwinter Boulevard, one that had been built by a mining tycoon during Moose County's boom years. Though the exterior was forbidding, the interior had been styled by Amanda's Design Studio. Plush carpet, grasscloth walls, and raw silk draperies were in pale seafoam green, accented with eighteenth-century mahogany furniture and benign oil paintings in expensive frames. The decor was so widely admired that most of the fashionable residences in Pickax were decorated in Dingleberry green.

When Qwilleran arrived on Tuesday evening the large parking lot in the rear was filled and all the legal parking spaces on the boulevard were taken, as well as some of the illegal ones. Entering the establishment he heard a respectful babble of voices in the adjoining rooms. Susan Exbridge, handsomely dressed as usual, quickly approached him in the foyer.

"Dennis is darling!" she said in a subdued voice, restraining her usual dramatics of speech and gesture. "I feel so sorry for him. He thinks Iris would still be alive if he had arrived a day earlier, but I did my best to ease his mind. I took him to lunch at Tipsy's and then drove him around the county. He was quite impressed! When he saw the Fitch estate—it's for sale, you know—he said the big house could be converted into condos, and he'd like to live in the other house himself. I didn't mention it to him, but if he inherits Iris's money he could afford to buy the Fitch property and we could get him into the Theatre Club. He's interested in acting, and we could use a handsome man for leading roles—of his age, I mean. I told him Moose County is a good place to raise a family. Of course, I can't imagine why anyone would want to live in St. Louis anyway, can you?"

"You should be selling real estate," Qwilleran said.

"I may do that if the antique shop isn't a big success. How will I ever be able to swing it without Iris? I had the connections, but she had the know-how. Exbridge and Cobb! It sounded so right! Like Crosse and Blackwell or Bausch and Lomb. Would you like to see her? She looks lovely."

Susan accompanied Qwilleran into the Slumber Room, where visitors were gathered in small groups, speaking in low but animated voices. One entire wall was banked with pink flowers, plus a few red and white blossoms for accent, and Iris Cobb in her pink suede suit lay at peace in a pink-lined casket with her rhinestone-studded eyeglasses folded in one hand as if she had just removed them before taking a nap.

Qwilleran said, "Was the pink nail polish your idea, Susan? I never saw her wear nail polish."

"She said she couldn't because she had her hands in water so much, but she won't have to cook any more, so I thought the polish was a nice touch."

"Don't kid yourself. At this moment she's happily concocting some ethereal delicacy for the angels."

"Have the attorneys called you?" she asked.

"No. Why should they?"

"Thursday morning is the reading of the will. They've asked Larry and me to attend. I wonder why. I'm getting nervous."

Qwilleran said, "Perhaps Iris left you her General Grant bed."

A new group of visitors arrived, and Susan excused herself to return to her greeting post in the foyer. Qwilleran sought out the chief mourner, who was eager to see him.

"Did you read her letters?" Dennis asked.

Qwilleran nodded dolefully. "Her decline was very rapid. It was a damn shame."

"I asked Doctor Halifax if the noises she heard could be the result of taking medication. He wouldn't say yes and wouldn't say no, but I saw the results of her tests, and she had really let herself get in bad shape. He said she had a 'crippling fear' of surgery. I knew that. She had been resisting eye surgery, although her vision was beginning to impair her driving."

"When would you like to see the farmhouse?"

"How about tomorrow after the funeral? I'm curious about—"

Dennis was interrupted by a loud voice at the entrance, and he looked toward the foyer. Everyone turned toward the foyer. The Boswells had arrived and were headed toward the bier, the man carrying their small child. For the first time Qwilleran noticed that he walked with a pronounced limp.

"Look, Baby," he was saying in the voice of a sideshow barker. "This is the nice lady who used to give you cookies. She's gone to live in heaven, and we came to say goodbye."

"Say goodbye to Mrs. Cobb, Baby," said the mother's soft voice.

"Bye-bye," said Baby, curling her fingers in a childish gesture.

"Iris looks so . . . *pretty*? Doesn't she, Baby?"

"Why is she in a box?" For a child of her age she was remarkably articulate, Qwilleran thought.

The father set her down and turned to see Qwilleran watching them. "They've got a good turnout here tonight. Parking lot was all parked up," he said in a voice that could be heard throughout the Slumber Room and adjoining areas. "Biggest visitation I ever went to! Will you take a look at those flowers! She was one popular lady! She didn't act like she had much on the ball, but people liked her. You can tell by the big crowd."

Mrs. Boswell, who was clasping her daughter's hand, said, "Baby, this is the nice man who's living at . . . the *museum*? Say hi to Mr. Qwilleran."

"Hi!" said Baby.

Qwilleran looked down at the creature four feet below his eye level, pathetically puny in her short blue velvet coat and hat and wrinkled white tights. The outfit had obviously been homemade in a hurry. Before he could reply with a stiff "How do you do," the parents had spotted the Lanspeaks and descended on them, leaving him with Baby.

She looked up in wonder at his moustache and said in her clear, precise speech, "What's that thing on your face?"

"That's my nose," said Qwilleran. "Doesn't your father have a nose?"

"Yes, he has a nose."

"How about your mother? Does she have a nose?"

"Everybody has a nose," said Baby with disdain, as if dealing with a dolt.

"Then you should recognize a nose when you see one."

Baby was not fazed by his evasive logic. "Where do you work?" she asked.

"I don't work. Where do you work?"

"I'm too little. My daddy works."

"Where does he work?"

"In the barn."

"What does he do in the barn?"

Baby scuffed the toe of her doll-size shoe. "I don't know. I don't go to the barn."

"Why not?"

"I'll get dirty."

"A likely story," said Qwilleran, glancing around and hoping to be rescued soon.

"They have kitties in the barn," Baby volunteered.

"If you don't go to the barn, how do you know they have kitties?"

This animated dialogue had attracted the rapt attention of surrounding groups, and Mrs. Boswell swooped in and snatched her daughter away. "Don't pester Mr. Qwilleran," she scolded softly.

It was a relief for him to circulate among the adults. The guest register was a who's who of Pickax: civic leaders, wealthy antique collectors, politicians running for office, and members of the Historical and Genealogical societies—the two most important organizations in a county that took pride in its heritage. The Old-Timers Club, which admitted only lifelong residents of advanced age, was represented by numerous white-haired members, many of them dependent upon canes, walkers, and wheelchairs. Qwilleran thought it commendable that Mitch Ogilvie, the young desk clerk from the hotel, paid lavish attention to these oldsters, listening to their stories and encouraging them to talk.

Arch Riker was there, clutching the arm of the unsteady Amanda. Polly Duncan, in the company of library boardmembers, exchanged glances with Qwilleran across the crowded room; they were always discreet in public. The lively Homer Tibbitt, age ninety-four, was accompanied by an elderly woman with well-coifed hair of a surprisingly youthful brown.

Riker said to Qwilleran, "Who's that old fellow who walks like a robot?"

"When you're his age, you won't be able to get out of bed without a derrick," said Qwilleran. "That's Homer Tibbitt, retired school principal, ninety-four and still doing volunteer work for the museum."

Amanda said, "That eighty-five-year-old woman with the thirty-year-old hair is Rhoda Finney. She's been chasing him for years, even before his wife died. She's one of the Lockmaster Finneys, and we all know about *them*!" Amanda's pronouncements always blended rumor, imagination, and truth in no known proportion. "The old fellow that Homer's talking to is Adam Dingleberry, oldest mortician in three counties." She referred to a frail, stooped figure dependent upon a walker. "He's buried more secrets than a dog buries bones. I'll bet some of them come back to haunt him. Look at the two old fogeys with their heads together, snickering like fools! You can bet

Adam's telling dirty stories and Homer made his girlfriend turn off her hearing aid."

Riker tugged at her arm. "Come on, Amanda; it's time to go."

Qwilleran maneuvered about the room until he caught Polly's eye, then tilted his head three degrees toward the front door. She said good night to her boardmembers and then followed him.

In the lobby Riker said, "Shall we go to the Old Stone Mill? They stay open later than Stephanie's."

"We'll meet you there," said Qwilleran. Then he and Polly walked to their separate cars.

At the picturesque mill the party of four asked for a quiet table and were conducted to a secluded corner overlooking the waterwheel. They were a motley foursome: the Klingenschoen heir with the overgrown moustache; Arch Riker with the equanimity, thinning hair, and paunchy figure of a lifelong newspaper deskman; Polly Duncan, the pleasant-faced, soft-voiced, well-informed administrator of the Pickax public library; Amanda Goodwinter of the Drinking Goodwinters, as her branch of the prominent clan was known. Polly had a matronly figure, a penchant for plain gray suits, and graying hair that was noticeably unstyled, but she was a paragon of fashion compared to Amanda, on whom every new garment looked secondhand and every hair looked purposely out of place. Nevertheless, Riker enjoyed her crotchety company for perverse reasons that Qwilleran could not fathom.

Amanda had her usual bourbon; Polly asked for dry sherry; Riker wanted Scotch; and Qwilleran ordered pumpkin pie and coffee.

Polly said, "Qwill, that was a beautiful obituary you wrote for Iris. In everyday life she was so self-effacing that one tended to forget all her skills and knowledge and admirable qualities."

Amanda raised her glass in a toast. "Here's a wet one to Saint Iris of the Hummocks!" Then she winced and scowled at Riker, who had kicked her under the table.

Polly raised her glass and quoted from *Hamlet*: "And flights of angels sing thee to thy rest."

The two men nodded and sipped in silence. Riker asked,

"How was your summer in England, Polly? Did you floor them with your knowledge of Shakespeare?"

She smiled pleasantly. "I had no chance to show off, Arch. I was too busy answering their questions about American movies."

"At least," Qwilleran said, "the English know that the Bard of Avon is an Elizabethan playwright and not a cosmetics distributor."

"Here come the big guns," Amanda muttered as another foursome arrived.

On the way to their table the Lanspeaks, Dennis Hough, and Susan Exbridge stopped to speak to Qwilleran's group, and Polly said to them, "That was a remarkable display at Dingleberry's. All color-coordinated! Even to the pink nail polish!"

"Give Susan the credit for that," Carol Lanspeak said.

"I might have guessed!" said Polly sweetly in what passed as a compliment to Susan's exquisite taste, except that she raised her eyebrows slightly. Qwilleran and Riker exchanged knowing glances. Polly's dim regard for Susan was no secret.

As the new arrivals went on to their table Riker asked, "Is it true that Dingleberry will bury you free if you're a hundred or older?"

"They can afford to," Amanda grumbled. "They're making money hand over fist, but I've had a helluva tough time collecting my decorating fee."

"They expect to take it out in trade," Qwilleran said.

"The Dingleberry enterprise," said Polly, "involves five generations. Adam Dingleberry's grandfather was a coffin maker. The next generation combined a furniture store with an undertaking parlor, as it used to be known. The present operation is run by Adam and his sons and grandsons."

Amanda said, "Who was that cretin with a jack-hammer voice that came in and disturbed the peace?"

"You made a hit with his kid, Qwill," said Riker. "Who are they?"

"My neighbors at the museum. He's cataloguing the printing presses for the Historical Society... Incidentally, Arch, the obituary I submitted referred to visiting hours at the funeral home. Someone changed it to 'visitation' hours. I know it's considered genteel in certain circles, but it's a ridiculous euphemism that doesn't belong in a newspaper with any class. A 'visitation' is a divine manifestation."

"Or a spirit communication," added Polly. "Shakespeare refers to the visitation of Hamlet's father's ghost."

"Speaking of ghosts," Qwilleran said, "has there ever been a rumor that the Goodwinter farmhouse is haunted?"

Belligerently, Amanda said, "If it isn't, it should be! Three generations died violent deaths, starting with that old tightwad Ephraim, and they all deserved it!"

Her escort rebuked her with quiet amusement. "You're speaking of your blood relatives, Amanda."

"That's not my branch of the family tree. We're crazy but Ephraim's branch has always been rich and mean."

"Quiet, Amanda. People are staring at you."

"Let them stare!" She glowered at surrounding tables.

Still protesting, Riker said, "Our managing editor is a direct descendent of Ephraim, and he's neither rich nor mean. Junior is poor and likable."

"He's only a kid," Amanda growled. "Give him time! He'll turn out rotten like all the rest."

Winking at Qwilleran and gently changing the subject, Riker asked, "Does anyone at this table believe in ghosts?"

"They're hallucinations caused by drugs, delirium, and other physical and mental disorders," Qwilleran said.

"But they've been around for thousands of years," said Polly. "Read the Bible, Cicero, Plutarch, Dickens, Poe!"

Riker said, "When our kids were young we took a vacation in a rented cabin in the mountains. Our dog went with us, of course. He was a big fearless boxer, but every night that animal would grovel on the cabin floor, whining and cringing like a coward. I never saw anything like it! Later we found out that a former tenant had been murdered by a tramp."

"I have a tale to relate, too," said Polly. "I was traveling in Europe when my mother died. I didn't even know she was ill, but one night I woke up and saw her standing by my bed as clear as could be—in her gray coat with two silver buttons."

"Did she speak?" Riker asked.

"No, but I sat up in bed and said, 'Mother! What are you doing here?' Immediately she vanished. The next morning I learned she had died several hours before I saw her image."

Qwilleran said, "That's known as a delayed crisis apparition, a kind of telepathy caused by intense emotional concentration."

"Hogwash!" said the lovely Amanda.

Qwilleran and Polly murmured a discreet good night in the parking lot of the Old Stone Mill and drove home in separate cars after an affectionate "I'll call you" and "à bientôt."

It was another one of those dark nights when cloud cover hid the moon. Unlike the reckless drive to answer Iris Cobb's cry for help, this journey was taken in a leisurely manner as Qwilleran thought about Polly Duncan and her melodious voice, her literate background, her little jealousies, and her haughty disdain for Susan Exbridge. (Susan had her hair done at Delphine's, spent money on clothes, drove an impressive car, wore real jewelry, lived in Indian Village, served on the library board of directors even though she never read a book—all things of which Polly disapproved.) It surprised him, however, that Polly accepted supernatural manifestations; he thought she had more sense.

He could see a light in the Fugtree farmhouse, and the TV was flickering in the Boswell cottage, but the museum yard was dark. What it needed was a timer to turn on lights automatically at dusk. He parked and reached for the flashlight in the glove compartment, but he had left it in the house. Turning on his headlights he found his way to the entrance, at the same time catching a glimpse of shadowy movement in one of the windows. The cats, he surmised, had been on the windowsill watching for him and had jumped down to meet him. When he opened the door, however, only Yum Yum made an appearance. Koko was elsewhere; he could be heard talking to himself in a musical monologue interspersed with yiks and yowls.

Stealthily Qwilleran stole to the rear of the apartment and observed the cat meandering about the kitchen with his nose to the floor like a bloodhound, sniffing here and there as if detecting spilled food. Mrs. Cobb's cooking habits had been casual. A handful of flung flour often missed the bowl; a vigorously stirred pot splashed; a wooden spoon dripped; a tomato squirted. Yet the floor looked clean and freshly waxed. Koko was following the memory of a scent; he was investigating something known only to himself; and he was giving a running commentary on his discoveries.

Qwilleran changed into night attire before making another attempt to hear the recording of *Otello*. The Siamese joined him in the parlor, but at the first crashing chords they flew out of the room and remained in hiding throughout the storm scene. At one point they thought it safe to come creeping back, but then the trumpets sounded, and they disappeared again.

Just as the triumphant Othello was making his dramatic entrance, the telephone rang. Qwilleran groaned his displeasure, turned down the volume, and took the call in the bedroom.

"Our office has been trying to reach you, Qwill," said the genial attorney who handled legal matters for the Klingenschoen Fund. "As attorneys for Mrs. Cobb we would like to suggest that you attend the reading of her will on Thursday morning."

Qwilleran huffed into his moustache with momentary annoyance. "Do you have a good reason for asking me to be there?"

"I'm sure you will find it interesting. Besides the major bequests to her family, she wished to leave certain remembrances to friends. Eleven o'clock Thursday morning in my office."

Qwilleran thanked him with little enthusiasm and went back to *Otello*. He had been following the libretto in English, and now he had lost his place and lost the drift of the opera. He rewound the tape and punched Play. Again the Siamese staged their absurd pantomime of wild flight and stealthy return; it was becoming a game. This time the tape unreeled as far as the opening scene of Act Two. The villainous Iago was launching into his hate-filled *Credo* when ... the telephone rang again. Qwilleran shuffled into the bedroom once more.

A woman's voice said, "Mr. Qwilleran, your lights are on."

Lost in the mood of the opera, he hesitated. Lights? What

lights? Yardlights? *"My car lights!"* he yelped. "Thanks. Who's calling?"

"Kristi at the Fugtree farm. I can see your place from an upstairs window."

After thanking her again Qwilleran dashed outdoors and turned off his headlights. The beam had faded to a sick yellow, and he knew the battery was down. He was right; the motor refused to turn over. Leaning back in the driver's seat he faced the facts: Country garages close at nine o'clock; It is now past midnight; The funeral is at ten-thirty in the morning; I have to pick up my suit at nine; My battery is dead.

There was only one thing to do. Disagreeable though it might be, it was the only solution to the problem.

CHAPTER 6

Early Wednesday morning Qwilleran clenched his teeth, bit his lip, swallowed his pride, and telephoned the cottage at the top of Black Creek Lane. It was important, he realized, to strike the right tone—not too suddenly friendly, not too apologetic, yet a few degrees warmer than before, with a note of urgency to mask embarrassment.

"Mr. Boswell," he said, "this is Qwilleran. I have a serious problem."

"How can I be of service? It's a privilege and a pleasure," said the voice that knifed the eardrums.

"I neglected to turn off my headlights last night, and my car won't start. Are you, by any chance, equipped to give my battery a jump?"

"Sure thing. I'll run down there pronto."

"I hate to bother you so early, but I have to be in Pickax at nine o'clock . . . for funeral preliminaries."

"No problem at all."

"I'll reimburse you, of course."

"Wouldn't think of it! That's what neighbors are for—to help each other. Be there in a jiffy."

Qwilleran loathed the man's syrupy sentiments and hoped he would not be expected to repay the favor by baby-sitting some evening while they went to a movie in Pickax.

Painful though he found it, Qwilleran survived the Boswell brand of friendliness and thanked him sincerely, though not effusively. As he started his drive to Pickax it occurred to him that some small token of appreciation would be in order, since Boswell refused remuneration. A bottle of something? A box of chocolates? A potted plant? A stuffed toy for Baby? He vetoed the toy immediately; such an avuncular gesture would be misconstrued, and Baby would start hanging around, asking questions, and expecting to pet the "kitties." She might even start calling him Uncle Qwill.

As he passed the Fugtree farm he remembered he owed Kristi Waffle a debt of gratitude as well. Chocolates? A potted plant? A bottle of something? He had not even met the woman. She sounded young and spirited. Apparently she had children, but of what age? Did she have a husband? If so, why was he not cutting the grass? They were hardly well-off. The inevitable pickup truck in the driveway was ready for the graveyard. By the time he arrived at Scottie's he was still in a quandary. A fruit basket? A frozen turkey? A bottle of something?

Qwilleran picked up his dark blue suit and rushed to his apartment over the garage. Across the Park Circle the mourners were already gathering at the Old Stone Church. Traffic was detoured, the cars of the funeral procession were lining up four abreast, and the park itself was filled with curious bystanders. Dressing hurriedly he found black shoes and a white shirt and dark socks, but all his ties were red stripes or red plaid or simply red, so it was back to Scottie's for a suitable tie.

When he finally arrived at the church, properly cravatted, he observed three generations of Dingleberry morticians in charge: old Adam propped up in the narthex, his sons handling details with inconspicuous efficiency, and his grandsons marshalling the procession. Within the church the organ was groaning sonorous chords, the pews were filled, the pink flowers were banked in front of the altar, and Iris Cobb lay in a pink casket in her pink suede suit. This was what she would have wanted for her farewell to Pickax. Although she had always appeared modest, she gloried in the attention and approval of others. Qwilleran felt a surge of joy for his former landlady, his former housekeeper, his eager-to-please friend—who had achieved such status.

After the interment he attended a small luncheon in a private room at Stephanie's. Conversation was in a minor key as guests endeavored to say the right thing, dropping crumbs of comfort, sweetly sad regrets, and nostalgic reminiscences.

Dennis Hough was the first to break the pattern. He said, "I've met some good people up here. No wonder my mother was so happy! I wouldn't mind relocating in Moose County."

"It would please Iris immensely," said Susan Exbridge.

"But I don't know how Cheryl will react to the idea. It's so far away from everything. How's the school system?"

Carol Lanspeak spoke up. "Thanks to the K Fund, we've been able to expand our facilities, improve the curriculum, and hire more teachers."

"The K Fund?"

"That's our affectionate nickname for the Klingenschoen Memorial Fund."

Larry Lanspeak said, "The county has several industrial and commercial builders, but we need a good residential builder. I think you should consider it."

After the luncheon, when Qwilleran and Dennis were driving to North Middle Hummock, the younger man asked, "How does the K Fund operate?"

"It manages and invests the Klingenschoen fortune and disburses the income in ways that will benefit the community—grants, scholarships, low-interest business loans, and so forth."

"If I started a business up here, would I stand a chance of getting a loan?"

"I have no doubt, if you applied to the Fund and presented a good case."

"My mother told me the Klingenschoen fortune is all yours."

"I inherited it, but too much money is a burden," Qwilleran explained. "I solved the problem by turning everything over to the Fund. I let them worry about it."

"That's very generous."

"Not generous; just smart. I have all I need. I used to be quite happy living out of two suitcases and renting a furnished room. I still don't require a lot of possessions."

As they passed a hedged field Qwilleran said, "This is where a flock of blackbirds rose out of the bushes and spooked a man's horse. He was thrown and killed. The blackbirds stage guerrilla warfare against the human population at certain times of year."

"Who was the man?"

"Samson Goodwinter. It happened more than seventy-five years ago, but the natives still talk about it as if it were last week."

"My mother's letters said that all the Goodwinters met with violent deaths."

"Let me explain the Goodwinter family," said Qwilleran. "There are forty-nine of them in the latest Pickax phone book, all descended from four brothers. There are the much-admired Goodwinters, like Doctor Halifax, and the eccentric Goodwinters, like Arch Riker's friend Amanda. Another branch of the family specializes in black sheep, or so it would seem. But the unfortunate Goodwinters that your mother mentioned are all the progeny of the eldest brother, Ephraim. He jinxed his whole line of descendents."

"How did he do that?"

"He was greedy. He owned the Goodwinter Mine and the local newspaper and a couple of banks in the county, but he was too stingy to provide safety measures for the mine. The result was an explosion that killed thirty-two miners."

"How long ago did that happen?"

"In 1904. From then on, he was violently hated. To thirty-odd families and their relatives he was the devil incarnate. He tried to make amends by donating a public library, but his victims' families wouldn't forgive. They threw rocks at his house and tried to burn down his barn. His sons and the hired man took turns standing guard with shotguns after dark."

"What did he look like? Do you know?"

"The museum has his portrait—a sour-looking villain with side whiskers and hollow cheeks and a turned-down mouth." They were now driving through the hilly terrain known as the Hummocks. "Around the next bend," Qwilleran pointed out, "you'll see a grotesque tree on a hill. It's called the Hanging Tree. It's where they found Ephraim Goodwinter dangling from a rope on October 30, 1904."

"What happened?"

"His family maintained it was suicide, but the rumor was circulated via the Pickax grapevine that he was lynched."

"Was there ever any proof, one way or the other?"

"Well, the family produced a suicide note," Qwilleran said, "so there was no investigation, and no charges were brought. And if the lynching story is true, it's curious that no one ever squealed on the vigilantes and there were no deathbed confessions. Today there's a fraternal order called the Noble Sons of the Noose. They're supposed to be direct descendents of the lynch mob."

"What do they do? Have you ever met one of them?"

"No one knows who belongs to the order; not even their wives know. The mayor of Pickax might be a Noble Son. Or the Dingleberry boys. Or Larry Lanspeak. It's a secret that has been handed down for three or four generations, and—believe me!— it's not easy to keep a secret in Moose County. They have a gossip network that makes satellite communication look like the pony express. Of course, they don't call it gossip. It's *shared information*."

"Fantastic!" said Dennis with wonder in his face. "This is interesting country!"

When they reached Black Creek Lane Qwilleran drove slowly to let his passenger enjoy the beauty of the foliage and the approach to the quaint farmhouse. A rusty van was leaving the barnyard as they arrived.

"Brace yourself," said Qwilleran. "Here comes the loudmouth who livened things up at the funeral home last night."

The van stopped, and Vince Boswell leaned out. "Sorry I couldn't get to the funeral," he said. "I'm trying to finish work on the presses before snow flies. How many cars went to the cemetery?"

"I didn't count them," Qwilleran snapped, and then—remembering Boswell's assistance in getting his car started—he amended his curt reply in a more cordial tone. "There was a marching band, very impressive. The church was filled."

"Must've been quite a sight. I wish I could've been there to say goodbye to the lady." He peered at Dennis. "I don't believe I've been formally introduced to your friend."

Qwilleran made the introductions briefly.

Boswell said, "Coming to pick up some of your mother's things, I suppose. She had a cookbook that my wife would like to have if you don't want it—just as a remembrance, you know. She's always looking for new things to cook. If you two gentlemen would like to come and have supper with us tonight, you'd be very welcome. It won't be fancy, but it'll be home-cooked."

"That's kind of you," said Qwilleran, "but Mr. Hough's time is limited. He simply wants to see the farmhouse."

"Be glad to show you the printing presses in the barn, sir."

"Not this time, thanks."

"Well, let me know if I can be of any assistance," said Boswell.

As the van drove away, Dennis said, "Do you think he's a Noble Son of the Noose?"

"He's a son of *something*," said Qwilleran, "but he bailed me out of a tight situation this morning, and I should be grateful. Maybe that's why he was hinting for your mother's cookbook."

"At the funeral home last night he asked Larry for my mother's job as resident manager. Sort of premature, don't you think?"

"Vince Boswell isn't noted for his finesse."

First they walked around the grounds, Qwilleran pointing out the features of the house. The original section was built of square logs measuring fourteen by fourteen inches, chinked with mortar made of clay, straw, and hog's blood. The east and west wings were added later, and the whole structure was covered with cedar shingles, now weathered to a silvery gray.

Dennis showed no sentiment when they entered his mother's

apartment. He strolled about with his hands in his pockets, commenting on the wide floorboards, the extravagant use of milled woodwork, and the six-over-six windows, many of the panes having the original wavy glass. He said nothing about the General Grant bed or the Pennsylvania *Schrank* or the pewter collection in the kitchen—all considered rare treasures by Iris Cobb.

When they entered the kitchen, Koko rose from his huddle on the windowsill, stretched his long body in a hairpin curve, and made a flying leap to the top of the freezer-chest, six feet away.

"Too early for dinner," Qwilleran told him.

"Is that Koko?" Dennis asked. "My mother told me about him. She said he's very smart."

Koko was now on the floor, tracing abstract patterns with his nose, moving his head from right to left, covering the entire room systematically.

"This is his bloodhound act," Qwilleran explained.

As the cat neared the telephone he became excited, hopped to the seat of the old school desk and sniffed the desktop with moist snorts.

"What's in that desk?" Dennis asked.

Qwilleran lifted the lid. "Papers," he said. There were scribbled notes in Iris Cobb's illegible hand, newspaper clippings, index cards, a magnifying glass, and a battered looseleaf notebook, its black covers now gray with waterspots and flour and hard use.

Dennis said, "That looks like her personal cookbook. She told me it was the only thing she saved from the fire last year. That's because it was in her luggage at the time. She was taking it on her honeymoon, if you can believe that."

"Knowing your mother, I can believe it," said Qwilleran as he returned the book to the desk. "There are women in Moose County who would sell their souls to the devil if they could get their hands on this collection of recipes. Would you like to see the museum now?"

Dennis glanced at his watch. "Sure."

The main section of the house was furnished with trestle tables, rope beds, a pie safe, banister-back chairs, iron-strapped chests and other trappings of a pioneer home. The east wing was devoted to collections of textiles, documents, lighting fixtures and the like. Dennis ignored the stenciled walls that had thrilled his mother, and the window curtains that had required so much research, and the heirlooms she had begged from old families in the area.

"It was the basement where she first heard the knocking," he said.

"Okay, let's go downstairs," said Qwilleran.

A sign at the top of the basement stairs explained that the "cellar" originally had a dirt floor and was used for storing root vegetables and apples in winter, and possibly milk and cream from the family cow. Later a coal bin had been added, and a fruit closet for home canning. The basement now had a concrete floor and the latest in heating and laundry equipment, but the exposed joists overhead were fourteen-inch logs with the bark still in evidence.

Qwilleran found a door leading to a storeroom under the west wing, where damaged furniture and household cast-offs were piled without plan or purpose, among them a wooden potato masher. The stone walls were a foot thick, one of them roughly covered with cracked plaster. Had Iris cracked it, Qwilleran wondered, when she tapped out an answer to the ghostly visitor?

"Nothing here to explain the knocking," said Dennis. "The house is built like Fort Knox. Let's go back upstairs. Susan is picking me up and taking me to see the Fitch property. The real estate broker is meeting us there."

"Are you serious about moving to Moose County?"

"I won't know until I talk it over with Cheryl, but when I tell her about the Fitch estate she might get excited."

Don't tell her about Susan, Qwilleran thought. There was an obvious rapport developing between Dennis and the vivacious divorcée. He had observed it at Dingleberry's and at the luncheon following the funeral, and he noticed it again when Susan arrived and whisked the young man away to the Fitch estate. He was at least fifteen years her junior but tall like her former husband and with the same rugged good looks.

When he had waved the couple on their way he went indoors,

flicking the hall lights out of sheer curiosity. The previous flick had activated four candles. Now it was three again. Qwilleran huffed into his moustache.

He had expected to spend the afternoon with Dennis, examining the museum exhibits and looking at the printing presses in the barn, after which they might have had drinks at the Shipwreck Tavern in Mooseville, dinner at the Northern Lights Hotel overlooking the lake, and dessert at the colorful Black Bear Café.

Somewhat disappointed he telephoned Polly at the library. "Would you like to go out tonight? We could have dinner at the Northern Lights and finish up at the Black Bear."

"How would you like to come to my place instead?" she asked.

"You shouldn't have to cook after working all day," he protested.

"Don't worry. I can whip up something very easily."

He knew what it would be. They had recently read a play aloud—*The Cocktail Party* by T. S. Eliot—and since then Polly had been whipping up curried dishes instead of broiling fish or pan-frying chops. He liked Indian fare, but Polly was whipping a good idea to death. Her cottage was beginning to have a permanent aroma of Bombay, as if it had seeped into the carpet and upholstery. "Are you sure you want to take the trouble?" he asked.

"Of course I do! Besides, I have a surprise for you."

"What is it?" Qwilleran hated to be surprised.

"If I tell you, it won't be a surprise, will it? Come at six-thirty. That will give me time to go home and change clothes."

And find the curry powder, he thought. Reluctantly he agreed. He would have preferred broiled whitefish or stuffed porkchops at the Northern Lights.

Now he had time to kill, and it occurred to him that he had never raked leaves. He had interviewed kings; he had been strafed on a Mediterranean beach; and briefly he had been held hostage by a crazed bank robber, but he had never raked leaves. He changed into jeans and a red plaid shirt and went to the steel barn to find a rake.

A year ago the barn had been the scene of an auction when the Goodwinters' household goods were liquidated. Now it functioned as a garage and utility shed, housing garden tools, a work bench, odds and ends of lumber, and stacks of firewood. Mrs. Cobb's station wagon was parked there, and he assumed it would be sold. It was larger than his downscale compact and would more easily accommodate the cats' carrier and their commode. It might be enjoyable to take them on a few trips around the country. The Lanspeaks had been raving about the Blue Ridge Mountains. He wondered if the altitude would hurt their ears.

Finding a rake, Qwilleran embarked on a new experience— pleasant exercise that activated the muscles without engaging the mind. It gave him time to think about the irritating Vince Boswell, Koko's discovery of Iris Cobb's cookbook, the all-too-obvious attraction between Susan Exbridge and Dennis Hough, Polly's promised surprise, and the prospect of another dinner of curried something-or-other.

From the corner of his eye he was aware of someone small approaching him.

"Hi!" said Baby.

Qwilleran grunted a reply and raked faster.

"What are you doing?"

"Raking leaves."

"Why?"

"For the same reason you brush your teeth. It has to be done."

She considered this analogical reasoning briefly and followed up with, "How old are you?"

"That's classified information. How old are you?"

"Three in April."

"What kind of car do you drive?" Qwilleran asked.

"I don't have a car," she said with a pretty pout. He had to admit she was a pretty child as well as articulate.

"Why not?"

"I'm too little."

"Why don't you grow up?"

As Baby pondered an answer to this baffling question her mother came running down the lane. "Baby? Baby?" she called out in her gentle and ineffectual way. "Daddy doesn't want you to come down here. I'm sorry, Mr. Qwilleran. Was she bothering you? She's always asking annoying . . . *questions?*"

"She's training to be a journalist," Qwilleran said, raking industriously.

He finished his chore with satisfaction, heaping the leaves in piles for the yard crew to remove. Then he went indoors to feed the Siamese. The freezer-chest contained, he estimated, a two-month supply of spaghetti sauce, chili, macaroni and cheese (his favorite), vichyssoise, pot roast, turkey tetrazzini, shrimp gumbo, deviled crab, Swedish meatballs and other Cobb specialties—nothing in curry sauce, he was glad to note.

He thawed some pot roast for the cats, and while they were devouring it he took Mrs. Cobb's personal cookbook from the small desk and looked for his favorite coconut cream cake with apricot filling, but the handwriting defeated him. Over the years the pages had been spotted with cook's fingerprints and smeared with tomato, chocolate, egg yolk, and what appeared to be blood. He thought, One could boil this and make a tasty soup. Koko had probably smelled the presence of the book and tracked it to its hiding place in the desk. Remarkable cat! Sniffing the book himself, he could detect no noticeable scent. He returned it to the desk and dressed for dinner.

Polly lived in a small house on the old MacGregor farm. The last of the MacGregors had died, the main farmhouse was for sale, and the intelligent goose that used to patrol the property was no longer around. For one dark moment as he parked the car Qwilleran envisioned curried goose as Polly's surprise, but when he approached the front door the aroma of curried shrimp assailed his nostrils and he half expected to hear raga music.

"Don't tell me! I can guess what's for dinner," he said.

Her greeting was unusually ardent. She bubbled with an excitement unlike her normal air of subdued happiness.

"Shall we have an Attitude Adjustment Hour before dinner?" she asked, blithely jingling ice cubes in glasses. She served him Squunk water with a twist and passed a plate of olive-and-cheese hors d'oeuvres. Then, raising her sherry glass she said, "Eat thy bread with joy and drink thy Squunk water with a merry heart."

"You're in a good mood tonight," he said. "Did the library board vote you a raise?"

"Guess again."

"They approved a new heating system for the library?"

Polly jumped up. Ordinarily she rose gracefully, but she jumped up saying, "Close your eyes," as she hurried to the bedroom. When she returned he heard a faint squeak, and he opened his eyes to see her holding a small basket in which lay a small white kitten with large brown ears, large brown feet, a dark smudge on his nose, and the indescribably blue eyes of a Siamese.

"Meet my little boy," she said proudly. "He came all the way from Lockmaster on the bus today, traveling by himself."

"Is this what Siamese look like when they're young?" Qwilleran asked in astonishment. He had adopted both Koko and Yum Yum after they were grown.

"Isn't he adorable?" She lifted him from the basket and nuzzled her face against his fur. "We love him to pieces! He's such a sweetheart! . . . Are you my little sweetheart? . . . Yes, he's my little sweetheart. Listen to him purr."

She placed the kitten carefully on the floor, and he lurched across the carpet like a windup toy, his skinny legs splayed at odd angles and his large brown feet flopping like a clown in oversize shoes. Polly explained, "He's still unsteady on his legs, and he doesn't quite know what to do with his feet. Of course, he's a little dismayed, being away from his mother and siblings . . . Aren't you, sweetums?"

Qwilleran had to admit he was an appealing little creature, but he found Polly's commentary cloying. He occasionally called Yum Yum his little sweetheart, but that was different. It was a term of endearment, not maudlin gush. "What's his name?" he asked.

"Bootsie, and he's going to grow up to be just like Koko."

Fat chance, Qwilleran thought, with a name like that! Koko bore the dignified cognomen of Kao K'o Kung, a thirteenth-century Chinese artist. He said, "You told me you didn't want a pet. You always said you were too busy and too often out of town."

"I know," she said, sweetly sheepish, "but the librarian in Lockmaster had a litter, and Bootsie was just too irresistible. Do you want to hold him? First I have to give him a kiss-kiss so that he knows he's loved."

Qwilleran accepted the small bundle gingerly. "He must weigh about three ounces. What's he stuffed with? Goose down?"

"He weighs exactly one pound and eight and a half ounces on my kitchen scale."

"Do you feed him with an eyedropper?"

"He gets a spoonful of nutritional catfood four times a day. It doesn't take much to fill up his little tum-tum."

Bootsie was quite content on Qwilleran's lap, his loud purr shaking his entire twenty-four and a half ounces. Occasionally he emitted a small squeak, closing his eyes in the effort.

"He needs oiling," Qwilleran said.

"That means he likes you. He wants you to be his godfather. Give him a kiss-kiss."

"No thanks. I have jealous cats at home." He was glad when Bootsie was returned to the bedroom and dinner was served.

It was curry again—and hot enough to send him catapulting out of his chair after the first forkful. "Wow!" he said.

"Hot?" Polly inquired.

"Like Hades! What happened?"

"I learned how to mix my own curry powder—fourteen spices, including four kinds of pepper. Would you like some ice water?"

Every few minutes Polly peeked into the bedroom to check the kitten. Asleep or awake? In or out of the basket? Happy or unhappy? Qwilleran could hardly believe that an intelligent, sophisticated, middle-aged woman with an executive position in a public library could be reduced overnight to a blithering fool.

For dessert she served a welcome dish of sherbet and suggested having coffee in the living room. "Would you like Bootsie to join us?" she asked coyly.

"No," he said firmly. "I have a serious matter to discuss with you."

"Really?" She said it with a distracted glance at the bedroom door, having heard a squeak, and he knew he would have to drop a bomb to galvanize her attention.

"It's my theory," he said, "that Iris Cobb's death was a case of murder."

Chapter 7

When Polly heard the word "murder," she was aghast. In Moose County homicide was traditionally considered the exclusive property of the cities Down Below. "What leads you to that conclusion, Qwill?"

"Observation, speculation, cerebration," he replied, smoothing his moustache slyly. "At the Old Stone Mill last night, you may remember, I asked if the Goodwinter farmhouse has the reputation of being haunted. I wasn't simply making conversation. Prior to her death Iris complained about noises in the walls—knocking, moaning, and even screaming. In her last letter to her son she was almost deranged by her fears, hinting that there were evil spirits in the house. Then, just before she died, she saw something outside the kitchen window that terrified her."

"How do you know?"

"She was talking to me on the phone at the time. Shortly after, I arrived and found her dead on the kitchen floor. Strangely, all the lights were turned off, inside and outside the house. A heart attack, the coroner said, but I saw the look of terror on her face, and I say it was not a heart attack pure and simple. She was frightened to death, purposely or accidentally, by something outside the window. It could be the same something that turned off the lights, either before or after she collapsed."

Polly gasped and forgot to look at the bedroom door. "Are you implying—a phantom? You've always scoffed at such things."

"I'm simply saying *I don't know*. Something is going on that I don't understand. Koko spends hours gazing out the very window where Iris saw the frightening vision."

"What is the view from that window?"

"After dark, nothing, unless cats can see things that we don't. In the daytime there's only the barnyard and the old barn beyond. The birds have gone south, it appears, and the squirrels are all up on Fugtree Road, raiding the oak trees. Yet something rivets Koko's attention. He also prowls the kitchen floor, sniffing and mumbling to himself."

"Have you heard any of the noises that disturbed Iris?"

"Not as yet. There's a light fixture that flashes on and off mysteriously, but that's the only spooky occurrence."

Polly said, "I've heard stories about Ephraim's ghost but considered them nonsense. This is a terrible development, Qwill! Why should it happen to that dear woman?"

"There's a possibility that her medication made her susceptible to certain influences in the house that would not disturb anyone else—or even Iris if her health had been normal."

"Should anything be done about it?"

"I don't see how we can act without more evidence," Qwilleran said. "Give me time. After all, it happened only three days ago."

Polly's brow was creased in puzzlement and concern. Not once had she mentioned Bootsie nor glanced in the direction of the bedroom door. With an agreeable feeling of satisfaction Qwilleran made excuses for leaving early.

Driving home to North Middle Hummock he did some serious thinking about Polly and the way she fussed over that kitten. He himself admired and respected his cats—and God knows he indulged them—but he was not sentimental, he told himself. Polly's fatuous prattle was entirely out of character for a sensible woman. Reviewing the course of their friendship he recalled that it was her intelligence that first attracted him. On certain subjects she was quite erudite. After getting off to a slow start, because of her inherent reserve, their relationship had blossomed. Then, with familiarity she became possessive and slightly officious and sometimes jealous. All of this he could understand, and he could handle it, but her gushing over the kitten was more than he could stomach. There would be no more relaxing country weekends at Polly's cottage with just the two of them—reading Shakespeare aloud and playing music— not while Bootsie diffused her attention. Bootsie! It was a vile name for a Siamese, Qwilleran insisted. Considering her passion for Shakespeare, why didn't she name him Puck?

The reading of Iris Cobb's will took place in the office of Hasselrich, Bennett and Barter on Thursday morning in the presence of Dennis Hough, Larry Lanspeak, Susan Exbridge, and Qwilleran, who attended reluctantly. The senior partner was noted for his affability and buoyant optimism. He was the kind of attorney, Qwilleran had once said, who made it a pleasure to be sued, or divorced, or found guilty—an elderly, balding man with quivering jowls and a slight stoop.

When all were assembled Hasselrich remarked, "I well remember the day Iris Cobb Hackpole came to me to draft her last will and testament. This was three months before her health started to decline. There was nothing morbid about the occasion. She was happy in the knowledge that her possessions would go to those she loved and respected, and to causes she embraced."

He opened cabinet doors behind his desk, rolled out a video screen and touched a remote control. There on the screen was Iris Cobb in her pink suede suit and rhinestone-studded eyeglasses. She was smiling. Her round face was glowing. A hush fell on the viewers.

From the speaker came the cheerful voice: "I, Iris Cobb Hackpole, a single woman of Pickax City in Moose County, being of sound mind and memory but mindful of the uncertainties of life, do hereby declare this instrument to be my last will and testament, hereby revoking any and all wills made by me at any time heretofore."

Swift looks passed between the listeners as she went on to bequeath her extensive financial holdings to her son and his family. To Susan Exbridge she left her share of the assets of Exbridge & Cobb. She wished the Historical Society to liquidate her antique collection, her car, and her personal belongings, the proceeds to benefit the museum. Excluded were only two items: She wished James Qwilleran to have the Pennsylvania German *Schrank*—for reasons he would understand—and her personal recipe book.

The image on the screen faded, and there was a moment of silence followed by appropriate exclamations and some murmured platitudes from Hasselrich.

Susan said to Qwilleran, "I'll make a deal. You give me the cookbook, and you can have Exbridge and Cobb." To Dennis she said, "Now you can move up here and take over the Fitch property."

"I like the idea," he said, and Qwilleran observed a meaningful stare lingering between them.

When a clerk appeared with a silver tray, Hasselrich himself poured coffee and passed the cups, pointing out proudly that they were his maternal grandmother's Wedgwood.

Larry said to Qwilleran, "I didn't know you were a cook."

"I know as much about cooking as I do about black holes in the universe," he replied, "but Iris had a sly sense of humor. The joke is that no one can read her handwriting. As for the *Schrank*, I'm glad she left me that and not the General Grant bed."

"How's everything at the farmhouse?"

"I'm learning to live with pink sheets and pink towels, but there is one problem. The closets and dressers are filled with Iris's clothing. With my shirts and pants and sweaters draped over chairs and doorknobs, I wake up at night and think I'm surrounded by spectres."

"Just move her things out of your way, Qwill," said Larry. "You'll find some empty cartons in the basement. Our donation committee will take it from there."

"Another thing, Larry. Either we have gremlins or we have faulty wiring in the hall light fixture. It should be investigated by an electrician."

"I'll alert Homer. He'll get a repairman out there right away."

Larry went to the attorney's desk and used the phone. Quick decisions and immediate action were his trademark.

Qwilleran had a second cup of coffee, congratulated the heir, and offered him a ride to the airport.

"Thanks, Qwill, but I've decided to stay over until Sunday," said Dennis. "The formal opening of Exbridge and Cobb was scheduled for Saturday, and Susan is going ahead as planned."

Susan said, "The invitations went into the mail last week, Qwill, and I know Iris wouldn't want us to cancel. She'll be with us in spirit, but I feel it's appropriate to have Dennis represent her in the flesh."

Uh-huh, Qwilleran thought.

"People may think the shop is going to limp along on one leg without Iris," she went on, speaking with animation, "but Dennis's presence will give the venture some stability, don't you think? It's terribly kind of him to offer to stay a few more days."

Uh-huh, Qwilleran thought. She was looking unusually happy; her dramatic gestures were more expansive than ever, and Dennis glanced at her too often.

Before leaving, Qwilleran asked Hasselrich if he proposed to notify the newspaper about the terms of the will.

"It has never been our policy to do so," said the attorney.

"In this case you should reconsider. The Hackpole money is news, and Iris was a V.I.P.," Qwilleran argued. "If you don't make an official statement, the Pickax grapevine will start distorting the facts."

"I'll have to cogitate about that," said Hasselrich.

Qwilleran left him cogitating and drove to the office of the *Moose County Something*, where he found the publisher in his richly decorated office.

"Arch, I never noticed this before," said Qwilleran, "but your walls are Dingleberry green."

"That's where I'll end up—at Dingleberry's—so I'm getting used to it a little at a time. What's on your mind? You look purposeful."

"The Cobb-Hackpole bequests have been announced. You ought to send Roger to the attorney's office to get the story."

"Who are the beneficiaries?"

"Her family, her business partner, the Historical Society, and—to a lesser extent—myself."

"You? What do you need? You own half the county already."

"She left me the seven-foot wardrobe that I gave her for a wedding present. Koko always enjoyed sitting on top of it."

"Let Koko sit on a stepladder. That's a Pennsylvania German *Schrank* and worth a small fortune," said Riker, who knew something about antiques. He touched the intercom button and barked, "Iris Cobb's will has been read. Qwill tipped us off. Get someone over to HB and B."

Qwilleran said, "She also left me a looseleaf notebook containing all her personal recipes, but you don't need to mention that in the story."

"I thought you were opposed to censorship," said Riker. "I see it as a provocative headline: MILLIONAIRE WIDOW BEQUEATHS COOKBOOK TO BILLIONAIRE BACHELOR. That has all kinds of interesting implications."

The intercom buzzer sounded, and a voice squawked, "Is Qwill there? Ask if he has any copy for us. We've used up his backlog."

"Did you hear that?" Riker asked. "Has the *Qwill Pen* run dry?"

"Straight from the Qwill Pen" was the name of the column that Qwilleran had agreed to write for the *Something*. "It's like this," he explained to Riker. "I planned some interviews, but Iris's death has kept me off the beat for a few days."

"That's okay. Just give us a quick think-piece for tomorrow," Riker said. "Remember Mrs. Fisheye."

Driving back to North Middle Hummock Qwilleran did his quick thinking. Both he and Riker remembered their high school English teacher who regularly assigned the class to write a thousand words on such subjects as the weather, or breakfast, or the color green. Fisheye was not her name, but it was her misfortune to have large, round, pale, watery eyes. As a student Qwilleran had done his share of groaning and protesting, but now he could write a thousand words on any subject at a moment's notice.

Surveying the landscape as he drove out on Ittibittiwassee

Road and through the Hummocks he decided on his topic: fences! Moose County was crisscrossed with picket fences, hand-split snake fences, barbed wire, four-bar corral, even root fences, each delivering its own message ranging from Welcome to Keep Out. In the fashionable Hummocks there were low stone walls by the mile as well as six-foot grapestake stockades around swimming pools. In the blighted town of Chipmunk there was a fence constructed of old bedsprings. Qwilleran was prepared—if those observations added up to fewer than a thousand words—to quote Robert Frost, allude to Cole Porter, and trace "fence" to its Latin root. He might even dedicate the column to Mrs. Fisheye.

As he drove past the Fugtree farm he noticed that their white fence needed a coat of paint, and he regretted that he had not adequately thanked the woman who had notified him about his headlights. He would like to buy her a paint job for the fence, but such largess might give the wrong impression. Perhaps, he decided, he should simply write a note of thanks.

Turning into Black Creek Lane he spotted two vehicles parked in the museum yard. One was a conservative dark blue four-door, about ten years old. The other was a van from Pickax Power Problems, Inc. The electrician was preparing to leave, and Homer Tibbitt was accepting his bill.

"Get the lights fixed?" Qwilleran called out to them.

"Nothin' wrong but loose lightbulbs," said the electrician. "If you get a lotta vibration it can shake the bulbs loose—make 'em flicker on and off—'specially them flame types. Screw 'em in tight—no problem."

"What could cause vibration?" Qwilleran asked.

"Who knows? Furnace, pump, appliances—any blame thing that's off-balance. Well, so long! Call me again when you gotta soft job like this."

Qwilleran frowned. He could imagine what Pickax Power Problems would charge for a run all the way out to North Middle Hummock. When he unlocked his door and the cats came to greet him, he said, "You heavyweights have got to stop stamping your feet!"

The Siamese were unusually alert and active for midafternoon, which was their scheduled naptime, but that was understandable. Koko as chief security officer had been keeping a wary eye on the electrician, and Yum Yum had been inspecting his shoelaces. In addition, Homer Tibbitt had accompanied the repairman, and the cats had never seen a human who walked like a robot. The chairman of maintenance, remarkably agile for his age, walked briskly with angular flailing movements of arms and legs.

Mr. Tibbitt had returned to the museum, and Qwilleran followed him to apologize. He found the chairman and an elderly brown-haired woman in the exhibit area.

"No need to apologize," said Tibbitt in his high-pitched voice. "It gives me an excuse to come out here and look things over. *She* drives me," he explained with a nod toward his companion. "They won't renew my license any more. That's the advantage of hooking up with a younger woman. Only trouble with Rhoda is her danged hearing aid. She won't get the blasted thing fixed. *Rhoda, this is Mr. Qwilleran.* This is Rhoda Finney. She taught English in my school when I was principal."

Qwilleran bowed over Ms. Finney's hand, and she beamed at him with the serenity of one who has not heard a word that has been said.

Tibbitt said, "Let's go into the office and have some coffee. *Rhoda, do you want some coffee?*"

"Sorry, I don't have any, dear," she said, rummaging in her handbag. "Would you like a throat lozenge?"

"Never mind." He waved her away and led Qwilleran into the bleak office. It was furnished with oak filing cabinets, scarred wooden tables, mismatched chairs, and shelves of reference books. One table was piled with dreary odds and ends under a sign specifying To Be Catalogued. Another table held an array of instant-beverage jars, paper cups, and plastic spoons.

"I'll do a little cleaning," said Ms. Finney, taking a feather duster from a hook and toddling from the room.

The old gentleman heated water in an electric kettle and measured out instant-coffee crystals for Qwilleran and coffee substitute for himself. "This insipid stuff is all Doctor Hal will let me drink since my last birthday," he explained, "but it's greatly improved with a few drops of brandy." He showed Qwilleran a silver hip flask engraved with his initials. "Leftover from Prohibition days," he said. "Comes in handy now and then . . . What did you think of the funeral? It was a decent send-off, I thought. Even old Dingleberry was impressed. Larry tells me you're living here till they find a manager. Have you noticed anything unusual?"

"Of what nature?" Qwilleran asked, grooming his moustache with a show of nonchalance.

"They say old Ephraim walks around once in a while. Never saw him myself because I've never been here overnight, but he has some kind of secret up his ghostly sleeve. Old Adam Dingleberry knows what it is, but he's not telling. I've twisted Adam's arm five different ways, but he won't budge, for love nor money."

"My cats have been acting strangely since we moved in," Qwilleran said. "I thought they might be searching for Iris Cobb. She invited them here to dinner a couple of times."

"No doubt they're seeing an invisible presence," said Tibbitt in all seriousness.

"Do you know anyone who has actually seen Ephraim's so-called ghost?"

"Senior Goodwinter told me something shortly before his accident. He said the old man came straight through the wall one night, carrying a rope. He was as silent as the grave. That was almost ninety years after Ephraim died, mind you! It gave Senior a suffocating feeling. Then the vision disappeared into the same wall he'd come from, and a few days later, Senior was dead."

"Which wall?" Qwilleran asked as his thoughts went to Iris Cobb and the potato masher. "Do you know which wall?"

"He didn't tell me that."

"Did any of the family ever see Ephraim looking in a window at night?"

"No one ever mentioned it, but the Goodwinters were inclined to be hush-hush about the whole matter. I was surprised when Senior confided in me. I'd been his teacher in the early grades, and so I guess he trusted me."

"I get the impression that people up here are strong believers in the spirits of the dead."

"Yes indeed! This is good ghost country—like Scotland, you know. We have a lot of Scots here. Didn't you tell me you're a Scot?"

"My mother was a Mackintosh," Qwilleran informed him with an air of pride, "and she never saw a ghost to my knowledge. Certainly she never talked about ghosts in my presence."

"You need sensitivity and an open mind, of course. Skeptics don't know what they're missing."

"Did you ever see an apparition?"

"I certainly did! Thirty-two of them! You've heard of the explosion at the Goodwinter Mine in 1904? Thirty-two miners blown to bits! Well . . . twenty years after that disaster I had a curious experience—twenty years to the day, May thirteenth. I'd been visiting a young lady who lived in the country. I lived in Pickax, a distance of six miles, and I was walking home. Not many folks in Moose County had automobiles in those days, and I didn't even have a bicycle. So I was walking home around midnight along North Pickax Road. It wasn't paved in those days. Do you know where that hill rises just north of the mine? It was only a slag heap then, and when I reached it I saw some shadows moving across the top of the heap. I stopped and stared into the darkness and realized they were men—plodding along with pickaxes and lunch buckets and with never a sound. Then they disappeared over the hill. I counted; there were thirty-two of them, and every one had a light on the front of his head. In my mind I can still see those bobbing lights as the column of men trudged along. There was no wind that night, but after they passed by, the leaves of the trees rustled and I felt a chill."

Qwilleran was respectfully quiet for a few moments before he said, "Did you say that was in 1924? Prohibition was in effect. Are you sure you hadn't been taking a nip of white lightning from that silver flask?"

"I'm not the only one who saw them," Homer protested. "And it was always on the anniversary of the explosion—May thirteenth."

"Are they still being seen?"

"Not very likely. Now that the road's paved and cars are whizzing by at seventy miles an hour, who could see anything as ephemeral as a ghost? But I'll tell you what! Next year, on the night of May thirteenth, you and I will go out to the Goodwinter Mine site, park the car, and wait for something to happen."

"I'll mark it on my calendar," Qwilleran said, "but don't forget to take your flask along."

At that moment Rhoda Finney entered the office with her feather duster. Seeing the coffee cups she said, "You naughty men! You didn't tell me you were having coffee!"

Homer glanced at Qwilleran and shrugged hopelessly. Hoisting himself out of his chair, he prepared to measure an instant beverage from the row of jars on the table. *"What kind?"* he shouted.

Ms. Finney looked at her watch. "Seventeen minutes after two, dear." She whisked a few items of office furniture with the duster before sitting down.

Qwilleran said, "This museum operation seems to be very well organized."

"Yes indeed," said Homer. "Larry runs a tight ship. We have twelve active committees and seventy-five volunteers. I ride herd on the maintenance staff. We have high school students doing the yard work, earning points for community service. We have twenty able-bodied volunteers doing the cleaning, if you count Rhoda with her blasted feather duster. We hire professionals—like Pickax Power Problems—to do repairs. For window washing the county sends us jail inmates."

"Do you ever find any loose shutters banging in the wind? Any loose shingles on the side of the house?"

"Nothing's been reported, and if it's not broken, we don't fix it."

"Did you know the plaster is cracked in the basement under the west wing?"

Homer dismissed the matter with an angular wave of the hand. "You mean the magpie nest? That's a repository for junk donated to the museum: broken furniture, rusty tools, moldy books, cracked crockery, stained slop jars and potties."

"The poppies were beautiful this year," Rhoda interrupted. "Too bad they don't have a longer blooming season."

"*I said potties—not poppies!*" Homer shouted in his reedy treble. "*Chamber pots! Thunder mugs! The things they put under beds!*"

Rhoda turned to Qwilleran and explained sweetly, "The garden club maintains our flower beds. Don't you think the rust and gold mums are lovely? We haven't had any frost yet."

"I give up!" said Homer, throwing up his bony hands. "She's a sweet woman, but she'll be the death of me!" With disjointed movements of arms and legs he stomped from the room.

Rhoda asked with a radiant smile, "Was he giving his lecture on old barns again?"

"No, he was giving his *lecture on ghosts*!" Qwilleran replied loudly.

"Oh . . . yes," she said as she hung the feather duster on a hook behind the door. "They have quite a few at the Fugtree farm, you know."

Qwilleran bowed out quickly, shouting that the phone was ringing in the west wing.

It was Roger MacGillivray, reporter for the *Moose County Something*, who was calling. "Qwill, I got the info on Iris Cobb's will," he said, "but there's one thing that isn't clear. What is this cookbook she left you?"

Qwilleran, who was adept at extemporaneous prevarication, said, "That is her personal collection of recipes that she wished to have published posthumously." He spoke with the deliberation of one who is authorized to make a statement for publication. "The Klingenschoen Fund will underwrite the printing costs, and proceeds will go to the Iris Cobb Memorial Scholarship. For home economics studies," he added as an afterthought.

"Great!" said Roger. "That wraps it up. Thanks a lot."

Qwilleran dashed off his column for Friday's paper and phoned it in to the copydesk. It was late, therefore, when he started thinking about dinner, but he found one of his favorite dishes in the freezer—lamb shank cooked with lentils—and he thawed a hearty portion in the microwave. It was a large piece of meat, and before sitting down to eat, he sliced off a generous chunk for the Siamese, dicing it and putting it on their plate under the telephone table. Yum Yum attacked it with enthusiasm, but Koko was virtually glued to the kitchen windowsill, staring at the darkness outside.

"We've had enough of this ridiculous performance, young man!" Qwilleran said. "We'll find out what's bugging you!" With flashlight in hand he stormed out of the building, beaming the light around the exterior, in shadowy places not illuminated by the yardlights. He saw nothing unusual, nothing moving. A slight tremor on his upper lip made him wonder, What are cats seeing when they're gazing into space? Koko had left the windowsill, and Qwilleran was ready to give up the search when the flashlight beam picked out some depressions in the ground under the kitchen window. They looked like footprints. That rules out disembodied spirits, he told himself. It could have been some kid from Chipmunk . . . a juvenile Peeping Tom . . . a window washer from the county jail.

He hurried indoors and looked up Homer Tibbitt's phone number. He wanted to know when the windows had last been washed.

The maintenance chairman lived at October House, a residence for seniors, and the operator said, "I'm sorry, but I can't ring Mr. Tibbitt at this hour. He retires at seven-thirty. Do you wish to leave a message?"

"Just tell him Jim Qwilleran called. I'll try again tomorrow morning."

Both cats seemed to have enjoyed their portion of lamb; they were washing their masks, whiskers, and ears with satisfaction. Qwilleran popped his own dinner plate into the microwave for another shot of heat and immediately pulled it out again, staring at it in disbelief. All that remained on his plate was a mess of lentils and a shank bone, gnawed clean.

Chapter 8

As Qwilleran prepared breakfast for the Siamese on Friday morning his mind was still on the footprints outside the kitchen window. If the window washers had been there since last weekend, the footprints could be theirs. If not, the telltale depressions had doubtlessly been left in the soft soil Sunday night, when Iris Cobb was making her last phone call. It had rained earlier that evening; since then the weather had been dry.

He placed the plate of tenderloin tips on the floor under the telephone table and once again called October House.

"Mr. Tibbitt," said the operator, "is not available. Would you care to leave a message?"

"This is Jim Qwilleran."

"Oh, yes, Mr. Qwilleran. You called last night."

"Will Mr. Tibbitt return soon?"

"I'm afraid not. He's gone to Lockmaster."

"Is he all right?" Qwilleran asked hastily. Lockmaster, in the county to the south, had a medical center noted for its geriatric department.

"Oh, yes, he's fine. Ms. Finney drove him down there to see the autumn color in horse country. They say it's gorgeous."

"I see," Qwilleran mused. "When do you expect them to return?"

"Not until Sunday afternoon. They're visiting friends down there. Shall I have him call you?"

"No. Don't bother. I'll catch up with him at the museum."

Qwilleran now faced an uncomfortable task—packing Iris Cobb's personal belongings in cartons from the basement. He had done it once before, after his mother died, and it was a heart-wrenching chore. He had done it often when he worked in a nursing home during college days, and in that situation it was a routine job. But it was an embarrassingly intimate rite to perform for a woman who had been his former landlady and housekeeper. He felt like a voyeur as he gathered her pink pantsuits, pink robes, pink underwear, and pink nightgowns from closets and dresser drawers. Most painful of all was the invasion of the top drawers with their jumble of smeared lipsticks, broken earrings, used emery boards, pill bottles, a hair brush with stray hairs clinging to the bristles, and the magnifying glass with silver handle that he had given her on her last birthday.

When the cartons were packed, he labeled them and carried them to the museum office. Koko wanted to accompany him.

"Sorry," Qwilleran said. "The sign stipulates no smoking, no food or beverages, and no bare feet."

When the chore was completed, however, Koko was still bouncing up and down at the door to the museum, trying to turn the doorknob. He had been allowed in the exhibit area once before when Mrs. Cobb was alive, and on that occasion he had been attracted to some model ships.

Qwilleran finally acquiesced. "All right, but you'll be disappointed," he told the cat. "The ship exhibit has been dismantled."

As soon as the connecting door was opened, Koko bounded into the museum, ignoring the pioneer rooms and heading for the east wing, which housed the theme exhibits, study collections, and the museum office. He scampered directly into the office, looked behind the door, and started jumping to reach Ms. Finney's feather duster.

"You devil!" Qwilleran said. "How did you know it was there?" He removed the cat and closed the office door, then watched him closely as he explored.

Koko bypassed the room that had formerly featured model

ships; the door was closed, and a sign announced a new exhibit opening soon. He showed no interest in historic documents or the distinguished collection of early lighting devices. What fascinated this remarkable cat was an exhibit that everyone considered the most boring in the museum: textiles. It consisted of bed linens and table linens yellow with age; quilts faded from laundering with lye soap; handwoven blankets perforated with moth holes; hand-hooked rugs dingy with wear; dreary dishtowels made from flour sacks; a stained mattress stuffed with straw; curtains dyed with berries and onion skins. Yet, the identification cards stated proudly the names of the early settlers who had woven, quilted, hooked, dyed, and stuffed these artifacts. Koko especially liked a bed pillow made from a flour sack and filled, according to the ID card, with chicken feathers from the Inchpot Centennial Farm. He sniffed it intently.

"Chicken feathers! I might have known!" said Qwilleran. "Let's go home." He picked up the cat, who squirmed from his grasp and rushed back to the Inchpot pillow. Curiously, a similar pillow from the Trevelyan Farm, dating somewhat earlier in Moose County history, was totally overlooked. Qwilleran got a stranglehold on Koko and wrestled him back to the apartment.

They were met by Yum Yum, who touched noses with Koko and proceeded to groom the historical odors out of his fur. This business finished, Koko undertook a new mission: staring at the freezer compartment at the top of the refrigerator.

"There's nothing in that freezer for cats," Qwilleran advised him. "You're barking up the wrong tree. You can have some meatloaf from the big freezer, but not until dinnertime."

Koko persisted, prancing on his hind legs. To prove his point, Qwilleran opened the freezer door, exposing stacks of cinnamon doughnuts, blueberry muffins, chocolate brownies, banana nutbread, and other confections. It was then that an idea flashed into his mind: A package of Mrs. Cobb's pecan rolls would make an ideal thank-you for the family at the Fugtree farm, a gift beyond price and with a touch of sentiment. Later he might present a cherry pie to the Boswells, if he could do so without getting involved in neighborly chitchat. Mrs. Boswell was all right, but her husband's voice made Qwilleran's blood curdle, and Baby was a little pest.

It was early afternoon, a suitable time to pay an impromptu visit. He thawed the pecan rolls and drove to the Fugtree farm. Although it was within walking distance, he reasoned that dropping in on foot would suggest back-fence familiarity, and even the obligatory sharing of refreshments. Arriving by car appeared more businesslike, and he could make a quick getaway. He decided to drive.

At close hand the neglected farmhouse was even more dilapidated than it appeared from the highway. Obviously the front door had not been used for years; even the steps were sprouting weeds. He drove around to the side door, and as he did so a young woman came walking from the nearest barn, wearing grubby coveralls and a feed cap. She had a designer figure, but they were not designer coveralls; rather, they had the air of the Farmers' Discount Store in North Kennebeck.

"You're Mr. Qwilleran," she greeted him. "I recognized you from your picture in the paper. Excuse the way I look; I've been mucking the barn."

Her manner and her speech seemed incompatible with mucking barns, and Qwilleran's curiosity was kindled. Stepping out of the car he handed her the package of pecan rolls. "I came to thank you for telling me about my car lights Tuesday night. This is something from Mrs. Cobb's freezer. I thought your family might enjoy it."

"Thank you, I don't have a family," she said, "but I love Iris's baking. I'm sorry we've lost her. She was such a neat lady."

Qwilleran was puzzled. "When you first called about Iris . . . you mentioned . . . that your youngsters were ill," he said hesitantly.

Her face went blank for a moment and then brightened. "I guess I said I was taking care of my sick kids. I meant . . . baby goats."

"Pardon my ignorance. I'm a recent refugee from Down Below and I haven't mastered the vocabulary up here."

"Please sit down," she said, waving toward some rusty garden chairs. "Would you like a glass of wine?"

"Thanks, Ms. Waffle, but alcohol isn't on my list of vices."

"Kristi," she said. "Call me Kristi, spelled K-r-i-s-t-i. Then how about some fresh lemonade made with honey from local bees?"

"Now you're speaking my language."

He sat down carefully in one of the infirm garden chairs and surveyed the farmyard. It was a scene of unfinished chores, uncut grass, unpainted barns, unmended fences. What was she doing here alone? he wondered. She was young. About thirty, he guessed. But serious in her mien. She was cordial, but only her lips smiled. Her eyes were heavy with sorrow, or regret, or worry. An interesting face!

Along with the lemonade came crackers and a chunk of soft white cheese. "Goat cheese," she explained. "I make it myself. Are you going to be staying at the museum?"

"Only until they find a replacement for Mrs. Cobb." Trying not to stare at the neglected grass and shabby house, he said, "How long have you had this place?"

"Ever since my mother died, a couple of years ago. I grew up here, but I've been away for ten years. When I inherited the house, I came back to see if I could make a living with goats. I'm the last of the Fugtrees."

"But your name is Waffle."

"That was my married name. After my divorce I decided to keep it."

Qwilleran thought, Anything is better than Fugtree.

"Anything is better than Fugtree," she said as if reading his mind.

"I'm not familiar with your family history, although I understand Captain Fugtree was a war hero."

Kristi sighed ruefully. "My earlier ancestors made a lot of money in lumbering, and they built this house, but the captain was more interested in being a war hero, which doesn't pay the bills. When my parents inherited the house, they struggled to keep it up, and now that they're gone, I'm trying to make it go. People tell me I should sell the land to a developer for condominiums, like the ones in Indian Village, but it would be a crime to tear down this fabulous house. At least, I want to give farming a try," she said, smiling sadly.

"Why goats?"

"For several reasons." She brightened perceptibly. "They're really sweet animals and not expensive to feed, and there's a growing market for goat products. Did you know that? I raise dairy goats now, but someday I'd like to have some Angoras and spin their hair and weave it. I studied weaving in art school."

"This sounds like material for the 'Qwill Pen' column," said Qwilleran. "May I make an appointment with you and the goats?"

"That would be neat, Mr. Qwilleran!"

"Please call me Qwill," he said. He was feeling comfortable and somewhat captivated. The lemonade was the best he had ever tasted, and the goat cheese was delectable. Kristi's soft, sad eyes were mesmerizing. He had no desire to leave. Looking up at the house, he said, "This is a unique example of nineteenth-century architecture. What was the reason for the tower? Was it simply a conceit?"

"I don't know exactly. My ancestors were gentlemen farmers, and my mother thought they used the tower as a lookout—to spy on the field hands and see if they were loafing."

"And what do you use it for?"

"I go up there to meditate. That's how I knew you'd left your car lights on."

"What's up in the tower?"

"Mostly flies. Flies love towers. Spraying doesn't do much good. They're always buzzing and sunning and multiplying. Would you like to see the house?"

"Very much so."

"I should warn you. It's a mess. My mother was an absolutely mad collector. She went to auctions and bought all kinds of junk. It's a disease, you know, bidding at auctions."

"I had an acute attack of auctionitis—once," said Qwilleran, "and I can see how the germ could get into anyone's blood and cause a chronic condition for which there is no cure."

They entered the house through the side door, picking their

way among shopping bags stuffed with clothing, shoes, hats, dolls and umbrellas; rusty tricycles and a manual lawnmower; open cartons loaded with dented pots and pans, chipped platters, bar trays and old milk bottles; wooden buckets and galvanized pails; an oak icebox and a wicker fern stand; stacks of magazines and bushels of books. Having been too long in attics and basements, these relics were giving their musty scent to the entire house.

Kristi said with a rueful smile, "I've been trying to thin out her accumulation—selling some and giving some away, but there's tons of it!"

The dining room alone harbored two large tables, twenty chairs, three china cabinets, and enough china to start a restaurant.

"See what I mean?" she said. "And this is only the beginning. The bedrooms are worse. Try not to look at the clutter. Look at the carved woodwork and the sculptured ceilings and the stained glass windows, and the staircase."

From the foyer a wide staircase angled up to the second floor. The newel post and handrail were massive, and the balusters were set extravagantly close together, harking back to the days when lumber was king. It was all black walnut, Kristi said.

"But this is not the original staircase," she pointed out. "The first one spiraled up into the tower and was very graceful. My great-grandfather replaced it and sealed off the tower."

"Too many flies?" Qwilleran asked. "Or too hard to heat?"

"That's a long story," she said, turning away. "Do you feel like climbing four flights?"

After they reached the third floor she unbolted a door leading to the tower. Here the stairs were plain and utilitarian, but they ended in a small enchanting room no bigger than a walk-in closet, with windows on four sides and windowseats cushioned in threadbare velvet. On a shabby wicker table there were binoculars, a guttered candle, and a book on yoga in a brown paper cover. Iridescent bluebottle flies were sunning on the south window.

Qwilleran picked up the glasses and looked to the north, where the big lake shimmered just below the horizon. To the west a church spire rose out of a forest of evergreens. To the east was the Goodwinter property with Boswell's van in the barnyard, a blue pickup in the museum drive, and half a dozen energetic young persons raking leaves, bagging them, and loading them in the truck.

Qwilleran asked, "What is the purpose of the diagonal line of trees cutting across the fields?"

"That's Black Creek," Kristi said. "You can't see the stream, but trees thrive on its banks, and there are some very old willows hanging over the water."

"This house," Qwilleran said as they went back down the four flights of stairs, "should be registered as a historic place."

"I know." Kristi's eyes filled with melancholy. "But there's too much red tape, and I wouldn't have time to do research and fill out the forms. And then the house and grounds would have to be fixed up, and that's more than I could afford to do."

Qwilleran patted his moustache smugly, thinking, This might be a project for the Klingenschoen Fund to underwrite. The Fugtrees were pioneers who helped develop the county, and their house is an architectural showplace worthy of preservation. Eventually it might be purchased by the Historical Society and opened to the public as a museum. He could visualize Fugtree Road becoming a "museum park" with the Goodwinter farmhouse demonstrating the life of the early settlers and the Fugtree mansion showing Moose County during its boom years. Even the antique presses in the barn had possibilities as a "Museum of the Printed Word." Qwilleran liked the name. One or two good restaurants might open in the vicinity, and the ghost town of North Middle Hummock would rise again, with the inevitable condominiums on the other side of Black Creek. The fact that Kristi was an attractive young woman had nothing to do with his enthusiastic speculations, he told himself.

"Would you like another glass of lemonade?" she asked to break the silence that fell after her last statement.

"No thank you," he said, snapping out of his reverie, "but how about two o'clock tomorrow afternoon for the interview?"

As she walked with him toward his car, he mentioned casually, "The Klingenschoen Fund might help you with the historic registration. Why don't you write a letter to the Fund in care of Hasselrich, Bennett and Barter? And see what happens."

Her eyes lost their melancholy for the first time. "Do you really think I'd stand a chance?"

"No harm in trying. All you have to lose is a postage stamp."

"Oh, Mr. Qwilleran—Qwill—I'd hug you if I hadn't been mucking the barn!"

"I'll take a raincheck," he said.

Arriving back at the farmhouse Qwilleran ignored the Siamese and looked up "goat" in the unabridged dictionary. Then he called Roger MacGillivray at the newspaper office. "Glad I caught you, Roger. I have a favor to ask. Are you free for dinner tonight?"

"Uh . . . yeah . . . but it would have to be early. I promised to be home by seven o'clock to baby-sit."

"I'll buy your dinner at Tipsy's if you'll stop at the Pickax library and bring me some books on goats."

There was a pause. "Spell that, Qwill."

"G-o-a-t-s. I'll meet you at Tipsy's at five-thirty."

"Let's get this straight, Qwill. You want books on *goats*?"

"That's right! Horned ruminant quadrupeds. And Roger . . ."

"Yes?"

"You don't need to let anyone know the books are for me."

CHAPTER 9

Tipsy's was a popular restaurant in North Kennebeck that had started in a small log cabin in the 1930s and now occupied a large log cabin, where serious eaters converged for serious steaks without such frivolities as parsley sprigs and herbed butter. Potatoes were peeled and Frenched in the kitchen without benefit of sodium acid pyrophosphate. The only vegetable choice was boiled carrots. The only salad was cole slaw. And there was a waiting line for tables every night.

Qwilleran and his guest, being pressed for time, used their press credentials to get a table, and they were seated directly below the large portrait of a black-and-white cat for whom the restaurant was named.

Roger slapped a stack of books on the table: *Raising Goats for Fun and Profit, Debunking Goat Myths,* and *How to Start a Goat Club.* "Is this what you want?" he asked incredulously.

"I'm interviewing a goat farmer," Qwilleran said, "and I don't want to be totally ignorant about which sex gives milk and which sex has B.O."

"Find out if it's true they eat tin cans," Roger said. "Who's the farmer? Do I know him?"

"Who said anything about *him*? It's a young woman at the Fugtree farm next to the Goodwinter museum. Her name is Kristi, spelled with a *K* and an *I*."

"Sure, I know her." Having grown up in Moose County and having taught school for nine years before switching to journalism, Roger's acquaintance was vast. "We were in high school together. She married a guy from Purple Point with more looks than brains, and they moved away—somewhere Down Below."

"She's moved back again, and she's divorced," Qwilleran said.

"I'm not surprised. He was a jerk, and Kristi was a talented girl. Flighty, though. She hopped from one great idea to another. I remember when she wanted to make macramé baskets for the basketball hoops."

"She seems to have her feet on the ground now."

"What is she like? She had big serious eyes and wore weird clothes, but then all the art students wore weird clothes."

"Now she wears dirty coveralls and muddy boots, and her hair is tied back under a feed cap. She still has big serious eyes. I think she has worries beyond her ability to cope."

The steaks were served promptly, and the two men applied themselves with concentration. The beef at Tipsy's required diligent chewing, but the flavor was world-class. It was homegrown, like the potatoes and carrots and cabbage. There was something in Moose County soil that produced flavorful root vegetables and superior browse for cattle.

Qwilleran said, "I suppose you know I'm living at the Goodwinter farmhouse until they find a new manager."

"Be prepared to dig in for the winter," Roger advised him. "They'll have a tough time replacing Iris Cobb."

"Did you know any of the Goodwinters when they were living there?"

"Only the three kids. We were all in school at the same time. Junior is the only one left around here. His sister is on a ranch in Montana, and his brother is somewhere out West."

"Did they ever say anything about the place being haunted?"

"No, their parents wouldn't let them mention the ghost rumor ... or their grandfather's murder ... or their great-grandfather's 'sudden death,' as it was called. The whole family acted as if nothing unusual had ever happened. Why do you ask? Are you seeing spooks?"

Qwilleran touched his moustache gingerly, undecided how much he should confide in Roger. He said, "You know I don't buy the idea of ghosts and demons and poltergeists, but ... Iris was hearing unearthly noises in the Goodwinter house before she died."

"Like what?"

"Like knocking and moaning and screaming."

"No kidding!"

"And Koko's behavior has been abnormal since we moved in. He's always talking to himself and staring into space."

"He's talking to ghosts," Roger said with a straight face.

Qwilleran could never be sure whether the young reporter was serious or not. He said, "Iris had a theory that a house exudes good or evil, depending on its previous occupants."

"My mother-in-law preaches the same thing," said Roger.

"How is Mildred, by the way? I haven't seen her lately."

"She's up to her eyebrows in good causes, as usual. Still trying to lose weight. Still carrying the torch for that husband of hers. I think she should get a lawyer and untie the knot."

"And how's Sharon and ... the baby?"

"Sharon's gone back to teaching. And that kid! I never knew a baby could be so much fun! ... Well, I can't stay for dessert. I've got to get home so Sharon can go to her club meeting. Thanks, Qwill. Best meal I've had in a month!"

Qwilleran remained and ordered Tipsy's old-fashioned bread pudding with a pitcher of thick cream for pouring, followed by two cups of coffee powerful enough to exorcise demons and domesticate poltergeists. Then he drove back to North Middle Hummock to cram for his interview with the goatherd.

After skimming through chapters on breeding, feeding, milking, de-horning, castrating, hoof trimming, barn cleaning and manure management, he made a decision: It would be better to walk the plank than to raise goats. Furthermore, there was the danger of such diseases as coccidiosis, demodectic mange, bloat, and foot rot, not to mention birth defects such as sprung pasterns, pendulous udder, blind teat, leaking orifice, and hermaphroditism. It was no wonder the goat-girl looked worried.

After this briefing he knew, however, what questions to ask, and he felt a growing admiration for Kristi and her choice of career. Perhaps, as Roger said, she was flighty in high school, but who isn't at that age? He was looking forward to the interview. When Polly Duncan called to ask if he planned to attend the reception at Exbridge & Cobb, Qwilleran was glad he had an honest excuse. He said, "I'm interviewing a farmer at two o'clock."

Kristi greeted him on Saturday afternoon in white coveralls. She had been assisting at a kidding, she said. "Buttercup had trouble, and I had to help. Geranium is ready, too, and I have to check her every half hour. You can hear her bleating, poor thing."

"Do you name all your goats?"

"Of course. They all have their own personalities."

As they walked toward the goat barns Qwilleran asked how many kids Buttercup had produced.

"Two. I'm building up my own herd instead of buying animals. It takes time, but it costs less."

"How much does a kid weigh at birth?"

"About six pounds. For a while I'll feed them from a bottle three to five times a day."

Qwilleran said, "There's one gnawing question on my mind. How or why did you get involved with goats?"

Kristi said gravely, "Well, I met a goat named Petunia, and it was love at first sight, so I took a correspondence course and then got a job at a goat farm. We were living in New England then."

"What was your husband doing all this time?"

"Not much of anything. That was the problem," she said with a bitter grimace.

They were approaching an area of small barns, sheds and wire-fenced yards in which were small shade trees with protected trunks. A barncat was squirming to get under the fence. In the nearest yard a dozen goats of different colors were nuzzling each other's heads, lounging on the ground, or standing motionless with passive expressions. They turned sad, gentle eyes to the two visitors, and Qwilleran glanced quickly at Kristi's eyes, which were also sad and gentle.

"I like that big black one with a striped face," he said. "What kind is he?"

"She," Kristi reminded him. "These are all does. That one is a Nubian, and I call her Black Tulip. Notice her Roman nose and elegantly long ears. She's from very good stock. The white one is Gardenia. She's a Saanen. I really love her; she's so feminine. The fawn-colored one with two stripes on the face is Honeysuckle."

"What's that structure in the middle of the yard?"

"A feeder. They get nutritional feed, but they also graze in the pasture. The farmer who leases the Fugtree acreage manages my pastureland. Students come in after school to clean the milking parlor and the feeders and things like that. And then I have a friend who comes out from Pickax on weekends to help."

There was a commotion in the farthest field. Two goats were butting heads, and a third was butting a barrel. "They're bucks," Kristi explained. "We keep them away from the milking area because of the odor."

"Then 'smelling like a billy goat' is not just a figure of speech?"

Kristi was forced to agree. "Would you like to pet the does?"

she asked. "They like attention. Don't make any sudden moves. Let them smell your hand first."

The does came to the fence and rubbed against the wire, then turned drowsy eyes toward Qwilleran, purring in a gentle moan, but their coats felt rough to a hand accustomed to stroking cats.

Next Kristi showed him the milking parlor. "I have the milk commercially pasteurized," she explained. "Then it's sold to people who are allergic to cow's milk or find it hard to digest. Would you like a cup of tea and some cheese?"

They went into the house and sat at the table in the kitchen, the only room in the house that appeared habitable. Even so, the table was cluttered with collectibles, including a large leather-bound family bible. Kristi said her mother had bought it at an auction, and the museum might like to have it.

Qwilleran said, "You didn't tell me why your great-grandfather rebuilt the staircase."

"There was scandal involved."

"All the better!"

"You won't put this in your column, will you?"

"Not if you object."

"Well," she began, "it happened early in this century. My great-grandfather had a beautiful daughter named Emmaline, and she fell in love with one of the Goodwinter boys, Ephraim's second son. His name was Samson. But her father disapproved, and Emmaline was forbidden to see her lover. Being a spunky girl she used to climb the spiral staircase to the tower and flash a light, which could be seen from the Goodwinter house, and Samson would meet her on the bank of the Black Creek under the willows. Then tragedy struck! Samson was thrown from his horse and killed. A few months later, Emmaline gave birth to a child, a horrible disgrace in those days. Her family despised her, and her friends deserted her. Then, one night during a thunderstorm, she climbed the spiral staircase and threw herself from the tower."

"A tragic story," Qwilleran said. "Is that why her father remodeled the stairs?"

"Yes, he ripped out the lovely spiral staircase and substituted the angular one we have now. When I was growing up, the door to the tower was always locked."

"How do you know the spiral staircase was lovely. Do you have a photograph?"

"No . . . I just know," she answered mysteriously.

"What happened to Emmaline's child?"

"Captain Fugtree brought him up as his own son. He was my father."

"Then Emmaline was your grandmother!"

"Oh, she was so beautiful, Qwill! I wish I had her looks."

"I'd like to see a picture of her."

"Her photos were all destroyed after she killed herself. Her family pretended she had never existed."

"Then how do you know she was beautiful?"

Kristi cast her sad eyes down and was slow in answering. When she looked up, her face was radiant. "I don't know whether I should tell you this . . . I see her whenever there's a thunderstorm." She waited to see Qwilleran's reaction, and when he looked sympathetic she went on. "She walks upstairs in a flowing white robe, very slowly, up into the tower—and then disappears . . . She walks up the spiral staircase that's not there!"

Qwilleran stared at the granddaughter of the phantom Emmaline and searched for the right thing to say. She had paid him a compliment by confiding this personal secret, and he had no desire to spoil her story by asking hard-nosed questions. He was saved by the telephone bell.

Kristi reached for the kitchen phone. "Hello?" Then she turned pale, staring straight ahead as if paralyzed. After listening for a few moments, she hung up without another word.

"Trouble?" Qwilleran asked.

She gulped and said, "My ex-husband. He's back in town."

He sensed from her distracted air that there would be no more interview, no more tea. "Well," he said, standing up, "perhaps I should leave now. It's been an instructive afternoon. Thank you for your cooperation and the refreshments. I may call you again to check on details. And let me know if there's anything I can do for you."

She nodded and moved toward the refrigerator like a sleepwalker. "Here's some cheese to take home," she said in a trembling voice. "And don't forget to take the bible for the museum."

As Qwilleran drove the short distance to the Goodwinter place he had more than goats on his mind. He wondered about the Emmaline story. Kristi was quite emotional about her grandmother; perhaps she only imagined that she saw her walking upstairs in flowing white robes. He would like to be there during the next thunderstorm . . . But more serious at the moment was the phone call and Kristi's terrified reaction. He hesitated to intrude in her personal affairs, but he was definitely concerned. She lived there alone. She could be in danger.

As he was about to turn into Black Creek Lane he heard a truck approaching from the west, and he looked back in time to see a pickup turning into the Fugtree drive. As soon as he arrived at the museum he dropped the cheese and the bible on the dining table and immediately called Kristi's number. To his relief she answered in a normal voice.

"This is Qwill," he said. "I forgot to ask how much milk a goat can produce in a day."

"Black Tulip is my best doe, and she gives three thousand pounds a year. We always figure annual weight, not volume per day." She was brief and businesslike in her answer. "And you can say that she was a Grand Champion at the county fair."

"I see. Well, thank you. Is everything all right over there?"

"Everything's okay."

"That phone call just before I left seemed to upset you, and I was concerned."

"That's kind of you, Qwill, but my friend is here from Pickax, and everything's under control."

"Good! Have a nice evening," said Qwilleran.

Was the phone message really from her ex-husband? he wondered. And who was this "friend" who suddenly appeared and made everything right? He turned back to the table where he had dropped Kristi's two donations. Yum Yum was eating one of them, and Koko was sitting on the other.

Chapter 10

Qwilleran had a reason for inviting Roger's mother-in-law to dinner. He wanted to know more about Kristi Fugtree Waffle—not to flesh out his goat interview but to satisfy his curiosity—and Mildred Hanstable was the one to ask. A lifelong resident of Moose County, she had taught school for almost thirty years, and she knew two generations of students as well as their parents and grandparents, the past and present members of the school board, the county commissioners—in short, everyone.

When Qwilleran phoned her in Mooseville she squealed with her usual exuberance, "Qwill! So good to hear from you! Roger tells me you're house-sitting at the museum. That was such a shock—losing Iris! She always looked so healthy, didn't she? Perhaps she was a little overweight, but . . . oh, Lord! so am I! I'm going on a diet right away."

"Start your diet tomorrow," he said. "Are you free to have dinner tonight?"

"I'm always free to have dinner. That's my problem."

"I'll pick you up at six-thirty, and we'll go to the Northern Lights Hotel."

Qwilleran thawed some lobster meat for the Siamese, wondering if the waterfront hotel in Mooseville would offer anything half as good. Then he showered and dressed in something he considered commendable for the occasion. When dating Polly Duncan, who was not attuned to fashion, he wore what was readily available, and clean. Mildred, on the other hand, taught art as well as home ec, and she had an eye for color, design, and coordination. For Mildred he tried harder. For Mildred he wore a camel's-hair cardigan over a white open-neck shirt and tan pants, an ensemble that enhanced the suntan he had acquired during recent months of biking. Admiring himself in Mrs. Cobb's full-length mirror, a nicety that was lacking in his Pickax apartment, he noted that the shades of tan flattered his graying hair and luxuriant pepper-and-salt moustache.

In a mood of self-congratulation he drove from the rolling hills and cultivated fields of the Hummocks to the wild, wooded lakeshore, experiencing once again the miraculous change in atmosphere near the lake. It was not merely the aroma of a hundred miles of water and a fleet of fishing boats; it was an indescribable element that elevated one's spirit and made Mooseville a vacation paradise.

Mildred greeted him with a platonic hug. "You're looking wonderful! And I love your tan and white combination!" She was licensed to hug platonically, being not only Roger's mother-in-law but Qwilleran's former neighbor and the food writer for the *Moose County Something* and the loyal wife of an absentee husband.

Qwilleran returned the compliment, admiring whatever it was she was wearing. "Did you design it, Mildred?"

"Yes, it's intended to be a flattering cover-up for a fat lady."

"Nonsense! You are a handsome mature woman with a mature figure," he said with a declamatory flourish.

"I always love your choice of words, Qwill."

As they drove toward downtown Mooseville there were signs that the vacation season was coming to a close. They encountered less tourist traffic, fewer recreation vehicles, and almost no boats on trailers. Summer cottages were boarded up for the winter. There were not many fishing boats bobbing alongside the municipal piers that bordered Main Street, and the seagulls were screeching their last hurrah of the season.

"It's kind of sad," Mildred observed, "but it's pleasant, too. October belongs to us and not to those loud, swaggering tourists from Down Below. Fortunately they throw their money around and keep our economy going. I just wish they had better manners."

The Northern Lights Hotel was a barracks-like building with three floors of plain windows in dreary rows, but it was a historic landmark that had served the community in the nineteenth century when sailors and loggers—likewise lacking in manners—patronized the free-lunch saloon and rented a room for two bits.

As Qwilleran and his guest seated themselves in the dining room at a window table overlooking the docks, Mildred said, "A hundred years ago people looked out this very same window and saw three-masted schooners taking on passengers in bustles and top hats, and new-fangled coal steamers taking on cargoes of lumber and ore." She glanced at the menu. "And a hundred years ago this hotel served slumgullion to deckhands and prospectors, instead of broiled whitefish and petite salads to dieters. What are you having, Qwill? You never have to worry about calories."

"Since the cats are having lobster tonight, I think I'm entitled to French onion soup, froglegs, Caesar salad, and pumpkin pecan pie."

"How do the cats like their new environment?" she asked.

"They've okayed the blue velvet wing chair, the Pennsylvania German *Schrank*, and the kitchen windowsill. About the General Grant bed, when polled they voted 'undecided.' Gastronomically they're in seventh cat heaven, chomping their way through Iris's twenty-four-cubic-foot freezer."

"I read about Iris's will in yesterday's paper. Did she really want to have her recipes published? Or did you invent that? To me it sounded suspiciously like a Qwilleranism."

"If you read it in the *Something*, it's true," he said.

"Well, when her cookbook is published, I want to buy the first copy."

"I was hoping you'd consent to be the editor, Mildred. The recipes will need editing and testing, I imagine. Iris was one of those casual cooks—a fistful of this, a slug of that. I'll volunteer to be your official taster."

"I'd be honored!" said Mildred.

"Let me warn you: her handwriting looks like Egyptian hieroglyphics."

"After correcting school papers for thirty years, Qwill, I can read anything."

He wanted to quiz her about Kristi but thought it prudent to defer the subject until the dessert course. Whenever he invited Mildred to dinner, it seemed, his motive was to pry information from her incredible memory bank, although he tried to be subtle about it. So he asked her about the new exhibit at the museum, soon to be unveiled. She was chairman of the exhibit committee.

"It was finished three weeks ago," she said, "but we postponed the opening to coincide with the autumn color season—sort of a double feature, you know. The show is all about disasters in Moose County history. The public likes disasters. I'm sure you know that. Didn't the circulation of the *Daily Fluxion* always go up after a major plane crash or earthquake?"

"How do you celebrate a disaster in a small room in a museum?" he asked.

"It takes a certain amount of ingenuity, if I say so myself. We're covering the walls with photo blowups, and I must tell you about the violent controversy that arose. A member of our committee, Fran Brodie, for your information, found a questionable photo in the museum files with no information as to origin or donor, only a date scribbled on the back: October 30, 1904. Does that ring a bell?"

"Isn't that when Ephraim Goodwinter's body was found?"

"A date that will live forever in coffee-shop gossip! It was just a snapshot—a ghoulish picture of the Hanging Tree with (presumably) a body dangling from a rope. Fran wanted to enlarge it to three by four feet. I said that would be pure sensationalism. *She said* it was local history. *I said* it was pandering to bad taste. *She said* it was objective reportage. *I said* it was probably a roll of carpet trussed up to look like a body."

"Why would anyone take the trouble to do that?"

"Ephraim-haters have gone to great lengths, Qwill, to 'prove' that he was lynched by a posse of men draped in white sheets. In fact, the museum even has a sheet with two eyeholes burned in it, allegedly found near the Hanging Tree on October 30, 1904, by the pastor of the Old Stone Church. I suspect it was planted there for the good reverend to find."

"I detect a note of skepticism in your remarks, Mildred."

"If you want to know, it's my opinion that the lynching story is a hoax. Ephraim's suicide note is in the possession of Junior Goodwinter, and the handwriting checks out. Junior has allowed us to photocopy it for the exhibit. Of course, Fran Brodie—who can be a pain in the you-know-what—said the suicide note could be a forgery. So the hassle began all over again, and Larry had to come in to arbitrate. The result was a compromise. We're calling the Goodwinter Mine disaster "Truth or Myth?" with a big banner to that effect. We're showing the alleged suicide note and the alleged hanging snapshot, but in actual size. No lurid blowups!"

"I'm glad you stood by your guns, Mildred. You always do! Was Fran ever a student of yours?"

"Ten years ago, yes. And now that she's an interior designer, she likes to challenge her old teacher. She's talented—I'll admit that—but she was always a brat in school and she's still a brat."

The entrees were served, and Qwilleran asked, "Did you attend the Exbridge and Cobb reception this afternoon?"

"It was fabulous!" she said. "You should have been there. They served excellent champagne and hors d'oeuvres. All the important people were there. Everyone dressed up for the occasion. Susan was looking smashing in a designer original, but then she always does; I wish I had that woman's figure. I met Iris's son; he's very personable. And the antiques—you wouldn't believe! They had a $10,000 Chippendale chair! A side chair! It didn't even have arms! And a $90,000 highboy!"

"Who's going to pay those prices in Moose County?"

"Don't kid yourself, Qwill. There's plenty of old money up here. They don't flaunt it, but they've got it—people like Doctor Zoller, Euphonia Gage, Doctor Halifax, the Lanspeaks, and how about you?"

"I've explained that before, Mildred. I'm not the acquisitive type. If I can't eat it or wear it, I don't buy it. Iris and Susan must have invested a fortune in that shop."

"They did," Mildred said, "and now Susan has it all. She really lucked out." Lowering her voice she added, "Don't repeat it, but—from what I noticed this afternoon—she's got her sights on Iris's son, too. I happen to know that he checked out of the hotel Thursday night but isn't leaving town until tomorrow. The hotel auditor is married to our school counselor, and I saw them both in Lanspeak's store today."

"I would have gone to the reception," Qwilleran said, "but I was interviewing an interesting young woman—Kristi Fugtree."

"I remember her," said Mildred. "I had her in art class—a very good weaver. She had intriguing eyes, like some movie star I've seen, but I can't remember who. She married and moved away. Is she back again?"

"She's back again and living on the family farm, raising goats and selling goat's milk."

"Well, that's different, isn't it? Kristi was always different. When my other students were weaving acrylic and chenille, Kristi was weaving cornhusks and milkweed."

"Do you know the fellow she married? His last name was Waffle."

"I knew him only by sight and reputation, and I thought Kristi made a bad choice. He was a good-looking kid and popular with the girls. Kristi was the only one who didn't run after him, so naturally he pursued her. Probably thought she had Fugtree money. If he had had any brains he would have known that the family fortune was thrown away by Captain Fugtree, who was very well-liked, but he was a snob and a loafer with a large ego. If Kristi's raising goats, at least she has more ambition than her illustrious forebear."

Qwilleran said, "The house has been neglected for years, but it's an architectural gem."

"Especially the tower! In my nubile days, when we used to hang out in the Willoway, we could see the tower above the trees, and we thought it looked haunted."

"What's the Willoway?"

"Haven't you discovered the Willoway? You're slipping, Qwill," she said with a mischievous smile. "It's a lover's lane under the willow trees that grow on the banks of the Black

Creek. The trail starts at the bridge near the museum and then angles across the back of the Goodwinter and Fugtree property. It's notoriously romantic! You should explore it, Qwill—with a suitable companion!"

On Sunday morning Qwilleran explored the Willoway, alone—although not so alone as he expected.

The expedition was not premeditated. He had been strolling about the grounds of the museum with his hands in his pockets, inhaling deeply, enjoying the riotous autumn color, when he received the distinct impression that he was being watched. He looked in all directions in a casual way, as if admiring the view.

Had he looked toward the farmhouse he would have discovered two pairs of intensely blue eyes fastened on him, but that did not occur to him. He glanced toward the east and saw farmland; to the north was the barn, minus Boswell's van; to the west one could see the tower of the Fugtree mansion rising above the treetops. Perhaps, he thought with pleasure, Kristi was watching him through the binoculars. It was amazing, he thought, how one could sense the fact from such a distance. He groomed his moustache and straightened his shoulders and decided to explore the Willoway.

The crisp, bright October day was so clear that one could hear the faint sound of church bells in West Middle Hummock three miles away. First he walked up Black Creek Lane, then east on Fugtree Road to the bridge, where he slid down an embankment to the stream. Although narrow and shallow, the creek rippled and gurgled briskly over the stones under the drooping branches of willows, while the trail—soft with decades of humus and now gaudily patterned with fallen leaves—was shaded by maples and oaks.

He found it an engagingly private place and he wondered if Iris had discovered this tranquil spot. Probably not; she was a confirmed indoorswoman. Ambling along the trail that meandered to follow the stream, he occasionally caught a glimpse of the Fugtree tower, which loomed larger as he drew closer. Here in the Willoway Emmaline and Samson had kept their ill-fated trysts.

Except for the bubbling water it was hauntingly quiet, as an October day can be, the dew-drenched trail muffling his footsteps. Once he paused to marvel at the picturesque scene, wishing he had brought his camera, and as he stood there he heard the crackling of underbrush. It was followed by indistinct voices. The inflections suggested the ritual of greeting, but not a joyous meeting. There were fragments of dialogue that he could not catch.

Qwilleran moved cautiously toward the source. Rounding a bend in the trail he ducked quickly behind a tree and listened. A woman was speaking angrily.

"I don't *have* any money!"

"Then get some!" a man said threateningly. "I need a car, too. They're after me."

"Why don't you steal one? You seem to know how." This was followed by a small cry of pain. "Don't you touch me, Brent!"

Qwilleran threw a rock into the stream, and the splash halted the hostile interchange for a few seconds.

"What's that?" the man asked in alarm.

"A fish . . . And you can't stay at the house, Brent, so get that out of your head."

There was incoherent whimpering about "no place to go."

"Go back where you came from, or I'll tell the police you're here!"

The man made a retort that sounded vicious, and Qwilleran threw another rock into the stream.

"Somebody's around," the man said.

"Nobody's here, stupid! And now I'm leaving, and I never want to see you again or hear from you! And I'm warning you, Brent: Don't try anything funny. I have a gun at the house!"

"Kristi, I'm hungry." The voice was pleading. "And it's cold at night."

There was a moment of silence. "I'll leave some bread and cheese on the big stump, but that's the end! Go back to Lockmaster and give yourself up."

Her final words faded away as she turned her back. Qwilleran ventured a stealthy peek around the trunk of an oak tree and saw her running along the trail with noiseless steps. He also saw a man in a dark green jacket with stenciling on the back. Then, hearing the sounds of a zipper and urinating in the stream, Qwilleran turned and made his own retreat, climbing the bank to a dirt access road that led to the rear of the Goodwinter property.

His first action was to move his car to the steel barn and lock the door. Then he phoned Kristi's number. Her voice was shaking when she answered.

"It's Qwill calling again," he said. "You must think I haven't got it all together, but I forgot to ask the names of the bucks."

"Oh . . . yes . . . They're Napoleon . . . and Rasputin . . . and Attila," she said.

"Very appropriate! Thank you, Kristi. It's a beautiful day. How's everything at the farm?"

"Okay." Her reply was not convincing.

"You can expect a lot of traffic on Fugtree Road this afternoon. The museum is opening a new exhibit. I hope the activity won't throw the animals off their feed."

"It won't bother them."

"Let me know if there's any problem, any problem at all. Do you hear?"

"Yes," she said weakly. "Thank you."

Hardly reassured by this conversation, Qwilleran wandered aimlessly about the apartment. Kristi's plight troubled him, but she gave the impression that his intervention was neither needed nor wanted. After all, she had a friend in Pickax with a pickup truck who seemed to be available in emergencies. Qwilleran combed his moustache with his fingers.

What he needed was a strong cup of coffee and something distracting to read—something to pass the time until one o'clock when the museum opened to the public. In Pickax he had been reading Kinglake's *Eothen* aloud to the cats, and there were three secondhand Arnold Bennetts he was eager to start, but he had neglected to bring his books to North Middle Hummock. Mrs. Cobb's magazines were not to his taste; he knew all he wanted to know about brown Rockingham ware and early Massachusetts glass-blowers and Newport blockfronts. As for her bookshelves, they were filled with figurines and cast-iron toys and colored glass. The few books on the shelves were paperback titles that he had read at least twice. He was in no mood for *Gone With the Wind* again.

His rambling thoughts were interrupted by a familiar sound: *thlunk!* Then again, *thlunk!* It was the unmistakable evidence of a paperback book hitting an Oriental rug. Qwilleran could recognize it anywhere. He strode into the parlor in time to see Koko making an exit with the low-slung body and drooping tail that spelled mischief. Two books had been knocked off the shelf. Qwilleran read the titles and went directly to the telephone. The time had come, he concluded, to discuss Koko's behavior with an expert.

There was a young woman in Mooseville who seemed to know all about cats. Lori Bamba was also the freelance secretary who handled Qwilleran's correspondence when the fan mail became too heavy. He called her number, using the kitchen telephone and taking care to close the door. Otherwise, Koko would make himself a pest. He liked Lori Bamba, and he knew when she was on the line.

Lori answered in the blithe way that made it a pleasure to hear her voice, and Qwilleran opened with the amenities. "Haven't seen you for a while, Lori. How's the baby?"

"He's crawling now, Qwill. Our calico thinks he's a kitten and tries to mother him."

"And how's Nick?"

"Well, he hasn't found a new job yet. Let us know if you have any ideas. He has an engineering degree, you know."

"I'll do that, but tell him not to quit until he's lined up something else. And how about you? Do you have time to write some letters for me?"

"Sure do! Nick goes to Pickax on Wednesdays. He can pick up your stuff."

"I'm not in Pickax, Lori. The cats and I are staying in Iris Cobb's apartment at the museum for a few weeks."

"Oh, Qwill! That was terrible news! We'll miss her."

"Everyone misses her, including the Siamese."

"How do they react to living in a museum?"

"That's why I'm calling you, Lori. Something is bothering Koko. The bird population has gone south, and yet he sits on the windowsill for hours, watching and waiting. One day when I took him into the exhibit area he went directly to a bed pillow stuffed with chicken feathers before World War I, and a few minutes ago he knocked two books off the shelf: *To Kill a Mockingbird* and *One Flew Over the Cuckoo's Nest*."

Without hesitation Lori asked, "Is there enough poultry in his diet?"

"Hmmm . . . We've been using up the food in Iris's freezer," Qwilleran said, "and now that you mention it, I believe it's mostly meat and seafood."

"Try serving more poultry," she advised.

"Okay, Lori, I'll give it a shot."

Qwilleran went in search of the Siamese. Standing in the central hall he called out, "Hey, you gastronomes, wherever you are! Doctor Purrgood wants you to eat more duckling, pheasant, and Cornish hen!"

Yum Yum could be heard scratching the gravel in the commode; it made a characteristic sound when flicked against the metal sides of the turkey roaster. Koko had done his famous vanishing act, however.

"Koko! Where are you?"

The cat had an exasperating way of making himself invisible when the occasion demanded, and Qwilleran always worried when he was out of sight.

Yum Yum soon emerged from the bathroom, walking delicately pigeon-toed. She went directly to one of the Oriental rugs in the parlor. There was a suspicious-looking hump in the middle of it, which she sniffed ardently. The hump wriggled.

Throwing back the rug Qwilleran demanded, "What's wrong with you, Koko? Is the thermostat set too low? Are you hiding from something? What are you trying to tell me?"

Koko drew himself up to his full height, as only a Siamese can do, and stalked loftily from the room.

CHAPTER 11

The first cars to arrive at the museum for the opening of the disaster exhibit were those of Historical Society members, looking well-dressed in their church clothes: the men with coats and ties, the women with skirts and heels. Mitch Ogilvie as traffic director instructed them to unload the elderly and infirm at the museum entrance and then park in the barnyard, leaving the regular parking slots for the public. A good turnout was expected following the story on the front page of the *Moose County Something*:

GOODWINTER MUSEUM REOPENS
FEATURING MAJOR DISASTERS

The Goodwinter Farmhouse Museum in North Middle Hummock will resume regular hours Sunday with a new exhibit featuring memorable events in Moose County history. The museum has been closed for a week following the death of Iris Cobb Hackpole, resident manager.

The new show displays photographs and artifacts from lumbering, shipping, and mining days, according to spokesperson Carol Lanspeak. Photo murals portray dramatic views of shipwrecks, forest fires, mine disasters, logjams and other mishaps, including a 1919 "disaster" when the sheriff poured gallons of bootleg liquor on the dump at Squunk Corners. Of special interest, Lanspeak said, is a vignette titled "Truth or Myth?" exploring the controversial death of Ephraim Goodwinter in 1904.

"The Goodwinter farm and surrounding countryside are at the height of autumn brilliance," Lanspeak said. "The color show makes a trip to the Hummocks doubly enjoyable." Regular hours are 1 to 4 P.M., Friday through Sunday. Groups may be accommodated by appointment.

At one o'clock Qwilleran dressed for the occasion, wearing a new paisley tie that Scottie had cajoled him into buying by burring his *r*'s. With Kristi's bible tucked under his arm he went directly to the museum office, where Larry was punching keys on the computerized catalogue.

"How's it going, Larry?"

"Good publicity always pays off," said the president. "What's that under your arm? Are you planning to deliver a sermon?"

"It's a bible donated by the young woman at the Fugtree farm. What shall I do with it?"

"Is it the Fugtree bible, I hope?"

"No, just something her mother bought at an auction."

"Too bad. Well, write the donor's name on this card and leave the bible on the catalogue table. The registrar will take care of it."

"Any luck, Larry, in finding a successor for Iris?"

"We've had a couple of nibbles. Iris, as you know, wouldn't take a penny, but we're prepared to pay a decent salary plus the apartment, including utilities. Mitch Ogilvie has applied for the job. He likes antiques, and God knows he's enthusiastic, but he's rather young, and the young ones stay a year and then take off for greener pastures. Susan thinks Vince Boswell would be good. He used to conduct antique auctions Down Below, and he's handy with tools. He could make minor repairs that we're having to pay for now."

"In my opinion," Qwilleran said, "Mitch has the better personality for the position. Being on the desk at the hotel he's accustomed to meeting people, and I've observed how he gets along with the elderly. Boswell comes on too strong and too loud. He turns people off. Besides, the manager's apartment is hardly large enough for a family of three."

Larry glanced around the office before answering. "Actually, Verona isn't his wife. If we give him the job he'll ship her and the kid back to Pittsburgh."

"How'd he get his bad leg?"

"Polio. That happened way back before they had the vaccine. Considering he has pain, he does pretty well."

"Hmmm . . . Too bad," Qwilleran murmured. "But Mitch, at least, has clean fingernails."

Larry shrugged. "Well . . . you know . . . Vince is doing all that dirty work in the barn. Some of those presses are filthy with an accumulation of ink and grease."

Qwilleran filled out the donation card and then asked, "What happens out here when snow flies?"

"We keep Black Creek snowplowed, and the county takes care of Fugtree Road. No problem."

"Does anyone visit the museum in winter?"

"Definitely! We schedule busloads of students and seniors and women's clubs, and we stage special events for Thanksgiving, Christmas, Valentine's Day, and so forth. For Halloween we have a marshmallow roast for the kids, and Mitch Ogilvie tells ghost stories. As for the snow, it makes this place really beautiful."

"Incidentally," Qwilleran said, "you should consider putting the yardlights on a timer, to turn on automatically at dusk. Also one or two interior lights for security reasons."

"Good idea," said Larry, taking a small notebook from his pocket and making an entry.

"Another matter I want to draw to your attention is the land grant signed 'Abraham Lincoln' in the document exhibit."

"That's the most valuable document we have," Larry said proudly.

"Except that it was not actually signed by Lincoln."

"You mean it's a forgery? How do you know?"

"I wouldn't suspect any felonious intent. I daresay there were thousands of certificates issued, and Secretary Seward was authorized to sign for the president. He did it with a flourish. Lincoln's signature was small and controlled, and he didn't spell out his first name."

"Glad you told me, Qwill. We'll put that information on the ID card." Out came Larry's notebook again. "The value of the document has just dropped a few thousand dollars, but thanks anyway, old pal."

At that moment Carol Lanspeak burst into the office. "Something's missing in the new exhibit, Larry," she said. "Come and see!"

She left immediately, with her husband close behind. Qwilleran followed but was intercepted every step of the way. Mildred Hanstable and Fran Brodie, chatting together like the best of friends, stopped him to comment on his paisley tie.

Mildred said to Fran, "How does he stay so svelte?"

Fran said to Mildred, "How does he stay so young?"

"I stay sober and single," Qwilleran advised them before moving on.

Susan Exbridge whispered in his ear, "Good news! Dennis Hough has made an offer on the Fitch property. He's going to open a construction business up here."

The bad news, Qwilleran thought, is that he's bringing his wife.

Next, Homer Tibbitt and Rhoda Finney approached him, and Homer said in his high-pitched voice, "Were you trying to reach me? We went down to Lockmaster to see the horse races and fix her hearing aid, and while we were there we got married so it wouldn't be a total loss."

"We've had the license for weeks, but he's a terrible stick-in-the-mud," the new Mrs. Tibbitt said, smiling fondly at the groom.

Qwilleran extended his felicitations and pressed on through the crowd, most of whom were trying to get into the crowded room featuring disasters.

Polly Duncan tugged at his sleeve and said in a half-whisper, "I have a great favor to ask, Qwill."

"I'll do anything," he said, "except cat-sit with a three-ounce kitten."

Reprovingly she said, "That's exactly what I was going to ask you to do. There's a seminar in Lockmaster, and I hoped I could leave Bootsie with you for one overnight."

"Hmmm," he mused, searching for good reasons to decline. "Wouldn't two big cats with loud voices frighten him?"

"I doubt it. He's a well-adjusted little fellow. Nothing bothers him."

"Yum Yum might think he's a mouse."

"She's smart enough to know better. He won't be any trouble, Qwill, and you'll love him as much as I do."

"Well . . . I'll give it a try . . . but if he expects me to kiss-kiss, he's grievously mistaken."

Qwilleran pushed his way through the growing crowd, noting the presence of attorney Hasselrich and his wife, Dr. Zoller and his latest blond, Arch Riker and the lovely Amanda, the Boswells with Baby, and several politicians whose names would be on the November ballot. Vince Boswell's voice could be heard above all the rest. "Are they going to have refreshments? Iris used to make the best damned cookies!"

Eventually Qwilleran reached the disaster exhibit. As Mildred had said, the dramatic impact was created with photo murals. They depicted the 1892 logjam that took seven lives, the 1898 fire that destroyed Sawdust City, the wreck of a three-masted schooner in the 1901 storm, and other calamities in Moose County history, but the dominating display was the "Truth or Myth?" vignette, which revived old questions about the mysterious end of Ephraim Goodwinter.

The story of the mine explosion and its aftermath was presented graphically without commentary. Photo blowups and newspaper clippings were grouped under four dates:

May 13, 1904—Photo of rescue crew at Goodwinter Mine. Headlines from Down Below say: 32 KILLED IN MINE EXPLOSION.

May 18, 1904—Photo of weeping widows and children. Excerpt from *Pickax Picayune* of that date: "Mr. and Mrs. Ephraim Goodwinter and family left today for several months abroad."

August 25, 1904—Architect's rendering of proposed library building. Feature story in the *Picayune*: "The city soon will have a public library, thanks to the munificence of Mr. Ephraim Goodwinter, owner and publisher of this newspaper."

November 2, 1904—Photo of Ephraim's funeral procession. Report in the *Picayune*: "Mourners accompanied the earthly remains of the late Ephraim Goodwinter to the grave in the longest funeral procession on record. Mr. Goodwinter died suddenly on Tuesday."

Interspersed with the enlarged photos and clippings were miners' hats, pickaxes, and sledgehammers—even a miner's lunchbucket with reference to the meat-and-potato "pasties" that they traditionally carried down the mine shaft. A portrait of the sour-faced philanthropist showed the knife slash it received while on display in the lobby of the public library. A fuzzy snapshot of the Hanging Tree with its grisly burden was identified as "unidentified." There was also a photocopy of the alleged suicide note in handwriting remarkably similar to that of A. Lincoln. A ballot box invited visitors to vote: Suicide or Murder?

Qwilleran's elbow was jostled by Hixie Rice, advertising manager for the *Moose County Something*. "I get one message from all this," she said. "What Ephraim needed was a good public relations counselor."

"What he needed," said Qwilleran, "was some common sense."

He retraced his course through the crowd and found the Lanspeaks in the office. "You said something was missing. What is it?"

"The sheet," said Carol.

"What sheet?"

"We displayed a white sheet that the Reverend Mr. Crawbanks found near the Hanging Tree after Ephraim's death."

"Do you mean to say that someone stole it?" Qwilleran asked.

Larry said somberly, "It's the only thing that has ever been removed from our exhibit space, and we've had some valuable stuff on display. Obviously we have a crackpot in our midst. And we know it's an inside job because it was missing when the doors first opened to the public at one o'clock. It's no great loss. The sheet had dubious value even as a historic artifact. But I don't like the idea that we have a petty thief on the staff."

Qwilleran asked, "How many people have keys to the museum. Homer tells me you have seventy-five volunteers."

"No one has a key. The volunteers let themselves in with the official key hidden on the front porch."

"Hidden where? Under the door mat?"

"Under the basket of Indian corn hanging above the doorbell," said Carol.

"We've always considered our people completely trustworthy," said Larry.

Qwilleran excused himself and went in search of the exhibit chairperson. He found Mildred in conversation with Verona Boswell, who was saying, "Baby talked in complete sentences by the time she was eight months old." She was clutching the hand of the tiny girl in blue velvet coat and hat.

"Excuse me, Mrs. Boswell," said Qwilleran. "May I borrow Mrs. Hanstable to explain one of the exhibits?"

"Why, of course . . . Baby, do you know who this is? Say hi to Mr. Qwilleran."

"Hi!" she said.

"Hi," he replied more graciously than usual.

He steered Mildred into the deserted textile room. "It's a quiet place to talk," he explained. "I have yet to see a single visitor looking at this godawful exhibit."

"It's grim, isn't it?" she agreed. "We tried to spark it up with colored backgrounds and clever signs, and we roped it off to make it look important, but everyone loves the red velvet roping and hates the textiles. What's on your mind, Qwill?"

"I'd like to compliment you on the disaster exhibit. It's attracting a lot of attention."

"I thank you, and Fran Brodie thanks you. It will be interesting to see the result of the voting."

"Have you looked at the exhibit today?"

"I haven't been able to get near it. Too many people. Did someone take another poke at Ephraim's portrait?"

"No, Mildred, someone walked off with the Reverend Mr. Crawbanks' sheet."

"Really? You wouldn't kid me, would you?"

"Carol discovered that it was missing. She and Larry are surprised to say the least. They have no idea who might have pilfered it. Have you?"

"Qwill," she said, "I don't pretend to understand anything that's going on in today's society. Why don't you ask Koko whodunit? He's smarter than either of us."

"Speaking of Koko," he said, "I wish you would look at that Inchpot bed pillow. Do you see anything unusual about it?"

She studied the limp pillow critically. "Only that it's been moved." She stepped over the velvet roping, plumped the pillow and arranged it more artfully. "There! Does that look better?"

"Is it a normal occurrence for displayed objects to be moved?"

"Well . . . no. The volunteers are told never to disarrange the exhibits. Why do you ask?"

He lowered his voice. "I brought Koko in here the other day, and he zeroed in on that pillow and sniffed it. He wouldn't leave it alone until I ejected him bodily from the museum. Now, don't tell me it's stuffed with chicken feathers, because the pillow from the Trevelyan farm is also stuffed with chicken feathers, but he ignored it completely."

"Let's see what it says on the ID card," Mildred said, stepping over the roping again and picking up the hand-printed label. "It was used on the Inchpot farm prior to World War I . . . The cover is a washed flour sack . . . It's stuffed with chicken feathers from the Inchpot coops . . . It was donated by Adeline Inchpot Crowe."

"Did you say *Crow*?"

"With an *e* on the end."

"Let's get out of here, Mildred. These seventy-five-year-old chicken feathers give me an acute case of depression. How would you like to have a look at Iris's cookbook while you're here?"

Qwilleran ran interference through the throng and suggested a cup of coffee when they entered the kitchen of the west wing.

"Or a little something else?" Mildred said coyly. "Large crowds make me nervous unless I have a glass in my hand."

"I'll see what I can find. Iris didn't maintain a well-stocked bar."

"Anything will do if it has a little buzz."

Qwilleran started rattling ice cubes. "The cookbook is in the school desk under the telephone. Lift up the lid ... I find dry sherry, Dubonnet and Campari. What'll it be?"

There was no response.

"Did you find it?" he asked. "It's just a looseleaf notebook, mixed in with a lot of clippings and scraps of paper."

Mildred was bending over the small desk. "It's not here."

"It's got to be there! I saw it a couple of days ago."

"It's not here," she insisted. "Come and look."

Qwilleran hurried to peer over her shoulder. "Where could it have gone?"

"The cats stole it," she said archly. "Koko lifted the lid, and Yum Yum heisted it with her famous paw."

"Not likely. They're larcenous, but a looseleaf notebook two inches thick is out of their class."

"You may have mislaid it."

"I looked at the handwriting for about ten seconds and then put it back in the desk. Someone came in here and pinched it—someone who knew where Iris kept it. Did she ever invite the museum staff in for coffee or anything?"

"Yes, often, but—"

"There's no lock on the door between here and the museum. Someone had three days to do the job. I've been out every day. We've got to get a lock on that door! What's to stop anyone from coming in and snatching the cats?" He stopped and looked around. "Where are they? They're usually in the kitchen. I haven't seen them. *Where are they?*"

Chapter 12

After the Siamese had been found asleep on a pink towel in the bathroom (insulated from the museum hubbub), and after Mildred had finished her Campari, and after the crowd had thinned out, Qwilleran went in search of Larry Lanspeak. The president was in the office conferring with a few directors of the museum.

"Come in, Qwill," said Larry. "We were just discussing the incident of the missing sheet."

"Now you can discuss the incident of the missing cookbook," Qwilleran said. "Iris's collection of recipes has disappeared from her desk."

"The cookbook I can understand," said Susan, "but who would take a sheet with holes in it?"

Carol suggested posting a large sign on the volunteers' bulletin board. "We could say, 'Will the volunteers who borrowed the sheet from the disaster exhibit and the cookbook from Iris Cobb's desk please return them to the museum office immediately. No questions asked.' How does that sound?"

Qwilleran said, "The time has come to install a lock on the connecting door between the museum and the manager's apartment. Iris had a large collection of valuable collectibles—small items, easy to pick up. People who wouldn't steal from the living think it's okay to steal from the dead. It's a primitive custom, practiced for centuries."

"Yes, but not around here," said Susan.

"How do you know? The dead never report it to the police. Moose County may have computers and camcorders and private planes, but there are plenty of primitive beliefs. Ghosts, for example. I keep hearing that Ephraim walks through the walls occasionally."

Larry smiled. "That's a popular joke, Qwill, just something to talk about over the coffee cups." He reached for the phone, at the same time glancing at his watch. "I'll call Homer about the lock. I hope he's still up. It's only five-thirty, but his bedtime keeps getting earlier and earlier."

"His new bride will change his habits," Qwilleran said. "She's a live one!"

"Yes," Larry said with a chuckle, "they'll be sitting up watching television until eight o'clock at night . . . Why are we laughing? When we're Homer's age, we won't even be here!" He completed the call and reported that Homer would round up a locksmith first thing in the morning.

Qwilleran said, "I have another suggestion to make, apropos of locks and valuables. Iris had a lot of private papers in her desk in the parlor. They should be bundled up, sealed, and turned over to her son."

"I'll be happy to do that," said Susan. "I'll be seeing Dennis this week."

Qwilleran gave her an expressionless stare and then turned to Larry.

The president said, "I propose we do it right now. Susan, you and Qwill and I can take care of it. How big a box will we need?"

The three of them trooped to the west wing, carrying a carton, sealing tape, and a felt marker. Koko and Yum Yum met them at the door.

"Hello, cats," said Larry jovially.

The Siamese followed them into the parlor, where the desk occupied a place of prominence.

"This is the ugliest desk I've ever seen," Qwilleran commented. It was basically a flat box with one drawer and a pull-out writing surface, perched on tall legs and topped with a cupboard.

"This is an original handmade Dingleberry, about 1890," Larry informed him. "Iris bought it at the Goodwinter auction. I was bidding against her, but I dropped out when the bidding reached four figures."

Behind the doors of the cupboard were shoeboxes labeled in large block letters with a felt marker: Bills, Letters, Financial, Medical, Insurance, and Personal. In the drawer were the usual pens, scissors, paper clips, rubber bands, memo pads, and a magnifying glass.

Qwilleran said, "She had magnifying glasses all over the house. She even wore one on a chain around her neck."

"Okay," said Larry. "Let's lock this stuff up in the museum office and have Dennis sign for it when he comes."

"Good idea," said Qwilleran.

Susan had nothing to say. She seemed to be sulking. As they were leaving the parlor she almost tripped over a rug.

Qwilleran caught her. "Sorry," he said. "There's a cat under the rug. This is the second time he's crawled under an Oriental."

"He has good taste," Larry said. "These are all antiques and museum-quality."

"Do you have any more booby traps around?" Susan said testily as she followed Larry back to the museum.

Qwilleran thawed some chicken à la king for the Siamese, who devoured it hungrily, carefully avoiding the pimento and the slivered almonds. He watched the fascinating ritual absently, thinking about the missing sheet, the misplaced pillow, the purloined cookbook, and Susan's eagerness to handle Iris Cobb's private papers.

Something had happened to Susan Exbridge after her husband divorced her for another woman. While she was the wife of a successful developer she had been an active clubwoman, serving on the board of every organization and working diligently for the common good. Since that blow to her ego she had concentrated on working for Susan Exbridge. In a way she was justified. According to the Pickax grapevine, her ex-husband had so maneuvered the divorce settlement that Susan was rich on paper but short of cash, and if she liquidated the securities, she would be liable for a large tax bite.

Rumor also had it that ninety percent of the Exbridge & Cobb venture was financed by Iris. If that were true, Qwilleran pondered, Susan's inheritance would be substantial. Granted, the two women were good friends as well as business partners, but that was a situation that aroused Qwilleran's suspicion. A more unlikely pair of chums could hardly be found. Iris was neither chic nor sophisticated nor glib, yet Susan had engulfed her with friendship, and Iris was flattered to be taken up by a woman so distinguished in manner, dress, and social connections.

It irritated Qwilleran to think that Iris Cobb had been used; it was her know-how as well as her money that had established the new antique shop. It irritated him also to see Susan making a play for Dennis Hough, who had a wife and infant son as well as the bulk of the Cobb-Hackpole fortune.

He worked off his resentment by concocting a sandwich for himself, using caraway rye bread from one freezer, corned beef from the other, and mustard and horseradish from the refrigerator. The Siamese watched him eat, and he shared the meat. "The spirit of Mrs. Cobb is still with us," he told them.

It was true. Her presence was palpable, invoked by the food she had cooked, the friendly kitchen, her taste in antiques, the pink sheets and towels, and even her magazines and paperback novels. At any moment she might walk into the room and say, "Oh, Mr. Q, would you like some of my chocolate coconut macaroons?"

He looked up from his sandwich and almost thought he could see her. Was this the invisible presence that engaged Koko in conversation?

Qwilleran jumped up and went outdoors, taking a brisk walk around the grounds to restore some semblance of peace to his life.

It was Sunday night. A week ago he had been listening to *Otello* when Mrs. Cobb's frantic phone call had interrupted Act One. Since then he had made two more attempts to hear the opera in its entirety. He would try again. Sunday evening was usually quiet in Moose County, and it was doubtful that anyone would be calling. Briefly he considered silencing the two phones, but communication was his life, and the idea of willfully missing an incoming call struck him as a moral lapse.

With a mug of coffee in his hand and two cats in the blue velvet wing chairs, the comfortable scene was set. He pressed the Play button. Again the crash of the opening chords catapulted the Siamese out of the parlor, but they returned and withstood the trumpets, although they laid their ears back.

All went well until Act Three and the aria that Polly had called gorgeous. Just as Othello began the poignant *Dio! mi potevi* . . . the telephone rang. Qwilleran tried to ignore it, but the insistent ringing ruined the music. Even so, he was determined to let it ring itself out. He turned up the volume. The tenor agonized, and the telephone rang. Qwilleran clenched his teeth. Ten rings . . . fifteen rings . . . twenty! Then it occurred to him that only a desperate person would persist so long, only someone who knew he was at home. He turned down the volume and went to the bedroom phone.

"Hello?" he said with apprehension.

"Qwill, this is Kristi," said a nervous voice. "Don't run the column about my goats."

"Why not, Kristi?"

"Something terrible has happened. Eight of them are dead, and the others are dying."

"My God! What happened?"

"I fed them at five o'clock and they were okay. Two hours later I went out there and three were lying dead." There was a catch in her voice. "The rest were struggling to breathe, and one of them fell over right at my feet. I can't—I can't—" Her words turned into sobs.

Sympathy welled up in Qwilleran's throat as his thoughts flew to Koko and Yum Yum. He knew how precious animals can be. "Easy now, Kristi," he said. "Easy! What did you do?"

She sobbed for a while and sniffed moistly before saying, "I called the vet's emergency number, and he came right away, but by that time all the kids were gone and most of the does." She choked up again.

He waited patiently for her to recover.

"The bucks are all right," she said. "They were penned separately."

"Do you have any idea what caused it?"

"The vet says it's poison—probably insecticide in the feed. Their lungs—" She stopped and cried again. "Their lungs filled with fluid, and they suffocated. The vet is sending samples to the lab. It's almost more than I can bear! The whole herd!"

"How could it possibly have happened?"

"The police call it vandalism."

Qwilleran felt a tingling sensation on his upper lip, and he knew the answer to his next question. "Do you have any idea who would commit such an unthinkable crime?"

"I know who did it!" Her grief gave way to anger. "The stupid fool I used to be married to!"

"Did you tell that to the police?"

"Yes. They've been looking for him ever since he walked away from a minimum-security camp near Lockmaster. He thought he could hide out here, or else I'd give him money and a car. I told him he was out of his mind. I didn't want anything to do with him! *Oh, why didn't I turn him in?*" she cried, ending with a heart-rending wail.

"This is shocking, Kristi! Did you have any idea he'd sabotage the farm?"

"He threatened me this morning, and I warned him I had a gun. I didn't expect anything like this. I could kill him! It's not just the loss of two years' work, but . . . all those sweet animals! Buttercup . . . Geranium . . . Black Tulip! They were so dear to me!" she said with a whimper.

"I wish there were something I could do. Is there anything I can do?" he asked.

"There's nothing anyone can do," she sighed. "Just don't run the column. The poisoning will be in the paper tomorrow. One of the reporters called me."

"Phone me, Kristi, if any trouble develops, no matter what it is."

"Thank you, Qwill. Good night."

Qwilleran turned off the stereo. He had heard enough tragedy for one night.

Early Monday morning his telephone began to ring, as the grapevine went into operation. Mildred Hanstable, Polly Duncan, Larry Lanspeak and others called to say, "Did you hear the newscast this morning? . . . Do you know what happened to your neighbor? . . . Isn't that the woman you were going to interview? . . . The board of health has removed all goat products from the market . . . They think it was poison."

It was a rude start to another busy day. Even before he had prepared his first cup of coffee Qwilleran saw Mr. and Mrs. Tibbitt drive up in their ponderous old car, followed closely by Al's Fix-All truck. That was the accepted system in Moose County; workmen always arrived six hours late, or before breakfast. Qwilleran greeted them moodily.

"I'm going to do a little dusting," Rhoda announced.

"I'm going to have a cup of coffee," said Homer.

"Will you join me?" Qwilleran asked, waving a coffee mug.

"No, thanks. I'll mix a cup of my own blend in the office." Homer patted his hip pocket and maneuvered his angular limbs briskly in the direction of the office.

Great guy! Qwilleran thought. He gulped a roll and coffee while the locksmith worked on the door and then joined Tibbitt in the museum office.

"Someone swiped my feather duster," Rhoda complained.

"I did!" said her husband. "I threw it in the trash. You can use a dustrag like everyone else. Spray it with that stuff that's supposed to pick up dust."

"Once a principal, always a principal," she explained to Qwilleran. "He likes to be boss." She took a duster from the cleaning closet and left the office, flicking it temperamentally at chairs and filing cabinets as she passed.

Qwilleran said to Homer, "Someone once told me there's no such thing as a locksmith in Moose County because there are no locks. So who's the guy working on my door?"

"A locksmith would starve to death in these parts," said Homer, "but this fellow fixes refrigerators, phonographs, typewriters—anything. Why do you want a lock between you and the museum? Has old Ephraim been bothering you? A door won't stop him, you know. Not even a stone wall."

"I don't worry about dead prowlers," Qwilleran said. "I worry about the live ones."

"Halloween's coming, and you can expect pranksters. When I was a young lad we used to spook houses around Halloween, especially if it was someone we hated, like a strict teacher or the town skinflint."

"How do you spook a house? That wasn't in our bag of tricks in Chicago, where I grew up."

"As I recall," said the old man, "you stick a big nail or something under a loose board on the outside of a house, with a long string attached. Then you pull the line taut and run a stick over it like bowing a violin. It reverberates all through the house. Screaming in the attic! Moaning in the walls! I doubt whether it would work with the aluminum siding and plywood they use nowadays. They're eliminating all life's little pleasures. Everything's synthetic, even our food."

"One of life's little pleasures, I gather, was carving initials on school desks," said Qwilleran. "Mrs. Cobb's telephone stand is an old desk with the initials H.T. carved on the top. Would you know anything about that?"

"In the lower righthand corner? That's my desk!" Homer exulted. "It came from the old Black Creek School. The teacher gave me what-for with a cane for carving that little masterpiece. If I'd been smart I would have carved someone else's initials. Adam Dingleberry had that desk before I did—he was four years ahead of me—and he carved the initials of the preacher's son. He had a madcap sense of humor. Still does! Got expelled from school for playing practical jokes. No one gave him credit for originality and creativity. Are there any other initials on the desk?"

"Quite a few. I remember B.O. I suppose those letters didn't have any significance in those days."

"That's Mitch's grandfather, Bruce Ogilvie. He came after me. He won all the spelling bees with his eyes closed—couldn't spell with 'em open."

Qwilleran said, "In this north country it seems that lives are interwoven. It gives the community a rich texture. Life in the cities Down Below is a tangle of loose threads."

"You should write a 'Qwill Pen' column about that," Homer suggested.

"I think I shall. Speaking of the 'Qwill Pen,' Rhoda tells me you know something about old barns."

"Yes, indeed! That's another tradition that's disappearing. They build steel things that look like factory warehouses. You can't convince me that the cattle are happy in those contraptions! But there's still a good barn on this property." He crooked an arm toward the north window. "It'll still be standing long after the steel barns have blown away."

"I haven't had a chance to look at it," Qwilleran admitted.

"Then let's go out there. It's a beauty!" Homer stood up slowly as if unlocking his joints one by one. "Contrary to popular opinion I'm not put together with plastic bones and steel pins. What you see is all original parts. Rhoda," he called out, "tell Al to leave his bill and we'll send him a check."

Walking toward the barn the two men made slow progress, although Homer's flailing arms and legs gave an impression of briskness. Qwilleran looked back toward the farmhouse and saw a small fawn-colored bundle on the kitchen windowsill; he waved a hand.

The Goodwinter barn was a classic style with a gambrel roof, its boards once painted red and now a red-streaked silvery gray. A lean-to had been added on one side, and the remains of a squat stone silo stood at the opposite corner like a gray ghost.

They walked in silence. "Can't walk . . . and talk . . . at the same time," said Homer, flinging his limbs rhythmically.

The barn was farther from the house than Qwilleran had realized, and larger than he had imagined. The closer they approached it, the loftier it loomed. A grassy ramp led up to enormous double doors.

He said, "Now I know what they mean by big as a barn door."

They were pausing at the foot of the ramp for Homer to catch his breath before attempting the ascent. When he recovered from the exertion he explained, "The doors had to be large so a loaded hay wagon could drive into the barn. The man-size door cut in the big door is called the eye of the needle."

As he spoke, a corner of the latter flapped open, and a pregnant cat stepped through the cat-hatch and waddled away.

"That's Cleo," he said. "She's on my committee in charge of rodent control. Looks like another litter of mousers is on the way. You can never have too many barncats."

"What's the function of the lean-to?" Qwilleran asked.

"Ephraim built it to house his carriages. He had some elegant ones, they say. Later his son kept his Stanley Steamer in there. After Titus Goodwinter was killed, his widow bought a Pierce Arrow—with windshield wipers, mind you! Everyone thought that was the cat's pajamas!"

The weathered wood barn perched high on a fieldstone foundation, and as the land sloped away to the rear, the foundation became a full story high.

"That's what they called a byre in Scotland," Homer said. "The Goodwinters kept cattle and horses down there in the old days." They climbed the grassy ramp slowly and entered the barn through the eye of the needle, the old man pointing out the door hardware—simple hooks and eyes of hand-wrought iron, the work of a local blacksmith.

The interior was dark after the sunshine outdoors. Only a few shafts of light slanted in from unseen windows high in the gables. All was silent except for the muted cooing of pigeons and beating of wings.

"Better open the big doors so we can see," said Homer. "This place gets darker every year."

Qwilleran suddenly realized he had never been inside a barn. He had seen them in the distance while speeding down a highway, and an apple barn was included with the Klingenschoen property, but he had not inspected it. Now, gazing upward at the vast space under the roof, crisscrossed with timbers, he felt the same sense of awe he had experienced in Gothic cathedrals.

Homer saw him gazing upward. "That's a double haymow," he explained. "The timbers are sixty feet long, fourteen inches square. Everything's put together with mortise-and-tenon construction—no nails. All white pine. You don't see white pine any more. It was all lumbered out."

He pointed out the marks of the hand axe and hewing adze. "The main floor was called the threshing floor. The boards are four inches thick. It takes a solid floor like this to support a loaded hay wagon—or those danged printing presses."

It was then that Qwilleran noticed the contents of the barn. Wooden packing crates and grotesque machines resembling instruments of torture stood about the straw-strewn floor.

"This is only part of it," the old man went on. "The rest of the crates are down in the stable. Senior Goodwinter was obsessed with handprinting. Every time an old printshop went out of business or modernized, he bought their obsolete equipment. Never got around to taking inventory or even opening the crates. He just kept on collecting."

"That's where I come in!" said a jarring voice behind them. Vince Boswell stood silhouetted in the open doorway. "My job is to find out what's in those crates and catalogue the stuff so they can start a printing museum," he said in his penetrating voice. It was easy to believe he had been an auctioneer. "Yesterday I uncrated a wooden press that's eighteenth century."

"You carry on," Homer told him. "I want to go back to the house before my legs give out. I'm getting a pain in my knees." He retreated down the grassy ramp.

At that moment a doll-size figure came trudging toward the ramp, wearing doll-size blue jeans and a wisp of a red sweater. She carried a green plastic pail in one hand and a yellow plastic spade in the other. She was followed by an anxious mother, running and calling in a small voice, "Baby! Baby! Come back here!"

Vince looked at them and stiffened. "Can't you control that kid?" he demanded. "Get her out of here. It isn't safe."

Verona scooped the child into her arms, the pail and spade flying in opposite directions.

"My pail! My shovel!" Baby screamed.

Qwilleran gathered them up and handed them to her.

"Say thank you," Verona murmured.

"Thank you," said Baby automatically. As they retreated up the lane she looked back toward the barn with longing. There was something disturbingly adult about her, Qwilleran thought, and she was so unhealthily thin.

With a shrug Boswell said, "I'll show you what I've found here, if you're interested." He pointed to a contraption with fancy legs. "That's a Washington toggle press, 1827. I've found old typecases, composing sticks, a primitive cylinder press, woodblocks—all kinds of surprises. I open a crate and never know what I'll find." He picked up a crowbar and wrenched the top off a wooden box. It was packed with straw. "Looks like a hand-operated papercutter."

"I'm vastly impressed," said Qwilleran as he edged toward the door.

"Wait up!" Boswell said in piercing tones. "You haven't seen the half of it yet."

"I must confess," said Qwilleran, "that I'm not greatly interested in mechanical equipment, and some of those presses look diabolical." He nodded toward something that seemed half sewing machine and half guillotine.

"That's a treadle press," said the expert. "And this one's an Albion. And that one's a Columbian. When the counterpoise lever moves, the eagle goes up and down." The Columbian was a cast-iron monster embellished with eagle, serpents, and dolphins.

"Amazing," said Qwilleran in a minor key. "You must tell me more about this fascinating subject some other time." He consulted his watch and headed for the ramp.

"Would you care to have a bowl of soup with the wife and me?"

"Thank you for the invitation, but I'm expecting an important phone call."

Boswell picked up a walkie-talkie from the top of a crate.

"Coming home to lunch, Verona," he said. "How about some tomato soup and a hot dog?"

The two of them closed the big doors, latching them with the crude hook and eye, and walked down the grassy ramp. Then Boswell drove away in his rusty van and Qwilleran strolled back to the house, grateful to escape the stilletto-voiced expert with the textbook patter. Why did he need a walkie-talkie? Why didn't he simply stand on the ramp and yell? How could the delicate Verona endure that deafening delivery? It irked him that she and Baby were expendable, that they could be shipped back to Pittsburgh like unwanted merchandise if Vince was named Mrs. Cobb's successor. That he should even presume to follow in her footsteps was obscene, Qwilleran told himself.

As he opened the door to the west wing, a furry blur whizzed past his ankles and flew off the steps. With a roar Qwilleran made a flying tackle, grabbing the cat's slippery body in both hands. They landed in a pile of leaves.

"Oh no, you don't, young man!" Qwilleran scolded as he carried him back into the house. "Where do you think you're going? To the Jellicle Ball with the barncats? Or are you interested in printing presses?"

As he spoke the words he dropped the cat on the floor, and Koko made a surprised four-point landing. As for Qwilleran, the idea that flashed across his mind at that moment made his moustache curl.

Exactly what, he asked himself, is in those unpacked crates? Printing presses? Or something else . . .

Chapter 13

Qwilleran's new-found suspicions regarding the printing presses were relegated to the back burner as he faced the exigencies of the day. There was a long telephone conversation with the CEO of the K Fund and then a follow-up call to Kristi at the Fugtree farm.

"Nothing to report," she said wearily. "The police keep dropping in. They've put up roadblocks around the county, expecting Brent to make a getaway in a stolen car, but no car thefts have been reported. Where's your car? I looked for it with the binoculars, and it wasn't in the yard. I was just going to phone you."

"It's locked up in the steel barn, but I appreciate your concern."

"The board of health is here again, and the men who do dead stock removal. It's too painful to watch. I can't bear to see them hauling away my beautiful Black Tulip and my sweet little Geranium."

"It's a terrible thing," Qwilleran said, "but you must put it behind you and think about your next step."

"I know. I must think constructively. That's what I've been trying to do. My friend says he'll help me fix up the house if I want to open a restaurant or bed-and-breakfast. But first I've got to unload all my mother's junk. I don't know whether to have a big garage sale or a big bonfire. And it will take money to get the house into shape. I don't know how much I'll get from the insurance. Oh, God! I don't want the insurance money! I just want to wake up and find Gardenia and Honeysuckle waiting to be milked and looking at me with those soulful eyes. I love goat farming!"

"I know you do, Kristi, but whether you start another herd or a B-and-B, the Klingenschoen Fund would like to help you register the house as a historic place. If you're interested, they're prepared to offer you a grant to cover research and renovation."

"Am I interested! Am I interested! Oh, Qwill, that would be neat—really neat! Wait till I tell Mitch."

"Mitch? Do you mean Mitch Ogilvie, by any chance?"

"Yes. He says he knows you. And Qwill, could I ask you a big favor? He's applied for the job of resident manager at the museum. Would you put in a few good words for him? He feels about the museum the same way I feel about goats. And he can't be a desk clerk at the hotel forever. He has too much to offer."

"Isn't he the one who tells ghost stories to the kids at Halloween?"

"Yes, and he really makes their teeth chatter!"

"I'd like to talk to him. Why don't you bring him over to the west wing for some cider and doughnuts?"

"When?"

"How about tonight?" Qwilleran suggested. "About eight o'clock."

"I'll bring some goat cheese and crackers," she said in great excitement. "And don't worry—the cheese isn't poisoned."

Next Qwilleran phoned Polly at the library. He said, "I'm driving into Pickax to do errands. Would you care to join me there for dinner?"

"Delighted," she said, "provided it's early. I must go home, you know, to feed my little sweetheart. He has four meals a day on a regular schedule."

Qwilleran recoiled. Many a time he had said, "I've got to go home and feed the cats," but Polly's simpering was intolerable.

"Why don't you come to my apartment when the library closes?" he suggested. "I'll have the Old Stone Mill send over some food. What shall I order for you?"

"Just a green salad with turkey julienne and some melba toast. I'll take some of the turkey home to my sweetheart. He eats like a little horse."

Qwilleran winced, forgetting how many doggie bags he had toted home to the Siamese, forgetting how the pocket of his old tweed overcoat had once smelled of turkey gravy. True, he often called Yum Yum "my little sweetheart," but he did it in private.

He spent that afternoon writing a "Qwill Pen" column on the museum's new disaster exhibit. About the missing sheet he was mum, but he questioned why there was no mention of the miners lost in the explosion. On display was a photo of a granite monument in the cemetery, erected by public subscription to the memory of the thirty-two, but they were not identified.

He filed his copy at the office of the *Something* and bought cider and doughnuts for his soirée with Kristi and Mitch, arriving at his Pickax apartment in time to order dinner.

Although home delivery was not an advertised service of the Old Stone Mill, the chef catered meals for the Siamese when they were in town, and a busboy named Derek Cuttlebrink was used to making daily visits with sushi, shrimp timbales, braised lamb brains and other delicacies.

Polly arrived on foot. Leaving her car in the library parking lot she cut through the rear of the property to the former Klingenschoen carriage house, an ounce of the discretion that she found wise to practice as head librarian in a gossipy town, although it fooled no one. The carriage house, now a four-car garage, was a sumptuous fieldstone building with arched doors and eight brass carriage lanterns posted at the corners. Using her own key, Polly unlocked what had been the servants' door and climbed the narrow stairs to Qwilleran's quarters. There was a warm moment of greeting that would have titillated the Pickax grapevine, and then he inquired about the health of her new boarder.

"He's becoming more adorable every day!" cried Polly. "The things he does are so darling, like sleeping on my pillow with his nose buried in my hair and purring his little heart out. He's gained five ounces, imagine!"

Qwilleran shuddered and picked up a decanter. "May I pour the usual?"

As Polly sipped her sherry she asked about the goat poisoning. "Any more news?"

"Nothing official. We also have a couple of mysteries at the museum. You may not have noticed it during the festivities yesterday, but the Reverend Mr. Crawbanks' sheet has disappeared from the disaster exhibit. Also missing is Iris Cobb's cookbook."

"Really? That's most unusual! The cookbook I can understand, but why the sheet? The young people used to flit about the countryside in white sheets around Halloween, trying to frighten people, until the county outlawed it with what they call the pork-and-beans ordinance."

"And what might that be?"

"It was the result of an incident near Mooseville. A woman sent her teenage son to buy groceries at a crossroads store, and he was walking home on a country road after dark. As he approached the bridge over the Ittibittiwassee, a white-sheeted figure rose out of the dark riverbed and started moaning and screaming. The intrepid youth kept on walking until he was a few yards from the ghost. Then he reached into his grocery sack and hurled a can of beans at the spectre—right between the eye holes. It was a young woman under the sheet, and she went to the hospital with a concussion."

"And I presume the youth went to the majors," Qwilleran said.

Just then the doorbell sounded, and Polly thought it prudent to retire to the bathroom to fix her hair. A tall lanky busboy arrived with Polly's salad and Qwilleran's lambchop—plus two servings of pumpkin chiffon pie with the compliments of the chef.

"Where are the cats?" the busboy asked.

"On vacation," Qwilleran said as he handed him a tip. "Thanks, Derek."

"They've got it made. I never get to go anywhere."

"I thought you were going away to college this fall."

Derek shrugged. "Well, you see, I got this good role in the next play at the theatre, and I met this girl from Lockmaster who's a blast, so I decided to work another year."

"Thanks again, Derek," said Qwilleran, ushering him to the door. "I'll look forward to seeing you in the November play. Don't tell me anything about your role; it's bad luck. The Siamese send you their regards. Give my thanks to the chef. Watch your step with that girl from Lockmaster. Don't trip on the stairs." In slow stages he maneuvered the gregarious Derek Cuttlebrink from the apartment.

Polly emerged from the bathroom, looking not much different. "He's a nice boy, but he hasn't found himself yet," she said.

"He's looking in the wrong place," Qwilleran muttered.

They dined at the travertine table, and Polly inquired how he liked the *Otello* recording.

"A stunning opera! Even the cats have enjoyed it. I've played it several times." Not all the way through, but he withheld that detail.

"How did you like Iago's *Credo*?"

"Unforgettable!"

"And don't you agree with me that *Dio! mi potevi* is gorgeous?"

"My word for it exactly! . . . And what did you think of the disaster exhibit?" he asked, changing the subject deftly.

"The girls accomplished a miracle! That was a difficult subject to dramatize. And the balloting idea was very clever."

"In my opinion they missed the boat. They should have honored the thirty-two victims by name, and I said so in my column."

"No one knows who they were, except for an occasional family recollection," Polly informed him. "There is no official list. We have old copies of the *Picayune* on microfilm, but the issues of May thirteenth to eighteenth are missing, oddly enough."

"Where did you get this film?"

"Junior Goodwinter turned everything over to us when the *Picayune* ceased publication. We also checked the county courthouse files, but death records prior to 1905 were destroyed in a fire that year."

"It would be interesting to know who threw the match," Qwilleran said. "It's doubtful that all the records were destroyed accidentally. Who would want the victims' names forgotten? The Goodwinters? Or would their names give a clue to the identity of the lynch mob? There were probably thirty-two in the gang, one to avenge each victim. A ritualistic touch, don't you think? They were draped in sheets so no one would know the identity of the actual hangman. I imagine they drew straws for the privilege."

"An interesting deduction," Polly said, "assuming that the lynching story is true."

"If Ephraim committed suicide, why would he do it in a public place? He had a big barn. He could have jumped off the haymow. Actually, does anyone really care—at this late date—about the exact fate of the old scoundrel? Why do the Noble Sons of the Noose persist generation after generation?"

"Because Ephraim Goodwinter is the only villain Moose County ever had," said Polly, "and people love to have a bête noire to hate."

She declined the pumpkin pie, and Qwilleran had no difficulty in consuming both pieces. Then he said, "What do you know about Vince and Verona?"

"Not much," Polly said. "They suddenly appeared a month ago and proposed a deal, which the museum board was delighted to accept. Vince offered to catalogue the presses, in return for which they gave him the cottage rent-free. Those presses were a white elephant, so Vince's arrival on the scene was considered a blessing from heaven."

"Don't you consider his offer unusually generous?"

"Not at all. He's writing a book on the history of printing, and this is a unique opportunity for him to see actual equipment that was used a hundred or two hundred years ago."

"I wouldn't mind knowing how he found out about the presses."

"He seems quite knowledgeable about printing."

Qwilleran said, "During my career, Polly, I've interviewed thousands of persons, and I can detect the difference between (a) those who know what they're talking about and (b) those who have memorized information from a book. I don't think Boswell is an 'a.'"

"No doubt the project is a learning experience for him," she persisted stubbornly. "He's always checking out books on the subject. Thanks to Senior Goodwinter, our library has the definitive collection on handprinting in the northeast central states."

Qwilleran huffed into his moustache. "Coffee?" he asked.

"Vince was an auctioneer Down Below," Polly added.

"Or a sideshow barker. His voice would wake the dead. There's one thing about Boswell's operation that puzzles me. Every time I return to the museum from somewhere else, his van is pulling away from the barn. Today I discovered that he uses a walkie-talkie to tell Verona when he's going home to lunch, and I suspect she uses it to tip him off when I turn into Black Creek Lane. One of these days I'm going to trick him—drive away from the museum, park my car somewhere, and sneak back on foot, coming in the back way."

"Oh, Qwill, you're a born gumshoe!" Polly laughed. "All you need is a deerstalker cap and a magnifying glass."

"You may laugh," he retorted, "but I'll tell you something

else: Koko spends most of his waking hours watching the barn from the kitchen window."

"He's looking for barncats or fieldmice."

"That's what you may think, but that's not the message I'm getting from the feline transmitter." He smoothed his moustache significantly. "I have a theory, not fully developed as yet, that Boswell is up to no good in that barn. He's looking for something other than printing equipment in those crates. And when he finds it, he drives around to the livestock doors, loads his van, and delivers the goods."

"What kind of goods?" Polly asked with an amused smile.

"I have no evidence," Qwilleran said, "and I'm not prepared to say. If I could spend an hour in that barn with a crowbar, I might have some answers. Bear in mind that Boswell is the first person to touch those crates since Senior Goodwinter's death a year ago. How did he know about them? Someone in Moose County tipped him off and is probably collaborating in the distribution."

Polly glanced at her watch. Still smiling she said, "Qwill, this is very interesting—confusing, but provocative. You must tell me more about it next time. I'm afraid I must excuse myself now. Bootsie has been alone all day, and the poor thing will want his din-din."

Qwilleran huffed into his moustache. "When do you leave for Lockmaster?"

"Early tomorrow evening. I'll drop off Bootsie on the way. He'll have his special food and his own little commode and his brush. He'll appreciate it if you give him a brush-brush and a kiss-kiss once in a while. He's so affectionate! And he's housebroken, of course. It's adorable to see the little dear scratching in the litterbox and then sitting down with a beatific expression on his smudged-nose face."

Polly returned to her car in the library parking lot, glancing about casually to see who was watching. Qwilleran waited a few discreet minutes and then loaded his bike in the trunk of his own car and headed for North Middle Hummock, where two Siamese were anxiously watching the freezer-chest.

"Guess who's coming to dinner tomorrow," he announced. "Bigfoot!"

Chapter 14

At approximately eight o'clock Monday evening Qwilleran was preparing for his guests, chilling the cider, finding paper napkins, piling a plate with doughnuts enough for ten, and laying a fire in each of the two fireplaces. Without warning Koko came racing into the kitchen from nowhere and hopped onto the windowsill that faced the barn. To Qwilleran's eye the window was nothing but a reflective black rectangle after dark, but Koko saw something that excited him.

Qwilleran cupped his eyes and peered into the blackness. wo lights were bobbing in the barnyard, and his mind flashed back to the bobbing lights on the hats of Homer's ghostly miners. But these lights were different; they darted erratically and swung in wide arcs. As they came closer he could distinguish two faces, and then he recognized Kristi and Mitch. They had walked from the Fugtree farm with flashlights—walked along the Willoway—and were approaching the museum property from the rear.

Qwilleran met them at the entrance, accompanied by the chief security officer.

Kristi said, "It's such a nice night that we decided to walk. The trail alongside the creek is a shortcut but kind of scary at night. Mitch ought to take the kids down there for the Halloween ghost stories this year." She gave Qwilleran an enthusiastic hug and a plastic tub of goat cheese. "I've been high," she said, "ever since you told me about the Klingenschoen offer."

The men shook hands, and Qwilleran said, "You have a fine old Scottish name. My mother was a Mackintosh."

"Yes, the Ogilvie clan goes back to the twelfth century," said Mitch with obvious pride. "My family came here from Scotland in 1861."

"And I happen to know that your grandfather won all the spelling bees with his eyes closed."

"You've been talking to Homer. That old guy has *some memory*!"

Kristi said to Qwilleran, "I'll weave you a scarf in the Mackintosh tartan as soon as I dig out my loom from under my mother's junk . . . Oooooh! What a beautiful cat! Is he friendly?"

"Especially to persons who come bearing goat cheese. Where would you like to sit? In the parlor or around the big table in the kitchen? In either place we can have a fire."

They elected the kitchen. While Qwilleran poured the cider, Mitch put a match to the kindling in the fireplace and Kristi lighted the pink candles that Mrs. Cobb had left on the table. "This is so cozy," she said. "Iris used to invite us over for lemonade and cookies. Mitch, wouldn't you love to live here?"

"Sure would! I'm living over the Pickax drug store right now," he explained to Qwilleran. "I wonder if they've had many applications for Iris's job."

"What are your qualifications, Mitch?"

"Well, I've belonged to the Historical Society ever since high school, and I've read a lot about antiques, and I'm on Homer's committee, supervising the kids who do the yardwork. Plus I have some ideas for special events I could stage if I lived here full time."

"And he gets along with *everybody*," Kristi said. "Even Amanda Goodwinter. Even Adam Dingleberry."

Mitch said, "Old Adam won't be around much longer. He's moved into the Senior Care Facility, but his mind is still sharp."

"And he still gropes girls," Kristi said.

"You should interview him for your column, Mr. Qwilleran, before it's too late."

"Call me Qwill, Mitch. Does Adam have any ghost stories to tell?"

"Everyone around here has had at least one supernatural experience," he said, looking pointedly at Kristi, but she ignored the hint.

"Unfortunately I haven't joined the club as yet," said Qwilleran. "How about the stories you tell the kids on Halloween? Are they classics? Or do you invent them?"

"They're all true, based on events in Moose County and Scottish history. Naturally I add a few hair-raising details."

"Have you ever seen the thirty-two miners?"

Mitch nodded. "About three years ago. I was coming back from a party in Mooseville, and I stopped at the side of the road for a minute, you know. It was near the Goodwinter hill—the old slag pile—and I saw them."

"What did they look like?"

"Just shadows of men, slogging along. I knew they were miners because they had lights on their hats."

"Did you count them?"

"I didn't think of it until some of them had disappeared over the hill, but here's something funny: It was May thirteenth, the anniversary of the explosion."

"Did you say you were coming home from a party?"

"That had nothing to do with it, I swear."

"Okay, I'll square with you. I've always been skeptical of these stories. I always thought there was some logical explanation. I still do, in the back of my mind, but I'm beginning to be skeptical of my own skepticism. Let me tell you what's been happening here."

He told them about Iris Cobb's terrified call in the middle of the night, about the knocking in the basement and the moaning in the walls, and about her "seeing something" just before her death. He said, "I've been told that Senior Goodwinter—just before he died—saw Ephraim walking through a wall. I'm trying to sort out the evidence, you understand."

Kristi said, "There are lots of rumors about Ephraim. They say he stashed away a lot of gold coins in case he wanted to make a quick getaway, but he died suddenly and now he comes back looking for them."

"The old miser!" said Mitch. "He never gives up!"

"One of my cats," Qwilleran said, "has been acting strangely since we moved here. He talks to himself and stares out the window where Iris saw the thing that frightened her."

"Cats are always doing crazy things," Kristi said.

"Koko," said Qwilleran, "is not your ordinary cat. He always has a damned good reason for doing what he does."

Hearing his name, the cat walked into the kitchen, looking elegant and vain.

"God! He's a beautiful animal," said Mitch.

"He looks so intelligent," Kristi added.

"Koko is not only intelligent but remarkably intuitive. I won't say that he's psychic, but he senses when something is out in left field, and if Ephraim's ghost is prowling around here, Koko is going to find him!"

All three turned to look at the remarkable cat. Unfortunately Koko had taken that moment to attend to the base of his tail.

Qwilleran said quickly, "Would you like to see the basement where Iris first heard the knocking? It's just a junkroom for the museum. Do you know the one I mean?"

"I know about it, but I've never been down there. I'd like to see it," Mitch said.

"I'll take Koko along. He can hear earthworms crawling and butterflies pollinating, and if there's anything irregular down there, he'll sniff it out. I'll put him on a leash so that I have a little control."

He strapped the cat into a blue leather harness and coiled a few yards of nylon cord that served as the leash, and the four of them went to the basement, Koko quite willingly.

In the storeroom a few bare lightbulbs threw garish light over the broken furniture, rusty tools, moldy books, cracked crockery, and cobwebs.

"My mother would love this!" Kristi said.

"This is what Homer calls the magpie nest," said Qwilleran. "Iris was looking for a broken bed warmer when she first heard the knocking in the wall. Here's the potato masher she used to reply." He picked up the small wooden club and rapped the Morse code for SOS on the plastered wall—the only skill he remembered from his year in the Boy Scouts—and followed it with the burlesque tattoo, "shave and a haircut, two bits." Neither message called forth a response, but the plaster cracked a little more.

Meanwhile Koko was snapping at cobwebs instead of investigating.

"Cats never cooperate," Qwilleran explained. "The trick is to ignore him for a while. Let's find something to sit on."

Kristi found a platform rocker that no longer rocked; Mitch perched on a barrel; Qwilleran sat on a kitchen chair with three rungs missing, all the while keeping a furtive eye on Koko, who was beginning to move around stealthily.

"I hear rumbling," Kristi said.

"That's thunder," Mitch told her, "but it's a long way off. It's not supposed to rain tonight."

Koko sniffed a wicker baby buggy without wheels. "Some kid cannibalized it to make a go-cart," Mitch guessed.

When the cat sniffed the potato masher, Qwilleran said, "We're getting warm. He knows Iris handled it. Now watch him!"

Koko was making his way to the cracked plaster wall, hopping over a coal skuttle, slinking under a three-legged chair, climbing up on the monstrous sideboard that stood against the plaster wall. It was a hodgepodge of shelves, mirrors, and carved ornament.

"My mother bought two of those dumb things," Kristi said. "Listen! Thunder again! It's coming closer!"

Koko was standing on his hind legs and stretching to see the wall behind the sideboard.

"He senses something," Qwilleran whispered.

Mitch said, "I think he sees a spider walking up the wall."

"I hate spiders," said Kristi.

With one swift movement Koko jumped up, swatted the

insect, brought it down in the cup of his paw, and chomped on it with satisfaction.

"Ugh!" she said.

"Let's go," said Qwilleran, grabbing the cat. "He's not in good form tonight."

"We should think about leaving," Mitch said as they emerged from the basement and saw the sky illuminated with blue lightning.

"I'll drive you home," Qwilleran offered, "so have another glass of cider before you go." The four paraded back to the kitchen.

"This is good stuff," said Mitch. "Did it come from Trevelyan's cider mill? They throw in bruised apples, windfalls, worms and everything. My grandfather insisted on using perfect apples, and it was the flattest cider anybody ever tasted."

The two men talked about leaf raking, the hotel business, and Scottish history, but Kristi was quiet and introspective. Finally she said softly, "Emmaline will walk tonight."

The men glanced at each other and then at her.

She said, "Qwill, would you like to see Emmaline? Mitch has seen her twice."

"Yes, I would," he said.

The downpour had started. They collected their jackets and ran for the steel barn. As they drove up Black Creek Lane torrents of water slapped the windshield. As they turned into the Fugtree drive, flashes of lightning silhouetted the Victorian house against an electric blue sky. No one spoke. They dashed for the side door and arrived in the kitchen wet. Still there was no conversation. Wordlessly Kristi draped their wet jackets over kitchen chairbacks. She turned on no lights, but she beamed a flashlight at the floor to lead them into the foyer. Groping through the incredible clutter they found their way to the massive staircase and sat on the stairs to wait in the dark, smelling the mustiness of the house, feeling the vibration from thunderclaps overhead, hearing the rain slap against the tall narrow windows, seeing the panes glow blue with each lightning flash. They waited.

"She's coming!" Kristi whispered.

No one dared to breathe.

The men stared in rapt silence.

Kristi shuddered and gasped.

Qwilleran found his blood running cold.

The minutes ticked away.

Then Kristi broke into tears. "Wasn't she beautiful?" she sighed.

"Beautiful!" Mitch said in a half-whisper.

"Incredible!" Qwilleran said under his breath.

The three sat quietly for a while, each with private thoughts. The rain relented; the tumult subsided; and Qwilleran brought himself to murmur, "What can I say? . . . Thank you . . . Good night." He squeezed Kristi's hand, touched Mitch's shoulder, and found his way out of the house. "My God!" he said aloud, sitting in the driver's seat, reluctant to turn on the ignition.

At home he dropped into his wing chair and fell into a reverie so deep that he didn't hear the vehicle pulling up to the door. The brass knocker startled him. He jumped up and opened the door, saying, "Mitch! Did you forget something?"

"Just wanted to talk for a minute—without Kristi."

"Come into the kitchen and get that wet jacket off. Do you want a cup of coffee before you drive home?"

"It might be a good idea."

"Put another log on the fire while I make the coffee."

"Sorry to come back so late."

"Forget it! What's on your mind?"

Mitch gave him a searching look. "Tell me honestly, Qwill. Did you see Emmaline?"

"Did you?" Qwilleran asked, returning the intent gaze.

"I've never seen her," the young man confessed.

"To tell the truth," Qwilleran said, "I didn't see her either, but I felt a chill. I sensed an invisible presence. Perhaps I was reacting to Kristi's emotion. Whatever, it was a memorable experience."

They drank coffee for a while without talking. Then Qwilleran said, "Have a doughnut." He pushed the plate across the table.

"Thanks. These are pretty good doughnuts."

"Kristi's an interesting young woman," Qwilleran said.

"I worry about her—with Brent still at large."

"Is he dangerous?"

"Worse still, he's stupid! He was okay until they went Down Below and he started doing drugs. He fell apart. Used to be a good-looking guy, too. At least, Kristi thought so, I guess."

"If he's that far gone," Qwilleran speculated, "it won't take the police long to track him down. It takes a modicum of intelligence and some animal instinct to be a fugitive."

"You're right!" Mitch pushed the plate back across the table. "Doughnut?"

"Yes. They're not bad."

"Up front, Qwill, do you think I stand a chance of getting the museum job?"

"I'm on your side, Mitch, but it's in the hands of the museum board."

"I've been doing some lobbying, and most of them pledged their support, but Larry and Susan are dragging their feet—that's what it seems like."

"I'll see what I can do on your behalf."

"Sure appreciate it." Mitch stared into his coffee cup and fidgeted.

"Another doughnut, Mitch?" The plate went back across the table.

"Thanks."

Qwilleran read the signals. "Is there something else on your mind?"

"Well, when you were telling us about Iris hearing the noises, I thought of something I should tell you, something I heard recently from one of the old-timers. He got the story from an old blacksmith who used to shoe the Goodwinter horses . . . You know about the big funeral they had for Ephraim?"

"I certainly do! Thirty-seven carriages, fifty-two buggies, or was it the other way around?"

"This blacksmith told the old-timer that Ephraim wasn't in the coffin!"

"Why? Did he know why?"

"The family of the old miser was afraid he'd be dug up—by his enemies, you know—so they went through the motions of burying him in the cemetery, but actually he was secretly buried, here on the farm."

"Where? Do you know?"

"Under the house!"

"Now I've heard everything, Mitch. Do you believe that story?"

"I'm only telling you what I heard, Qwill, on account of what you said about Iris, and the way your cat is acting."

"Hmmm," Qwilleran said, stroking his moustache. "How about another cup of coffee?"

"Thanks, but I've got to be going. I'm on the day shift this week."

Qwilleran and Koko walked their guest to the door and watched the blue pickup drive away. The rain had stopped, but the trees were still dripping, and the night was dark. Koko was sniffing and peering into the blackness, and Qwilleran made a lunge for the cat before he could cross the threshold and disappear into the night.

Chapter 15

At midnight Qwilleran retired to the General Grant bed with a paperback novel that Koko had twice knocked off the shelf. He had read *One Flew Over the Cuckoo's Nest* some years before and had seen the movie but he was willing to read it again. He tried, but his eyes only processed the words automatically while his mind reviewed the evening with Kristi, Mitch, and Emmaline. He particularly relished the rumor about Ephraim's burial under the house. Mitch apparently believed the story, but the old-timer who revealed it may have imagined the whole thing, or the blacksmith who related it may have taken a swig after a hard day at the anvil. Nevertheless, Qwilleran liked the story.

The Siamese were curled up on the foot of his bed. In Pickax they had their own room, complete with all conveniences, but at the museum they wanted to sleep on the foot of Qwilleran's bed, a quirk that made him wonder about subliminal influences in the place. All was quiet except for an occasional twitching paw or delicate snore. Shortly after he had turned off the bedside lamp and rolled over, he felt the animals snap out of their deep sleep. Koko was grunting. He turned on the lamp in time to see them listening with ears pricked, necks extended, and heads swiveling like periscopes as they strained to see into the adjoining hall. Then, with one accord, they jumped from the bed with fluid grace and scampered toward the kitchen. They had heard something.

Qwilleran had heard it, too, but he assumed the refrigerator motor had kicked on, or the electric pump was refilling the tank, as it sometimes did in the middle of the night for reasons of its own. Nevertheless, he slipped into his moose-skin moccasins and groped his way to the kitchen, where he heard the gentle sound of a cat lapping a drink of water. That was Yum Yum. Koko was on the windowsill, chattering as he did at squirrels—unusual behavior in the middle of the night.

Qwilleran looked out the window and saw nothing, but he thought it prudent to check the museum. Without turning on lights—simply low-beaming a flashlight on and off—he inspected the exhibit rooms and the office. Whimsically he thought, it would be a joke on a skeptic like me if Ephraim Goodwinter were to materialize through a wall—and what a column it would make for the "Qwill Pen"! Hopefully he sat down in the office. Once he thought he saw, from the corner of his eye, a wisp of movement, and he turned quickly, but there was nothing there. If he had been less skeptical he might have been more patient, but he declined to spend more than five minutes on ghost watching.

Returning to his apartment he locked the connecting door and went back to bed, where he turned on the radio and heard WPKX signing off for the night. Yum Yum again nestled against his feet, although her partner had not returned. Qwilleran picked up his book and tried to resume reading, but Koko's absence made him uncomfortable. Once more he padded to the kitchen and called him without hearing a reply. The entire apartment was silent, and it was not the living, breathing silence that means a furry body is hiding and listening; it was the dead silence that falls on a place when a missing cat is simply *not there*.

Grumbling under his breath, Qwilleran returned to the museum and found Koko sitting on the registrar's table with other uncatalogued items: a stoneware jug, a hand-cranked apple peeler, an embroidered pillow celebrating the Columbian Exposition of 1893, a wooden blueberry picker, an old print of sailing ships—and Kristi's bible. The merest quiver in the roots of Qwilleran's moustache told him to carry both the cat and the bible back to the apartment.

This time, with two cats pressing against his feet, he had no trouble falling asleep. He slept soundly until the darkest hour of night, when he found himself sitting up in bed and staring at the face of the stern-eyed, sour-faced miser. He tried to speak, but no words came. He tried to shout. Ephraim came closer and closer, and then the General Grant headboard began to topple. He raised both hands in a futile attempt to stop it from crushing him . . .

The dream ended, and Qwilleran found himself sitting up in bed with both arms raised and his head throbbing. The cats were blissfully asleep; the headboard was firmly in place; but his skin was clammy, his throat was sore, and his eyes burned.

After taking aspirin and a large glass of water he finished the night on the sofa and succumbed to deep sleep until the telephone rang and the familiar voice of Arch Riker barked, "Did you hear the news on the radio?"

"No, dammit! I was sound asleep!" Qwilleran complained in a hoarse croak. "With a friend like you, who needs an alarm clock? What time is it?"

"Nine-fifteen. Do you want to go back to sleep or do you want to hear some hot breaking news?" asked the publisher of the *Something*, knowing well what the answer would be.

Qwilleran was instantly awake. "What happened?" he asked in full voice.

"It was on the nine o'clock news. They found the body of a man near where you're living. Were you involved in any fights last night?"

"Who? Who's the man?"

"For an innocent bystander you sound unusually anxious, my friend. They're not releasing his name until they've notified next of kin."

"Where was the body?"

"On Fugtree Road near the Black Creek bridge. That's all I know. Roger's over at the police station getting something for the *Something*."

Qwilleran had no sooner hung up than Polly Duncan called him with the same news.

He said, "Both the cats and I were alerted last night. Something was happening in the neighborhood, but I couldn't figure it out. After that, I had a nightmare. I saw Ephraim's ghost. I was wishing I had a can of beans. When I woke up I was having a peculiar physical reaction." He described the symptoms.

"It sounds to me," Polly said, "like an allergy attack, probably caused by all those fallen leaves and the heavy rain. Drink a lot of water."

Qwilleran opted for coffee, then called the *Moose County Something*. Roger had just returned from the civic center.

"What did you find out, Roger?" he asked.

"Talk about poetic justice! The murdered man is Brent Waffle," the young reporter said. "He's the guy Kristi Fugtree divorced, and he was the prime suspect in the poisoning of her goats."

"How was he killed?" Qwilleran held his breath, remembering that Kristi had a gun and she was emotional enough to use it.

"Hit on the head with a blunt instrument, but it didn't happen at the bridge. He was dumped there. They can tell by the bleeding or something that he was killed elsewhere."

"Do they know the time of death?"

"The medical examiner figures between five and six P.M. yesterday."

"Who found the body?"

"A road crew going to work on the bridge."

"How about suspects?"

"They're talking to people around your neighborhood. They'll get to you soon, so you'd better rehearse your alibi . . . I've got to go and file my story now. Keep this under your hat till the paper hits the street."

Qwilleran leafed through Mrs. Cobb's phone book, but before he could make another call there was a commotion on the windowsill. Koko was agitated, pacing back and forth on the sill like a caged tiger, uttering a sharp "ik ik ik."

"What's all the fuss about?" Qwilleran asked. He went to the window in time to see something disappearing through the cat-hatch in the barn door, and it was not a cat. On the grassy ramp outside the hatch lay a small bright green object.

Qwilleran rang the Boswell cottage. "This is Qwilleran. I think Baby's in the barn. Better send your husband down to get her."

"Oh dear! . . . I didn't know . . ." said a confused voice. "Vince isn't here . . . I'll get dressed . . ."

"Are you feeling all right, Mrs. Boswell?"

"I was lying down . . . I didn't know . . . I'll get dressed . . ."

"Stay where you are. I'll find her and send her home."

"Oh, thank you . . . I'm sorry . . . I didn't know . . ."

Qwilleran skipped the civilities, pulled on some clothes and ran to the barn. Opening the eye of the needle and squinting into the darkness, he called "Baby! Baby!"—his voice reverberating in the vaulted space. Then he opened the big barn doors, and the flood of light revealed the small girl trudging down an aisle between the crates, clutching a kitten, its four legs protruding awkwardly like a scarecrow.

"I found a kitty," she said.

"Be careful! He might scratch. Put him down gently—very gently—that's the way!"

Baby did as she was told. That was to her credit, Qwilleran thought. She listened to reason and she was obedient.

"I like kitties," she said.

"I know you do, but your mother wants you to go home. She isn't feeling well. Pick up your pail, and we'll walk back to your house."

With a backward look at the kitten as it staggered away on wobbly legs, Baby walked out of the barn and picked up the green pail and yellow spade. Qwilleran closed the barn door, and they started down the ramp.

"That's a nice pail," he said. "Where did you get it?"

"My mommy bought it for me."

"What color is it?"

"It's *green!*" she said impatiently as if she considered her questioner mentally deficient.

"What do you do with your pail?"

"Dig in the sand."

"There's no sand around here."

"We went to the *beach*," she said with a two-year-old's frown.

They were walking slowly across the barnyard, and Qwilleran realized that the legs of small children are uncommonly short; it would take half an hour to traverse Black Creek Lane. He doubted that he could maintain a dialogue with Baby for half an hour without insulting her intelligence and sounding like a fool himself.

She broke the silence by saying, "I want to go to the bathroom."

"Can you wait till you get home?"

"I don't know."

Dire possibilities flashed through Qwilleran's mind. This was a situation he had never been called upon to face.

Baby had a solution, however. "Do you have a bathroom?" she asked.

Devious child! he thought; she's determined to get in to see the cats. Thinking fast, he said, "It's out of order."

"What does that mean?"

"It's broken."

They walked on, Qwilleran clutching her hand and dragging her along.

"I want to go to the bathroom," she repeated.

Qwilleran took a deep breath. "Okay, I'll get you home in a hurry. Hang on to your pail." He scooped her up as he had seen Verona do, reflecting that she weighed not much more than Yum Yum. With rapid strides, being careful not to jiggle her, he hurried up the lane.

Verona was waiting on the porch, wearing a shabby robe, her hair uncombed, and her face pale. One eye was swollen shut, and there was a purple bruise on her cheek.

"Thank you, Mr. Qwilleran. I'm sorry to trouble you."

Baby tugged at her mother's bathrobe, and a wordless understanding passed between them.

"Excuse me," Verona said.

Qwilleran waited. The black eye aroused his curiosity. When she returned, he said, "Where's Vince?"

"Gone to Lockmaster . . . to the *library?* To do some *research?* He left yesterday *noon?*" The fascinating lilt had returned to her speech.

"What happened to your eye?" Qwilleran asked.

"Oh, stupid me! I walked into a cupboard *door?*"

Qwilleran huffed into his moustache. He had heard that one before. "I found your little girl playing with kittens in the barn. They may be wild. She could get scratched or bitten."

"Poor Baby doesn't have anyone to play with," said Verona pathetically.

"Why doesn't your husband make a sandbox for her? She likes to dig."

"I'll ask him, but he works hard and gets so *tired?* His bad leg, you know, gives him *pain?*"

"When do you expect him?"

"I think he'll be home for *supper?*"

Jogging back to the museum Qwilleran thought, Why would Boswell go to the Lockmaster library when the Pickax library has the definitive collection of material on handprinting? What else might attract him to Lockmaster? The medical center? The race track? Or some covert business in connection with the crates in the barn? His fleeting suspicion about the content of the crates returned, and he thought, I'd like to spend an hour with a crowbar in that barn!

Upon arriving home he found Koko on the telephone table, an indication that it had been ringing. Kristi might have tried to phone. He called the Fugtree farm.

"I've heard the news!" he said to her. "I don't know what to say!"

She spoke with surprising belligerence. "I know damn well what to say. Why didn't someone kill him before he poisoned my goats?"

"Do the police have a suspect?"

"Of course," she said bitterly. "I'm the prime suspect, and Mitch is a close second."

"How do I get on the list?" Qwilleran asked. "I was on the Willoway Sunday morning, and I heard him threatening you. I threw a rock into the stream, but I felt like throwing it at his head."

"Well, I imagine the police will be talking to you as a matter of course."

"I'll keep in touch. Let me know if there's anything I can do."

Soon afterward, Larry Lanspeak phoned. "What the devil is happening in North Middle Hummock, Qwill? First Iris's death, then two thefts in the museum, then a herd of goats poisoned, and now a mysterious dead body."

"Not guilty!"

"We've had an application for Iris's job from a woman in Lockmaster who's highly qualified, but she's too old, considering she's already had one heart attack. God knows we don't want another manager dropping dead on the kitchen floor."

"I still think Mitch is your man, Larry," said Qwilleran. "I spent some time with him last evening, and I'm impressed. He has good ideas, and he'd bring some youthful spirit to the job. Old people like him and young people like him."

"I value your opinion," said Larry, "but—taking the long view—I still favor Boswell, and Susan goes along with my thinking. As manager he can continue cataloguing the presses, help us set up a Museum of Handprinting and assume the title of curator. In its scope I daresay it will be unique in the United States, if not the world! Of course, the final decision is up to the board of governors. We're having a meeting this week."

Qwilleran said, "Excuse me, Larry. There's a sheriff's car pulling up at the door. I'll talk to you later."

The deputy standing on the doorstep was the one who had responded to Qwilleran's call ten days before. "Mr. Qwilleran, may I ask you a question or two?" he asked politely.

"Certainly. Will you step inside? I don't want the cats to run outdoors." Both of them were standing beside him, sniffing the fresh air.

The deputy asked, "Did you see or hear anything suspicious, sir, in the vicinity of Fugtree Road?"

"I can't say that I did. This old house is built like a fort, you know, and the windows were closed. I had friends in during the evening, and we were talking and not paying much attention to the outside world . . . although . . . there was one thing I might mention," Qwilleran added as an afterthought. "Sometime after midnight I was reading in bed when the cats alerted me to a faint rumbling sound. I checked the apartment and also the museum and found everything in order."

"Did you look outdoors?"

"Briefly, but everything was quiet so I went back to my reading."

"What time was that?"

"WPKX was signing off."

At that moment there was a rumbling sound in the hallway, and both men turned to look for its source. It was coming from the floor at the far end of the hall. One of the Oriental rugs was humped in the middle, and the hump was heaving.

"That's my cat," Qwilleran explained. "He burrows under rugs and talks to himself."

The deputy produced a photograph of a man, full-face and profile. "Have you seen this person in the vicinity in the last two or three days?"

"Can't say that I've ever seen this face." It was the face of a once-handsome but now debauched thirty-year-old. "Is he the man you're looking for?" Qwilleran asked with feigned innocence.

"This is the victim. We're interested in his movements in the last few days."

"I'll let you know if anything comes to mind."

"Appreciate it."

Qwilleran closed the door after the deputy, straightened the crumpled rug, and went to look for Koko. This time he was on the dining table, guarding the bible and twitching his whiskers.

"Aha! Leather!" Qwilleran said aloud. The binding was elaborately embossed cowhide with gold-tooling, and the fore-edges of the pages were gilded. Probably a hundred years old, he guessed. Opening the bible to check the date of publication, he went no farther than the flyleaf. The page was covered with hand-written family records, and some of the names and dates demanded Qwilleran's immediate attention.

CHAPTER 16

While the cowhide binding of the historic bible may have attracted Koko, it was the flyleaf that occupied Qwilleran's attention for the next few hours. He forgot to have lunch, and the Siamese respected his concentration and refrained from interrupting, although Koko stood by for moral support. This grand book had once rated a place of importance and reverence on someone's parlor table. More recently it had been relegated to the Fugtree jumble of relics, acquiring some of the mansion's moldy aroma. It was this fustiness that had caused Koko's whiskers to twitch, Qwilleran assumed.

Inside the cover was a salescheck from the Bid-a-Bit Auction House dated August of 1959, stating that Mrs. Fugtree had paid five dollars for the "Bosworth Bible." Making a quick check of the Moose County telephone book, Qwilleran found no Bosworths listed, the family had either died out or moved away. Also inside the cover was an envelope of yellowed newspaper clippings, obviously from the old *Pickax Picayune*. In typical nineteenth-century style the news items, obituaries, and social notes all resembled classified ads, and the typefaces were microscopic, suggesting that readers had better eyesight in those days.

He scanned the clippings and laid them aside, then turned his attention to the flyleaf. Having heard members of the Genealogical Society talk at great length about their adventures in tracing their lineage, he knew it was customary to keep family records in the bible. He knew nothing of his own ancestry except that his mother's maiden name was Mackintosh, yet he found the Bosworth family tree fascinating.

Unfortunately the generations were not charted in the scientific way. Births, deaths, marriages, and calamities were recorded as they occurred, with the year noted. A house burned down in 1908; a leg was amputated in 1911; someone drowned in 1945. It was a chatty journal as much as a family tree. In the early years entries were written with a wide-nibbed pen dipped in ink that had faded somewhat—later, with a fountain pen that occasionally leaked—and finally, it appeared, with a good-quality ballpoint.

The handwriting suggested that the same person had kept the records for more than fifty years, and the dainty script led Qwilleran to believe it was a woman. The last entry was dated 1958, a year before the bible was sold at auction, no doubt in the liquidation of her estate. No member of the family had claimed the nostalgic document. He soon guessed her identity and decided that he liked her. She included squibs of news: A bride had a large dowry or tiny feet; a newborn had red hair or big ears; a death notice was followed by a terse comment, "drank." There was no room on the flyleaf for wasted words, but the newspaper clippings enlarged on the vital statistics.

Qwilleran tackled the investigation with the same gusto he applied to a good meal, and Koko knew something exciting was taking place. He sat on the table and watched intently as the clippings were sorted in neat piles: weddings, births, christenings, business announcements, obituaries, accidents, etc., occasionally putting forth a bashful paw to touch, then withdrawing it when Qwilleran said, "No!"

What first flagged his attention was a date. The first name on the page was Luther Bosworth, born 1874. The similarity to Vince's surname was noted and dismissed; the important factor was the date of death—1904. If Luther died on May 13 in that year, he was obviously one of the explosion victims, only thirty years old. But would a miner own such a pretentious bible? The cottages provided for miners were little more than shacks, and the mine owners operated company stores that kept the workers constantly in debt.

A further check showed that Luther married in 1898. His bride, Lucy, was only seventeen. Six years later she was widowed and left with four small children. What did single parents do in those days? Send their children to an orphanage? Take in washing?

"I think Lucy is the one who kept these records," Qwilleran said to Koko. "Damnit! Why didn't she state exact dates? And how did she get this expensive bible?"

"Yow!" said Koko, ambiguously.

"Okay, let's see if we can figure out what happened to Lucy's four kids." The flyleaf provided the following information:

One son died in 1918. "France" was the notation, making him a World War I casualty.

A daughter died in 1919. "Influenza." A cross-reference in the *Picayune* revealed that seventy-three residents of Moose County died in that post-war epidemic, including two doctors who "worked until they dropped."

Two children, Benjamin and Margaret, survived to carry on the family lineage, but only Benjamin could carry on the family name. Qwilleran traced his line first, and what he found had him pounding the table with the excitement of discovery.

Benjamin Bosworth had three children. One of them, named Henry, died in 1945. "Navy—drowned at sea" was his grandmother's notation. Henry's widow moved to Pittsburgh in 1956, taking her son. The boy had suffered an accident in 1955, and the *Picayune* file elucidated in its usual terse style: "A farmhand employed by the Trevelyan Orchard fired a shotgun to deter youths from robbing the apple trees Wednesday night, resulting in three scared boys and one broken leg. Vincent Bosworth fell from a tree and sustained a compound fracture."

In obvious glee Qwilleran pounded the table and said, "Well, Koko, what do you deduce from that?"

The cat shuffled his feet self-consciously and made no comment.

"I'll tell you what I deduce! Vincent Bosworth, still suffering from a badly repaired fracture—not polio!—returns from Pittsburgh after many years with his name changed. Why did he come back? And why did he change his name? And why does he blame his limp on polio? Vince is the great-grandson of Luther and Lucy!"

Qwilleran was so elated that he had to get out of the house and walk. He took two turns around the grounds, taking care not to shuffle his feet through the fallen leaves. The damp earth exuded a heady aroma; the garden club's rust and gold mums were still blooming stubbornly; a barncat was sunning on the grassy ramp; there was no sign of Boswell and his van. Altogether it was a pleasant day.

Returning to his genealogical investigation he said to Koko, "This is more fun than panning for gold. Now let's see what happened to Luther's daughter Margaret."

According to the flyleaf, Margaret married one Roscoe DeFord. Lucy's proud comment was "Lawyer!" The *Picayune* mentioned a reception for two hundred guests at the Pickax Hotel and a honeymoon in Paris—not bad for a miner's daughter, Qwilleran thought, if that's what Luther was. The DeFord name was still evident in Pickax, although not in the practice of law.

Working faster, driven by suspense, he identified the progeny of Roscoe and Margaret DeFord: four children, ten grandchildren. One of the latter was named Susan, born 1949.

"Well, I'll be damned!" said Qwilleran. He remembered the gold lettering on the Exbridge & Cobb window. In one corner were the names of the proprietors: Iris Cobb and Susan DeFord Exbridge.

"So Susan Exbridge and Vince Boswell are second cousins!" he said to the faithful Koko. "Who would guess it? She's so suave, and he's such a boor! But blood is thicker than water, as they say, and that's why she's backing him for the museum job. Obviously she doesn't care to have it known that they're related."

This discovery called for a celebration. He prepared coffee and thawed a couple of chocolate brownies from the bountiful freezer, and he gave the Siamese a handful of something crunchy that was said to be nutritious and good for their teeth. He was eager to resume his search now. There was one more clue to pursue: the fate of Luther's widow.

"When we last heard from her," he said, "she was a twenty-three-year-old widow with four young children and an impressive bible. Was she deeply religious? Was she pretty? Too bad we don't have a picture of her."

His enthusiasm was contagious, and both cats were now in attendance, seated on the table in statuesque poses. Yum Yum's notorious paw occasionally disturbed the order of the clippings.

"Ple-e-ease! If you're going to participate, do something constructive . . . Listen to this! In the same year that Luther died, Lucy went into business—and she wasn't taking in washing!"

A business announcement in the *Picayune* stated: "Lucy Bosworth, widow of Luther Bosworth, announces that she has purchased the Pickax General Store from John Edwards, who is retiring because of ill health. Mrs. Bosworth will continue to handle the best quality edibles, apparel, hardware, sundries, notions and homemade root beer at reasonable prices. Open daily 7 A.M. to 10 P.M. Closed Sundays until noon."

"The party store of 1904!" Qwilleran exclaimed. "With checkers around the pot-bellied stove instead of video games . . . Wait a minute! What do we have here?"

A written comment in the margin of the clipping, in Lucy's recognizable hand, said, "Cash."

"Interesting," said Qwilleran. "If Luther was a miner, where did Lucy get the money to pay cash for a going business? Miners didn't carry insurance in those days—*that* I know! Did Ephraim make restitution to the victims' families? Not likely, unless forced to do so. Did Lucy sue? Victims weren't big on litigation in the good old days. Did she blackmail the old tightwad? And if so, on what grounds?"

"Yow!" said Koko with an emphasis that reinforced Qwilleran's conjecture.

He continued deciphering the entries on the flyleaf. In 1904 Lucy bought the store. In 1905 she remarried. Her new husband was Karl Lunspik, and her parenthetical remark in the bible was "Handsome!"

"Ah!" he said. "Handsome man marries widow with four small children! For love? Or because she owns a successful business and an expensive bible?" The next facts caused his moustache to bristle:

In 1906 Karl and Lucy Lunspik had a son, William.

In 1908 their name was legally changed to Lanspeak.

In 1911 the Pickax General Store was re-named Lanspeak's Dry Goods.

In 1926 their son, William, joined the business, and it became Lanspeak's Department Store.

William had five children and eleven grandchildren, one of the latter being Lawrence Karl Lanspeak, born 1946.

"Fantastic!" yelled Qwilleran, to the alarm of the Siamese, who scattered. "They're all second cousins—Larry and Susan with their country club connections and status cars . . . and Vince Boswell with his rusty van and irritating manners. Larry is the great-grandson of the unsinkable Lucy Bosworth!"

He picked up the phone and called the store. As soon as Larry heard Qwilleran's voice, he said, "Have you seen today's paper? They've identified the body. The guy that poisoned the goats!"

"I know," said Qwilleran. "The police have been around asking questions."

"I hope you didn't give your right name," Larry quipped.

"Speaking of names, I've made a discovery at the museum. When do you plan on coming out here?"

"Tomorrow, but why don't you come into town tonight and have dinner with Carol and me? Meet us at Stephanie's."

"Sounds good," Qwilleran said, "but I'm tied up tonight. Thanks just the same. See you tomorrow." He refrained from mentioning that Polly was bringing Bootsie to spend the night.

Turning away from the phone he heard a faint knocking in the front of the apartment that startled him. The usual summons from that direction was the clanging of the brass door knocker.

The Siamese froze with their ears forward, and when he left the kitchen to investigate, they hung back. Walking down the hall, he heard the knocking again. He glanced through the glass in the front door but saw no one standing there and no car parked in the yard. It was true, he told himself, that old houses make strange noises.

As he turned his back, the knocking was repeated. Even in broad daylight it was eerie, and to Mrs. Cobb's ears in the middle of the night it must have been terrifying. He strode back to the front door and yanked it open. There on the top step was Baby, carrying her green pail and raising her yellow spade, ready to strike again.

"Hi!" she said.

Qwilleran groaned with relief and annoyance. "What are you doing here? Does your mother know where you are?"

She offered him the green pail. "This is for you."

There was a note in the pail, as well as a chunk of something wrapped in waxed paper. The note said, "Just thought you'd like some meatloaf for a sandwich. Made it yesterday. It's better the second day."

"Tell your mother thank-you," he said, handing back the pail.

Baby was peeking around his legs. "Can I see the kitties?"

"They're having their nap. Why don't you go home and have your nap?"

"I had my nap," she said, turning away and gazing speculatively toward the barn.

"Go home now," he said sternly. "Go right home, do you hear?"

Without another word Baby walked down the steps and marched up the lane on her short legs, carrying her green pail. He watched her until she was almost home. She never looked back.

Qwilleran prepared a meatloaf sandwich for himself and gave some to the cats. All three devoured it as if they had been on a week-long fast. Then he hauled his bike out of the steel barn and went for a ride.

There was an unusual amount of traffic on Fugtree Road—

gawkers, driving out to see where the body was found, hoping to see blood. A county road crew was working on the bridge, and a blatant orange sign warned that the road was closed for construction, but Qwilleran wheeled past the barrier and talked to the foreman, a burly man in a farm cap, with a cheekful of snuff. The foreman recognized the famous moustache.

"Right down yonder," he said, pointing to the rocky slope where Qwilleran had first scrambled down to the Willoway. "Dry blood all over his face. Looked like one o' them Halloween get-ups."

"Do the police have any idea who did it?" It was a truism in Moose County that anyone in a farm cap possessed inside information or was willing to invent some.

"I hear they gotta coupla suspects, but they didn't charge anybody yet. He was killed somewheres else and dumped. There was a lotta muddy tire tracks on the pavement when we come on the job."

"Who was the murdered man?"

"The guy that poisoned the goats—escaped con, local kid—went Down Below and got inta trouble. I'm tellin' ya," said the foreman with an emphatic spit, "if it was my goats, I'da went after 'im myself with a shotgun!"

Chapter 17

Qwilleran returned from his bike ride just as Polly was parking her car in the farmyard. "I'm a little early," she apologized, "because I want to reach Lockmaster before dark." She handed him a cardboard cat carrier. "Here's my precious darling. Take him indoors before he catches cold. I'll collect his impedimenta."

The carrier had a top handle and round airholes and a printed message on the side: "Hi! My name is Bootsie. What's your name?" From one of the holes a wet button-size nose protruded, then quickly withdrew, only to be replaced by a brown paw that might have belonged to a cocker spaniel.

Polly entered the apartment carrying a can of clinical-looking catfood with much fine print on the label, a cushioned basket, a brush, and a shallow litterbox containing shreds of torn paper. "This is his own commode," she said. "He's trained to paper. I use paper toweling—not newsprint because the ink might come off on his little derrière . . . And here's his special food, a formula computerized to suit his needs. Give him three level tablespoons, no more, no less, for each meal, and don't let him have anything else. Spread it thinly over a saucer, and I suggest you place the saucer in a secluded corner so he won't feel threatened."

"How about drinking water? Can he have the stuff out of the tap?"

"Tap water will be satisfactory," she said with a serious nod, "and here's his sleeping basket. Put it in a warm place, elevated a foot or two off the floor . . . And thank you so much, Qwill! Now I must dash. Let me say goodbye to the little dear." Tenderly she lifted Bootsie from the carrier and touched her nose to his wet one. "Kiss-kiss, sweetums. Be a good kitten." To Qwilleran she added, "Tomorrow is his birthday, by the way; he'll be eleven weeks old."

She gave Qwilleran a fond but hasty farewell, handed him the innocent kitten, and hurried out to her car. He stood holding the handful of purring fur, wondering what had become of the Siamese. They had avoided the opening ceremonies, as well they might, and until he knew their whereabouts he was reluctant to let the kitten out of his grasp.

Koko and Yum Yum, it was eventually discovered, were on top of the seven-foot Pennsylvania German *Schrank*, sitting side by side in compact bundles, looking petrified.

"Oh, there you are!" Qwilleran said. "Come down and meet Bigfoot."

He placed the kitten carefully on the floor. The tiny thing looked vulnerable with his skinny white neck, skinny brown tail, floppy feet and smudged nose, but once he found himself free of restraints he took a few staggering steps and then shot out of the room like a missile. By the time Qwilleran found him he was on the kitchen counter, eating the leftover meatloaf, waxed paper and all. Seeing the big man, he raced to the front of the apartment with exaggerated leaps like a grasshopper, bouncing from chair to table to desk to bed to dresser. Koko and Yum Yum were still on top of the *Schrank*, gazing down in apparent disbelief.

For the next few hours Bigfoot created chaos with his wild flight—slamming into furniture, breaking a piece of antique glass, leaping and falling and landing on his back, climbing Qwilleran's pantleg and pouncing on his lap. After a nerve-wracking dinner hour he telephoned Lori Bamba in Mooseville and cried "Help!"

He wasted no time inquiring about the baby's health or Nick's job-hunting. He said, "I don't know how I fell into this trap, Lori. Polly Duncan has a new kitten and I agreed to cat-sit, but he turned out to be a wound-up, hyperactive, jet-propelled maniac! He's driving us all crazy with his whizzing around and pouncing, and all the time he's purring like a Model T with two cylinders missing."

"How old is he?" asked Lori.

"Eleven weeks tomorrow. I'm supposed to sing 'Happy Birthday' to him."

"Remember, Qwill, he's very young, and he's being exposed to a strange house with two big cats. He's apprehensive. Fright causes flight."

"Apprehensive!" Qwilleran shouted. "Koko and Yum Yum are the ones who are apprehensive. They're on top of the seven-foot wardrobe and won't come down, even to eat. Bigfoot ate his own medically approved food, and then he ate their turkey loaf with olives and mushrooms, and then he swooped in and knocked a piece of salmon right off my fork! . . . And let me tell you something else. Instead of claws he has needles. When I sit down he pounces on my lap and sinks those eighteen needles. Propriety prevents me from describing the effect. Ask your husband to tell you."

Lori was listening sympathetically. "Where is the kitten now?"

"I finally locked him up in his carrier, but I can't leave him in that cramped box for twenty-four hours. Isn't there some kind of feline Mickey Finn?"

"With all that food in his stomach and with the security of the carrier, he should go to sleep soon, Qwill. Leave him there until he calms down. Then at bedtime shut him up in the kitchen with his water dish and litterbox and something soft to sleep on."

"I'll try it. Thanks, Lori."

She was right. Bigfoot was quiet for an evening of serenity, and the Siamese ventured down from their safe perch. The domestic peace was short-lived, however.

Shortly before midnight Qwilleran took the carrier to the kitchen, closed the door and released Bigfoot. For a while the kitten staggered about the floor like a drunken plowman, squeaking and purring at the same time. Then he became quiet and mysteriously absent from view. It should have been obvious that he was lurking in ambush.

Qwilleran was preparing the kitten's bedtime meal—three tablespoons of unappetizing gray hash smeared thinly on a saucer—when he was suddenly attacked from the rear. Bigfoot had pounced on his back and was clinging to his sweater.

"Down!" he yelled, shrugging his shoulders in an attempt to dislodge his attacker, but his sweater was a chunky knit pullover, and Bootsie was firmly hooked into the yarn and squealing at the top of his minuscule lungs.

"Down! . . . Ow-w-w-w!" Every time he yelled, the needles sank deeper into his flesh and the squeals accelerated.

"Shut up, you idiot!"

Qwilleran reached behind his back, first over his shoulders and then around his midriff. The former approach netted him a handful of ears; the latter, only a wisp of a tail. He pulled gently on the tail. "Ow-w-w-w! Damnit!"

Hearing the commotion, the Siamese ventured down from the top of the *Schrank* and yowled outside the kitchen door.

"And you shut up, too!" he bellowed at them.

Stay calm, he told himself and tried sitting quietly on the edge of a chair. It worked, to a degree. Bootsie stopped squealing and gouging but made no attempt to disengage his claws. He was content to spend the night, suspended like a papoose.

After five minutes of inactivity Qwilleran reached the end of his patience. As Lori said, fright causes flight. He jumped to his feet, roaring the useful curse he had learned in North Africa, flapping his arms and galloping about the kitchen like a witch doctor. The curse ended in a prolonged howl of pain as Bigfoot gripped Qwilleran's back for the wild ride.

It was after midnight. In desperation he telephoned the Boswells' number. When he heard Verona's gentle hello, he shouted, "Let me talk to Vince! I'm in bad trouble! This is Qwilleran."

"Oh, dear! Vince hasn't come home," said the soft voice with an overtone of alarm. "Is there anythin' I can do?"

"I've got a cat on my back—with his claws hooked into my sweater! I need someone to pry him loose . . . Ow-w-w-w!"

"Oh, gracious! I'll come right away."

He walked slowly to the front door, trying not to upset Bigfoot, and turned on the yardlights. In a matter of minutes that seemed like hours Verona appeared, running and clutching a flashlight. A heavy jacket was thrown over her shabby bathrobe.

Opening the door in slow motion, he warned her, "Don't make any sudden movement. See if you can grasp him about the middle and raise him gently to unhook the claws. Try releasing one paw at a time."

Verona did as she was told, but when one paw was freed, another clutched with renewed determination.

"I'm afraid it's not workin'. May I make a suggestion?" she asked in her deferential way. "We could take your sweater off over your *head?* If I roll it up in the back, we should get the kitten and all."

"Okay. Take it easy. Don't alarm him."

"Oh, he's a nice kitty. He's such a nice kitty," Verona cooed as she rolled the sweater over the little animal and then over Qwilleran's head. "Oh, gracious!" she said. "Your shirt is all *bloody?*"

He ripped it off.

"And your back is a mess of bloody *scratches?* Do you have an antiseptic?"

"There's something in the bathroom, I think."

Leaving Bigfoot rolled cozily in the sweater, they trooped to the bathroom and found a liquid which Verona applied liberally to the scratches while Qwilleran winced and grunted.

"Does it smart? We don't want to get an infection, do we? There now, put on somethin' so you don't take a *chill?*" Her voice was music to his ears.

"I don't know how to thank you, Mrs. Boswell," he said as he put on a fresh shirt. "I was reluctant to bother you at this late hour, but my only other recourse was the volunteer fire department in North Kennebeck."

"No bother. No bother at all. Do you have any more scratches that need antiseptic?"

"Uh . . . I don't think so," Qwilleran said. "Where's Vince?"

"Stayin' in Lockmaster a bit longer. He didn't finish at the *library?*"

He looked down at the pathetic little woman with her hair uncombed, her black eye turning yellow, her ridiculous garb—khaki jacket, faded bathrobe, old sneakers. "Would you like a cup of coffee?"

"I should go home," she said. "I left Baby sleepin' and she might wake up . . . but . . . do you have any milk?"

"Milk? I'm afraid not. I'm not a milk drinker. Mrs. Cobb left a carton but it turned sour and I threw it out."

"I've run out of milk for *Baby?* I thought Vince was comin' home and could do some *shoppin'?*"

"There's a package of that powdered stuff here. Could you use that?"

"Oh, I'd appreciate it so *much?*"

"If Vince isn't home tomorrow morning, I'll pick up some groceries for you. Make a list of what you need."

Verona redded with embarrassment. "He didn't leave me any money."

"That's unforgivable! Let's see what we can find here." Taking a shopping bag from the broom closet he filled it with cheesebread, blueberry muffins, banana-nut bread, vegetable soup, tuna casserole, chili, and—reluctantly—his favorite dish, macaroni and cheese. "I'll drive you home," he said, picking up a jacket and feeling for his keys.

It was a short ride, hardly more than two city blocks. After a brief silence Verona said, "I saw your big *kitties?* They're beautiful! I'd love for Baby to see them someday."

"All right," he said. "Bring her over on Thursday afternoon. And thanks again, Mrs. Boswell, for coming to my rescue."

"Call me Verona," she said as she climbed out of the car. He waited until she was in the house and then drove away, asking himself how a nice woman like Verona could get mixed up with a cad like Boswell.

Back at the apartment Bigfoot was still rolled up in the sweater, and when Qwilleran unrolled him the kitten remained in deep slumber with an angelic look on his smudge-nosed face. He was purring in his sleep.

CHAPTER 18

Bigfoot and the Siamese were socializing politely when Qwilleran rode away on his bicycle Wednesday morning, headed for West Middle Hummock. As he passed the Fugtree farm he wondered when the police would return to question him about his Monday evening visitors.

Brent Waffle was killed before eight o'clock, according to the medical report. Kristi and Mitch arrived via the Willoway promptly at eight. They might have encountered Waffle on the trail, argued violently, bashed him with a flashlight—or two flashlights—and left his body on the bank of the stream. Perhaps they remembered the Buddy Yarrow case on the Ittibittiwassee River, when the coroner ruled that Buddy slipped and hit his head on a rock. Then, after midnight, Mitch would drive down one of the access roads to the Willoway and remove the body to the public highway, a site farther removed from the Fugtree property. The rumbling that Qwilleran had heard at a late hour could have been Mitch's truck on the gravel road.

If this scenario were true, he reflected, the amateur murderers had been remarkably cool during the evening. And if it were true, why would the body—left on the Willoway during the torrential rain—be covered with dried blood when found by the road crew? More likely, Waffle had been killed indoors. Perhaps the guy had returned to the scene of his crime and was hiding in one of the vacant goat barns, perhaps eyeing Kristi as his next victim. Perhaps the bucks—Attila, Napoleon and Rasputin—had created a disturbance and alerted her. Then she and Mitch went to investigate, and it was two against one.

Qwilleran hoped his speculations were wrong. They were good kids, with promising lives ahead of them. It was the mesmerizing effect of pedaling his bike that produced such fantasies, he told himself.

At a country store in West Middle Hummock he bought apples, oranges, and milk and dropped them off at the Boswell cottage. Verona, still in a bathrobe, was tearfully grateful.

"Where's Vince?" he asked.

She shrugged and shook her head sadly.

"Call me if any problem arises."

Baby, clutching her mother's bathrobe, said, "I'm going to see the kitties tomorrow."

When Qwilleran arrived at the museum the yard was filled with cars: the Tibbitts' old four-door, Larry's long station wagon, and Susan's gas-guzzler (part of her divorce settlement) among others. It appeared that the board of governors was in session, no doubt deciding on a new manager.

Qwilleran changed quickly from his thermal jumpsuit, counted the noses of three sleeping bundles of fur, and joined the group in the museum. The meeting had not yet been called to order. Some of the officers and committee heads were milling about the exhibit area; others were having coffee in the office.

"Join us, Qwill!" Larry called out. "Have a doughnut!"

"First, a word with you, Larry." Qwilleran beckoned him out of the office and conducted him to the apartment. "I want you to see something I've discovered."

"What is it?"

"Something that belonged to your great-grandmother."

"Which one? I had four. So did you, as a matter of fact."

"Mine didn't write family secrets on the flyleaves of their bibles," Qwilleran retorted. "Have a chair."

They sat at the big table, and Qwilleran picked up the large, leather-bound, gold-tooled book. "This rare artifact was sold at a Bid-a-Bit auction to Mrs. Fugtree, whose daughter presented it to the museum. It was identified as the Bosworth Bible, because the first name recorded on the flyleaf was Luther Bosworth, who died in 1904."

"Let me see that!" Larry held out his hand.

"Not so fast! From studying the inscriptions I deduce that Luther's widow, Lucy, kept the family records in the bible. She apparently died around 1958, because there are no entries beyond that date, and Mrs. Fugtree made her purchase in 1959."

"You've been a busy boy," said Larry, "but what's the point?"

"The point is that, according to Lucy, you and Susan and Vince Boswell are second cousins, but of course you know that; everyone in Moose County is a genealogy nut."

"I believe there is some sort of relationship," Larry said evasively. "Ow-w-w-w! *What's that?*" He was shaking his leg.

"Sorry. That's Bigfoot. I'll lock him up. He's Polly's cat." Qwilleran put Bootsie in the broom closet.

"Okay, Sherlock, what else did you discover?" Larry asked. "You look smug."

"I learned some facts about your store. Your great-grandmother bought the Pickax General Store in 1904, shortly after Luther died. She paid cash for it. Soon after, she married Karl what's-his-name and changed the store name to Lanspeak's Dry Goods. It would make a newsy column for the 'Qwill Pen.' I'm sure you could fill in the details."

Good actor though he was, Larry could not keep his face from flushing nor his forehead from perspiring. "Let me see that thing!"

Qwilleran clutched the bible possessively. "One more thing, Larry, and then I won't delay you any longer. You and Susan have been pushing Vince Boswell—or Bosworth, as the case may be—for Iris's job, but are you sure he projects the image you want for the museum? Even though he's your relative he lacks a suitable personality and lacks class, to put it bluntly, and there may be other marks against him if my hunches check out." He smoothed his moustache in a significant gesture. "If the board is meeting today to discuss the matter, it might be wise to postpone your decision."

"What are you trying to say, Qwill? What's the big mystery?"

"Vince has gone to Lockmaster, leaving Verona without transportation, without money, and even without milk for the child. He left Monday, and there's no telling when he'll return. Does he play the horses? The race season just opened in Lockmaster."

"I don't know about that."

"Obviously the man has little sense of responsibility. Is that the kind of manager you want? By the way, why did he change his name from Bosworth?"

"To tell the truth, I never asked him," said Larry.

"Was Luther Bosworth a miner? Was he a victim of the May thirteenth explosion?"

"No, he was sort of a handyman—a caretaker on the Goodwinter farm. All I know is what my great-uncle Benjamin said. Ephraim thought very highly of Luther."

"But you're not descended from Luther; your great-grandfather was Karl."

"Correct."

"Karl was a handsome man."

"How do you know?"

"Read your family bible, and you'll find out." Qwilleran presented it to Larry with a flourish, unaware of some clattering and thumping in the broom closet.

"Now let me ask you a question," Larry said. "According to

the paper, the murder victim was Kristi Fugtree's ex-husband. Everyone says he's the one who poisoned her goats. She's now seeing a lot of Mitch Ogilvie. Do you think Mitch had anything to do with it?"

"Not very likely. He and Kristi were here Monday night, drinking cider and discussing the restoration of the Fugtree mansion as a historic place."

"I hope to God he's not involved," said Larry. "Now I've got to go back to the office and start the meeting."

"One more question, if you don't mind, Larry. What do you know about sandboxes for kids?"

"People around here make them with two-by-fours and get free sand on Sandpit Road. Why do you ask?"

"We have a budding archaeologist at the Boswell cottage with no place to dig."

Out came the reliable notebook. "The yard crew can rig something up. There might be some two-by-fours in the steel barn. I'll take care of it."

As he left there was a minor explosion in the broom closet, accompanied by the sound of shattering glass. Qwilleran yanked open the door. Bootsie was sitting on the shelf with the light bulbs, purring.

Polly Duncan returned earlier than expected to pick up the kitten. "When the meeting ended, I didn't stay to socialize," she explained. "I was lonesome for my little sweetheart. Was he a good boy?"

"No problem. I have a few scars, and the value of the Cobb glass collection is down a few hundred dollars, and the Siamese will never be the same, but . . . no problem."

Polly paid no attention. "Where is he? I can hardly wait to see him. *Where is he?*" Both she and Qwilleran searched the apartment, checking all the warm places and soft places. They found Koko and Yum Yum on the blue velvet wing chair but not a hair of the kitten. Qwilleran could tell by Polly's terrified expression that she thought the Siamese had eaten Bigfoot.

"Here he is!" he called from the bathroom, just in time to save Polly from nervous collapse.

Bootsie was in the turkey roaster that served as a commode for the Siamese, sound asleep in the gravel.

Polly seized him. "Bootsie darling! What are you doing there? Were you lonesome? Did you miss me? Kiss-kiss . . . Did he use his litterbox, Qwill?"

"He seemed to prefer the turkey roaster."

"I hope he wasn't too frightened to eat."

"No, he ate *very well*, let me assure you. Did you run into Vince Boswell down there? He's supposed to be doing research at the library."

"I didn't see anyone from Pickax. If they were there, they were all at the track. The races are on this week. Now we must pack our luggage and go home."

Qwilleran produced Bootsie's basket, litterbox, brush, and carrier with alacrity.

"Say goodbye to Uncle Qwill, Bootsie," said Polly, lifting the kitten's thin foreleg and waving the floppy brown paw. "Look at that lovely paw—just like a beautiful brown flower. Do you think I should clip his claws?"

"Don't do anything rash," said Qwilleran.

When they had left, he heaved a sigh of relief, and the Siamese walked around, stretching. The three of them enjoyed a peaceful dinner of chicken cordon bleu from the freezer, and at dusk they settled down in the parlor for some music—the cats on the blue wing chair and Qwilleran on the brown lounge chair opposite, a mug of coffee in his hand. Both telephone bells had been turned off. No matter what the crisis or emergency, he was determined to hear Polly's opera cassette without interruption.

As the first three acts unreeled he realized he was actually enjoying this music. Whatever sardonic remarks about opera he had made in the past, he was willing to rescind. The Siamese were listening, too, possibly hearing notes and nuances that escaped his ear. He was following the English libretto, and the suspense was mounting in the fourth act. During the poignant "Willow Song" Desdemona cried, "Hark! I hear a wailing! Hush! Who is knocking at that door?" And Emilia replied, "It is the wind."

At that precise moment a rumbling growl came from the depths of Koko's chest. He jumped to the floor and ran into the hall. A moment later there was a frantic pounding at the front door, the brass knocker clanging and fists beating the door panels.

Qwilleran rushed to open it.

"*Help me find Baby!*" screamed Verona, wild-eyed with anxiety and gasping for breath. "She got out! Maybe the barn!"

He grabbed a jacket and the battery-operated lantern, and they ran across the barnyard. A mercury-vapor lamp on a high pole flooded the entire yard, but Verona had run all the way down the lane without a flashlight. She had forgotten it in her panic.

"How long has she been gone?" Qwilleran shouted.

"I don't know." She was short of breath.

"Where's Vince?"

"Not home yet."

They raced up the grassy ramp to the eye of the needle.

"Step inside, but don't go any farther," Qwilleran ordered. "It's dark in there. Too many obstacles. Call her name."

"Baby! Baby!" Verona called in a terrified voice.

"Louder!"

She started forward.

"Stay back! And I mean it! Call her name!"

"Ba-aby! Ba-aby!"

Qwilleran flashed his light up and down the straw-covered aisles between the crates and presses. There was no movement except for a barncat darting to cover. In one corner of the barn an industrial palette was leaning against the wall. Qwilleran had seen this wooden platform on his previous visit, flat on the floor, and he had wondered if Boswell used a forklift. Now it was leaning against the wall.

"Stay where you are!" he warned Verona as he went to investigate. "Don't stop calling."

The up-ended palette had been covering a square opening in the threshing floor, and a ladder led down into the stable. Qwilleran flashed his light down the hole and saw a green pail. He climbed down the ladder and quickly up again.

Putting his arm around Verona he said, "Come back to the house. We have to call the ambulance."

"*She's hurt!* Where is she? I've got to see her!"

"You can't. Wait till the ambulance comes."

Verona fainted.

Qwilleran carried her back to the apartment and placed her on the bed, where she lay—awake but motionless and staring at the ceiling. He covered her with a blanket and elevated her feet, then called the emergency number and Dr. Halifax.

"Doc, I've got a mother and child here. The baby's unconscious," he said. "I think the mother's in shock. I've called the ambulance. What should I do in the meantime?"

"Keep them both warm. Have the ambulance bring them both to the Pickax hospital. I'll be there. What's the name?"

"Boswell. Verona Boswell."

"Don't know the name. That's not a Moose County name."

The paramedics put Baby on a stretcher and told the sheriff's deputy who was standing by, "Looks like she fell down a ladder and landed on the stable floor. Stone floor. Possible broken neck, looks like."

Such a puny neck, Qwilleran thought. Hardly bigger than Koko's.

After Verona had been carried out on a stretcher, Qwilleran went to the barn again with his lantern and flashed it down into the stable. The green pail was still there. He closed the eye of the needle and returned to the museum. As soon as he opened the apartment door, something whizzed past his feet and disappeared around the corner of the house faster than the eye could discern. He dashed off in pursuit, bellowing, "Koko! Come back here!"

The cat was headed for the barn at a speed four times faster than Qwilleran's fifty-yard dash. Clearing the ramp in two leaps Koko disappeared through the cat-hatch as if he had been a barncat in one of his other lives. Qwilleran swung the great doors open to take advantage of the lightpole and called his name.

A twinge on his upper lip told him that Koko would leap down the ladder. Qwilleran followed. The stable was a low-ceilinged, stone-floored room with more crates and more presses and more straw. He flashed the light around the stalls and listened intently until he heard a familiar rumbling growl ascending the scale and ending in a shriek. He traced it to the far end of the stable, near the back doors where the horses and cows would have been led into their stalls. Koko was there, hovering over something wedged between two crates—a litter of squirming newborn kittens and a mother cat, bedded down on a piece of soiled cloth.

Qwilleran seized Koko about the middle, and the cat seemed quite willing to be seized. As they headed for the ladder he almost tripped over the crowbar that Boswell used to open crates. He flashed his lantern around the floor. In one corner a pile of straw was hollowed as if someone had slept there. He saw beer cans and empty cigarette packs. That fool Boswell! Qwilleran thought. Goofing off and *smoking* in a bed of dry straw!

The cat under his arm was wriggling to get free, and he let him go. With his nose to the floor Koko followed a scent that led him into the pile of straw, led him to a bundle of something rolled to make a pillow, led him to a patch of dried blood on the pillow and the straw. The bundle was the same dark green Qwilleran had seen on the Willoway, stenciled LOCKMASTER COUNTY JAIL.

Clutching Koko and the lantern Qwilleran hurried back to the apartment and made three phone calls: first to the night desk of the *Moose County Something*, then to the sheriff's department, and finally to the president of the Historical Society.

Chapter 19

The early-morning newscast on WPKX included this announcement: "A suspect in the bludgeoning murder of Brent Waffle is being sought by police in several northern counties following the discovery of incriminating evidence and the suspect's disappearance from the area. According to the sheriff's department, the name of the suspect will not be released until he is apprehended and charged."

There followed brief reports on a three-car accident at the blinker in downtown Kennebeck and a controversy at the Pickax city council meeting regarding a Halloween curfew. The newscast ended with the following: "A two-and-a-half-year-old child fell and was seriously injured on the property of the Goodwinter Farmhouse Museum last evening. A trap door in the barn floor was left uncovered, and the child fell to the stone-paved floor of the stable below."

After that eye-opening news hit the airways, Qwilleran received phone calls from all the usual operators on the local grapevine, one of the first being Mr. O'Dell, the white-haired janitor who serviced Qwilleran's apartment in Pickax. He said, "It's the windows I'm thinkin' of washin' if you'll be comin' back to the city soon."

"I have no immediate plans," Qwilleran said. "I promised to stay here until they find a new manager."

"A pity it is, what's happenin' out there," said Mr. O'Dell. "First Mrs. Cobb, a good woman, God rest her soul! And herself barely cold in her grave when the little one, innocent as a lamb, fell. Sure an' it's a black cloud that hangs over the Goodwinter farm, an' I'm givin' you some advice if you've a mind to take it. No good will come of it if you take it into your head to stay there. The divil is up to tricks for eighty or ninety year since, I'm thinkin'."

"I appreciate your advice, Mr. O'Dell," said Qwilleran. "I'll give it some serious thought."

"An' shall I be washin' the windows?"

"Yes, go ahead and wash the windows." Qwilleran was in no hurry to move back to Pickax, devil or no devil, but he knew it would relieve Mr. O'Dell's mind if the windows were clean.

Arch Riker had other ideas. "Why don't you move back to town and stop playing detective?" the publisher said. "Readers are complaining. They expect to see the 'Qwill Pen' on certain days."

"It's been nothing but emergencies, obstacles, and distractions for the last two weeks," Qwilleran said. "I was all set to write a goat column when the herd was poisoned and the front page got the story. I was planning to do a piece on the antique printing presses, but the so-called expert has left town and will wind up in prison."

"Excuses, excuses! Find an old-timer and rip off some memoirs for Monday," Riker suggested. "Do it the easy way until you get back on the track."

Taking the publisher's suggestion and Mitch Ogilvie's tip, Qwilleran called the Senior Care Facility in Pickax and asked to interview Adam Dingleberry. The nurse in charge recommended a late-morning visit, since the old gentleman was always drowsy after lunch, and she specified a time limit of thirty minutes for the nonagenarian, by doctor's orders.

Arriving at the Facility, Qwilleran found the lobby bright with canaries—those yellow-smocked volunteers wearing "We Care" lapel buttons. They were fluttering about, greeting visitors, wheeling patients, tucking in lap blankets, adjusting shawls, smiling sweetly, and showing that they cared, whether the patients were paying guests like Adam Dingleberry or indigent wards of the county. There was no hint that the cheerfully modern building was descended from the County Poor Farm.

One of the canaries ushered Qwilleran into the reading room, a quiet place equipped with large-print books and cleverly adjustable reading lamps. He had been there on previous occasions to conduct interviews and had never seen anyone reading. Patients who were not confined to their beds were in the lounge, watching television.

"He's a little hard of hearing," said the canary who wheeled the elderly mortician into the room, a wizened little man who had once been the tallest boy in school and a holy terror, according to Homer Tibbitt.

The volunteer took a seat apart from them, near the door, and Qwilleran said in a loud, clear voice, "We've never met, Mr. Dingleberry, but I've seen you at meetings of the old-timers, and Homer Tibbitt tells me he went to school with you."

"Homer, eh? He were younger than me in school. Still is.

He's only ninety-four. I'm ninety-eight. How old are you?" His voice had the same high pitch as Homer's, and it cracked on every tenth word.

"I'm embarrassed to say," Qwilleran replied, "that I'm only fifty."

"Fifty, eh? You have to walk around on your own legs. When you're my age, you get trundled around everywhere."

"That gives me something to look forward to."

In spite of his shrunken form and leathery wrinkles, Adam Dingleberry had sharp birdlike eyes that darted as fast as his mind. "The city fathers are tryin' to outlaw Halloween," he said, taking the lead in the conversation. "In the old days we used to wax windows and knock over outhouses till hell-won't-have-it. One year we bricked up the schoolhouse door."

Qwilleran said, "May I turn on my machine and tape some of this?" He placed the recorder on the table between them, and the following conversation was preserved for posterity:

The museum has a desk from the Black Creek School, carved with initials. Would any of them be yours?

Nope. I always carved somebody else's initials. Never finished the grades. They kicked me out for smearin' the teacher's chair with cow dung. My paw give me a whuppin' but it were worth it.

Is it a fact that the Dingleberry family has been in the funeral business for more than a hundred years?

Yup. My grampaw come from the Old Country to build shafthouses for the mines. Built coffins, too. When some poor soul died, Grampaw stayed up all night whittlin' a coffin—tailor-made to fit. Coffins warn't like we have now. They was wide at the top, narrow at the foot. Makes sense, don't it? It took a heap o' skill to mitre the joints. Grampaw were mighty proud of his work, and my paw learned coffin-buildin' from him, only Paw started buildin' furniture.

What kind of furniture, Mr. Dingleberry?

Wal, now, he used to build a desk with long legs and a cupboard on top. Sold tons of 'em! The Dingleberry desk, it were called. They was all a bit different: doors, no doors, one drawer, two drawers, false bottom, built-in lockbox, pigeonholes, whatever folks wanted.

Did your father sign his work?

Nope. Folks knowed who built their desk. No sense in puttin' a name on it. Like today, they slap names all over. My grandsons have names on the outside of their shirts! Next thing, they'll be puttin' the Dingleberry name inside the casket!

How did your father become a mortician?

Wal, now, his desk—it were such a good seller, he hired fellas to build 'em and tables and beds and coffins—whatall folks wanted. So Paw opened a furniture store. Gave free funerals to folks that bought coffins. He had a fancy black hearse and black horses with black feathers. Funerals were a sight in them days! When me and my brothers come along—they're all dead now—we opened a reg'lar funeral parlor, all proper and dignified but not highfalutin, see? Got rid o' the horses when automobiles come in. Folks hated to see 'em go. Then my sons took over, and my grandsons. They went away to school. I never finished.

Do you remember the Ephraim Goodwinter funeral?

(Long pause.) Wal, now, I were a young lad, but my folks talked about it.

Was his death a suicide or a lynching?

(Long pause.) All I know, he were strung up.

Do you know who cut down the body?

Yup. My paw and Ephraim's son, Titus. They had a preacher there, too. Forget his name.

Mr. Crawbanks?

That's him!

How do you know all this?

(Long pause.) I warn't supposed to be there. My paw told me to stay to home, but I hid in the wagon. The preacher, he said some prayers, and Paw and Titus took off their hats. I crossed myself. I knew I'd get a whuppin' when we got home.

Did you see the corpse? Were the hands tied or not?

Couldn't see. It were near daybreak—not much light.

Did anyone have a camera?

Yup. Titus, he took a picture. Don't know what for.

How was the corpse dressed?

That were a long time ago, and I were too bug-eyed to pay attention. They throwed a blanket over him.

A suicide would have to stand on a box or something and then kick it away. Do you remember seeing anything like that?

(Long pause.) Musta sat on a horse and give it a kick. Horse went home all by itself. Empty saddle. That's when they come lookin' for the old man. That's what Titus said.

Did you believe that?

I were a young boy then. Didn't stop to figger it out.

Did your father ever talk about it?

(Long pause.) Nope. Not then. (Long pause.) What d'you want to know all this for?

Our readers enjoy the memoirs of old-timers. I've interviewed Euphonia Gage, Emma Huggins Wimsey, Homer Tibbitt . . .

Homer, eh? I could tell you some things he don't know. But don't put it in the paper.

I'll turn off my tape recorder.

Qwilleran flipped the button on the machine and placed it on the floor.

"I want a drink of water," the old man demanded in his shrill voice. As the canary hurried from the room, he said to Qwilleran. "Don't want her to hear this." With a leer he added, "What d'you think of her?"

"She's an attractive woman."

"Too young for me."

When the canary returned with the glass of water, Qwilleran took her aside and said, "May I have a few minutes alone with Mr. Dingleberry? He has some personal matters to discuss."

"Certainly," she said. "I'll wait outside."

Nervously Adam said, "Where'd she go?"

"Right outside the door. What did you want to tell me, Mr. Dingleberry?"

"You won't print it in the paper?"

"I won't print it in the paper."

"Never tell a living soul?"

"I promise," said Qwilleran, raising his right hand.

"My paw told me afore he died. Made me promise not to tell. If folks found out, he said, we'd both be strung up. But he's gone now, and I'll be goin' soon. No percentage in takin' it to the grave."

"Shouldn't you be passing this secret along to your sons?"

"Nope. Don't trust them whippersnappers. Too gol-durned cocky. You've got an honest face."

Qwilleran groomed his moustache with a show of modesty. Strangers had always been eager to confide in him. Looking intensely interested and sincere, he said, "What did your father reveal to you?"

"Wal, now, it were about Ephraim's funeral," old Adam said in his reedy voice. "Longest funeral procession in the history of Pickax! Six black horses 'stead of four. Two come all the way from Lockmaster. They was followed by a thirty-seven carriages and fifty-two buggies, but . . . *it were all a joke*!" He finished with a cackling laugh that turned into a coughing spell, and Qwilleran handed him the glass of water.

"What was the joke?" he asked when the spasm had subsided.

Adam cackled with glee. "Ephraim warn't in the coffin!"

Qwilleran thought, So Mitch's story is true. He's buried under the house! To Adam he said, "You say Ephraim's body wasn't in the coffin. Where was it?"

"Wal, now, the truth were . . ." Adam took a sip of water, which went down the wrong throat, and the coughing resumed so violently that Qwilleran feared the old man would choke. He called for help, and a nurse and two canaries rushed to his aid.

When it was over and Adam was calm enough to leer at the nurse, Qwilleran thanked the staffers and bowed them out of the room. Then he repeated his question. "Where was Ephraim's body?"

Cackling a laugh that was almost a yodel, the mortician said, *"Ephraim warn't dead!"*

Qwilleran stared at the old man in the wheelchair. There was a possibility that he might be senile, yet the rest of his conversation had been plausible—that is, plausible by Moose County's contrary standards. "How do you explain that bit of deception?" he asked.

"Wal, now, Ephraim knowed folks hated his guts and they was hell-bent on revenge, so he fooled 'em. He sailed off to Yerp. Went to Switzerland. Used another name. Let folks think he were dead." Adam started to cackle.

Qwilleran handed him the glass of water in anticipation of another attack of convulsive mirth. "Take a sip, Mr. Dingleberry. Be careful how you swallow . . . What about the rest of the Goodwinter family?"

"Wal, now, Ephraim's wife moved back east—that were the story they told—but she followed him to Yerp. In them days folks could disappear without no fuss. Damn gover'ment warn't buttin' in all the time. Way it turned out, though, the joke were on Ephraim. When he writ that suicide note, he never knowed his enemies would take credit for lynchin' him!"

"What about his sons?"

"Titus and Samson, the two of 'em lived in the farmhouse and run the business—run it into the ground mostly." His voice soared into a falsetto and ended with a shriek of hilarity.

"If your father participated in this hoax, I hope he was amply rewarded."

"Two thousand dollars," said Adam. "That were big money in them days—mighty big! And five hun'erd every quarter, so long as Paw kep' his lip buttoned. Paw were a religious man, and he wouldn'ta done it but he were in debt to Ephraim's bank. He were afraid of losin' his store."

"How long did the quarterly payments continue?"

"Till Ephraim kicked the bucket in 1935. Paw always told me it were an investment he made, payin' off. He were on his deathbed when he told the truth and warned me not to tell. He said folks would be madder'n hell and might burn down the furniture store for makin' fools of 'em." Adam's chin sank on his chest. The half hour was almost up.

"That's a thought-provoking story with interesting ramifications," Qwilleran said. "Thank you for taking me into your confidence."

The old man showed another spurt of energy. "There were somethin' else on Paw's conscience. He buried the Goodwinters' hired man, and they paid for the funeral—paid plenty, considerin' it were a plain coffin."

Qwilleran was instantly alerted. "What was the hired man's name?"

"I forget now."

"Luther Bosworth? Thirty years old? Left a wife and four kids?"

"That's him!"

"What happened to Luther?"

"One o' the Goodwinter horses went berserk. Trampled him to death—so bad they had a closed coffin."

"When did this happen?"

"Right after Ephraim left. Titus said he shot the horse."

There was a tap on the door, and the canary opened it an inch or two. "Visiting time almost up, sir."

"Don't let her in," Adam said.

Qwilleran called out, "One more minute, please." The door closed, and he said to Adam, "Do you know why the Goodwinters paid extra for the funeral?"

Adam wiped his mouth. "It were hush money. Paw wouldn'ta took it if he warn't beholden to the bank. Paw were a religious man."

"I'm sure he was! But what were the Goodwinters trying to hush up?"

Adam wiped his mouth again. "Wal, Titus said the man were trampled to death, but when Paw picked up the body, there were only a bullethole in the head."

There was another tap on the door. The old man's chin sank on his chest again, but he revived enough to make a swipe at the skirt of the canary when she came in to wheel him to his room.

Driving back to North Middle Hummock Qwilleran was thinking, Mitch Ogilvie was right on one point: Old Adam knew a thing or two. The story of the double hoax was plotted with enough dovetailing details to make it convincing—in Moose County, at any rate, where the incredible is believable ... And yet, was it really true? Adam Dingleberry had a reputation as a practical joker. Telling a cock-and-bull story about Ephraim could be his final joke on the whole county. Telling it to the media would be a virtual guarantee that it would be leaked. What headlines it would make! GOODWINTER HANGING A HOAX! MINE OWNER DIED ABROAD IN 1935! The wire services would pick it up, and Qwilleran's byline would once more be flashed nationwide. But how would Moose County react? The Noble Sons of the Noose—whoever they were—might trash the Dingleberry funeral home with all its lavish decor, not yet paid for. They might even go after Junior Goodwinter, managing editor of the *Something*, a nice kid in spite of being the great-grandson of the original villain. Qwilleran had a responsibility here, and a decision to make. The double hoax might be a triple hoax.

CHAPTER 20

Arriving at the farmhouse, Qwilleran made straight for the stereo, followed by two Siamese with waving tails. "Adjust your ears," he instructed them. "You're about to hear an astounding tale."

If the cats were expecting Verdi, they were disappointed. Adam's high-pitched voice crackled from the speakers: "Yup. My grampaw come from the Old Country to build shafthouses for the mines ..."

Their ears swiveled nervously until they heard a deep voice saying, "What kind of furniture, Mr. Dingleberry?" At the familiar sound Koko rose on hind legs and pawed the player while Yum Yum purred enthusiastically.

"Thank you," Qwilleran said to them. "I admit I was in good voice."

The old man was saying, "They was all a bit different: doors, no doors, one drawer, two drawers, false bottom, built-in lockbox, pigeonholes, whatever folks wanted."

"Yow!" said Koko, and Qwilleran felt a familiar quiver in the roots of his moustache. He turned off the sound.

Mrs. Cobb's ugly desk was a Dingleberry; no matter what its value on the local market, Qwilleran still thought it ugly. It had tall legs, a cupboard with doors, no pigeonholes, one drawer, not two. Did it have a false bottom? He removed the drawer and inspected it, shook it, pressed the bottom in several places, felt around the perimeter with his fingertips, hit the sides with the flat of his hand, shook it again. The bottom was thicker than normal, and something was shifting inside it.

"I may need some help here," Qwilleran said, and the cat sniffed and pawed while the man ran his hand over the surfaces and pressed experimentally at vital points. Unaccountably the bottom of the drawer popped up at one end, and Qwilleran pried it out.

There were no jewels concealed in the false bottom; no doubt Mrs. Goodwinter had taken them to Switzerland. There were documents, however, that gave him a psychological chill, as if he were invading a tomb, and he built a fire in the fireplace before spreading the musty papers on the hearth rug. There were bills, receipts and promissory notes. He recognized the writing on one such document:

Rec'd of Titus Goodwinter the sum of three thousand dollars ($3,000) in compensation for the accidental death of my husband. Signed this day of Oct. 31, 1904.

Lucy Bosworth

Had Titus dictated it? Had Lucy written it under duress? Or had she been an accomplice in the plot? The receipt led Qwilleran on a wild gallop of speculation regarding the young woman's relationship with her husband and, for that matter, with Titus, who was a notorious womanizer. It was clear that the payoff financed the purchase of the Pickax General Store, $3,000 being an enormous sum in the days when a family of six could live nicely on five dollars a week. The blood money, so to speak, may have paid for the impressive bible as well, a status symbol of its day.

There were other documents of historic interest if one had the time to study them, including promissory notes at abnormally high interest rates, signed by names well-known in Moose County, among them the thriftless Captain Fugtree. Ephraim's banks may have operated legitimately, but in his private money-lending he was guilty of usury.

The handwriting on a receipt dated October 28 caught Qwilleran's attention. It was the same small bold script found in Ephraim's suicide note, but it was signed by the financially captive storekeeper and undertaker, Adam Dingleberry's "Paw." Driven by debt to set aside his religious scruples, he had signed the following:

> *Rec'd of Ephraim Goodwinter, the sum of two thousand dollars ($2,000) in consideration of which the undersigned agrees to bury an empty coffin with full ceremony in the Goodwinter plot in the Pickax Cemetery, payee to conceal the arrangements noted above from all living souls and future descendants, on condition of which payer agrees to make quarterly payments of five hundred dollars ($500) until such time as payer departs this life. Signed and accepted this day of Oct. 28, 1904.*
>
> *Joshua Dingleberry*

A similar agreement with Titus Goodwinter, covering the interment of Luther Bosworth, also bore Joshua's signature.

The Siamese, attracted by the heat from the burning logs or the stale aroma of the documents, were in close attendance, and Koko was particularly interested in a folded sheet of paper that had been handled by dirty hands. It was a rough diagram with measurements and other specifications noted in faded penciling that Qwilleran could not decipher even with his reading glasses. Using a magnifying glass from the telephone desk he was able to identify the central element as a half-circle with dimensions given in feet. Two rectangles connected by a pair of parallel lines were marked SW and NW, but no dimensions were specified. Folded in with the diagram was a misspelled bill from the Mayfus Stone Quarry on Sandpit Road: "4 lodes stone to pave carage house." The date was May 16, 1904, and it was marked "pd."

"Three days after the explosion!" Qwilleran observed. "What do you two sleuths make of that? The carriage house is not paved; it's plank like the threshing floor. And what's this?"

Folded in with the diagram was a small slip of paper in Ephraim Goodwinter's unmistakable hand:

Rec'd of Ephraim Goodwinter the sum of one thousand dollars ($1,000) in consideration of which the undersigned agrees to do stonework as specified, privately and without help and without revealing same to any living soul, work to be completed by August 15 of the current year. Signed and accepted this day of May 16, 1904.

Luther Bosworth
X (his mark)

"Luther couldn't even write his name!" Qwilleran exclaimed. "How do you like that?"

Hearing no reply he looked for the cats. Yum Yum was asleep on the hearth rug with her tail curled comfortably over her nose. A hump in one of the other Orientals indicated that Koko was in hiding again. In consternation Qwilleran went to the telephone and called a number in Mooseville.

"Hello, Lori. This is Qwill," he said. "How's everything? . . . Glad to hear it. How's the baby? . . . Are you sure he isn't eating the cats' food? . . . Speaking of cats, I'm sorry to trouble you again, but I'd like to ask you a question about Koko's latest aberration. He's accustomed to wall-to-wall carpet in our Pickax apartment, you know, but here we have bare wood floors scattered with small rugs, and he's always hiding under them—something he's never done before . . . Well, there are different kinds: Orientals in the parlor and entrance hall, hooked rugs in the bedroom, braided rugs in the kitchen and dining area—all old and handmade. Koko prefers the Orientals, which are the thinnest and the most valuable. He's always been a snob . . . No, he tunnels under them in a neat, workmanlike way, making a hump in the rug. *Wait a minute!* Excuse me, Lori. I just got an idea! I'll call you back."

Qwilleran hung up, tamping his moustache with fervor. He grabbed a flashlight, rushed out to the barn, barged through the eye of the needle, frightening a barncat, plunged down the ladder into the stable, flashed his light into the southwest corner. There he found another wooden palette like the one on the threshing floor above. This one also leaned against the wall, but it was surrounded by rubble. When he pulled it aside he was gaping at a hole in the foot-thick stone wall. The opening was about four feet wide and three feet high, an arched tunnel of crumbling masonry with a floor of hard-packed clay. The arch was roughly mortared quarry stone. As far as the beam of the flashlight penetrated there was arched stone.

Qwilleran dropped to his knees and started to crawl. This was Ephraim's escape tunnel, he realized, evidently planned when public outcry alarmed him. The bill for the stone was dated three days after the explosion—the same day that Luther signed his *X* and agreed to build the tunnel secretly while the family traveled abroad.

Had Ephraim actually used this escape hatch on the night of October 29? It was quite possible. Qwilleran imagined furious hordes shouting obscenities in front of the farmhouse and throwing rocks at the windows, while Ephraim craftily crawled through the tunnel. No doubt, the trusted Bosworth had a horse ready—two horses, one for Ephraim's son—the saddlebags packed with valuables. Under cover of darkness the pair would ride along the Willoway, heading for Mooseville, where Ephraim would board a passenger boat to Canada across the lake. His wife, meanwhile, was taking refuge at the parsonage with Mr. and Mrs. Crawbanks. A deal had already been made with Enoch Dingleberry, and Ephraim's sons would carry out the remainder of the charade: killing Luther, who knew too much, then blaming the horse; staging the hanging with a hastily rigged effigy; announcing the suicide and producing the suicide note;

mourning at their father's funeral. Little did they know that the rumor mill would go into operation, with their enemies taking credit for Ephraim's demise. What started the rumor, of course, was Mr. Crawbanks' discovery of the white sheet, recently left there by some Halloween prankster.

Composing this melodrama occupied Qwilleran's mind while he crawled slowly and painfully through the tunnel. It was rough on the hands, and he had a bad knee dating back to his years in the armed service. He sat down and pondered. What he needed was a pair of heavy gloves and some padding for his knees.

Carefully he backed out of the cramped space, brushed himself off and climbed the ladder. He could hear the playful shouts of the teenage yard crew as they raked leaves, bagging them and loading the bags in Mitch's blue pickup. They were working on the north side of the house, and Qwilleran sauntered through their midst en route to the west wing.

Mitch hailed him. "Hi, Qwill! Nice day for a walk."

Once inside the apartment he contemplated his strategy. Gloves were no problem; he had brought a pair of lined leather gloves from Pickax, and he was willing to sacrifice them for the tunnel investigation. How to pad his knees presented a challenge, however. He canvassed the apartment looking for likely material. All he could find was a stack of pink terry towels with Iris Cobb's monogram. They would have to do. Now he needed some kind of heavy cord to bind the towels around his knees.

Koko was following him around, sensing an adventure, and his eager presence gave Qwilleran an idea. It might be advantageous to take the cat to the tunnel, letting him walk ahead, prudently restrained by a leash. Miners used to lower canaries down the mineshaft to test for toxic gasses. If Koko sniffed any noxious fumes, he wouldn't succumb; he would raise holy hell as only an outraged Siamese can do. Koko had a blue leather harness, and the leash was a twelve-foot length of nylon cord, some of which could be used to bind the pink towels. Congratulating himself on his ingenuity, Qwilleran cut the leash down to a manageable six feet and reserved the remainder for binding.

The yard crew was rapidly working its way around to the west side, and he hesitated to walk to the barn wearing leather gloves, leading Koko on a leash, and carrying an armful of pink towels. After pacing the floor for a while he went outdoors and asked Mitch for a plastic leaf bag.

"Going to do some raking, Qwill?"

"No, just bundling up some stuff to store in the barn."

Now he was all set. Into the plastic bag he threw the pink towels, a second flashlight, gloves, the harness and two short lengths of cord. He stuffed Koko inside his shirt and added a loose jacket for camouflage. "This won't take long," he explained to the cat, "and I would appreciate your cooperation. Keep your mouth shut and don't exercise your claws."

Qwilleran waited until the volunteers gathered around Mitch's truck for a guzzle break. Then he slung the sack over his shoulder and headed for the barn. He could feel some wriggling inside his shirt, and he heard a few muffled yiks, but the barnyard was traversed without arousing suspicion. Avoiding exposure on the grassy ramp, he scuttled around the east side of the barn and entered the stable through the livestock door in the rear. So far, so good!

First he trussed Koko, purring, into his harness and tied him to a printing press. Then he applied himself to wrapping legs with bath towels and cord, an idea that proved less achievable than it sounded. In fact, after the first attempt he found it impossible to bend his knees, and it was necessary to untie the cords and start again. Koko, becoming impatient, uttered some piercing yowls.

"Quiet!" Qwilleran growled. "I'm working as fast as I can."

At last they were ready. Koko in his blue harness and Qwilleran in his pink kneepads entered the tunnel, the cat leading the way and the man crawling after him. It was slow work. The clay floor of the tunnel was scattered with stones and chunks of mortar. Tossing them aside with one gloved hand and wielding the flashlight with the other, Qwilleran was obliged to hold Koko's leash in his teeth, trusting the cat not to make a sudden leap forward.

It was a slow crawl and a long crawl. After all, the original diagram showed the tunnel extending from the stable, under the carriage house and across the barnyard to the basement of the west wing. Qwilleran had read about such a tunnel in Europe, connecting a convent with the outside world: the convent was haunted, and human bones were eventually found in the tunnel. There were no bones in the Goodwinter tunnel, only beer cans and gum wrappers and some unidentified items that Koko saw fit to sniff. Qwilleran found the air in the tunnel stuffy, smelling of mold and mice, but Koko was experiencing a catly high.

They crawled on. The farther they progressed, the more rubble they encountered, and the faster the cat wanted to travel, yikking and tugging at his leash.

"Arrgh!" Qwilleran growled through his teeth.

"Yow!" replied Koko impatiently.

They were nearing the southwest terminal, but there was no light at the end of the tunnel—just a wall of chipped stone. Scattered about were broken rocks, chunks of mortar, and a few discarded tools—chisels, hammers, and a drill. Also there was a great deal of dust. They crawled to the end, Qwilleran choking and trying to cough without unclenching his teeth.

Koko was the first to find it—a small, square, boxlike object in a dark corner of the tunnel.

A bomb! Qwilleran thought. *Dynamite!*

Twisting the end of the leash around one gloved hand, he used the other to flood the contraption with light. Then he moved toward it on his knees and found a button to press. For a moment there was dead silence in the tunnel, then . . . a hair-raising screech . . . an angry growl ending in a vicious snarl . . . the moans of the dying . . . the bong of a death knell . . . ghostly wailing and rattling . . . *screams!*

Koko shot off like a rocket, and Qwilleran on the other end of the leash went sprawling on the clay.

Chapter 21

When Qwilleran emerged from the barn with his sackful of pink towels and yowling cat, Mitch Ogilvie cupped his hands and yelled across the barnyard, "Your phone's ringing!"

For two hours Qwilleran had been on hands and knees with hunched back, and he responded stiffly. Nevertheless, he made his way to the apartment quickly enough to catch the caller before she hung up.

"Oh, there you are, Qwill!" said Carol Lanspeak. "I let it ring fifteen times because I thought you were outdoors on a nice day like this. Were you outdoors?"

"Yes," he said, breathing hard.

"I've been to the hospital to see Verona. Baby is going to make it—and Verona's pregnant."

"I didn't know. How is she?"

"Not too good. She wants to go 'down home' and have Baby convalesce there. Larry's taking care of her expenses and giving her something to live on. Vince left her without a cent! That brute!"

"Have they found him?"

"I don't think so. The police have been talking to Verona, and Larry has asked his attorney to advise her."

"I feel sorry for Verona."

"So do I. We never really got to know her. She was so quiet and retiring. She volunteered for our cleaning committee and was very reliable. The reason I'm calling, Qwill—she has something she wants to tell you. She says it's important. Do you think you could go to the hospital tonight? I'm taking her to the airport tomorrow."

"I'll go. Thanks for letting me know."

"By the way, the board has voted to give Mitch the job," said Carol.

Polly Duncan was the next to call. "They've found him!" she said without any formalities. "Somewhere in Ohio. My assistant's mother-in-law heard it on the air and phoned the library."

"He's guilty of more than just killing a hophead, I surmise."

"What do you mean?"

"I'd like to drop in to see you tonight—and discuss a few things," Qwilleran said.

"Come for dinner, and I'll whip up a curry."

"Uh ... thanks, Polly, but I have an appointment in Pickax. See you after eight o'clock."

"Don't have dessert," she said. "We'll have pumpkin pie and coffee."

On the way to Pickax Qwilleran experienced a pang of remorse that he had not allowed Baby to visit the cats; it was pure selfishness on his part, he admitted. And now it wouldn't ever happen. It was perhaps a need for penance that led him to have dinner at the Dimsdale Diner. After some watery soup and oversalted cabbage rolls and unrecognizable coffee, he drove to the hospital.

He found Verona in a private room, sitting in a chair and picking at a meal tray. "I'm sorry to interrupt your dinner," he said.

"I don't feel like eatin' anythin'," she said, pushing the tray away. "Have they caught him?" Her soft voice had lost its lilt and was now a dreary monotone.

"They found him somewhere in Ohio."

"I'm glad."

"Cheer up. Baby is going to be all right, and your eye is looking better. The bruise is fading."

She touched her face. "I didn't bump into a door. We were arguin' and he hit me."

"When did it happen?"

"When he was leavin'—Monday night."

"You told me he left Monday noon."

"That's what he told me to say." She turned away and looked out the window.

"Carol Lanspeak said you have something you want to tell me, Mrs. Boswell."

"That's not my name. I'm Verona Whitmoor."

"I like that better. It has a pleasant musical sound, like your speaking voice," he said.

She looked flustered and lowered her head. "I'm so ashamed. I was cleanin' the museum, gettin' it ready for Sunday, and I went in Iris's kitchen when you weren't there and took the cookbook."

"I knew you were the one," said Qwilleran, "after you sent me the meatloaf. It was her recipe."

"Vince liked her meatloaf so much, and I was tryin' to please him."

"I'm surprised you could read her handwriting."

"It was hard, but I figured it out. I meant to take it back, but then everythin' happened." She looked pitifully vulnerable and undernourished.

"Ms. Whitmoor, shouldn't you have something to eat? That apple pudding looks good."

"I'm not hungry."

"How did you happen to meet Vince?" Qwilleran asked.

"I was workin' in a restaurant in Pittsburgh, and he used to come in. I felt sorry for him because he was always in pain—with his bad leg, you know. He was wounded in Vietnam."

Qwilleran huffed scornfully into his moustache.

Verona went on. "We got friendly, and he invited me to come up here on a vacation. He said I could bring Baby. He didn't tell me about the money—not then."

"What money?"

"His mother came from here, and she told him about some money hidden under the barn, but he had to dig for it. His grandfather knew all about it. But the diggin' was hard, and he was always afraid someone would find out what he was doin'. That's why he killed the man in the barn." Verona put her face in her hands, and her thin shoulders shook with her sobbing. Such an outburst of emotion over the murder of a tramp caused Qwilleran to ask:

"Did you know the man who was killed?"

She shook her head, and the tears continued to pour forth. He placed the tissue box on her lap and waited patiently. What could he say? Perhaps her emotions were a confused combination of grief and relief that she and Baby were free of Vince. It was a long, painful scene. When he finally persuaded her to talk, her faltering voice mumbled a few words at a time.

He described the emotional ordeal when he arrived at Polly's cottage at eight o'clock. Bursting into the house he said, "I knew that guy was a fraud! He was no expert on printing presses, and he lied about his bad leg—told Larry it was polio, told Verona he got it in Vietnam. Actually it was the result of a boyhood escapade. And get this! He and Larry and Susan are second cousins!"

"Sit down and have some pie," Polly said, "and start from the beginning."

"I've just been to the hospital to see Verona," he said.

"Did she know anything about the murder of Waffle?"

"Not until the police told her, but she knew what Boswell was doing in the barn. He was digging for Ephraim's gold coins!"

"How naive! Where did he hear that hoary fable?"

"His great-grandfather was Ephraim's hired man, and the story had been handed down in the family. He believed it. Changed his name so the town wouldn't connect him with the original Bosworth. Cataloguing the presses was only a cover. It happily presented itself when he contacted Larry about a vacation up here with his 'wife and child.' But he was constantly afraid someone would blow his cover. So when Brent Waffle hid out in the stable, I suppose Boswell considered him a threat and killed him with a crowbar."

"What happened to your contraband crate theory, Qwill?" Polly said teasingly.

"Forget it. I was off-base."

In his state of animation Qwilleran failed to notice that the pumpkin pie had been frozen and insufficiently thawed, or that

Bigfoot was sitting on his knee. He said, "On the night the body was dumped, the cats heard a noise, and so did I—a rumbling sound. It was Boswell's van, driving around the far side of the barn to pick up the body in the stable. After that, he took off, having instructed Verona to lie for him. He also gave her a poke in the eye."

Polly offered him more pie, and he declined. "One slice is more than enough, but I'll have another cup of coffee." After a few gulps he said, "Boswell was using a drill in his search for the loot, and the vibration was loosening lightbulbs. I believe it also cracked the plastered wall in the basement. That's where Iris first heard sounds of knocking. He was using a hammer and chisel to gouge out the mortar . . . Are you ready for the worst?"

"Is there more?"

"Plenty, but it took me awhile to get it out of Verona. She was on a crying jag, and I thought she was upset about Baby and her condition. Actually she was agonizing over Iris's death. I happened to have a small inconspicuous recorder with me. Would you like to hear my conversation with Verona firsthand?"

Polly demurred. "It doesn't seem quite decent. It was a private conversation."

"Would it be more decent if I repeated it verbatim?"

"Well . . . if you put it that way . . ."

Verona's faltering speech was punctuated with sniffles and whimpers, but Qwilleran's voice was the first on the tape, and he grimaced when he heard himself repeating Boswell's corny line. "My God! Did I say that?" he said.

🐾 *Don't be afraid to talk to me about your grief, Ms. Whitmoor. That's what neighbors are for.*

I feel terrible about it. When Iris died, I wanted to die, too.

She was a wonderful woman. Everyone loved her.

She was so kind to Baby and me. No one else . . . (long pause).

Did you know she had a heart condition?

She never talked about herself, but I knew she was worried about somethin'.

Did she tell you about the mysterious noises in the house?

Yes, she did. And when I told Vince he got nervous. He said she was too nosy. He was poundin' and drillin', and she could hear it and thought it was ghosts or somethin'. (Soft crying.)

What did he do about it?

He tried to figure out ways to get her out of the house, so he could work, but she loved the museum and loved her kitchen. She was always cookin' and bakin'. (Long pause.)

Go on, Ms. Whitmoor.

One day he came home with a Halloween cassette—spooky sounds, you know. He said he had an idea. He said she was a silly woman, and he could frighten her enough so she would quit the job, and then we could live in the manager's apartment and he could dig all he wanted to.

Did his idea work?

She got very upset, but she didn't leave. Vince talked about it all the time. He was like a crazy man, and when he got into a tantrum like that, his leg would hurt worse.

Do you remember the night Iris Cobb died?

(Prolonged wailing.) I'll never forget it! Not till I die!

What happened?

(Whimpering.) He gave me a sheet with two holes in it. (Sobs.) He told me to get under the sheet . . . and stand outside her window . . . and he would play the spooky sound effects. I didn't want to, but he said . . . (long pause).

What did he say?

He said some threatenin' things, and I was afraid for Baby, so I did what he wanted. (Anguished wailing.) I didn't know what he was goin' to do! . . . Oh, Jesus forgive me! . . . I didn't know he was goin' to smother Iris with that pillow! (Hysterical sobs.)

Qwilleran switched off the tape. He said to Polly, "Her crying went on until I thought she was going into convulsions. In fact, the nurse came in and gave her something to drink and said I'd better leave. So I did, but I waited in the visitors' lounge and after a while I went back. I thanked her and told her she was a good woman and she should go down south and start a new life. I held both her hands, and she almost smiled. Then I asked her a question: Why was Iris's apartment in darkness? That question had been nagging me ever since I found her body on the kitchen floor."

"Did Verona have an answer?"

"She said she was the one who went in and turned off lights and the microwave. Homer Tibbitt had impressed upon the cleaning volunteers that they should always turn everything off—because of the danger of fire."

Polly said, "I feel limp! This is an unnerving story—and bizarre!"

"You want to hear something really bizarre?" Qwilleran said. "When I first took Koko into the museum, he went directly to a certain bed pillow in the textile collection. I didn't know it at the time, but that pillow had been removed from the exhibit without authorization and then returned . . . And that's not all. When he ran out to the barn last night he found a litter of kittens on a soiled white sheet with burn holes. Obviously Boswell had stuffed it between the crates after it had been used to frighten Iris. It had been raining, and the sheet had dragged on the wet ground; the edges were muddy . . . And one more incredible instance, Polly! Twice—not once, but twice—Koko knocked a novel off the bookshelf in which a character is smothered with a pillow!"

When Qwilleran returned to the farmhouse, the Siamese met him with yowling complaints and bristling fur. It was chilly in the apartment. "Is the thermostat too low?" he asked them, "or has Ephraim's shade been drifting around?" He started a crackling blaze in the parlor fireplace, got into his old Mackintosh bathrobe, and dropped into a lounge chair for contemplation.

He had refrained from telling Polly about Adam Dingleberry's story and about the documents he had found to confirm it. The papers were returned to the false bottom of the old

Dingleberry desk, and the secret would be safe for a few more decades. Moose County could go on believing that Ephraim died on October 30, 1904—one way or the other—and the Noble Sons of the Noose could continue their fraternal shenanigans. Qwilleran suspected that the Noble Sons, thirty-two of them with lights on their caps, staged a ghostly march across the Goodwinter slag heap every year on May 13.

In the blue wing chair, the Siamese were indulging in a mutual grooming session. Had they chosen that chair because it was Mrs. Cobb's favorite or because they knew the upholstery enhanced the blue of their eyes? Qwilleran watched them—beautiful creatures, vain, and mysterious.

He said to Koko, "When you sat in the kitchen window, staring at the barnyard, did you know something irregular was happening out there?"

Koko, intent on flicking a facile tongue around Yum Yum's left ear, paid no attention. Why, Qwilleran asked himself, are cats either smotheringly attentive or infuriatingly indifferent? He went on—doggedly:

"When you tunneled under rugs were you trying to tell me something? Or were you just amusing yourself?"

Koko extended his services to Yum Yum's snowy throat, and she raised her chin in ecstasy. Qwilleran could remember when Koko expected the female to do the laundering. Times had changed.

"And how about all that muttering and mumbling?" he demanded. "Were you talking to yourself or conversing with an invisible presence?"

Both cats settled down with paws tucked under in contentment, totally oblivious.

As Qwilleran sat brooding in his chair and dimly perceiving the blue wing chair opposite, he could almost feel Iris Cobb's presence. At that precise moment two brown noses lifted, four brown ears swiveled, two sets of whiskers twitched. Something was about to happen. Qwilleran braced himself for a pink apparition, bearing cookies. Ten seconds later, the telephone rang.

Qwilleran took the call in the bedroom. "Hello? . . . Of course

I remember you! How's everything Down Below? . . . I don't know. What's the proposition? . . . A penthouse, did you say? Sounds good, but I'll have to discuss it with my bosses. Where can I reach you? . . ."

He returned to the parlor and addressed the blue wing chair. "How would you guys like to spend the winter in the Crime Belt instead of the Snow Belt?"

The chair was vacant. They had sensed another change of address. Qwilleran's eyes automatically rose to the top of the Pennsylvania German *Schrank*. Not there. But he noticed a hump in the hearth rug and another hump in the rug before the sofa. Both humps were eloquently motionless.

THE CAT WHO LIVED HIGH

Chapter 1

The news that reached Pickax City early on that cold November morning sent a deathly chill through the small northern community. The Pickax police chief, Andrew Brodie, was the first to hear about the car crash. It had occurred four hundred miles to the south, in the perilous urban area that locals called Down Below. The metropolitan police appealed to Brodie for assistance in locating the next of kin.

The victim, they said, had been driving through the heart of the city on a four-lane freeway when the occupants of a passing car, according to witnesses, fired shots at him, causing him to lose control of his vehicle, which crashed into a concrete abutment and burned. The driver's body was consumed by the flames, but through the license plates the registration had been traced to James Qwilleran, fifty-two, of Pickax City.

Brodie smashed his leathery fist down on the desk, and his face contorted in grief and anger. "I warned him! I warned him!" he shouted.

Qwilleran had no living relatives; a phone call to his attorney confirmed that fact. His family consisted of two Siamese cats, but his extended family included the entire population of Moose County. The genial personality and quirky philosophy of the retired journalist endeared "Mr. Q" to everyone. The column he wrote for the local newspaper had won him a host of admirers. His luxuriant moustache and drooping eyelids and graying temples were considered sexually attractive by women of all ages. And the fact that he was the richest bachelor in three counties and an unbridled philanthropist made him a civic treasure.

Brodie immediately called Arch Riker, Qwilleran's lifelong friend and current publisher of the Moose County newspaper. "Dammit! I warned him about that jungle!" the chief shouted into the phone. "He's been living up here for three years, and he forgot that life Down Below is like Russian roulette!"

Shocked and searching for something to say, Riker mumbled soberly, "Qwill knew all about that. Before moving up here he lived in cities for fifty years. He and I grew up in Chicago."

"Things have changed since then," Brodie snapped. "God! Do you know what this means?"

The fact was that Qwilleran had inherited vast wealth from the Klingenschoen estate—on one condition: He must live in Moose County for five years. Otherwise, the Klingenschoen millions—or billions—would go to the alternate heirs out of state.

Riker listened glumly to Brodie's tirade and then phoned Polly Duncan, the woman in Qwilleran's life, who was prostrated by the news. He himself made immediate plans to fly down to the city. By the time the publisher had notified his own news desk and the local radio station, the telephone lines were spluttering with the bad tidings, and Moose County was caught up in a frenzy of horror and grief. Thousands would miss Qwilleran's column on page two of the newspaper. Hundreds would miss the sight of Mr. Q riding his bicycle on country roads and walking about downtown Pickax with a long stride and a sober expression, answering their greetings with a courteous salute. And everyone realized the community would now lose scholarships, grants, and interest-free loans. Why, they asked each other, had he been so rash as to venture Down Below? Only one person thought to worry about the Siamese. His part-time secretary, Lori Bamba, cried, "What will happen to Koko and Yum Yum?"

There were cats galore in Moose County—barn mousers, feral cats, and pampered pets—yet none so pampered as the two thoroughbreds who lived with Qwilleran, and none quite so remarkable as Kao K'o Kung, whose everyday name was Koko. With his noble whiskers, aristocratic ears, sensitive nose, and inscrutable gaze Koko could see the invisible, hear the inaudible, and sense the unknowable. His companion, Yum Yum, was a charmer who captivated Qwilleran with shameless wiles, reaching out a paw to touch his moustache while squeezing her eyes and purring throatily. They were a handsome pair—fawn-furred, with seal-brown extremities and mesmerizing blue eyes. What would happen to them now? Where were they? Would anyone feed them?

Then came the gripping question: Were they still alive? Had they been in the car when it burned?

About two weeks before the metropolitan police called Brodie with the fateful news, Qwilleran and his two feline companions were spending a quiet evening at home in Moose County—the man, a husky six feet two, sprawled in the second-best easy chair with nothing much on his mind; the cats lounging on the best chair, as was their due, meditating and looking exquisite. When the raucous bell of the telephone disturbed the domestic peace, Qwilleran reluctantly hoisted himself to his feet and went to the phone in the adjoining room. It was a long-distance call from Down Below.

He heard an unfamiliar voice say, "Hello, Mr. Qwilleran. You'll never guess who this is! . . . Amberina, from the Three Weird Sisters in Junktown! Do you remember me?"

"Of course I remember you," he said diplomatically, at the same time thinking fast. The three women had an antique shop, but which of the sisters was Amberina? The giddy young blond or the man-crazy redhead or the unimpressive brunette? "How's everything Down Below?" he asked. "I haven't been there for quite a while—three years, as a matter of fact."

"You'd never recognize Junktown," she replied. "We're being gentrified, like they say. People are buying the old townhouses and fixing them up, and we're getting some first-class restaurants and antique shops."

"Do you still have your shop?"

"No, we gave it up. Ivrene finished art school and got a job in Chicago. Cluthra married money—wouldn't you know?—and moved to Texas. And I'm working for an auction house. From what I hear, Mr. Qwilleran, your life has changed, too, with the inheritance and everything."

"Much to my surprise, yes . . . By the way, did you hear about Iris Cobb?"

"Gosh, were we ever shocked! When she was in Junktown she was such a live wire."

"Does Mary Duckworth still have the Blue Dragon?"

"She sure does! It's the best antique shop on the street—the most expensive, that is. Robert Maus has opened a classy restaurant, and Charlotte Roop is his manager. You know both of them, I think."

Why, Qwilleran thought, is this woman calling me after three years? His momentary silence brought her to the point.

Amberina said, "Mary wanted me to call you because she's going out of town. She has something she'd like to suggest to you."

"Well, fire away!"

"Do you know the big old white apartment building called the Casablanca? It's sort of run-down, but it's a landmark."

"I vaguely remember it."

"It's a tall building between Junktown and the reclaimed area where they're putting up the new office towers and condos."

"Yes, now I know the one you mean," he said.

"Well, to make a long story short, some developers want to tear it down, which would be a crime! That building is really built! And it has a lot of history. Junktown has formed a task force called SOCK—Save Our Casablanca Kommittee—spelled with a K, you know."

"Does SOCK have any clout?" Qwilleran quipped.

"Not really. That's why we're calling you."

"What's the proposition?"

She drew a deep breath. "The Casablanca used to be the best address in town. SOCK wants you to buy it and restore it . . . There! I said it! It wasn't easy."

It was Qwilleran's turn to take a deep breath. "Now wait a minute, Amberina. Let me straighten you out. I'm no financier, and I don't get involved in business ventures. Nothing is further from my mind. In fact, I've turned my inheritance over to the Klingenschoen Memorial Fund. I have nothing to do with it." Actually he made suggestions to the Fund, but he saw no need to mention that.

"We all remember what you did for Junktown when you wrote for the *Daily Fluxion*, Mr. Qwilleran. Your series of articles in the paper really woke us up and started our comeback."

He stroked his moustache as he remembered his memorable winter in that slummy part of town. "I admit my Junktown experience whetted my interest in preservation," he said, "and theoretically I endorse your cause, although I'm in no position to know whether it's feasible."

"Oh, but you should see the Casablanca!" she said with enthusiasm. "The experts tell us it has great possibilities." Qwilleran was beginning to remember her now. Amberina was the least weird of the Three Weird Sisters. "The building used to be very grand," she was saying. "Some changes have been made, but the architects say they're reversible. It could go back to being a fashionable place to live, and that would be a real boost for Junktown. Right now the Casablanca is . . . well, the tenants are a mixed bag. But they're interesting! Mostly singles, but a few couples, not necessarily married. Whites, blacks, Asians, Hispanics . . . yuppies, artists, truck drivers, wealthy widows, college students, a couple of stunning call girls, and a few bums and crazies, but they're harmless."

"You make it sound irresistible."

"I live at the Casablanca myself," she said with a small hysterical laugh.

Quill now remembered more about Amberina. She had dark hair, very attractive blue eyes (probably wore contacts), and a husband. Yet she now spoke as if she lived alone. "I'd like to see the place," he said.

"Mary said to tell you the penthouse apartment is available for sublet, and it's very well furnished. Maybe you'd like to come down and stay for a while."

"Well, I don't know..."

"You should decide fast, Mr. Qwilleran, because the developers are putting pressure on the owner of the building to sell it to them. SOCK is getting kind of antsy."

"Who is the owner?"

"We call her the Countess. She's seventy-five years old. She's lived in the building all her life and still has her original apartment. I'm sure you could talk her into selling to your Memorial Fund, Mr. Qwilleran. You're a very charming man."

"Not always," he protested in mock modesty, grooming his moustache. He was well aware of his success in winning over women, especially older ones. "If I were to drive down there," he said slowly and thoughtfully, "I'd have to take my cats. Are pets permitted?"

"Cats are okay, but not dogs. In fact, there are cats all over the place." Amberina giggled. "Some people call it the Casablanca Cathouse."

"Did you say there's a penthouse available?" he asked with increasing interest.

"You'd love it! It's really very glamorous. There's a large sunken living room with a skylight and indoor trees... and a marvelous view... and a terrace..."

"Let me call you back tomorrow. I'll have to discuss it with my bosses," Qwilleran said facetiously, meaning the Siamese.

"Don't lose any time," she warned. "If anything happens to the old lady, Mary says, the building will be sold to the developers so the heirs can be paid off."

After hanging up the phone he rationalized fast. One: He had been confined to Moose County for three years, except for one flying trip Down Below to have dinner at the Press Club. Two: Winter was on its way, and winters in Moose County were not only cruel but interminable. Three: The imperiled Casablanca would be a convenient excuse to escape the glacial pavements and ten-foot snowbanks of Pickax. At least, he thought, there's no harm in driving down and checking out the building's potential.

First he broke the news to the Siamese. Living alone, he made it a practice to converse with his cats, often reading aloud to them and always discussing his problems and plans. They seemed to enjoy the sound of his voice, whether or not they knew what he was saying. More importantly, verbalizing his thoughts helped him to make decisions.

"Listen, you guys," he called out to them, "how would you like to spend the winter in the Crime Belt instead of the Snow Belt? . . . Where are you?"

His companions had deserted their comfortable chair and were nowhere in view.

"Where did you brats go?" he demanded.

There was not a murmur from either of them, although he could feel their presence, and he could guess where they were. Koko had burrowed under the hearth rug, and Yum Yum was hiding under the rug in front of the sofa. Their silent comment was readily interpreted: They abhorred a change of address, and they sensed what Qwilleran had in mind.

He paced the floor with growing eagerness. Despite the reaction of his housemates, he relished the idea of a winter in the big city. He missed the Press Club. He missed the camaraderie of the staffers at the *Daily Fluxion*, where he had been a popular feature writer. He missed the stage shows, the hockey and pro basketball, and the variety of restaurants. There was one drawback: He would have to forgo the companionship of Polly Duncan. He had become very fond of Pickax City's head librarian. They shared the same interests. She was his own age— an intelligent and loving woman. And since neither had a desire to marry, they were a compatible pair.

Polly was the first one he wanted to consult about his proposed venture, and he phoned her little house in the country, but before he could break the news, she quelched his elation with a cry of distress.

"Oh, Qwill! I was just about to call you. I've had some dreadful news. I'm being evicted!"

"What do you mean?" For years she had been the tenant of a snug cottage in farming country, and he had spent many idyllic weekends surrounded by cornfields and deer habitat and a hemisphere of blue sky.

"I told you the farm had been sold," she said, almost in tears.

"Now I learn that the new owner wants my cottage for his married son. Winter's almost here! Where can I go? Landlords don't permit cats, and I can't give up Bootsie! What shall I do?" she wailed. Here was a woman who could devise a swift solution to the most complex problem arising at the public library; her panic over this personal setback was disturbing. "Are you there?" she cried impatiently. "Did you hear me, Qwill?"

"I heard you. I'm thinking," he said. "It so happens that I'm invited to spend the winter months Down Below—in a penthouse apartment. That means . . . you could put your furniture in storage and stay at my place in Pickax while you scout for a new house." Whimsically he added, "I have no objection to cats." There was silence at the other end of the line. "Are you there, Polly? Did you hear me?"

"I'm thinking," she said. "It sounds like an ideal solution, Qwill, and it's certainly very generous of you, and of course it would be handy to the library, but . . ."

"But what?"

"But I don't like the idea of your spending all that time Down Below."

"You went to England for an entire summer," he reminded her. "I didn't care for that idea, either, but I survived."

"That's not what I mean. Cities are so unsafe! I don't want anything to happen to you."

"Polly, may I remind you that I lived in large cities all my life before moving up here."

"What is the penthouse you mentioned?" she asked warily.

"Let's have dinner tomorrow night, and I'll explain."

Next he phoned his old friend, Arch Riker, now publisher of the local paper. He said, "I've just had an interesting call from Down Below. Do you remember the Casablanca apartments on the edge of Junktown?"

"Sure," said Riker. "Rosie and I lived there when we were first married. They'd cut up most of the large apartments into efficiencies and one-bedroom units. We had a few good years there. Then the kids started coming, and we moved to the suburbs. What about the Casablanca? I suppose they're tearing it down."

"You guessed right," Qwilleran said. "Some developers want to take it over."

"They'll need a nuclear bomb to demolish that hunk of masonry. It's built like the Rock of Gibraltar."

"Well, hold on to your hat, Arch. I've been thinking it might be a good public relations ploy for the Klingenschoen Fund to buy it and restore it."

"What! You mean—restore it all the way? That would be a costly operation. You're talking about megamillions!"

"That's what I mean—restore the apartments to their original condition and go condo. The Fund is making money faster than the board of directors can give it away, so what if it's a financial loss? It will be a triumph for the cause of preservation—and a feather in the Klingenschoen cap."

"I have to think about that. Offhand, it sounds like a madcap gamble. Have you suggested it to the board of directors?"

"I heard the news only half an hour ago, Arch. I'll need more particulars, but see what you think of this: If I spend the winter down there, investigating the possibilities, I can write a weekly column for you on the horrors of city living. Moose County readers will lap it up!"

"Are you sure you want to go down there?" Riker asked apprehensively. "It's a dangerous place to live, what with muggings and break-ins and murders."

"Are you telling *me?* I wrote the book!" At the height of his career Qwilleran had written a best-seller on urban crime. "You may remember, Arch, there were muggings and break-ins and murders when you and I worked for the *Daily Fluxion,* and we took them for granted."

"From what I hear and read, conditions are much worse now."

"There's no coward so cowardly as a city dweller who has moved to the boondocks, my friend. Listen to this: I can get the penthouse at the Casablanca, furnished."

"Sounds good, I guess, but don't rush into anything," Riker advised. "Think about it for a couple of weeks."

"I can't wait a couple of weeks. The K Fund will have to sneak in a bid ahead of the wrecking ball. Besides, we can expect snow any day now, and it won't stop snowing until March. I won't be able to get out of here."

"What about the cats?"

"I'll take them with me, of course."

"They won't like living high up. We were on the ninth floor, and our cats hated the elevator."

"They'll adjust. There's a terrace, and where there's a terrace there are pigeons. Koko is a licensed pigeon watcher."

"Well . . . do it if you want to take the gamble, Qwill, but wear a bulletproof vest," Riker warned, and said good-bye.

Qwilleran found it difficult to settle down. He tried reading aloud to the Siamese to calm his excitement, but his mind was not on the printed page. He was impatient to learn more about the Casablanca. Unable to wait until morning, he phoned Down Below.

"I hope I'm not calling too late, Amberina," he said. "I need more information before I can broach the subject to the board of directors."

"Sure," she said distractedly, as if watching something attention-riveting on television.

"First, do you know anything about the history of the building? When was it built?"

"In 1901. The first high-rise apartment building in the city. The first to have an elevator."

"How many stories?"

"Thirteen."

"Who lived there originally? What kind of people?"

"Well, Mary says there were financiers, government officials, railroad tycoons, judges, heiresses—that kind. Also, they had suites for visiting royalty, opera stars, and so forth. After the stock market crash in 1929, more millionaires jumped off the roof of the Casablanca than any other building in the county."

"An impressive distinction," Qwilleran said wryly. "When did the place start to go downhill?"

"In the Depression. They couldn't rent the expensive apartments, so they cut them up, lowered ceilings—anything to cut costs and bring in some rent money."

"What can you tell me about the structure itself?"

"Let's see . . . SOCK put out a brochure that's around here somewhere. If you don't mind waiting, I'll try to find it. I'm not a very well-organized person."

"Take your time," he said. He had been making notes, and while she searched for the brochure, he sketched out his approach to the board of directors, scheduled his departure, and made a list of people to notify.

"Okay, here I am. I found it. Sorry to keep you waiting," Amberina said. "It was with my Christmas cards."

"Aren't you early with Christmas cards?"

"I haven't sent out *last year's* cards yet! . . . Are you ready? It says the exterior is faced with white glazed brick. The design is modified Moorish . . . Marble lobby with Persian rugs . . . Elevators paneled in rosewood . . . Mosaic tile floors in hallways. Apartments soundproof and fireproof, with twelve-foot ceilings and black walnut woodwork. Restaurant with terrace on the top floor. Also a swimming pool up there . . . this is the way it was in 1901, you understand. How does it sound, Mr. Qwilleran?"

"Not bad! You'd better reserve that penthouse for me."

"Mary told me to say that you'll be the guest of SOCK."

"I can afford to pay my own rent, but I appreciate the offer. How's the parking?"

"There's a paved lot with reserved spaces for tenants."

"And what's the crime situation in Junktown?"

"Well, we finally got the floozies and winos and pushers off the street."

"How did you do that?"

"The city cooperated because the Pennimans were behind it—"

"—and the city realized a broader tax base," Qwilleran guessed.

"Something like that. We have a citizens' patrol at night, and, of course, we don't take any chances after dark."

"How about security in the building itself?"

"Pretty good. The front door is locked, and there's a buzzer system. We had a doorman until a year ago. The side door is locked except for emergencies."

"Apparently the elderly woman who owns the building feels safe enough."

"I guess so. She has sort of a live-in bodyguard."

"Then it's a deal. Count on me to arrive next weekend."

"Mary will be tickled. We'll make all the arrangements for you."

"One question, Amberina. How many persons know that SOCK is inviting me to go down there?"

"Well, it was Mary's idea, and she probably discussed it with Robert Maus, but she wouldn't gab it around. She's not that type."

"All right. Let's keep it that way. Don't broadcast it. The story is that I want to get away from the abominable snow and ice up north, and the Casablanca is the only place that allows cats."

"Okay, I'll tell Mary."

"Any instructions for me when I arrive?"

"Just buzz the manager from the vestibule. We don't have a doorman anymore, but the custodian will help with your luggage. It will be nice to see you again, Mr. Qwilleran."

"What happened to the doorman?" he asked.

"Well," she said apologetically, "he was shot."

CHAPTER 2

The senior partner of the Pickax firm of Hasselrich Bennett & Barter, legal counsel for the Klingenschoen Memorial Fund, was an elderly man with stooped shoulders and quivering jowls, but he had the buoyant optimism and indomitability of a young man. It was Hasselrich whom Qwilleran chose to approach regarding the Casablanca proposal.

Before discussing business, the attorney insisted on serving coffee, pouring it proudly from his paternal grandmother's silver teapot into his maternal grandmother's Wedgwood cups, which rattled in the saucers as his shaking hands did the honors.

"It appears," Qwilleran began after a respectable interval for pleasantries, "that all of the Fund's ventures are on the East Coast, and it might be advisable to make ourselves known in another part of the country. What I have to suggest is both an investment and a public beneficence."

Hasselrich listened attentively as Qwilleran described the gentrification of Junktown, the unique architecture of the Casablanca, and the opportunity for the K Fund to preserve a fragment of the region's heritage. At the mention of the marble lobby and rosewood-paneled elevators, the attorney's jowls quivered with approval. "Many a time I have heard my grandfather extolling that magnificent building. He knew the man who built it," said Hasselrich. "As a young boy I was once treated to lunch in the rooftop restaurant. Unfortunately, I remember nothing but the spinach timbales. I had a juvenile aversion to spinach."

Qwilleran said, "The rooftop restaurant is now a penthouse apartment, and I plan to spend some time there, investigating the possibilities and persuading the owner to sell, if it seems wise. You know what will happen if developers are allowed to acquire the property; the building will be razed."

"Deplorable!" said Hasselrich. "We must not let that happen. This must be added to the agenda for the directors' meeting next week."

"I plan to drive down there in a few days—to beat the snow," said Qwilleran. "If you will be good enough to make the presentation in my absence, I'll supply a fact sheet." He welcomed any excuse to avoid meetings with the board of directors.

"Do you find it quite necessary to attend to this research yourself?" asked the attorney. "There are agencies we might retain to make a feasibility study."

"I consider it highly advisable. The owner is being pressured by the developers, and it will require some personal strategy to persuade the lady to sell to us."

The elderly attorney's lowered eyes and twitching eyelids were making broad inferences.

"She's seventy-five," Qwilleran added hastily, "and if she dies before deciding in our favor, we're out of luck and the Casablanca is doomed."

Hasselrich cleared his throat. "There is one consideration that gives me pause. You have indicated a profound interest in the welfare of Moose County, and that entails a responsibility to remain in good health, so to speak. You understand my meaning, do you not?"

"Moose County's interest in keeping me alive is no greater than my own desire to live, and I might point out another fact," Qwilleran said firmly. "When I go Down Below I am not a naive tourist from the outback; I've been city-smart since childhood."

Hasselrich studied his desktop and shook his jowls. "You seem to have made your decision. We can only hope for your safe return."

That same afternoon, the *Moose County Something*, as the local newspaper was waggishly named, carried the regular Tuesday column headed "Straight from the Qwill Pen," with an editor's note stating that Jim Qwilleran would be on a leave of absence for an indefinite period, pursuing business Down Below, but he would file an occasional column on city living, to appear in his usual space.

As soon as Qwilleran read this he recognized a conspiracy on the part of Arch Riker, the publisher, and Junior Goodwinter, the managing editor. The two guessed what the result of such an announcement would be, and they were right. Qwilleran's telephone started to ring, and the citizens of Moose County tried to dissuade him from braving the perils Down Below. When told that the trip was important and necessary, they offered advice: "Wear a money belt . . . Don't take your best watch . . . Get a burglar alarm for your car . . . Lock yourself in when you drive in the city."

Police Chief Brodie said, "Och, mon, you're a bit daft. I happen to hear a few things that don't get in the papers, but if you insist on going, stay home after dark and buy one of them gadgets that lock the brake pedal to the steering wheel."

From Susan Exbridge, a member of the Theatre Club, there was a melodramatic phone call: "*Darling*, don't *walk* anywhere!

Take a taxi, even if you're only going a block. I have friends Down Below, and they tell me it's *hell!*"

Dr. Goodwinter warned of respiratory ailments caused by airborne pollutants, and Eddington Smith, the timid dealer in secondhand books, offered to lend his handgun.

Lori Bamba was concerned chiefly about the cats. "If you're taking Koko and Yum Yum," she said, "don't let it be known that you have pedigreed animals. Kitnapping is big business Down Below. Also, you should feed them extra B vitamins to combat stress, because they'll sense menacing elements."

Even Qwilleran's cleaning man was worried. "It's prayin' I'll be," said Mr. O'Dell, "until you be comin' safe home, Mr. Q."

Nevertheless, Qwilleran stubbornly shopped for the journey. He bought a cagelike cat carrier that was more commodious and better ventilated than the picnic hamper in which the Siamese had formerly traveled. For their meals en route he laid in a supply of canned crabmeat, boned chicken, and red salmon. He also bought two blue leather harnesses—one medium and one large—with matching leashes. For himself he would take whatever he happened to have on hand. There were two suits in his closet—a gray flannel that he had worn once to a wedding and a dark blue serge that he had worn once as a pallbearer. These—with two white shirts, a couple of ties, and a raincoat—were his concessions to city dressing. Otherwise, he would take flannel shirts, sweaters, and his comfortable tweed sports coat with leather patches on the elbows.

During Qwilleran's final days in Pickax, farewell scenes with friends and associates had the solemnity of a deathbed vigil. Polly Duncan, on their last evening together, was lachrymose and in no mood to be comforted or to quote Shakespeare, although Qwilleran rose to the occasion with "parting is such sweet sorrow."

"Promise you'll call me as soon as you arrive" were her final words. He had hoped for less wifely anxiety and more amorous sentiments.

Even the Siamese sensed that something dire was afoot, and they sulked for twenty-four hours before their departure. When taken for rides in their new carrier, as rehearsal for the trip, they reacted like condemned nobility on the way to the guillotine—stoic, proud, and aloof.

None of this heightened Qwilleran's anticipation of the expedition, but he packed the car on Saturday morning with grim determination. Two suitcases, his typewriter, the unabridged dictionary, and his computerized coffeemaker went into the trunk. On the backseat were two boxes of books, the new cat carrier, and a blue cushion. The cats' water dish and their commode—a turkey roaster with the handles sawed off—were on the floor of the backseat.

The car was a small, energy-efficient, preowned four-door that Qwilleran had bought in a hurry, following his accident on Ittibittiwassee Road. The paint finish, a metallic purplish-blue, was not to his liking, but the used-car dealer assured him it was a color ahead of its time, called Purple Plum, and it would increase in acceptance and popularity.

"It looks better on fruit," Qwilleran remarked. The price was right, however, and the gas mileage was said to be phenomenal, and he had retained thrifty habits despite his new financial status, so he bought it. This was the car he packed for the four-hundred-mile journey, which he intended to stretch over two days for the comfort of the Siamese.

"All aboard the Purple Plum for Lockmaster, Paddockville, and all points south!" he announced to his two reluctant passengers. Grudgingly they allowed themselves to be stuffed into the carrier.

As the three of them pulled away from their home on Park Circle, the pair in the backseat maintained their funereal silence, leaving Qwilleran long, quiet hours to reflect on his sojourn in the north country. Despite the king-size mosquitoes, poison ivy, skunks, and hazardous deer crossings, Moose County afforded a comfortable life among good people. Most of them were rampant individualists and non-stop gossips, but that merely made them more interesting in the eyes of a journalist. How, he questioned, would he adjust to city life with its mask of conformity, guarded privacy, and self-interest?

His ruminations were interrupted by a demanding shriek from the backseat—so loud and so sudden that he gripped the steering wheel to keep the car on the road. Yum Yum was merely making a suggestion. How a creature of such delicacy and gentleness could produce this vulgar screech was beyond his comprehension, but it was effective. At the next crossroads he stopped for a coffee break and released the Siamese from their coop to stretch, peer out the windows, lap a tongueful of water, and examine the gas pedal.

After six hours of driving (Yum Yum objected to speeds in excess of fifty miles per hour), Qwilleran could not fault his passengers. They were behaving like mature, sophisticated travelers. At the motel that night—a less-than-deluxe establishment that welcomed pets—the Siamese slept soundly throughout the night, although Qwilleran was disturbed by barking dogs, slamming doors, and a growling ice machine outside his room. This appliance was located at the foot of wooden steps, up and down which the second-floor guests thumped frequently, shouting to each other:

"Where's the gin?"

"In the trunk under the spare tire!"

"I can't find the peanuts!"

It was Saturday night, and travelers were partying late. They also took an undue number of showers in Qwilleran's estimation. The force of the water hitting the fiberglass tubs in neighboring rooms thundered like Niagara, while he lay awake waiting for the tumult to end.

Meanwhile, the Siamese slept peacefully on top of his feet, and when he wriggled to relieve the numbness, they moved farther up and draped their soft bodies across his knees. Then late arrivals slammed their car doors and ran up the wooden steps, exchanging shouts:

"Bring my zipper bag up with you!"

"Which one?"

"The blue one!"

"Do you have the key?"

"Yes, but I can't find 203."

"Who's going to take Pierre for a walk?"

After that they all took showers, and the cascading water in the rooms above drowned out the television in the rooms on either side. Qwilleran heaved the cats off his knees, and they crawled farther up without opening their eyes.

So it continued until four o'clock in the morning, at which time he managed an hour's sleep before the early risers started taking showers, slamming car doors, and revving motors. He could have been excused for greeting the new day with a colossal grouch, but he exhibited a purposeful and admirable calm. All of Moose County had advised against this trip, and he was determined to prove them wrong from start to finish. He was, he told himself repeatedly, having a good time.

On the second day of driving, the panorama of woods and open fields and farmyards gave way to a scattering of billboards, gas stations, auto graveyards, and party stores, followed by strip malls and housing developments with fine-sounding names, and finally the freeway. Heavy traffic and increased speed began to put the backseat passengers on their guard, their noses lifting to register the density of emissions, while Yum Yum complained bitterly. For Qwilleran the sight of sweeping interchanges and incoming jets and the jagged skyline produced an urban high that he had relished in the past and had almost forgotten. Even the Purple Plum looked less offensive in the smoggy atmosphere.

He left the freeway at the Zwinger exit. On this late Sunday afternoon, downtown was virtually deserted. Zwinger Street, formerly a blighted area, was now Zwinger Boulevard—a continuous landscaped park dotted with glass towers, parking structures, and apartment complexes. Then the boulevard narrowed into the nineteenth-century neighborhood known as Junktown, with the Casablanca standing like a sentinel at the approach.

"Oh, no!" Qwilleran said aloud. "It looks like a refrigerator!" The Casablanca was indeed white, although in need of cleaning, and it had the proportions of a refrigerator, with a dark line across the facade at the ninth floor, as if delineating the freezer compartment. Modified Moorish, the SOCK brochure had called it. True, there were some arches and a marquee and two large ornamental lanterns of Spanish persuasion, but on the whole it looked like a refrigerator. Not so in 1901 perhaps, when iceboxes were made of golden oak, but now . . .

Qwilleran made a U-turn and pulled up to the curb, where the city permitted twenty-minute parking. He unloaded the cat carrier and the turkey roaster and then, taking care to lock all four doors, approached the shabby entrance. Broken glass in the two lanterns exposed the light bulbs, and the glass sidelights of the door were walled up with plywood that no one had bothered to paint. Carefully he picked his way up the cracked marble steps and set down the carrier, opening the heavy black door and holding it with his foot while he maneuvered into the dark vestibule.

"Help ya?" called a voice from the gloom. A jogger was about to leave the building.

"How do I ring the manager?" Qwilleran inquired.

"Right over here." A young man with a reddish moustache almost as imposing as Qwilleran's pressed a button on the apartment directory panel. "You moving in?"

"Yes. Where do you jog around here?"

"Around the vacant lots behind the building. Two times around is a mile—and not too much carbon monoxide."

"Is it safe?"

The man held up a small tube and pointed it at Qwilleran. "Zap!" he said, looking wise. "Hey, nice cats!" he added, squinting at the carrier. When a voice finally squawked on the intercom the obliging jogger yelled, "New tenant, Mrs. Tuttle." A buzzer released the door, and he sprang to open it. "Manager's desk straight down the hall, opposite the second elevator."

"Thanks. Good running!" Qwilleran wished him. The inner door slammed behind him, and he found himself in an empty lobby.

It was narrower than he had expected—a tunnel-like hall with a low ceiling and a lingering odor of disinfectant. Fluorescent tubes were spaced too far apart to provide effective light. The floor was well-worn vinyl, but clean, and the walls were covered with something that looked like sandpaper. When he reached the first elevator, however, he stopped and stared; the elevator door was burnished bronze sculptured in low relief, representing scenes from *Don Quixote* and *Carmen*.

As he studied the unexpected artistry, the door slid open, and a man in black tie and dinner jacket stepped out, saying coolly, "This is a private elevator," at the same time flinging a contemptuous glance at the turkey roaster.

With the top handle of the carrier in one hand and the roaster under the other arm, Qwilleran walked slowly toward the rear of the building, observing and sniffing. Someone on the main floor was cooking, and he knew Portuguese garlic soup when he smelled it. Lined up in the tunnel were a cigarette machine, a soft-drink dispenser, and an old wooden telephone booth. Some attempt had been made to brighten the hall by painting apartment doors in jellybean colors, but the paint was scratched and dreary with age.

As he reached the phone booth, a body tumbled out onto the floor. It was a woman of indefinite age, wearing a red cocktail dress, and she was clutching a pint rum bottle, uncapped. "Oops!" she said.

Gallantly, Qwilleran set down his baggage and went to her assistance. "Hurt yourself?"

She slurred an apology as he helped her up, propped her on the seat of the phone booth, and closed her safely inside, leaving only a puddle on the floor.

He picked up the cat carrier and commode and walked on. As he approached the manager's desk, there was sudden activity within the carrier, which started jiggling and swinging, the reason being that two felines—a calico and a tiger with a chewed ear—had wandered out from nowhere and were eyeing the new arrivals. Although the host cats were not hostile, Qwilleran thought it advisable to place the carrier on the scarred counter where a homemade sign announced: "Mrs. Tuttle, manager. Ring for service." Separating the manager's desk from the tenants' counter was a window of thick, bulletproof acrylic.

He rang the bell, and a large, powerful-looking woman with a broad smile on her ebony face bounded out from the inner office. "Oh, you've got two Siamese!" she exclaimed joyously. Despite her genial greeting, she studied Qwilleran with a stern and forbidding eye, and he imagined that she tolerated no nonsense from the tenants or the resident cats.

"Good afternoon," he said. "Are you Mrs. Tuttle? My name is Qwilleran. The penthouse apartment has been reserved for me."

"Yes, SIR!" she said. "We're expecting you! Glad to have you here. Did you have a good trip?"

"Fine, thank you. Do you also have a parking space for me?"

"Yes, SIR!" She produced a ledger and flipped the looseleaf pages to Q. "First we need one month security deposit and one month rent, and the parking is payable by the quarter . . . What are they called?"

"Uh . . . what?" Qwilleran was concentrating on his checkbook. He considered the rent high, even though utilities were included.

"Do your kitties have names?"

"Uh . . . the larger one is Koko, and the . . . uh . . . female is Yum Yum." He had put the turkey roaster on the floor, and it was being sniffed by the calico and the tiger. "I see you have a welcoming committee down on the floor."

"That's Napoleon and Kitty-Baby," she said. "They live on the main floor. Your kitties will be the only ones on Fourteen."

"Fourteen? I thought the building had thirteen stories."

"They skipped Thirteen. Bad luck, you know. On the top floor there are two apartments, 14-A and 14-B. Yours is the nice one, all furnished. You'll be very comfortable. Here is your receipt and your key to 14-A. And here's your mailbox key; the boxes are through the arch. Mail is delivered around three or four o'clock. Your parking slot is #28 on the west side of the lot. The elevator's right behind you. Ring for the one with the red door. Old Red, we call it. A nice old elevator. Old Green is out of order."

"What's the one with the bronze door, near the entrance?" he asked.

"A private elevator for the owner of the building. Bye-bye, kitties! Glad to have you here, Mr. Qwilleran."

The Siamese had not uttered a sound. He picked up the roaster and the carrier and moved to the elevator bank, accompanied by Napoleon and Kitty-Baby. Two doors, one painted red and one painted green, were closed, displaying an abstract design of scratches and gouges made by impatient tenants carrying doorkeys. He pressed the button, and noises in the shaft indicated that Old Red was descending . . . slowly . . . very slowly. When the car finally arrived, it could be heard bouncing and leveling. Then the door opened with a convulsive jerk, and a tiny Asian woman with two small, doll-like children stepped out and scurried away as if glad to escape safely.

Qwilleran boarded, signaled for the fourteenth floor, and waited for the door to close, while Napoleon and Kitty-Baby stayed in the lobby staring into the car as if they would not be caught dead in Old Red. The Siamese were still ominously silent.

There was a bulletin board on the rear wall of the elevator, where manager and tenants had posted notices, and Qwilleran amused himself while waiting for the door to close by reading the messages. Two signs were neatly lettered with a felt marker and signed "Mrs. T."

IF DOOR IS OPEN, DO NOT JUMP!
ATTENTION ALL CATS! MONDAY IS SPRAY DAY!

There was also a handwritten message on a note card with an embossed W, offering a baby grand piano for sale in apartment 10-F. Scribbled on a scrap of brown paper was an ad for a tennis racquet for twenty-five dollars, spelled T-E-N-I-S-R-A-C-K-E-T. Qwilleran was a born proofreader.

Mystified by the first two notices and questioning the market for baby grands in such a building, he failed to notice that the elevator door was still standing open. It was hardly the latest model in automatic equipment, and he looked for a suitable button to press. There was one labeled OPEN and a red button labeled HELP; that was all. The red button, he observed, showed signs of wear. Out in the lobby all was quiet. Mrs. Tuttle had left her post behind the bulletproof window, and the only signs of life were Napoleon and Kitty-Baby.

In Qwilleran's lean and hungry days, when he lived for a brief time at the decrepit Medford Manor, there was a stubborn elevator door that responded to a vigorous kick. He tried it, but

Old Red only shuddered. Then he heard running footsteps approaching from the front door and a voice calling "Hold it!" A short man in a yellow satin jacket, with the name "Valdez" on the back, slid into view like a base runner approaching first.

"No hurry," Qwilleran told him. "The door won't close."

The fellow gave him a scornful glance and jumped up and down on the elevator floor. The door immediately closed, and the car proceeded slowly upward, clanking and shuddering as it passed each floor. Valdez got off at Five, and as he left the car he turned and said, "You jump."

Qwilleran jumped, the door closed, and Old Red ascended at the same snail-like pace, with groaning and scraping added to the clanking and shuddering. The Siamese had been patient, but suddenly Yum Yum emitted her ear-splitting screech, and immediately the car stopped dead. According to the floor indicator over the door they were not yet at Fourteen. According to the floor indicator they were not anywhere.

"*Now* what have you done?" Qwilleran scolded.

He pressed the button for his floor, but the car did not budge. He jumped, Valdez-style, and nothing happened. He pressed the button labeled OPEN, and the door slowly obliged, revealing the black brick wall of the elevator shaft.

"Ye gods!" Qwilleran shouted. "We're trapped between floors!"

CHAPTER 3

The Siamese, who had been more or less uncommunicative for four hundred miles, became vociferous when told they were trapped between floors in the Casablanca elevator shaft. Qwilleran pressed the HELP button and could hear a bell like a fire alarm ringing in some remote precinct of the old building, but the longer he leaned on the red button and the longer the bell pealed, the louder Koko howled and Yum Yum yodeled.

"*Quiet!*" Qwilleran commanded, and gave the bell another prolonged ring, but in Siamese cat language "quiet" means "louder."

"Shhhh!" he scolded.

Somewhere an elevator door was being forced open; somewhere a distant voice was shouting.

Qwilleran shouted back, "We're stuck between floors!"

"Where y'at?" came the faint query.

"YOW!" Koko replied.

"Quiet, you dumbbell! I can't hear what he's saying . . . *We're stuck between floors!*"

"What floor?" The voice sounded hollow, suggesting that hands were being cupped for a megaphone effect.

"YOW!"

"I can't hear you!" Qwilleran shouted.

"What floor?" The voice was coming from overhead.

"YOW!"

"*Shut up!*"

"What you say down there?"

"We're between floors! I don't know where!" Qwilleran bellowed at his loudest.

There was the sound of a heavy door closing, followed by a long period of silence and inactivity.

"You really blew it!" Qwilleran told Koko. "They were coming to our rescue, and you wouldn't keep your mouth shut. Now we may be here all night." He looked around the dismal cell with its soiled walls and torn floor tiles. One of the fluorescent tubes had burned out leaving half the car in shadow. "At least you've got your commode," he said to his disgruntled companions, "which is more than I can say." He rang the emergency bell again.

There was another wrenching sound in the shaft above, and a voice overhead—somewhat closer this time—yelled, "You gotta climb out!"

"YOW!" Koko replied.

"How?" Qwilleran shouted.

"What?"

"YOW!"

Qwilleran gave the cat carrier a remonstrative shove with his foot, which only accelerated the howls. "How do I climb out?"

"Push up the roof!"

In the tan ceiling of the car there was a metal plate, black with fingerprints.

"Push it all the way!" came the instructions from on high.

Qwilleran reached up, gave the metal plate a forceful push, and it flopped open with a clatter. Through the rectangular opening he could see a bare light bulb, dazzlingly bright in the black shaft, and a ladder slowly descending. He wondered if he could squeeze through the hole in the roof; he wondered if the carrier would go through.

"I've got luggage down here!" he yelled.

There was another long wait, and then a rope came dangling through the trapdoor.

"Tie it on the handle!" called the rescuer.

Qwilleran quickly knotted one end to the top handle of the cat carrier and watched it rise off the floor and ascend in jerks that annoyed the occupants. It disappeared into the hole above.

"Anythin' else?"

Qwilleran looked speculatively at the turkey roaster. Its handles had long ago been sawed off to fit on the floor of the car. Furthermore, it contained slightly used kitty gravel.

"Nothing else!" he shouted, kicking the pan into a dark corner of the elevator. Then he started up the ladder. Above him he could see a pale face and a red golf hat clapped on a head of sandy hair.

The custodian was waiting for him at the top. "Sorry 'bout this."

On hands and knees Qwilleran crawled out of the black hole onto the mosaic tile floor of a hallway, a performance that interested the waiting cats enormously; they were always entranced by unusual behavior on his part.

"Where are we?" he asked.

"On Nine. Gotta walk up. We got both cars broke now—Old Red and Old Green. Serviceman don't come till tomorrow. Costs double on Sundays."

Their rescuer was a thin, wiry man of middle age, all elbows and knees and bony shoulders, wearing khaki pants and a bush jacket, its large pockets bulging with a flashlight and other tools of his trade. Judging by his prison pallor, it was doubtful that he had ever bushwhacked beyond the weedy landscaping of the Casablanca. The man picked up the cat carrier and headed for the stairwell.

"Here, let me take that," Qwilleran offered. "It's heavy."

"I seen heavier. Lady on Seven, she's got two cats, must weigh twenty pounds apiece. You in 14-A?"

"Yes. My name's Qwilleran. What's your name?"

"Rupert."

"I appreciate your coming to our rescue."

After that brief exchange, the two men plodded silently up the four long flights to the fourteenth floor, which was really the thirteenth. At the top of the stairs they emerged into a small lobby with a marble floor and marble walls, a relic of the rooftop restaurant in the Casablanca's illustrious past. There were two elevator doors, closed and silent, and two apartment doors with painted numbers.

Qwilleran glanced at his key and opened 14-A. "I guess this is it."

"Yep, this is it," said Rupert. "Doorbell's broke." He touched the pearl button to prove it. "All the doorbells are broke."

They walked into a spacious foyer handsomely furnished in the contemporary style, with doorways and arches leading to other equally lavish areas. This was more than Qwilleran had expected. It explained why the rent was high. A bank of French doors overlooked a large room with a lofty ceiling and a conversation pit six feet deep. "Is that the sunken living room?" he asked. "It looks like a carpeted swimming pool."

"That's what it was—a swimmin' pool," said the custodian. "Not very deep. Didn't do much divin' in them days, I reckon."

An exceptionally long sofa doglegged around one end of the depression, and around the ceramic-tiled rim of the former pool there were indoor trees in tubs, some reaching almost to the skylight twenty feet overhead.

Qwilleran noticed a few plastic pails scattered about the room, and there were waterstains on the carpet. "Does the skylight leak?" he asked.

"When it rains," Rupert said with a worried nod. "Where'd you park?"

"At the front door in a twenty-minute zone. I may have a ticket by now."

"Nobody bothers you on Sunday. Gimme your keys and I'll haul up the rest of your gear."

"I'll go with you," Qwilleran said, remembering the advice showered on him in Pickax. "I suppose we have to walk down thirteen flights and up again."

"If we can find the freight, we'll ride up."

"Then let's go."

The custodian looked at the cat carrier standing in the middle of the foyer. "Ain'tcha gonna let 'em out?"

"They can wait till we get back." Qwilleran always checked the premises for hazards and hidden exits before releasing the Siamese.

The two men began the tedious descent to the main floor, down marble stairs with ornamental iron banisters, each flight enclosed in a grim stairwell. "Good-looking staircases," Qwilleran commented. "Too bad they're enclosed."

"Fire department made 'em do it."

"What's that trapdoor?" In the wall of each stairwell, toward the top of the flight, there was a small square door labeled DANGER—KEEP OUT.

"That's to the crawl space. Water pipes, heat, electric, and all stuff like that," Rupert informed him.

Halfway down they met the tiny Asian woman shepherding her two small children from one floor to another. She seemed unaware of their presence.

"Are there many children in the building?" Qwilleran asked.

"Mostly kids of the doctors that work at the hospital. From all different countries."

At last they reached the main floor, and as they walked past the manager's desk, Mrs. Tuttle, who was knitting something behind the bulletproof window, sang out cheerfully, "Why didn't you two ride the elevator?" She motioned toward Old Red, which was standing there with its door hospitably open. Qwilleran squinted into the dim back corner of the car and quickly retrieved the turkey roaster, carrying it away triumphantly.

Farther down the hall Valdez, still in his yellow satin jacket, was beating his fists against the soft-drink dispenser, and Napoleon was sniffing a puddle near the phone booth, critically. There was no activity around the elaborate bronze door of the private elevator.

"Quiet on Sundays," Rupert commented.

In front of the building the Purple Plum was still parked at the curb, neither stolen nor ticketed, and Qwilleran drove into the parking lot while Rupert went to the basement for a luggage cart. The lot was an obstacle course dotted with potholes, and his #28 parking slot was occupied by a small green Japanese car.

"Park in #29," Rupert told him. "Nobody cares."

"This lot is in terrible condition," Qwilleran complained. "When was it last paved? In 1901?"

"No use fixin' it. They could tear the place down next week."

Rupert wheeled the suitcases, typewriter, dictionary, books, and coffeemaker into the basement, Qwilleran following with the turkey roaster and the cats' water dish. They rode up in the freight elevator, a rough enclosure of splintery boards, but it worked!

"How come this one works?" Qwilleran asked.

"It's never broke," the custodian said. "Tenants don't get to use it, that's why. They're the ones wreck the elevators. Wait'll you see how they wreck the washers and dryers! There's a coin laundry in the basement."

"What do we do about rubbish?"

"Put it out in the hall at night. Boy picks up startin' at six in the mornin'. Any problem, just ring the desk. Housephone's on the kitchen wall in 14-A."

Qwilleran tipped him liberally. Although frugal by nature, he had developed a generous streak since inheriting money. Now he bolted the door, cat-proofed the rooms, and released the Siamese. "We're here!" he said. They emerged cautiously, swiveling their fine brown heads, pointing their ears, curving their whiskers, and sensing the long broad foyer. Koko walked resolutely to the far wall where French doors led to the terrace; he checked for pigeons and seemed disappointed that none appeared. Meanwhile Yum Yum was putting forth an experimental paw to touch the art rugs scattered about the parquet floor.

Art was everywhere: paintings on the walls, sculpture on pedestals, crystal and ceramic objects in lighted niches. The canvases were not to Qwilleran's liking: splotches of color and geometric studies that seemed meaningless to him; a still life of an auto mechanic's workbench; a bloody scene depicting a butcher block with work in progress; a realistic portrayal of people eating spaghetti.

Then he noticed an envelope with his name, propped against a bowl of fruit on a console table. Nestled among the winesap apples, tangerines, and Bosc pears, like a Cracker Jack prize, was a can of lobster. "You guys are in luck," he said to the Siamese. "But after your shenanigans in the elevator, I don't know whether you deserve it."

The accompanying note was from Amberina: "Welcome to the Casablanca! Mary wants me to take you to dinner at Roberto's tonight. Call my apartment when you get in. SOCK had your phone connected."

Qwilleran lost no time in phoning. "I accept with pleasure. I have a lot of questions to ask. Where's Roberto's?"

"In Junktown, a couple of blocks away. We can walk."

"Is that advisable after dark?"

"I never walk alone, but . . . sure, it'll be okay. Could you meet me inside the front door at seven o'clock? I won't ask you to come to my apartment. It's a mess."

He opened the can of lobster for the Siamese, arranging it on a Royal Copenhagen plate. All the appointments in the apartment were top-notch: Waterford crystal, Swedish sterling, German stainless, and so on. After unpacking his suitcases he wandered about the rooms, eating an apple and marveling at the expensive art books on the library table, the waterbed in the master bedroom, the gold faucets in the bathroom. He looked askance at the painting of the bloody butcher block; it was not something he would care to see early in the morning on an empty stomach, yet it occupied a prominent spot on the end wall of the foyer.

When the Siamese had finished their meal and groomed their paws, whiskers, ears, and tails, he introduced them to the sunken living room. In no time at all they discovered they could race around the rim of the former pool, chase each other up and down the carpeted stairs leading to the conversation pit, climb the trees, and scamper the length of the sofa-back. For his own satisfaction he paced off the length of the dogleg sofa and found it to be an incredible twenty feet. Though few in number, the furnishings were large-scale: an enormous onyx cocktail table stacked with art magazines; an eight-foot bar; an impressive stereo system with satellite speakers the size of coffins.

The most dramatic feature was the gallery of paintings that covered the upper walls. They were large still lifes, all studies of mushrooms—whole or halved or sliced, tumbled about in various poses. The jarring effect, to Qwilleran's eye, was not the size of the mushrooms—some two feet in diameter—but the fact that each arrangement was pictured with a pointed knife that looked murderously sharp. He had to admit that the knife lifted the still lifes out of the ordinary. Somehow it suggested a human presence. But he could not imagine why the owner of the apartment had hung so many mushrooms, unless . . . he had painted them himself. Who was this talented tenant? The signature on the work was a cryptic logo: two Rs back-to-back. Why did he specialize in mushrooms? Why did he leave? Where had he gone? When would he return? And why was he willing to sublet this lavishly furnished apartment to a stranger?

There were no windows in the room—only the skylight, and it admitted a sick light on this late afternoon in November. Apart from the potted trees and the green and yellow plastic pails strategically placed in case of rain, the interior was monochromatically neutral. Walls, upholstered sofa, and commercial-weave carpet were all in a pale gray-beige like the mushrooms.

He checked his watch. It was time to dress for dinner. At that moment he heard a door slam in the elevator lobby; the occupant of 14-B was either coming in or going out. He soon discovered which.

When 14-A had been carved out of the former restaurant, space was no object, and the master bathroom was large enough to accommodate a whirlpool bath for two, a tanning couch, and an exercise bike. The stall shower was large enough for three. At the turn of a knob, water pelted Qwilleran's body from three sides, gentle as rain or sharp as needles. He was luxuriating in this experience when the water abruptly turned ice cold. He yelped and bounded from the enclosure. Dripping and cursing and half-draped in a towel, he found the house telephone in the kitchen. Mrs. Tuttle's businesslike voice answered.

"This is Qwilleran in 14-A," he said in a politely shocked tone. "I was taking a shower and the water suddenly ran cold, ice cold!"

"That happens," she said. "It's an old building, you know. Evidently your neighbor started to take a shower at the same time."

"You mean I have to coordinate my bathing schedule with 14-B?"

"I don't think you need to worry about it too much," she said soothingly.

That's right, he thought. The building may be torn down next week. "Who is the tenant in 14-B?"

Mrs. Tuttle said something that sounded like Keestra Hedrog, and when he asked her to repeat the name, it still sounded like Keestra Hedrog. He huffed into his moustache and hung up.

After toweling and donning his old plaid bathrobe in the Mackintosh tartan (his mother had been a Mackintosh), he was in the process of eating another apple when he heard incredible sounds from the adjoining apartment—like a hundred-piece orchestra tuning up discordantly for Tchaikovsky's *1812 Overture*. The cats' ears swiveled nervously, the left and right ears twisting in opposite directions. He realized that they were hearing a composition for the synthesizer, a kind of music he had not yet learned to appreciate. He also realized that the walls between 14-A and 14-B were regrettably thin—one of the

Casablanca's Depression economies. By the time he had finished dressing, however, the recording ended, a door slammed again, and his neighbor apparently went out for the evening.

He checked out the cats as he always did before leaving and found Yum Yum in the bedroom, sniffing the waterbed, but Koko was not in evidence. He called his name and received no response. For one sickening moment he wondered if the cat had discovered a secret exit. Hurrying from room to room he called and searched and worried. It was not until he went down into the conversation pit that he found the missing Koko.

The eight-foot bar in the pit was situated rather conspicuously in the middle of the floor, and Koko was sniffing this piece of furniture, oblivious of everything else. Qwilleran himself had not touched alcohol for several years, and when he served spirits to his guests, Koko showed no interest whatever unless he happened upon a stray anchovy olive. So why was he so intent upon investigating this leather-upholstered, teak-topped liquor dispensary? Koko always had a sound reason for his actions, although it was not always obvious.

Qwilleran opened the drawers and cabinets of the bar and found decanters, glassware, jiggers, corkscrews, muddlers, napkins, and so forth. That was all.

"Sorry, Koko," he said. "No anchovies. No mice. No dead bodies."

The cat ignored him. He was sniffing the base of the bar, running his twitching nose along the line where the furniture met the carpet, as if some small object had found its way underneath. Qwilleran touched his moustache questioningly, his curiosity aroused. It was a heavy bar, but by putting his shoulder against one end of it he could slide it across the tightly woven carpet. As it began to move, Koko became agitated, prancing back and forth in encouragement.

"If this turns out to be an anchovy-stuffed olive," Qwilleran said, "you're going to be in the doghouse!" He shoved again. The ponderous bar moved a few inches at a time.

Then Koko yowled. A thin dark line had appeared on the pale carpet. It widened as Qwilleran lunged with his shoulder—wider and wider until a large dark stain was revealed.

"Blood!" Qwilleran said.

"Yow!" said Koko. He arched his back, elongated his legs, hooked his tail, and pranced in a circle. Qwilleran had seen the dance before— Koko's death dance. Then from the cat's innards came a new sound: less than a growl yet deeper than a purr. It sounded like "Rrrrrrrrr!"

CHAPTER 4

Before leaving for dinner with Amberina, Qwilleran made a long-distance phone call. It was Sunday evening, and Polly Duncan would be at home waiting for news. He deemed it advisable to keep the report upbeat: Yes, he had enjoyed the trip . . . Yes, the cats behaved well . . . The manager and custodian were helpful. The apartment was spacious and well-furnished, with a magnificent view of the sunset. He mentioned nothing about the malfunctioning elevator nor the leaking skylight nor the bulletproof window at the manager's desk nor the bloodstain on the carpet, and he especially avoided reference to his dinner date with Amberina. Polly was a wonderful woman but inclined to be jealous.

Then he said goodbye to the Siamese, having placed their blue cushion on the bed in the small bedroom. "Be good kids," he said. "Have a nap and stay out of trouble. I'll be back in a couple of hours, perhaps with a doggie bag." He turned off all the lights except the one in the bathroom, where they had their commode, thinking that the darkness would encourage them to nap and stay out of mischief.

Leaving 14-A, he spotted a namecard tacked on the door of 14-B, and he sauntered close enough to read it. His neighbor's name was indeed Keestra Hedrog, as Mrs. Tuttle had said. It looked like something spelled backward and he considered tacking a namecard to his own door: Mij Narelliwq.

What, he asked himself, had happened to nomenclature in

recent years? Strange new words had entered the language and strange new names were popping up in the telephone directory. Mary, Betty, and Ann had been replaced by Thedira and Cheryline. Even ordinary names had tricky spellings like Elizabette and Alyce, causing inconvenience to all concerned, not to mention the time lost in explaining and correcting. (His own name, spelled with the unconventional QW, had been the bane of editors, typesetters, and proofreaders for thirty years, but that fact escaped him.)

He signaled for the elevator and heard evidence of mechanical torment in the shaft—noises so threatening that he chose to walk downstairs. Feeling his way through the poorly lighted stairwells, he encountered bags of trash, unidentified odors and—between the seventh and sixth floors—a shrouded figure standing alone on the stairs and mumbling.

On the main floor he passed two elderly women in bathrobes, huddled in conference. One of them was saying in a croaking voice, "I've been mugged five times. How many times have you been mugged?"

"Only twice," said the other, shrilly, "but the second time they knocked me down."

Both of them squinted suspiciously at Qwilleran as he passed.

He found Rupert hanging around the manager's desk, still with the red golf hat on the back of his head, while three boisterous students practiced karate chops in front of the elevators.

"Knock it off," Rupert warned them, "or I'll tell Mrs. T."

The youths clicked their heels, clasped their hands prayerfully, and bowed low, then made a dash for Old Red when it arrived.

"Crazy college kids," Rupert explained to Qwilleran. "Everything okay on Fourteen?"

"So far, so good." He started for the front door but returned. "There's something I wanted to ask about, Rupert. In my living room there's a huge piece of furniture—a serving bar—right in the middle of the floor. Do you happen to know why?"

"Mrs. T said to put it there," said the custodian. "I didn't ask no questions. Me and the boy had to move the thing. It's mighty heavy."

"How long have you been working here, Rupert?"

"Twenty years next March. Good job! Meet lotsa people. And I get an apartment in the basement thrown in."

"What will you do if they tear down the building?"

"Go on unemployment. Go on welfare, I reckon, if I can't find work. I'm fifty-six."

Qwilleran had a long wait for Amberina, but the time was not wasted. While standing at the front door he watched a circus parade of tenants and visitors coming in and going out. He tried not to stare at the outlandish clothing on the young ones, or the pathetic condition of some of the old ones, or the exotic beauty wearing a sari, or the fellow with a macaw in a cage.

When two well-dressed young men arrived, carrying a small gold tote bag from the city's most exclusive chocolatier, he watched them go to the burnished bronze door and ring for the private elevator, and he began to conjecture about the "Countess." The mysterious seventy-five-year-old who was visited by men wearing dinner jackets or bearing gifts sounded like Lady Hester Stanhope in Kinglake's *Eothen*, a book he had been reading aloud to the Siamese. Lady Hester lived in a crumbling middle-eastern convent, subsisting on milk and enjoying the adulation of desert tribes. Was the Countess the Lady Hester of the crumbling Casablanca?

His flights of fancy were interrupted when Amberina came running down the hall. "Sorry I'm late. I lost my contact lens, and I couldn't seem to get myself together."

He said, "Who are the well-dressed men who ride up and down on the Countess's elevator?"

"Her bridge partners," she explained. "She loves to play cards."

Amberina had changed since their last meeting three years before. Her strikingly-brunette hair was a different color and a different style—lighter, redder, and frizzier. She had put on weight and her dimples were less beguiling. He was disappointed, but he said, "Good to see you again, Amberina. You're looking great!"

"So are you, Mr. Qwilleran, and you look so countrified!" He was wearing his tweed coat with leather patches and his chukka boots.

They left the building and zigzagged down the broken marble slabs with care. "These steps should be repaired before someone trips and sues the Countess," he remarked.

"No point in making repairs when the whole place may be torn down next week," she said with a touch of bitterness. We're all keeping our fingers crossed that nothing terrible will happen. Mary says the city would love it if the elevator dropped and killed six tenants, or a steam boiler blew up and cooked everyone on the main floor. Then they'd condemn the place and start collecting higher property taxes on a billion-dollar hotel or something. I do hope your people decide to buy the Casablanca, Mr. Qwilleran."

Now they were strolling down Junktown's new brick sidewalks, recently planted with small trees and lighted with old-fashioned gaslamps.

Qwilleran said, "This is exactly what C. C. Cobb wanted three years ago, and the city fought him every step of the way."

The jerry-built storefronts that previous landlords had tacked on to the front of historic townhouses had been removed. One could never guess where the old fruit and tobacco stand had been, or the wig and fortune-telling shop. New owners had miraculously restored the original stone steps, iron railings, and impressive entrance doors. A brightly lighted coffee house occupied the premises of the former furniture-refinishing shop in an old stable, now named the Carriage House Café.

"Tell me about this restaurant we're going to. What is Roberto's?" Qwilleran asked.

"You know—don't you?—that Robert Maus wanted to open a restaurant when he gave up the law business. Well, he went to Italy and worked in a restaurant in Milan for a year. When he came home he was cooking Italian and had changed his name to Roberto."

"I hope he didn't change his last name to 'Mausolini.'"

Amberina let out an involuntary shriek. "Wait till Mary hears that! She won't think it's funny. She's very serious, you know."

"I know. So is he."

"Well, anyway, he opened this Italian restaurant in one of the old townhouses—Mary talked him into it, I think—and he lives upstairs. I've never eaten there—too expensive—but Mary says it's fabulous food."

"Everything Robert prepares is fabulous. Will he be there tonight?"

"You're supposed to call him Roberto, Mr. Qwilleran. No, he's off on Sundays, and they're closed on Mondays, but he personally supervises the kitchen five nights a week. Imagine! A law degree! And he's cooking spaghetti!"

An unobtrusive sign on the iron railing of a townhouse announced "Roberto's North Italian Cuisine." As they climbed the stone steps Qwilleran knew what to expect. He had lived in Junktown long enough to be familiar with old townhouses. Even though they became rooming houses they had high ceilings, carved woodwork, ornate fireplaces (boarded up), and gaslight chandeliers (electrified)—all of these in various degrees of shabbiness. With Robert Maus's taste for English baronial he would add red velvet draperies and leather chairs studded with nailheads. *Ecco!* North Italian!

Qwilleran was shocked, therefore, when they entered the restaurant. The interior had been gutted. Walls, ceiling, and arches were an unbroken sweep of smooth plaster in a custardy shade of cream. The carpet was eggplant in hue; so was the upholstery of the steel-based chairs. Silk-shaded lamps on the tables and silk-shaded sconces on the walls threw a golden glow over the cream-tinted table linens.

Before he could splutter a comment, a white-haired woman armed with menus approached in a flurry of excitement. "Mr. Qwilleran! Do you remember me? I'm Charlotte Roop," she said in a reedy voice.

She had been his neighbor three years before on River Road—a strait-laced, spinsterish woman obsessed with crossword puzzles—but she had changed drastically. Where was her disapproving scowl? Her tightly pursed lips? Had she had a facelift? Could she possibly have found love and happiness with a good man? Qwilleran chuckled at the idea. Instead of her usual nondescript garb smothered in costume jewelry, she was wearing a simple beige dress with a cameo at the throat—a cameo brought from Italy by her new boss, Qwilleran assumed.

"Of course I remember you!" he exclaimed. "You're looking . . . you're looking . . . What's a six-letter word for beautiful?"

"Oh, Mr. Qwilleran, you remembered!" she cried with pleasure, adding in a lower voice, "But I don't do crossword puzzles anymore. I have a gentleman friend." She flushed.

"Good for you! He's a lucky fellow!"

Miss Roop touched the cameo self-consciously. "I'm the one who's lucky. I have a lovely apartment at the Casablanca and a lovely job with our wonderful Roberto. Let me show you to our best table."

"This is a handsome place," Qwilleran said. "Very warm, very friendly, yet surprisingly modern."

"Roberto wanted it to be the color of zabaglione. He brought Italian artisans over to do the plastering." She handed them menus and recommended the *tagliatelle con salmone affumicato* and the *vitello alla griglia*. Her boss, always a perfectionist, had coached her on the pronunciation. She added, "Roberto wishes you to be our guests tonight. Would you like something from the bar?"

Considering Miss Roop's former attitude toward anything stronger than weak tea, this was a right-about-face. She suggested Pinot Grigio as an apéritif. Amberina shrugged and accepted. Qwilleran asked for mineral water with lemon. Meanwhile, a waiter displaying professional éclat draped napkins across their laps—*heated* napkins.

"Real flowers," Amberina whispered as she fingered the rosebuds in a Venetian glass vase. "I wonder how many of these vases they lose."

There was little general conversation as they adjusted to the elegance of the room and the awesomeness of the menu. Finally she said, "Tell me honestly, Mr. Qwilleran. What do you think of the Casablanca?"

"It's a dump! Does anyone really think it's worth restoring? Does anyone think it's even *possible* to restore such a ruin?"

"SOCK is positive," she replied earnestly. "Mary Duckworth

and Roberto are officers, and you know they don't waste their time on a lot of baloney. They've had an architect make a study for SOCK, and he knows exactly what has to be done and how to do it and how much it will cost. I don't have the exact facts, but Mary can fill you in on that stuff."

"Where is she?"

"Right now she's flying back from Philadelphia. There was a big antique show there, and she took a double booth. Her porters drove a truckload down, and she expected it would return empty. Mary has that snooty manner, you know, and she can sell anything and get a good price for it. People *believe* her! I wish I had her class. But that's the way it goes! The rich get richer. Her family is in banking, you know."

"Does she still wear kimonos embroidered with dragons when she waits on customers?"

"No, she's gone back to being preppy, pearls and everything . . . EEK! Did you see these prices?" she squealed when she saw the right-hand side of the card. "I'm glad I'm not paying for this! I'm going to order the most expensive thing on the menu. The chances are I'll never come here again."

They each ordered an antipasto, soup, and a veal dish. Then Qwilleran said, "I have a few questions to ask, Amberina. Is the elevator service always as bad as it was today?"

"I wish you'd call me Amber," she said.

"And you seem to have forgotten that you used to call me Qwill."

"I didn't forget," she said sheepishly, "but now that you've got all that money, I thought I should call you mister . . . What were we talking about?"

"The elevators."

"Oh, yes . . . You just happened to hit a bad weekend. Usually they break down one at a time, and that's not so bad. Or if it happens during the week, we're in luck, because the serviceman comes right away—if it's during the day. It's time and a half after five o'clock, you know, and the management doesn't go for that."

"I should have taken an apartment on a lower floor," Qwilleran said. "Another question: What's the meaning of the notice in the elevator about cats and spraying? It doesn't sound good."

"Oh, *that!* Mrs. Tuttle posts a notice every time the exterminator is scheduled. He sprays the hallways, plus any apartments that request it, so people keep their cats locked up on Spray Day."

"My cats never go out under any circumstances."

"That's a good idea. They can get on the elevator and just . . . disappear. There's a big turnover in cats at the Casablanca."

"Do you have one?"

"No, I have fish. They're cheaper and they don't have to go to the vet. They just die."

"Frankly, I fail to understand the roving-cat policy at the Casablanca."

"It's for rodent control."

"Does the building have rats in addition to everything else?"

"Only around the back street, where they keep the dumpsters. I've had mice in my apartment, though. I don't know how mice get up to the eighth floor."

"On Old Red," Qwilleran suggested.

The antipasti were served: breaded baby squid with marinara sauce, and roasted red peppers with anchovies and onion.

"I wish my sisters could see me now!" said Amber. "Eating squid at Roberto's with a millionaire!"

"Getting back to the notices in the elevator," he said, "is there a large market for baby grand pianos at the Casablanca?"

"You'd be surprised! There's still some money floating around the building—and a few good-sized apartments. We have elderly widows who are *loaded!* They don't move out because they've always lived here."

"Who's selling the piano? The sign says apartment 10-F."

"That's Isabelle Wilburton. Her rooms are crammed with family heirlooms, and she sells them off one at a time to buy booze."

"What does she look like? I saw a middle-aged woman in a cocktail dress, tippling in the phone booth when I moved in."

"That's our Isabelle! Her family made a killing in the furniture business, and they pay her basic living expenses, so long as she stays out of their sight. I warn you! Don't let Isabelle latch onto you! She'll drive you crazy."

The antipasto plates were whisked away, and the proficient waiter—who was always there when needed and absent when not—served the soup, a rich chicken broth threaded with egg and cheese.

"What do they call this?" Amber asked Qwilleran. "I wish I had written it down so I can tell my sisters."

"*Stracciatella alla romana*. What will happen to tenants like Isabelle if the building is restored to its original grandeur?"

"What will happen to any of us?" said Amber with a shrug. "I'll have to find a rich husband and move to the country. Maybe he'll set me up in a shop of my own." She had a suggestive twinkle in her eyes, which he ignored.

He said, "You had a husband the last time I saw you."

She twisted her lips in an unattractive smirk. "Husbands come and go like the Zwinger Boulevard bus."

"You've changed your hair color, too."

"This is my natural color. I dyed it for him because he liked brunettes. I suppose you're having a tough time staying single now that you've got all that money."

"So far I've been successful without trying very hard," he said, and then added to keep the record straight, "but I have a good friend up north who shares my interests and tastes. I hope she'll come down for a visit while I'm here."

"That must be nice," said Amber. "We weren't so compatible. I don't know why we ever happened to get married. I'm a slob around the house, but my ex liked everything *just so*. A place for everything and everything in its place, you know. If he repeated that remark *once more*, I swore I'd shoot him, and I didn't want to go to prison, so I filed for divorce. I hope he marries a computer. Mary tells me you're divorced."

"Right." He popped a chunk of crusty roll into his mouth to preclude further elaboration.

Amber was not easily put off, however. "What happened?"

"Nothing worth mentioning." He gobbled another morsel. "What do you do at the auction house?"

"Just clerical work. It doesn't pay much, but I'm working with antiques, so I like it. You should come to one of our auctions. Last month a painting went for $2.3 million—right in your class, Qwill."

He huffed into his moustache and ignored the remark. "Here comes the veal."

She had ordered the top-price rib chop with wine and mushroom sauce, and now she asked for a bottle of Valpolicella, explaining, "What I don't drink, I can take home."

As Qwilleran knifed his medium-priced *vitello alla piccata*, sautéed with lemon and capers, he inquired about Mrs. Tuttle. "She seems to have a remarkable blend of motherly concern and military authority."

"Oh, she's wonderful! Can you believe that she was actually born in the Casablanca basement?" Amber replied. "Her father was the custodian. They lived in the basement, and she grew up playing in the boiler room and on the stairs. By the time she was twelve she knew the building inside out, and it was always her ambition to be manager. She's very obliging, as long as you don't break the rules. Ask her for anything you need. You may not get it, but she'll smile a lot."

"I might need some more pails. The skylight leaks. Also, the hot water in the shower is unpredictable."

"We all have that problem," said Amber. "You get used to it."

"Do you know the person in 14-B?"

"No, she's new, but I've seen her on the elevator—sort of wild-looking." Amber was gobbling her food hungrily.

"I hope she doesn't take too many showers," Qwilleran said. "What can you tell me about the Countess?"

"I've never met her. I've never even seen her! I'm not in her class. Mary knows her. Mary gets invited to the twelfth floor because her father is a banker and she went to one of those eastern colleges." Amber was well into her bottle of Valpolicella and was losing what little reticence she had. "When you lived here before, Qwill, we all thought you had a thing for Mary and couldn't get anywhere because you worked for a newspaper and she thought she was too good for you."

"It's gratifying to know that all the gossips aren't in Pickax

City," he said. "Shall we have dessert? I recommend gelato and espresso." Then he launched the subject that was uppermost in his mind. "Why is the penthouse apartment being sublet—with all those valuable furnishings?"

"The former tenant died, and the estate is going through the courts," Amber said. "Mary had to pull strings to get you in there. If it wasn't for all your money—"

"Who was the tenant?"

"An art dealer—part owner of a gallery in the financial district, Bessinger-Todd."

"Apparently he was very successful, although I don't concur with his choice of art."

"It was a woman, Qwill. Dianne Bessinger. We called her Lady Di."

"Why was she living in a broken-down place like the Casablanca?"

"I guess she thought the penthouse was glamorous. She was the one who founded SOCK."

"Did you ever see her apartment? It's filled with mushroom paintings."

"I know. She gave a party for SOCK volunteers once, and I asked her about the mushrooms. I don't pretend to know anything about art. She said mushrooms are sexy."

"What happened to her?"

"She . . . well, she died unexpectedly." For the first time that evening, Amber was speaking guardedly.

"At what age?"

"In her forties. Forty-five, I think it said in the paper."

"Was it drugs?"

"No." Amber was fidgeting nervously. "It's something we don't like to talk about. Ask Mary when you see her."

Ah! It was AIDS, Qwilleran thought, but immediately changed his mind. That would hardly explain the large bloodstain on the carpet, and people never died "unexpectedly" of AIDS. Or did they? "You say she was the founder of SOCK?" he said.

"Yes, she felt very strongly about the Casablanca," said Amber, relieved to veer away from the unmentionable subject.

"Anybody who's ever lived here feels that way—kind of emotional about the old building."

"And what happened to your doorman? You said he was shot. What were the circumstances? Was he mixed up in something illegal?"

"No, nothing like that," she said, relaxing over her cup of espresso. "Doesn't this have a wonderful aroma?"

"So what happened to him? What's the story?"

"Well, he was a nice old joe who had lived in the basement forever. Then he went on social security, and we really didn't need a doorman any longer, but he liked to put on his old uniform once in a while and open car doors and collect a few tips. It was a long coachman's coat down to his ankles—made him feel important, I guess. But it had turned green with age, and the gold braid was tarnished, and some of the buttons were missing. Also he'd forget to shave. We called him Poor Old Gus. He was a sad sight, but he sort of fitted the Casablanca image, you know—a character! People used to drive past and laugh. He was written up in the *Daily Fluxion* once. Then one night some kids—high on something, I guess—drove by and shot Poor Old Gus dead!"

Qwilleran frowned and shook his head in abhorrence.

"Is everything all right?" asked an anxious voice at his elbow.

"The food and service were perfection, Miss Roop," he assured her. "Give my compliments to Roberto."

"Oh, thank you. That will make him very happy. Do you still have your kitties, Mr. Qwilleran?"

"I certainly do! And I brought them to the Casablanca with me."

"Would they like a treat from our kitchen?"

"I feel safe in saying that they would be overjoyed."

Qwilleran and Amber walked home under the gaslights—she carrying a half-empty bottle of wine and he carrying a foil package folded decorously into a cream-colored napkin. They walked along a street almost deserted except for a woman airing a pair of Dobermans and two men walking together with purposeful stride, swinging long-handled flashlights.

"That's our Junktown patrol," Amber said. "They're volunteers. You might like to take a turn some night, just to see what it's like."

"Be glad to," said Qwilleran, recognizing a subject for his newspaper column. "Are they ever called upon to handle any... incidents?"

"I don't think so. Mostly they discourage crime just by being there. They shine their flashlights, you know, and blow their whistles, and talk on their portable phones."

When they reached the Casablanca and entered through the heavy black doors, Qwilleran noticed the black paint-covered brass fittings that the management no longer cared to keep polished. Only the bronze door of the Countess's elevator retained its original burnished beauty.

Amber said, "I'd invite you in for a nightcap, but my apartment's a disaster area. I'm ashamed of it."

"Thanks anyway," he said. "I've had a long hard day on the road and in the elevator shaft, and I'm ready to turn in." He was glad of an excuse; he had had enough of Amber's company for one evening. He would have preferred the preppy Mary, or the mysterious Countess, or even the affable, dictatorial Mrs. Tuttle. He pictured her as a subject for his column.

Old Red was in operation, and it took them to the eighth floor, where he walked Amber to her door and said a courteous goodnight, thanking her for her company and the indoctrination.

"Sorry I couldn't give you much information," she said, "but Mary will call you tomorrow. We're awfully glad you're here, Qwill." She gave him a lingering look that he pretended not to notice.

He walked up the remaining flights, and when he arrived at Fourteen (which was really Thirteen), the door of Old Red was slowly closing. Someone was going down... or had just come up. Unlocking his door and reaching for the light switch, Qwilleran discovered that the foyer and other rooms were already lighted, although he distinctly remembered leaving the apartment in darkness, except for the bathroom.

"*Who's here?*" he demanded.

Koko and Yum Yum came running. They showed no symptoms of terror, no indication that an intruder had threatened them. They were simply aware that Qwilleran was carrying a packet of veal, scallops, and squid. Yum Yum rubbed against his ankles voluptuously, while Koko stood on his hind legs and pawed the air.

Ignoring them, he moved from room to room, warily. In the library both the desk lamp and a floor lamp were unaccountably lit—as were a pair of accent lamps on the foyer console, the buffet lamp in the dining room, and the bedlamps in both sleeping rooms. The French doors to the living room were closed, as he had left them, and the area was in darkness, likewise the kitchen. He examined closets, then went out on the terrace and explored its entire length, passing the French doors of 14-B. His neighbor's blinds were closed, but light glowed through dimly. The huddled mass in a dark corner of the terrace turned out to be a cluster of large empty plant pots.

Qwilleran stroked his moustache in puzzlement and returned to 14-A. Who could have entered—and why? Did someone know he was being taken to dinner by SOCK? Did they have a key to his apartment? But why would they leave all the lights blazing? ... unless they were interrupted and made a quick getaway.

At that moment he heard the door of 14-B open and close. He rushed out to the elevator lobby, but there was no one there—merely the evidence that Keestra Hedrog had put her rubbish container outside the door.

Mystified, Qwilleran returned to the kitchen to give the Siamese a taste of squid; the chef had wrapped enough food for three days. But he was too late. The cream-colored napkin lay on the floor, and the foil wrapper was open and licked clean, while two satisfied gourmands sat nearby, washing up, with not the slightest indication that they felt any guilt. On the contrary, they seemed proud of themselves.

Chapter 5

"You guys had a picnic last night!" Qwilleran said grudgingly on Monday morning as he opened a can of boned chicken for the Siamese. "After stuffing yourselves with all that food, you don't deserve breakfast!"

Yet, Koko was prowling as if he had fasted for a week, and Yum Yum was clawing Qwilleran's pantleg.

"What I want to know is this: Which one of you two turned on all the lights?"

While he was dining at Roberto's with Amber, Koko or Yum Yum or both of them had discovered that most of the lamps in 14-A had touch-switches, and the scamps had run from one to the other making them light up. No doubt they expected to make this a nightly romp, but Qwilleran foiled them. Before retiring he cat-proofed all the lamps by turning off thumb-switches or disconnecting plugs, at the same time making the observation that touch-switches were not practical in households dominated by felines.

After that he had some difficulty in falling asleep. He was not accustomed to a waterbed, and he lay there expecting to drown . . . listening to the periodic clanking of the radiators as the boilers sent up another burst of steam . . . hearing the drone of traffic on the nearby freeway . . . counting the number of police and ambulance sirens . . . wondering why the helicopter was hovering overhead . . .

recognizing an occasional gunshot. He had lived too long in the country.

Eventually he fell asleep and slept until the yowling outside his bedroom door told him to shuffle out into the kitchen and open that can of boned chicken. While searching for the can opener, he discovered a Japanese slicer with a tapered blade and light wood handle, similar to those in the mushroom paintings. He carried it into the gallery—as he preferred to call the sunken living room—to compare, and he was right. Koko followed him and sniffed the bloodstain, opening his mouth and showing his teeth.

"Get away from that!" Qwilleran ordered, and put his shoulder to the bar once more to cover the stain. Then he changed his mind. It was an awkward location for a bar. He nudged it back again into a more suitable position and covered the stain with a rug from the library—an Indian dhurrie in pale colors that blended with the mushroom carpet. Shooing the cat from the gallery, he closed the French doors.

Yum Yum was now batting some small object about the floor of the foyer. Koko might have a notably investigative nose, but Yum Yum had a notably meddlesome paw. Rings, watches, and coins—as well as bottle caps and paper clips—were within her realm of interest, and any sudden activity that gave her pleasure was suspect. This time it was an ivory-colored tile less than an inch square—not exactly square but slightly rectangular, and not ivory or ceramic but a lightweight wood in a smooth, pale finish. Qwilleran confiscated it, to Yum Yum's disappointment, and dropped it in his sweater pocket.

While waiting for the computerized coffeemaker to perform its morning magic, he ate a tangerine and speculated that the bowl of fruit had been Mary Duckworth's idea; she remembered that winesaps were his favorite apple and that lobster sent the Siamese into orbit. Did she have romantic memories of their previous association? Or was this thoughtful gesture a political move on behalf of SOCK? He could never be sure about that woman. Circumstances had thrown them together in Junktown three years before, and she was haughty and aloof at first, but she had relaxed briefly on one unforgettable Christmas Eve. After that they went their separate ways. At what point they would resume their acquaintance remained to be seen. Three years ago he had been a stranger in town, down on his luck and trying to make a comeback. Now he was in a position to buy the entire inventory of her antique shop, as well as the Casablanca and most of Zwinger Boulevard.

When she phoned him that morning, however, there was no hint that she entertained sentimental memories. She greeted him in the crisp, impersonal way that was her normal manner of speech.

"Good to hear your voice, Mary," he said. "How was your Philadelphia trip?"

"Immensely successful. And your journey down here, Qwill?"

"Not bad. It's hard to get used to the smog, though. I'm used to breathing something called fresh air."

"In Junktown," she said loftily, "we don't call it smog. We call it opalescence. Are you comfortably settled in your apartment?"

"Settled but not necessarily comfortable. More about that later. But the cats and I appreciate your welcoming gift, and I don't need to tell you that dinner at Roberto's was superb."

"Yes, Roberto is a perfectionist. He uses only the best ingredients and takes infinite pains with the preparation. He actually imports water from Lake Como, you know, for baking the rolls."

"I noticed the distinction," Qwilleran said, "but I traced it to one of the Swiss lakes. That shows how wrong one's palate can be." He said it facetiously, knowing that the literal antique dealer would take him seriously, and she did.

She said, "You're wonderfully knowledgeable about food, Qwill."

"When can you and I get together, Mary. I have a lot of questions to ask."

"The sooner the better. Could you come to my shop this afternoon around four o'clock? We can have a private talk. The shop is closed on Mondays, so we won't be interrupted."

Qwilleran agreed. That would give him time to buy supplies for the cats, reorient himself in the city, and have lunch at the Press Club. But before leaving the apartment, he brushed the silky fawn-colored coats of the Siamese, all the while plying them with compliments on their elegantly long brown legs, their gracefully slender brown tails, their incredibly beautiful blue eyes, and their impressively alert white whiskers. They listened with rapture displayed by their waving tails.

Then he tuned in the radio to check the weather prediction. In doing so he learned that four houses on a southside block had been torched by arsonists over the weekend; a co-ed had been strangled backstage at the university auditorium; and a man had killed his wife and three children. The weather would be clear but chilly.

"They call this clear?" Qwilleran said scornfully as he peered out the window at the smog-filtered sunlight.

He walked to the Carriage House Café for ham and eggs, wearing a Nordic sweater and field jacket and his Aussie hat. Its brim had a dip in the front that complemented his large drooping moustache and made women turn to look at him.

At the restaurant he found not a single familiar face. The patrons—gulping breakfast or reading the *Morning Rampage* with their coffee—were all strangers, and they were better-dressed than the former denizens of Junktown. Much had changed in three years, but that was typical of inner cities. In Moose County nothing ever changed unless it blew away in a high wind. The same families went on for generations; the same storekeepers managed the same stores; and everyone knew everyone else. Not only that, but the eggs tasted better up north, and when Qwilleran paid his check at the Carriage House he noted that ham and eggs cost two dollars less in Pickax.

On one of the side streets he found a grocery store where he could buy a ten-pound bag of sterilized gravel for the cats' commode, gourmet canned goods for their meals, and white grapejuice for Koko—further evidence that Junktown had upscaled.

He was becoming accustomed to surprises, but when he walked back to the Casablanca he was shocked to see a painted sign on the vacant property across the street where a row of old buildings had been demolished. The sign featured an artist's rendering of a proposed building spanning Zwinger Boulevard—actually two towers connected by a bridge across the top, somewhat like the Bridge of Sighs in Venice.

"Site of the new Gateway Alcazar," the sign proclaimed. "Offices, stores, and hotel. Space now leasing."

One of the two towers obviously occupied the Casablanca site, and Qwilleran considered it an example of gross nerve! He made a note of the firm promoting the project: Penniman, Greystone & Fleudd. He knew of the wealthy Pennimans and the civic-minded Greystones, but Fleudd was a new name to him. He could not even pronounce it.

At the Casablanca a stretcher was being loaded into an ambulance, and Qwilleran inquired about it at the manager's desk.

"An old gentleman on Four had a heart attack," said Mrs. Tuttle as if it were a routine occurrence.

"May I leave my groceries here while I go for a walk?"

"Certainly," she said. "Be careful where you go. Stay on the main streets."

Qwilleran had acquired the walking habit up north, and he headed for downtown on foot, proceeding at a studious pace in order to evaluate the streetscape. Ahead of him stretched the new Zwinger Boulevard with its trendy buildings: glass office towers like giant mirrors; an apartment building like an armed camp; the new Penniman Plaza hotel like an amusement park. The thought crossed his mind that the Klingenschoen Fund could buy all of this, tear it down, and build something more pleasing to the eye.

He was, of course, the only pedestrian in sight. Traffic shot past him in surges, barreling for the next red light like race horses bursting out of the gate. At one point a police car pulled up. "Looking for something, sir?" asked an officer.

If Qwilleran had said, "I'm thinking of buying all of this and tearing it down," they would have sent him to the psychiatric ward, so he flashed his press card and told them he was reporting on the architecture of inner cities in the northeast central United States.

Next, discovering an office building with shops on the main

floor, he bought a handbag for Polly and had it gift-wrapped and shipped with an affectionate enclosure. It was called a "Paris bag," something not to be found in Moose County, where a "Chicago bag" was considered the last word.

He also entered a bookstore called "Books 'n' Stuff," that stocked more videos and greeting cards than books. Furthermore, its supermarket lighting and background music discouraged browsing. Qwilleran had his own ideas about the correct ambiance for a bookstore: dim, quiet, and slightly dusty.

Downtown he passed the *Daily Fluxion* and would have dropped in to banter with the staffers, but the formidable new security system in the lobby was inhibiting. He kept going in the direction of the Press Club.

This venerable landmark on Canard Street had been remodeled and redecorated. It was no longer the hangout where he and Arch Riker used to lunch almost every day at the same table in the same corner of the bar, served by the same waitress who knew exactly how they liked their burgers. None of the old crowd was there. Everyone seemed younger, and there was a preponderance of ad salesmen and publicity hacks on expense accounts—a suit-and-tie crowd. He was the only one in the place who looked as if he had arrived on horseback. He ate at the bar, but the corned beef sandwich was not as good as it used to be. Bruno, the bartender, had quit, and no one remembered Bruno or knew where he had gone.

As Qwilleran was leaving the bar, he recognized one familiar face. The portly and easygoing Lieutenant Hames of the Homicide Squad was lunching with someone who was obviously a newsman and probably the new reporter on the police beat; Qwilleran could identify the breed instantly. He stopped at their table.

"What brings you down from the North Pole?" the detective asked in his usual jocular style.

"The developers are evicting me from my igloo," Qwilleran replied. "They're building air-conditioned condos."

"Do you guys know each other?" Hames introduced Matt something or other from the *Fluxion*'s police bureau. The name sounded like Thiggamon.

"Spell it," Qwilleran requested as he shook hands with the young reporter.

"T-h-i-double g-a-m-o-n."

"What happened to Lodge Kendall?"

"He went out west to work on some new magazine," said Matt. "Aren't you the one who gave the big retirement bash for Arch Riker? I missed it by two days."

"You're entitled to a raincheck."

"What are you doing here anyway?" asked Hames.

"Spending the winter with crime and pollution instead of snowdrifts and icebergs. I'm staying at the Casablanca."

"Are you nuts? They're getting ready to bulldoze that pile of rubble. Do you still have your smart cat?"

"I sure do and he's getting smarter every day."

"I suppose you still indulge his taste for lobster and frog legs."

Qwilleran said, "I admit that he lives high, for a cat, but he saved my neck a couple of times, and I owe him."

Hames turned to the new reporter. "Qwill has this cat that can dig up clues better than the whole Homicide Squad. When I told my wife about him, she bugged me until I got her a Siamese, but ours is more interested in breaking the law than enforcing it. Pull up a chair, Qwill. Have some coffee. Have dessert. The *Fluxion*'s picking up the tab."

Qwilleran declined, saying that he had an appointment, and went on his way, thinking about the proliferation of Hedrogs and Thiggamons, like names out of science fiction. Moreover, the bylines at the *Fluxion* were getting longer and more complicated. Fran Unger had been replaced by Martta Newton-Ffiske. At the *Morning Rampage* Jack Murphy's gossip column was now written by Sasha Crispen-Schmitt. Try saying that fast, he thought: Try saying it three times.

In a critical and slightly grouchy mood he pushed through the lunch-hour crowds on the street, finding most of the pedestrians to be in a mad rush, tense, and rude. The women he evaluated as chic, glamorous, and self-consciously thin, though not as pretty or as healthy-looking as those in Moose County.

Returning to the Casablanca too early for his appointment with Mary Duckworth, he went for a ride, extricating the Purple

Plum from the parking lot's tire-bashing cracks and craters and driving to River Road, his last address before moving up north. His old domicile and the tennis club next-door had been replaced by a condo complex and marina, and he could hardly remember how either of the original buildings looked. Too bad! He chalked up another score for the developers and drove back to the Casablanca, hoping it would still be there. What he found was a revised situation in the parking lot. His official slot, #28, was still occupied—not by the green Japanese car but by a decrepit station wagon with a New Jersey license plate. Someone else had pulled into #29, so he wheeled the Purple Plum into #27. After a morning of disappointment, indignation, and other negative reactions, Qwilleran was none too happy when he left for Mary Duckworth's antique shop.

The Blue Dragon still occupied a narrow townhouse, handsomely preserved, and a large blue porcelain dragon (not for sale) still dominated the front window bay. That much had not changed. Nor had the entrance hall with its Chinese wallpaper, Chippendale furniture, and silver chandeliers. There was a life-size ebony carving of a Nubian slave with jeweled turban that had not yet sold, and Qwilleran glanced at the price tag to see if it had been marked down. It had gone up another two thousand dollars, Mary's credo being: If it doesn't sell, raise the price.

As for Mary herself, she still had the sleek blue-black hair and willowy figure that he remembered, but the long cigarette holder and the long fingernails were no longer in evidence. Instead of an Oriental kimono, she wore a well-tailored suit and pearls. She shook his hand briefly and glanced at his Nordic sweater and Aussie hat. "You look so *sportif*, Qwill!"

"I see you haven't sold the blackamoor," he said.

"I'm holding it back. Originally it stood in the lobby of the Casablanca, and it will appreciate in value, no matter what happens to the building."

"Do you still keep that unfriendly German shepherd?"

"Actually," said Mary, "I don't feel the need for a watchdog, considering the new atmosphere in Junktown. I was able to find him a good home in the suburbs, where he's really needed. Come into the office." She motioned him to sit in a wing chair.

Its tall, narrow proportions labeled it an antique, and he glanced at the price tag. He looked twice. At first reading he thought it was $180.00, then realized it was $18,000. He sat down carefully.

"Before we say another word," he began, "would you explain the dark line that makes the Casablanca look like a refrigerator? It's just above the ninth floor."

"There was a projecting ledge there," she said, "and the city ordered it removed. Portions of it were falling down on the sidewalk and injuring passersby. Our architect maintains it can be safely restored, and it should be restored, being an integral part of the design. Meanwhile, the building management is reluctant to spend money on cosmetic improvements because—"

"Because the building may be torn down next week," Qwilleran interrupted. "Everyone chants that excuse like a Greek chorus, and they may be right. This morning I saw the sign announcing the Gateway Alcazar. The developers seem to be supremely confident."

"Aren't you appalled?" Mary said with a shudder. "The audacity of those people is unthinkable! They've even contrived a publicity story in the *Morning Rampage* comparing their arched monstrosity to the Arc de Triomphe!"

"Well, the Pennimans own the *Rampage*, don't they?"

"Nevertheless, Roberto wrote a letter to the editor calling it the 'Arc de Catastrophe.' If your Klingenschoen Fund comes to our rescue, we shall be eternally grateful."

"What do you know about Penniman, Greystone and F-l-e-u-d-d? I don't know how to pronounce it."

"Flood."

"What's their track record?"

"Fleudd has recently joined them, but the Penniman and Greystone firm has been in real-estate development for years. They're the ones who wanted to tear down the Press Club."

"The media clobbered that idea in a hurry," Qwilleran recalled. "Has the *Daily Fluxion* come to the support of SOCK?"

"Not with any conviction. They merely fuel the controversy. The mayor and the city council have made statements in favor of the Gateway Alcazar, but the university and the art community support SOCK."

"How about your father? What does he think about saving the Casablanca?"

Mary raised her eyebrows expressively. "As you know, he and I are always at odds on every issue, and his bank has already agreed to lease space for a branch office in the Gateway building. Ironic, isn't it?"

"Tell me about the Countess," he said. "So far no one has mentioned her name."

"She is Adelaide St. John Plumb. Her father was Harrison Wills Plumb, who built the Casablanca in 1901. She was born on the twelfth floor of the Casablanca seventy-five years ago, with a midwife, a nurse, and two doctors in attendance, according to the story she tells and tells and tells. She's inclined to be repetitive."

"Did she ever marry?"

"No. She was engaged at an early age but broke it off. She adored her father, and they were very close."

"I see . . . How does she react to all this brouhaha over her birthplace?"

"That's a curious situation," Mary admitted. "I believe she enjoys being the center of attention. The promoters make her large offers and ply her with gifts, while SOCK appeals to her better instincts and makes pointed references to her father—her 'dear father.' She procrastinates, and we stall for time, hoping to find an angel. Do you play bridge?"

Jolted by this non sequitur, Qwilleran said, "Uh . . . no, I don't."

"How about backgammon?"

"Frankly, I've never liked games that require any mental effort. What is the reason for this interrogation, may I ask?"

"Let me explain," said Mary. "The Countess has one interest in life: table games—cards, Parcheesi, checkers, mah-jongg, anything except chess. Roberto and I stay in her good graces by playing once a week."

"Does much money exchange hands?"

"There's no gambling. She plays for the pleasure of competition, and she's really very good. She should be! She's been playing daily all her life, beginning as a young child. Did Amber tell you that the Countess is a recluse?"

"No, she didn't." Qwilleran's vision of Lady Hester Stanhope flashed across his mind.

"Yes, she lives in a world of her own on the twelfth floor, with three servants."

"Surely she goes out occasionally."

"She never leaves the building or even her own apartment, which occupies an entire floor. Her doctors, lawyers, hairdresser, dressmaker, and masseuse all make house calls."

"What's her problem? Agoraphobia?"

"She claims to have trouble breathing if she steps outside her door . . . You don't play dominoes?"

"No! Especially not dominoes."

"Scrabble?"

He shook his head. "Does this woman know I'm here—and why?"

"We told her you're a writer who inherited money and retired to the country, and you're spending the winter here to escape the bad weather up north."

"What was her reaction?"

"She asked if you play bridge."

"Does she know I used to write for the *Fluxion?*"

"There was no point in mentioning it. She never reads newspapers. As I said before, she has created a private world."

Qwilleran was convinced he had discovered Lady Hester in the flesh. He said, "Does anyone know of my interest in buying the Casablanca?"

"Only Roberto and myself and the architect. And we confided in Amber, of course, when I had to leave town."

"Since the Klingenschoen board of directors won't even hear about this until Thursday, I don't want my possible involvement to leak out."

"We understand that."

"I'll be filing stories for the Moose County paper while

I'm here, and I'm thinking that a column on the Casablanca would make a good kickoff. Will the Countess object to being interviewed?"

"I'm sure she'll enjoy the attention, although she'll want to talk mostly about her dear father."

"Who handles the business end of the Casablanca?"

"A realty firm, with her lawyers as intermediaries."

"Is she interested in the tenants?"

"Only if they have good manners and good clothes and play bridge. To break the ice, I'd like to take you to tea on Twelve. She pours every afternoon at four."

"First," Qwilleran said, "I want to know your architect's appraisal of the building. As of this moment I don't believe it shows much promise."

Mary handed him a bound copy of a report. "There it is! Two hundred pages. Most of it is technical, but if you read the first and last chapters, you'll have all the necessary information."

Qwilleran noted the name on the cover: Grinchman & Hills, architects and engineers. It was a well-known firm. Magazines had publicized their projects around the country: an art museum, a university library, the restoration of a nineteenth-century government building. "Not a bad connection," he said. "I'll study this thing, and if I have any questions, whom do I call? Grinchman or Hills?"

"They're both deceased," Mary said. "Only the name remains, and the reputation. The man who prepared the report for SOCK, virtually gratis, is Jefferson Lowell. He's totally sympathetic to the cause. You'll like him."

Qwilleran rose. "This discussion has been enjoyable and enlightening, Mary. I'll let you know when I'm ready for tea with the Countess."

"Time is of the essence," she reminded him. "After all, the woman is seventy-five, and anything can happen." She accompanied him to the door, through a maze of high-priced pedigreed antiques. "Do you still have your Mackintosh coat of arms?"

"I wouldn't part with it. It's the first antique I ever bought, and it's incorporated into my apartment up north." He drew a small object from his pocket. "Can you identify this?"

"Where did you get it?"

"My cat was batting it about the floor in the penthouse."

"It's a blank tile from a Scrabble set. Blanks are wild in Scrabble. The former tenant was an avid player."

"She was an art dealer, I understand, and that explains some of the peculiar artwork, but why so many mushrooms? Who painted them? They're signed with a double R."

Mary's eyes wavered as she replied, "He was a young artist by the name of Ross Rasmus."

"Why did he put a knife in every picture?"

She hesitated momentarily. "Roberto says there's sensuous pleasure in slicing a mushroom with a sharp knife. Perhaps that's what it's all about."

With a searching look Qwilleran said, "I hear she died unexpectedly. What was the cause of death?"

"Really, Qwill, we avoid talking about it," Mary said uncomfortably. "It was rather—sordid, and that's not the image we want for the Casablanca."

"You don't have to be cagey with me, Mary. Since I'm subletting the apartment, I deserve to know."

"Well, if you insist . . . I have to tell you that she was . . . murdered."

He stroked his moustache smugly. "That's what I surmised. There's a sizable bloodstain on the carpet. Someone had placed a piece of furniture over it for camouflage, but Koko found it."

"How is Koko?" Mary asked brightly.

"Never mind Koko. Tell me what happened to the art dealer."

The words came out reluctantly. "She . . . her throat was cut."

"By the mushroom artist?"

She nodded.

"That figures. He was obsessed with knives. When did this happen?"

"On Labor Day weekend."

"Why is so much of this Ross fellow's work hanging in the apartment?"

"Well," said Mary, selecting her words with care, "he was a young artist . . . and she thought he had promise . . . and she promoted him in her gallery. He was her protégé, you might say."

"Uh-huh," said Qwilleran knowingly. "Where is he now? I assume he was convicted."

"No," Mary said slowly. "He was never brought to trial . . . You see, he left a confession . . . and took his own life."

Chapter 6

Qwilleran felt in better spirits when he left the Blue Dragon. Koko's discovery was pertinent: 14-A had been the scene of a murder. That cat had an infallible sense when it came to turning up evidence of criminal activity.

Carrying the Grinchman & Hills report Qwilleran headed for home with a brisk step, eager to start reading. Instead of wasting time on dinner in a restaurant, he stopped at the Carriage House Café to inquire about take-out food.

"We don't usually . . . do . . . take-outs," said the cashier in a distracted way. She was staring at Qwilleran's oversized moustache. "Are you on television?"

Regarding her with mournful eyes under drooping lids, he said in a rich, resonant tone reserved for such occasions, "At this moment I am live—in person—talking with an attractive woman behind a cash register, regarding the possibility of a take-out dinner."

"I'll see what I can do," she called over her shoulder as she hurried into the kitchen. Immediately a man with long hair and a chef's hat peered through the small window in the kitchen door. Qwilleran gave him a cordial salute.

The cashier returned. "We don't have take-out trays, but the cook will put together a serving of today's special, if you don't mind carrying a regular plate. You can bring it back tomorrow. Are you driving?"

"I'm walking but I don't have far to go. What is your special?"

"Beef Stroganoff."

"It sounds most appetizing."

"We'll put some coleslaw and a dinner roll in foil," the cashier volunteered.

While retrieving his bill clip from his pocket, Qwilleran placed the Grinchman & Hills report on the counter and noticed the cashier trying to read it upside down.

"Grinch . . . man . . . and . . . Hills," she read aloud. "Is that the script for a movie?" she asked, wide-eyed.

"Yes, but keep it quiet," he replied in a low voice with a swift glance to either side. "It's going to be a buddy movie like *Bonnie and Clyde* or *Harold and Maude*. I'm playing Grinchman."

Leaving a sizable tip for a happy and flustered cashier, he departed with the bulky report under one arm and a plate of hot food covered with foil, on top of which were balanced two foil packets. "Your coleslaw and buttered roll," the cashier told him with an expansive display of hospitality. "Open the door for him," she called to the busboy.

Qwilleran covered the distance to the Casablanca quickly, and a young man held the two heavy doors for him, saying, "Somebody's gonna eat tonight."

On the main floor there was activity suitable for late afternoon on a Monday. The person seated in the phone booth was telephoning and neither swigging nor snorting. An elderly man using a walker moved down the hall slowly and with extreme concentration. Kitty-Baby, having picked up the scent of the beef Stroganoff, was dogging Qwilleran's feet. In the vicinity of the desk a young man was swinging a mop across the floor, while Mrs. Tuttle sat at her post, knitting, and Rupert lounged about in his red hat. Despite the tools in his jacket pocket, he never seemed to do much work. Among the persons waiting for the elevator were employed tenants with gaunt end-of-day expressions, the Asian mother with her children, elderly souls complaining about Medicare, and students with an excess of youthful energy, talking loudly about bridges, professors, and final exams. Probably engineering students, Qwilleran guessed.

Rupert caught his eye and nodded toward the elevators. "Both workin' today."

"A cause for celebration," Qwilleran replied.

While the passengers waited in suspense, reassuring knocks and whines could be heard in both elevator shafts. Old Green was the first to appear, immediately filling with passengers and going on its way. Then the door of Old Red opened, and two of the waiting students rushed aboard. Qwilleran stood back, allowing a white-haired woman with a cane to go next. Slowly, one faltering step at a time, she approached the car, and just as her head and one foot were inside, the heavy door started to close.

"Hold it!" he yelled.

One student lunged for the door; the other lunged at the woman, pushing her from danger. As she toppled backward, Qwilleran dropped everything and caught her, while Old Red closed its door and took off.

Instantly Mrs. Tuttle and Rupert were on the scene, the custodian retrieving the woman's cane and the manager saying, "Are you all right, Mrs. Button?"

Set back on her feet but shaking violently, the woman raised her cane as if to strike and screamed in a cracked voice, *"That man grabbed me!"*

"He saved you, Mrs. Button," explained the manager. "You could have fallen and broken your hip."

"He grabbed me!"

"Wheelchair," Mrs. Tuttle mumbled, and Rupert quickly brought one from the office and took the offended victim upstairs in Old Green, while Qwilleran surveyed the gooey hash on the floor.

"I'm so sorry, Mr. Qwilleran," said Mrs. Tuttle. "Is that your dinner?"

"It *was* my dinner. Anyway, the plate didn't break, but I'm afraid I messed up your floor."

"Don't worry about that. The boy will take care of it."

"I don't think that will be necessary," he said. Kitty-Baby had been joined by Napoleon and two other cats, and the quartet was lapping it up, coleslaw and all.

"At least let me wash your plate," Mrs. Tuttle offered.

"It looks as if Old Red is my nemesis," said Qwilleran as he nodded his thanks to a child who handed him his buttered roll and a man who picked up the Grinchman & Hills report, straightening its rumpled pages.

"Could the boy go out and bring you something to eat?" the manager suggested.

"I think not, thank you. I'll go upstairs and feed the cats and then go out to dinner."

When he opened the door of 14-A, Koko and Yum Yum came forward nonchalantly.

"How about showing some concern?" he chided them. "How about displaying a little sympathy? I've just had a grueling experience."

They followed him into the kitchen and watched politely as he opened a can of crabmeat. They were neither prowling nor yowling nor ankle-rubbing, and Qwilleran realized that they were not hungry.

"Has someone been up here?" he demanded. "Did they give you something to eat?"

When he placed the plate of food on the floor, the cats circled it and sniffed from all angles before consenting to nibble daintily. Then Qwilleran was sure someone had been feeding them. He inspected the apartment for signs of intrusion and found no evidence in the library or in either bedroom. The doors to the terrace were locked. Both bathrooms were undisturbed. Only in the gallery was there anything different, and he could not imagine exactly what it was. The Indian dhurrie still covered the bloodstain on the carpet; no artwork was missing; the potted trees had all their leaves, but something had been changed.

At that moment Koko entered the gallery and embarked on a businesslike program of sniffing. He sniffed at the foot of the stairs, alongside the sofa, on the gallery level between trees, and in front of the stereo.

"The pails!" Qwilleran shouted. "Someone took the pails!" He hurried to the housephone in the kitchen and said to a surprised Mrs. Tuttle, "What happened to my pails?"

"Your what?" she asked.

"This is Qwilleran in 14-A. There were plastic pails standing around my living room to catch drips when the skylight leaks. What happened to them? It might rain!"

"Oh, I forgot to tell you," she apologized. "The man was here to fix the skylight today, so Rupert collected the pails. I forgot to tell you during the trouble with Mrs. Button."

"I see. Sorry to bother you." He tamped his moustache. He would have to speak firmly to Rupert about feeding the animals. But his annoyance at the custodian was erased by his admiration for Koko. That cat had known the exact location of every pail!

Now Qwilleran was twice as hungry. Carrying the clean plastic plate he returned to the Carriage House Café.

"Oh, it's you again!" cried the cashier in delight. "How did you like the special? You didn't need to bring the plate back right away."

"It was so good," Qwilleran said, "that I'd like to do it all over again, including that delicious coleslaw and perhaps two rolls if you can spare them." He sat on a stool at the counter, and the cashier insisted on serving him herself, while the cook waved a friendly hand in the small window of the kitchen door and later sent out a complimentary slice of apple pie.

Thus fortified, Qwilleran returned to the Casablanca, where he found the red-hatted Rupert sitting at the manager's desk, reading a comic book. "I notice that the skylight's been repaired," he said to the custodian.

"Yep. No more leaks." The man held up crossed fingers.

"How did you get along with the cats when you picked up the pails?"

"Okay. I gave 'em a jelly doughnut. They gobbled it up."

"Jelly doughnut!" Qwilleran was aghast.

Rupert, misunderstanding his reaction, excused the apparent extravagance by explaining that it was a stale doughnut that had been lying around the basement for several days.

Controlling himself, Qwilleran said in a friendly way, "I'd rather you wouldn't give the cats any treats if you have occasion to enter the apartment, Rupert. They're on a strict diet because of . . . because of their kidneys."

"Yeah, cats always have trouble with their kidneys, seems if."

"But thanks for collecting the pails, friend. You're right on the ball!"

Then Qwilleran rode up to Fourteen on Old Red and confronted the Siamese. "Stale jelly doughnut!" he said in indignation. "You ate a stale jelly doughnut! And yet you guys turn up your nose at a fresh can of salmon if it's pink! You hypocrites!"

Changing into a warm-up suit, he locked himself into the library to study the Grinchman & Hills report. It appeared to be a formidable task, and he wanted no one sitting on his lap or purring in his ear.

The introduction described the original structure, as Amber had quoted from the SOCK brochure. Then came the chapter on necessary improvements, which Qwilleran condensed on a legal pad as follows:

- Clean and repair exterior and restore ornamentation.
- Restore grassy park on west side and porte cochere on the east.
- Acquire property behind building for parking structure.
- New roof and skylight.
- New triple-glazed windows throughout, custom-made.
- Mechanical update: elevators, heating and air-conditioning, plumbing, wiring, TV cables, and intercom.
- Remove superimposed floorings, false walls, and dropped ceilings.
- Restore former apartment spaces with maids' rooms.
- Update bathrooms in the character of the original.
- Restore marble, woodwork, paneling, mosaic tile.
- Duplicate original light fixtures, custom-made.
- Furnish lobby as before: Spanish furniture, Oriental rugs, oil paintings.
- Reinstate restaurant on Fourteen, converting pool area into sidewalk café.
- Landscape terrace in 1900 style.

- Update basement apartments for staff.
- Redesign kitchen and laundry facilities.
- Preserve owner's apartment on Twelve as refurbished in 1925.

After compiling this ambitious list, Qwilleran blew into his moustache—an expression of incredulity. Turning to the final chapter he had greater cause for disbelief; the bottom line was in nine digits. He emitted an audible gulp! Such a sum was beyond his comprehension. Despite his inheritance, he still bought his shirts on sale and telephoned long distance during the discount hours. Nevertheless, he knew that the Klingenschoen Fund was accustomed to disbursing hundreds of millions without blinking, and he managed not to blink, although he gulped audibly.

As he mused on the possibilities and problems of such an extensive restoration, the hush of the library was broken by the sound of drumbeats. They were coming through the wall from 14-B. *Thump thump thump dum-dum thump dum-dum thump BONG!* The final beat reverberated like a Chinese gong. Then he heard a shrill voice, although the words were inaudible, followed by a repetition of the drumbeats.

He went out on the terrace and walked past the French doors of 14-B, but the blinds were closed as before. Next he went out to the elevator lobby and listened at his neighbor's door. He could hear a voice chanting, then more thumps and a BONG! He was standing with his ear close to the door when noises in the elevator shaft alerted him, and he sprang back just as Old Red debouched a creature with spiky hair, wearing black tights, black boots, a black poncho, and black eye makeup.

"Good evening," he said to the creature, giving his greeting a neighborly inflection.

Without replying, he or she darted past him, hammered on the door of 14-B, and was admitted amid birdlike shrieks.

The charivari had no effect on the Siamese, who were sleeping soundly somewhere, full of crabmeat and stale jelly doughnut. Qwilleran spent the next two hours in the gallery, however, with the French doors closed and the stereo volume turned to high.

Toward the end of the evening, when the thumps and bongs had subsided, he heard a commotion in the hall: the door of 14-B slamming, a cacophony of shrill voices. He grabbed his wastebasket and opened his front door on the pretext of putting out his rubbish. As he did so, he caught sight of more creatures in black, chattering and shrieking like inhabitants of a rain forest as they boarded Old Red. When they saw him, they fell silent and stared with black-rimmed eyes. The elevator door closed and Old Red descended. Qwilleran told himself with a chuckle that they were members of some kind of satanic cult, and Old Red was taking them down to the infernal regions.

Perhaps it was the sudden silence that roused the Siamese, or their internal clock told them it was time for their eleven o'clock treat. Whatever alerted them, they wandered out from wherever they had been sleeping and performed the ritual of yawning and stretching, first two forelegs and then one hind leg. Koko jumped to the desktop and nosed the Grinchman & Hills report. Yum Yum stood on her hind legs and placed her paws on the edge of the wastebasket, peering into its depths in hope of finding a crumpled paper or piece of string.

"I don't know about you," Qwilleran said to the pair, "but I've had a most interesting evening. If we do what the architects suggest, this building will no longer look like a refrigerator, and it won't be a sore thumb on Zwinger Boulevard. The lobby will be a showplace; the apartments will be palatial; the rooftop restaurant will be exclusive; and they'll no longer allow cats. How do you react to that?"

"Yow," said Koko, who was now examining the library sofa. It was covered with fake leopard, and he knew it was not the real thing. Industriously, with vertical tail, he sniffed the seams, pawed the button tufting, and reached down behind the seat cushions. Some of his memorable discoveries had been made behind seat cushions: cocktail crackers, paper clips, folding money, pencils, and small articles of clothing. Now he was scrabbling so assiduously that Qwilleran went to his aid. He removed one of the seat cushions, and there—tucked in the crevice between the seat platform and the sofa-back—was an item of gold jewelry.

"Good boy!" he said. "Let me see it."

Engraved discs were linked together to make a flexible bracelet, but the clasp was broken. One disc was engraved in cursive script: "To Dianne." Another was inscribed: "From Ross." The remainder bore the numerals: 1-1-4-1, 5-1-1-1, 4-1-3-5, etc. Obviously it was a secret code between the two.

"Okay, this is enough excitement for tonight," Qwilleran said, "but tomorrow we do a little research on the Labor Day incident."

On Tuesday morning Qwilleran called Jefferson Lowell at Grinchman & Hills, inviting him to lunch at the Press Club, and the architect accepted. There was a certain mystique about the Press Club, and most persons jumped at an invitation.

Before going out to breakfast, he checked the weather report on the radio and learned that the Narcotics Squad had rounded up fifty-two suspects in a drug bust; a judge had been indicted for accepting bribes; and a cold front was moving in.

On his way out of the building Qwilleran was flagged by the manager. She said, "I'm sorry about that commotion last night. Mrs. Button is very old and a little confused at times."

"I understand, Mrs. Tuttle."

"Last year she had an attack, and the paramedics gave her CPR. The next day she accused them of rape. It even went to court, but of course it was thrown out."

"I'm glad you warned me," Qwilleran said. "Next time I'll let her fall."

If Mrs. Tuttle appreciated his sly humor, she gave no indication. "I also wanted to tell you, Mr. Qwilleran, that some of our tenants do cleaning—those that are on social security, you know. They like to keep active and earn a little extra. Let me know if you need help with your apartment."

"I'll take you up on that," he said, "but don't send me Mrs. Button."

Then he walked downtown. It was a good day for walking—by urban standards; a light breeze diluted the emissions from cars and trucks and diesel vehicles. En route he stopped for pancakes and sausages, observing that they were twice the price of a similar breakfast in Pickax, and the sausages were not half so good. Moose County had hog farms, and independent butchers made their own sausages. He was spoiled.

At the *Daily Fluxion* he braved the security cordon and gained admittance to the library, where he asked to see clips on the Bessinger murder. The film bank produced three entries, the first dated the day after Labor Day. Although the victim's name was spelled differently in each news item, that was not unusual for the *Daily Fluxion*.

MURDER-SUICIDE JOLTS ART WORLD

The violent deaths of an art dealer and an artist Sunday night, apparently murder and suicide, have shocked the local art world and the residents of the Casablanca apartments.

The body of Diane Bessinger, 45, co-owner of the Bessinger-Todd Gallery, was found in her penthouse apartment Monday morning. Her throat had been cut. The body of Ross Rasmus, 25, a client of Bessinger, was found earlier atop a car in the parking lot below the murdered woman's terrace.

Rasmus apparently jumped to his death after leaving a contrite confession daubed on a wall. His body landed on the roof of a car owned by a Casablanca tenant, who found it at 12:05 A.M. Monday and notified the police.

"I went out for some smokes and beer," said Jack Yazbro, 39, "and the top of my car was all bashed in. He wasn't that big of a guy, but it's a long way down."

Bessinger died between 11 P.M. and midnight Sunday, according to the medical examiner, although the body was not discovered until Monday morning when her partner, Jerome Todd, phoned and was unable to get an answer.

"I heard about Ross's suicide on the radio and tried to call her," Todd said. "When she didn't answer, I got worried and called the building manager."

The gallery had mounted a one-man exhibit of Rasmus's mushroom paintings in June. "They sold poorly," said Todd, "and Ross blamed us for not publicizing the event enough."

Rasmus rented a loft apartment adjoining Bessinger's lavish penthouse at the Casablanca. Jessica Tuttle, manager of the building, called him a good tenant. "He was a nice, quiet, serious young man," she said. "We rented to him at Ms. Bessinger's recommendation."

It was Tuttle who found the murdered woman's body. "Mr. Todd called me about not getting an answer on the phone. He was sure she was home, because she had guests coming for a holiday brunch. So I took my keys and went up there. Her body was on the living room floor, and there was a lot of blood on the carpet."

Bessinger had been in the news frequently in connection with the Save Our Casablanca Kommittee, of which she was founder and leader.

Following the news item, a brief obituary had been published in the Wednesday edition of the *Fluxion*, with a half-column photo of the deceased, a vivacious-looking woman with dark shoulder-length hair. Diane had become Diana.

BESSINGER, DIANA

Diana Bessinger, 45, of the Casablanca apartments died Sunday at her home. She was co-owner of the Bessinger-Todd Gallery, founder of the Save Our Casablanca Kommittee, an officer of the Turp and Chisel Club, and an active worker in local art projects.

A native of Iowa, she was the daughter of the late Prof. and Mrs. Damon Bessinger. She is survived by one brother and two daughters.

Private services will be held Thursday. Memorials may be made to the Turp and Chisel scholarship fund.

The following Sunday, the art page of the *Fluxion* carried a commentary by art writer Ylana Targ, with yet a third spelling of the victim's name. A photo taken by a *Fluxion* photographer at the Rasmus opening in June showed a smiling "Dianne" Bessinger and a shy Ross Rasmus, posed with one of the mushroom paintings. The byline, Qwilleran noted, was another one of those names that was just as logical spelled backward or forward.

MUSHROOM MURDER HAS NO ANSWERS
by Ylana Targ

There is only one topic of conversation in the galleries and studios as Dianne Bessinger is tearfully laid to rest and the ashes of the "mushroom painter" are shipped ignominiously to his hometown—somewhere.

Why did he do it? What caused this talented, thoughtful artist to turn violent and commit such a heinous crime? His suicide is easier to explain; it was the only possible escape from intolerable guilt. Desperate remorse must have driven him over the parapet of the Casablanca terrace.

"Lady Di" was his patron, his enthusiastic press agent, his best friend, who saw merit in his work when no other gallery would take a chance on his monomania for mushrooms. Once, when asked why he never painted broccoli or crook-neck squash, Ross said meekly, "I haven't said all I have to say about mushrooms."

Granted, mushrooms are erotic, and he captured their mushroomness succinctly. Pairing the fleshy fungus with the razor-edge knife, as he did, bordered on soft porn.

Dianne said in an interview last June, "There have been artists who painted softness, crispness, silkiness, or mistiness sublimely, but only Rasmus could paint sharpness so sharp that the viewer cringes."

The knife he portrayed in the paintings was always the same—a tapered, pointed Japanese slicer with a pale wooden handle and a provocative shapeliness of its own.

One shudders to think too much about the actual crime. The motive is all one can safely or sanely contemplate, and that is a question that will never be answered.

Dianne Bessinger was the founder and president of SOCK. It was a passion with her, and she would not want her worthwhile cause to be overshadowed by the notoriety surrounding her tragic death. She would say, "Let the matter fade away now, and get on with the business of saving the Casablanca."

Qwilleran finished reading the clips and patted his moustache. It would be a challenge, he thought, to uncover that hidden motive. It might be buried in 14-A.

CHAPTER 7

On an impulse, after reading the murder-suicide clips in the *Fluxion* library, Qwilleran walked to the Bessinger-Todd Gallery in the financial district. It had the same address as the old Lambreth Gallery that he knew so well, but the interior had changed dramatically. At that morning hour the place had a vast emptiness, except for a business-suited man supervising a jeans-clad assistant perched on a stepladder. He turned in surprise as Qwilleran entered, saying, "We're closed. I thought the door was locked."

"Am I intruding? I'm Jim Qwilleran, formerly of the *Daily Fluxion*. I used to cover the art beat when Mountclemens was the critic."

"How do you do. I'm Jerome Todd. I've heard about Mountclemens, but that was before my time here. I'm from Des Moines."

"I've been away for three years. I see you've enlarged the gallery."

"Yes, we knocked out the ceiling so we could exhibit larger works, and we added the balcony for crafts objects."

Qwilleran said, "I'm retired now and living up north, but I heard about the tragic loss of your partner and wanted to extend my condolences."

"Thank you . . . Is there anything I can do for you?" Todd asked in an abrupt change of subject. He was a tall, distinguished-looking man with one disturbing mannerism—the habit of pinching his nose as if he smelled an unpleasant odor.

Qwilleran was adept at inventing impromptu replies. "I happen to be staying at the Casablanca," he said, "and I would like to propose a memorial to Ms. Bessinger that would help the cause she championed."

Todd looked surprised and wary in equal proportions.

"What I envision," Qwilleran went on smoothly as if he had been planning it for months, "is a book about the historic Casablanca, using old photos from the public library. For text I would rely on interviews and research."

"That would be costly to put together," said the dealer, withdrawing slightly as he began to anticipate a touch for money.

"There are grants available for publishing books on historical subjects," Qwilleran said coolly, "and revenue from the sale of the books would go to the Bessinger Memorial Fund. My own services would be donated."

Instead of being relieved, Todd showed increased wariness. "Who would be interviewed?" he asked sharply.

"Local historians, architects, and persons who have recollections of the early Casablanca. You'll be surprised how many of them will come forward when we broadcast a request. My own attorney remembers eating spinach timbales in the rooftop restaurant as a boy."

"I wouldn't want anyone to go digging into the circumstances of my partner's death. There's been too much notoriety and gossip already," the dealer said, pinching his nose.

"There would be nothing like that, I assure you," said Qwilleran. At that moment a glimpse of movement overhead caused him to look up; a Persian cat was walking along the railing of the balcony. "By the way," he said, "I'm subletting Ms. Bessinger's apartment while the estate is in probate, and I admire her taste in furniture and art."

Todd nodded in silent agreement.

"How long were you in partnership, Mr. Todd?"

"Eighteen years. We came here to take over the Lambreth Gallery when Zoe Lambreth moved to California."

"Do you happen to have any Rasmus paintings?"

"I do not! And I'm weary of the talk about that fellow! There are plenty of *living* artists." Todd pinched his nose again.

"The only reason I asked is that I'm in the market for large-scale art for a house I'm building up north." Qwilleran was exercising his talent for instant falsehood.

"Then you must come to our opening on Friday night," said the dealer, visibly relieved as he anticipated cash flow. "We're in the process of mounting the show, so the walls are vacant, but you'll see some impressive works at the vernissage."

"I'm converting a barn into a residence," said Qwilleran, embroidering his innocent lie, "so I'll have large wall spaces, and I was hoping for a mushroom painting. Mushrooms seem appropriate for a barn."

Stiffly Todd said, "All his work sold out immediately after his suicide. If I'd had my wits about me, I would have held some back, but I was in shock. They didn't sell well at all in June. He's worth more dead than alive. But if you come here Friday night you'll see the work of other artists you might like. What kind of barn are you remodeling?"

"An apple barn. Octagonal." The barn on the Klingenschoen property had indeed stored apples, and it really was eight-sided.

"Spectacular! You might consider contemporary tapestries. Do you know the sizes of your wall spaces?"

"Actually, the job isn't off the drawing board as yet," said Qwilleran, being completely truthful.

"Come anyway on Friday. There'll be champagne, hors d'oeuvres, live music, and valet parking."

"What are the hours?"

"From six o'clock until the well runs dry."

"Thank you. I'll be here." Qwilleran started toward the door and turned back. "Tell me frankly. How do you feel about the future of the Casablanca?"

"It's a lost cause," said Todd without emotion.

"Yet your partner was convinced it could be saved."

"Yes ... but ... the picture has changed. The building is being razed to make way for the new Gateway Alcazar, which will be the missing link between the new downtown and the new Junktown. I'm moving the gallery there. I've signed up to lease space twice the size of what I have here."

Qwilleran consulted his watch. It was time to meet the architect at the Press Club. "Well, thanks for your time, Mr. Todd. I'll see you on Friday."

As he walked to the Press Club he told himself that the book project, born on the spur of the moment, was not a bad idea. As for converting the apple barn, that sounded good, too. It would be ten times roomier than his present apartment in Pickax, and the Siamese could climb about the overhead beams.

The Press Club occupied a grimy stone fortress that had once been the county jail, and as a hangout for the working press it had maintained a certain forbidding atmosphere for many years. The interior had changed, however, since Qwilleran's days at the *Daily Fluxion*. It had been renovated, modernized, brightened and—in his estimation—ruined. Yet it was a popular place at noon. He waited for the architect in the lobby, observing the lunch-time crowd that streamed through the door: reporters and editors, advertising and PR types, radio and TV personalities.

Eventually a man with a neatly clipped beard entered slowly, appraising the lobby with curiosity and a critical set to his mouth. Qwilleran stepped forward and introduced himself.

"I'm Jeff Lowell," said the man. "So this is the celebrated Press Club. Somehow it's not what I expected." He gestured toward the damask walls and gilt-framed mirrors.

"They redecorated a couple of years ago," said Qwilleran apologetically, "and it's no longer the dismal, shabby Press Club that I loved. Shall we go upstairs?"

Upstairs there was a dining room with tablecloths, cloth napkins, and peppermills on the tables instead of paper placemats and squeeze bottles of mustard and ketchup. They took a table in a secluded corner.

"So you're interested in the Casablanca restoration," said the architect.

"Interested enough to want to ask questions. I've done my homework. I spent last evening reading the Grinchman & Hills report. You seem quite sanguine about the project."

"As the report made clear, it will cost a mint, but it's entirely feasible. It could be the most sensational preservation project in the country," Lowell said.

"What is your particular interest?"

"For one thing, I lived in that building for a few years before I was married, and there's something about the place that gets into a person's blood; I don't know how to explain it. But chiefly, my firm is interested because the Casablanca was designed by the late John Grinchman, and we have all the original specs in our archives. Naturally that facilitated the study immeasurably. Grinchman was a struggling young architect at the turn of the century when he met Harrison Plumb. Plumb had a harebrained scheme that no established architect would touch, but Grinchman took the gamble, and he Casablanca made his reputation. In design it was ahead of its time; Moorish didn't become a fad until after World War One. The walls were built two feet thick at the base, tapering up to eighteen inches at the top. All the mechanical equipment—water pipes, steam pipes, electric conduits—were concentrated in crawl spaces between floors, for easy access and to help soundproof the building. And there was another feature that may amuse you: The occupants could have *all the electricity they wanted!*"

"What do you know about Harrison Plumb?" Qwilleran asked.

"His family had accumulated their fortune in railroads, but he was not inclined to business. He was a dreamer, a dilettante. He studied for a while at L'Ecole des Beaux Arts, and while he was in Paris he saw the nobility living in lavish apartments in the city.

He brought the idea home. He dreamed of building an apartment-palace."

"What was the reaction from the local elite?"

"They tumbled for it! It was a smash hit! For families there were twelve-room apartments with servants' quarters. There were smaller apartments for bachelors and mistresses. Horses and carriages were stabled in the rear and available at a moment's notice, like taxis. Curiously there were no kitchens, but there was the restaurant on the top floor, and the residents either went upstairs to the dining room or had their meals sent down."

"What about the swimming pool?"

"That was for men only—and somewhat of a conceit. On the main floor they had a stockbroker, jeweler, law firm, and insurance agency. In the basement there were laundresses and cobblers. Barbers, tailors, seamstresses, and hairdressers were on call to the apartments."

"And Plumb kept the best apartment for himself?"

"The entire twelfth floor. It was designed to his specifications in Spanish style and then redesigned in the 1920s in the French Modern of its day. If the building is restored, the Plumb suite could eventually be a private museum; it's that spectacular!"

Qwilleran said, "Suppose the Klingenschoen Fund undertook to restore the Casablanca to its original character, would there be a demand for the apartments?"

"I have no doubt."

"I suppose you've met Harrison Plumb's daughter?"

"Only twice," said Lowell. "The first time was when I asked permission to make the study. I buttered up the old girl, invoked the memory of her dear father, indulged in some architectural double-talk, and got her okay. The second time was when I presented her with a copy of the report—leather-bound, mind you—which I'm sure she hasn't opened, even though we bound in a photo of her father, arm in arm with John Grinchman. Unfortunately, I'm not a bridge player, so I was never invited back."

"I have yet to meet the lady," said Qwilleran. "What is she like?"

"Nice enough, but an absurd anachronism, living in a private time capsule. She doesn't give a damn if the front steps are pulverizing and the tenants' elevators are shot. If someone doesn't shake some sense into her, she'll hang on to the place until she dies, and that'll be the end of the Casablanca. I don't want to be there on the day they blast."

They ordered the Press Club's Tuesday special, pork chops, and talked about the metamorphosis of Zwinger Boulevard, the proposed Gateway Alcazar, and the gentrification of Junktown. Then over cheesecake and coffee they reverted to the subject of the Casablanca.

"Let's draw up the battlelines," said Qwilleran. "On the one side, the developers and the city fathers want to see it demolished."

"Also the financial backers for the Gateway Alcazar. Also the realty firm that manages the Casablanca. The building is a headache for them; in spite of the low rents, it's only half-occupied, and the mechanical equipment is constantly breaking down because of age and mishandling."

"Okay. And on the other side we have SOCK and G&H, right?"

"Plus the art and academic sector. Plus an army of former tenants in all walks of life who've contributed to SOCK for the campaign. Strange as it may seem, there are people who are sentimental about the Casablanca in the same way they love the memory of—say—Paris. It has almost a living presence. It's too bad what happened to Di Bessinger. She had a lot of drive and—as you probably know—she was set to inherit the building."

"That's news to me," Qwilleran said.

"You might say she had a vested interest in the Casablanca. That's not to discount her genuine love for it, of course."

"Are you telling me that the Countess had named Bessinger in her will?"

"Yes, Di spent a lot of time up on Twelve, and it must have been appreciated by the older woman, who—let's face it—lives a lonely life."

"Tell me this," said Qwilleran. "If the Klingenschoen Fund

makes an offer—and at this point I'm not sure they will—can we be certain that the Countess will sell?"

"That I can't answer," said the architect. "Mary Duckworth thinks the woman is craftily playing cat and mouse with both sides. She can't possibly want to see her home demolished, and yet she's related to the Pennimans on her mother's side, and they're financial backers for the Gateway. Do you know the Pennimans?"

"I know they own the *Morning Rampage*," said Qwilleran, "and as an alumnus of the *Daily Fluxion* I don't think highly of their paper."

"Also they're big in radio, television, and God knows what else. Penniman is spelled P-O-W-E-R in this town. It would give me personally a lot of satisfaction to see that crew get their blocks knocked off."

"This is going to be an interesting crusade," said Qwilleran. "You understand, of course, that the Klingenschoen board doesn't meet till Thursday, and at this point it's just pie in the sky."

The two men shook hands and promised to keep in touch.

From the Press Club Qwilleran wandered over to the public library, one of the few buildings in town that had not changed, except for the addition of a parking structure. It was forty times the size of the library in Pickax, and he wondered if Polly Duncan had ever seen it. She crossed his mind more often than he imagined she would. What would she think of the Casablanca elevators? The tenants? The conversation pit? The mushroom paintings? The gold faucets? The waterbed? He doubted that she had the objectivity to appreciate a building that looked like a refrigerator.

Browsing through the library's local history collection, he was gratified to find abundant material on the Casablanca in the years when Zwinger Boulevard was crowded with horses and carriages—later with Stanley Steamers and Columbus Electrics. Photos in sepia or black and white depicted presidents, financial wizards, and theater greats standing on the front steps of the building, or stepping from a Duesenberg with the assistance of a uniformed doorman, or dining in the Palm Pavilion on the roof. Women in satin hobble skirts and furs, escorted by men in opera cloaks and top hats, were shown departing for a charity ball. In the grassy park adjoining the building a bevy of nursemaids aired infants in perambulators, and overdressed children batted shuttlecocks with battledores. There was even a photo of the undersized swimming pool with male bathers wearing long-legged bathing suits.

What interested Qwilleran most were the pictures of Harrison Plumb with his little moustache, probably a souvenir of his Paris days. He was shown sometimes with his friend Grinchman, often with visiting dignitaries, frequently with his wife and three children, the boys in knee pants and little Adelaide with ringlets cascading below the brim of a flower-laden hat. In later photos Adelaide and her father posed in a Stutz Bearcat or at a tea table on the terrace. Qwilleran recalled hearing that the personalities and events of the past seep into the brick and stones and woodwork of an old building, giving it an aura. If true, that accounted for the Casablanca magic that Lowell had tried to describe.

Following his two-hour immersion in the gentle, elegant past, Qwilleran found the whizzing traffic hard to take. He walked home briskly because a cold breeze was blowing, and Zwinger Boulevard, with its high buildings, functioned as a wind tunnel. It had been called Eat Street by the *Fluxion* food editor, and Qwilleran counted a dozen ethnic restaurants not to be found in Moose County: Polynesian, Mexican, Japanese, Hungarian, Szechuan, and Middle Eastern, to name a few. He intended to try them all. He wished Polly were with him.

It was the end of the day, and tenants were converging on the Casablanca by car, bus, and taxi. Qwilleran, the only one to arrive on foot, checked the parking lot, hoping that his space might be vacant, but this time a 1975 jalopy was parked in #28.

As he joined the miscellaneous crew trooping through the front door, a man with a reddish moustache hailed him. "Hi! Did you move in?"

"Yes, I've joined the happy few," Qwilleran acknowledged.

"What floor?"

"Fourteen."

"Does the roof still leak?"

"I'll know better when it rains, but they claim to have fixed it yesterday."

"You must have connections. They never fix anything around here." He ran ahead to catch the elevator, and only then did Qwilleran realize that he was the friendly jogger who had helped him on his arrival Sunday afternoon.

In the lobby were workmen in coveralls carrying six-packs, boisterous students with bookbags, women dressed for success and carrying briefcases, and elderly inmates with canes and bandages and swollen legs. Together they created the atmosphere of a bus terminal and a hospital corridor.

Most tenants stopped in the mailroom to unlock their mailboxes, after which they looked sourly at what they found there. Upon entering the crowded cubicle, Qwilleran had to dodge a large hairless man wearing a T-shirt imprinted "Ferdie Le Bull." Next, a middle-aged woman in a sequin-studded black cocktail dress, looking anxiously at a handful of envelopes, collided with him.

"Sorry," he mumbled.

"Well, hello!" she said in a girlish voice, regarding his moustache appreciatively. "Where have they been hiding *you?*"

There was no mail in Qwilleran's box. It was too soon to hear from Polly, and other letters were being intercepted by his part-time secretary.

Rupert was standing by as if expecting an emergency, his red hat having the visibility of a fire hydrant. Mrs. Tuttle was sitting behind her desk, knitting, but keeping a stern eye on the engineering students. And among those waiting for the elevator was Amber, carrying a bag of groceries and looking tired.

Qwilleran asked her, "Is there an engineering school in the vicinity? These kids are always talking about bridges."

"They're from the dental school," she said. "Qwill, meet my neighbor on Eight, Courtney Hampton. Courtney, this is Jim Qwilleran. He's got Di's apartment on Fourteen."

The young man she introduced had square shoulders, slim hips, and a suit of the latest cut. He glanced at Qwilleran's boots and tweeds and said with a nasal twang, "Just in from the country?"

Amber said, "Courtney works at Kipper & Fine, the men's clothing store. What have you been doing all day, Qwill?"

"Walking around. Getting oriented. Everything has changed."

"The Casablanca will be the next to go," her neighbor predicted. "Don't unpack your luggage."

"I wonder what's on TV tonight?" Amber said with a weary sigh.

"As for me," said Courtney with a grandiose flourish of eyebrows, "if anyone is interested, I . . . am playing bridge . . . with the Countess tonight."

"La di da," said Amber.

Both elevators arrived simultaneously, and the crowd surged aboard, separating Qwilleran from the other two. As Old Green reluctantly ascended, it performed a sluggish ritual at each floor, first bouncing to a stop, then listlessly opening its door to unload a passenger, after which it waited a long minute, closed its door in slow motion, and crept upward to the next floor. No one spoke. Passengers were holding their collective breath.

It had been a long day, and Qwilleran was glad to be home, but when he opened the door of 14-A he was met by a blast of heat. The radiators were hissing and clanking, and both cats were stretched full-length on the floor, panting.

"What happened?" he demanded. "It must be 110 in here!" He hunted for a thermostat and, finding none, grabbed the housephone. "Mrs. Tuttle! Qwilleran in 14-A. What happened to the furnace? We're suffocating! The cats are half cooked! I expect the window glass to melt!"

"Open the windows," she said calmly. "Your side of the building heats up when a cold wind comes from the east. We don't have much control over it. The apartments on the east side are freezing, and the furnace works overtime to try to get them a little heat. Just open all your windows."

He did as he was told, and the Siamese revived sufficiently to sit up and take a little nourishment in the form of a can of red salmon. As for Qwilleran, he lost no time in going out to dinner. It occurred to him that he should invite Amber; she looked too tired to thaw whatever was in her grocery bag, and the temperature in her apartment might be insufferable, whether she lived on the frigid or sweltering side of the building. Yet, he disliked her line of conversation, and he believed that too soon an invitation might encourage her. In his present financial situation he had to be careful. Women used to be attracted to his ample moustache; now he feared they were attracted to his ample bank account.

Feeling guilty, he went to the nearest restaurant on Eat Street, which happened to be Japanese—a roomful of hibachi tables under lighted canopies, against a background of shoji screens and Japanese art. Each table seated eight around a large grill, and Qwilleran was conducted to a table where four persons were already seated.

He often dined alone and entertained himself by eavesdropping and composing scenarios about the other diners. At the hibachi table he found a young couple sipping tea from handleless gray cups and giggling about the chopsticks. The man was cloyingly attentive, and his companion kept admiring her ring finger. Newlyweds, Qwilleran decided. From the country. Honeymooning in the big city. They ordered chicken from the low end of the menu.

At the opposite end of the table two men in business suits were drinking sake martinis and ordering the lobster-steak-shrimp combination. On expense accounts, Qwilleran guessed. (He himself ordered the medium-priced teriyaki steak.) Upon further study, pursued surreptitiously, he decided that the man wearing a custom-tailored suit and ostentatious gold jewelry was treating the other man to dinner, his guest being a deferential sort in a suit off the rack and a shirt too loose around the neck. Also, he had a bandage on his ear. They were a curious pair—employer and employee, Qwilleran thought, judging by their respective attitudes. He had a feeling that he had seen that ear patch at the Casablanca—in the lobby or in the elevator. The man in question suddenly glanced in Qwilleran's direction, then mumbled something to his host, who turned to look at the newcomer with the oversized moustache. All of this Qwilleran observed from the corner of his eye, enjoying it immensely.

Conversation at the table halted when the Japanese chef appeared—an imposing figure in his stovepipe hat, two feet tall, and his leather knife holster. He bowed curtly and whipped out his steel spatulas, which he proceeded to wield with the aplomb of a symphony percussionist. The audience was speechless as he manipulated the splash of egg, the hill of sliced mushrooms, and the mountain of rice. Steaks, seafood, and chicken breasts sizzled in butter and were doused with seasonings and flamed in wine. Then the chef drew his formidable knife, cubed the meat and served the food on rough-textured gray plates. With a quick bow he said, "Have a nice evening," and disappeared.

Qwilleran was the only one who used chopsticks, having acquired virtuosity when he was an overseas correspondent.

Watching him in admiration, the bride said, "You're good at that."

"I've been practicing," he said. "Is this your first time here?"

"Yes," she said. "We think it's neat, don't we, honey?"

"Yeah, it's neat," said her groom.

When Qwilleran left the restaurant it was dark, and he took the precaution of hailing a taxi. It was mid-evening now, and the main floor of the Casablanca was deserted. Most of the tenants were eating dinner or watching TV. The students were doing their homework, and the old folks had retired for the night.

As Qwilleran waited for Old Red, the door opened. The young woman who stepped out could only be described as a vision! She had a model's figure and an angel's face, enhanced by incredibly artful makeup. He stared after her and confirmed that she had also a model's walk and an heiress's clothing budget. He blew copiously into his moustache.

After Old Red, scented with expensive perfume, had transported him to Fourteen, which was really Thirteen, he greeted the Siamese in a daze, saying, "You wouldn't believe what I've just seen!"

"Yow!" said Koko, rising on his hind legs.

"Sorry. No samples tonight. How's the temperature? A little better? I apologize for the sauna. How would you guys like a read?"

Shedding his street clothes gratefully and getting into his pajama bottoms, Qwilleran intended to read another chapter of Kinglake's *Eothen*. It may have been his imagination, but the Siamese seemed to enjoy the references to camels, goats, and beasts of burden. Their ears always twitched and their whiskers curled. It was uncanny.

So the three of them filed into the library, Koko leading the way with tail erect as a flagpole, followed by Yum Yum slinking sinuously, one dainty foot in front of the other, exactly like that girl in the lobby, Qwilleran thought. He brought up the rear, wearing the bottoms of the Valentine-red pajamas that Polly had given him the previous February.

The library was the most livable room in the apartment, made friendly with shelves of art books and walls of paintings. The furniture was contemporary teakwood and chrome created by big-name designers whose names Qwilleran had forgotten. He dropped into an inviting chair and turned to chapter ten, while Yum Yum turned around three times on his lap and settled down with chin on paw. Koko had just assumed his posture of eager listener when a slight noise elsewhere catapulted both cats out of the library and into the foyer. Qwilleran followed and found Koko scratching at something under the door. An envelope had been pushed halfway underneath.

There was no name on it, but it contained a sheet of heavy notepaper embossed with a W, and the following message had been written with an unsteady hand:

"Welcome to the Casablanca. Come down and have a drink with me—any time." It was signed by Isabelle Wilburton of apartment 10-F, the one who wanted to sell her baby grand piano.

Qwilleran growled into his moustache and tossed the note into the wastebasket, being careful not to crumple it. Crumpled paper was like catnip to Yum Yum, and she would retrieve it in three seconds. All his life it had been his compulsive habit to crumple paper before discarding it, but those days were gone forever. Amazing, he thought, how one adjusts to living with cats. A few years before, if anyone had suggested such a thing, he would have called that person a blasted fool.

Back in the library he turned once more to chapter ten, but a slight quiver on his upper lip caused him to put the book down. He passed a hand over his moustache as if to calm the disturbing sensation. "Let's sit quietly and think for a while," he said to the waiting listeners. "We've been here for forty-eight hours and I'm getting some vibrations."

The fact that someone had been murdered on the premises did not bother Qwilleran; it was Koko's interest in the incident that alerted him. That cat knew everything! First he found the bloodstain under a heavy piece of furniture, and then he found the gold bracelet buried in the upholstery of a sofa. Koko had an instinct for sinister truths hidden beneath the surface.

Qwilleran himself, after reading the newspaper accounts, questioned the motive of the "nice, quiet, young man" who brutally knifed his benefactor, his "best friend," to whom he had given a gold bracelet inscribed with an intimate code. Ross may have blamed the gallery because his paintings failed to sell, but that was a weak excuse for murder. It was Todd who gave the *Fluxion* that frail scrap of information, Todd with his nervous habit of nose-pinching. What did *that* signify?

The news that Di Bessinger had been named heir to the Casablanca also raised suspicions in Qwilleran's mind. Many powerful interests opposed her. It was definitely to their advantage to have her out of the picture. Even her own partner disagreed with her on the preservation of the old building and was now planning to move the gallery to the Gateway Alcazar. But none of this explained the role of Ross Rasmus as the hit man.

"What's your opinion, Koko?" Qwilleran asked.

The cat was not listening. He was craning his neck and staring toward the foyer. A moment later there was a frantic banging on the front door. Qwilleran hurried to the scene and yanked the door open, catching a wild-eyed woman with fists raised, ready to pound the door panels again. She screamed, "The building's on fire!"

Chapter 8

Just as the woman from 14-B screamed "Fire!" Qwilleran smelled smoke and heard the sirens.

"Don't take the elevator!" she cried as she dashed for the stairwell in a terrycloth robe.

He jammed the cats unceremoniously into their carrier, grabbed his pajama top, and started down the stairs, assuming that the boilers had overheated in their battle with the bitter east wind. Other tenants joined the downward trek at every floor, most of them grumbling and whining.

"Why are we doing this? The building's fireproof," one protested.

"My husband's watching football on TV, and he won't budge," said a woman. "I say: Let him burn!"

"Smells like burning chicken to me," said another.

"Did they ring the firebell? I didn't hear it. My neighbor banged on my door. They're supposed to ring the firebell."

"Betcha ten bucks the Countess ain't walkin' down."

By the time the disgruntled refugees reached the main floor, the lobby was filled with a hubbub of voices raised in alarm or indignation, while Mrs. Tuttle tried to calm them. They were a motley assemblage in various states of undress: women with hair curlers and no makeup; hairy-legged men in nightshirts; old tenants without their dentures; bald tenants without their hairpieces. Qwilleran was conspicuous in his red pajamas. A few persons were clutching treasured possessions or squawling cats, and the Siamese in their carrier yowled and shrieked in the spirit of the occasion. Among the refugees was a man in a washed-out seersucker robe that might have been purloined from a hospital. He had thinning hair, a pale face, and a white patch where his right ear should be; Qwilleran recognized his fellow diner from the hibachi table.

Fortunately for the underclad residents, the lobby was on the warm side of the building. Those from the cold side were threatening to bring their mattresses and sleep on the lobby floor. Mrs. Tuttle was doing a heroic job of controlling the crowd.

Then an elevator door opened, and firemen in black rubber coats and boots, carrying red-handled axes, stepped out. "Go back to bed, folks," they said, grinning. "Only a chicken burning."

The tenants would have been happier if it had been a real fire.

"What! I walked down six flights for a chicken?"

"I knew it was a chicken. I know burning chicken when I smell it."

"Somebody put it in the oven to thaw and went out to the bar and forgot it."

"Whoever done it, they should kick 'em out."

"They're gonna kick us all out pretty soon."

The crowd began to disperse, some boarding the elevators and some heading for the stairwells, while others hung around the lobby, welcoming the opportunity for social fellowship.

The Siamese, following their rude experience among angry tenants and complaining cats, were understandably upset. Qwilleran, too, was restless and perhaps slightly lonesome, although he would not have admitted it. He considered it too late to call Polly but took a chance on phoning Arch Riker. "How's everything in Pickax?" he asked his old friend.

"I wondered when you were going to report in," said the editor. "Everything's just the way you left it—no snow yet."

"Any world-shaking news?"

"We had some excitement today. One of the conservation officers spotted a bald eagle near Wildcat Junction."

"What did you do? Put out an extra?"

"I'll blue-pencil that cynical remark. You talk like city folks."

"Have you seen Polly?"

"Yes—at a library meeting tonight. She showed slides of her trip to England. She told me she'd heard from you."

"What's happening at the paper?"

"Hixie sold a full-page ad to Iris Cobb's son. He's going into business up here."

"Watch her! He's happily married," Qwilleran said.

"And we ran a notice in the sick column that old man Dingleberry is in the hospital for observation."

"Of the nurses, no doubt. That old roué is ninety-five and thinks he's twenty-five."

"What about you?" asked Riker. "What have you been doing?"

"Nothing much. Dropped into the *Flux* office today . . . Had lunch twice at the Press Club . . . Bumped into Lieutenant Hames. There's a whole string of new restaurants on Zwinger that you'd like, Arch. So far I've tried North Italian and Japanese. Why don't you fly down for a few days?"

"Can't right now. There's a special edition coming out for deer season, and we're sponsoring a contest for hunters. What do you think of the Casablanca?"

"Not bad for an old building, and the sunsets from the fourteenth floor are spectacular."

"That's one thing the city does well," said Riker. "Sunsets! That's because of the dirt in the atmosphere."

"My apartment has a skylighted living room, a terrace, a waterbed, gold faucets, and a library of art books that you wouldn't believe."

"How do you do it, Qwill? You always luck out. How do the cats react to the altitude?"

"No complaints, although I think Koko is disappointed by the scarcity of pigeons."

"Have you decided about the restoration?"

"I've done some research and had a couple of conferences. Today I met with the architect, and next I'm going to meet the owner of the building, so it's coming right along. You know, Arch, what we have here is King Tut's tomb, waiting to be excavated."

"Well, stay out of trouble, chum," said Riker, "and don't forget to send us some copy."

After delivering this upbeat report, Qwilleran felt better, and he retired, allowing the Siamese to share the waterbed because of their disturbed state of mind. Yum Yum particularly liked the sensation.

On Wednesday morning he telephoned Mary Duckworth. He said, "I've read the Grinchman report and I'm ready to meet the Countess. When can you arrange it?"

"How about this afternoon at four?"

"How do I dress?"

"I'd suggest a suit and tie. And she doesn't permit smoking."

"No problem. I've given up my pipe," Qwilleran said. "I found out the smoke is bad for the Siamese."

"I've given up cigarettes," she said. "My doctor finally convinced me the smoke is bad for antique furniture. Have you talked to Jefferson Lowell?"

"We had lunch. Nice guy."

"Are you convinced, Qwill?"

"I don't know as yet. Where shall we meet?"

"At the front door a few minutes before four. One is always prompt when calling on the Countess."

Before having his hair cut, his moustache trimmed, his good gray suit pressed, and his shoes shined, Qwilleran checked the weather on the radio and learned that a woman shopper had been abducted from a supermarket parking lot; a jogger had been beaten by hoodlums in Penniman Park; and rain was predicted, clearing in midafternoon. He taxied around town to do his errands, had a quick lunch at the Junktown deli, and returned to 14-A early enough to spend a little quality time with the Siamese. He proposed another chapter of *Eothen*, and the cats followed him into the library, but Koko had other ideas. He jumped to the library table and started pawing furiously.

Koko was known to be a bibliophile, and on the six-foot library table there were large-format art books reproducing the work of Michelangelo, Renoir, Van Gogh, Wyeth, and others, although the cat usually preferred small volumes that he could easily knock off a bookshelf.

"What are you doing, you crazy animal?" Qwilleran said.

Koko had found a long flat box among the art books. It looked like leather, and it was labeled "Scrabble." The blank tile found by Yum Yum had obviously strayed from this box. Opening it, Qwilleran found a hundred or so small tiles, each with a single letter of the alphabet. The sight was like a B-12 shot to one who had won all the spelling bees in grade school and had been an orthographic snob ever since. He sat down at the desk, opened the game board, and read the rules out of sheer curiosity.

"This is easy," he said. Scooping up a handful of tiles at random he spelled words like QADI and JAGIR. Years of playing a dictionary game with Koko had given him a vocabulary of esoteric words that he had little opportunity to use. Soon he was building a crossword arrangement on the board. It began with CAD, grew to CADMIUM, and intercepted with SLUMP. This connected with EGRETS and OLPE.

The Siamese watched, patiently waiting for their quality time, but Qwilleran was fascinated by the lettered tiles and the small numerals that gave the value of each letter. All too soon it was time to put on his gray suit and meet Mary Duckworth on the main floor. Before leaving the apartment, he slipped a piece of fruit in his suitcoat pocket.

"You look splendid!" she said when they met, although she gave a brief qualifying glance at the bulge in his pocket.

They rang for the private elevator at the bronze door and rode up to Twelve in a carpeted car with rosewood walls and a velvet-covered bench. The ride was no faster than Old Red or Old Green, but it was smoother and quieter.

On the way up, Qwilleran mentioned, "You knew that Di Bessinger was going to inherit the Casablanca?"

Mary nodded regretfully.

"Who gets it now?"

"Various charities. Qwill, I don't know what you're expecting, but the Plumb apartment may come as a surprise. It's done in vintage Art Deco."

They stepped off the elevator into a large foyer banded in horizontal panels of coral, burgundy, and bottle green, defined by thin strips of copper, and the floor was ceramic tile in a metallic copper glaze. Everything was slightly dulled with age. A pair of angular chairs flanked an angular console on which were two dozen tea roses reflected in a large round mirror.

Mary pressed a doorbell disguised as a miniature Egyptian head, and they waited before double doors sheathed in tooled copper. When the doors opened, they were confronted by a formidable man in a coral-colored coat.

"Good afternoon, Ferdinand," said Mary. "Miss Adelaide is expecting us. This is Mr. Qwilleran."

"Sure. You know where to go." The houseman waved a ham-like hand toward the drawing room. He had the build of a linebacker, with beefy shoulders, a bull neck, and a bald head. The Countess's live-in bodyguard, Qwilleran guessed, doubled as butler. "She was late gettin' up from her nap," the man said, "and then she had to have her hair fixed. She fired the old girl that fixed it, and the new girl is kinda slow."

"Interesting," said Mary stiffly.

The drawing room was more than Qwilleran could assimilate at a glance. What registered was a peach-colored marble floor scattered with geometric-patterned rugs, and peach walls banded in copper and hung with large round mirrors.

Mary motioned him to sit in a tub-shaped chair composed of plump rolls of overstuffed black leather stacked on chrome legs. "You're sitting in an original Bibendum chair from the 1920s," she said.

His gaze went from item to item: The tea table was tortoiseshell; all lamps had bulbous bases; the windows were frosted glass crisscrossed with copper grillwork. Everything was somewhat faded, and there was a sepulchral silence.

Ferdinand followed them into the drawing room. "You never been here before," he said to Qwilleran.

"This is my first visit."

"You play bridge?"

"I'm afraid not."

"She likes to play bridge."

"So I have heard," said Qwilleran with a glance at Mary. She was sitting tight-lipped and haughty.

"She likes all kinds of games," said the houseman. "Is it still raining?"

"It stopped about an hour ago."

"We had some good weather this week."

"Very true."

"I used to wrestle on TV," said the big man.

"Is that so?" Qwilleran wished he had brought his pocket tape recorder.

"I was Ferdie Le Bull. That's what they called me." The houseman unbuttoned his coral coat and exhibited a T-shirt stenciled with the name. "You never saw me wrestle?"

"I never had that pleasure."

"Here she comes now," Ferdinand announced.

Adelaide St. John Plumb was a small unprepossessing woman who carried her head cocked graciously to one side and spoke in a breathy little-girl voice. "So good of you to come." Brown hair plastered flat against her head in uniform waves contrasted absurdly with her pale aging skin, a network of fine wrinkles. So did the penciled eyebrows and red Cupid's-bow mouth. She was wearing a peach chiffon tea gown and long strands of gold beads.

Her guests rose. Mary said, "Miss Plumb, may I present James Qwilleran."

"So happy to meet you," said their hostess.

"*Enchanté!*" said Qwilleran, bending low over her hand in a courtly gesture. Then he drew from his pocket a perfect Bosc pear with bronze skin and long, curved stem, offering it in the palm of his hand like a jewel-encrusted Fabergé bauble. "The perfect complement for your beautiful apartment, Mademoiselle."

The Countess was a trifle slow in responding. "How charming . . . Please be seated . . . Ferdinand, you may bring the tea tray." She seated herself gracefully on an overstuffed sofa in front of the tortoiseshell tea table. "I trust you are well, Mary?"

"Quite well, thank you. And you, Miss Adelaide?"

"Very well. Did it rain today?"

"Yes, rather briskly."

The hostess turned to Qwilleran, inclining her head winningly. "You have recently arrived from the east?"

"From the north," he corrected her. "Four hundred miles north."

"How cold it must be!"

Mary said, "Mr. Qwilleran is spending the winter here to escape the snow and ice."

"How lovely! I hope you will enjoy your stay, Mr . . ."

"Qwilleran."

"Do you play bridge?"

"I regret to say that bridge is not one of my accomplishments," he said, "but I have a considerable aptitude for Scrabble."

Mary expressed surprise, and the Countess expressed delight. "How nice! You must join me in a game some evening."

Ferdinand, wearing white cotton gloves, placed a silver tea tray before her—cubistic in design with ebony trim—and the hostess performed the tea ritual with well-practiced gestures.

"Mr. Qwilleran is a writer," said Mary.

"How wonderful! What do you write?"

"I plan to write a book on the history of the Casablanca," he said, astonishing Mary once more. "The public library has a large collection of photos, including many of yourself, Miss Plumb."

"Do they have pictures of my dear father?"

"Quite a few."

"I would adore seeing them." She tilted her head prettily.

"Do you have many recollections of the early Casablanca?"

"Yes indeed! I was born here—in this very suite—with a midwife, a nurse, and two doctors in attendance. My father was Harrison Wills Plumb—a wonderful man! I hardly remember my mother. She was related to the Pennimans. She died when I was only four. There was an influenza epidemic, and my mother and two brothers were stricken. All three of them died in one week, leaving me as my father's only consolation. I was four years old."

Mary said, "Tell Mr. Qwilleran how you happened to escape the epidemic."

"It was a miracle! My nurse—I think her name was Hedda—asked permission to take me to the mountains where it would be healthier. We stayed there—the two of us—in a small cabin, living on onions and molasses and tea . . . I shudder to think of it. But neither of us became ill. I returned to my home to find only my father alive—a shattered man! I was four years old."

Ferdinand's clumsy hands, in white gloves the size of an outfielder's mitt, passed a silver salver of pound cake studded with caraway seeds.

The Countess went on. "I was all my father had left in the world, and he lavished me with attention and lovely things. I adored him!"

"Did he send you away to school?" Qwilleran asked.

"I was schooled at home by private tutors, because my father refused to allow me out of his sight. We went everywhere together—to the symphony and opera and charity balls. When we traveled abroad each year we were entertained royally in Paris and always dined at the captain's table aboard ship. I called Father my best beau, and he sent me tea roses and cherry cordials . . . Ferdinand, you may pass the bonbons."

The big hands passed a tiny footed candy dish in which three chocolate-covered cherries rested on a linen doily.

Qwilleran took the opportunity to say, "You have a handsomely designed apartment, Miss Plumb."

"Thank you, Mr. . . . ."

"Qwilleran."

"Yes, my dear father designed it following one of our visits to Paris. A charming Frenchman with a little moustache spent a year in rebuilding the entire suite. I quite fell in love with him," she said, cocking her head coquettishly. "Artisans came from the Continent to do the work. It was an exciting time for a young girl."

"Do you remember any of the people who lived here at that time? Do you recall any names?"

"Oh, yes! There were the Pennimans, of course. My mother was related to them . . . and the Duxbury family; they were bankers . . . and the Teahandles and Wilburtons and Greystones. All the important families had complete suites or *pieds-à-terre*."

"How about visiting celebrities? President Coolidge? Caruso? The Barrymores?"

"I'm sure they stayed here, but . . . life was such a whirl in those days, and I was only a young girl. Forgive me if I don't remember."

"I suppose you dined in the rooftop restaurant."

"The Palm Pavilion. Yes indeed! My father and I had our own table with a lovely view, and all the serving men knew our favorite dishes. I adored bananas Foster! The captain always prepared it at our table. On nice days we would have tea on the terrace. I made my debut in the Palm Pavilion, wearing an adorable white beaded dress."

"I enjoy that same view from my apartment," Qwilleran said. "I'm staying where Dianne Bessinger used to live. I understand you knew her well."

The Countess lowered her eyes sadly. "I miss her a great deal. We used to play Scrabble twice a week. Such a pity she was struck down so early in life. She simply passed away in her sleep. Her heart failed."

Qwilleran shot a glance at Mary and found her frowning at him. Furthermore, Ferdinand was standing by with arms folded, looking grim.

Mary rose. "Thank you so much, Miss Adelaide, for inviting us."

"It was a pleasure, my dear. And Mr. Qwillen, I hope you will join me at the bridge table soon."

"Not bridge," he said. "Scrabble."

"Yes, of course. I shall look forward to seeing you again."

Ferdinand followed the two guests to the foyer and whipped out a dog-eared pad and the stub of a pencil. "Friday, Saturday, and Sunday is full up," he said. "Nobody's comin' tomorrow. She needs somebody for tomorrow." He looked menacingly at Qwilleran. "Tomorrow? Eight o'clock?" It sounded less like an invitation and more like a royal command.

"Eight o'clock will be fine," Qwilleran said as they stepped into the waiting elevator. Once in its rosewood and velvet privacy they both talked at once.

He said, "Where did she find that three-hundred-pound butler?"

Mary said, "I thought you didn't play games, Qwill."

"Her hair is like Eleanor Roosevelt's in the Thirties."

"I almost choked when you handed her that pear."

"She doesn't even know that Dianne was murdered!"

As they stepped out of the rosewood elevator on the main floor, the workaday crowd was pouring through the front door. They stared at the privileged pair.

Qwilleran said, "I'll walk out of the building with you, Mary. I want to check the parking lot. I've been here since Sunday, and five different cars have been parked in my space." As they approached the lot he asked, "May I ask you a question?"

"Of course."

"What do you think was the artist's motive for killing his patron?"

"Jealousy," she said with finality.

"You mean he had a rival?"

"Not just one," she replied with a knowing grimace. "Di liked variety."

"Were you friendly with her?"

"I admired what she was trying to accomplish, and I admit she had charisma, or people would never have rallied around SOCK the way they did."

Qwilleran stroked his moustache. "Could there have been anything political about her murder?"

"What do you mean?"

They had arrived at the entrance to the parking lot, and Mary was looking at her wristwatch.

"We'll talk about it another time. Perhaps we could have dinner some evening," he suggested.

"If we arrange it for a Sunday or Monday," she said, adopting her usual businesslike delivery, "I'm sure Roberto would like to join us."

Qwilleran said it would be a good idea. He had lost his personal interest in Mary. Yet, it was a remarkable fact that she was the only woman Koko had ever actively approved. The cat discouraged Melinda, antagonized Cokey, and feuded openly with Rosemary. As for Polly, he tolerated her because she had a soothing voice, but he endorsed Mary Duckworth because she was an opportunist, and so was he! Koko knew a kindred spirit when he sniffed one. Also in her favor was the entire case of canned lobster she had given the Siamese three years before. That's the way it was with cats!

While Mary returned to the Blue Dragon, Qwilleran zigzagged his way through the parking lot, avoiding potholes filled with rainwater. To his surprise, slot #28 was finally vacant. Now he could move the Purple Plum into its rightful space. He pulled out his car keys, but there was something wrong with the purplish-blue metallic four-door parked in #27. It appeared to have sunk into the ground! Actually, it had four flat tires.

Chapter 9

Whether the tires of the Purple Plum were slashed or the valves were loosened, it made no difference to Qwilleran. In high dudgeon he strode toward the building entrance. Halfway there he stopped and considered: If he left the scene, someone could pull into the lot and turn into his legal parking space. He returned to #28 and stood between the yellow lines—or lines that had been yellow once upon a time. He took up his position with a belligerent stance and folded arms and fierce expression made more intimidating by his rambunctious moustache.

The first car to pull into the lot was a BMW. Hmmm, Qwilleran murmured to himself. What was a BMW doing in the Casablanca parking lot? The driver parked several slots away and walked slowly toward the building entrance. It was a woman. She walked seductively. She was dressed exquisitely. She was the vision he had seen in the lobby the night before.

"Excuse me, miss," he said in his richest, most mellifluent tones. "Are you going into the building?" He was glad he was wearing a suit and tie.

"That was my intention," she replied in a silky voice.

He had no time for pleasurable reactions. "Kindly do me a favor," he asked. "Tell Mrs. Tuttle to send Rupert out here. Someone has slashed my tires." He gestured toward the dejected vehicle slumped in the adjoining slot.

"Who would have the temerity to perpetrate such a reprehensible act?" she replied.

Qwilleran thought, She's not real; she's a robot; she's programmed; she's from outer space. Calmly he said, "I was parked in his—or her—space because my own was occupied by someone else, and I suppose he—or she—resented it. Have you had any trouble like that?"

"Fortunately I seem immune to hostility," she replied. "I shall be happy to send the custodian to your assistance."

"Watch out for the puddles," he advised. "They're a foot deep."

She gave him a languid smile and walked toward the building. In a state of transfixion Qwilleran watched her go, breathing lustily into his moustache.

When Rupert arrived a few minutes later, it was determined that the tires were not slashed. Someone had tampered with the valves, and Rupert knew a garage that would come right over with portable airtanks.

"Who pays for #27?" Qwilleran demanded.

"I dunno."

"Well, as soon as the tires are inflated, I'm going to move my car into my own slot and leave it there for the rest of the winter. I'll walk, or take the bus . . . By the way, who is the woman who drives the BMW?"

"Winnie Wingfoot," said Rupert. "She's a model. Lives on Ten."

"Is that her real name?"

"I dunno. I guess so."

If Qwilleran entertained any thoughts of revenge against the reprehensible perpetrator, they were mollified by thoughts of Winnie Wingfoot. He floated up to Fourteen on Old Red, changed absentmindedly into red pajamas instead of his gray warm-up suit, and fed the cats twice. For his own dinner he phoned for pizza.

"Casablanca? What floor?" asked the order taker.

"Fourteen."

"We don't deliver in that building any higher than Three."

"Send it over. I'll meet the delivery man at the front door," Qwilleran said.

He walked down to the main floor for the sake of the exercise and encountered the jogger between Eleven and Ten. The man was running up the stairs. Between aerobic gasps he explained, "Too muddy . . . round the . . . vacant lots." Then he added, "You going . . . to bed early?"

Only then did Qwilleran realize his Freudian slip. He returned to the penthouse and changed from red pajamas into gray warm-ups.

In the lobby a white-haired man was taking his constitutional by walking briskly the length of the hallway and back, swinging his arms and taking exaggerated strides. A few stragglers were picking up their mail. The Asian woman was coming in with her two children, and Amber was on her way out.

"I've been trying to get you on the phone," she said. "Courtney wants me to bring you to dinner at his place Saturday night. You remember—the Kipper & Fine salesman."

"What's the occasion?"

"Nothing. He just likes to show off. He can be a nerd sometimes, but the food's always good—better than I cook—and he knows all the gossip."

"I accept," said Qwilleran without further deliberation.

"Cocktails at six. Come as you are," she said. "Are you waiting for someone?"

"The pizza man. By the way, Amber, I'm ashamed to admit I don't know your last name."

She said something like "Cowbell."

"Spell it."

"K-o-w-b-e-l. Here comes your pizza, Qwill. Gotta dash. I'm late."

The pizza was good—better than any he had found in Moose

County, he had to admit. He gave the Siamese a taste of the cheese and a nibble of the pepperoni. Then he pushbuttoned a pot of coffee and carried it into the library. He intended to study his Scrabble—particularly the scoring rules and the value of the various letters—in preparation for his forthcoming joust with the Countess. He unfolded the board and deployed the tiles on the teakwood-and-chrome card table, then started building crosswords, playing for premium squares as well as high-value words. Koko was on hand, watching the process in his nearsighted way. Abruptly the cat lifted his head and listened. A minute or so later, there was a knock at the apartment door.

No one had buzzed from the vestibule, so it was obviously a resident, and a fantasy flashed through Qwilleran's mind: It was the beauteous Winnie Wingfoot! Then again, he reflected, it might be Rupert. Nevertheless, he gave the mirror a quick glance, smoothed his moustache, and finger-combed his hair before opening the door.

A woman was standing there, wearing a fur coat, and it was not Winnie Wingfoot. It was Isabelle, the middle-aged tippler, and she was carrying a bottle. He regarded her without speaking.

"Hello," she said.

"Good evening," he replied coolly.

"Like a drink?" she asked, looking flirtatious and waving the bottle. Her other hand clutched the coat, and he hesitated to guess what she might have under it, if anything.

"No thanks, I'm on the wagon, but thanks for the offer," he said in a monotone intended to discourage her.

"Can I come in?" she asked.

"You must forgive me, but I'm working and I have a deadline."

"Don'cha wanna take your mind off your work?" She opened her coat, and Qwilleran's wildest surmise was confirmed.

He said, "You'd better bundle up before you catch cold." Gently he closed the door, hearing a vulgar remark as he did so.

Huffing into his moustache, he returned to the library. "That was Isabelle," he told Koko. "Too bad it wasn't Winnie. She has a better vocabulary."

At that moment he felt an uncomfortable desire to talk with Polly Duncan in Moose County, even though the eleven o'clock discount was not yet in effect. He dialed anyway.

"I'm so glad you called, Qwill," she said. "I was just thinking about you. How is life in the wicked city?"

"You'd be surprised how wicked," he said. "Today someone let the air out of my tires, and tonight a female flasher presented herself at my door."

"Oh, no! Qwill, you must have been encouraging her!"

"All I did was pick her up off the floor when she fell out of the phone booth. How are things in Moose County?"

"I'm starting to pack things to go into storage. Bootsie is helping me by jumping into every carton. He's adorable, but he's a monomaniac about food, Qwill—tries to steal it right off my fork!"

"He's growing. He'll get over it. Koko and Yum Yum have gone through all kinds of phases."

"How do they like it down there?"

"Yum Yum has discovered the waterbed and gets some kind of catly thrill out of it. Koko and I are learning to play Scrabble. I have a Scrabble date with the Countess tomorrow night."

"Is she very glamorous?" Polly inquired anxiously.

"Not exactly. She's a gracious hostess but out of touch with reality. I don't know how I'm going to talk real-estate business with her."

"Is the Casablanca as wonderful as you thought?"

"Yes and no, but I'd like to write a book about its history. I wish you were here, Polly, so we could discuss it."

"I wish I were, too. I miss you, Qwill."

"There are some interesting restaurants we could explore."

"Qwill, something has been worrying me. Suppose I move into your apartment—"

"Hold it!" he shouted into the phone. "I can't hear you!" There was a prolonged wait during which a helicopter circled overhead. "Okay, Polly. Sorry. What were you saying? A helicopter was hovering over the building and creating pandemonium. The cats hate it!"

"What's happening?" she asked.

"Who knows? They're up there every night, sometimes shining their searchlight into my window."

"Why, that's terrible! Isn't that unconstitutional?"

"Now what were you saying about moving into my apartment?"

"Suppose I move in, and then the Casablanca project falls through and you decide to come home!"

"We'll cross that bridge when we come to it," Qwilleran said. "Call me if anything interesting happens, or even if it doesn't."

"I will, dearest."

"*A bientôt,*" he said with feeling.

"*A bientôt.*"

Sometimes he wished he could find the words to express what he wanted to say to Polly. Though a professional wordsmith, he was tongue-tied with this woman of whom he was so fond, but she understood. Feeling suddenly bereft of human companionship, he considered calling Amber Kowbel but decided he was not as bereft as all that.

On the Scrabble table Koko was sitting tall in his impudent pose, with ears askew and whiskers tilted. He had been up to some kind of mischief; Qwilleran could read the signals. A brief search revealed a scattering of Scrabble tiles on the floor under the table.

"You joker! You think that's funny!"

"Rrrrrrrrrrrr," said the cat.

"What's this new noise you're making? It sounds like a Scrabble tile stuck in your throat."

Qwilleran stooped to gather up the tiles, and at the same instant Koko jumped from the table with a flip of his tail that struck the man on the cheek, stinging like a whip.

"Please! Watch your tail!"

Koko walked stiff-legged from the room, turning once to look scornfully over his shoulder. Koko's scorn had an edge like a knife.

Qwilleran wondered, Did I say something wrong? Is he trying to tell me something?

Compulsively he tried to make a word out of the tiles that Koko had dislodged: H, R, O, S, B, X, and A. On the first try he came up with SOAR, but that was worth only four points. BOAR was good for six. (He was beginning to think in terms of scoring.) HOAR was even better—seven points—but HOAX added up to fourteen. Qwilleran congratulated himself; he was getting the hang of it.

Out in the foyer Koko was warbling his new tune: "Rrrrrrrrrrr!"

Chapter 10

On Thursday morning, when Qwilleran was brushing the Siamese and giving them their daily dose of flattery, he was interrupted by a phone call from Jeff Lowell of Grinchman & Hills. "I hear you're going to do a book on the Casablanca," he said.

"News travels fast."

"I saw Mary Duckworth last night. The reason I'm calling—we have photographs in our archives of both exterior and interior, taken in 1901. You're welcome to use them. We even have shots of Harrison Plumb's Moorish suite on Twelve with its carved lattices and decorative tiles and iron gates—fantastic!"

"Was the Art Deco renovation ever photographed?"

"Not to my knowledge. Our firm wasn't involved with that."

"It should be photographed. Could you recommend someone to do it?"

"Sure could!" He mentioned a name that sounded like Sorg Butra.

"Spell it," Qwilleran asked.

"S-o-r-g B-u-t-r-a. Want me to tell him you're interested?"

"Just give me his phone number. I haven't broached the subject to the Countess as yet. Did Mary mention anything else I discussed? About the Bessinger murder?"

"No, I just saw her briefly in a theater lobby."

"I have a theory I'd like to try out on you, whenever we can get together."

"Well, I'm leaving for San Francisco right now, but I'll get in touch when I get back. Enjoyed lunch on Tuesday, Qwill."

"So did I. Have a good trip, Jeff."

"Nice guy," he said to the cats when he resumed the brushing. "I never met an architect I didn't like."

"Ik ik ik," said Koko.

"Now what does that mean?"

The phone rang again, and this time it was from the *Daily Fluxion* police bureau.

"Sure, Matt, I'm always interested in ideas," Qwilleran said. "What's on your mind? . . . Well, I don't know about that. Hames is a smart cop, but he goes overboard about Koko . . . Yes, I admit he's a remarkable cat, but . . . Okay, Matt, let me think about it. Why don't we have lunch? . . . See you at the Press Club at noon."

"That was Matt Thiggamon," he explained to the cats afterward. "He wants to do a story on you, Koko—on your sleuthing. How does that grab you?"

Koko rolled over, thrust one leg skyward, and proceeded to groom the base of his tail.

"I assume you're giving him the leg. I agree with you. We don't want any publicity, but I'm taking him to lunch anyway. I wonder what the weather is going to be."

He tuned in the newscast and learned that a law clerk who had been fired returned and shot his boss and the boss's secretary; a city councilman was found to have more than a hundred unpaid parking tickets; and the weather would be cold and overcast with a slight chance of showers. In Pickax, he reflected, WPKX would be announcing that a bow-hunter had bagged an eight-point buck, and a fourteen-year-old girl had won the quilt contest.

To create a stir at the Press Club, Qwilleran wore a plaid flannel shirt, a field jacket, and his Aussie hat. Matt said enviously, "You're really living the life, Qwill!"

They sat at a table in a far corner of the bar. "I wish I had a nickel," Qwilleran remarked, "for every time Arch Riker and I had lunch at this table."

"I hear he was a great guy," said Matt. "He left just before I joined the staff. What's he doing now?"

"He's editor and publisher of our small newspaper up north. It's called the *Moose County Something*."

"And what do you do up there?"

"I'm busier in my retirement than I was when I wrote for the *Fluxion*. Merely keeping up with the local gossip can be a full-time occupation in a small town."

They ordered French onion soup and roast beef sandwiches, and Qwilleran specified horseradish. There had been a time when every waitress in the club knew that Qwilleran liked horseradish with beef, but those days were past.

Matt said, "Is that your cat's picture in the lobby?"

"Yes, that's Koko. He's a lifetime member of the Press Club, and he has his own press card signed by the chief of police."

"Hames says he's psychic."

"All cats are psychic to a degree. If you pick up a can opener, they know whether you're going to open a can of catfood or a can of green beans. They can be sound asleep at the other end of the house, but all you have to do is *think about salmon*, and they're right there! I have to admit, though," Qwilleran said with thinly veiled pride, "that Koko goes the average cat one better. Perhaps you've heard about the pottery murders on River Road. Koko solved that case before the police knew a crime had been committed. Prior to that there was a major theft in Muggy Swamp, and then a shooting at the Villa Verandah, and later a high death rate among antique dealers in Junktown. Koko investigated all those incidents successfully—not that he did anything uncatlike. He just sniffed and scratched and shoved things around, coming up with pertinent clues. I don't want him to have any publicity, however; it might go to his head and cause him to give up sleuthing. Cats are perverse and unpredictable, like wives."

"Are you married?" Matt asked.

"I was at one time."

"For how long?"

"Long enough to become an authority on the subject."

The young reporter said, "I just got married last June and I think it's the only way to live."

"Good for you!"

The roast beef sandwiches were served, and Qwilleran had to ask for horseradish a second time. He said to Matt, "Where are you living?"

"Happy View Woods."

All young couples, Qwilleran had discovered, were paying mortgages in Happy View Woods, raising families, and worrying about crabgrass in their lawns. He himself had always preferred to live in apartments or hotels, being somewhat of a gypsy at heart. He said, "I'm staying in the penthouse apartment at the Casablanca. Does that ring a bell?"

"That's where the art dealer was murdered a couple of months ago."

"Did you see the scene of the crime?"

"No, the coverage was cut-and-dried," said the police reporter. "The murderer left a confession and killed himself. Also, there was a major airline crash at the airport on the same day, and that took precedence over everything for two weeks."

"Do you know anything about the murderer?"

"His name was Ross Rasmus, an artist. He specialized in painting *mushrooms*. Can you swallow that? He must have been crazy to begin with! He daubed his confession on a wall with red paint."

"Which wall?"

"I don't think anyone ever mentioned which wall."

The chances were, Qwilleran reasoned, that the artist went back to his studio, where he kept his paints, and daubed it on his own wall. That would be 14-B. Keestra Hedrog might know something about it. "Was there any speculation about motive?" he asked Matt.

"Well, they were lovers, you know. That was pretty well-known. She liked to discover young talent—young male talent. Everybody figured she discovered a successor to Ross Rasmus, and he was jealous. The autopsy turned up evidence of drugs. He was stoned when he did it."

"What was the weapon?"

"I don't believe the actual weapon was ever identified."

"The reason I ask: The penthouse has a lot of his paintings on the walls, each with a knife included with the mushrooms. It's a Japanese slicer, and there's one exactly like it in the kitchen."

"Oh, yeah," said Matt. "There's plenty of those around. My wife has one. She's into stir-fry."

They munched their sandwiches in silence, Qwilleran wishing he had some horseradish. After a while he said, "The artist's body landed on some guy's car. He was quoted in your story. Do you remember the name?"

"Gosh, no, I don't. That was two months ago."

At that moment a young woman in boots and a long skirt wandered over to their table, and Matt introduced her as Sasha Crispen-Schmitt of the *Morning Rampage*.

Qwilleran rose and said cordially but not truthfully that he had read her column and enjoyed it.

"Thanks. Please sit down," she said, looking at his moustache. "I've heard about you. Don't you live up north in a town with a funny name?"

"Pickax, population three thousand. And if you think that's funny, we also have a Sawdust City, Chipmunk, and Brrr, spelled B-r-r-r. Will you join us for coffee or a drink?"

"Wish I could," said Ms. Crispen-Schmitt, "but I have to get back to the office for another *paralyzing* meeting. What are you doing down here?"

"I just wanted to spend one winter away from ten-foot snowbanks and wall-to-wall ice."

Matt said, "He's staying at the old broken-down Casablanca."

"Really?" she said. "I lived there for a while myself. Why did you choose that grungy place?"

"They allow cats," Qwilleran said, "and I have two Siamese."

"How do you like the building?"

"It's interesting, if you're a masochist."

"What floor are you on?"

"Fourteen."

"Well, it's better if you're high up."

"Not when both elevators are out of order at the same time," Qwilleran told her.

"Isn't Fourteen where they had a murder a couple of months ago?"

"So they tell me."

"Well, look, I'd love to stay, but . . . maybe we can have lunch while you're here."

"By all means," said Qwilleran. When she had walked away, he said to Matt, "Attractive girl. Married?"

The reporter nodded. "To one of our sportswriters."

"Shall we have dessert, Matt? Today's special is pumpkin pie with whipped cream. I wonder if it's the real thing. One gets spoiled living half a mile from a dairy farm."

The waitress who had not brought his horseradish was now unable to say whether the whipped cream was actually from a cow.

"If you don't know, it probably isn't," Qwilleran said. "Bring me apple pie with cheese. Is it real cheese? Never mind; I'm sure it isn't. Bring me frozen yogurt."

After coffee and dessert they left the Press Club, Matt to return to police headquarters and Qwilleran to ride the Zwinger bus to the Casablanca.

"Thanks," said Matt. "I enjoyed the lunch."

"My pleasure," said Qwilleran. "And say, would you do me a favor? Check your story on the Bessinger murder and see whose car was damaged in the parking lot, will you? Then give me a ring. Here's my number."

It was quiet around the Casablanca in the early afternoon. Before climbing the crumbling steps he had a look at the parking lot. The Purple Plum was safe in slot #28, but what he really wanted to check was the row of parking spaces adjacent to the building. They were numbered 1 to 20, and directly above them was the parapet of the terrace from which Ross had jumped. Slots 21 to 40 were on the west side of the lot. Both rows were inadequately lighted after dark; a single floodlight was mounted on the side of the building midway between front and back—only one light for a very large lot. It was another management economy.

Qwilleran could not say why, but his hand went to his moustache. This luxuriant facial feature was notable not only for its size but for its response to various stimuli. Reactions of doubt or apprehension or suspicion were always accompanied by a tremor on his upper lip. He pounded his moustache with his fist as he entered the building.

Upstairs he found another envelope under his door, and he groaned, presuming that Isabelle had been there again, but this time it was a heavy ivory-colored envelope with his name inscribed in very proper handwriting. Perhaps it was from Winnie Wingfoot, he thought hopefully as he tore it open. The message, obviously written with a fountain pen and not a ballpoint, read as follows: "Would you do me the honor of dining with me tonight at seven o'clock?—Adelaide Plumb." In the lower left-hand corner she specified RSVP and gave a telephone number.

Somewhat deflated, Qwilleran called to accept.

Ferdie Le Bull answered. "Okay, I'll tell her," said the houseman. "She's having her nap. It'll be chicken hash tonight. D'you like chicken hash? I don't call that real food, but she always has chicken hash on Thursday."

"Whatever the menu, Ferdinand, please convey my message: Mr. Qwilleran accepts with pleasure."

Hanging up the phone he called out to the Siamese, "You guys will eat better than I will tonight . . . Where are you?"

Koko was sitting quietly in the foyer, gazing out the French doors to the terrace, waiting patiently for the pigeons that never came in for a landing. Yum Yum was asleep on the waterbed; she slept entirely too much since arriving at the Casablanca, Qwilleran thought.

In preparation for his soirée with the Countess he threw some shirts and socks into a shopping bag and ventured down to the basement laundry room for the first time. As Old Red slowly descended he read the following notices on the bulletin board:

WANTED TO BUY—guitar—Apt. 2-F.
FREE KITTENS—Apt. 9-B.
REWARD! Who stole cassettes from parking lot?
See mgr.

At the fourth floor Old Red came to a grinding stop, and a woman carrying a laundry bag started to board the car. Catching sight of the moustached stranger with a shopping bag, she started to back off but apparently decided to take a chance. There was no eye contact, but roguishly Qwilleran started to breathe heavily, causing her to edge closer to the door. He was feeling playful following his stimulating lunch at the Press Club and his brief dialogue with the Countess's absurd butler. When the elevator reached the bottom with a crash, the other passenger scuttled off the car, and he followed her with deliberately heavy footfalls.

The laundry room was large and dreary with one row of washers and another row of dryers, many of them labeled out of order. The peeling masonry walls had not known a paintbrush for perhaps sixty years. At that time—when family laundresses did the washing, ironing, and mangling—a cheerful environment was not thought necessary. Now the somber workplace was enlivened by a veritable gallery of prohibitions and warnings neatly printed with red and green felt markers and lavished with exclamation marks:

NO SMOKING! NO LOUD RADIO!
NO HORSING AROUND!!!
HAVE RESPECT FOR OTHERS!
CANADIAN COINS DON'T WORK!
NOT RESPONSIBLE FOR LOST WASH!
STAY WITH YOUR THINGS!!!
BALANCE YOUR LOAD!!!

Machines were churning and spinning, and one thumped noisily; not everyone had balanced his or her load. Several persons were patiently staying with their things: an old man jabbering to himself, the woman with two small children—speaking in their native tongue—another woman in a housedress and sweater, glowering at a student with his nose in a textbook who had not balanced his load. Qwilleran studied the signs for instructions:

TOO MUCH SOAP MESSES UP MACHINES!!
DON'T FEED THE MICE!!!
MOTHERS WITH BABIES—
NO DIAPERING ON MACHINES! USE RESTROOM!!

Although no stranger to laundromats, Qwilleran found sadistic pleasure in asking his fearful fellow passenger from Old Red how to use the washer, explaining in a graveyard voice that he was new in the building. She obliged without looking at him, then moved away quickly.

He balanced his load, inserted a coin, and studied the posted messages for further inspiration, no doubt from the motherly Mrs. Tuttle:

BE A GOOD NEIGHBOR! CLEAN LINT TRAP!
DON'T HOG THE DRYERS!!
NO LIQUOR! NO LOITERING!
THIS IS NOT A SOCIAL HALL!!!
ONLY ONE PERSON AT A TIME IN THE RESTROOM
OR IT WILL BE LOCKED!!!

The benches were hard and backless and not likely to encourage loitering, but Qwilleran sat down and scanned the newspapers he had brought along until—from the corner of his eye—he caught a flash of red. Rupert had sauntered into the room and was surveying it for violations.

Qwilleran beckoned to him and asked, "May I ask a question, Rupert? Why are there no pigeons on the terrace? My cats like to watch pigeons."

"Them dirty birds!" said the custodian in disgust. "Lady that lived there before, she used to feed 'em, and the parkers in the lot raised holy hell. Don't let Mrs. T catch you feedin' 'em or she'll be after you with a rollin' pin!"

Qwilleran resumed reading Sasha Crispen-Schmitt's column in the *Morning Rampage*, a shallow recital of gossip and rumors. When another tenant entered the room carrying a laundry basket, he made the mistake of looking up. It was Isabelle Wilburton, wearing a soiled housecoat.

She came directly to him. "Sorry if I offended you last night."

"No harm done," he said, returning to his newspaper.

She loaded one of the washers, and he wondered if she would remove her housecoat and throw it in, but she was still decently clothed when she sat down beside him on the uncomfortable bench.

"I get so lonely," she said. "That's my trouble. I don't have any friends except the damned rum bottle."

"The bottle can be your worst enemy. Take it from one who's been there."

"I used to have a wonderful job. I was a corporate secretary."

"What happened?"

"My boss was killed in a plane crash."

"Couldn't you get another job?"

"I didn't . . . I couldn't . . . The heart went out of me. I'd been with him twenty years, ever since business school. He was more than a boss. We used to go on business trips together, and a lot of times we'd work late at the office and have dinner sent in. I was so happy in those days."

"I suppose he was married," Qwilleran said.

Isabelle heaved an enormous sigh. "I used to shop for gifts for his wife and children. When he died, everybody felt sorry for them. Nobody felt sorry for me. Twenty years! I used to have beautiful clothes. I still have the cocktail dresses he bought me. I put them on and sit at my kitchen table and drink rum."

"Why aren't you drinking today?"

"My check hasn't come yet."

"Did he leave you a trust?"

She shook her head sadly. "It comes from my family."

"Where do they live?"

"In the suburbs. They have a big house in Muggy Swamp."

"Apparently you haven't sold your piano."

"Winnie Wingfoot looked at it, but she can't make up her mind. Do you know Winnie?"

"I've seen her in the parking lot," Qwilleran said.

"Isn't she gorgeous? If I had her looks, I'd have a lot of friends. Of course, she's younger. Could you use a piano?"

"I'm afraid not."

"Is that your washer? It stopped," Isabelle informed him.

Qwilleran transferred his clothes to a dryer and returned to the bench. "Aren't you friendly with your family?"

"They won't have anything to do with me. I guess I embarrass them. Do you have a family?"

"Only a couple of cats, but the three of us are a real family. Did you ever think of getting a cat?"

"There are lots of them around the building, but . . . I've never had a pet," she said with lack of interest.

"They're good company when you live alone—almost human."

Isabelle turned away. She looked at her fingernails. She looked at the ceiling.

Qwilleran said, "Someone on Nine is offering free kittens."

"If I just had one friend, I'd be all right," she said. "I wouldn't drink. I don't know why I don't have any friends."

"I can tell you why," he said, lowering his voice. "I had the same problem a few years ago."

"You did?"

Although he had a healthy curiosity about the secrets of others, Qwilleran was loathe to discuss his own personal history, but he recognized this was an exception. "Drinking ruined my life after I'd had a successful career in journalism."

"Did you lose someone you loved?" she asked with sympathy in her bloodshot eyes.

"I made a bad marriage and went through a shattering divorce. I started drinking heavily, and my ex-wife cracked up. Two lives ruined! So then I had a load of guilt added to my disappointment and resentment and murderous hate for my meddling in-laws. I lost my friends and couldn't hold a job. No newspaper would hire me after a couple of bad incidents, and I didn't have any convenient checks coming in the mail."

"What did you do?"

"It took a horrifying accident to make me realize I needed help. I was living like a bum in New York, and one night I was so drunk I fell off a subway platform. I'll never forget the screams of onlookers and the roar of the train coming out of the tunnel. They hauled me out just in time! Believe me, that was a sobering experience. It was also the turning point. I took the advice that had been given me and got counseling. The road back was slow and painful, but I made it! And I've never again touched alcohol. That's my story."

Isabelle's eyes were filled with tears. "Would you like to have dinner at my place tonight?" she asked hopefully. "I could thaw some spaghetti."

"I appreciate the invitation," he said, "but I have an important dinner date—so important," he added with an attempt at drollery, "that I'm washing my shirt and socks." He was relieved to see his dryer stop churning. Putting his shirts on hangers and throwing his socks and undershorts in the shopping bag, he escaped from the laundry room.

His telephone was ringing when he unlocked the door to 14-A. The caller was Matt Thiggamon. "Sorry to take so long," he said. "I got the guy's name. It's Jack Yazbro."

"Spell it."

"Y-a-z-b-r-o."

"Thanks a lot, Matt."

"Any time."

Qwilleran lost no time in going downstairs to the desk. "Mrs. Tuttle," he said, "I want to compliment you on the way you run this building. I've seen you handle a variety of situations in a very competent manner and deal with all kinds of tenants."

"Thank you," she said with her hearty smile, although it was partially canceled out by her intimidating gimlet stare. "I do my best but I didn't think anyone ever noticed."

"Even your signs in the laundry room are done with a certain flair."

"Oh, my! That makes me feel real good. Is everything all right on Fourteen?"

"Everything's fine. The skylight doesn't leak. The radiators are behaving. The sunsets are spectacular. Too bad this building is going to be torn down. Do you know when?"

She shrugged. "Nobody tells me a thing! I just take one day at a time and trust in the Lord."

"One question: Do you happen to know where Mr. Yazbro parks his car?"

"Wait a bit. I'll look it up in the rent book." She leafed through a loose-leaf ledger. "I remember he changed his parking space a while back. He always liked to park against the building, but . . ."

"But what?" Qwilleran asked when she failed to finish the sentence.

"Something fell on his car, and he asked to be changed."

"Do things often drop on cars parked near the building?" he asked slyly.

Mrs. Tuttle glanced up sharply from the ledger. "We used to have trouble with pigeons. Don't you go feeding them, now! Here it is—Mr. Yazbro. He was in #18. Now he has #27." She slapped the book shut.

Twenty-seven, she said.

"Thank you, Mrs. Tuttle. Keep up the good work!"

Qwilleran made a beeline for the parking lot. He had been parked in #27 when someone tampered with his tires. Now there was a minivan parked there. The slot had been vacant during the afternoon. Yazbro had just come home from work—that is, if the minivan belonged to Yazbro. It was impossible to be certain considering the disorganized parking system. He recorded the license number on a scrap of paper and returned to the front desk, waving it at Mrs. Tuttle.

"Sorry to bother you again," he said, "but is this Mr. Yazbro's license number?"

She consulted the ledger again, and the two numbers tallied. "Is anything wrong?" she asked.

"There certainly is! Yazbro is the snake who let the air out of my tires yesterday, and I'd like to discuss it with him. What's his apartment number?"

"He's in 4-K. I hope there won't be any trouble, Mr. Qwilleran. Do you want Rupert to go up with you?"

"No, thank you. It won't be necessary."

CHAPTER 11

Riding Old Red up to Yazbro's apartment on Four, Qwilleran had plenty of time to plan his confrontation with the man who had deflated his tires. He had dealt with villains before, and he knew how to bring them to their knees without incurring hostility. He was a good actor and could always carry it off. The trick was to open with friendly small talk, throw in a little prevarication, and then catch them off-base with an accusation and a warning that was sinister but not too threatening. He knocked on the door of 4-K with authority but not belligerence; that was another important detail. Then he waited. He knocked again.

A voice from within shouted, "Who zat?"

"Your neighbor, Mr. Yazbro," he replied in an ingratiating voice.

Qwilleran, standing six feet two and weighing a solid two twenty, did not consider himself a small man, but the giant with bulging muscles and aggressive jaw who answered his knock—totally filling the doorway, grasping a beer bottle by the neck, and stripped to the waist—made him feel like a pygmy.

"Mr. Yazbro?" he asked with poise that was admirable.

"Yeah."

"Do you drive a minivan and park in #27?"

"Yeah."

No one had ever called Qwilleran a coward, but he knew the better part of valor, and he was a master at inventing the quick lie. "I believe you left your parking lights on," he said agreeably. "Just thought you'd like to know." Then, without waiting to hear Yazbro's grunts of rage, he walked casually to the elevator and pressed the UP button for Old Green. The giant soon followed, rattling his car keys and muttering to himself, and pressed the DOWN button for Old Red.

"We've had a lot of rain lately," Qwilleran said pleasantly.

"Yeah," said Yazbro, as Old Green opened its door and transported Qwilleran, inch by groaning inch, to Fourteen.

The Siamese met him at the door. "Time for dinner?" he asked them.

A reply of sorts rattled in Koko's throat. "Rrrrrrrrrrrr."

"Does that mean you want roast raccoon rare . . . or ragout of rabbit?"

"Rrrrrrrrrrrr," Koko gargled, and Qwilleran opened a can of red salmon, reflecting that he might have to take the cat to the veterinarian for a laryngoscopy.

While they devoured the salmon with rapt concentration, he analyzed Koko's current behavior. Besides making ugly noises in his throat, he prowled restlessly and followed Qwilleran everywhere, patently bored. It was understandable. Yum Yum was sleeping a lot and providing little companionship; there were no pigeons for entertainment; and Qwilleran himself had been absent a great deal or preoccupied with matters like Scrabble or the Grinchman & Hills report.

"Okay, you guys," he said. "Let's have some fun." He produced the new leather harnesses, jiggling them tantalizingly.

Koko had been harnessed before and was eager to buckle up, but Yum Yum resisted the collaring and girdling. Although usually susceptible to blandishments, she disregarded remarks that the blue leather matched her eyes and enhanced her fawn-colored fur. She squirmed; she kicked; she snapped her jaws. When Qwilleran tugged the leash, she refused to walk or even to stand on her four feet. He tugged harder and she played dead. When he picked her up and set her on her feet, she toppled over as if there were not a bone or muscle in her body and lay there, inert, not moving a whisker.

"You're an uncooperative, unappreciative, impossible wench!" he said. "I'll remember this the next time you want to take possession of my lap."

Meanwhile Koko was prancing about the room, dragging his leash. He was a veteran at this. Some of his greatest adventures had happened at the end of a twelve-foot nylon cord. Now he made it clear that he wanted to explore the terrace.

"It'll be cold," Qwilleran warned him.

"Yow," Koko replied.

"And there are no pigeons."

"Yow!"

"And it's getting dark."

"YOW!" Koko said vehemently, tugging toward the exit.

On the terrace he led the way impatiently, pulling Qwilleran toward the front of the building and then all the way back to the rear. At one point the cat stopped abruptly and turned toward the parapet. Qwilleran tightened his hold on the leash as Koko prepared to jump on the stone baluster. Teetering on the railing with his four feet bunched together, he peered over the edge. Holding the leash taut, Qwilleran also looked over the railing. Directly below was parking slot #18, the number painted on the tarmac in faded yellow paint.

"Incredible!" said Qwilleran.

"Rrrrrrrrrrrr," said Koko.

"Let's go inside. It's chilly."

Koko refused to move, and when Qwilleran grabbed him about the middle, his body was tense and his tail curled stiffly.

Why, Qwilleran wondered as he carried the cat back indoors, did Ross walk, run, or stagger a hundred feet down the terrace in order to jump on Yazbro's car? Even more mystifying was the next question: How did Koko know the exact spot where it happened?

Back in the apartment he found Yum Yum asleep on the waterbed—harness, leash and all. Gently Qwilleran rolled her over, unbuckling the strap and drawing the collar over her head. Without opening her eyes she purred. And why not? She had won the argument. She had had the last word.

"Just like a female!" Qwilleran muttered.

It was time to dress for dinner with the Countess, and he brought his dark blue suit and white shirt from the closet, marveling that he had worn suits twice in two days. In Moose County he had worn them twice in three years, once for a wedding and once for a funeral. To his funeral suit he now added a red tie to elevate its mood. A striped shirt would have had more snap, but sartorial niceties were not in Qwilleran's field of interest.

This social event was one he hardly approached with keen anticipation. Nevertheless, years of carrying out unattractive assignments for tyrannical editors had disciplined him into automatic performance of duty. Also, there was the prospect of a book on the Casablanca—a coffee-table book in folio format with large photographs on good paper. The K Fund would underwrite it.

This was the afternoon, he remembered, that the Klingenschoen board was scheduled to meet, Hasselrich presenting the Casablanca proposition with quivering excitement and anecdotes about spinach timbales. As if his thoughts were telepathic, the phone rang at that moment, and Hasselrich was on the line, advising him that the board had voted unanimously to foot the bill for saving the Casablanca, leaving the amount entirely to Qwilleran's discretion.

"This may not be the last," said the attorney. "A resolution was passed to pursue similar ventures in the public interest as a means of enhancing the Klingenschoen image."

Qwilleran consulted his watch. The invitation was for seven o'clock, and it was not yet six. He telephoned Mary Duckworth. "Are you busy? Do you have a few minutes? I'd like to drop in for a briefing before I ascend to Art Deco heaven in the rosewood chariot. Also, I have good news!"

"Yes! Come along," she said. "Ring the bell. The shop's closed."

In his dark blue suit, with a raincoat over his arm, Qwilleran rode down on Old Green. A red-haired woman boarded the car at Nine, and he could feel her staring at him. He straightened his shoulders and concentrated on watching the floor indicator.

Since some of the lights were inoperative, the car descended from eight to five to two to one. In the lobby Mrs. Tuttle looked up from her knitting with a smile of admiration. Two old ladies in quilted bathrobes squinted at him without scowling. It was the dark suit, he decided; he should wear it more often instead of waiting for another funeral.

As he strode down Zwinger Boulevard toward the Blue Dragon, he was stopped by a woman walking a Dalmatian. "Excuse me, do you know what time it is?" she asked.

"My watch says six-ten."

"You're new in the neighborhood."

"Just visiting," he said as he saluted courteously and went on his way.

Next it was Mary Duckworth's turn to exclaim. "You look tremendously attractive, Qwill!" she said. "Adelaide will be swept off her feet! She phoned me today—first time she has ever called—and said how much she enjoyed your company. She thanked me for taking you to tea."

"It's only because I play Scrabble."

"No, I think she liked your moustache. Or it was the Bosc pear. Whatever it was, you've kindled a light in the old girl's eyes."

"From the appearance of the old girl's eyes," Qwilleran said, "she has cataracts. Why doesn't she have surgery?"

"It may be that she doesn't want to see any better than she does. Did you notice that the windows have frosted glass? She wants time to stand still, circa 1935. But she can see the playing cards well enough—and the game board! . . . What's your good news?"

They sat in the shop, Qwilleran in a genuine Chippendale corner chair and Mary on a Chinese ebony throne inlaid with mother-of-pearl.

He said, "The Klingenschoen Fund has given me carte blanche for the Casablanca preservation."

"Wonderful! But I'm not surprised. After all, it's your own money, isn't it? My father says that's no secret in financial circles."

"It won't actually be mine for another two years. But that's neither here nor there. The crucial question is: Will I be able to convince the Countess to sell?"

"The way things look," said Mary, "you should have no problem. Are you looking forward to the evening?"

"I find the prospect challenging but the environment depressing, like a glamorous old movie palace that hasn't shown films since World War Two."

"You must remember," she said, "that an interior acquires a certain patina after sixty years, and the Plumb apartment is museum quality. There's a large vase in the drawing room, decorated with flowers and nude women. I don't know whether you noticed it—"

"I noticed it."

"That piece alone is worth thousands of dollars on today's market. It's a René Buthaud."

"Spell that."

"B-u-t-h-a-u-d. We have a shop in Junktown that specializes in Art Deco, and the lowest price tag is in four figures."

"I've been meaning to ask you, Mary," he said. "How long have you known the Countess?"

"I didn't meet her until I joined SOCK and Di Bessinger enlisted me for backgammon, but I've heard the Adelaide legend all my life."

"And what might that be?" Qwilleran's curiosity caused his moustache to bristle.

"Not anything you'd want to put in your book, but it was common gossip in social circles in the Thirties, according to my mother."

"Well, let's have it!"

"This is a true story," she began. "Soon after Adelaide made her debut she became affianced to a man who was considered a great catch, provided a girl had money. He was penniless but handsome and charming and from good stock. Adelaide was the lucky girl and the envy of her set. Then . . . the economy collapsed, the banks closed, and Harrison Plumb was in desperate straits. He had never been financially astute, my father said, and he had thrown away millions on the Art Deco renovation. But now half the units of Casablanca were vacant, and the remaining tenants lacked the cash to pay the rent. The building had been his passion for thirty years, and he was about to lose it. Suddenly three astounding things happened: Adelaide broke her engagement; her father was solvent once more; and one of her Penniman cousins married the jilted man."

"Are the obvious deductions true?" Qwilleran asked.

"There's no doubt about it. Adelaide bartered her fiancé for millions to save the Casablanca and save her dear father from ruin. And in those days a million was a lot of money."

"That says something about Adelaide, but I'm not sure what," Qwilleran remarked. "Was it noble sacrifice or cold calculation?"

"We think it was a painful, selfless gesture; right afterward she dropped out of the social scene completely. Sadly, her father died within months, and the Casablanca never regained its prestige."

"How old was she when this happened?"

"Eighteen, I believe."

"She gives the impression of being satisfied with her choice. Who handles her financial affairs?"

"After her father's death her Penniman relatives advised her to invest his life insurance and exploit the Casablanca. Naturally the Pennimans are now advising her to sell—"

"—to Penniman, Greystone & Fleudd, of course. And you expect me to buck that kind of competition? You're a dreamer."

"You have a strong ally, though, in her love for the building and for her father's memory. You can do it, Qwill!"

Huffing into his moustache, he stood up to leave. "Well, wish me luck . . . What's that thing?" He pointed to a small decorative object.

"It's art glass—a pillbox—Art Deco design, probably seventy-five years old."

"Would she like it?"

"She'd love it! Even more than the Bosc pear."

"I'll buy it," he said.

"Take it, with my compliments." Mary removed the price tag. "I'll put it in a velvet sack."

With the velvet sack in his pocket, Qwilleran paid his second visit to the Plumb Palace on Twelve. As he waited for the elevator at the bronze door, the feisty Mrs. Button came hobbling down the hall with her cane.

"My! You do look handsome!" she said in a high, cracked voice. "My late husband always looked handsome in a dark suit. Every Thursday evening he would put on his dinner coat and I would put on a long dress, and we would go to the symphony. We always sat in a first-tier box. Are you going up to play cards with Adelaide? Have a lovely evening."

Mrs. Button hobbled as far as the front door, then turned and hobbled back again—one of several ambulatory invalids who took their prescribed exercise in the hallways of the Casablanca. Qwilleran thought, If the building reverts to its original palatial character, what will happen to the old people? And the students? And Isabelle? And Mrs. Tuttle and Rupert?

Pondering this he rode up to Twelve in the rosewood elevator and was admitted by Ferdinand, looming huge in his coral-colored coat. "It's not gonna be chicken hash," were the houseman's first words. "It's gonna be shrimp. I dunno why. It's always chicken hash on Thursday."

The hostess came forward with hands extended and head tilted prettily to one side. She had been tilting her head prettily for so many years that one shoulder was now higher than the other. Yesterday Qwilleran thought her posturings and obsessions were ludicrous; today, having heard the Adelaide legend, he found her a pathetic figure, despite her turquoise chiffon hostess gown with floating scarfs and square-cut onyx and diamond jewelry.

"So good to see you again, Mr. Qwillen," she said.

He sat in the Bibendum chair, and Ferdinand served heavily watered grapejuice in square-cut stemware. Qwilleran raised his glass in a toast. "To gracious ladies in enchanted palaces!"

The sad little Countess inclined her head in acknowledgment. "Have you had an interesting day?" she asked.

"I spent the day looking forward to this evening and selecting this trinket for you." He presented the velvet sack.

With cries of delight she extracted the Art Deco pillbox. "Oh, thank you, Mr. Qwillen! It's French Modern! I shall put this in my boudoir."

"I thought it would be in keeping with the stunning ambiance you have created. Is that a René Buthaud vase on the mantel?" he asked, flaunting his newly acquired knowledge.

"Yes, and it means so much to me. It contains the ashes of my dear father. He was such a handsome and cultivated gentleman! How he loved to take me to Paris—to the opera and museums and salons!"

"Did you meet Gertrude Stein?"

"We attended her salon. I was a very young girl, but I remember meeting some dashing young men. I think they were writers."

"Hemingway? Fitzgerald?"

She raised her hands in a gracefully helpless gesture. "That was so long ago. Forgive me if I don't remember."

At that moment Ferdinand made his menacing appearance and announced in a muscle-bound growl, "Dinner's served."

It was served on square-cut dinnerware on a round ebony table in a circular dining room paneled in black, turquoise, and mirror, its perimeter lighted with torchères. The entrée was shrimp Newburgh, preceded by a slice of pâté and followed by that favorite of the Twenties, Waldorf salad. Then Ferdinand prepared bananas Foster in a chafing dish with heavy-handed competence and a disdainful expression meaning that this was not real food.

During dinner the conversation lurched rather than flowed, their voices sounding hollow in the vaultlike room. Qwilleran was relieved when they moved to the library for coffee and Scrabble. Here he proceeded to amaze his hostess by spelling such high-scoring words as ZANY and QIVIUT, and once he retripled. She was a good player and she seemed to relish the challenge. She was a different woman at the game table.

At the end she said, "This has been a most enjoyable evening. I hope you will come again, Mr. Qwillen."

"Enough of formality," he said. "Could you bring yourself to call me Qwill. It's good for seventeen points."

"I must correct you," she said merrily. "Fourteen points."

"Seventeen," he insisted. "I spell it with a QW."

"Then you must call me Zizou, my father's pet name for me. It's worth twenty-three!" Her laughter was so giddy that Ferdinand made an alarmed appearance in the doorway.

"May I beg a favor of you, Zizou?" Qwilleran asked, taking advantage of her happy mood. "Yesterday I mentioned writing a book about the Casablanca. Would you consent to having your apartment photographed?"

"Would you take my picture, too?" she answered coyly.

"By all means. Sitting on the sofa, pouring tea."

"That would be quite exciting. What should I wear?"

"You always look beautiful, whatever you wear."

"Do you have a camera?"

"Yes, but not good enough for this. I'd hire an architectural photographer. He could take some striking views of these rooms."

"Would he photograph all of them?"

"All that you wish to have photographed."

"Oh, dear! I wonder if my dear father would approve."

Qwilleran launched his proposal. "He would approve enthusiastically, and there is something else that your father would want you to do. He would realize that buildings, like people, get tired in their old age. They need rejuvenation. If he were here, he would know that the Casablanca is badly in need of repair, from the roof to the basement."

Shocked at the suggestion, the Countess fluttered her hands about her jewelry. "I find my suite quite—quite satisfactory."

"That's because you don't venture beyond your magnificent copper doors, Zizou. This may be painful for you to contemplate, but your palace is in bad condition, and there are people who think it should be torn down."

She stiffened. "That will never happen!"

"Some of the people who play bridge with you are asking to

buy the building, are they not? If you sell to them, they'll tear it down. To save the Casablanca you need a partner—someone who appreciates the building as much as you do." (Careful, he thought; it sounds like a marriage proposal. Ferdie Le Bull was around the corner, listening.) "You need a financial partner," he went on, "who will put money into its renovation and restore it to its original beauty. Your father would approve of a partnership. When he built this palace in 1901, he had an architect for a partner. A financial partner would be the beginning of a new life for the Casablanca."

The expression in her clouded eyes told him that the concept was beyond her comprehension. Her brain was geared for grand slams and retriples. Her face was a blank. She was withdrawing.

As if sensing a crisis, Ferdinand made his clumsy entrance. "Want me to bring the tea?"

Once more the Countess cocked her head prettily and said in her debutante voice, "Would you like a cup of camomile tea before you leave, Mr. Qwillen?"

"No, thank you," he said rising. "It has been an enjoyable evening, but I must say good night, Miss Plumb." He bowed out, and the glowering houseman showed him to the door.

Nibbling at his moustache, Qwilleran rode down to the main floor in luxury and rode up to Fourteen in the dismal clutches of Old Green. Ignoring Koko's greeting at the door he went directly to the telephone and called Polly Duncan.

"I crashed!" he announced without preamble. "I broached the subject of restoration to the Countess and hit a stone wall."

"That's too bad," she said soothingly but not earnestly.

"She's been out-of-touch for sixty years. She doesn't know what's happening and doesn't want to know. One can't reason with her."

"Perhaps you should consider this setback a signal from your tutelary genius, telling you to forget the Casablanca and come home."

"I can't give up so easily. The K Fund okayed the investment today, and it would be embarrassing—"

"Sleep on it," Polly advised. "Tomorrow it will be clear what you should do, but I wish you would seriously consider coming home. Today on the radio they reported a shooting in an office building down there. A man killed a lawyer and his secretary."

"That was a disgruntled law clerk who had been fired," Qwilleran explained.

"Next time it could be a disgruntled motorist who doesn't like the way you change lanes on the freeway," she said sharply. "You have a duty to play it safe, like English royalty."

"Hmff," Qwilleran grumbled. He took time to groom his moustache with his fingertips before changing the subject. "How's everything with you?"

"I may have some good news, Qwill. There's a chance that old Mrs. Gage on Goodwinter Boulevard will rent her carriage house."

"What about Bootsie?"

"She doesn't object to cats. How are the Siamese?"

"Yum Yum is rather lethargic and Koko is acting strangely," he said.

"They're homesick for Pickax," Polly said cunningly, adding weight to her argument. She knew he would return for the cats' well-being if not for his own. "What else did you do today?"

"I had lunch at the Press Club, but the service was terrible, and the food isn't as good as it used to be. I took Koko for a walk on the terrace, and I did some laundry in the basement of the building."

They rambled on like comfortable old marrieds until Polly ended the conversation with, "Think about what I said, dearest, and call me about your decision." She knew that Qwilleran liked to limit his long-distance calls to five minutes.

"*A bientôt.*"

"*A bientôt.*"

His frustration was subsiding, and he was about to relieve it further with a large dish of ice cream, when he received an urgent phone call from Amber, asking if he had seen the night edition of Friday's *Morning Rampage*. "You're in Sasha Crispen-Schmitt's column!" she announced.

"I haven't seen the paper. Read it to me."

"You won't like it," she said, and then read: " 'Guess who's staying at the Casablanca in the penthouse apartment of the late Diane Bessinger! None other than Jim Qwilleran, former *Daily Fluxion* writer who inherited untold millions and moved to a small town that no one ever heard of. Would anyone care to put two and two together? Our guess: Qwill is here to bankroll the preservation of the Casablanca, which so many local bigwigs want to tear down. Get your ringside tickets for the Battle of the Bucks!' "

Chapter 12

Early Friday morning Qwilleran called Mary Duckworth. "Have you seen the *Morning Rampage*?" he asked abruptly.

"I've just finished reading about you. I loathe that kind of journalism! Where did they get their information?"

"I was lunching with a *Fluxion* reporter at the Press Club, and Sasha what's her name came to our table. The guy told her I'm staying at the Casablanca. In retrospect I'm convinced her appearance at our table was not accidental. It somehow leaked out that the Klingenschoen Fund is interested in backing SOCK, and she was snooping for information."

Mary said, "I wonder what effect the item will have."

"No doubt the developers will step up their campaign. The city might find an excuse for condemnation proceedings. Or— and this is a wild supposition—Adelaide's Penniman cousins might conspire to find her mentally incompetent. With their unholy influence in this town, they could swing it! But here's the real setback, Mary. I got nowhere with Adelaide last night, although the evening started well. After Scrabble we were on first-name terms. Then I started to talk business, as diplomatically as I could, and she retired into her shell. It's like trying to save a sailor from drowning when he doesn't know his boat is leaking."

"What can we do?"

"I'd like to discuss it with Roberto. He used to be her attorney, you told me. Surely he learned how to get through to her. Can we pry him loose from his kitchen long enough for a conference?"

"Sunday evening is his night off."

"Then let's get together on Sunday. You line it up. Let me know when."

Qwilleran was in a bad humor. He paced the floor for a while, accidentally stepping on a tail or two, before deciding that ham and eggs would improve his disposition. But first he tuned in the radio station that offered round-the-clock news and weather. He learned that the thirty-seventh youth had been shot in a local high school and the temperature would be mild with high humidity resulting in increased smog.

On the way out of the building he was passing the manager's desk when a commotion at the rear of the main floor indicated that something or someone was being brought down on the freight elevator. He watched while ambulance attendants whisked a covered body to the front door.

"Who's that?" he asked Mrs. Tuttle.

"Mrs. Button, the dear soul."

"She talked to me last night, and she was in fine shape."

"That's the way it goes. The ways of the Lord are mysterious. Have you decided whether you'd like cleaning help, Mr. Qwilleran? Mrs. Jasper is available on Mondays."

"Okay, send her up," he said.

"Oh, look what we have here!" Old Green had arrived at the main floor, and Isabelle Wilburton stepped out of the car, cradling a kitten in her arms—white with orange head and tail.

"Isn't this the cutest, funniest thing you ever saw?" she gushed.

"He's so sweet! What are you going to call him?" asked Mrs. Tuttle.

"It's a girl. I'm going to call her Sweetie Pie. I got her from the people in 9-B."

"How old is she?"

Qwilleran edged away from the desk and went out to breakfast.

Putting the Countess out of his mind, he spent most of the day writing a column on the Casablanca for publication in the *Moose County Something*. The problem was: How to make the subject credible to north country readers when he could hardly believe it himself. While working, he evicted the Siamese from the library, an unfriendly act that aroused the indignation of Koko. The cat prowled outside the closed door muttering his new intestinal "Rrrrrrrrr" as if he were about to regurgitate. After listening to the unsettling performance for half an hour, Qwilleran yanked open the library door.

"What's your problem?" he demanded.

Koko ran to the end of the foyer, where the French doors led to the terrace, but it was not the outdoors that interested him; it was the bloody butcher block painting. Standing on his hind legs with his head weaving from left to right like a cobra, he uttered his gagging guttural.

"Frankly, I feel the same way about it," Qwilleran said. Not only was the subject matter nauseating but the canvas was hung in a makeshift way, off-center and too low. With suspicion teasing his upper lip, he lifted the painting down from its hanger.

Immediately Koko stretched to his full length and sniffed the mushroom-tinted wall. Compared with the adjoining walls it looked freshly painted. Qwilleran, examining it closely, detected some unevenness enough to feel with his fingertips, and when the cat started prancing in circles with his back arched and his tail bushed, it was time to take the matter seriously. Qwilleran removed the shade from a table lamp and used the bare bulb to sidelight the wall surface. His suspicions were confirmed. The oblique light accentuated some crude daubing under the recent paint job. Large block letters in three ragged lines spelled out:

FORGIVE
ME
DIANE

There was a signature: two Rs, back to back.

So this was the confession! The management, in preparation

for Qwilleran's arrival, had painted over it and hung a picture for further camouflage. Did Koko smell fresh paint? Or did he know it concealed something of interest? He was adept at detecting anything out of order or out of place.

"You're a clever fellow," he said to the cat, who bounded away to the kitchen and looked pointedly at his empty plate. As Qwilleran was giving him a treat, the telephone rang, and he took the call in the library. It was a familiar voice from Moose County.

"Hey, Qwill, I've just been reading about you in the out-state edition of the *Rampage*," said Arch Riker.

"Dammit! I didn't want the competition to know why I'm here," Qwilleran replied. "My story is that I'm here to write a book on the Casablanca, which is more or less true, and to get away from the severe winter up north."

"Skip the book and send us some copy," said the editor.

"I'm working on it. I was interrupted a few minutes ago by our resident investigator. He dredged up some evidence in connection with a murder-suicide incident in this apartment."

"What murder? What suicide? You didn't tell me anything about a crime."

"It was a lovers' quarrel, so they say, but when Old Nosey starts sniffing around in that significant way of his, my suspicions start working overtime."

"Now, back up, Qwill. Don't go charging into something that doesn't concern you," Riker warned him. "Just bear down on completing your original mission and hightail it back here while the roads are still open. We've been lucky so far—no snow—but it's on the way down from Canada. I wish they'd export more cheese and less weather."

Qwilleran said neither yes nor no; he disliked being told what to do. "If you talk to Polly, don't mention the murder," he said. "She worries, you know. She thinks murder is contagious, like measles."

When he concluded the phone call, Koko was sitting tall on the desk, looking hopeful, yearning for attention, and Qwilleran felt sorry for him. In the old days they had invented a game with the unabridged dictionary, which amused them both. "Okay, let's see what you and I can do with Scrabble," he said to the cat, as he scattered the tiles over the surface of the card table. "You fish out some letters, and I'll see if I can make a word."

Koko looked down at the assortment of small squares in his nearsighted way and did nothing until Qwilleran pawed at the tiles himself. Then the cat got the idea and withdrew E, H, I, S, A, P, and W. In a matter of seconds Qwilleran had spelled WHIPS.

"Those letters add up to thirteen points," he explained, "and the ones I didn't use add up to two. That's thirteen to two in my favor. If you want to score high, you have to choose consonants like X and Q and not too many vowels."

As if he understood, Koko proceeded to improve his game, and the score was a near-tie when it was time for Qwilleran to quit and dress for the evening. "Nothing personal," he said to the cat, "but I found the game more stimulating with the Countess."

He taxied downtown and dined at a middle-eastern restaurant before heading for the vernissage at the Bessinger-Todd Gallery. In the canyons of the financial district the Friday night hush as disturbed by a commotion around the gallery as cars pulled up one after the other. Three valets in red jumpsuits were kept hopping, and the hubbub within the building could be heard out on the sidewalk. Guests were pouring through the front door into an exhibit space already packed with art lovers, although art was not their prime interest. They milled about, drinking champagne, and shouting to be heard above the clangor of the music, while the musicians increased their volume in order to be heard above the din of voices. The center of attention seemed to be a young man with shoulder-length blond hair, who stood head and shoulders above all the rest.

Qwilleran saw no one he knew, apart from Jerome Todd and the sour-faced critic from the *Daily Fluxion*. He was not interested in the bar, and the buffet was engulfed by hungry guests, four deep. As for the art, he saw nothing he would care to hang on the walls of his remodeled barn, if he had one. The focal point of the exhibition was a trio of large canvases depicting ravenous eaters devouring fast food, obviously by the same artist who had painted the spaghetti orgy in 14-A.

On the balcony, away from the press of bodies, he found a more intimate collection of ceramics, blown glass, stainless steel sculpture and bronzes, as well as more breathing space. He was particularly curious about some ceramic discs displayed on small easels. Looking like limp piecrust, paper-thin, they were embellished with wavy sheaves of paper-thin clay and fired in smoky mushroom tones.

As he studied them with baffled interest, a hearty voice behind him said, "I'll be damned if it isn't the best-looking moustache east of the Mississippi!"

He turned to see a tall, gaunt woman with straight gray hair and gray bangs, and he recognized the city's dean of potters. "Inga Berry!" he exclaimed. "What a pleasure!"

"Qwill, I thought you were dead until I read about you in today's paper. Is it true what they said?"

"Never believe anything you read in the *Morning Rampage*," he cautioned. "Will you explain these things to me?" He pointed to the ceramic discs.

"Do you like this goofy stuff?" she asked with a challenging frown. Inga Berry was known for her large-scale ceramic pots thrown on the wheel and intricately glazed.

"They appeal to me for some obscure reason," he said, "probably because they look like something to eat. I wouldn't mind buying one."

The potter pounded his lapel with her fist. "Good boy! These are my current indiscretions in clay. I call them floppy discs."

"What happened to your spectacular pots?"

She held up two misshapen hands. "Arthritis. When your thumbs start to go, you can't throw pots on a wheel, but these things I can do with a rolling pin."

"Congratulations on your indiscretions. How do you get the appetizing effect?"

"Smoke-fired bisque."

"Your glass is empty, Inga. May I bring you some champagne?"

She made a grimace of distaste. "I can drink a gallon of this stuff without getting a glow. Let's get out of this madhouse and get some real hooch." She pushed back her bangs with a nervous hand.

Qwilleran shouldered a way through the crowd, the potter following with a slight limp. "Good show, Jerry!" she called out to Todd as they left, and Qwilleran threw the proprietor a complimentary hand signal that was more polite than honest.

Out on the sidewalk Inga said, "Whew! I can't stand crowds anymore. I must be getting old. The Bessinger-Todd openings never attracted a crowd like this before all the lurid publicity."

"Do you have a car, Inga?" he asked.

"I came on the bus. A car's too much of a problem in the city, especially at my age."

"Then we'll take a taxi . . . Valet! Cab, please."

"I'm going on eighty, you know," said Inga, smoothing her ruffled bangs. "That's when life begins. Nothing is expected of you, and you're forgiven for everything."

"Are you still teaching at the arts and crafts school?"

"Retired last year. Glad to get out of that cesspool of twaddle. When I was young we had something to say, and we were damn good at saying it, but today . . ."

Qwilleran handed her into a taxi. "How about going to my place at the Casablanca? I happen to have some bourbon."

"Hot diggity! You're speaking my language. I spent some giddy hours at the Casablanca in the Thirties. The rents went down, and a lot of artists moved in and gave wild parties—beer in the bathtubs and nude models in the elevators! Those were the days! We knew how to have fun." When the cab pulled up in front of the building, she said, "This place will be gone soon. I signed a petition for SOCK, but it won't do any good. If the Pennimans and the city fathers get their heads together and want the building torn down, it'll disappear overnight."

"You ride the elevator at your own risk," he warned as they boarded Old Green.

"Do you still have your beautiful cats?"

"More accurately, they have me. At this moment Koko knows we're on the way up to Fourteen, and he'll greet us at the door. Did you ever see the Bessinger apartment?"

"No, but I've heard a lot about it. Her murder was something I can't get through my noodle. She was a good woman. I don't know about her private life, but she was always honest and fair with artists, and that's more than I can say about most dealers. And more than I can say about her husband."

"I didn't know she was married, although I think the obituary mentioned daughters."

"Oh, sure! She and Jerome Todd were married for years in Des Moines. They divorced after they came here."

"Apparently it was amicable."

"Yes and no, according to scuttlebutt. To tell the awful truth, I never knew what she could see in Todd. He's such a cold fish! But they stayed together as business partners. She took care of the talent; and he was a good businessman—good for himself, that is; not so good for the artists he represents."

Old Green finally stumbled up to the top and stopped with a bang as if it had hit the roof, and when Qwilleran unlocked the door to 14-A and switched on the foyer lights, Koko walked to greet them with stately gait and lofty ears.

"Hello, you swanky rascal," said Inga. "Look at that noble nose! Look at that tapered tail! Talk about line and design! Where's the other one?"

"Probably asleep on the waterbed."

The potter gazed around the foyer with an artist's eye. "Pretty posh!"

"Wait till you see the gallery!" Qwilleran opened the French doors and turned on the track lights that illuminated the mushroom paintings, the conversation pit, and the well-stocked bar. "We'll have our drinks in the library, but I wanted you to see the artwork."

Inga nodded. "I knew Ross when he was in art school, before he got into mushrooms and found himself. Those paintings are worth plenty now . . . What's the cat doing?" Koko was burrowing under the dhurrie in front of the bar.

"Merely expressing his joy at seeing you again, Inga." He was loading a tray with bourbon, mineral water, glasses, and an ice bucket. "Go into the library and look at the art books while I get ice from the kitchen."

When he carried the tray into the library, Inga was exclaiming over the collection. "If they have an estate sale, I'll be the first in line. That's the only way I can afford books like these."

Qwilleran poured the drinks. "There won't be any bargains, Inga. The murder will give all of this stuff a juicy provenance, and the prices will skyrocket."

"Disgusting, isn't it?" she said. "Murder used to be shocking. Now it's an opportunity for profiteering." She raised her glass. "Here's to the memory of two good kids. I don't understand how Ross could do it."

"The autopsy showed drug use."

She shook her head woefully. "I can't picture Ross as a druggie. He was kind of a health nut, you know. He didn't go in for weight lifting or jogging or anything like that, but he had definite ideas about food. He was the next best thing to a vegetarian."

"What about his relationship with Lady Di?"

"Ah, there's the fly in the soup!" Inga said. "From what I hear, that's what broke up her marriage."

"They say Ross's motive was jealousy. Di had found a new protégé."

Inga scowled into her gray bangs. "Rewayne Wilk. He was there tonight."

"Spell it," Qwilleran requested.

"R-e-w-a-y-n-e W-i-l-k. Big blond with long hair and a cleft chin. Maybe you saw his three masterworks. He calls them *The Pizza Eaters*, *The Hot Dog Eaters*, and *The Wing Ding Eaters*. All I can say is . . . Van Gogh did it better with potatoes."

"May I freshen your drink, Inga?"

"I never say no."

"I suppose you've heard about Ross's confession painted on the wall," he said as he poured. "I found it today. It had been painted over, but the lettering shows through faintly."

"Where? Let me see it."

They went to the end of the foyer, Koko trotting ahead as if he knew their destination. Qwilleran removed the butcher block painting and sidelighted the wall with a bare lamp bulb.

Inga said, "It looks like he used pigment right out of the tube, and his brush was a #12 bright, but he spelled her name wrong. Poor kid! He had talent and a future, and he threw them both away."

"Speaking of wasted lives," Qwilleran said, "do you know Adelaide Plumb?"

"We've never met, but I've known about her for years."

"Do you know the story about her—how she sold her fiancé for millions to save the Casablanca?"

"It wasn't her idea," said Inga. "She did it under duress."

"What are you implying?"

"Her father set it up! That's not the conventional wisdom, but I happen to know that it's true. I was around in the Thirties, don't forget ... What time is it? Here I am, babbling like an idiot, and it's time for me to go home. I live at the Senior Towers, and if I'm not in by eleven o'clock, they check the morgue."

"I'll take you home," Qwilleran said.

"Just call me a taxi."

Firmly he said, "Inga, I'm not letting you out of my sight until I deliver you to the Senior Towers and get a signed receipt."

"Well, I guess this is one of the perks when you're eighty," she said, patting her gray bangs smugly.

Koko followed them to the door. "Back in a few minutes," Qwilleran promised, and when he returned, the cat was waiting expectantly. He led the way into the library and massaged the Scrabble box eagerly with his front paws.

"No games tonight, old boy," said Qwilleran. "We have matters to discuss."

Koko sat on the library table, tall and alert, as Qwilleran opened the covers of several large art books. Then he opened a desk drawer and examined the bracelet that Koko had found behind a sofa cushion.

"Inga is right," he said, addressing the cat. "Lady Di signed herself D-i-a-n-n-e on her bookplates. The Van Gogh was a gift from Ross, and he inscribed it 'To D-i-a-n-n-e from Ross.' The bracelet he gave her was engraved with the same double N. Why would he paint D-i-a-n-e on the wall?"

"Yow!" said Koko encouragingly.

"And why would he sign his so-called confession with his professional logo? He was 'Ross' on the bracelet and 'Ross' in the gift book." Qwilleran patted his moustache. "It looks to me as if the suicide was a hoax. Someone drugged him and threw him off the terrace, then went into his studio and got a tube of red paint."

"Rrrrrrrrrrrrrr," said Koko.

"Tomorrow we'll have a talk with Lieutenant Hames and let him figure out who really killed Lady Di, and who dumped her lover from the rear end of the terrace, where the floodlight doesn't reach."

The cat slapped the table with his tail—twice.

"There may have been two of them involved in the crime."

Chapter 14

Author's note: There is no Chapter 13 in this book.

Early Saturday morning Qwilleran placed a telephone call to the Homicide Squad and left a message for Lieutenant Hames. When the phone rang a few minutes later, he was prepared to greet the detective but heard instead the soothing voice of Polly Duncan.

"Where were you last evening?" she began. "I tried to reach you."

"What time did you call?"

"At eleven, when the rates dropped."

To taunt her he replied, "I was taking a woman home. I met her at an art gallery, and we came here for a few drinks."

There was a worried pause. "Who was she?"

"An artist."

"Did you just . . . pick her up?"

"No, we'd met before. You don't need to worry, Polly. She's eighty years old and crippled with arthritis. Why were you trying to reach me?"

"To tell you that I read about you in the *Morning Rampage*. The library subscribes, you know. But mostly to thank you for the beautiful handbag. It's the nicest I've ever owned! That was very thoughtful of you, dearest, although it only makes me miss you more."

"I wanted you to know I'm thinking of you, in spite of being surrounded by female flashers and arthritic octogenarians and eccentric heiresses." He made no mention of Winnie Wingfoot, although he moistened his lips as her image flashed through his mind. "How's the kitten with a hollow leg?"

"Absolutely incorrigible! Last night I brought home two little lamb chops for my dinner, and as soon as I unwrapped them, he swooped in and dragged one down to the floor."

"Any news about the carriage house?"

"Yes, Mrs. Gage is letting me have it with the idea that I'll keep an eye on the big house while she's in Florida. So you can have your apartment, Qwill, if you come home. What did you decide?"

"I have eighteen more restaurants to try before I can return to face Moose County goulash."

"Oh, Qwill! It's not that bad! Where did you have dinner last night?"

"At a middle-eastern place downtown—hummus, pita, kabobs and tabbouleh."

"Alone?"

"Alone, and I have a receipted guest check to prove it."

After more affectionate banter Polly said, "Do be careful, dearest. If anything happened to you, it would break my heart, you know that."

"I'll be careful," he promised.

When he went out to breakfast, he discovered that Saturday morning was carnival time in the Casablanca lobby as the tenants turned out to shop for groceries, do laundry, pay the rent, pick up their dry cleaning, stock up on videos for the weekend, return books to the library, jog around the vacant lots, and do all the other busywork that occupies working people and students on their day off. Even the old and infirm were circulating; the two elderly women who usually drifted through the halls in quilted robes were fully dressed, explaining to everyone that they were being taken to visit a friend in a nursing home. Mrs. Tuttle was busy handling complaints and writing rent receipts. Rupert was directing a youth who was trying to mop the floor. Napoleon and Kitty-Baby were dodging feet.

After picking up a few treats for his roommates at a neighborhood deli, Qwilleran returned to the building and was heading for the elevator when he encountered the person he least wanted to meet. Surprisingly, Isabelle Wilburton presented a neat and appropriate appearance in a white blouse and khaki skirt. On previous occasions he had seen her in a spotted housecoat or a cocktail dress or a fur coat or less. She was carrying her kitten, nestled in a blue towel.

"Mr. Qwilleran, I took your advice," she said. "Isn't she adorable? Her name is Sweetie Pie."

"She's an appealing little cat," he agreed, "and she'll be good company for you."

"Would you like to have dinner with us tonight? I'm cooking a pot roast. I hope it will be good. I haven't really cooked anything for ages."

"I appreciate the thought," he said, "but I've already accepted another invitation."

"How about tomorrow night?" she asked hopefully.

"Unfortunately I've agreed to keep Sunday open for a meeting with the officers of SOCK. You see, I'm writing a book on the historic Casablanca."

"Oh, really? I could tell you a lot about that. My grandparents had an apartment here back in the 1920s, when it was so exclusive. My grandmother used to tell me stories about it."

"I'll keep that in mind. Thank you for the suggestion," he said, inwardly recoiling. "Has the mailperson been here?"

Isabelle waved an envelope. "Yes, the mail just came in." She appeared quite happy about it. No doubt the envelope contained her subsistence check.

Qwilleran went to the mailroom and found the door blocked by Ferdie Le Bull, his imprinted T-shirt stretched across his enormous chest. He confronted Qwilleran with the menacing scowl that was his idea of social grace. "When you gonna take the pictures?" he demanded.

"Of Miss Plumb's apartment? Whenever she gives her approval."

"Any time's okay. She never goes out."

"All right. I'll notify the photographer, and he'll call you to make an appointment."

"She's all het up about it," said the houseman. "Is he gonna take my picture, too?" He passed a hand over his bald head.

"Probably."

"Does he play bridge?"

"You'll have to ask him," said Qwilleran.

Encouraged by this positive development he determined to go ahead seriously with the book. As he waited for the elevator he visualized about thirty percent text and seventy percent black-and-white photos: views of the opulent lobby and Palm Pavilion, pictures of celebrities, old cars, and residents in nostalgic fashions—from Edwardian to Flapper Era to Early Thirties. In the center, a color section would feature overall shots of the Art Deco rooms as well as close-ups of the rare vase containing Harrison Plumb's ashes, the Cubist rugs and pillows, a tooled copper screen inset with ebony, tables with angular legs, club chairs with voluptuous curves, and walls of framed French art photos of the 1920s. It was all lush and otherworldly. The frontispiece would be Adelaide St. John Plumb with her plucked and penciled eyebrows and her marcelled hair, sitting on the overstuffed sofa and pouring tea, looking like a living relic of the Casablanca's dim past.

For the text he would like to interview old-timers; surely there were such persons tucked away in odd corners of the building, living in faded splendor. It was a pity that Mrs. Button had not survived a little longer. Even Isabelle Wilburton might have to be interviewed.

As he pondered the possibilities, the door of Old Red opened, and the white-haired manager of Roberto's restaurant stepped from the car, accompanied by a pale-faced man who was much younger. He was the fellow with a bandage where his right ear should be.

Charlotte Roop was looking buoyantly happy. "Oh, Mr. Qwilleran!" she cried. "I want you to meet my friend, Raymond Dimwitty . . . Ray, this is Mr. Qwilleran who I've told you so much about."

Not believing what he had heard, Qwilleran said, "I didn't catch the last name. Spell it for me."

"D-u-n-w-o-o-d-y," said the man.

Qwilleran made heroic attempts not to stare at the ear patch as they exchanged polite words.

Charlotte said, "We always go out to lunch on Saturday and then to a movie. There's a discount if you go early, and I don't have to be at the restaurant until four."

"I hope you have an enjoyable afternoon. You have good weather for it," Qwilleran said courteously.

Old Red had gone up without him, and now he waited for Old Green, wondering how this unlikely couple had met: Charlotte with her fluttery, spinsterish manner and white hair like spun sugar, a woman well past retirement age, and Raymond Dunwoody with his ear patch and blank expression, a man not over forty-five. When the elevator arrived and opened its reluctant door, a cheerful passenger with a laundry basket, on her way up from the basement, crowed, "Oh, wow! We have somebody rich and famous living here now!" This was followed by a gusty laugh.

"If I were rich and famous, I wouldn't be living at Ye Olde Broken-down Casablanca," Qwilleran said with forced geniality that concealed his irritation. He disembarked at Three and walked the rest of the way up to Fourteen, silently cursing Sasha what's her name for revealing his financial status. He enjoyed the role of a retired journalist; he did not enjoy the role of a millionaire. Briefly, he considered moving to the Penniman Plaza until he remembered that hotels did not accept cats.

On the way upstairs he heard an ambulance siren winding down in front of the building. Another casualty! Who was it this time?

Arriving at 14-A he found a newspaper clipping under his door with a note from Amber scrawled in the margin: "Did you see this?" It came from the business page of Saturday's *Morning Rampage*—an interview with one of the principals of Penniman, Greystone & Fleudd. Rexwell Fleudd stated that the proposed Gateway Alcazar was fifty percent leased, and ground would be broken sooner than expected. A one-column head shot of the developer showed a long narrow face with high cheekbones and blow-dried hair. Qwilleran crumpled it in disgust and tossed it in the wastebasket.

Immediately the delicate thud of velvet paws could be heard, bounding out of the bedroom, and Yum Yum, the sleeping beauty, made a nosedive into the wastebasket to retrieve the crumpled clipping. The crumpling of paper was a sound she could hear in her dreams. Qwilleran took it away from her, not wanting her to chew it and ingest printer's ink. As he did so, he had another look at that arrogant face and wondered where he had seen it before.

Yum Yum was peeved, and to assuage her ruffled feelings he stroked her fur and paid her a few lavish compliments on her pulchritude, her sweetness of disposition, and her nobility of character. She purred—and went back to bed.

Why does she loll around so much? he asked himself. Is it the smog? Or some kind of stress?

Meanwhile, Koko was waiting for action on the Scrabble table, and he won the first few draws so handily that Qwilleran changed the rules to permit proper nouns, slang, and foreign words. Even with a handicap the cat won, but the man had the satisfaction of spelling such words as IXION, MERCI, CIAO, and SNAFU. Toward the end of the game he spelled a word that proved to be prophetic: OOPS.

As it happened, he intended to spend the afternoon at the

library, and on his way downtown he stopped at the Penniman Plaza for lunch. The coffee shop was on the mezzanine, and he was stepping on the upward-bound escalator when he heard a cracked voice directly behind him crying, "Help me!"

He half-turned and caught a glimpse of a dirty white beard. At the same moment someone grabbed his arm. What happened next seemed to be in slow motion: his hand reaching for the handrail . . . the handrail moving beyond his grasp . . . his body sinking backward . . . his feet continuing to move upward . . . the steps behind him rising to meet his spine . . . the whole escalator ascending relentlessly as he lay on his back, riding to the mezzanine feetfirst.

The absurdity of his position stunned him momentarily until screams from onlookers recalled the episode on the subway tracks and marshalled his wits. In a matter of seconds he had to swing his legs around in the narrow space, maneuver his feet lower than his head, scramble to his knees, stand up. Just as the moving steps telescoped into the floor above, he was upright, and hands were helping him step onto terra firma.

"Are you hurt, sir?" a security man asked.

"I don't think so," Qwilleran replied. "Only a trifle surprised."

"Let me take you to the manager's office, sir."

"First I want to sit down and have a cup of coffee and figure out what happened."

"You can get coffee right here in the bar, sir. Are you sure you're all right?" The uniformed guard conducted Qwilleran into a dimly lighted lounge. "I'll notify the manager, sir. He'll send someone down."

"Mr. Qwilleran! What happened?" the bartender called out. He had a reddish moustache, and Qwilleran recognized the jogger from the Casablanca.

"I don't know exactly."

Another security guard arrived on the scene. "I was down there. I seen it. One of them kooks that wanders around—kind of unsteady on his feet—wanted to get on the escalator, and I told him not to. He grabbed this man's arm."

"I rode up feetfirst," Qwilleran explained to the bartender.

"I've gone feetfirst into worse situations than this, but I'll admit this was a peculiar sensation."

"You need a stiff drink. What'll it be?"

"My days as a stiff drinker are over, but I could use a strong cup of coffee."

"Coming right up."

Qwilleran sipped the brew gratefully while security personnel hovered about to prevent his escape, pending the arrival of a hotel official. He said to the bartender, "You know my name but I don't know yours."

"Randy. Randy Jupiter. I remember reading your column when you wrote for the *Fluxion*—the reviews about restaurants, I mean. I clipped every one and then checked them out on my day off. You were always right on!"

Qwilleran smoothed his moustache. Having his column clipped was his favorite kind of compliment. "A lot of new eating places have opened since then," he said. "I've been away for three years."

"They sure have! It looks like nobody stays home and cooks anymore. How long are you going to be here? I could recommend a few good ones."

"My plans aren't definite. I'm here to write a book on the Casablanca, and it will depend on what luck I have with research."

"The *Rampage* said you're going to buy the building," Jupiter said with a grin.

"No one believes the *Rampage*. Stick with the *Fluxion*, boy."

"Didn't you say you're on Fourteen?"

"In 14-A."

"That must be the Bessinger apartment. I've never seen it, but I hear it's something else."

"It's unique," Qwilleran agreed.

The assistant manager appeared, and Qwilleran assured her he was not hurt and saw no reason to hold the hotel responsible. He willingly supplied the personable young woman with the information she needed for her report and accepted vouchers good for dinner and dry cleaning. When the transaction was completed the bartender said to Qwilleran, "That's not too shabby."

"She might have offered to go to dinner with me. Then it would be worth the indignity of riding up feetfirst. How long have you lived at the Casablanca?"

"Just a few months. Do you like jazz?"

"I was a jazzhound in college but I haven't done much listening lately." Qwilleran felt comfortable with the bartender. It was his private theory that men with large moustaches tend to gravitate toward other men with large moustaches. Likewise, fat men get together. Men with beards or long hair like to talk to men with beards or long hair.

Jupiter said, "I've got a super collection of old jazz artists. Any time you want to hear some great sounds like Jelly Roll, the Duke—"

"Do you have Charlie Parker?"

"I have everything. Just knock on my door. I'm in 6-A."

"My apartment has a fantastic stereo system and spectacular acoustics," Qwilleran said. "Perhaps you'd like to bring some recordings upstairs."

"I'd go for that."

"I'll get in touch with you."

"Call me here or at home." Jupiter scribbled two phone numbers on a cocktail napkin.

"Okay. Now I'm ready for lunch."

Lunch at the Penniman coffee shop was agreeably uneventful. Qwilleran also welcomed the scholarly silence of the library's history department, where he selected photos and signed an order for copies to be made.

Back at the Casablanca, 14-A was equally quiet. Too quiet! Koko seemed preoccupied as he waited for the mincing of the roast beef from the deli, and Yum Yum did not report at all until Qwilleran went to the bedroom and said, "Would Cleopatra consent to rise from her divan and repair to the dining salon for a light repast?"

He should have known that Koko's distracted demeanor was the countdown before the blast-off.

Chapter 15

Koko's abnormal behavior during the preparation of his dinner meant that mischief was hatching in that fine brown head. But Qwilleran had other matters on his mind, such as: what to wear for his dinner engagement at Courtney Hampton's apartment. Amber had specified that dress would be casual. Remembering the clothing salesman's supercilious gibe ("Just in from the country?"), he deliberately chose to wear his cashmere pullover, a garment that would impress anyone who knew the price of sweaters. At the appointed time he walked downstairs to the eighth floor and knocked on Amber's door. When she opened it he caught a glimpse of a room piled high with cardboard cartons and shopping bags.

"How recently did you move in?" he asked as they walked down the hall to the front of the building.

"I've been here two years, but it seems I never get around to unpacking," she said with a humorously hopeless shrug. "Now— let me tell you about Courtney's place, so it won't come as a total shock. He has one of the big old apartments, and he puts on the dog when he entertains, even hiring a woman to cook and a man to serve. But he doesn't have any furniture!"

"If the food is good, I'm prepared to eat off the floor," Qwilleran said. "Incidentally, I have yet to see an apartment in this building other than the penthouse and the Art Deco extravaganza on Twelve."

"I meant to ask, how did you get along with the Countess?"

"Very well. We played Scrabble, and I let her win a little."

"You men are so gallant—when you lose."

A pair of topiary trees flanked the entrance to 8-A. "He only puts them out when he's having company," Amber explained as she clanged the door knocker.

"I hope he also takes in the brass knocker when he goes to bed," Qwilleran said. "Someone stole my plastic rubbish container last night."

The door was opened by an emaciated gray-haired man in a white duck coat—someone Qwilleran had seen in the lobby, or on the elevator, or possibly in the laundry room. Not far behind him was the host, wearing a coolie suit in black silk and making gestures of Oriental welcome.

"Well, look at you!" Amber exclaimed.

"Just in from the rice paddy?" Qwilleran asked.

They entered a large room with dark walls lighted only by candles, Amber remarking, "I see Mrs. Tuttle cut off your electricity again."

Courtney reproached her with flared nostrils. "What you see here," he said to Qwilleran, loftily, "is one of the original suites, occupied for sixty years by a bachelor judge. All I did was paint the walls Venetian red. The black walnut woodwork and the hardwood floors are original. I apologize for the lack of furniture. Special-order items take an *unconscionably* long time."

"They're growing the trees," Amber said.

As Qwilleran's eyes became accustomed to the dim light, he realized he was in a room at least fifty feet long and bare enough to be a ballroom. In one corner was a compact seating arrangement: two couches right-angled against the wall, covered with fringed Spanish rugs and heaped with pillows of some ethnic origin. The couches were actually army cots, he later decided. For a cocktail table there was a large square of thick plate glass supported by concrete blocks, and under it was a worn Persian rug, the only floor covering in the room. Three long-stemmed white carnations in a tall crystal vase looked aggressively contemporary. In candlelight the corner was almost glamorous.

"You have a new rug," Amber observed.

"A semi-antique Tabriz, my dear—this month's acquisition from our friend Isabelle."

She explained to Qwilleran, "He means Isabelle Wilburton. He's systematically stripping the poor woman's apartment."

"I am keeping the poor woman *afloat*," Courtney said with hauteur. "Last month's acquisition was that painting over the sideboard—American, of course—probably of the Hudson River school. A curator from the art museum is coming here tomorrow to identify it incontrovertibly." The misty landscape in an elaborate gilded frame was hanging above a sideboard composed of two large, wooden packing cases, on which stood a silver teaset. "Would we all like a margarita?"

"Qwill doesn't drink," Amber announced.

"Evian?" asked the host.

"Evian will do," Qwilleran said, "if you don't have Squunk water."

The other two gave him a brief questioning glance. No one outside of Moose County had ever heard of Squunk water. Then Courtney turned to the white-coated server. "Hopkins, bring us two margaritas and an Evian for the gentleman." The white coat disappeared into the gloom at the far end of the room, and the host went on. "Originally the suite consisted of this drawing room plus a large bedroom totally without closets plus a *huge* bathroom. *Where* did they hang their clothes in 1901? And *what* did they do in the bathroom that required so much space? Fortunately the judge added closets and a kitchenette."

Amber said to Qwilleran, "You should see Court's previous apartment. It was like a cell at Leavenworth."

"*Courtney!*" he corrected her with a frown.

The drinks and a silver bowl of macadamia nuts were served by Hopkins, moving as if in a trance.

Qwilleran asked, "How was your card game Wednesday night?"

"Not too excruciating, although I could manage nicely without the camomile tea and caraway seed cake. The Countess was my partner. Considering that she acts like a ghost of the 1920s, she's a *killer* at the bridge table."

"Who else was there?" Amber asked.

"Winnie Wingfoot and that *pushy* Randy Jupiter. He probably *bribed* Ferdie to include him," Courtney said with a curled lip.

"I think Randy has a lot of personality," Amber said in his defense.

"*Too much* personality. I don't trust that kind. And he *jogs*."

"You're such a snob, Court."

"*Courtney*, please!"

"At least Randy is friendly and alive," she persisted. "Most of the people in this building are half dead."

The host said, "That reminds me, guess who died today?"

"Okay, twenty questions," Amber said. "Was it a man?"

"No."

"Then it was a woman. Did she wear a hearing aid?"

"No."

"Was she in her eighties?"

"No."

"In her seventies?"

"No. You'll never guess, Amber."

"Did she live on Seven?"

"No."

"Did she break her hip last year?"

"Give up, Amber. Give up! You'll never guess," said Courtney. "According to Madame Defarge—who sits behind her bulletproof window, knitting and counting bodies—it was *Elpidia* that they carried out."

"What!" cried Amber.

"Who's Elpidia?" Qwilleran asked.

"The Countess's personal maid," she said. "What happened, Courtney?"

"They say it was food poisoning, but I think it was an O.D. Being personal maid to the Countess would drive *anyone* to pills."

Qwilleran said, "I never saw the maid or the housekeeper."

"The maid was kind of weird, but the housekeeper's nice,"

Amber informed him. "She's Ferdie's mother. She has her own apartment on Two, but Ferdie lives in."

"She commutes daily to Twelve, where she bakes her *famous* caraway seed cake," Courtney added. "Incidentally, I've asked Winnie to drop in for a drink before she goes out for the evening . . . Have you met Winnie, Qwill? May I call you Qwill?"

"By all means . . . I haven't met Ms. Wingfoot but I've seen her. A beautiful girl!"

"When I look at Winnie," Amber said, "I want to go home and take an O.D. myself."

The door knocker resounded, and Qwilleran's pulse quickened. He smoothed his moustache and jumped to his feet as Hopkins admitted the satin-clad model. She glided into the room, glittering and dragging a fur jacket.

"Winnie, my angel," said the host, "this is Qwill Qwilleran, who is going to buy the Casablanca."

"Not true," said Qwilleran, taking the hand that was extended languidly in his direction.

"Our paths have crossed," said Winnie. "In the car park, under inauspicious circumstances. I trust your difficulties were satisfactorily resolved."

"Thanks to your prompt assistance, Ms. Wingfoot."

"Winifred," she corrected him.

"Would you like a margarita, angel?" the host asked.

"It would pleasure me immensely."

She sat on the army cot next to Qwilleran, who was aware of a heady scent and long silky legs.

"The weather turned out to be quite pleasant today," he said, knowing that it was a dumb remark.

"Quite revivifying," she said.

"Did you buy Isabelle's piano?" Courtney asked her. "She told me you were looking at it."

"I have it under consideration."

"Do you play?" Qwilleran inquired.

"Yes, rather well," she replied, bestowing a sultry glance on his moustache.

Courtney said, "Mrs. Button died this week, and Madame

Defarge says there's going to be a tag sale. I hope it's true. I have my sights on a small Rubens Peale."

Hopkins materialized from the dark end of the room with a tray of margaritas.

Amber said, "Isabelle has adopted a cat, and I may have to break down and get one myself. I had another mouse last night."

"If you would clean up your apartment, Amberina dear," said Courtney, "you would solve your problem. The little things are *incubating* in those eighty-four shopping bags . . . When is the Bessinger estate going to be liquidated, Qwill?"

"I have no idea. I'm just subletting while I work on a book about the Casablanca."

Courtney explained to Winnie, "Qwill is a noted journalist."

"How delicious!" she said.

"I'm hoping to interview old-timers who remember something about the early days. Any recommendations?"

"Mrs. Jasper!" said Courtney and Amber in unison.

"She did housework in the Casablanca way back when," Amber said, "and she can tell you all kinds of stories."

Winnie, upon finishing her drink, uncrossed her incredible legs and rose, saying, "I regret I must wrench myself away from this stimulating group, but I have a dinner date."

As the host escorted her to the door, Qwilleran remarked quietly to Amber, "I imagine she has no trouble getting dinner dates."

"I'm in the wrong business," she whispered.

Courtney lighted candles at the dark end of the room, where planks were laid across columns of concrete blocks to form a long narrow table. "Hopkins, tell Cook we wish to serve now," he said.

The seats were upended orange crates, each with a velvet cushion weighted at the four corners with tassels. "Watch out for splinters," Amber warned Qwilleran.

For a table centerpiece white carnations were arranged with weeds from the parking lot. Pewter service plates and goblets were set on the bare boards, and there were four tall pewter candlesticks.

"Where did you steal these?" Amber asked, and Courtney reproved her with a withering glance.

The soup course was cream of watercress, followed by crabcakes with shitake mushrooms, baby beets in an orange glaze, and wild rice. A salad of artichoke hearts and sprouts was served on Lalique plates as a separate course, and the meal ended with a chocolate soufflé. Not bad, Qwilleran thought, for a crate-and-block environment.

Amber said to him, "Every year on the Fourth of July Courtney gives a party on the roof with picnic baskets full of chicken and wine and cherry tarts. The roof is a super place to watch the fireworks."

"How do you get up there?"

"There's a stairway from Fourteen. The door says No Admittance, but it's never locked. It's a nice place to sun in the summer."

Qwilleran said, "As an expert on the Casablanca scene, perhaps you could answer some questions, Courtney. How come Rupert never seems to do any work? He just hangs around."

"Actually he's a security guard," said the host, "and he has an *arsenal* under that ill-fitting jacket."

"How about this guy Yazbro on Four?"

"He's a furniture mover with one claim to fame: Ross's body landed on his car, and he got his name in the paper. Shall we have coffee in the lounge area? And would we all like to hear some Noel Coward?" He moved toward a stack of strawberry crates containing cassettes and compact discs.

"Play the tape of your own show, Courtney," said Amber. She turned to Qwilleran. "He's producing an original musical called *The Casablanca Cathouse*, and the opening number is a blast!"

"I'm doing the book and lyrics, but I haven't found a composer yet," said the impresario. "Keestra is doing the choreography. You may have heard, Qwill, about Keestra Hedrog and her Gut Dancers. She lives in 14-B."

"Are they belly dancers? I've heard some strange bumps coming through the wall."

"They're non-disciplinary, non-motivational interpreters of basic sensibilities," Courtney explained patronizingly.

"Play the opening number, Court," Amber urged.

"*Courtney!*" he rebuked her. "You'll have to imagine the music."

The tape started to unreel, and his voice, with an affected British accent, announced, "Presenting a musical in two acts by Courtney Hampton. *The Casablanca Cathouse*—Act one, Scene one." The lyrics followed:

There's a spot that has been libeled as an odious address
Because it's old and battered and the lobby is a mess.
True . . .
The roof may leak, the hallways reek,
The elevators fail to rise, the ceilings drop before your eyes,
But it's really not as squalid as you'd guess.
The window sills may start to rot, the taps run dry (both cold and hot),
And occasionally the kitchen sink develops a peculiar stink,
But it's really not as nasty as you think.
Yes . . .
The Casablanca Cathouse is a marvelous place to live,
Tenants getting more exclusive all the time!
The strippers from the Bijou were evicted the first night.
We've lost the drunken deadbeats who had that bloody fight.
There's a madam on Eleven, but she seems a bit all right,
And the window washer fell and gave up crime.
Yes . . .
The Casablanca Cathouse is a MARVELOUS place to live!
The mice are getting smaller every year.
We're just a tad Bohemian with a decadent kind of chic.
We pass each other in the halls and never, never speak.
Whenever we get mugged, we simply turn the other cheek.
To be normal, good, or rational is queer.
Oh . . .
We've got intriguing clutches of folks with canes and crutches,
And lonely wraiths and elderly voyeurs,

*And male and female flashers and flocks of aging mashers,
And gorgeous broads in diamonds and furs.
Yes . . .
The Casablanca Cathouse is a MA-A-ARVELOUS place to live!
All others by comparison seem dead.
It has a reputation as a seedy sort of spot.
No one runs for Congress, and no one owns a yacht,
But things are getting better since Poor Old Gus was shot,
And the helicopter's always overhead!*

There was a long pause, Courtney pressed a button, and he and Amber looked expectantly at their guest.

"It'll never play Broadway," Qwilleran said, "but you might do a season on the Casablanca roof."

"The plot," the author explained, "is based on the Bessinger murder."

Qwilleran was staring into space. He cupped a hand around his moustache. He jumped to his feet. "I've got to get upstairs! Excuse me," he blurted, heading for the door. "Great evening! Great dinner!" He was out in the hall when he finished his explanation, and he ran upstairs to Fourteen. A tremor on his upper lip warned him of trouble.

As he unlocked the door to 14-A, he heard water running and splashing. He dashed down the bedroom hall, flipping wall switches as he went. When he reached the master bedroom he found the floor wet. *The Waterbed!* he thought . . . No, the gushing and splashing came from the bathroom. He turned on the light. The floor was flooded! The washbowl was overflowing; the faucet was running full force; and there on the toilet tank sat Koko, surveying his achievement.

Chapter 16

When Qwilleran rushed into 14-A and found the bathroom flooded and the culprit sitting on the toilet tank, he had no time to analyze motives. He tore off his shoes and socks, threw bath towels on the floor, then squeezed them out—a performance that Koko found diverting. Qwilleran growled into his moustache but realized the futility of a reprimand. If he said "Bad cat!" Koko would merely gaze at him with that no-speak-English expression.

The mopping job finished, he took the towels to the basement to put in the dryer, but the laundry room was locked for the night. It gave him time, however, as he rode down on sluggish Old Red and up again on laggard Old Green, to think about Koko's misdemeanor. The cat had rubbed his jaw against the lever-type faucet. It was obviously neurotic behavior; he was bored and lonely and wanted to attract attention. With Yum Yum in her indolent mood, Koko missed the chasing, frolicking, wrestling, and mutual grooming sessions that are so important to Siamese pairs.

It's my fault, Qwilleran said to himself; I dragged them to the city when they wanted to stay in the country.

Koko was waiting for him when he returned with the pail of wet towels. "I'm sorry, old friend," he said. "Tomorrow's Sunday. We'll spend the day together. We'll find something interesting to do. If the weather permits, how would you like to go for a walk on the roof?"

"Yow," said Koko, squeezing his eyes.

He gave the cats a bedtime snack—a morsel of smoked salmon from the deli—and was getting into his pajamas when he had reason to pause and listen. Something could be heard crawling under the floor.

"That's no mouse," he said aloud. "That's a rat!"

The cats heard it, too, Koko scurrying around with his nose to the floor, and even Yum Yum sniffing in a lackadaisical way.

Qwilleran strode to the housephone in the kitchen and rang the manager's night number. Rupert answered.

"Rupert! This is Qwilleran on Fourteen. We've got rats up here under the floor! . . . Rats! That's what I said. R-a-t-s! Yes, I can hear them under the floor in the master bedroom. The cats hear them, too . . . Oh! Is that so? . . . Hmmm, I see. That's too bad . . . Well, sorry to bother you, Rupert. Good night."

He returned to the bedroom. "It's a plumber in the crawl space," he informed the Siamese. "He's investigating a leak. Water's dripping down into the Countess's bedroom. Does that make you feel guilty, Koko?"

The cat laundered a spot on his chest with exasperating nonchalance.

If it had happened to any apartment but that of the Countess, Qwilleran reflected, the management would have waited until Monday.

True to his word he spent Sunday with the Siamese, first grooming them both with a new rubber-bristled brush he had found in a pet shop. Then he read aloud to them from *Eothen*, Yum Yum falling asleep on his lap during the chapter on the Cairo plague. Around noontime he strapped the harness on Koko and took him for a walk—out of the apartment, across the elevator lobby, through the door marked No Admittance, up two flights of stairs, and out onto the roof, Koko marching with soldierly step and perpendicular tail.

It was glorious on the rooftop. There was a dramatic view of the downtown skyline and the river curving away to the south. The cat sniffed the breeze hungrily and tugged on the leash; he wanted to walk to the edge. Qwilleran had other ideas; he pulled Koko to the skylight and peered down into the penthouse apartment. Although the glass was clouded with age, certain panes had been replaced in recent times, and it was possible to see the long sofa, the large paintings, and some of the potted trees. At night, with the gallery lighted, anyone on the roof could look down and see whatever was happening in the conversation pit.

Qwilleran thought, What if . . . ? What if someone on the roof had witnessed the murder of Di Bessinger and knew the true identity of the murderer? Why wouldn't he come forward with the information? Because he would fear for his own life, or because he would recognize an opportunity for blackmail? But that was the way it happened in mystery novels, not in real life.

The skylight held no attraction for Koko, who preferred to walk on the low parapet that edged the roof. Together they made one complete turn around the perimeter before going downstairs for the next activity, which was Scrabble.

Hardly had the game started when the telephone rang. Qwilleran hoped it might be Winnie Wingfoot; he had a hunch she would follow up their brief acquaintance of the evening before. Instead, it was the disappointing, reedy voice of Charlotte Roop.

"Are you busy, Mr. Qwilleran? I hope I'm not interrupting anything."

"I was just thinking of going for a walk," he said, "but that's all right."

"I wondered if I could go up and see your beautiful pussycats a little later on, if it wouldn't be too much of an imposition."

She had shown no interest in the Siamese when they lived on River Road. "Sure," he said without enthusiasm. "What time would be convenient?"

"Well, I'm due at the restaurant at four, and if I went up there about three thirty . . ."

"That's good," he said, thinking that she would be unable to stay long. "I'll expect you at three thirty. I'm in 14-A."

"Do you mind if I bring my friend?"

"Of course I don't mind." What else could he say?

To Koko he said, "Your old pal Charlotte is dropping in at three thirty. Try to act like a gentleman." During their previous acquaintance, which had been brief, the cat had gone out of his way to shock and embarrass the woman. Charlotte was easily shocked and embarrassed in those days.

They went back to their Scrabble. Koko was partial to the letter O, and Qwilleran was building words like FOOT, ROOF, TOOT, and DODO when the telephone rang again. This time he was sure it was Winnie Wingfoot, but it was Isabelle Wilburton, and she was inebriated.

"Watcha doin'?" she asked in a sleepy voice.

"I'm working at my desk," he said coolly.

"Mind if I . . . come up?"

"I'm afraid this is not a good time to visit. I'm concentrating on a problem."

"Wanna come down here?"

"I've just told you, Miss Wilburton, that I'm extremely busy and cannot leave my work at this time," he said with a touch of impatience.

"Why don'cha call me Isabelle?"

"All right, Isabelle. As I said, I can't interrupt what I'm doing."

"Don'cha like me?"

He had a great desire to hang up, but he said as graciously as he could, "It's not that I don't like you; it's simply that you are calling at an inopportune time."

"Don'cha wanna see my cat?"

"I've seen your cat, Isabelle. I saw her in the lobby yesterday. She's a nice little kitten and I told you so."

"Wanna come and have dinner?"

He tried to speak kindly. "Perhaps you don't remember, but I told you yesterday that I have a dinner meeting with the officers of SOCK."

"Nobody wants to eat with me," she whined. "I don't have any friends. I'm gonna jump off the roof."

"Now, wait a minute, Isabelle. Don't talk like that. You have a good life ahead of you. How old are you?"

"Forty-two. Forty-three. Don't remember."

"Do you remember the conversation we had in the laundry room? I had the same experience when I was your age, so I know how you feel and what you're going through. I also know you can get help, the way I did, and start enjoying a good life again. There are groups you can join, where you'll meet people who have the same problem as yours."

"Don't have any problem. Just don't have any friends. No reason to live anymore. Gonna go up on the roof and jump off."

"Isabelle, the last time I saw you in the lobby you were carrying your kitten in a blue blanket, and you seemed very happy. What's the name of your kitten?"

"Sweetie Pie." Her speech was slurred.

"Is she good company?"

There was no answer. He thought he heard a glug and a swallow.

"What do you feed her?"

"Stuff out of a can."

"Do you play with her? Kittens like to play. You should tie a twist of paper on a string and swing it around—let her jump for it and chase it." It was an asinine conversation, but he was trying to distract her from her grisly intention. "Where does she sleep?"

"On my bed."

"Is she a happy cat?"

"Guess so."

"Does she purr a lot?" He hoped that something would capture her interest.

"I dunno."

"Kittens need love and attention. They like to be brushed, too. Have you tried brushing her?" Qwilleran mopped his brow. Why was he perspiring? Why was he working so hard? She wasn't even listening.

"Wanna come down . . . have a drink?" she mumbled.

"Have you had anything to eat today, Isabelle?"

"Gonna jump off the roof . . . end it all."

"Listen, Isabelle, you can't do that. Think of Sweetie Pie! She needs you! What would she do without you? She's just a helpless kitten."

"Gonna take her with me."

He paused for an instant. Then, "Hold the line a minute, Isabelle. Don't hang up! I'll be right back!"

Hurrying to the kitchen he rang the housephone. "Isabelle Wilburton's threatening to jump off the roof!" he shouted. "I've got her on the phone!"

"Keep her on the line," Mrs. Tuttle said. "I'll go up to her apartment."

He rushed back to his phone in the library but heard only a dial tone. Was she on the way to the roof—with the kitten? Running out of the apartment and slamming the door, he sprinted up two flights of stairs, three at a time; there was no one up there. He waited for a while, but Isabelle didn't appear. Could she have arrived before him? Impossible! Yet he looked over the edge apprehensively. A wind had sprung up, and he stepped inside the stairwell for protection.

What am I doing here at the Casablanca? he asked himself. It had been nothing but stress in the last week: cranky elevators, cold showers, runaway radiators, the Gut Dancers, trouble in the parking lot, the crazy Countess, and now Isabelle! After ten or fifteen minutes he was sure she had been intercepted, and he started downstairs. At the bottom of the second flight he received a harsh surprise. The steel door shutting off the stairwell was locked!

At first he refused to believe it. Then he realized that Mrs. Tuttle had sent Rupert up to lock the door and foil the would-be suicide. He banged on the door with a fist, hoping that Keestra Hedrog would be spending a quiet Sunday afternoon at home and would hear him. The only response was a muffled "Yow!" from behind the door of 14-A. Koko knew he was in trouble, but a lot of good that did!

Qwilleran returned to the roof and looked over the edge, doubting that he could signal for help from that height. There was no one in the parking lot, Sundays at the Casablanca being as quiet as Saturdays were hectic. He circled the roof, hoping to see a pedestrian walking a dog on Zwinger Boulevard, or a jogger behind the building, or someone throwing rubbish into the dumpster. There was no one in sight, and it was getting cold.

Slowly he started down the two flights to Fourteen. In the stairwell he could hear the machinery in the elevator housing, as well as a certain familiar clanking and banging that meant Old Red or Old Green was approaching Fourteen. He ran down the stairs and was pounding on the door and calling for help when the elevator arrived.

"Oh, dear!" said a timid voice. "Who's that?"

"I'm locked in the stairwell! Get the manager to open the door!"

"Oh, dear! This is Charlotte, Mr. Qwilleran. We were just coming to see you . . . Raymond, go down to the desk and tell them. I'll stay here."

There were sounds of an elevator descending.

"How did you get locked in there, Mr. Qwilleran?" asked the reedy voice that now sounded so welcome, so comforting.

"You'll never believe my story," he said on the other side of the door. "I'll tell you when I get out."

"Roberto is expecting you for dinner tonight. He said to send you up to his apartment when you arrive."

"Am I holding you up? I don't want you to be late for work."

"Oh, no, it's only twenty-five minutes to four. I'm sure Raymond will get someone right away."

Qwilleran had always found conversation with Charlotte to be strained, even without a heavy door between them, and he was relieved when the elevator made its noisy arrival and Rupert unlocked the door.

"Nobody told me you was on the roof," he said.

"Nobody knew. Thanks, Rupert. I wasn't looking forward to spending the night in the stairwell. You'll have to let me into 14-A, too. I forgot my key."

Standing by were Charlotte Roop and her friend with the ear patch. Qwilleran felt momentarily grateful to both of them, and he felt a flash of sympathy for Dunwoody, wondering why he wore such a noticeable badge of his deformity. Perhaps he could not afford a prosthetic ear.

"Come in," he said. "Welcome to the garden spot of the Casablanca."

The two entered, gazing in wonder.

"Were you never here before?" he asked.

"No," said Charlotte. "I never was."

"Where did it happen?" Dunwoody asked.

"Where did what happen?"

"The murder."

"I don't know," Qwilleran said untruthfully. He opened the French doors to the gallery. "This is the former swimming pool, now a combination living room and art gallery. Won't you go in and sit down? Be careful going down the steps. I'll try to find the cats."

Awestruck, the couple wandered into the skylighted wonderland of potted trees and gargantuan mushrooms.

Qwilleran found Yum Yum in the bedroom, dozing on the waterbed, and he found Koko in the bathroom, sitting in the turkey roaster—just sitting there. "No comment, please," he said to the cat. When he returned to the gallery with an animal under each arm, his visitors were huddled close together on the twenty-foot sofa like babes in the wilderness.

"Here they are! This one is Koko, the male, and this is Yum Yum, the female," he said, aware of the inanity of the statement.

"What kind are they?" asked Dunwoody.

"Siamese. Very intelligent."

Yum Yum demonstrated her intelligence by scampering up the stairs, through the French doors and back to the waterbed. Koko scratched his ear with a hind foot, a trick that required him to cross his eyes and show his fangs—the least attractive pose in his entire repertory.

"May I offer you a drink?" Qwilleran asked.

"Nothing for me," said Charlotte.

"Wouldn't mind a beer," Dunwoody said, his impassive face showing a glimmer of interest.

Excusing himself, Qwilleran went to the kitchen and returned with a tray. "Just in case you want to change your mind," he said to Charlotte, "here is a glass of white grapejuice." He refrained from saying that it was Koko's private stock; the notion would have offended her. Dunwoody reached for his glass of beer gingerly; it was doubtlessly the only beer he had ever drunk from Waterford cut crystal. "Cheers!" Qwilleran said grimly as he raised his own glass of grapejuice.

"Unusual room," said Dunwoody.

"The entire apartment was created from a former restaurant called the Palm Pavilion. The building has an interesting history. I'm thinking of writing a book about it."

Charlotte said to her friend, "Mr. Qwilleran is a brilliant writer." They both gazed on him in wonder.

"Are you also in the restaurant business?" Qwilleran asked the man.

"No, I work for the city."

"He's an engineer," said Charlotte proudly. "How do you like living in the country, Mr. Qwilleran?"

"Now that I've adjusted to the fresh air, safe streets, and lack of traffic, I like it."

"I've always lived in the city. So has Raymond, haven't you, dear?" She turned and beamed at her companion.

Qwilleran resisted a desire to look at his watch. "How long have you lived at the Casablanca?"

"Ever since they tore down our old building on River Road. Raymond moved in . . . when did you move in, dear?"

"Four months ago."

"It's convenient to our work," she explained.

"That's a definite advantage," said Qwilleran.

"The bus stops in front." This was Dunwoody's contribution.

The three looked at each other, Qwilleran trying desperately to think of something to say. It was the longest ten minutes in his memory.

Dunwoody spoke again. "What's that cat doing?"

Koko was burrowing under the dhurrie in front of the bar.

"Stop that, Koko!" Qwilleran scolded. He dragged the cat from under the rug and straightened it to cover the bloodstain.

"It's a bad habit he's picked up. Another beer, Mr. Dunwoody?"

"It's time for me to go to work," said Charlotte. "Come, Raymond. Thank you, Mr. Qwilleran."

"My pleasure, I assure you. It's fortunate that you happened along when you did." He had been so relieved to see them arrive, and now he was so relieved to see them leave!

His guests climbed out of the conversation pit, murmured their goodbyes, and left the apartment. If Qwilleran had been a drinking man, he would have poured a double scotch. Instead he scooped a large dishful of Neapolitan ice cream for himself and a spoonful for the Siamese. They lapped up the vanilla but showed their disapproval of the chocolate and strawberry by pawing the air in sign language that said, "Take it and bury it!"

Considering the events of the afternoon, Qwilleran was glad when it was time to dress and go to dinner at Roberto's. Out came the gray suit again, and at six thirty he walked to the Blue Dragon to pick up Mary Duckworth.

On the way to the restaurant she said, "Will you explain something, Qwill? Last Monday you told me you didn't play table games, and three days later you were beating the Countess at Scrabble."

"It astounds me, too, Mary. First, Yum Yum found that blank tile, and then Koko found the Scrabble box, so I read the instructions and decided to give it a try. If I happened to win, it was beginner's luck," he said modestly. "Incidentally, there are several tiles missing in the Scrabble set. I wonder what happened to them."

"Di had a cat who used to steal them and push them under the refrigerator," she said.

"I didn't know she had a cat."

"A Persian named Vincent—after Van Gogh, you know."

"What happened to him?"

"Her ex-husband took him. Vincent lives at the gallery now."

"Did she like Scrabble, or did she play to humor the Countess?"

"She was an avid player. It was a Sunday night ritual. I used to make a foursome occasionally."

"Were you there . . . on the Sunday night . . . when she died?"

Mary nodded. "That's a painful memory. When I left the party around eight o'clock, everything was fine."

Qwilleran had another question to ask, but they had arrived at the restaurant, and two other couples were preceding them up the steps, creating congestion in the foyer where Charlotte was official greeter.

"We'll go right upstairs, Charlotte," said Mary.

Chapter 17

The eggplant-color carpet of Roberto's restaurant continued up the stairs to his apartment. "You'll find that his taste has changed radically, Qwill," said Mary, raising the eyebrows that were so accustomed to being raised. "In Italy he discovered International Modern!" As a purveyor of Chippendale and Ch'ien-lung, she obviously disapproved.

"I like Modern, myself," he said. "I've liked it ever since I sublet Harry Noyton's apartment at the Villa Verandah."

"Noyton's place was Victorian Gothic compared to what you are about to see," she replied.

The carpet ended at the top of the stairs, and the floor from there on was a glossy expanse of amber marble. Here and there on this mirrorlike surface stood constructions of steel rods or tubes combined with geometric elements of glass or leather, apparently tables and chairs. Roberto made his entrance from the far end, where Qwilleran supposed he did his actual living in a baronial snuggery furnished with cushioned couches and red velvet.

This attorney who preferred to be a chef was an impressive figure of a man, his shoulders rounded from bending over lawbooks and the chopping board. In dress he was still conservative, and he still had a slow, judicial manner of speech punctuated by thoughtful pauses, but he used his hands more eloquently, something he had not done before living in Italy for a year.

"Good . . . to see you again," he said. There was no effusive Continental embrace; that would be too much to expect from the former Robert Maus.

"Roberto, this is a great occasion," Qwilleran said. "It's been three years since we last met, but it seems like three decades. Let me tell you that your restaurant is handsome, and the food is superb."

"I have learned a few things," said the host. "Sit you down. We shall have an apéritif . . . and some private conversation . . . and then go down to dinner."

Qwilleran selected an assemblage of rods and planes that seemed least likely to assault his body and found it not only surprisingly substantial but remarkably comfortable. The other two members of the party seated themselves at some distance from each other and from Qwilleran. Space was part of the design in this cool, calm, empty environment.

"The service downstairs," Qwilleran went on, "is excellent. Where do you find such good waiters?"

"Law students," said the restaurateur. "I tell them to consider our customers . . . as the ladies and gentlemen of the jury."

"I'm glad you've hired Charlotte Roop as your manager. She seems very happy and not quite so strait-laced."

Mary said, "You can't give all the credit to the job. She has a male companion, probably for the first time in her life."

"I know," said Qwilleran. "I've met him. Does anyone know what happened to his ear?"

"Dynamite explosion," said Roberto. "The poor fellow . . . is lucky to be alive."

"He's had extensive plastic surgery," Mary added.

They discussed the metamorphosis of Junktown, Zwinger Boulevard, River Road, and the city in general. Then Roberto said, "I understand you have a problem, Mr. Qwilleran . . . concerning the Casablanca."

"I do indeed, and it has nothing to do with ways and means, since the Klingenschoen Fund has agreed to underwrite the restoration. The obstacle is Miss Plumb herself. I thought I had established a rapport with her, but as soon as I mentioned the possibility of a restoration, she dropped the curtain. Perhaps you know how to get through to her. After all, you were her attorney for—how many years?"

Roberto took a deep breath and emphasized his words with the hand gestures of desperation. "Twelve years! Twelve frustrating, thankless years. I much prefer to be . . . stuffing tortellini."

Mary said, "How does she react to your proposal to write a book, Qwill?"

"I doubt whether she grasps the concept, but she likes the idea of having her picture taken. Leaving the book aside, there is one aspect of this entire project that alarms me. SOCK has powerful opponents, and now that the news has leaked that SOCK has a source of funding, they may take desperate measures. All they need to do is pray for Miss Plumb's demise, you know, and their goal is accomplished. If their prayers are answered, Providence might deal her a sudden heart attack or a cerebral hemorrhage or salmonella poisoning."

"A rather . . . ghastly . . . hypothesis," said Roberto.

"Did you know that her maid died suddenly yesterday?"

"Elpidia?" Mary asked in surprise.

"Elpidia. Food poisoning, they said. Was it the chicken hash? Or did she sneak some chocolates intended for the Countess?"

Roberto said stiffly, "If you suspect attempts on Miss Plumb's life . . . I see no foundation whatever . . . for your line of reasoning."

"A great many interests would benefit from the Countess's death: the developers, the banks, the city treasury . . ."

"But we are talking about reputable businessmen and civic leaders . . . not the underworld."

"I know the Pennimans and the Greystones are fine old families, patrons of the arts, and all that, but who is Fleudd?"

Roberto and Mary exchanged glances but neither ventured a reply. Mary said, "Qwill's hunches have been right in the past, Roberto, even when they seemed farfetched."

"I'm not making any accusations," Qwilleran said. "I'm just throwing out a few questions. Who, for example, is the grotesque houseman who works for the Countess? Can he be trusted?"

"Ferdinand," Mary said earnestly, "is a very loyal and helpful employee, no matter how absurd he may appear. His mother has been housekeeper for the Countess for years."

"And who handles her legal affairs now that you're out of the picture, Roberto? Who drew up her new will after the Bessinger murder?"

"My former law firm."

"Why did they steer her bequests to miscellaneous charities? Are they unsympathetic to the Casablanca cause?"

Mary said, "They were obviously influenced by the Pennimans—"

"What I am saying is this," Qwilleran interrupted. "The cards are stacked against us. Ordinarily I don't give up easily, but now I'm convinced that the Casablanca restoration is hopeless. What concerns me is the safety of that pathetic little woman on the twelfth floor. What can be done to protect her?"

Roberto was frowning and withdrawing in a display of incredulity.

"You may think my suspicions unfounded," Qwilleran went on, "but you said the same thing three years ago on River Road, and you remember what happened there!"

"Qwill may be right," Mary said.

"I would also like to submit that the ruthless forces endangering the Countess have already committed two murders in pursuit of their goal."

"What . . . are you . . . saying?" Roberto demanded.

"I have reason to believe that Bessinger, as heir to the Casablanca, was murdered by someone hired to eliminate her, and Ross Rasmus was framed."

"What evidence do you have?"

"Enough to discuss with a friend of mine at Homicide." Qwilleran smoothed his moustache confidently. "At this particular moment I'm not at liberty to reveal the nature of the evidence or the identity of my source." He had no intention of telling this unimaginative dealer in torts and tortellini about the significant bristling of his moustache or Koko's propensity for unearthing crimes.

At that juncture a waiter appeared and announced that their table was ready, and Roberto ushered them downstairs, obviously relieved to terminate the disagreeable topic of conversation.

In the restaurant, surrounded by other diners—one of whom was a man in a dinner jacket, a man with a long thin face and high cheekbones—they talked about Italian food, the antique show in Philadelphia, and life in Moose County, and at the end of the meal Roberto said, "The matter you mentioned upstairs, Mr. Qwilleran . . . allow me to give it some thought."

As Qwilleran escorted Mary Duckworth back to the Blue Dragon, he was carrying a foil packet wrapped in a napkin. They walked in silence for a while—past a woman walking a Great Dane, past the citizens' patrol swinging flashlights. Then he said, "Tell me about the night she was killed. Who was there playing Scrabble earlier in the evening?"

"It was a holiday weekend," Mary said, "and she had invited a lot of people in for snacking and grazing at five o'clock. Roberto refused to go. He is quite opinionated about food, as you know, and he abhors snacking and grazing. So I went alone. Ross was there, of course. And Ylana Targ, who writes the art column for the *Fluxion*. And Jerome Todd. And Rewayne Wilk, Di's latest discovery; he paints disgusting pictures of people eating. And there were some other artists." She mentioned names that meant nothing to Qwilleran. "And there was that *pill*, Courtney Hampton, whom I cannot stand! Di thought he was terribly clever. And there were some others who live at the Casablanca."

"How long did the party last?"

"It started thinning out at eight o'clock, and I left. Di wanted me to stay for Scrabble, but I had promised to meet Roberto for dinner. He has become a good and dear friend."

Qwilleran told himself that these two stuffed shirts deserved each other. He said, "No one answered my question when I asked about Fleudd. Who is he anyway?"

"He's supposed to be an idea man. Penniman & Greystone took him in a few months ago. They were always rather conservative, you know, and Fleudd is supposed to shake them up."

"Was the Gateway Alcazar his idea?"

"I suppose so."

"Does he eat at Roberto's often?"

"I don't know. I've never seen him there."

"Well, he was there tonight."

Qwilleran stroked his moustache as they said goodnight in front of the Blue Dragon, and he made a mental note to call Matt Thiggamon in the morning.

Chapter 18

Early Monday morning Qwilleran received a phone call from Homicide, but it was not Lieutenant Hames on the line. It was the nasal voice of his partner, Wojcik, a by-the-book cop who lacked Hames's imagination and had a lip-curling scorn for meddling journalists and psychic cats.

"Wojcik here," he snapped. "You called Hames. Anything urgent?"

"I owe him a lunch, that's all. Is he around?"

"Out of town for a couple of days."

"Thanks for letting me know. I'll call him later."

It was a promise Qwilleran was destined not to keep.

For the cats' breakfast he minced baked shrimp stuffed with lump crabmeat and placed the plate on the floor. "*Gamberi ripieni alla Roberto,*" he announced, "with the compliments of the chef. *Buon appetito!*" The Siamese plunged into their breakfast with gusto. Their current behavior might be abnormal, but there was nothing wrong with their gustatory connoisseurship.

As he watched them devour the repast with gurgling murmurs of ecstasy, there was a knock at the door. Before he could respond, a key turned in the lock, the door opened, and a gray-haired rosy-cheeked woman in a faded denim smock bustled into the foyer.

"Oh, you still here? Mornin' to you. I be Mrs. Jasper," she said. "Mrs. Tuttle said I were to clean on Mondays."

"Happy to have you. I'm on my way out to breakfast, so I won't be in your way. Do you know where everything is?"

"That I do! I cleaned for Miss Bessinger, and I handle everythin' careful, like she said, and clean the rugs with attachments, them bein' handmade. *You moved one!*" she exclaimed with a frown, as she peered into the gallery where the dhurrie covered the bloodstain.

"I prefer to have it there," Qwilleran said. "Will you water the trees? They haven't had any attention for a week."

"Water trees, change beds, put sheets and towels through laundry, turn on dishwasher, push vac around, and dust a bit," she recited. "I don't do windows." She marched into the kitchen and poked her head into the dishwasher, which was empty.

"I take my meals out," Qwilleran explained. "That's the cats' plate on the floor. There may be some cat hairs around the apartment. I have two Siamese."

It hardly needed mentioning. Koko was circling the woman with intense interest and sniffing her shoes.

"No bother. Miss Bessinger had a Persian, and I have a tom of my own, though his tomcattin' days be over. You've seen Napoleon, like as not. We live on the main floor, and he be a sociable critter."

She headed for the gallery with the vacuum cleaner and attachments, which Qwilleran offered to carry. Her regional speech reminded him of certain longtime residents of Moose County. "May I ask where you came from originally, Mrs. Jasper? You're not city bred."

"Aye, I come from a small town up north, name of Chipmunk. My paw had a potato farm."

"I know Chipmunk very well," he said. "I live in Pickax City."

"Aye, Pickax! Paw used to drive the wagon to Pickax to buy feed and seed. Sundays we went fishin' at Purple Point. Once we see'd a minstrel show at Sawdust City. It were good livin' up there, it were. A body felt safe. On the radio this mornin' they was three people shot to death at the Penniman Hotel, and a man in a car shot another driver on the freeway. It warn't like that in Chipmunk!"

"When did you leave Moose County?" Qwilleran asked as he plugged in the vacuum for her.

"I were fifteen year old. I be seventy-six next birthday but more strong and able than some young ones be. On the farm I hoed potatoes and kept chickens and milked the cow and growed vegetables for the table—afore I were ten year old."

"Why did you leave Chipmunk?"

"I were itchin' to see the big city, so my paw let me come and live with my aunt Florrie. She were a cook for some folks livin' here, and she got me a job as a housemaid. Worked here seven year afore I married my Andrew and raised a family. He were a mailman. Three boys and two girls we had, and one born dead. I cooked and cleaned and washed and ironed and made everythin' they wore on their backs till they growed up and moved away. Then I went back to housekeepin' for folks, and when my Andrew died—that good man!—I moved in here, main floor, and kep' right on workin'."

"Was Miss Bessinger nice to work for?"

"Aye, she were very tidy. Some folks is terrible messy, but not her! It were a great pity what happened."

"Did you clean for the man next door also?"

"Aye. He were messy, but he were a nice man. Come from the country, he did. Them tubs of dirt on the porch—he growed tomatoes, corn, and beans out there last summer, and the hellycopter were always flyin' over, disturbin' the peace. Didn't know corn plants when they saw 'em."

"Were you shocked to hear he had murdered Miss Bessinger?"

"I were that! I were up late that night, watchin' TV, and I heard screamin' outside the window and then a big bang. That were when he landed on a car. I looked out, but it were dark back there. Then the police and ambulance come, and I went out in the hall—everybody out there in their nightclothes and Mrs.

Tuttle tellin' them to go back to bed. It were awful! No one knowed she were lyin' dead upstairs."

Mrs. Jasper turned on the vacuum cleaner, putting an end to her monologue, and Qwilleran went in search of the Siamese. Yum Yum was on the waterbed, gazing into middle distance; Koko was prowling restlessly, talking to himself in guttural rumblings and curling his tail into a corkscrew—something he had never done before. Qwilleran called the desk and inquired about an animal clinic.

"Are the kitties sick?" Mrs. Tuttle asked.

"No, just acting moody, and I want to have them checked."

"The nearest vet is out River Road eight miles." She gave the name and number of the clinic. "You have to call for an appointment. How is Mrs. Jasper doing?"

"She's a vigorous woman for her age."

"Don't know where she gets her pep. She'll talk your ear off, too, if you let her. Hope there's nothing wrong with the kitties."

He called the clinic and said he would like the doctor to examine two Siamese.

"What is the nature of the problem?" asked the receptionist.

"We're from out of town, and since arriving in the city the cats have not been themselves. I want to be sure there's nothing radically wrong with them. They're very important to me."

"In that case we could squeeze you in this afternoon—say, at four o'clock. What are their names?"

"Koko and Yum Yum. My name is Qwilleran. I'm at the Casablanca."

"We have a lot of patients from there."

"See you at four."

It was another promise he would not keep.

Before going to breakfast he tuned in the radio—not only for the weathercast but to corroborate Mrs. Jasper's report about three murders at the Penniman Plaza. Oddly, the shooting on the freeway was mentioned, but there was no word about the triple killing at the hotel. His mounting curiosity led him to the Plaza for breakfast. On a newsstand he picked up a copy of the *Morning Rampage* and found that the paper had not covered the incident.

Not all the homicides in a large city are reported in the press—of that he was well aware—but when three persons are shot to death in a large downtown hotel with deluxe pretensions, it should be front-page news.

At the coffee shop he ordered a combination of steak, eggs, and potatoes that would have been called a Duck Hunter's Breakfast in Moose County; at the Penniman Plaza it was the Power Brunch. He waited until the waitress had poured his third cup of coffee before he asked her about the triple killing. She had no idea what he was talking about.

On the way out of the building he stopped at the bar. It opened at eleven, and Randy Jupiter was in the process of setting up. Qwilleran perched on a barstool. "I hear you had some excitement here over the weekend, Randy."

"We did? I've been off since Saturday afternoon."

"There were three murders in the hotel. Didn't you hear about it?"

The bartender shook his head.

"It was on the radio."

"Are you sure? It could've been some other hotel." Jupiter glanced quickly around the bar and then wrote "can't talk" on a cocktail napkin. He said, "The coffee's brewing. Want a cup?"

"No, thanks," said Qwilleran. "I had three in the coffee shop." He slid off the stool. "If you're still interested in a jazz session, how about tonight?"

"Sure! Any requests?"

"Your choice, but no screaming trumpet. It sends the cats into fits. I like sax myself. Shall we say eight o'clock?"

Before stepping onto the escalator Qwilleran checked the vicinity for possible hazards, then rode slowly down on the moving stairs, reflecting that the radio station he had tuned in, as well as the *Morning Rampage*, were Penniman-owned. For information on the triple murder he would have to wait for the *Daily Fluxion* to hit the street, or for the bartender to arrive with his jazz recordings, or for Hames to come back to town.

Returning to 14-A he found Mrs. Jasper in the kitchen, with Koko watching her every move.

"The boss, he be tellin' me what to do," she said. "Now I'll take the towels and things down to the laundry and have a bit of lunch afore I come up again."

Qwilleran went into the library to peruse his notes gleaned from photo captions at the public library. Koko followed and leaped to the library table, where he took up his post on the volume of Van Gogh reproductions. He could have chosen Cézanne, Rembrandt, or one of the other masters, but he always elected to sit on the Van Gogh, complacently washing up. It occurred to Qwilleran that Vincent, the Bessinger Persian, might have elected to sit in that spot while waiting to steal a Scrabble tile.

From his notes he could reconstruct the romantic past of the Palm Pavilion. Harrison Plumb had celebrated his daughter's birthday with a musicale featuring a string quartet from the Penniman Conservatory. The Wilburtons hosted a reception for a visiting professor of anthropology who was lecturing at the university. The Pennimans entertained the French ambassador. Mr. and Mrs. Duxbury gave a dinner for the governor. No amount of restoration and no amount of Klingenschoen money, he had to admit, would ever recall the magic of the Casablanca's first quarter of a century. It could only be captured in a book, with pictures and text, a thought which reminded him to line up the photographer. He called Sorg Butra's number and was informed that the photographer was out of town on assignment. Qwilleran left a message for Butra to call him.

It was a call he would never receive.

When Mrs. Jasper returned with her laundry basket, he flagged her down at the library door, saying, "When did you first come to work at the Casablanca, Mrs. Jasper?"

"Just afore the 1929 Crash. That's when folks was jumpin' off the roof. It were terrible."

"Come in and sit down. Do you remember the names of any people you worked for?"

She sat on the edge of a chair with the basket on her lap, her rosy cheeks glowing. "I only worked for one family, and they was just two of 'em—father and daughter. He were a nice man with a little moustache. Mr. Plumb were his name."

"His daughter still lives here!"

"Aye, on Twelve. Miss Adelaide. Her and me was the same age."

"Here, let me take that basket. Make yourself comfortable," he said with a sudden surge of hospitality. "Would you like a cup of coffee?"

"I just had a nice cup o' tea downstairs, thankee just the same."

"What kind of work did you do for the Plumbs?"

"I were backstairs maid. I had a room of my own—imagine!—and me just a young girl from Chipmunk. They hired a lot of help in them days. We had a good time."

"What was Adelaide like when she was young?"

"Oh, she were a sassy girl, that one! Mr. Plumb spoiled her somethin' terrible. Bought her an automobile for her birthday, and the houseman used to drive her up and down Zwinger Boulevard like a princess. I remember her comin'-out party and the dress she wore—all beads and feathers and way up above her knees. That were the style then. After that the young men came callin' and bringin' chocolates and flowers. First thing we knowed, she were engaged to the handsomest of the lot." Mrs. Jasper shook her head sadly. "But it were too bad the way it worked out."

"What happened?"

"Well, now, the weddin' were all set, invitations and all, weddin' dress ordered special from Paris. Then somethin' happened suddenlike. Mr. Plumb were upset, and Miss Adelaide were poutin', and the help was tiptoein' around, afraid to open their mouth. I asked Housekeeper and she said Mr. Plumb were short of money. Next thing, he sold the automobile and let some of the help go, and Miss Adelaide stayed in her room and wouldn't come out, no matter what. Housekeeper said Mr. Plumb made her break her engagement. After that he got sickly and died." Mrs. Jasper leaned forward, wide-eyed. "It be my notion that Miss Adelaide poisoned him!"

Qwilleran, who had been lulled into a reverie by the singsong quality of the woman's voice, fairly jumped out of his chair. "What makes you think so?"

"She talked to me chummylike, us bein' the same age."

"What did she tell you?"

"Oh, she hated him for what he did! That were what she told me, stampin' her feet and throwin' things and screamin'. She were spoiled. Always got what she wanted and did what she wanted. I wouldn't put it past her to poison her own father."

"How would she get her hands on poison?"

"There were rat poison in the basement. The janitor had it in his cupboard with a big skull and crossbones on it."

"Come on, Mrs. Jasper," Qwilleran chided. "Can you picture the belle of the Casablanca prowling around the basement to steal rat poison?"

"Not her. It were the houseman, to my way o' thinkin'. He were a young man what looked like a movie star, and she smiled at him a lot. Housekeeper said no good would come of it."

"Very interesting," said Qwilleran, huffing into his moustache. He had a sympathetic attitude that encouraged confidences, true or false, and persons in all walks of life had poured out their secrets, but servants' gossip hardly qualified for the Casablanca history.

"Aye, it were interesting," Mrs. Jasper went on. "After Mr. Plumb died and she got the insurance money, the houseman bought hisself an automobile! Where would a young whippersnapper get money for an automobile in them days?"

"How many times have you told this story, Mrs. Jasper?"

"Only to my Andrew after we was married, and he said not to talk about it, but the Countess be old now, and it don't matter, and I always wanted to tell somebody."

"Well, thank you," he said. "It's after three o'clock now, and I must take the cats to the doctor."

"I'll water the trees and then I be through," said Mrs. Jasper.

Qwilleran paid her and said he would see her the following Monday—another promise he would be unable to keep.

Both of the Siamese were on the waterbed. "Everyone up!" he called out cheerfully. "Get your tickets for a ride in the Purple Plum!" He made no mention of the clinic, and yet they knew! No amount of coaxing would convince them to enter the carrier.

First he tried to push Koko through the small door, beginning with the forelegs, then the head, but the cat braced his hind legs against the conveyance, straddling the door and lashing his tail like a whip. Even employing all his cunning, Qwilleran still could not engineer four legs, a head, a lashing tail, and a squirming body into the carrier simultaneously. In frustration he abandoned the project and had a dish of ice cream, and when he returned to the scene some minutes later, both animals were huddled in the carrier contentedly, side by side.

"Cats!" Qwilleran grumbled. "CATS!"

He carried the coop from the apartment and rang for the elevator.

"Don't shriek when the car is in operation," he cautioned Yum Yum. "You know what happened last time." He held his breath until Old Green landed them safely on the main floor.

"Bye-bye, kitties," called Mrs. Tuttle, looking up from her knitting as they passed the bulletproof window.

The two old women in quilted robes had their heads together as usual, scowling and complaining. "Moving out?" one of them croaked in a funereal voice.

"No, just going to the doctor," he replied. It was a mission he never accomplished.

A brisk breeze was blowing down Zwinger Boulevard, whipping around the Casablanca and whistling through the cat carrier, and Qwilleran removed his jacket and threw it over the cage. As fast as possible he zigzagged through the parking lot, sidestepping the potholes. Not until the obstacle course was half negotiated did he look up and realize that slot #28 was vacant. The Purple Plum had vanished.

CHAPTER 19

Qwilleran tore back into the building with two confused Siamese bumping around inside the carrier. "Mrs. Tuttle!" he called out at the desk. "My car is gone! It's been stolen!"

"Oh, dearie me!" she said, not as perturbed as he thought she should be. "Did you lock your doors? Someone had cassettes stolen, but he left his doors—"

"I always lock my doors!"

"Was it a new car?"

"No, but it was in excellent condition."

Rupert, hearing the commotion, sauntered over and leaned on the counter. "Don't pay to keep a nice car."

Mrs. Tuttle offered to call the police.

"Never mind," Qwilleran said in annoyance. "I'll go upstairs and call them myself. I just wanted you to know." Although he had no affection for the Purple Plum, he resented having it stolen.

Riding up in Old Green he said to the occupants of the carrier, "You two will be happy about this development. Now you don't have to go to the doctor."

He telephoned the clinic and canceled his appointment. "My car has been stolen," he explained.

"I've had two stolen," said the receptionist comfortably. "Now I drive an old piece of junk."

Next he called the precinct station, and a bored sergeant took the information, saying they would try to send an officer to the building.

Then he called Mary and broke the news.

"I sympathize," she said. "I don't own a car anymore. I take taxis or rent a car when I need transportation."

"They're sending an officer over here."

"Don't count on it too much, Qwill."

Suddenly he was enormously hungry. He fed the cats hurriedly and went out to dinner, riding down on Old Red. When it stopped at Four, Yazbro stepped aboard, squinting at Qwilleran with a glimmer of hostile recognition.

"My car has just been stolen," Qwilleran said to enlist the man's sympathy.

Yazbro grunted something unintelligible.

"It was parked in #28, next to your slot. Was it there when you left this morning?"

"Di'n't notice."

Qwilleran went to the deli for an early dinner. All he wanted was a bowl of chicken soup with matzo balls, a pastrami sandwich two inches thick, a dish of rice pudding, and some time to sort out his feelings about life in the big city. The Press Club was not what it used to be. The staffers at the *Daily Fluxion* were all new and uninteresting. There was no one whose company he enjoyed half as much as that of Polly Duncan and Arch Riker, not to mention Larry Lanspeak, Chief Brodie, Junior Goodwinter, Roger MacGillivray, and a dozen others. The Casablanca itself was a disaster, and the Countess would never agree to sell to the Klingenschoen Fund. And the last straw was the theft of his car.

Even the prospect of writing a book on the Casablanca was losing its appeal. At this moment he had only one reason to stay. He wanted to have lunch with Lieutenant Hames as soon as the detective returned to town. He wanted to tell him about Koko's discoveries: first the bloodstain, then the bracelet, and finally the confession on the wall. He would relate how the cat found the exact spot where the artist was said to have jumped from the terrace. Then he would advance his theory that special-interest groups were resorting to criminal means to clear the way for the Gateway Alcazar: knifing the heir to the Casablanca and throwing her lover from the terrace, after drugging them both. But in attempting to frame Ross they had used an unlikely signature on his alleged confession and had misspelled Dianne. Furthermore, one tenant heard screams as the body plummeted to earth. As a newsman Qwilleran had seen suicides jump off high buildings and bridges, and they jumped in desperate silence.

He walked home slowly and found the crumbling front steps a disgrace, the lobby grim, the tenants depressing, and Old Red an affront to human dignity. Koko met him at the door as usual and trotted to the library as usual, where he took up his position on the Van Gogh volume as usual, tensing his tail like a corkscrew.

"What are you trying to tell me?" Qwilleran asked him. "Was that Vincent's favorite perch?" The thought crossed his mind that Vincent had witnessed the murder, and he had an irrational desire to visit the Bessinger-Todd Gallery once more.

When he phoned, he was answered in a hurry. "Is the gallery still open?" he asked. "This is Jim Qwilleran at the Casablanca."

"I've just locked the door. This is Jerry Todd. What can I do for you?"

"I never had a chance to talk with you about artwork for my barn, and I may be leaving soon."

"If you want to come over, I'll wait," the art dealer suggested.

"Be right there."

Qwilleran ran downstairs, thinking it quicker and easier than taking the elevator. He hailed a cab and arrived at the gallery within minutes.

Todd unlocked the door. "That was fast."

"I see you've sold a lot of things since Friday night," said Qwilleran, observing the empty walls.

"Very successful opening," the dealer said cheerfully, pinching his nose in the odd way he had. "*The Pizza Eaters*, *The Wing Ding Eaters* and *The Hot Dog Eaters* all went to one buyer, a fast-food chain. They wanted them for their corporate headquarters. It will occupy an entire floor of the Gateway Alcazar. Did you see anything you liked at the opening?"

"Nothing suitable for a barn, to tell the truth."

"Perhaps you should consider contemporary tapestries if you're going to have a lot of wood surfaces. We have one rtist who does abstract weavings in nature themes. I can show you pictures of her work." He produced an album of color slides.

Qwilleran, who truthfully had no plans to convert his barn, was captivated. "How large are they?"

"She takes commissions to order, including some huge tapestries for hotel lobbies. You'd never guess it, but she's just a tiny little thing. Here's her picture."

The artist had a roguish pixie face that appealed to Qwilleran. "Your suggestion is certainly something for me to consider," he said. "I'll get back to you after I consult my architect."

"Architects approve of her tapestries. They complement rather than compete with the architecture, and her perception of dimension is outstanding. She shows great sensitivity with threads, and of course she dyes her own colors."

At that moment a mushroom-tinted Persian walked into the room waving a plumed tail. "Is that Vincent?" Qwilleran asked.

"Yes, that's Vincent. He was Dianne's cat and I adopted him. They don't allow pets where I live, but he's happy in the gallery, and customers like him," said Todd, pinching his nose. Vincent circled the two men with dignity and oscillating tail.

"Did he experience any psychological trauma as a result of the Labor Day incident?"

"Apparently not. She always locked him up in the bedroom when she had company. He liked the waterbed, so he didn't object. In fact, when he came to live at the gallery, I bought him a cat-size waterbed."

"You did? Where did you buy it? I have a cat who'd like a waterbed."

"From a mail-order catalogue. I can get the information for you if you're interested."

"I'd appreciate that. And by the way, when Vincent lived at the Casablanca, did he make a habit of sitting on any of the art books?"

"Not that guy! He always looks for the softest seat in the house!"

Qwilleran cleared his throat. "I have something to tell you, Mr. Todd, and I hope it won't be too distasteful. Since living in the penthouse I've found evidence that Ross did not commit the murder and did not take his own life."

Todd gulped and pinched his nose. "What kind of evidence?"

"That's something I can't discuss until I've talked with my friend at the Homicide Squad."

"Oh, God! Does that mean the case will be reopened? We've had enough notoriety! Nobody knows me as a gallery director anymore; I'm the ex-husband of a murdered woman. I swear there are people who think I did it!"

In a kindly vein Qwilleran went on. "I understand there was a cocktail party the evening before Labor Day. If you were there and can recall some of the other guests, it may help corroborate my suspicions."

"I was there!" Todd said grimly. "Di had invited a lot of people including the girl from the newspaper, so I felt I should make an appearance. Ylana Targ. She writes the art column."

"How late did you stay?"

"Till about ten o'clock. I wanted to leave earlier because one fellow had brought jazz records, and jazz drives me up the wall, but it started raining—a real cloudburst. The skylight started leaking, and we had to put pots and pans around to catch the drips."

"Who was there when you left?"

"Ross, of course. Di and Ylana and Ross and another fellow from the building were playing Scrabble. A few others were in the living room, drinking and passing smokes around. I don't remember who they were."

"The fellow who made a fourth for Scrabble—do you know his name, or what he looked like?"

"He was slick-looking . . . well-groomed . . . sort of like a male model."

"Well, I won't detain you any longer," Qwilleran said. "Thanks for staying open. I'll call you about the tapestries when I get back to Pickax. I think we can do business."

He returned home, changed into a sweatshirt, track-lighted the gallery, filled the ice bucket on the bar, and put a bowl of cashews on the cocktail table. "Care for a few rounds of Scrabble while we're waiting?" he asked Koko.

The cat was more than willing. (No wonder! Qwilleran thought. He always wins!) On this occasion Koko was choosing a preponderance of low-scoring consonants like R, S, L, T, and N, and Qwilleran was considering another change in the rules, when the velvet paw drew forth D, E, V, B, O, G, and J. Immediately Qwilleran spelled JOVE, which netted fourteen points, leaving only seven for Koko.

"By Jove!" he said to the cat. "I think we've got it!"

At that moment there was an awkward knock at the door. He swept the tiles into the Scrabble box and went to admit his guest.

The Penniman bartender was loaded down with cassette-caddies and LPs. "Relax!" he said. "I'm not planning to stay three days. I brought a whole bunch so you can take your pick."

"Come in. I've been looking forward to this."

"Man, this is not too shabby!" said Jupiter in admiration as he perused the foyer. "And it opens right onto the terrace!"

"You've never been here before?"

"Never got invited."

"Wait till you see the sunken living room." Qwilleran opened the French doors. "The stereo is down in the pit. Here, let me take some of that load."

They carried the recordings into the gallery and piled them on the giant cocktail table. The guest stood in the middle of the pit with his hands in his pockets, staring in every direction. "I should think you'd get fed up with mushrooms."

"Don't knock them," said Qwilleran. "Since the scandal, they've become gilt-edged securities. They don't belong to me, of course. I'm just subletting. Let's have a drink. What's yours?" Hearing the rattle of icecubes, Koko made his imposing entrance through the open French doors. "Here comes the lord of the manor."

"Good-looking cat," said Jupiter. "Better than most of the rat catchers around this building."

It was almost as if Koko resented being lumped with rat catchers. From that moment on, he devised ways of tormenting the visitor. But first he had his saucer of white grapejuice.

Jupiter with his vodka on the rocks and Qwilleran with his club soda took seats on the long sofa, and the latter said, "They stole my car from the parking lot today."

"Par for the course," said the other with a shrug.

"You people around here are so damned casual about car theft!" Qwilleran complained. "Even the old ladies in the lobby talk about muggings the way we talk about weather in Moose County."

Koko jumped on the back of the long sofa and walked its length like a model on a runway. On the way back he stopped to sniff the guest's hair.

"Hey, what's going on back there?" Jupiter said, slapping the back of his head.

"Sorry," said Qwilleran, pushing the cat off the sofa. "He likes your shampoo . . . Now, can you tell me what happened at the hotel over the weekend?"

"It was in the *Fluxion* this afternoon, so it's no secret any more. Two men and a woman in a suite on the top floor were gunned down execution-style, so you know it's drug-related. The hotel always tries to put the lid on anything like that. They think it'll scare off the tourists and conventions . . . *Hey, what's he doing?*"

Koko was on the cocktail table, biting the corners of record jackets. Qwilleran sent him flying with a gentle backhand, and the cat spent the next ten minutes licking his damaged ego.

"How'd you get your big jazz collection, Randy?"

"I was lucky. I had an uncle who was a bebop drummer—

never made it big, but he got me hooked, and then he died and left me all his records. D'you have any requests?"

"Well, I told you I like sax—Sidney Bechet, Jimmy Dorsey, Stan Getz, Charlie Parker, Coltrane. If I could play an instrument, that's what I'd like to play. It's almost like the human voice."

"Okay, we'll start with Charlie ... What's that thumping noise?"

"That's Keestra Hedrog and her Gut Dancers. They rehearse in 14-B every Monday night. I'll close the doors and it won't bother us."

Koko was standing in the doorway, half in and half out of the room, and when Qwilleran climbed out of the pit and tried to close the double doors, the cat stood as if glued to the threshold. "Are you coming in or staying out?" Qwilleran asked.

Koko deliberated, unable to make up his mind, until a slight tap from a size twelve shoe sent him catapulting into the gallery—down into the pit, up onto the rim, circling it like an indoor track, picking up speed and flying across the cocktail table, scattering cassettes in all directions.

"Cripes! He's like a tornado!" Jupiter said as he retrieved his collection.

"Sorry, he's wound up tonight for some reason. . . . Koko! You behave, or leave the room!"

The cat jumped to the top of the bar, among the bottles and decanters, where he could keep the visitor under surveillance, and the evening progressed uneventfully for a while.

Jupiter played a program that went from bebop to swing to Chicago jazz to big band to Dixieland to blues to rag. After his third drink he pantomimed a bebop drummer in sync with a recording, and the frenetic performance sent Koko burrowing under the dhurrie.

"Now what's he doing?" the man wanted to know.

"That rug covers the stain where Dianne Bessinger bled to death."

"No kidding!"

"I believe it was Labor Day weekend. How long have you lived here?"

"I moved in . . . let's see . . . Memorial weekend."

"Did you get to know Dianne or Ross?"

"No, they never came into the bar, and I don't go for this kind of stuff." Jupiter waved an arm around the gallery walls.

Qwilleran said, "Since moving into this apartment I've discovered some new twists regarding the murder. Did you know that there are prominent men in town who would profit by Dianne's death?"

"No kidding!"

"It's a fact."

Jupiter said he'd like another drink, and after pouring it Qwilleran said, "What's more, I happen to have evidence that Ross did not kill Dianne."

"You're kidding!" Koko had returned to the sofa-back and was sniffing the bartender's head again. His neck was reddening. He brushed the cat away like an annoying fly.

"Yes, there's no doubt in my mind that it was a frame-up. In fact, I have an appointment at the Homicide Squad tomorrow—to turn my information over to the detectives."

"How'd you find out?" The vodka was coloring Jupiter's face to match his moustache.

"I have a snoopy nature and a little experience in criminal investigation. There are tenants who heard screams just before Ross landed on Yazbro's car. Dianne's murderer tossed the artist over the parapet, after dragging him down to the dark end of the terrace." Qwilleran kept a sharp eye on his guest and saw his hand go into his sweater pocket. "Want any more ice?" he asked as he carried his own glass to the bar. Feeling secure behind the massive piece of furniture, he went on. "But here's the clincher: You see that skylight up there? Someone was on the roof when it happened. There was a witness!"

Jupiter struggled to his feet. Qwilleran thought, he's half-bombed! The man walked unsteadily to the bar and stood on the dhurrie, his hand still in his pocket. Wordlessly the two of them faced each other across the bar, until the heavy silence was broken by a clatter of glassware as something dropped between them. Koko had flown through the air, landing on the bar with arched back, bushed tail, flattened ears, and bared fangs.

Taking advantage of the distraction, Jupiter sneaked around the end of the bar, snatching a small tube from his pocket. As he raised it there was a *click* and a knifeblade shot out. Qwilleran, without taking his eye off the knife, grabbed a bottle by the neck. For one frozen moment they faced each other. At the same time a blur of fur passed between the two men, landing on the assailant's shoulder. A whiplike tail flicked twice. There was a yell of pain, and the man put a hand to his eyes. The other hand wavered, and Qwilleran smashed down hard on the knife, then brought the bottle down on Jupiter's head. As he collapsed, Qwilleran kicked the knife away and stood over him with the bottle.

The French doors burst open! Two figures appeared on the level above. One of them had a gun.

"Hold it! I got you covered!"

Qwilleran started to raise his hands before he realized that the man with the handgun was wearing a red golf hat. The man behind him had the paunchy figure of Arch Riker.

"Call the police!" Qwilleran yelled.

Riker's ruddy face turned pale. "Qwill! You're supposed to be dead!"

Chapter 20

"I need a drink!" said Arch Riker after the police and their prisoner had cleared out.

"First tell me what the hell you're doing here!" Qwilleran demanded of his friend.

"I came to feed the cats! And claim your remains at the morgue!"

"I don't get it."

Riker explained slowly and clearly. "The police here called Brodie in Pickax early this morning. They told him someone shot at you on the freeway. They said your car crashed and burned. They said you were incinerated along with all dentification. They traced the car to you through the license plates."

"Someone stole my car! That's what happened."

"Whatever. I picked up your dental records from Dr. Zoller and caught the first plane out of Pickax. The whole of Moose County is in mourning."

Qwilleran started for the telephone. "I'd better call Polly."

"Don't! She'll have a stroke. She thinks you're dead. I'll call Brodie and he can break the good news to her. Also, I should call my news desk and the radio station. If you're feeling generous, you can pour me a double scotch."

When the two men settled down in the library with their drinks, Qwilleran posed a question: "Was the episode on the freeway a random shooting? Or did they think they were taking a shot at me?"

"Why would anyone want to shoot you?"

"It's a long story."

Koko walked into the room with feline insouciance as if nothing had happened all evening. He jumped to the library table and sat on the Van Gogh.

"Where's Yum Yum?" Riker asked.

"In the bedroom, sleeping her life away. I've got to get the cats back to Pickax. Something here disagrees with them."

"If people are taking shots at you and threatening you with knives, you'd better get your own tail back to Pickax, friend. What have you been doing? Meddling again? Snooping where you have no business?"

"Do you want to hear the whole story, Arch? Or do you want to preach a sermon?" Qwilleran asked.

He related the murder-suicide myth as reported in the newspaper and described Koko's several discoveries. "Here's the bracelet," he said, drawing it from a desk drawer.

"What's the significance of the numbers?"

"It's obviously a private code between lovers. I think the numbers refer to the value of letters in a Scrabble set. The 1-1-4-1, for example, could stand for L-O-V-E. It could also stand for T-O-F-U, although I doubt that—"

"How do you know so much about Scrabble all of a sudden?"

"I've found out it's not a bad game, Arch. I also tried entertaining Koko with a kind of scratch-Scrabble because he was bored, and I kept spelling words that started a train of thought. HOAX, for example. I began to wonder if Ross had been framed. At first I suspected Dianne's ex-husband."

"Pity us ex-husbands," said Riker. "We're always the first suspects. I live in mortal fear that someone will murder Rosie."

"The guy had a habit of pinching his nose, and I attributed it to guilt, but later I decided he was sensitive to cat dander."

"I'm glad the ex-husband got off the hook."

"There's more to the story, Arch. Do you want me to go on?"

"Please do. This is better than television."

"Okay. Then I realized that the developers who wanted to tear down the Casablanca had a strong motive for eliminating Dianne, and I began to suspect one of them—a guy by the name of F-l-e-u-d-d, pronounced Flood. Koko put the idea in my head—I won't tell you how, because you won't believe it. Anyhow, I checked it out with a guy at the *Fluxion* and learned that Fleudd has a past history of dirty tricks—nothing felonious, so far, just unscrupulous. So I thought, Suppose Fleudd had an agent in residence at the Casablanca who committed the double murder and tipped him off to my purpose here! The word AGENT turned up on the Scrabble board, and tonight I came up with JOVE—which is another name for Jupiter, right?"

Riker said, "You spelled HOAX and AGENT and JOVE because the ideas were already lurking in your subconscious."

"Be that as it may, when Jupiter came up here for a jazz session, I caught him in a couple of lies that suggested he had something to hide, so I tried a little prevarication of my own. After he'd had a few drinks and was losing control, I told him that someone on the roof had witnessed Dianne's murder through the skylight. That brought him out in the open, and if Koko hadn't whipped his tail at the crucial moment, I probably wouldn't be here talking to you."

"Yow," said Koko, who liked to hear his name mentioned.

"Speaking of tails, Koko is beginning to convey information by means of *tail language*, just as humans express emotions with body language. In the last few days he's been twisting his tail like a corkscrew."

"Are you trying to tell me that Koko knew the murderer was a bartender? If so, his tail's not the only thing that's screwy around here! What does a cat know about bar accessories?"

"Cats are gifted with senses that transcend human intelligence—a fact that's hard for us to accept—and Koko's senses are becoming more acute every year."

"You're really wound up tonight!" Riker held out his glass. "How about another touch? And then I'll turn in. This whole day has been an unnerving experience, and I've got to catch an early plane tomorrow. How about you? What have you decided about the Casablanca?"

"I'm giving it up. I'll hang around long enough to turn my evidence over to Lieutenant Hames, and then I'll rent a car and drive the cats back to Pickax . . . See you in the morning, Arch. The guestroom is down the hall, first door on the right. Just throw the cats' cushion off the bed."

Qwilleran, having made his decision to forget the Casablanca and go home, slept well that night. He slept well until about three o'clock in the morning, at which time he dreamed someone was pounding him on the stomach. When he opened his eyes, he was sitting and Koko was having a catfit—jumping on and off the bed, pouncing on his body, yowling and growling. When the cat ran from the room like a crazed animal, Qwilleran followed him down the bedroom hall, past the guestroom where Riker was snoring quietly, and into the foyer. There Koko clawed at the parquet floor, his tail tense and twisted. Next he was racing madly about, knocking things over, crashing into furniture.

Qwilleran listened. He could hear what was alarming the cat! It was a rustling, crackling, creaking under the floor!

Bolting back to the guestroom he yelled, "Arch! Arch! Get up! Get up! Quick! We're getting out of here!" Then he ran to the housephone and rang the night number. "Ring the fire bell!" he shouted. "Get everyone out! Get the Countess out! Fire between Twelve and Fourteen!"

Riker appeared in the foyer, groggy with sleep. "What? ... What? ..."

"No questions! Throw on some clothes!" Qwilleran pushed Yum Yum into the carrier, and Koko followed her without bidding. "Don't pack! No time to lose!" He pulled on pants and a sweater over his pajamas and pointed Riker to the door. "Down the stairs! Take the cats and start down! Hurry!"

He delayed long enough to hammer at the door of 14-B.

"Who is it?" a voice screamed.

"Building's on fire! Get out fast!" he yelled, then dashed for the stairs. The fire bell had started its urgent clamor, and at the tenth floor tenants began stumbling into the stairwell, grumbling and questioning.

Qwilleran caught up with Riker and said, "Give me the cats and you go ahead. Try to get a cab out in front."

"What . . . ?"

"Don't ask. Just do it!"

On the main floor the tenants, clutching cats and other treasures, were in an uproar.

Qwilleran shouted to Mrs. Tuttle over the heads of the milling crowd, "Can you get Miss Plumb out?"

"We phoned and Rupert went up there!"

The emergency door was open, and sirens could be heard, converging from all directions. Not stopping to recognize faces in the lobby, Qwilleran pushed through to the front door and found Riker flagging a cab. He put the carrier in the front with the driver and shouted, "Penniman Plaza!" before climbing into the backseat.

Angrily Riker said, "Will you tell me what this is all about?"

"I don't know." Qwilleran pounded his moustache with his fist . . . *"Oh, my God!"*

A deafening explosion rocked the cab. A flash of light illuminated Zwinger Boulevard. Looking out the rear window they saw the Casablanca crowned with fire.

"Jeez!" yelled the driver. "Cracked my windshield!" He started to pull over.

"Don't stop! There'll be fallout."

Moments later, the roof of the cab was showered with debris. Sirens screamed. Red and blue flashing lights filled the street. At the hotel the security guards were out on the sidewalk, looking toward the west.

While the cab waited, Qwilleran ran in to the registration desk and came out with the word that the Airport Motel was the nearest facility that would accept pets. The driver headed for the freeway, and his passengers rode in silence, sickened by the enormity of the disaster and stunned by the thought of their near-extinction. All was quiet in the cat carrier.

Finally Qwilleran said, "The noise I heard . . . the noise Koko detected . . . under the floor . . . It sounded like someone in the crawl space, setting a fire . . . I didn't have time to think . . . Now I realize they were planting a time bomb." His thoughts went to those whose lives had touched his briefly:

The Countess . . . Had they been able to dislodge her from her palace? Rupert with his handgun and Ferdinand with his muscle could overpower her, if not convince her, but they had only minutes to act. It was questionable that all three could escape.

Isabelle . . . She lived on one of the upper floors. Was she sober enough to recognize the danger? If not, her troubles were over.

Winnie Wingfoot . . . She also lived on Ten, but she had probably stayed out all night.

Keestra Hedrog . . . No cause for concern. She would fly to safety on her broomstick.

Amberina Kowbel . . . Poor, disorganized Amber! At least she would never have to unpack the eighty-four shopping bags and the mountain of cartons.

Courtney ... He would get out all right, lugging his Hudson River painting.

But what about the nameless old ladies in quilted robes? And all the others with canes and crutches?

He said, "It would have been wrong, Arch, to evict all those people and revert the Casablanca to a ritzy enclave for the superrich."

"They're evicted now, that's for sure," said Riker.

The driver tuned in the round-the-clock news station on his radio. After a few words about a woman arrested for selling her children, and about the discovery of three bodies buried in Penniman Park, the announcer said: "Bulletin! An explosion rocked the near West Side at 3:18 this morning, destroying the top floors of the Casablanca apartment house. The cause has not been determined. Firefighters and rescue crew are on the scene, and survivors are being evacuated. The blast broke windows in Junktown, and debris fell on an area of several blocks. There is no report on the number of casualties at this time. Stay tuned."

The cause has not been determined, Qwilleran thought. He remembered Amber saying, "The city would love it if something terrible happened to the Casablanca." He remembered that Raymond Dunwoody worked for the city and had lost an ear in a dynamite explosion. Had he planted dynamite in the crawl space between Twelve and Fourteen? If so, at whose behest? Qwilleran felt a tingling sensation in the roots of his moustache—the old familiar feeling that meant he was on the right trail. It was the man with an ear patch, he recalled, who had been the dinner guest of an affluent businessman at the Japanese restaurant; the generous host, Qwilleran now knew, was Fleudd. He had joined Penniman & Greystone in the spring, and Dunwoody had been living with Charlotte Roop for the last four months, no doubt relaying information about SOCK when she innocently discussed conversations she had overheard at Roberto's. Furthermore, it was Memorial Day weekend when Jupiter moved into the Casablanca. They were both undercover agents for Fleudd!

Riker broke the silence as they approached the motel. "I had enough sense to grab my credit cards, but I don't have my socks or my razor or my partial!"

"I'm in the same boat," Qwilleran said. "I have my wallet but I've lost everything else, including the cats' turkey roaster."

The clerk at the motel said, "We have a few rooms with waterbeds."

"Not for me," said Riker.

"I'll take one," said Qwilleran. "And do you have a disposable litterbox for the cats?"

Once situated in the room, he opened the door of the carrier and threw himself on the bed, while the Siamese inspected the room like veteran travelers.

In a matter of minutes someone kicked the door, and Riker was standing there with two paper cups. "Turn on the TV! There's live coverage on 'All-night News' right after the commercials. And here's some free coffee."

An announcer in a parka—filmed against a background of fire trucks, ambulances, and police cars—was saying, "Firemen are still fighting the blaze at the Casablanca apartments following an explosion at 3:18 this morning. The blast, of unknown origin, destroyed three floors of the building, which is almost a hundred years old."

The camera zoomed to the top of the blackened, smoldering structure, while the voice-over continued: "Forty-two residents have been hospitalized with injuries, and many are missing. No bodies have been recovered. Jessica Tuttle, manager of the Casablanca, says it is impossible to tell how many persons were in the building at the time of the explosion."

The face of Mrs. Tuttle, grim and managerial, flashed on the screen with a microphone thrust in front of her. "We have about two hundred tenants," she said, "but we don't know who was in the building when it happened and who wasn't. We're grateful for the prompt rescue attempts. Everything's been handled very efficiently ... No, I don't know what could have caused it. Perhaps the Lord is trying to tell us something."

A cracked voice off-camera shouted, "He's tellin' ya to tear the place down!"

The video cut to a Red Cross van and then a bus being loaded with refugees in nightclothes, some huddled in blankets. Voice-over: "Survivors are being bused to temporary shelters. Residents who were not on the premises at the time of the explosion are urged to telephone the following number to assist in the search for the missing . . ."

Qwilleran said, "There's Mrs. Jasper with Napoleon, boarding the bus!" She raised the cat's paw to wave at the camera. "And there's Yazbro, the skunk who let the air out of my tires!"

A man in a red golf hat was helping elderly tenants into the bus. Then, as the camera panned the windows of the loaded vehicle, showing strained and frightened faces, Qwilleran caught a glimpse of plucked eyebrows, marcelled hair, and a head tilted prettily to one side. His sigh of relief was more like a groan.

He said, "I wonder if poor Charlotte got out safely. I wonder if her 'gentleman friend' got out in time. If not, he's lost more than an ear on this job."

"Yow!" said Koko. He was sitting tall on the TV and washing up—just as he had sat tall on the volume of Van Gogh, licking his right paw and washing his mask, his whiskers, and particularly his right ear.

"Remarkable cat!" Qwilleran murmured without elucidating to his skeptical friend.

"I've had all I can take," said Riker. "I'm going to bed."

As soon as he was out of the room the Siamese engaged in a sudden expression of joy, chasing each other wildly under and over the furniture; they knew they were going home. Qwilleran propped himself against the headboard and watched the steeplechase.

Eventually Yum Yum snuggled down on his lap. She had lost her apathy and moody aloofness. Had she been affected by the "opalescence" that hung over the city like a stifling blanket? Did she find it unsettling to live on the fourteenth floor (which was really the thirteenth)? Or was she simply using feline strategy to get her own way? Qwilleran stroked her soft silky fur and called her his little sweetheart, and she responded by raising a velvet paw to touch his moustache, all the while squeezing her eyes and purring deliriously.

As for Koko, he jumped on the bed and flopped down in an attitude of exhaustion. It had been a strenuous night. He had saved an estimated two hundred persons.

THE CAT WHO KNEW A CARDINAL

Chapter 1

September promised to be a quiet month in Moose County, that summer vacation paradise 400 miles north of everywhere. After Labor Day the tourists returned to urban turmoil in the cities Down Below; the black fly season ended; children went reluctantly back to school; and everyday life cranked down to its normal, sleepy pace. This year the siesta was short-lived, however. Within a week the community was jolted by news of the Orchard Incident, as it was headlined by the local newspaper.

Prior to the Orchard Incident there was only one item of scandal on the gossip circuit in Pickax City, the county seat (population 3,000). Jim Qwilleran, semi-retired journalist and heir to the vast Klingenschoen fortune, was living in a barn! An apple barn! Oh, well, the townfolk conceded with shrugs and wagging heads, Mr. Q was entitled to a few eccentricities, being the richest man in the county and a free-wheeling philanthropist.

"Apple barn's better'n a pig barn," they chortled over coffee mugs in the cafés. After four years they had become accustomed to the sight of Mr. Q's oversize moustache with its melancholy droop. They no longer questioned the unorthodox *W* in the spelling of Qwilleran. And most of them now accepted the fact that the middle-aged divorced bachelor chose to live alone—with two cats!

Actually the facts were these: After twenty-five years of chasing the news in the capitals of the United States and Europe, Qwilleran had succumbed to the attractions of rural living, and he was captivated by barns, particularly an octagonal structure on the Klingenschoen property. The hundred-year-old fieldstone foundation was still intact, and its shingled siding was weathered to a silvery gray. Rising majestically as high as a four-story building, it overlooked a field of grotesque skeletons—the tortured remains of what was once a thriving apple orchard. Now it was of interest only to birds, including one that whistled an inquisitive *who-it? who-it? who-it?*

Qwilleran had first discovered the barn during his rambles about the Klingenschoen estate, which extended from the main thoroughfare of Pickax to Trevelyan Road, almost a half mile distant. The mansion of the notorious Klingenschoens, facing Main Street, had been converted into a theatre for stage productions, with the extensive gardens in the rear paved for parking. Beyond was a high, ornamental fence of wrought iron. Then came a dense patch of woods that concealed the barn and the orchard. After that, the lane leading to Trevelyan Road was hardly more than a dirt trail, winding through overgrown pastureland and past the foundations of old cottages once occupied by tenant farmers. If anyone remembered the lane at all, it was known as Trevelyan Trail. At the end of it an outsize, rural mailbox on a post was identified with the letter *Q*.

Originally the barn had been used for storing apples, pressing cider, and making apple butter. In recent years, all that remained was a wealth of empty space rising cathedral-like to the octagonal roof. Drastic renovation was required to make it habitable, but after Mr. Q moved in he was pleased to learn that the interior—on a warm and humid day—still exuded the aroma of Winesaps and Jonathans.

On a certain warm and humid day in September—the tenth of the month, to be exact—Qwilleran's housemates continually raised noses to sniff a scent they could not identify. They were a pair of Siamese—strictly indoor cats—and it was partly for their benefit that the barn had been converted to its present design.

With ramps and catwalks spiraling upward around the interior walls, with balconies floating on three levels, and with a system of massive beams radiating under the roof, the design allowed this acrobatic couple to race wildly, leap recklessly, and wrestle precariously on timbers thirty or forty feet overhead. For their quiet moments there were window-walls through which they could watch the flight of a bird, the fall of a leaf, and the ballet of wind-swept grasses in the orchard.

Qwilleran himself, having lived for two years in an apartment above the Klingenschoen garage, was awed by the spatial magnificence of his new residence. He was a big man in his comfort-loving fifties, with wide shoulders and long legs, and nature had not intended him to live in cramped quarters. On that warm and humid Saturday evening he strode about his domain enjoying the feeling of spaciousness and the dramatic perspectives, all the while stroking his bushy salt-and-pepper moustache with satisfaction. The last rays of the sunset slanted into the interior through high triangular windows, so shaped to preserve the symmetry of beams and braces.

"This time we got it right," he said to the cats, who were following him, strutting elegantly on long slender legs. "This is where we belong!" The three of them had lived at several addresses—sometimes happily, sometimes disastrously. "This is the last time we're going to move, you'll be glad to hear."

"Yow!" was the male cat's reply in a minor key; one could almost detect a note of skepticism.

Qwilleran made it a policy to converse with the Siamese, and the male responded as if he understood human speech. "We have Dennis to thank for all of this," he went on. "I only wish Mrs. Cobb could see it." Chuckling over a private reminiscence, he added, "She'd be tickled pink, wouldn't she?"

"Yow," said Koko in a soft, regretful tone as if he remembered Mrs. Cobb's superlative meatloaf.

The renovation had been designed and engineered by the son of Qwilleran's former housekeeper. Dennis Hough was his name, pronounced *Huff*, and his arrival in Pickax from St. Louis had created a stir for three reasons: The barn project was a sensation; the young builder had given his construction firm a whimsical name that delighted the locals; and the man himself had a mesmerizing effect on the women of Moose County. It was Qwilleran who had urged Dennis Hough to relocate, giving him the barn as his first commission and arranging Klingenschoen funds to back his new venture.

On this quiet Saturday evening the three barn dwellers were on a lofty catwalk high under the roof, and Qwilleran was reveling in the bird's-eye view of the comfortably furnished main floor when a piercingly loud demand from Yum Yum, the female, told him she cared more about food than architecture.

"Sorry," he apologized with a swift glance at his watch. "We're running a little late. Let's go down and see what we can find in the freezer."

The Siamese turned and scampered down the ramp, shoulder to shoulder, until they reached the lower balcony. From there they swooped down to the main floor like flying squirrels, landing in a deep-cushioned chair with two soft thuds—a shortcut they had been swift to discover. Qwilleran took a more conventional route down a circular metal stairway to the kitchen.

Although he had been a bachelor for many years, he had never learned to cook even the simplest survival food for himself. His culinary skills were limited to thawing and coffeemaking. Now he dropped two frozen Alaska king crablegs into boiling water, then carefully removed the meat from the shells, diced it, and placed a plateful on the floor. The Siamese responded by circling the dish dubiously, first clockwise and then counterclockwise, before consenting to nibble.

"I suppose you'd prefer breast of pheasant tonight," Qwilleran said.

If he indulged them it was because they were an important two-thirds of his life. He had no other family. Yum Yum was a lovable pet who liked to sit on his lap and reach out a paw to touch his moustache wonderingly; Koko was a remarkably intelligent animal in whom the natural feline instincts were developed to a supranormal degree. Yum Yum knew when Qwilleran wore something new or served the food on a different plate, but Koko's twitching nose and bristling whiskers could sense danger and uncover hidden truths. Yum Yum had a larcenous paw that pilfered small objects of significance, but Qwilleran was convinced that Koko craftily planted the idea in her head. Together they were a wily pair of accomplices.

"Those devils!" he had recently remarked to his friend Polly. "I believe they have the Mungojerry-Rumpelteazer franchise for Moose County."

Tonight, as the cats nosed their way through the crabmeat without enthusiasm, the man observed the disapproving posture of the fawn-furred bodies, the critical tilt of the brown ears, and the reproachful contour of the brown tails. He was beginning to read their body language—especially their tail language. His concentration was interrupted when the telephone rang and there was no one on the line. Thinking nothing of it, he proceeded to thaw a pouch of beef stew for his own dinner.

Ordinarily, Saturday evening would have found him dining at the Old Stone Mill with Polly Duncan, the chief librarian in Pickax and the chief woman in his life. She was out of town, however, and he gulped down the beef stew without tasting it, after which he retired to his studio to write his "Straight from the Qwill Pen" column for the local newspaper. His upbeat topic was the success of an unusual experiment in Pickax. On that very evening the Theatre Club was presenting the final performance of *The Famous History of the Life of King Henry the Eighth*. It had been a controversial choice of play. Even devotees of Shakespeare predicted there would be more persons on the stage than in the audience. Yet, the production had achieved the longest run in Pickax theatre history: twelve performances over a period of four weekends, with virtually no empty seats.

Qwilleran had attended opening night in the company of Polly Duncan, fifth row on the aisle, after which he wrote a justifiably favorable review. Now that the final box office results were known, he wrote a wrap-up piece commending the audiences for their discerning appreciation of serious drama and complimenting the small-town performers for their believable portrayals of sixteenth-century English nobility. It was not entirely accidental that he neglected to mention the director until the last paragraph. Hilary VanBrook had offended Qwilleran's journalistic pride by refusing to be profiled in the "Qwill Pen" column—an opportunity that the rest of Pickax equated with winning the lottery. Now the journalist was getting the last word, so to speak, by relegating the director to the last paragraph.

Pleased with his handiwork, he concocted a cup of coffee in a computerized machine, thawed a doughnut, and prepared to relax with a book he had bought secondhand. Qwilleran was thrifty by temperament, and despite his new financial status he retained many of his old habits of frugality. He drove a pre-owned car, gassed up at the self-serve pump, winced when he looked at pricetags, and always sought out bargains in used books.

After getting into pajamas and his comfortable old threadbare plaid robe, he put a match to some dry twigs and applewood logs in the fireplace and was about to stretch out in an oversized armchair when the telephone rang again. Once more he heard an abrupt click-off followed by a dial tone, and this time he questioned it. In the cities where he had lived and worked Down Below, the incident would suggest a burglar lurking in a phone booth down at the corner. In Moose County, where break-ins were rare, he could suspect only curiosity-seekers. There had been so much gossip about Qwilleran's apple barn (where a fruit grower had hanged himself from the rafters in 1920) that townfolk had been prowling about the premises and peering in the windows.

Putting the phone call out of his mind, he settled down in his big chair with his feet propped on the ottoman. Immediately, the Siamese came running in anticipation of a reading session. He often read aloud to them. They seemed to appreciate the sound of his voice, whether he was reciting from his secondhand Walt Whitman or reading the major league scores in the newspapers from Down Below. He had a richly timbred delivery—the result of his diction classes while dabbling in college drama—and the acoustics of the barn added to its resonance.

As he opened Audubon's *Birds of America*—the so-called Popular Edition of the nineteenth-century best-seller—his audience arranged themselves in comfortable bundles of attention, Yum Yum on his lap and Koko at his elbow on the arm of the chair. Ornithology was not one of Qwilleran's interests, but Polly had given him binoculars for his birthday and was trying to convert him to bird watching. Moreover, a book with two hundred colorplates was an irresistible bargain at a dollar.

"It's mostly pictures," he explained to the attentive animals as he turned the pages. "Who thinks up these absurd names? Black-bellied plover! Loggerhead shrike! Pied-billed grebe! Don't you think they're absurd?"

"Yow," Koko agreed.

"Here's a handsome one! It's your friend, the cardinal. The book says it resides in thickets, tangles, and gardens as far north as Canada."

Koko, an experienced pigeon watcher from Down Below, now spent hours every day at the windows on the various levels of the barn, sighting myriad small birds in the blighted orchard. Recently he had struck up an acquaintance with a visitor distinguished by red plumage, a royal crown, and a patrician beak, who whistled a continual question: *who-it?*

As Qwilleran turned the page to the rose-breasted grosbeak, both cats suddenly stretched to attention and craned their necks in the direction of the front door. Qwilleran also sat up and listened. He could hear a menacing rumble in the orchard that sounded alarmingly like army tanks, and he could see lights approaching the barn. He jumped to his feet and switched on the yardlights. Peering down the Trevelyan Trail he could see them coming—a column of headlights, weaving and bouncing as vehicles maneuvered through the ruts of the dirt road.

"What the deuce is this?" he barked, palming his moustache in perplexity. "An invasion?" The alarming tone of his voice sent both cats bounding out of sight; they had no intention of being caught in the line of fire.

One by one the vehicles turned out of the lane and parked in the tall grasses between the old apple trees. Headlights disappeared, and dark figures piled out of dark cars and trucks, converging on the barn. Only when they reached the pool of light in the yard did Qwilleran recognize them as the cast and crew of *Henry VIII*. They were carrying six-packs, coolers, brown paper bags, and pizza boxes.

His first thought was: Dammit! They've caught me in my pajamas and old robe! His second thought was: They look like hoboes themselves. It was true. The troupe wore backstage attire: tattered jeans, faded sweatshirts, washed out plaids, bedraggled sweaters, and grimy sneakers—a drastic change from the court finery of an hour before.

"Happy barn warming!" they shouted when they saw Qwilleran in the doorway. He reached around the doorjamb and threw a master switch that illuminated the entire interior. Uplights and downlights were concealed artfully in timbers and under balconies. Then he stepped aside and let them file into the barn—all forty of them!

If their eyes popped and their jaws dropped, it was for good reason. The walls of the main floor were the original stone foundation, a random stack of boulders held together by hidden mortar—craggy as a grotto. Overhead were massive pine timbers, some of them twelve inches square. Sandblasted to their original honey color, they contrasted softly with the newly insulated walls, painted white. And in the center of it all stood the contemporary fireplace, a huge white cube with three chubby cylindrical white flues rising to the center of the roof.

For the first time in anyone's memory the members of the Pickax Theatre Club were speechless. They wandered about the main level in a trance, gazing upward at the interlocking braces and beams, then downward at the earthen tile floor where furniture was arranged in conversation groups on Moroccan rugs. Then they collected their wits and all talked at once.

"Do you actually *live here*, Qwill?"

"I utterly don't believe it!"

"Neat! Really neat! Must've cost plenty!"

"Did Dennis do all of this? He's a genius!"

"Man, there's room for three grand pianos and two billiard tables."

"Look at the size of those beams! They don't grow trees like that any more."

"Swell place for a hanging."

"Qwill, darling, it's shattering! Would you like to time-share?"

Qwilleran had met the entire troupe at one time or another, and some of them were his favorite acquaintances in Pickax:

Larry Lanspeak, owner of the local department store, for one. He had auditioned for Cardinal Wolsey but landed the King Henry role, and his slight build required fifteen pounds of padding to match the girth of the well-fed monarch.

Fran Brodie, Qwilleran's interior designer and also daughter of the police chief. She auditioned for Queen Katharine but was ultimately cast as the beauteous Anne Boleyn. Perfect casting, Qwilleran thought. During the coronation scene he had been unable to take his eyes from her, and he was afraid Polly would hear his heavy breathing.

Carol Lanspeak, president of the club and everyone's friend. She was another capable aspirant for Queen Katharine and was deeply disappointed when director VanBrook picked her as his assistant and understudy for the queen.

Susan Exbridge, antique dealer and recent divorcée. She looked younger than her forty years and desperately wanted to play Anne Boleyn. When the director assigned her to do the Old Lady, she was furious but quickly recovered upon learning that the Old Lady had some bawdy lines that might steal the show.

Derek Cuttlebrink, busboy at the Old Stone Mill. He played five minor roles and was outstanding—not for his acting but for his bean-pole stature. Derek was six feet seven and still growing. Each time he made an entrance as another character, the audience whispered, "Here he comes again."

Dennis Hough, building contractor and new man in town. He, too, wanted to play Cardinal Wolsey but had to settle for a lesser role. Nevertheless, as the Duke of Buckingham, unjustly sentenced to death, he made a farewell speech that plunged the audience into tears night after night.

Eddington Smith, dealer in used books. This shy little old man played Cardinal Campeius, although no one could hear a word he said. It hardly mattered, because Cardinal Wolsey had all the best lines.

Hixie Rice, advertising manager for the local newspaper. As volunteer publicist for the club, she sold enough ads in the playbill to defray the cost of the sumptuous court costumes.

Wally Toddwhistle, the talented young taxidermist. He built stage sets for Theatre Club productions, and for *Henry VIII* he worked miracles with used lumber, spray paint, and bedsheets.

Also present was the director, Hilary VanBrook, who wandered about by himself and had little or nothing to say. The rest of the company was sky-high after the heady experience of closing night: the standing ovation, the flowers, and the general relief that the whole thing was over. Now they were reacting noisily. The Siamese watched the crowd from a catwalk and twitched noses in recognition of the cheese, pepperoni, and anchovy wafting upward. The troupe appeared to be starved. They wolfed the pizza and washed it down with cold drinks and a strong brew from Qwilleran's computerized coffeemaker, all the while talking nonstop:

"Somebody missed the light cue, and I had to say my lines in the dark! I could have killed the jerk at the lightboard!"

"When Katharine had her vision tonight, the angels dropped the garland on her head. I could hardly keep a straight face."

"Everything goes haywire on the last night, but the audience doesn't know the difference."

"I was supposed to carry a gold scepter in the procession, you know, and tonight nobody could find the blasted thing!"

"At least nobody stepped on my train this time, thank God. For these small mercies we are grateful."

"Halfway through the treason trial he went up like a kite, and I had to ad-lib. That's tough to do in Elizabethan English."

"The audience was really with us tonight, weren't they? The Old Lady even got some belly laughs from the balcony."

"Why not? She played it like the side of a barn!"

Qwilleran moved hospitably through the group, jingling the ice in his glass of Squunk water. (It looked like vodka on the rocks, but everyone knew it was mineral water from a flowing well at Squunk Corners.) He was not surprised to see Dennis Hough surrounded by women. Among them were Susan Exbridge, her dark hair still sleek after wearing the Old Lady's wig . . . and Hixie Rice, tossing her asymmetrical page-boy cut, which was auburn this week . . . and Fran Brodie, whose soft, strawberry blond curls contrasted surprisingly with her steely gray eyes.

Carol Lanspeak nudged Qwilleran's elbow slyly. "Look at Dennis with his groupies. Too bad I'm happily married to Larry; I'd join the pack."

Qwilleran said, "Dennis is a good-looking guy."

"And he has an interesting quality," Carol said. "Masculine and yet sensitive. He looks cool, but he's wired to a very short fuse. There were quite a few blowups during rehearsals."

"He's impulsive, but I overlooked his mood swings when we were working on the barn because he was doing such a great job. He was on his way to be a registered architect, you know, before he went into the construction business. Notice how he incorporated the old loft ladders into the design." As he spoke, the lanky busboy was halfway up a ladder, waving an arm and leg at those below. "The catwalks are for washing the high windows. We're going to hang tapestries from the railings."

"You could hang quilts," said Carol, whose taste ran to country coziness.

"No quilts!" Qwilleran said sternly. "Fran has ordered some contemporary hangings. They should be here any day now."

"Everyone in town is aching to see this place, Qwill."

"That's why we're having a public open house. The admission charge to benefit the library was Polly's idea."

"Serve refreshments and the library will clean up! We have a very hungry population." Then casually she inquired, with the licensed nosiness of a Pickax native, "Where's Polly tonight?"

Everyone knew that the Klingenschoen heir and the chief librarian spent weekends together. During bull sessions at the Dimsdale Diner one of the men usually asked, "Do you think he'll ever marry her?" And women drinking coffee at Lois's Luncheonette always brought up the topic: "Wonder why she doesn't marry him?"

To answer Carol's question Qwilleran explained, "Polly's in Lockmaster, attending a wedding. The librarian down there has a son who's going off the deep end."

"Who's taking care of Bootsie?" Another well-known fact in Pickax was the librarian's obsessive concern for her young cat.

"I went over there tonight to feed him, and I'll go again tomorrow morning to fill up his four hollow legs and police his commode. I never saw a cat eat so much!"

"He's still growing," Carol said.

"Polly will be home in the late afternoon to tell me what the bride wore and who caught the bouquet and all that guff. I don't know why you women are so wild about weddings."

"You talk like a grouchy old bachelor, Qwill."

"I'd rather go to a ballgame. Do you realize that I haven't seen a major league game in four years? And I was born a Cub fan in Chicago."

"It's your own fault, Qwill. You know very well that Larry would love to fly you down to Chicago or Minneapolis. He's bought a new four-seater. Polly and I could go along for a shopping binge. Or maybe she'd like to see the game, too."

"Polly—does—not—like—baseball!" Qwilleran said with emphasis. Nor shopping, either, he thought, reflecting on her limited wardrobe assembled haphazardly at Lanspeak's Department Store during sales.

Carol's husband joined them. "Did I hear my services being volunteered?"

At first glance the Lanspeaks were a plain-looking middle-aged couple, but they had a youthful source of energy that made them civic leaders and genial company as well as excellent actors. Qwilleran often wondered what they ate for breakfast. He said,

"Larry, you were great onstage! The kingliest Henry I've ever seen!"

"Thanks, fella. Let me tell you, it's good to be thin again. Besides navigating Henry's belly around the stage, I had to *think fat!* That's quite an adjustment! And then there was that damned itchy beard! I shaved it off as soon as the final curtain fell."

Carol asked, "How did Polly like the play?"

"She gave it raves, and we both thought the crowd scenes were tremendously effective. How did you manage all those kids?"

"It wasn't easy—getting them into costume, keeping them quiet backstage, pushing them out on cue. They dressed at the school, you know, and we transported them on school buses. *Trauma time!* Fortunately, Hilary had directed the play before and knew all the tricks. As his assistant I learned a lot; I won't deny that." She turned her back to the other guests and lowered her voice. "But as president of the club and wife of the president of the school board, I wish to go on record as saying *I can't stand the man!*"

A large percentage of the Pickax population entertained a loathing for Hilary VanBrook, principal of the high school. At fault was his abrasive personality and unbearable conceit. The public even resented the turtlenecks he wore to school. In Moose County there was something subversive about an administrator who wore black turtlenecks instead of the expected white shirt and quiet tie. But chiefly annoying was his habit of being eminently successful at everything he proposed, no matter how preposterous it appeared to parents, teachers, the superintendent of schools, and the school board.

Principal-bashing, therefore, was a favorite pastime. He was an unattractive man, and behind his back he was called Horseface. Yet, everyone remained in awe of his capabilities and self-assurance. It was because of his brilliant record as a school administrator and his reputation as a brain that the Theatre Club had allowed him to mount a play that was considered too dull, on a stage that was too small, with a cast that was too large. And now *Henry VIII* was going into the books as another triumph for Horseface.

"Yes," Larry said grudgingly in a low voice, "that scurvy knave has done it again! Ticket sales were so good we actually made a profit. With all those kids in the cast, you know, the hall was filled with their relatives, friends, and classmates." He glanced to left and right to ascertain the director's whereabouts and continued in a stage whisper. "He made two political mistakes. He should certainly *not* have played Cardinal Wolsey himself, and he should definitely *not* have brought someone from the next county to play Queen Katharine. We have plenty of talent right here in Moose County."

Qwilleran scanned the scattered groups of guests. "What happened to the queen? I don't see her here tonight."

Carol said, "She left right after the curtain. Got out of makeup in a hurry and didn't even say goodbye to the cast."

"Well, we weren't very cordial to her, I'm afraid," Larry confessed, "although we told her about the party and how to get here, and she wrote it down. I thought she'd show up. Of course, she lives in Lockmaster, and that's a sixty-mile drive, so I guess she can be excused."

Carol squeezed her husband's arm. "How do you like the barn, honey?"

"Fantastic! What condition was it in, Qwill, before you started?"

"Structurally solid, but filthy! For years it had been a motel for birds, cats, bats, and even skunks. Fran hung those German prints as an apology to the dispossessed bats." He pointed to a group of four framed zoological prints of flying mammals, dated 1824.

"You should have the barn photographed, Qwill, for a magazine."

"Yes, I'd like to see it published—for Dennis's sake. And Fran did a great job with the furnishings, considering I'm not the easiest client to get along with. John Bushland is coming up from Lockmaster to shoot some pictures for insurance purposes. I'm curious to know how everything looks on film."

"Don't we have a good photographer here?" Larry asked sharply. There had been jealous rivalry between Pickax and Lockmaster for a century or more.

"No one with Bushy's talent and experience and equipment."

"You're right. He's good," Larry acknowledged.

Someone shouted "Last call for pizza!" and the crowd swarmed to the kitchen snack bar—all except Hilary VanBrook. While the others had mingled in shifting clusters, the director had stayed on the periphery. In his bottle-green corduroy sports coat and red turtleneck he was clearly the best-dressed individual in the largely raggle-taggle assemblage. With shoulders hunched, hands in pockets, and a saturnine expression on his gaunt and homely face, he appeared to be studying— with a critical eye—the handhewn and woodpegged framework of the building, the design of the fireplace, the zoological prints, and the printer's typecase half filled with engraved metal plates mounted on wooden blocks.

He was standing in front of a pine wardrobe, seven feet high, when Qwilleran approached and said, "That's a Pennsylvania German *schrank* dating 1850 or earlier."

"More likely Austrian," the director corrected him. "You can see the piece had painted decoration originally. It's been stripped and refinished, which lessens its value, as you probably know."

Qwilleran devoutly wished that Dennis's mother had been present to refute the man's pronouncement. VanBrook delivered it without looking at his listener. He had a disconcerting habit of rolling his eyes around the room while discoursing. Exercising admirable restraint, Qwilleran replied, "Be that as it may, let me congratulate you on the success of the play."

The director flashed a glance at the frayed lapels of Qwilleran's old plaid robe. "Its success came as no surprise to me. When I proposed doing the play, the opposition came from persons with little theatre experience or understanding of Shakespeare. A dull play, they labeled it. With competent direction there are no dull plays. Furthermore, *Henry VIII* addresses problems that are rife in our society today. I insist that our senior students study *Henry VIII*."

Qwilleran said, "I understand there was no Shakespeare taught in Pickax before you took the helm."

"Regrettably true. Now our freshmen are exposed to *Romeo and Juliet*, sophomores read *Macbeth*, and juniors study *Julius Caesar*. Not only do they read the plays; they speak the lines. Shakespeare is meant to be spoken."

Listening to VanBrook's theatrical voice and looking past his shoulder, Qwilleran could see the ramp leading down from the balcony. Koko was descending the slope to investigate, walking with a purposeful gait, his eyes fixed on the principal. Effortlessly and silently the cat rose to the top of the *schrank* and assumed a position above the man's head, gazing down with a peculiar stare. Qwilleran, hoping that Koko had no intentions that might prove embarrassing, gave the cat a stern glance and cleared his throat pointedly before inquiring of VanBrook, "What do you think of the job Dennis did with this great barn of a place?"

"Derivative, of course," VanBrook said with a lofty display of design acumen.

"According to Dennis, ramps are in keeping with barn vernacular. Any resemblance to the Guggenheim Museum is purely coincidental. Those ladders," Qwilleran went on, "are the original loft ladders; the rungs are lashed to the siderails with leather thongs."

Apparently the director could feel Koko's stare at the top of his head, and he passed his hand over his hairpiece. (That hairpiece was a topic of much discussion in Pickax, where men were expected to have the real thing or none at all.) Then VanBrook turned abruptly and looked at the top of the *schrank*.

Hastily Qwilleran said, "This is our male Siamese, Kao K'o Kung, named after a thirteenth-century Chinese artist."

"Yow!" said Koko, who knew his name when he heard it.

"The Yuan dynasty," the principal said with a superior nod. "He was also a noted poet, although that is not generally known by Westerners. His name means 'worthy of respect' or words to that effect. An exact translation is difficult." He turned his back to the Pennsylvania German *schrank*, which had suddenly become Austrian, and Qwilleran was glad that the cat staring at the hairpiece was Koko and not his accomplice. Yum Yum the Paw would snatch it with a lightning-fast grab and carry it up the ramp to the bedroom, where she would hide it under the bed or, worse still, slam-dunk it in the toilet.

VanBrook was saying, "Appreciation of all the arts is something I have introduced into the curriculum here, as I did when I was principal of Lockmaster High School. It is my contention that graduates who play instruments badly or draw still lifes poorly contribute nothing to the cultural climate of the community. The essence of a true education is an *appreciation* of art, music, literature, and architecture." He gazed about the barn speculatively. "I should like to bring grades nine to twelve over here, one class at a time, on field trips in the next few weeks."

Qwilleran blinked at the man's audacity, but before he could formulate a reply there was a murmur on top of the *schrank*, a shifting of paws, and a furry body swooped over the principal's head and landed on a rug ten feet away, after which Koko yowled loudly and imperiously.

Larry Lanspeak heard him and interpreted the message. "C'mon, you guys," he called out. "Chugalug! Qwill's cats need to get some sleep."

Reluctantly the guests started gathering paper plates and napkins, collecting empties, straightening chairs. Gradually they drifted out into the night, clowning and uttering war whoops.

As Fran gave Qwilleran a theatrical goodnight kiss, he said to her, "Was this party your idea? Did you ring my phone a couple of times and hang up?"

"We had to be sure you were here, Qwill. We thought you might be out with Polly. Where is Polly tonight?"

"In Lockmaster at a wedding."

"Oh, really? Why didn't you go?" she asked slyly. "Afraid you'd catch the bouquet?"

"Don't be cheeky, young lady," he warned her. "I haven't paid your bill yet." He watched her leave—a good designer, easy to like, half his age and refreshingly impudent, stunning even in grubby rehearsal togs. Dennis walked out with Susan, the two of them sharing a secret joke. Eddington Smith tagged along with the Lanspeaks, who were giving him a ride home.

VanBrook lingered long enough to say, "I'll have my assistant contact you about the student tours."

This time Qwilleran was ready with a reply. "An excellent idea," he said, "but I must make one stipulation. I insist that Dennis conduct the tours and explain the design and construction methods. If you will take the initiative and line him up, I'll consent gladly." He knew that the principal and the builder had been at odds during rehearsals.

VanBrook rolled his eyes around the interior once more, said a curt goodnight, and followed the others who were trooping to their parked cars, all of them laughing and shouting, reliving the play, hitching rides, making dates. Headlights were turned on and motors turned over, some of them purring and others backfiring or roaring like jets. Qwilleran watched the taillights bounce and weave as they followed the rutted lane to the highway.

Closing the door, he turned off the yardlights and most of the interior lights, then gave the Siamese a bedtime treat. "You two characters behaved very well. I'm glad you sent them home, Koko. Do you realize what time it is?"

The Siamese gloated over their morsel of food as if it were a five-course meal, and as Qwilleran watched them his mind wandered to his recent visitors. He envied them the experience of rehearsing, performing, bowing to applause, grieving over roles that got away, complaining about the director, agonizing over miscues and lost props. For a short time he had been an active member of the club, but Polly had convinced him that learning lines and attending rehearsals would rob him of time better spent on serious writing. Actually, he suspected, the middle-aged librarian who wore size sixteen was jealous of the svelte and exuberant young actresses in the club. Polly was an intelligent woman and a loving companion who shared his interest in literature, but she had one fault. Jealousy caused her to be overpossessive.

The Siamese, having licked their empty plate for several minutes, were now laving their brown masks and white whiskers with moistened brown paws, as well as swiping long pink tongues over their nearly white breasts. Then, in the midst of a swipe, they both stopped and posed like waxworks with tongues extended. Abruptly, Koko broke away and trotted to the front door, where he peered through the side windows into the darkness. Qwilleran followed, and Yum Yum padded along behind. As he stared into the blackness of the orchard he could see the last set of taillights disappearing down the trail and turning into Trevelyan Road.

The spill of light from the barn also picked up a metallic reflection that had no business being in the orchard. A car without lights was still parked among the trees.

He huffed into his moustache. "Can you beat that?" he said aloud. "I'll bet it's Dennis and Susan . . . Why don't they go to his place or her place?"

"Yow," Koko agreed.

Dennis's wife and child were still in St. Louis, and he had not seen them for several months, owing to the barn project and the play rehearsals.

"Oh, well, live and let live," Qwilleran said as he turned out yardlights and remembered his own reckless youth. "Let's screen the fireplace and go to bed."

He turned away from the front door and followed Yum Yum, who was scampering up the ramp, but Koko remained stubbornly at his post, a determined voyeur, his body taut and his tail pointed stiffly. Qwilleran heard a low rumble. Was it a growl?

"Cut that out," he called to him. "Just mind your own business and turn in. It's three o'clock."

Still the cat growled, and the rumble that came from his lower depths ended in a falsetto shriek. It was an ominous pronouncement that Koko never made without reason. Qwilleran picked up a jacket and a flashlight and started out the door, pushing the excited cat aside with a persuasive toe and shouting a stern "No!" when he tried to follow.

"Hey, you down there!" he called out as he crossed the barnyard, swinging the flashlight in arcs. "Any trouble?"

The night was silent. There was no traffic noise from Main Street at that hour. No wind whistled through the dying apple trees. And there was no movement in the vehicle, a well-kept late-model car. No one turned on the ignition or switched on the headlights.

Qwilleran flashed his light on the surrounding ground and between the trees. Then he beamed it into the car at an oblique angle to avoid reflections in the window glass. Only the driver could be seen, and he was slumped over the wheel.

Heart attack, Qwilleran thought in alarm. Only when he hurried to the other side of the car did he see the blood and the bullethole in the back of the head.

CHAPTER 2

Qwilleran's hand hovered over the phone for an instant before he lifted the handset and reported the homicide. As a hard-headed journalist Down Below he would have notified his newspaper first and then the police, but there was a sense of intimacy in a town the size of Pickax, and his loyalties had changed. He knew the victim, and the police chief was a personal friend. Without further hesitation he called Chief Brodie at home.

"Brodie!" was the gruff answer from a man who was accustomed to being roused from sleep at 3 A.M.

"Andy, this is Qwill, reporting a homicide in your precinct."

"Where?"

"In my orchard."

"Who?"

"Hilary VanBrook."

There was a momentary pause. "What was he doing in your orchard?"

"There was a party here for the Theatre Club, and he was the last to leave. He was shot before he had a chance to start his car."

Brodie shifted from gruff lawman to concerned parent. "Was Fran there?"

"The whole club was here."

"Be right over."

"Hold it, Andy! The driveway is probably full of tire tracks and footprints, if that concerns you. Come in the other way, through the theatre parking lot. I'll meet you there and unlock the gate."

Brodie grunted and hung up.

Qwilleran pulled pants and a sweater over his pajamas, picked up the flashlight once more, and headed at a run toward Main Street. The road through the woods had been freshly graded and graveled, and it was only a few hundred yards to the fence. Even so, when he arrived at the gate headlights were already illuminating the theatre parking lot. In a town the size of Pickax, everything was five minutes away from everything else.

He jumped into Chief Brodie's car and pointed the way through the woods, while other vehicles with flashing lights followed. He explained, "We've had trespassers lately, so I lock the gate at night."

"How'd you find out about VanBrook?" Brodie snapped.

"After everyone left the orchard, there was still one car parked among the trees. Then that cat of mine started howling suspiciously. I went out to investigate and found VanBrook slumped over the steering wheel."

"He wasn't a happy individual. No wife. No family. Could be suicide."

"Not with a bullethole in the back of his head," Qwilleran said. "It blew his hairpiece off." They had reached the rear of the barn. "Park here. All the activity was on the other side."

A Pickax prowl car and a state police vehicle pulled alongside, leaving room for the ambulance, which arrived immediately, and the medical examiner.

"Anything I can do?" Qwilleran asked.

"Stay indoors till we need you," Brodie ordered. "Leave the house lights on."

Qwilleran threw the master switch once more, and the entire barn glowed like a beacon, the light spilling out to illuminate the surrounding grounds.

The Siamese were nervous. They knew something was wrong. Strangers were milling about the yard, and police spotlights were turning the misshapen trees into frightening giants. Qwilleran picked up the cats and climbed the ramp with one squirming animal under each arm. In their own apartment on the top balcony there were comforting carpets and cushions, useful baskets and perches, a scratching post, and TV. Slipping a video of birdlife into the VCR to calm them, he returned to the main level, feeling mildly guilty; he had not yet called the newspaper.

He notified the night desk, asking if they had a reporter available. Yes, they said, Roger was subbing for Dave.

"Tell him to use the Main Street entrance," Qwilleran said.

Then he tried to reach Larry Lanspeak; as president of the school board Larry deserved to be notified immediately. It appeared, however, that the Lanspeaks had not yet arrived home. They lived in the country; Larry was a cautious driver; and they always drove Eddington Smith home first. Qwilleran gave them another fifteen minutes to reach the affluent suburb of West Middle Hummock before he punched their number again.

Larry answered on the tenth ring. "Just walked in the door, Qwill. What's up?"

"I have bad news for you, Larry. You'll have to shop around for another high school principal."

"What do you mean?"

"VanBrook has been killed."

"What happened? Car accident?"

"You won't believe this, Larry, but someone put a bullet through his skull. The police are here, combing the orchard with their spotlights."

"How did you find out? Did you hear the shot?"

"Didn't hear a thing, except someone's jalopy backfiring. After the gang pulled out, there was one car left. I went out to check it."

"This is a mess, Qwill. The police will assume it was one of us."

"I don't know what they'll assume, but we'd better be prepared to answer questions tomorrow."

Larry volunteered to call the superintendent of schools and alert him. "Otherwise he'll hear it on the radio, or the cops will bang on his door. I can't believe this is happening!"

A chugging motor in the yard caught Qwilleran's ear. "Excuse me, Larry. Another car just drove in. I think it's a reporter. I'll talk with you later."

The car parked alongside the police vehicles, and Qwilleran recognized Roger MacGillivray's ten-year-old boneshaker. He went out to meet the bearded young man who had given up teaching history in order to report living history for the local paper.

"What happened?" asked the reporter, slinging two cameras over his shoulder.

"We had a Theatre Club party here after the final performance, and at three o'clock everyone drove away except the director. That's all I know. If you want details, you'll have to get them from Brodie. He's down there where it happened."

Qwilleran watched the scene as Roger approached the chief and said a few words. Brodie turned and threw a scowl at the barn, then answered some questions tersely before jerking his thumb over his shoulder. Roger snapped a couple of quick shots before retreating to the barn.

"How come you're working tonight?" Qwilleran asked as he opened the door.

"Dave had to go to a wedding in Lockmaster, so I switched with him," Roger explained. "Hey, this place is fabulous! Sharon would love to see it!"

"Bring her down here for a drink some evening. Bring Mildred, too."

"One of us will have to baby-sit, so I'll send the girls alone. Don't let my mother-in-law drink too much. She's been hitting the bottle since Stan died. I don't know why. She's one hundred percent better off without him, but ... you know how women are!"

"How will Sharon and Mildred react when they hear about their principal's sudden demise?"

"They'll go into shock, but they won't be sorry. VanBrook did some good things for the curriculum and the school's academic standing, and they admired him in a grudging way, but none of the teachers liked the guy, and that included me. He treated us like kids. And then there were his meetings! Teachers don't like meetings anyway—they're nonproductive—and Horseface chaired meetings that were just boring ego trips. That's the chief reason I quit and went to work for the paper. After that, whenever I went to the school to cover a story, VanBrook made me feel like the plumber who'd come to fix the latrines . . . Any idea who shot him? It had to be one of your guests. Right?"

"I'm not hazarding any guesses, Roger, and certainly not for the rapacious press. Would you like a beer?"

"Might as well. Okay if I look around?"

"Go ahead. On the first balcony I have a sleeping room and writing studio. You can open the door and look in, but don't expect it to be tidy. On the second balcony is the guestroom. The cats have the third level. Don't disturb them; they've had a harrowing night."

"Don't worry. You know me and cats! Sharon says I'm an ailurophobe."

The phone rang, and it was Qwilleran's old friend on the line. Arch Riker, fellow journalist from Down Below, was now editor and publisher of the local newspaper. "What's going on there?" he demanded. "The night desk tipped me off. Why didn't you let me know?"

"There's nothing you can do, Arch. Go back to bed. Roger's here. You'll read about it on your front page Monday."

"Any suspects?"

"You can ask Roger."

"Put him on."

The reporter's remarks on the phone revealed that he had learned nothing from Brodie. After hanging up he said to Qwilleran, "How about telling me who was here at the party?"

"That information may be crucial to the investigation. I can't discuss it at this time," Qwilleran recited in a monotone.

"Whose side are you on, anyway?"

Before Qwilleran could answer there was an authoritative knock on the door, and Brodie was standing there with orders for Roger to clear out. The reporter made a routine protest but shouldered his cameras and drove away.

"Want a cup of coffee?" Qwilleran asked the chief.

"Hell, I wouldn't take my life in my hands by drinking the stuff you brew!" He strode into the barn with a lumbering swagger. Off duty he was a genial Scot who wore a kilt and played the bagpipe. Tonight he was the gruff, grumbling investigator, taking in the scene with a veteran's eye.

"Any clues out there?" Qwilleran asked. "Any evidence?"

"I'm here to ask questions, friend—not answer them." Brodie scanned the contemporary furniture upholstered in pale tweeds and leathers. "Got anything to sit on? Like kitchen chairs?"

Qwilleran led the way to the snack bar.

"I smell pizza," said the chief.

"Actors get hungry. You should know that, Andy. You've been feeding one."

"Not any more," said Brodie with a frown. "Fran's moved out. Wanted her own place. Don't know why. She had it comfortable at home." He looked troubled—a north-country father who thought daughters should either marry and settle down or live at home with the folks.

Qwilleran said, "It's normal for a young career woman to want her own apartment, Andy."

Brodie snapped out of his fatherly role. "Who was here tonight?"

"I happen to have a printed guestlist." He handed the chief one of the playbills, listing the cast of characters in order of appearance.

Brodie ran a thumb down the righthand side of the page. "Were all these people here?"

"All except the woman from Lockmaster who played the

queen. And of course the spear carriers left on the school bus right after the coronation scene. You saw the show, didn't you?"

Brodie grunted an affirmative. "What were they all doing here besides eating pizza?"

"Drinking beer and soft drinks and coffee . . . hashing over the run of the play . . . celebrating its success . . . making a lot of noise."

"Were they smoking anything they shouldn't?"

"No. Carol puts the clamps on that. She runs a tight ship. Fran can tell you."

"Any arguments? Any brawls?"

"Nothing like that. Everyone was in a good humor."

"Did you see anybody hanging around the orchard that didn't belong?"

"Not tonight, but we've had curiosity-seekers prowling around ever since we moved in."

"How come VanBrook honored the party with his presence? He was an unsociable cuss."

"He had an ulterior motive," said Qwilleran. "He wanted to bring the entire student body tramping through my barn on field trips. He didn't ask me; he told me!"

"That sounds like him, all right. How popular was he in the club?"

"Ask Fran about that. I'm not an active member."

"Did you hear gunfire in the orchard?"

"No, but the cats heard something, and when I looked out the window I saw the taillights of a car pulling onto the highway."

"Which way did it go?"

"Turned right."

"Notice anything about the taillights?"

"Now that you mention it, Andy, they weren't the horizontal ones you see on passenger cars. They were vertical and set wide apart, like those on a van or truck."

"How long has your mailbox been knocked over?"

"It was okay when I picked up my Saturday mail."

"Well, somebody sideswiped it and bent the post."

"That should make your job easier," Qwilleran said, thinking,

Somewhere there is a vehicle with a damaged fender over the right front wheel.

Brodie stood up. "No need to keep you up all night. I'll get back to you in the morning."

"Not too early—please!"

The chief walked to the door and turned to give the interior a final scowling appraisal. "I climbed many a ladder like that when I was a kid. What are the three white things that look like smokestacks?"

"Smokestacks. It's a contemporary idea for venting a fireplace. Bring your wife over some evening. She'll enjoy seeing Fran's work."

"Did my daughter pick out all this furniture?" Brodie asked, more in dismay than admiration.

"She gets all the credit. She has a good eye and good taste."

Brodie grunted and turned to leave, but he lingered with his hand on the door handle. "This fella that did over your barn—Dennis what's-his-name . . ."

"H-o-u-g-h, pronounced Huff. He's Iris Cobb's son."

"I hear Fran is kinda thick with him." He searched Qwilleran's face for verification. "He's married, you know."

"Don't worry," said Qwilleran. "All the women in town go for Dennis, but he dotes on his family, and when they move up here, the fringe element will cool off. Meanwhile, Fran and Dennis have merely collaborated on this project."

"I hope you're right . . . Well, good night. We've got the driveway blockaded at the far end, and we're leaving a man on duty. The crime lab is coming up from Down Below." Brodie walked away a few steps and added, "Something tells me this'll be an easy case to solve."

Qwilleran turned out the houselights and climbed the ramp to his bedroom, but he was in no mood to sleep. He perused a playbill and tried to imagine each actor with a smoking gun in hand. In each case it looked like bad casting. He wondered how soon Brodie would start ringing doorbells and rousing the party goers from their beds for interrogation. The chief would undoubtedly start with his own daughter, who lived in Indian Village, a popular apartment complex for singles. Susan, Dennis, and Hixie also had apartments there. The Lanspeaks lived farther out in a rambling country house. Poor Eddington Smith holed up downtown in the bookbinding workshop behind his bookstore. Other members of the club came from surrounding towns: bustling Kennebeck, quaint Sawdust City, ramshackle Wildcat, and as far away as the resort town of Mooseville. Only Wildcat lay to the south of Pickax; a driver heading for Wildcat would turn right on Trevelyan Road upon leaving Trevelyan Trail.

Lying there awake he remembered his houseman's prediction when he first saw the renovated barn. The white-haired and highly respected Pat O'Dell had been custodian of the Pickax high school before retiring and starting his own janitorial service. He gazed up at the lofty beams and said in a fearful voice, "Will yourself be livin' here?"

"Yes, I enjoy lots of space, Mr. O'Dell, and I'm counting on you and Mrs. Fulgrove to handle the maintenance as you did in my old apartment."

"The divil himself would be hard up to clean the windows way up there, I'm thinkin', or sweep the cobwebs down."

"That's one reason we built the catwalks. I hope you're not leery about heights."

Mr. O'Dell shook his head with foreboding. "An old farmer, they're tellin', was after puttin' a rope around his neck and swingin' from one of those rafters. It were seventy year since. Sure an' that's when a blight fell on the apple trees. It's troubled I'd be, Mr. Q, to live here."

"But life must go on, Mr. O'Dell. Let me show you where we hide the key, in case you want to work when I'm not here. Mrs. Fulgrove will do the light cleaning on Wednesdays."

"Saints preserve us!" was the janitor's parting remark as he ventured a final apprehensive look at the superstructure. That had been two weeks ago, and now Mr. O'Dell would be saying, "Sure an' I told you so."

When at last Qwilleran managed to doze off on Sunday morning, it seemed a mere fifteen minutes before he was jolted awake by the telephone, its ring sounding more urgent than usual.

Fran Brodie was on the line. "Dad just called and broke the news! This is terrible! What does it mean?"

"It means we'll all be questioned," Qwilleran replied sleepily.

"No one in the club would do such a thing, do you think? Dad refused to tell me if they had a suspect or if they found any evidence. He can be so exasperating when he's playing the cop. It must have been turmoil in your orchard last night."

"It was, and I've had about fifteen minutes' sleep."

"Sorry I woke you, Qwill. Go back to sleep. I'm going to call some of the others now."

Qwilleran looked at his bedside clock. In five minutes WPKX would feature the Orchard Incident on the eight o'clock newscast. He steeled himself for another misleading bulletin, WPKX style, with inflated prepositions and pretentious pauses:

"Hilary VanBrook, principal of Pickax High School, was found dead early this morning IN . . . a parked . . . car. Police say VanBrook was shot in the head AFTER . . . an all-night party held AT . . . a barn . . . occupied BY . . . James Qwilleran. Suicide has been ruled out, and robbery was apparently not the motive according TO . . . Police Chief . . . Andrew . . . Brodie. No further details are available AT . . . this . . . hour."

Qwilleran muttered, "I could punch that announcer IN . . . the teeth!" The reference to "a parked car" and "all-night party" would have tongues wagging all over the county, he predicted. It was Sunday. He could imagine the buzzing among church goers. Telephone lines would be jammed; restaurants would be crowded with folks who never dined out as a rule; neighbors who disliked yardwork would be raking leaves and spreading rumors across back fences. Immediately Qwilleran's own phone started to ring.

Larry Lanspeak was the first to call. "Heard anything more, Qwill?"

"Not a word."

"Okay if I drop in for a few minutes before church?"

"Sure. Come along."

"Carol's on the altar committee, so I'll have to drop her off at ten o'clock with a trunkful of mums."

"Come through the theatre parking lot," Qwilleran instructed him. "The lane's blockaded."

Next Eddington Smith called, speaking in the same trembling voice that had made him inaudible as Cardinal Campeius. "Do you think they'll suspect me?" he asked. "I've got a handgun in my workshop. Do you think I should get rid of it?"

"Has it been fired recently?" Qwilleran asked, knowing that Edd had never bought any ammunition.

"No, but it has my fingerprints. Maybe I should wipe them off."

"Don't do anything, Edd, and don't worry. The police wouldn't suspect you in a million years."

Shortly afterward, Susan Exbridge telephoned, opening with the brazen banter that she had affected since her divorce. "Qwill, darling, why don't you confess? With those sexy eyelids and that sinister moustache you look exactly like a killer."

In contrast, the next caller was frantically serious. It was Wally Toddwhistle's mother. "Oh, Mr. Q, I'm worried sick," she cried. "Do you think they'll suspect Wally?"

"Is there any reason why they should?"

"Well, he got into trouble in his last year of high school, and Horseface gave him a rotten deal. Don't you know about it?"

"No. What happened?"

"It was only a prank that the kids dreamed up. It wasn't even Wally's idea, but he took the blame and wouldn't tell on the others, and that damned principal expelled him a few weeks before graduation! I went to school and raised hell, but it didn't do any good. Wally never got his diploma. His dad was ill during all this trouble, and I think that's what killed him."

"Did you or Wally make any threats at that time?"

"Wally wouldn't threaten a fly! I guess I said a few things I shouldn't've, though. I speak my mind, but Wally is a sweet boy. He takes after his dad."

"When did this happen?"

"Two years ago last May."

"If you were going to shoot Mr. VanBrook, Mrs. Toddwhistle, you would have done it before this. Put your mind at ease."

She wanted to talk longer, but Larry Lanspeak arrived, and Qwilleran asked to be excused.

Larry, looking immaculate in his custom-tailored suit and highly polished wingtips, said, "Don't let me stay more than twenty minutes. I'm ushering today." The Lanspeaks attended the Old Stone Church across the park from the Klingenschoen Theatre—the largest, oldest, wealthiest congregation in town. He dropped into a chair in an attitude of dejection, saying, "I worry about this situation."

"Did Hilary attend your church?" Qwilleran asked as he poured coffee.

"I don't think he had church affiliations anywhere, but he seemed to be knowledgeable about Eastern religions."

"From what I observed, he seemed to be knowledgeable about everything."

"You can say that again! I remember seeing his résumé when we hired him. He'd spent quite some time in Asia and claimed to read and write Chinese—as well as Japanese, which he claimed to speak fluently. His housekeeper told our housekeeper that he had a lot of Oriental stuff around the house . . . But that's not all! According to the résumé, he had studied architecture and horticulture; he had been an Equity actor in New York; and he had assorted degrees in education. I suppose you can do all that if you're not tied down with a family and don't spend any time socializing. He never attended athletic events or any other school function, which is a faux pas in a small community. In fact, he was conspicuously invisible on Saturdays and Sundays, although a couple of persons reported seeing him driving south on Friday nights—toward Lockmaster, you know."

"Where he spent the weekend smoking opium and reading Chinese poetry, no doubt," Qwilleran quipped.

"He was shot in the head, according to the radio," Larry said. "Doesn't that sound like a Chinese execution?"

"Or someone was hiding in the backseat, waiting for him to get behind the wheel. That's how they do it in the movies."

"Don't take this too lightly, Qwill. It certainly looks as if the shooter was one of us."

"Or someone who wanted to make it look like one of us."

"I'll tell you one thing—straight. I've never seen a rehearsal period with so much antagonism . . . On the other hand, could it be some kind of drug connection?"

"I thought Moose County was free of influences from Down Below," Qwilleran said. "There are no fast-food chains. Not even garage sales!"

"But they're going to creep in," Larry predicted, "now that we've started promoting tourism."

Qwilleran refilled the coffee cups. "Were you able to reach the superintendent?"

"Yes, I woke Lyle around four o'clock this morning and broke the news."

"What was his reaction?"

"Well, you know Lyle Compton! He never minces words! He said he'd often felt like braining Hilary himself. That'll be the general reaction around town, believe me! We'll have enough collective guilt in Pickax to sink a battleship."

Qwilleran said, "I just heard that VanBrook expelled Wally Toddwhistle a few weeks short of graduation because of some schoolboy escapade."

"True. And it was a crime on Hilary's part. Wally is a nice quiet kid, and he was a pretty good student. As for the nature of the prank, most people around town got a kick out of it."

"What was the offense?"

"Well, it was like this. Wally's father was a taxidermist, you know, and Wally brought a stuffed skunk to school. Somehow it turned up on the principal's chair. Wally looked like the obvious culprit, although he swore he didn't do it. The whole school board went to bat for him, but VanBrook threw him out. He told the board he'd run the school his way or tear up his contract. Lyle was afraid to cross him."

"It seems like draconian punishment."

"Wally didn't really suffer, though. He'd been working with his father ever since he was a kid, so he just took over the taxidermy shop, and he's doing okay without a diploma. He's simply talented. Hunters all over the Midwest send him their skins."

"More coffee, Larry?"

"No, thanks. This is potent stuff. I'll be waltzing up the center aisle and spilling the offering plate." He looked at his watch. "I hear church bells. I'll talk to you later." On the way out he stopped to say, "Wait till Lockmaster hears about this! The people down there think we're barbarians, and this will confirm their opinion."

As Larry drove away, answering the summons from the tower of the Old Stone Church, another kind of summons could be heard from the third balcony, where the Siamese had been sleeping off the excitement of the night before. Qwilleran released them from their apartment and was feeding them when Polly Duncan telephoned. He assumed she had heard the shocking news on the air, but her greeting was unexpectedly blithe.

"Dearest," she said, "I'm still in Lockmaster. It was a lovely wedding, and we celebrated into the wee hours. Did you give Bootsie his breakfast this morning?"

"Uh—yes," he said, knowing when it was advisable to bend the truth a little. Under the circumstances he had forgotten Bootsie completely.

"How is my little darling? Did he eat well? Did you talk to him?"

"Yes, indeed. We had a stimulating discussion about American foreign policy and the value of the dollar. When will you be home? Don't forget we have a reservation for dinner at Tipsy's."

"That's why I'm calling, dear. I've been invited to brunch at the Palomino Paddock, and I think I should accept. It's a four-star restaurant, and I've never been there. Do you mind? We can dine at Tipsy's next Sunday." She sounded unusually elated.

"I don't mind at all," Qwilleran said stiffly.

"I'll be home in time to give Bootsie his dinner, and I'll call you then."

"By the way," he said, "obviously you haven't listened to the radio. We've had an unfortunate incident up here."

"No, I haven't heard. What happened?"

"Hilary VanBrook has been murdered."

"Murdered! Incredible! Who did it? Where did it happen?"

"I'll tell you when you return," Qwilleran said. "Enjoy your brunch."

As a point of honor he never broke a social engagement, and Polly's defection irked him considerably. She had been partying all night with that Lockmaster crowd; why did she need to stay down there for a mere brunch? If she wanted to eat at a four-star restaurant, *he* could take her there.

"What do you think of that development?" he asked Koko.

The cat murmured an ambiguous reply, his attention fixed on the berry bushes outside the window, where the cardinal usually made his morning call.

"I'd better hike over to the boulevard and feed the monster," Qwilleran said.

He walked briskly to Goodwinter Boulevard, where Polly's apartment occupied the second floor of a carriage house behind an austere stone mansion. All the houses on the street were built of stone—the coldly impressive castles of nineteenth-century mining tycoons and lumber barons. One such house had been leased by VanBrook, and Qwilleran wondered why the man had needed such grandiose living quarters with fifteen or twenty rooms. As he passed it he noticed that the draperies were drawn on all the windows.

Arriving at Polly's carriage house he unlocked the downstairs door and climbed the stairs to her apartment, where a yearling Siamese was complaining about his tardy breakfast.

"*Mea culpa! Mea culpa!*" said Qwilleran. "I've been involved in extraordinary circumstances. Here's an extra spoonful." He gave Bootsie fresh water and a quick brushing and then hurried back to the barn in time to catch the phone ringing.

The exuberant voice of Hixie Rice said, "Isn't this exciting, Qwill? We'll all be interrogated! I'm going to invent some lurid details—nothing incriminating—just something to add zest and color to the investigation and attract the media Down Below."

Hixie—a transplant from Down Below, where she worked in

advertising and publicity—took pleasure in manipulating the media, both print and electronic.

Qwilleran said sternly, "I suggest you curb your creative impulse in this case, Hixie. We're all faced with a serious situation. Stick to the facts, and don't spread any false rumors to confuse the constabulary or entertain the local residents."

"I love it when you're playing uncle," she laughed.

Relenting he said, "Would you like to discuss the matter over dinner? I have a table reserved at Tipsy's."

She made the obvious reply. "Where's Polly?"

"Out of town."

"Good! I'll have you all to myself. Shall I meet you at the restaurant?"

The place called Tipsy's Tavern was located in the town of Kennebeck northeast of Pickax. Driving there to meet his guest, Qwilleran passed through countryside that had seemed wild and mysterious four years before, when he was a transplanted city dweller. Now he felt comfortable with the Moose County scene: stony pastures, potato farms and sheep ranches . . . dark patches of woods providing habitat for thousands of white-tailed deer . . . dry autumn cornfields from which clouds of blackbirds rose and swirled in close-order formation as he passed . . . the rotting shafthouses of abandoned mines, now fenced and posted as dangerous.

The first sign of Kennebeck was a towering grain elevator in the distance, the skyscraper of the north country. Then the watertower came into view, freshly painted with the town symbol. Some enterprising artist, not afraid of heights, had canvassed the county, decorating watertowers. Every community flaunted its symbol: a pickax, a fish, a sailboat, an antlered buck, a happy face, a pine tree. Kennebeck's tower, like the welcome sign at the town limits, bore the silhouette of a cat. It was a prosperous community with a wide main street and curbstones, plus senior housing, condominiums, and other signs of the times. Yet, in the 1930s Kennebeck had been in danger of becoming a ghost town.

Then, providentially, a blind pig operator from Down Below,

hurt by the repeal of Prohibition, returned to his hometown of Kennebeck to open a legitimate bar and steakhouse. He brought with him a white cat with a deformed foot (it made her stagger) and a comical black patch on her head, like a hat slipping down over one eye. Appropriately her name was Tipsy. Her boozy antics and agreeable disposition made customers smile and attracted diners from far and wide. Tipsy's personality, along with the good steaks, put Kennebeck back on the map.

The original restaurant in a log cabin had been enlarged many times during the intervening years, but it still offered casual dining in a rustic setting, and Qwilleran's favorite table was in the main dining room within sight of a larger-than-life oil painting of the founding cat.

He arrived before Hixie and sat at the bar, sipping Squunk water with a twist of lemon. He was on his third drink when his guest arrived, looking harried and tossing her pageboy nervously.

"Quick! I need a martini!" she said. "Make it a double. Then I'll apologize for being late."

The bartender looked questioningly at Qwilleran, then at Hixie, then at Qwilleran again, as if to say, "Where's Mrs. Duncan?"

"You'll never believe this, Qwill," she said in her usual tragicomic style, "but I was driving out Ittibittiwassee Road with not a car in sight—anywhere! And I got in a two-car accident!"

"That's not easy to do."

"Let me tell you how it happened. When I reached Mayfus Road, a car came out of *nowhere* and ran the stop sign! There were only two of us within ten square miles—and we collided! Why do these crazy things happen to me?"

"You're disaster-prone, Hixie," Qwilleran said sympathetically. She had a long history of getting locked in restrooms, setting her hair on fire, picking the wrong men, and more. "It's fortunate you weren't hurt."

"I had my seat belt fastened, but the passenger side was wrecked, and I waited for Gippel's towtruck to come from Pickax."

"How did you get here?"

"The sheriff dropped me off. He was a real sweetheart, and I adore those brimmed hats they wear! After dinner you'll have to drive me to Gippel's, and they'll give me a loaner."

They sat at Qwilleran's table under the friendly eye of Tipsy and ordered from the no-nonsense menu chalked on a blackboard: steak or fish, take it or leave it. The soup of the day was the soup of the year: bean. The vegetable was always boiled carrots, but they were homegrown, small and sweet. The tiny Moose County potatoes, boiled in their skins, had an Irish flavor, and the steak always tasted like honest meat.

"Have the police knocked on your door?" Qwilleran asked.

"Not yet. Have you talked to anyone?"

"Larry. He worries that someone in the club is guilty, but I think he's wrong." Qwilleran patted his moustache.

"Do you know something that the rest of us don't know?"

"I have a hunch, that's all."

Qwilleran's hunches were always accompanied by a tingling in the roots of his moustache, something he could not explain and refused to discuss. His years on the police beat Down Below, coupled with a natural curiosity, had given him an interest in criminal investigation, and when he was on the right scent there was always that reassuring sensation on his upper lip.

At Tipsy's the food was served by plump, bustling, jolly, gray-haired women who admonished diners to eat everything on their plates.

Qwilleran said to Hixie, "Where do they get all these clones to wait on table? I suppose they advertise: WANTED: Plump, jolly, gray-haired waitpersons with bustling experience. Grandmothers preferred."

They ordered steak—and whatever happened to come with it. Over the bean soup Hixie said, "I have something exciting to discuss."

"Okay. Let's have it." Hixie's ideas were always novel and usually successful, except when they involved Koko; he declined to do TV commercials or endorse a line of frozen gourmet catfoods. It was she, however, who delighted local readers by naming the new newspaper the *Moose County Something*, and it was Hixie who convinced Dennis Hough to advertise his new construction firm as "Huff & Puff Construction Associates."

"First, have you seen the announcement of my new contest?" she asked.

"Yes. What gave you the idea?"

"Well, you see, Qwill, I drive around the county selling ads, and I see black-and-white cats by the thousand! People seem to think they're all descended from Tipsy. So I thought, Why not a Tipsy Look-Alike Contest? The Kennebeck Chamber of Commerce jumped at the opportunity! They're printing posters and T-shirts."

"And the *Something* is selling some extra advertising space," Qwilleran added.

"Of course! We have a good slogan. The original Tipsy, you know, was a very sweet cat as well as comic-looking, so our slogan is 'Sweeter and Funnier.' How do you like it?"

"It may be just what this county needs. Are you getting any entries?"

"Hundreds!"

The steaks arrived, and the conversation switched to food—also office gossip at the *Something* and the open house at Qwilleran's barn.

When the waitress served the bread pudding, he said, "One thing puzzles me. How will you judge the Tipsy contest?"

"Glad you asked, Qwill. People are sending in snapshots of their cats, and we'll narrow them down to the fifty best look-alikes. They'll come to Kennebeck for the final judging, and I'm hoping you'll be one of the judges."

"Hold on, Hixie!" he said. "You know I like to cooperate, but I would rather not have to judge fifty live cats."

"Your name on the panel will add a lot of prestige to the contest," she said, "and Lyle Compton has agreed to judge."

"Our school superintendent will do anything for public exposure. He might want to run for governor some day. Who else is on the panel?"

"Mildred Hanstable."

Qwilleran smoothed his moustache. Roger MacGillivray's newly widowed mother-in-law was one of his favorite women—and an excellent cook. He said, "All right. It's a foul prospect, but I'll do it."

Over the coffee, Hixie broached the subject of the murder again. "Hilary was infuriatingly uncooperative when I was trying to get publicity for *Henry VIII*. And everyone I talk to harbors some grudge against the guy."

"He's hurt someone more deeply than we know," Qwilleran said. "There are dark corners of his life that he's kept secret."

"Do you think it could be drug-related?"

"Not likely, although I'm sure the idea of a high school principal as drug dealer appeals to your imagination. Moose County has always been pretty clean; that's one advantage to living in the boondocks. We have an alcohol problem, but that's all—as yet."

"The sheriff's helicopter is always hovering over those desolate stretches between Chipmunk and Purple Point."

"They're looking for poachers, not marijuana plantings. What does Gary Pratt think about it? Do you still see a lot of Gary?"

"Not lately," Hixie said. "He's such a hairy ape, and since meeting Dennis I realize I go for clean-cut."

Qwilleran assumed his uncle role again. "I hope you know Dennis is happily married, Hixie. Don't walk into any more disappointments. He has a bright two-year-old who looks just like him, and his wife's trying to sell the house in St. Louis so the family can be together up here."

"She's not trying very hard," was Hixie's flippant retort. "Dennis says she doesn't want to live four hundred miles north of everywhere." She turned serious. "I don't know whether this means anything, Qwill, but ... I tried to call Dennis this morning after I heard the news on the radio, and he wasn't there. I got a recorded message."

"He was probably sleeping and didn't want to be disturbed," Qwilleran suggested. "None of us got much sleep last night."

"But I looked out the window at the carport, and his assigned parking space was empty."

"He might have gone home with someone. Did that occur to you?"

"I don't think he did. This afternoon, when his van was still missing, I mentioned it to the manager, and this is what she told me: According to the nightman at the gate, Dennis left before daybreak, right after he came in. He didn't say anything, but he looked worried, and he drove away from the gate very fast and turned onto the highway with tires squealing."

CHAPTER 3

Returning home from Tipsy's restaurant Sunday night, Qwilleran stepped on a small object in the foyer and kicked another one in front of the *schrank*. A third turned up under a rug. They were metal engravings mounted on wooden blocks—printing memorabilia that he had started to collect. In embarking on a new hobby, he had also provided a pastime for the Siamese: stealing typeblocks from the typecase where they were displayed. This time they had filched small cuts of a fish, a rabbit, and a rooster. Either the subject matter was appealing, or the blocks were the right size for a playful paw.

As Qwilleran entered the barn, the light on his answering machine was flashing, and he pressed the button to hear a brief recorded message from Polly: "Qwill, I arrived home from Lockmaster later than I planned. Don't call me back tonight. I'm very tired, and I'm going to bed early."

There were no intimate expressions of affection included in the message; Polly, he concluded, must be very tired, indeed. After brunch at the Palomino Paddock what else had she been doing?

He himself felt in high gear despite his fifteen minutes of sleep the night before. He was stimulated by the puzzle confronting Chief Brodie, although he had no intention of meddling in the case. His friend would not appreciate suggestions from an amateur investigator. While working the police beat Down Below Qwilleran had written a book on urban crime, now out of print, but it hardly entitled him to advise a pro like Brodie.

He prepared a cup of coffee and carried it to a comfortable chair, propping his feet on an ottoman. Yum Yum promptly took possession of his lap, and Koko assumed an attentive position at his feet. They were ready for some quality time.

"Well," he began, "what we have here is the kind of criminal case that is solved immediately—or never. What's your guess?"

Koko blinked his eyes, a signal that Qwilleran interpreted as "no opinion." Cats, he recalled, were never interested in generalities.

"I don't buy the theory that it was an inside job," he went on, grooming his moustache, "although I don't know why I feel that way. If Brodie expends too much time and effort in hounding the members of the club, he's wasting his time."

"Yow," said Koko.

"I'm glad you agree. The one individual he should be investigating is the victim himself. Who was he—really? Where did he get a name like Hilary VanBrook? We know he came here from Lockmaster, but where did he operate before that? He was obviously not a native of the north country, so why did this brilliant man with a cosmopolitan background and impressive credentials choose to live in the outback? Where did he disappear on weekends? Why did he need that large house on Goodwinter Boulevard?"

Qwilleran had forgotten that he himself was indirectly responsible for bringing the principal to Pickax. Four years before—four long and eventful years—Qwilleran had arrived in Moose County as the reluctant heir to the Klingenschoen fortune, reluctant because he had no desire for wealth. He was a dedicated journalist who enjoyed hacking a living on the crime beat. He was content with a one-room apartment, no car, and a meager wardrobe that packed in a jiffy when his newspaper sent him off on assignment. Finding himself suddenly encumbered with millions—yet with no interest in financial matters—he solved the problem very simply: He established the Klingenschoen Memorial Fund to give the money away. Immediately a board of trustees started awarding grants, scholarships, and loans to benefit the community.

In direst need, it so happened, was the local school system, known to operate on the lowest per-pupil expenditure in the state. As the Klingenschoen Fund poured money into school facilities and teacher salaries, this cornucopia of largesse gave superintendent Lyle Compton an idea: Money might lure the celebrated Hilary VanBrook away from Lockmaster High School where he had accomplished wonders in a few years. Although Lockmaster considered Moose County a primitive wilderness populated by savages who could not even win a football game, VanBrook accepted the Pickax challenge—and the lucrative contract. Under his leadership the Pickax high school earned accreditation, the curriculum was expanded, and more graduates went on to college. Although the athletic teams did no better, faculty and parents considered the new principal a miracle-worker—while loathing his overweening personality and heartless policies.

A few months before his murder VanBrook wrote a typically curt and scornful letter to the Theatre Club, proposing a Shakespeare production as a change from the light comedies, musicals, and mysteries favored by local audiences. He volunteered to direct it himself. The play he proposed was *The Famous History of the Life of King Henry the Eighth*, and the officers of the Theatre Club uttered a unanimous groan.

Carol Lanspeak called Qwilleran for his opinion. "I'm consulting you," she said, "because the K Fund may have to bail us out if it's a flop. No one likes the idea, and yet Horseface has a reputation as a no-fail genius. We're asking him to meet with our board of directors for further discussion, and we're inviting you to audit the meeting. You can bring your tape recorder if you wish; it might make a subject for the 'Qwill Pen' column—that is, if we decide to cut our throats."

It was a dinner meeting held in a private room at the New

Pickax Hotel, built in 1935, the year its predecessor burned down. After a dinner of meatloaf and scalloped potatoes (the hotel was not noted for its imaginative cuisine), the board waited for the guest of honor to arrive. VanBrook had declined to join them for dinner, a pointedly unfriendly gesture. When he finally arrived—late, without apology—Carol called the meeting to order and invited the principal to elucidate on his proposal. As if the board were composed of illiterates, he responded by reading a copy of the same letter he had mailed to them, spitting out the phrases with obvious disdain.

Qwilleran heard someone whisper, "Isn't he a pill?" Yet, the man had a rich, well-modulated voice; it was easy to believe he had been a professional actor. The principal finished reading and rolled his eyes at the walls and ceiling.

Officers and board members exchanged looks of dismay. The first to find nerve enough to speak was Scott Gippel, car dealer and treasurer of the club, whose girth was so enormous that he required two chairs. "The public won't go for that heavy stuff," he said.

Carol Lanspeak spoke up. "Since receiving Mr. VanBrook's letter I've read the play twice, and I regret to say that I can't find a single memorable or quotable line except the first one: *I come no more to make you laugh.*"

"That's when half the audience gets up and walks out," said Gippel good-naturedly, his not-too-solid flesh quivering with mirth over his own quip.

The chairman of the play-reading committee, a retired teacher of English, commented, "Mr. VanBrook has a point; it's time we attempted Shakespeare, but is this the right play for us? There is even some doubt that Shakespeare wrote *Henry VIII*. It reads—if you will pardon my candor—as if it were written by a committee."

Qwilleran stole a look at VanBrook, who was listening in supercilious silence, gazing at the ceiling and rolling his eyes as if searching for cracks in the plaster.

Fran Brodie said, "I'd like to make another objection. *Henry VIII* calls for a large cast, and we have limited space backstage and very few dressing rooms. The theatre was not designed for large productions."

"The cost of all those costumes will be prohibitive," Gippel added.

"And there are so few roles for women," Carol objected.

"If you ask me, it's too dull and too long," said Junior Goodwinter, the young managing editor of the *Moose County Something*. "And the last scene is a let-down, like the last half of the ninth in a 14–0 ballgame."

VanBrook rose to his feet. "May I speak?"

"Of course. Please do," said Carol with an artificial smile. She frowned at her husband, who had not opened his mouth during the objections. As president of the board of education he had helped convince VanBrook to leave Lockmaster, and he joined Lyle Compton in humoring the principal—who was doing so much good, and who was known to be temperamental, and whose contract was coming up for renewal. If VanBrook failed to sign again, he would undoubtedly return to the Lockmaster school system, and the good folk of Pickax would be left drowning in chagrin.

In a condescending manner VanBrook began. "*Henry VIII* is no longer than *Romeo and Juliet*, and it is shorter by far than *Hamlet* and *Richard III*. So much for *too long*." He darted a contemptuous glance at the editor. "As for *too dull*, the play has been captivating audiences for three centuries with its color and pageantry. Furthermore, it addresses such contemporary concerns as corruption, greed, power politics, and the abuse of women. As a morality play it deplores *the vain pomp and glory of this world* . . . Is everyone still with me?" His listeners wriggled uncomfortably, and he went on. "You say there are too few roles for women, and yet one of the strongest roles Shakespeare ever wrote for a woman is Katharine of Aragon, Queen of England. Anne Boleyn is another coveted role, and even the Old Lady is a small gem of a part. For those who fancy themselves in period costumes there are plenty of ladies-in-waiting sweeping on and off the stage. And if you think *Henry VIII* lacks great scenes, let me draw your attention to Buckingham's arrest, his unjust condemnation as a traitor, the roisterous party that King Henry crashes in disguise, the queen's court trial, her later confrontation with Cardinal Wolsey, Wolsey's repentant leave-taking, the coronation of Queen Anne, and the heart-rending death of Katharine."

He flashed a triumphant glance around the conference room and continued. "It so happens that I have staged this play before, and there are certain techniques that can be employed—notably the use of students as supernumeraries, to be costumed at the school and transported to the theatre in school buses. The Klingenschoen garage at the rear of the theatre can provide dressing rooms for actors playing small roles and making infrequent entrances."

Qwilleran thought, Wait a minute, bub! I'm still living in the garage!

"As for the final scene," VanBrook said, "this purely political indulgence was tacked on to flatter the monarchy, and let me assure you that it will be omitted. *Henry VIII* will end with Katharine's death scene, which has been called the glory of the play."

Everyone was silent until Carol said, "Thank you, Mr. Van-Brook, for your enlightening explanation ... Shall we make a decision now?" she asked the board. "Or do we need time to mull it over?"

Larry spoke up for the first time. "I move that we mount *Henry VIII* as our first fall show."

Fran Brodie seconded the motion. "Let's take a gamble on it," she said, and Qwilleran could imagine visions of Queen Katharine dancing in her steely gray eyes.

"Okay, I'll go along," said Gippel, "and hope to God we sell some tickets. There'll be more flesh on the stage than in the audience—that's my guess."

Hixie Rice said, "It has great publicity possibilities, with all those high school kids carrying spears."

Junior Goodwinter capitulated. "Count me in, so long as you lop off the last scene."

And so *The Famous History of the Life of King Henry the Eighth* went into production. Qwilleran was not further involved, although he knew that Carol and Fran were auditioning for Queen Katharine, and Larry and Dennis wanted to read for Cardinal Wolsey. Everyone assumed that Larry would get the choice role.

On the evening following the last audition, Qwilleran was going to a late dinner at the Old Stone Mill as the Lanspeaks were leaving. He intercepted them in the restaurant parking lot, saying to Larry, "I suppose I'm expected to kiss your ring."

"Oh, hell! I missed out on Wolsey," the actor said with a disappointed smirk. "Hilary wants me to play King Henry. Isn't that a bummer? I'll have to grow a beard if I don't want to use spirit gum. Scott should be doing Henry; he wouldn't need any padding."

Carol said, "Scott could never learn the lines. The only line he ever remembers is at the bottom of the page."

"So I suppose Dennis is doing Wolsey?" Qwilleran asked.

"NO!" Larry thundered in disgust. "Hilary's doing it himself! Of course, it's expedient, because he's done it before. He's also bringing a woman from Lockmaster to play Katharine. He directed her in the production down there a few years ago."

"When do rehearsals start? I might drop in some evening."

"Next Monday," Carol said. "Five nights a week, starting at six-thirty. We've always started at seven to give working people time to eat a decent meal, but Horseface has decreed six-thirty. He wants me as assistant director and understudy for Katharine. Since she lives sixty miles away, she'll come up only two nights a week, so I'll have to read her lines the rest of the time." She raised her eyebrows in a gesture of resignation. "I don't expect to enjoy it, but if I learn something, it won't be a total loss."

Qwilleran said, "I wanted to do a profile on VanBrook for my column, but he refused flatly. Wouldn't give a reason."

"Typical," said Larry with a shrug. "Where's Polly tonight?"

"Hosting a dinner meeting of the library board. What did you have to eat?"

"Red snapper—very good! And try the blue plum buckle—if they have any left. It's going fast."

The Lanspeaks went to their car, and Qwilleran entered the restaurant that had been converted from an old stone grist mill. The hostess seated him at his favorite table, and Derek Cuttlebrink filled his water glass and delivered the breadbasket with a flourish. Although Derek was the busboy, his six-foot-seven stature and sociable manner caused new customers to mistake him for the owner.

"I'm playing five parts," he announced. "I get my name in the program five times—for Wolsey's servant, the court crier, the executioner, the mayor of London, and a messenger. I like the executioner best; I get to carry the axe and wear a hood."

"You're going to be a busy boy with all those costume changes," Qwilleran said.

"I figure I can wear the same pants and just change the coat and hat."

"In Shakespeare they're called breeches, Derek."

"I've been thinking it over," said the busboy. "I've decided I'd like to be an actor instead of a cop. It would be more fun. You stay up all night and sleep late."

The waitress appeared, and Derek drifted away to clear some tables. Qwilleran ordered the red snapper. "And save me a piece of plum buckle if you have any left."

During the following week the number of cars in the theatre parking lot every evening indicated that rehearsals were in full swing, and one evening Qwilleran slipped into the auditorium to observe, thinking he might pick up some material for a "Qwill Pen" column. It was six-thirty when he took an aisle seat at the rear. The entire cast was on hand, except for the woman from Lockmaster; it was her off-night. The director had not yet made an appearance.

At six forty-five Carol said, "No point in wasting valuable time. Let's go over the scenes that Hilary blocked last night. We'll skip the prologue and start with the first scene as far as the dirty-look episode. Let's have the Duke of Buckingham, the Duke of Norfolk, and Lord Abergavenny on stage. Norfolk enters first, stage left. The others, stage right."

Three actors, carrying scripts and looking far from aristocratic in their rehearsal clothes, made their entrance.

Carol called out from the third row, "Norfolk, take a longer, more deliberate stride. You're a duke! . . . That's better! And Abergav'ny, show respect for your father-in-law but don't hide behind him. Let's do that entrance again and take it from *Good morrow and well met*." As the scene progressed, Carol made notes and occasionally interrupted. "Norfolk, don't just look at the speaker, listen to what he's saying. It'll show in your face . . . And Abergavenny, keep your chin up . . . Buckingham, take a couple of steps downstage when you say *O you go far*."

When Dennis reached Buckingham's clever line—*No man's pie is freed from his ambitious finger*—he stopped and laughed. "That's my favorite line."

There was a ripple of amusement as the actors in the front rows looked at each other with understanding.

Carol said, "Okay, take it again. And Norfolk, use your upstage hand so you don't hide your face."

When they reached the dirty-look episode and VanBrook had not yet arrived, Carol read Cardinal Wolsey's lines and walked through the scene with the others. Suddenly the doors at the rear of the auditorium burst open.

"What's going on here?" came the director's stentorian demand. Starting down the aisle in his green turtleneck jersey, he caught sight of Qwilleran. "What are you doing here?"

"Waiting for the six-thirty rehearsal to begin," said Qwilleran with a pointed look at his wristwatch.

"Out! Out!" VanBrook pointed to the door.

Dennis Hough walked to the stage apron and boomed, "He can stay, for God's sake! He owns the damned theatre!"

"Out! Out!"

Qwilleran obligingly left the auditorium, walked upstairs, and slipped into the dark balcony, while VanBrook proceeded without apology or explanation. Whatever had delayed him had also annoyed him, and he was impatient with everyone.

Brusquely he said, "Archbishop, stop looking at your wristwatch! This is the sixteenth century . . . You—the Old Lady—we're doing *Henry VIII*, not Uncle Wiggley! You're carrying your hands like a rabbit . . . Who's giggling backstage? Keep quiet or go home! . . . Suffolk, there are four syllables in 'coronation.' It's the crowning of a monarch, not something from the florist." None of this was said in good-natured jest; it was pure acrimony. "Campeius, can you act more like a Roman cardinal and less like a mouse?"

The actors waiting for their scenes glanced at each other uneasily. Eddington Smith, playing Cardinal Campeius, was a shy little old fellow who was always treated gently by members of the club, no matter how inadequate his performance.

When VanBrook told Anne Boleyn to stop simpering like an idiot, the flashing of Fran's steely gray eyes could be seen even from the balcony. As for Dennis, his square jaw was clenched most of the time. At one point Dave Landrum, who was playing Suffolk, threw his script at the director and walked out. Qwilleran doubted that anyone would return for rehearsal the following night. He doubted, moreover, that *Henry VIII* would ever open.

Nevertheless, the rehearsals stumbled along with a new Suffolk, and Qwilleran received reports on the play's progress from Larry, with whom he had coffee at the Dimsdale Diner twice a week.

Larry, whose royal beard was growing nicely, said, "Hilary's always picking on poor Edd Smith, who wouldn't be in the club at all if Dr. Halifax hadn't ordered it as therapy. Edd still doesn't project, even though Carol coaches him. He shouts the first two words, then trails off into a whisper. Dennis has come to his defense a couple of times. There's a real personality clash flaring up between Dennis and Hilary."

"How is Carol taking it?"

"She's being a saint! She puts up with Hilary because she hopes to learn something. If you ask me, she's learning what *not* to do while directing a group of amateurs. He works hard with some and ignores others. He butters up the woman from Lockmaster and insults everyone else."

"Is she good?"

"Sure, she's good, but Carol or Fran could have done as well."

"Who is she, anyway?" Qwilleran asked.

"Her name is Fiona Stucker. I don't know anything about her except that she played Katharine in the Lockmaster production of *Henry* five years ago."

"How are the student extras coming along?"

"Carol is working hard with the kids, getting them to walk like sixteenth-century nobles instead of couch potatoes. I think Derek, with his five roles and great height, is going to provide the comic relief in this play. He's so conspicuous that the audience will recognize him as the executioner even with a black hood over his head. And I'm afraid he's going to get a laugh during Katharine's death scene. When he enters as a messenger toward the end of the play—his fifth role, bear in mind—Katharine's line is *This fellow, let me ne'er see again.* We all have to struggle to keep a straight face, and the audience is going to crack up!"

"The play can use some comic relief," Qwilleran said.

"Yes, but not during Katharine's death scene."

On opening night the audience made all the right responses. They wept over Buckingham's noble farewell, gasped at the magnificence of the coronation, and suppressed their tittering over Derek's frequent entrances. There was a rumble of excitement during the crowd scenes, when their teenage sons and daughters paraded down the center aisle as guards with halberds, standard bearers with banners, officers with tipstaffs, noblemen with swords, countesses with coronets, and vergers with silver wands.

Onstage there were only two miscues and one fluff—not bad for opening night. Qwilleran, fifth row on the aisle with Polly Duncan as his guest, cheered inwardly when Dennis delivered his poignant speech, cringed when Eddington mouthed words that could not be heard, felt his blood pressure rising when Fran appeared as the beauteous Anne, and waited fearfully for Derek to ruin Katharine's death scene. Fortunately the director had deleted the lines that would get an inappropriate guffaw.

The next time Qwilleran met Larry for coffee, the actor said, "I have to admit that Hilary's good as the cardinal. Despite his built-in arrogance he manages to make Wolsey's repentance convincing. But I have a feeling that he resents the public's adoration of Buckingham. When they flock backstage after the show, it's Dennis they want to see. And when Dennis makes his first entrance and says *Good morning and well met,* you can hear the hearts palpitating in the auditorium."

Qwilleran said, "Your Henry is perfect, Larry—straight out of the Holbein portrait."

"That's what Hilary wanted." He rubbed his chin. "I'll tell you one thing: I'll be glad when I can shave off this beard."

Three weeks later he had shaved off the beard, VanBrook was dead, and Dennis had disappeared without explanation.

CHAPTER 4

The Monday following the Orchard Incident, as it came to be labeled by the *Moose County Something,* was a gloomy day suitable for the grim police business taking place in the barnyard. The comings and goings of officialdom ruined Koko's morning bird watch. He liked to take his post at the window-wall overlooking the orchard, from which he could see red, yellow, gray, blue, and brown birds flitting in the branches of the old trees and scrubby berry bushes, once cultivated but now growing wild.

Koko's particular favorite was the male cardinal who called every morning and evening in company with his soberly dressed mate. With his red plumage, kingly crown, and black face patch emphasizing his patrician beak, he conducted himself like a monarch of birds. There appeared to be mutual appreciation between the cardinal and the aristocratic cat. Koko sat almost motionless, with the last three inches of his tail fluttering to match the fluttering of the bird's tail feathers.

At one point during the overcast morning a van pulled into

the yard, and a photographer unloading camera cases, lights, and tripods was challenged by the police. Qwilleran assured them that this was John Bushland, commercial photographer from Lockmaster, who had an appointment to shoot the interior of the barn.

Bushy, as he was called, was an agile, enthusiastic, outgoing young man who joked about losing his hair early. *"Hair Today; Gone Tomorrow"* was the slogan on his sweatshirt. Seriously he said to Qwilleran, "I heard about the trouble. What's the latest?"

"Police are investigating. That's all I know. What's the reaction in Lockmaster?"

"To tell the truth, everyone's relieved. They were afraid he'd get tired of Pickax, and they'd get him back again. Got any idea who shot him?"

"I suspect it was someone from Lockmaster trying to make it look like someone from Pickax. Did you know VanBrook when he was principal down there?"

"Not personally. Not having kids, Vicki and I weren't involved in that scene."

Bushy regarded the octagonal mass of stone and silvery shingles with awe. "I like those triangular windows around the top. We should do some exteriors, but not while the police cars are here."

"Sorry it's not a sunny day," Qwilleran said.

"All the better for interiors. We won't have to contend with the glare."

"Come on in. Ready for a cup of coffee?"

"Not right now. I want to work first." When they carried the gear indoors, Bushy was amazed by the lightness of the interior. "I expected it to be dark. All these white walls, all this light-colored wood—it makes my job a lot easier."

"That's what I wanted—a minimum of dark corners and shadows. It's too easy for cats to make themselves invisible in a dark environment, and I like to know where they are at all times. Otherwise I worry." He handed Bushy the binoculars. "Up there on one of those radiating beams you can see the mark of the original builder: J. Mayfus & Son, 1881.

I'd like you to get a close-up of that if possible. Shall I lock the cats up in their loft?"

"It won't be necessary. Who did the furnishings?"

"Fran Brodie. I didn't want anything rustic, and she said that contemporary furniture would accentuate the antiquity of the structure."

In the lounge there were two sofas and an oversized chair upholstered in oatmeal tweed—all boldly designed, square-cut pieces. The tables were off-white lacquered cubes.

"You don't see anything like this in Lockmaster," Bushy said.

Qwilleran pointed out certain items that he wanted included in the pictures: the pine wardrobe, the bat prints, the printer's typecase, and the Mackintosh coat of arms. "My mother was a Mackintosh," he remarked.

"Sure. No problem. Anything you want." Bushy was wandering about, checking camera angles. "Everywhere you look, it's a picture! And there are lots of places to spot a light under a balcony or behind a beam if I want to light a corner."

"What can I do to help?"

"Nothing. You've got plenty of electric outlets, I see. I might have to move some of the furniture slightly."

"So if you don't need me, Bushy, I'll go out and do a few errands. Help yourself to cold drinks in the fridge. For coffee just press the Brew button. See you later! If the phone rings, my answering machine will pick it up. Be sure the cats don't run outdoors."

Leaving the barn, Qwilleran was intercepted by Brodie. "Where's Dennis Hough?" he demanded. He pronounced it *Howe*.

"I don't know," Qwilleran said. "I haven't been in touch with him since Saturday. Now that the barn's finished he won't be coming around any more."

"He hasn't been home since the party."

"Probably drove to St. Louis to see his family. Doesn't Fran know where he went?"

Brodie grunted unintelligibly. "This company called Huff & Puff doesn't even have an office."

Qwilleran explained patiently, "My barn was his first job. All he needed was a phone for lining up workmen and supplies, so he worked out of his apartment."

"Do you know how to reach him in St. Louis?"

"No, but I'm sure directory assistance can tell you. His name is pronounced *Huff*, but it's spelled H-o-u-g-h. Give him time to get down there; it's a long drive."

Qwilleran walked downtown. Most of Pickax was within walking distance, and he was accustomed to using his legs, being a former pavement pounder from the Concrete Belt. The rest of Pickax depended on wheels.

En route to Lois's Luncheonette for breakfast he stopped at the used bookstore, an establishment he could never pass without entering. This time he had a mission. Eddington Smith had recently acquired a large library from an estate, and Qwilleran was hoping to find a copy of his own best-selling book written eighteen years before. During the ups and downs of his life following those halcyon days he had not salvaged a single copy, but now that his fortunes had changed, he was always on the lookout for *City of Brotherly Crime* by James M. Qwilleran. He had used a middle initial in those days. Professional book detectives had been unable to unearth the book; public libraries no longer had the title in the stacks or in the catalogue. Yet, doggedly he continued the hopeless hunt, like a parent searching for a lost child.

The store called Edd's Editions was a gloomy cave filled with gray, dusty, musty hardcover books as well as paperbacks with torn covers and yellowed edges. Eddington materialized from the shadows at the rear of the store.

"Find my book?" Qwilleran asked.

"Not so far, but I haven't unpacked everything yet," said the conscientious old bookseller. "Did the police find any evidence?"

"You know as much as I do, Edd."

"I couldn't sleep last night. 'Other sins only speak; murder shrieks out.' " Eddington amazed his customers by having a quotation for every occasion.

"Who said that?"

"Webster, I think."

"Which one?"

"I don't know. How many are there?"

At that moment a smoky Persian, whose voluminous tail dusted the books, walked sedately toward Qwilleran and sat down on a biography of Sir Edmund Backhouse.

"Am I to consider that a recommendation?" Qwilleran asked. "Or is Winston just resting?"

"It looks like an interesting book," said the bookseller. "He was a British orientalist and sort of a mystery man."

"I'll take it," said Qwilleran, who could never walk out of a bookstore without making a purchase.

At Lois's Luncheonette he sat at the counter and ordered eggs over lightly, country fries extra crisp, rye toast dry, and coffee right away; no cream.

"Whatcha think of the murder, Mr. Q?" asked the waitress, whose nametag read Alvola.

" 'Other sins only speak; murder shrieks out,' " he recited with declamatory effect.

"Is that Shakespeare?" she asked. Thanks to *Henry VIII*, the Bard was the fad of the month among young people in Pickax. In October it would be a rock star or comic strip hero. "It sounds like Shakespeare," said Alvola knowledgeably.

"No, it was some other dude," Qwilleran said as he buried his nose in his book. Actually he was listening to the conversation at nearby tables. No one was mourning the principal; all were fearful that the killer might prove to be a well-known citizen, or a student, or a friend, or a neighbor. It was fear mixed with excitement, expressed with a certain amount of relish. Qwilleran thought, This case will never be solved; no one in Moose County wants it to be solved.

His next stop was Amanda's Design Studio, where he dropped in to see Fran Brodie. On the job she wore three-inch heels, and her skirts rose higher than most Pickax hemlines—facts that were not lost on her client. "Where's your boss?" he asked.

"Amanda's gone to a design center Down Below. Is anything happening at the barn?"

"Various authorities are there, doing their duty. No one is talking, of course. I keep my nose out of it."

"Dad told Mother that they found traces of foam rubber in the car, meaning it had been used as a silencer."

"But the cats heard it. They can hear a leaf fall."

"Want to hear something ironic?" the designer asked. "Hilary ordered custom-made treatments for twenty windows—the whole main floor—and they arrived by motor freight this morning. *This morning!* I called Amanda, and she had a fit."

"What does his house look like?"

"It's one of those stone houses on Goodwinter Boulevard, you know. The main floor is done in Japanese; he did it himself. The window treatments we ordered for him last month are shoji screens. I've never been upstairs, but he told me the bedrooms are filled with books."

Thinking of *City of Brotherly Crime* Qwilleran said, "I wouldn't mind seeing that place."

"I have the key, and Amanda wants the screens to be on the premises when we file our claim on the estate. Would you like to help me deliver them?"

"When?" he asked with unusual eagerness.

"I'll have to let you know, but it'll be soon."

As he was leaving the studio he said, "We've got to do something about the fish-bowl effect at the barn. The Peeping Toms are having a field day." What had once been the huge barn door was now a huge wall of glass.

"Mini-blinds would solve the problem," the designer said. "I'll drop in and measure the windows. I still have your key."

Qwilleran's planned destination was the public library, a building that looked like a Greek temple except for the bicycle rack and the book-drop receptacle near the front steps. As he walked through the vestibule he automatically turned his head to the left, where a chalkboard displayed the Shakespeare quotation of the day—one of Polly's pet ideas. He expected to see *Murder most foul.* Instead, he read: *Love is a smoke raised with the fume of sighs.* The wedding in Lockmaster had put her in a romantic mood.

In the main hall the clerks gave him the bright greeting due the richest man in the county who was also their supervisor's companion of choice. To delude them he first browsed through the new book shelves and punched a few keys on the computer catalogue before sauntering up the stairs to the mezzanine. Here the daily papers were scattered on tables in the reading room, and here Polly presided over the library operation in a glass-enclosed office. She was seated behind her desk, wearing her usual gray suit and white blouse, but she was looking radiant, and her graying hair still showed the special attention it had received in preparation for the wedding.

"You are looking . . . especially well!" he greeted her. "Evidently you enjoyed your weekend." He took a seat in one of the hard oak armchairs that had come with the building in 1904.

"Thank you, Qwill," she said. "It was an absolutely wonderful weekend, but strenuous. I'm not conditioned to all that partying. That's why I left the message not to call me. The wedding ceremony was absolutely beautiful! The bride wore her grandmother's lace dress with a six-foot train, and everyone was terribly emotional. The reception was held at the Riding and Hunt Club, and I danced with the bridegroom and the bride's father and—simply everyone!"

Qwilleran and Polly never danced. The opportunity seldom arose, and he was unaware that she liked to dance. "How many guests were there?" he asked.

"Three hundred, Shirley said. Her son made a handsome groom. He's just out of law school and has a job with the best law firm in Lockmaster. You've never met Shirley, have you? She's the one who had the litter of kittens and gave me Bootsie. We've been friends for twenty years. Her husband is in real estate. His name is Alan, spelled A-l-a-n."

She's chattering, Qwilleran thought; why is she chattering? Polly's manner of speech was usually reserved and often pedantic; she made a brief, pithy statement and waited for her listener's reaction. Today her speech bubbled with the exuberance of a younger woman—one who has been out on the town for the first time. He combed his moustache with his fingers. "So you had brunch at the Paddock! Do you consider it as good as its reputation?"

"Absolutely!" she said. "It's a marvelous restaurant, and I stayed longer than I anticipated."

He wondered about that "absolutely." It was not Polly's kind of word, and yet she had used it three times. Ordinarily she would say "definitely" or "without doubt," but never "absolutely."

"But tell me about Hilary VanBrook," she was saying. "Everyone is shocked—and worried about what the police will uncover."

"May I shut the door?" he asked. There were a few loiterers in the reading room, and everyone in Pickax had big ears.

"I heard on the radio," Polly said, "that you gave an all-night party!" She regarded him accusingly.

"WPKX has a talent for garbling the news to give the wrong impression," he said. "Actually the entire cast and rew of *Henry VIII* descended on me around midnight and stayed until 3 A.M. After they had left, Koko started creating a disturbance that aroused my curiosity. I went out and found the body. The shooter had used a silencer, and yet that cat heard the shot. Or perhaps he knew by instinct that something was wrong. During the party he was on top of the *schrank*, staring down at VanBrook's head, and I thought Koko recognized a hairpiece. He can always tell the difference between real and false. But now I believe he knew something was going to happen to the man—and that *he was going to get it in the back of the head!*"

"Oh, Qwill! Isn't that a trifle extreme? I know cats have a sixth sense, but I can't believe they're prescient."

"Koko is not your average cat."

"Weren't you surprised that Mr. VanBrook attended the party? He has a reputation for being asocial."

"He had an ulterior motive, Polly. He expected to line up a field trip for the entire student body, marching grades nine to twelve through my barn! A lot of nerve, I thought."

"He was a very arrogant man. No one liked him, but people don't kill simply because a person is socially unacceptable."

"Don't be too sure. A man shot his neighbor last month in an argument over dog-doo."

"Yes, but that was Down Below. They don't behave that way up here . . . Excuse me." Her telephone rang, and she answered briskly. "This is Mrs. Duncan . . . Well, good morning!" she added in a softer tone, her face suddenly aglow with pleasure. She glanced at Qwilleran as she said, "I'm just fine, thank you . . . Absolutely! . . . Well, I'm in a conference at the moment . . . Yes, please do." She hung up the phone, smiling to herself.

Who was that? Qwilleran wanted to ask but decided against it. If Polly wanted him to know, she would tell. He said, "I'd better hie myself home. Bushy is taking pictures of the barn this morning."

"That's nice," she said, straightening papers on her desk. "He was the official photographer at the wedding." She seemed preoccupied, and Qwilleran left without making any further remarks.

In walking back to the barn he took the long way around in order to pass the office of the *Moose County Something*. It occurred to him that their police reporter might have information withheld from the public. The press always had an inside story or was privy to the latest rumor.

Junior Goodwinter hailed him from the managing editor's office. "Hey, Qwill! Did they let you out on bail?"

"If I'm charged, Junior, I'm going to implicate you. Maybe we can be cellmates. What's the latest?"

"No one has been charged yet. The police aren't talking, but we pumped the Dingleberry boys and found out that the cremated remains are supposed to be sent to Lockmaster at the request of VanBrook's attorney."

"No funeral here? That's his final insult to the public." The citizens of Pickax dearly loved a celebrity funeral with a marching band playing a dirge and a long procession to the cemetery. It had been a cherished tradition since the nineteenth century.

"That's right. No funeral," said the editor. "We called Lyle Compton about the possibility of a memorial service, and he said no one would attend. He said VanBrook's assistant will be elevated to the job of principal, at least pro tem. The board will have to vote on it, but the guy's competent, and there's no reason why he shouldn't get the job.... That's all the news to this moment, but Arch wants to see you."

Arch Riker and Qwilleran had been lifelong friends Down Below, and they had worked together at the *Daily Fluxion*. During Riker's twenty-five years as an editor he had never rated more than a desk, a telephone, and a computer terminal. Now, as publisher of a backwoods journal, he sat in a large carpeted office with a desk the size of a Ping-Pong table. What's more—fellow staffers at the *Fluxion* would never believe this—he had draperies on the windows, installed by Amanda's Studio of Interior Design.

"Sit down," he said to Qwilleran. "Help yourself to coffee."

"Thanks, but I've just had three cups at Lois's."

"What's the scuttlebutt over there?"

"Everyone's on edge, fearing that some prominent member of the community is guilty. They overlook the fact that a brilliant man, who has done much for the education system, has been struck down in the prime of life. True, he was an outsider and not well-liked, but a crime is a crime, even if the victim is a pariah or even if the murderer is the publisher of the *Something*."

"While you're on your soapbox, why don't you do a column on the subject, Qwill?"

"No, thanks. It happened in my backyard, and I'm keeping out of it, but I suggest you write an editorial." His hand went involuntarily to his moustache.

Riker recognized the gesture. "Are you getting the investigative itch? Do you think you might do some private sleuthing?"

"Not this time. I have confidence in Brodie. He grew up here, and he's a walking file on everyone in the county. It wouldn't surprise me if he knows who pulled the trigger and is setting a trap for him—or her." He started to leave the office.

"Aren't you getting any vibrations from Koko?" Riker asked mockingly.

"He keeps pulling engravings from my typecase, but so far the message is only FOOD. See you later, Arch."

On the way out of the building Qwilleran stuck his head in an office where Hixie Rice was selling a full-page ad to the owner of a food market, exuding charm and enthusiasm into the instrument.

"Any word about Dennis?" he asked after she had hung up triumphantly.

"His parking space is still empty. Why didn't he tell *someone*— you or me or Susan or Fran? It worries me."

"If you infer that he's a fugitive from justice, get it out of your head, Hixie. We all know he's a decent guy, and I maintain he's on his way home to see his wife and child—possibly because of some sort of family emergency down there, or because his wife found a buyer for their house. She probably called while he was at the theatre and left a message on his answering machine."

"I hope you're right, Qwill."

He declined her invitation to have a microwaved sub in the staff lounge and left to complete his errands. At the post office he picked up his mail and told them to hold future deliveries until the battered mailbox could be repaired.

"Kids out your way must be bashing mailboxes with ballbats again," the clerk guessed.

"Looks like it," Qwilleran said.

Other postal patrons were picking up their mail or buying stamps, and most were standing around in neighborly huddles, discussing the murder. They lowered their voices or changed the subject when they caught sight of Mr. Q.

By the time he arrived home the official cars were thinning out, but the photographer's van was still there. "How's it going?" he asked Bushy.

The photographer was packing up his gear. "Wait'll you hear what happened! Remember how the cats behaved when you brought them to my studio for portraits last year?"

"I remember. They wouldn't leave their carrying coop," Qwilleran recalled. "I drove one hundred twenty miles round trip, and we couldn't get them out of their carrier even with a can opener."

"Well, today it was different. They wanted to be in every picture! Every time I set up a shot, one of them was *right there!* I shot the kitchen, and they were both perched on the circular stairs. Whichever way I aimed the camera, there was a cat sitting on a railing or climbing a ladder."

"I should have locked them up," said Qwilleran. "Cats are perverse. They figure out what you want and then do the opposite."

"What's the difference? These photos are only for insurance purposes, aren't they? It'll look as if you've got twenty cats, that's all."

Qwilleran watched the photographer pack, marveling how much equipment can be fitted into a small case where there is a place for everything.

"Now I'm ready for that coffee," Bushy said.

"Would you like a drink of Scotch and a bowl of chili first?"

"Sure would, but I'd rather have wine if you've got it."

"Name it, and we have it. This is the best bar outside of the Shipwreck Tavern. I have thirsty friends."

"And you never touch a drop," the photographer marveled. "How come?"

"Let's just say that I paid my dues when I was young and reckless, and I dropped out of the club ten years ago."

The two men sank into leather chairs with wide arms, deep seats, and welcoming cushions—near the bookshelves and the printer's typecase.

"You've got a nice setup," Bushy said. "You've really got space. We have, too, but it's all cut up into rooms. I see you collect old printing stuff. I have a friend—the editor of the *Lockmaster Logger*—who collects typefaces and old advertising posters. He has a playbill from Ford's Theatre dated April 14, 1865—the night Lincoln was assassinated."

The Siamese, aware that chili was in the offing, made a sudden appearance and settled on the ottoman.

Bushy said, "I'd still like to photograph those two characters in my studio. There's a market for cat photos right now. Now that they know me, perhaps we could try it again. Would you like to bring them down to Lockmaster once more?"

"I'm willing to give it another shot," Qwilleran said.

"Have you ever been to our famous steeplechase?"

"No. Horse racing never appealed to me. I'm no gambler. If I put out a dollar I expect a dollar's worth in return."

"This is different. It's like a big picnic, with horses jumping over hedges, and hounds baying, and carriages on parade. Here's what I thought: The September steeplechase is next weekend. Bring the cats down and stay at our house. We have lots of room. The cats can prowl around and get used to the studio."

"I'll have to think about that," Qwilleran said, "but I appreciate the invitation."

"There's a party Saturday night after the races, and on Sunday a lot of us go to brunch at the Palomino Paddock."

"I've heard about the brunch. My friend Polly was there yesterday."

"I know. I saw her there, and she was really enjoying herself. She was at the wedding reception, too—living it up. They had a terrific buffet and an open bar. You should have been there, Qwill." Bushy was talkative by nature, and a glass of burgundy enhanced this propensity. His range of topics covered his new boat, fishing conditions at Purple Point, his wife's disappointment at being childless, and the problems of living in a century-old house. Qwilleran was a good listener; he never knew when he might glean a tidbit for his column.

Just as Bushy was telling about his wife's grandmother, who lived with them, a sudden impulse triggered the Siamese and catapulted them off the ottoman, round and round the fireplace cube, up the ramp, spiraling toward the roof, racing across the beams, leaping from catwalk to balcony, pounding down the ramp with thundering paws, then swooping to the main level, landing on the ottoman, where they came to a sudden stop and licked their fur. Time: thirty-five seconds.

"What was that all about?" asked the stunned photographer.

"I think they're telling me to go to the steeplechase. I accept your invitation."

After the bowls of chili (hot) and coffee (strong), Qwilleran helped carry the photographic equipment to the van, and Bushy asked, "What are you going to do with your orchard? It's pretty well shot."

"I'll clear out the dead trees and plant something else," said Qwilleran.

"You could make it a bird sanctuary. Keep those berry bushes and wild cherries and plant some cedars and maples and things like that. Our yard is a conference center for birdlife. Vicki's grandmother is a nut about birds."

Qwilleran returned indoors to ask the Siamese if they were in favor of a bird sanctuary and was greeted by Koko in his impertinent pose: legs splayed, head cocked, tail crooked.

"You scoundrel!" Qwilleran said as he picked up the printing blocks scattered around the floor. This time he found a squirrel, a rabbit, an eagle, and a seahorse, two of them hidden under rugs, a trick he attributed to Yum Yum. They're both bored, he thought. "Would anyone like to go for an outing?" he asked.

When he produced the harnesses and jingled them invitingly, Yum Yum promptly disappeared, but Koko was ready for action. Harnessed and leashed and perched on Qwilleran's shoulder, he was soon riding toward the mailbox on the highway. Qwilleran avoided the rutted trail and waded through the weeds in the orchard. Small birds landed on the tips of tall grasses and bounced them up and down, and he could feel Koko's body trembling.

Toward the end of the property the cat struggled to get down. Was this the spot where the killer parked his truck or van? More likely, Qwilleran concluded, there was an abandoned bird's nest in the grass. Some nest builders, Polly had told him, are groundlings.

Arriving at the highway, he allowed Koko to walk, and the cat investigated tire tracks on the pavement and pebbles on the shoulder. The crime lab had removed the mailbox for analysis, but Koko found a piece of glass they had overlooked. A fragment of a headlight? Or a shard from a whiskey bottle aimed at the mailbox by a Saturday-night carouser?

Whatever it is, Qwilleran said to himself, we're staying out of this case. Yet, Koko was tugging on the leash urgently. He was tugging toward the south—the direction in which the last vehicle had turned after the fateful party.

Chapter 5

The day after Qwilleran accepted Bushy's invitation to the steeplechase, the sun was shining; the weather prediction was favorable; the Siamese were well and happy. Yet, he greeted the day with a mild depression. The triangular windows in the upper walls of the apple barn were performing their usual magic, throwing geometric patches of sunlight about the interior. As the earth turned, those distorted triangles of warmth and brightness moved from place to place, confusing the Siamese, who were always attracted to cozy spots. Ordinarily, Qwilleran was fascinated by this slow-motion minuet of sunsplashes, but on this day he was nagged by a vague uneasiness.

The morning started well enough with a phone call from Lockmaster. "Qwill, this is Vicki Bushland. I'm so glad you and the cats will be spending the weekend with us."

"It will be my pleasure," he assured her.

"I hope the weather will be fine. It's beautiful today. Is the sun shining up there?"

"It's working overtime," he said, making note of the bright triangles on the floor and walls and the front of the *schrank*. "Is there anything I may contribute to the weekend?"

"Just bring your binoculars and your camera for the races.

The Saturday night party at the Riding and Hunt Club is rather dressy. The women wear long dresses, but black tie is optional for the men. Otherwise, everything's casual. We have a tailgate picnic at the race course on Saturday."

"Sounds good," he said, more politely than truthfully. Meals alfresco had never appealed to him. The prospect entailed limp paper plates, plastic forks, stuffed eggs with fragments of eggshell mashed into the stuffing, tuna sandwiches gritty with sand, and ants in the chocolate cake. Nevertheless, the experience might produce worthwhile material for the "Qwill Pen," and he would have an excuse to absent himself from the apple barn during the public open house. On Saturday half of Moose County, at five dollars a head, would be tramping up and down the ramps, no doubt making disparaging remarks about the fireplace design and the contemporary furniture. But his underlying reason for accepting the Bushlands' invitation may have been his curiosity about the person who had brunched with Polly at the Palomino Paddock, sending her home late, tired, and starry-eyed. No doubt this was the caller with whom she had that brief and guarded conversation while Qwilleran squirmed in a hard oak chair.

"I'm looking forward to the whole weekend," he told Vicki.

"Could you arrive in time for dinner on Friday?" she asked. "We'd have cocktails at six. I'd like to give a little dinner party because my grandmother is dying to meet you. She adored your column when you were writing for the *Daily Fluxion*, and now we buy the Moose County paper every Tuesday and Friday so she can read 'Straight from the Qwill Pen.' Sometimes you switch days, and then the dear lady has a fit!"

"I'm sure I'll like your grandmother immensely," Qwilleran said.

"We'll invite a few others you might enjoy meeting. Everyone knows who you are, and all our friends have heard about the time you and Bushy were marooned on the island during a storm. So we'll all be looking forward to your visit."

"None more than I," he said in the graciously formal style he adopted on such occasions.

"Do you like pasta? We have to serve something my grandmother can swallow easily."

"I consider myself omnivorous—with the small exception of turnips and parsnips."

"How about the cats? What do they eat?"

"Don't worry about them. I'll take along some canned stuff."

Canned stuff to the Siamese meant red salmon, boned chicken, solid-pack white tuna, crabmeat, and lobster.

Although feeding the cats would be a simple matter, dressing for dinner at the Riding and Hunt Club would pose a problem. The navy blue suit that Qwilleran reserved for funerals had been lost in a fire. Furthermore, a dinner jacket would be preferable if only to dispel the Lockmaster notion that Moose County was populated with aborigines. He had never owned a dinner jacket. He had rented one for Arch Riker's wedding twenty-odd years before, and he assumed that the practice was still customary. He assumed that the young potato farmers and sheep ranchers whose wedding photos appeared in the *Something* were able to rent their dinner jackets and tailcoats from Scottie's Men's Shop.

Time was short. He headed downtown at a pace faster than usual, turning his head only to count the yellow posters in store windows—posters made brighter by the relentless September sun:

LIVING BARN TOUR
SAT., SEPT. 17, 10 A.M. TO 5 P.M.
TICKETS $5

Scottie greeted him at the door. "Weel, laddie, you've done it again!" he said, putting on the brogue that pleased his Scottish and part-Scottish customers. (Qwilleran's mother, everyone knew, had been a Mackintosh.)

"Meaning what?" Qwilleran asked.

"You found another dead body! Canna remember any dead bodies before you moved to town."

Qwilleran huffed into his moustache as dismissal of the

remark. "I want to rent a dinner jacket and everything that goes with it."

"Och! You want to *rent?* Is the Klingenschoen heir too hard up to buy one?"

"Look, Scottie, I've lived here for four years with no need for formal clothing, and I may never need it again. Waste not, want not."

"Spoken like a true Mackintosh! Or was your mother a Mackenzie?"

"Mackintosh," Qwilleran growled.

" 'Twill make a juicy bit of gossip when the word gets around that the richest man in Moose County is *rentin'* a dinner jacket. Every man in your position, laddie, should own a dinner jacket."

Reluctantly Qwilleran allowed himself to be sold, and as he was being fitted, the storekeeper brought up the subject of the murder again. "Let them say what they will about VanBrook, it were too bad. Aye, it were too bad."

"Was he a good customer of yours?" Qwilleran asked, assuming that Scottie's reactions would be related to the cash register.

"Not good, but frequent. He come in here reg'lar to look for turtlenecks in colors they don't make . . . The police have a suspect, I hear."

"I was not aware of that, Scottie. Who is it?" Qwilleran asked innocently.

"There's a rumor that Dennis Hough is in hidin'." He pronounced it *Hoe.* "The mayor's wife were in Mooseville to a ladies' social, and she saw the laddie comin' out of the Shipwreck Tavern, lookin' furtive and in want of a shave."

"What kind of refreshments were they serving at that ladies' social? Dennis is driving to St. Louis to see his family for the first time in several months! The gossips want to suspect him because he's an outsider from Down Below. The people around here, if you ask me, are a bunch of xenophobes."

"If you mean they're slow in payin' their bills, you hit the nail on the head, laddie."

Leaving Scottie's store, Qwilleran met Carol Lanspeak going into the family's emporium. "Heard anything?" she asked.

"Not a word," he replied. "How about you?"

"Wait till you hear! We just received a letter that Hilary mailed last Friday, the day before he died, billing us for mileage for that woman from Lockmaster! Eight rehearsals and twelve performances at one hundred forty miles a round trip. Do you realize what that amounts to at twenty-five cents a mile? Seven hundred dollars! I know she used a lot of gas to come up here, but the point is: *We didn't need her!*"

"Can the club afford it?"

"Well, it'll put us in the red again. It's just another example of Hilary's arrogance. He never gave us a hint that we'd be liable for her travel expenses. Scott Gippel thinks we should just ignore it. We don't know the woman's address, and we don't know who's handling the estate."

"What does Larry say about it?"

"He hasn't seen the letter yet. He'll hit the ceiling!" Her eye caught the yellow poster in the store window. "Your Living Barn Tour is being well publicized, but isn't a five-dollar admission kind of steep for Pickax pocketbooks?"

"They'll pay five dollars just to see the scene of the crime," he said.

"That's ghoulish, Qwill."

"But true. You wait and see."

Carol went into the store, and Qwilleran went on his way, thinking about the letter posthumously received. Who was VanBrook's executor? What was the extent of his estate? Who would inherit? Only one person in Pickax, he thought, would know anything about the principal's connections. The superintendent of schools would have a file on the man. Qwilleran had a sudden urge to lunch with Lyle Compton, and he knew that Compton always liked an excuse to get out of the office.

Qwilleran phoned the board of education and made a date for noon, then called the Old Stone Mill for a reservation. Thriftily he used the phone in Amanda's Studio of Interior Design.

"Have you heard anything new?" Fran asked him when he hung up the phone. "I haven't been able to pry anything out of Dad. He isn't talking, not even to Mother, but there's an ugly rumor circulating about Dennis."

"How do these baseless rumors get started?" Qwilleran asked irritably.

"He left town suddenly."

"No doubt headed for St. Louis on family business."

"That's what I think, too, although he didn't mention it to anyone . . . How did the shoot turn out yesterday?"

"Pretty good, I guess. Bushy took a lot of pictures and promised to print a complete set for you. I'll see them this weekend when I go down to Lockmaster. Have you ever been to the steeplechase?"

"No, but I hear it's quite a blast."

Qwilleran looked at his watch. "I'm meeting Lyle at noon. See you later."

"Wait a minute, Qwill. Want to help me make that delivery to Hilary's house tomorrow?"

"What time?"

"Is nine o'clock too early? I know you're a slow starter."

"Not on Wednesday mornings! Mrs. Fulgrove comes to dust, and I like any excuse to get out."

"Okay, then. Park behind the studio, and you can help me load the screens in the van. They're in flat cartons, large but not heavy. And," Fran added slyly, "we won't charge you for the two phone calls."

Stroking his moustache with satisfaction, Qwilleran left for lunch with a singularly buoyant step. He was going to see what was behind those drawn draperies on Goodwinter Boulevard.

The Old Stone Mill was a picturesque restaurant converted from a nineteenth-century grist mill, and its outstanding features were a six-foot-seven busboy who talked a lot and an old millwheel that turned and creaked and groaned continuously. The two men were shown to Qwilleran's favorite table: it had the best view and the most privacy and was comfortably removed from the incessant racket of the ancient wheel.

As Derek Cuttlebrink sauntered over with water pitcher and bread basket, the superintendent said with his usual cynical scowl, "Here comes our most distinguished alumnus."

"Hi, Mr. Compton," said the gregarious busboy. "Did you see me in the play?"

"I certainly did, Derek, and you were head and shoulders above all the others."

"Gee!"

"When are you going to complete your education, my boy? Or is your goal to be the oldest busboy in the forty-eight contiguous states?"

"Well, I've got this new girl that kinda likes me, and she doesn't want me to go away to college," Derek explained plausibly. "I see her three times a week. Last night we went roller skating."

The hostess, hurrying past with an armful of menu folders, nudged him. "Setups on tables six and nine, Derek, and table four wants more water."

As the busboy drifted away with his water pitcher, Compton said, "The Cuttlebrinks were the founders of the town of Wildcat, but their pioneer spirit is wearing thin. Every generation gets taller but not brighter ... What looks interesting on the menu? I don't want anything nutritious. I get all that at home." The superintendent was a painfully thin man who smoked too many cigars and scoffed at vegetables and salads.

Qwilleran said, "There's a cheese and broccoli soup that's so thick you could use it for mortar. The avocado-stuffed pita is a mess to eat, but delicious. The crab Louis salad is the genuine thing."

"I'll take chili and a hot dog," Compton told the waitress ... "So they finally eliminated VanBrook," he said to Qwilleran. "I always knew he'd get it someday. Too bad it happened on our territory. It makes Moose County look bad."

"If you found him so objectionable, why did you keep renewing his contract?"

"He was so damned good that he had us over a barrel. There are devils you can live with, you know."

"What happens to his estate? Did he have any family elsewhere?"

"The only personal contact listed in his file is an attorney in Lockmaster. When the police notified me, I talked to this man and asked if there was anything we could do. He told me that Hilary had opted for cremation, with his ashes to be sent to Lockmaster. Then he asked for the name of an estate liquidator, and I referred him to Susan Exbridge."

"Hilary was a mystery man, wasn't he? I'm reading the biography of Sir Edmund Backhouse, the British sinologist, and I see a similarity: A brilliant, erudite man of astounding accomplishments but also an eccentric who doesn't fit the social norm."

"Hilary was that, all right," Compton agreed.

"Even his name rouses one's curiosity, if not suspicion."

"Hilary VanBrook was his professional name, assumed when he was acting on the New York stage. It's not the one used for social security, federal withholding, and so forth, but you have to admit it has a touch of class. His real name was William Smurple—not an auspicious name for a Broadway star."

"Or a high school principal," Qwilleran said. "I hear he claimed to speak Japanese fluently. Was that true?"

"To all appearances. We had a Japanese exchange student up here one year, and they seemed to converse glibly. So that checked out. I never had any qualms about his credibility, although I often questioned his judgment. We lost a helluva good custodian because of him, and a good janitor is a pearl beyond price. Pat O'Dell had been in the school system for forty years, and you couldn't find a more conscientious worker or more charismatic personality. He was the unofficial student counselor; the kids flocked to him for advice—a grandfather figure, you might say. Well, Hilary blew the whistle on *that* unorthodox arrangement! I think he was jealous of the man's popularity. At any rate, he made it so uncomfortable for old Pat O'Dell that he quit."

"What about the Toddwhistle incident?"

"Kids have been putting things on teachers' chairs and in principals' mailboxes for generations! Hilary overreacted. Now that he's gone, we'll probably give Wally a diploma, if he wants it. But I'll bet he earns more money stuffing animals than I do hiring teachers."

They ordered apple pie, and Qwilleran asked, "With all VanBrook's talents and background, why did he choose to live in remote places like Lockmaster and Pickax? Did he ever explain?"

"Yes, he did, when we first interviewed him. He said he had seen the world at its best and at its worst, and now he wanted a quiet place in which to study and meditate."

Qwilleran thought: He could be running from someone or something. He could be an upscale con man on the wanted list. His murderer could be an enemy from Down Below, settling an old score.

Compton was saying, "He claimed to have ninety thousand books in his library. He listed his major interests as architecture, horticulture, Shakespeare, and baroque music. He had three academic degrees."

"Did you verify them before hiring him?"

"Hell, no. We took him on faith, knowing what an outstanding job he'd done as principal of Lockmaster. As a matter of fact, he turned out to be so damned good for Pickax that we never crossed him. We were afraid we'd lose him."

"Well, you've lost him now," Qwilleran said.

"I hear the police are looking for your builder, and he's skipped town."

"Lyle, if I were a doctoral candidate in communications, I'd write my thesis on the Moose County rumor mill. Let me tell you something. Dennis Hough had no more motive than you or I have, and I happen to know he's on his way home to see his family Down Below."

"I hope you're right," said Compton. He lighted a cigar, and that was Qwilleran's cue to excuse himself, grabbing the check and saying he had another appointment. Actually, since giving up pipesmoking, he found tobacco fumes offensive. Yet, in the days when he puffed on a quarter-bend bulldog, he went about perfuming restaurants and offices and cocktail parties with Groat and Boddle Number Five, imported from Scotland, thinking he was doing surrounding noses a favor.

Qwilleran did indeed have another appointment—with Susan Exbridge—who was chairing the library committee in charge of the barn tour. As he headed for her antique shop, he was struck by a chilling thought. Suppose Dennis did not go to St. Louis! Suppose he drove to some out-of-county collision shop to have the damage repaired on his van! Suppose the mayor's wife really did see him coming out of the Shipwreck Tavern! He dismissed the thought with a mental shudder.

The Exbridge & Cobb antique shop on Main Street was a class act. The clean windows, the gold lettering on the glass, the polished mahogany and brass on display—all sparkled in the afternoon sun, thanks to the ministrations of Mr. O'Dell and Mrs. Fulgrove.

When Qwilleran walked in, Susan turned, expecting a customer, but the proprietorial smile turned to dismay when she saw him. "Oh, Qwill!" she agonized. "Have you heard the news? They're hunting for Dennis, and he's *gone!*"

"Don't be alarmed," he said with diminished confidence. "He's on his way Down Below to see his family. I saw you two leaving the party together. What happened after that, if you don't mind my asking?"

"He walked me to my car, which was at the far end of the lane, and then returned to his van. He didn't say a word about going to St. Louis."

"Will you take offense if I ask you something personal?"

"We-e-ell . . ." she hesitated.

"What were you and Dennis giggling about when you left the barn?"

"Giggling?"

"You were enjoying some private joke. I'm not prying into your affairs, but it might give a clue to his next move."

"Oh," she said, recollecting the episode. "It was nothing. It was about one of the Old Lady's lines to Anne Boleyn. She says, *And you, a very fresh fish, have your mouth filled before you open it.* On the last night, I said it with a certain significant emphasis. Someone in the audience guffawed, and Fran glared at me murderously. I'd give anything to know who laughed."

"Hmff," Qwilleran said. "I didn't come here to quiz you, Susan. I came to ask about the Barn Tour. Is everything under control?"

"There's one problem, Qwill. Dennis was going to give me some facts about the remodeling, to help the guides answer questions. What shall we do?"

"I'll type something out for you. Who are the guides?"

"Members of the library board and a few volunteers."

"How many visitors do you expect?"

"We've printed five hundred tickets, and they're selling well. The ad runs tomorrow, and we're taking a few radio spots."

"I'm leaving town Friday for the weekend. Why don't you come over Thursday morning before you open your shop? You can pick up the key to the barn and see that everything's in order. And don't worry about Dennis, Susan. I'm confident that it'll straighten out all right."

Qwilleran believed what he was saying, more or less, until he later met Hixie Rice coming out of the bank. "I've been trying to reach you, Qwill!" she cried. "I was in Mooseville this morning, calling on customers, and I saw Dennis's van! I was driving east on the lakeshore road. He was just ahead of me, and he turned into your property. Don't you have a letter *K* on a post at the entrance to your log cabin?"

Qwilleran nodded solemnly.

"When he made the left turn, I saw him clearly, hunched over the steering wheel. He looked ghastly! Does he have a key to your cabin?"

"No, he returned it. I let him use the cabin last month when he was rehearsing. He wanted to learn his lines while walking on the secluded beach."

"What should we do?"

"I'll drive out there to see what's happening."

"Be careful, Qwill," she warned. "If he's cracked up—and if he has a gun—and if he's killed once—"

"Dennis doesn't own a gun, Hixie. In fact, he's anti-gun. But something's happened to him. I'll get my car and drive out to Mooseville."

"I'll drive you. My car's right here. I hope you don't mind riding in a piece of junk; it's a loaner."

The route to Mooseville, thirty miles away, was fairly straight, and they far exceeded the speed limit. There was little traffic at this time of year—after the tourist season and before the hunting season. The highway passed through a desolate landscape ravaged by early lumbering and mining operations. Although the sun was shining, the scene was bleak, and so was the conversation.

Qwilleran said, "If he's in trouble, why didn't he confide in me? I thought we were good friends."

"Me too. I was thinking of quitting the *Something* and going into partnership with him. I could line up contracts and get publicity."

When they reached the lakeshore, the vacation cottages on the beach had an air of desertion. Qwilleran said, "It's around the next curve. Slow down."

"I'm getting nervous," said Hixie.

The letter *K* on a post marked the entrance to the Klingenschoen property, and the private drive led through patches of woods and over a succession of dunes until it emerged in a clearing.

"There's no one here!" Qwilleran said. "This is where he'd have to park."

They found tire tracks in the soft earth, however, and on the beach at the foot of the dune there were footprints. Sand and surf had not yet disguised the traces. The cabin itself, closed for the season, was undisturbed.

"If he's been on the run, he's been sleeping in his van," Qwilleran said. "How well do you know the manager at Indian Village?"

"We have a good rapport, and she's high on my Christmas list."

"Could you get the key to Dennis's apartment?"

"I could think of something . . . I could say that he's out of town and called me to send him papers from his desk."

"Good enough."

In Indian Village there were eight apartments in each two-story building, with a central hall serving them all. Hixie admitted Qwilleran into her own apartment and then went to see the manager. She returned with the key.

"It's my contention," Qwilleran told her, "that Dennis returned from the party early Sunday morning and either found a message on his answering machine or found something in his Saturday mail that caused him to take off in a hurry. It would have to be serious business to make him hide out in his van—a threat perhaps."

Entering Dennis's apartment with caution and stealth, they went directly to the desk. It was cluttered with papers in connection with the barn remodeling. There was a pink or yellow order form for every can of paint and every pound of nails that went into the job. The only sign of recent mail delivery was an unopened telephone bill. Then Qwilleran pressed the button of the answering machine.

When he heard the first message, he reached for the pocket-size recorder that was always in his jacket along with his keys.

"We've got to tape this," he said. "I want to play it for Brodie. But don't say a word about this to *anyone*, Hixie. Let's get back to town."

Hixie drove to the theatre parking lot, and Qwilleran walked the rest of the way home—through the iron gate, through the woods. Approaching the barn, he could see a van parked at the back door—Dennis's van—and he quickened his step, torn between relief and apprehension.

The back door was unlocked, as he expected; Dennis knew where to find the key. Walking into the kitchen Qwilleran shouted a cheerful, "Hello! Anybody here?" The only response was a wild shrieking and guttural howling from the top balcony.

He had locked the Siamese in their loft that morning, troubled as he was by his gnawing sense of foreboding. The cacophony from the loft made his blood run cold, and an awareness of death made him catch his breath. He moved toward the center of the building and slowly, systematically, surveyed the cavernous interior.

The afternoon sun was slanting through the high windows on the west, making triangles on the rugs, walls, and white fireplace cube, and across one triangle of sunlight there was a vertical shadow—the shadow of a body hanging from a beam overhead.

Chapter 6

Dennis Hough—creator of the spectacular barn renovation and darling of the Theatre Club—had let himself into the apple barn Tuesday afternoon, using the hidden key. Then he climbed to the upper balcony, threw a rope over a beam, and jumped from the railing.

Brodie himself responded when Qwilleran made his grisly discovery and called the police. The chief strode into the barn saying, "What did I tell you? What did I tell you? This is the man who killed VanBrook. He couldn't live with himself!"

"You've got it wrong," Qwilleran said. "Let me play you a tape. Dennis arrived at his apartment early Sunday morning, following the party, and checked his answering machine for messages. This is what he heard."

There followed a woman's voice, bitter and vindictive. "Don't come home, Dennis! Not ever! I've filed for divorce. I've found someone who'll be a good daddy for Denny and a real husband for me. Denny doesn't even know you any more. There's nothing you can say or do, so don't call me. Just stay up north and have your jollies."

Qwilleran said, "Do you want to hear it again?"

"No," Brodie said. "How did you get this?"

"I had access to his apartment, just as he had access to this barn. I found the message this afternoon and taped it to disprove your theory. Dennis didn't know he was under suspicion—or even that VanBrook had been killed, probably. He was overwhelmed by his own private tragedy."

Brodie grunted and massaged his chin. "We'll have to notify that woman as next of kin."

"I'll be willing to do it," said Qwilleran, who prided himself on his comforting and understanding manner in notifying the bereaved. He punched a number supplied by directory assistance, and when a woman's voice answered he said in his practiced tone of sincerity and concern, "Is this Mrs. Hough?" The fact that he pronounced it correctly was in his favor.

"Yes?" she replied.

"This is Jim Qwilleran, a friend of your husband, calling from Pickax—"

"I don't want to talk to any friend of that skunk!" she screamed into the phone and banged down the receiver.

Qwilleran winced. "Did you hear that, Andy?"

"Gimme the phone." Brodie punched the same number, and when she answered he said in his official monotone, "This is the police calling. Your husband is dead, Mrs. Hough. Suicide. Request directions for disposition of the body . . . Thank you, ma'am."

He turned to Qwilleran. "I won't repeat what she said. The gist of it is—we can do what we please. She wants no part of her husband, dead or alive."

Qwilleran said, "His friends in the Theatre Club will handle everything. I'll call Larry Lanspeak."

"I'll take the tape," Brodie said. "Just keep it quiet. He was never declared a suspect, so there's no need to deny the rumor. Let the public think what they want; we'll continue the investigation."

While the emergency crew and medical examiner went about their work, Qwilleran notified one person about the suicide, and that was Hixie. "You'll hear it on the six o'clock news," he said. "Dennis has taken his life." He waited for her hysterical outburst to subside and then said, "Don't mention the message from his wife to *anyone*, Hixie. Those are Brodie's orders. When he finds the real killer, Dennis will be cleared."

At six o'clock a brief announcement on WPKX stated: "A building contractor—Dennis Hough, thirty, of St. Louis, Missouri—died suddenly today in ... a Pickax barn ... he had recently ... remodeled. No details ... are ... available." The name of the deceased was pronounced *Huck*. "Died suddenly" was a euphemism for suicide in the north country.

Qwilleran was loathe to imagine the anguish of his friend's private moments preceding his desperate act. He thought: If I had been here, I could have prevented it. Qwilleran's own life had once been in ruins. He knew the shock of a suddenly failed marriage, the pain of rejection, the guilt, the sense of failure, the hopelessness. He skipped dinner, finding the thought of food nauseating, and fed the Siamese in their loft apartment. Koko, who knew something extraordinary had been happening, was determined to escape and investigate, but Qwilleran brought him down with a lunging tackle.

Down on the main level he turned on the answering machine; he wished no idle gossip, no prying questions. Then he shut himself in his studio, away from the sight of those overhead beams, that fireplace cube, and those triangular windows. He tried to lose himself in the pages of a book. As he delved farther and farther into the Backhouse biography, it occurred to him that the life of the mysterious VanBrook would be equally fascinating. The mystery of the man's personality and background, whether resolved or not, would be intensified by his violent death. The search for the killer, sidetracked by false suspicions, would add another dimension of suspense.

There was a violent storm that night. Gale winds from Canada swept across the big lake and joined with heavy rain to lash the rotting apple trees. By morning, the orchard was a wreck, and Trevelyan Trail was a ribbon of mud. Qwilleran called the landscape service, requesting a clean-up crew and truckloads of crushed stone.

Then he showered and shaved in a hurry and fed the cats without ceremony. It was Wednesday, and he hoped to escape before the vigorous Mrs. Fulgrove arrived to dust, vacuum, polish, and deliver her weekly lecture. This week her topics would undoubtedly be murder and suicide, in addition to her usual tirade about the abundance of cat hair. He succeeded in avoiding her and even had time for coffee and a roll at Lois's Luncheonette before reporting to the back door of Amanda's Studio of Interior Design.

He was met by a distraught young woman. "Dad told me about it!" Fran cried. "He wouldn't discuss motive, but everyone says it means that Dennis killed VanBrook."

Irritably Qwilleran said, "What everyone in Pickax says, thinks, feels, knows, or believes is of no concern to me, Fran."

"I know how you must feel about it, Qwill. I'm distressed, too. Dennis and I worked so compatibly on the barn. I'll miss him."

"Larry is arranging the funeral. There'll be a private service in the Dingleberry chapel for a few friends, then burial next to his mother."

Fran asked, "How is Polly reacting?"

"We haven't discussed it," he said.

"Are you two getting along all right?" she asked with concern.

"Why do you want to know?" he asked sharply.

"Well, you know . . . she wasn't there at the barn Saturday night . . . and then someone saw you at Tipsy's on Sunday—with another woman, they said."

Qwilleran huffed into his moustache angrily. "Okay, where are the cartons? How many do you have to deliver? Let's get the van loaded!"

On the short drive to Goodwinter Boulevard the designer said, "Hilary's neighbors will have their telescopes out. They'll be sure I'm looting a dead man's house."

"I gather that snooping is a major pastime in Pickax."

"You don't know the half of it! There are two busybodies who make it their lifework to spy and pry and spread rumors. But if you meet them on the post office steps, they're *so sweet!*"

"Who are they?"

"I'll give you a couple of clues," Fran said teasingly. "One wears a plastic rainhat even when the sun is shining, and the other calls everyone Dear Heart."

"Thanks for warning me," Qwilleran said. "Was Hilary a good customer of yours?"

"He didn't buy much, but he liked to come in to the studio and look around and tell us things that we already knew. He considered himself an authority on everything. He bought a lamp once, and we upholstered a chair for him last year, but the screens are the first big order I wrote up. And then this had to happen!"

"I suppose your father got a search warrant and went into the house."

"I don't know," she said coolly.

"Does he know you're delivering merchandise?"

"No, but Dear Heart will see that he finds out. Actually, Qwill, Dad and I haven't been on good terms since I moved into my apartment."

"Too bad. Sorry to hear it."

Fran parked in the rear of the house, and they started to unload. The interior was similar to others on Goodwinter Boulevard: large, square rooms with high ceilings, connected by wide arches; heavy woodwork in a dark varnish; a ponderous staircase lavished with carving and turnings; tall, narrow windows. But instead of the usual heirloom furniture and elaborate wallcoverings, the main rooms were white-walled and sparsely furnished with tatami floor matting, low Oriental tables, and floor cushions. There were a few pieces of porcelain, two Japanese scrolls, and a folding screen decorated with galloping fat-rumped horses. The only false note was the use of heavy draperies smothering the windows.

Fran explained, "Hilary was replacing the draperies with shoji screens so he could have light as well as privacy. He was quite secretive about his life-style."

"How could he live like this?" Qwilleran himself required large, comfortable chairs and a place to put his feet up.

"I believe he slept on a futon down here, but he said he had a study upstairs as well as rooms for books and hobbies."

Hobbies! Qwilleran found himself speculating wildly. "Okay if I look around?"

"Sure, go ahead," she said. "I'll be opening the cartons and putting each screen where it belongs. They were all custom-made, you know. We're talking about ten thousand dollars here, and God knows how long we'll have to wait to collect."

Qwilleran walked slowly up the impressive staircase, thinking about the ninety thousand books Compton had mentioned. He wondered if the collection included *City of Brotherly Crime*. He wondered if the books were catalogued. When he started opening doors, however, his hopes wilted; the books had never been unpacked. He went from room to room and found hundreds of sealed cartons of books—or so they were labeled.

Only one room was organized enough to have bookshelves, and they covered four walls. This was evidently the principal's study, having a desk, lounge chair, reading lamp, and stereo system. As for the volumes on the shelves, they expressed Van-Brook's eclectic tastes: Eastern philosophy, Elizabethan drama, architecture, Oriental art, eighteenth-century costume, Cantonese cookery, botany—but nothing on urban crime.

The desktop in this hideaway had an excessive tidiness reflecting the influence of the Japanese style downstairs. A brass paperknife in the shape of a Chinese dragon was placed precisely parallel to the onyx-base pen set. The telephone was squared off with the lefthand edge of the desk, and a brass-bound box (locked) was squared off with the righthand edge. In between, in dead center, was a clean desk blotter on which lay a neat pile of letters. Apparently they had been received and opened on Saturday, at which time they were read and returned to their envelopes.

There was a muffled quiet in the study. Fran's footsteps could be heard downstairs, and occasionally the ripping of a carton.

Casually, with an ear alert to the activity below, Qwilleran examined the mail. There were bills from utility companies, magazine-subscription departments, and an auto-insurance agency. There were no death threats, he was sorry to discover. But one small envelope addressed by hand had a scribble in the upper lefthand corner that piqued his curiosity: F. Stucker, 231 Fourth Street, Lockmaster. After determining that Fran was fully occupied with her screens, he gingerly drew the letter from its envelope and read the following:

Dear Mr. VanBrook—Thanks a lot for the $200. I didn't expect you to pay for my gas. It was nice of you to ask me to be in your play. But I can sure use the money. I had to buy new boots for Robbie. So thanks again.
Fiona

"Two hundred bucks!" Qwilleran said softly to the surrounding bookshelves. "That faker was making five hundred on the deal!" Was petty cheating one of his "hobbies"? Qwilleran tried the desk drawers, but they were locked.

Then, as he carefully tucked the note back in its envelope, he heard a humming sound in the insulated silence. He had not heard it before. It seemed to come from the rear of the second floor, and he followed it down the hall. Ahead of him was a rosy light spilling from a doorway. He approached warily and peeked into the room. The humming came from a transformer; the ceiling was covered with a battery of rose-tinted lights, and a timer had just turned them on.

Under the lights were long tables holding trays of plants, greenhouse style, but they were beginning to wilt. Obviously no one had watered them since VanBrook's last day on earth. What were they? Qwilleran was no horticulturist, but he knew this was not *Cannabis sativa*. There were purple flowers among the greenery. He rubbed a leaf and smelled his fingers; there was no clue. He broke off a sprig and put it in his shirt pocket, thinking he would give Koko a sniff.

"Okay, Quill," Fran called from the foot of the stairs. "I've done all I can do. Let's go."

As they drove away from the house, with the empty cartons loaded in the van, she said, "Well, what did you think of the place?"

"Esoteric, to say the least. If the estate puts his books up for sale, I'd like to know about it. What are the plants he was growing upstairs?"

"I never saw any plants. I was never invited upstairs. When I came to measure for the screens, he gave me a cup of tea, and we sat cross-legged on the floor cushions. I sure hope Amanda can collect for those screens."

"Amanda won't let anyone cheat her, dead or alive."

"Can you stand some good news?" she asked. "Your tapestries have arrived, and we can install them tomorrow—in time for the open house!"

"How do they look?"

"I haven't opened the packages, and the suspense is killing me, but I'll wait till we deliver them."

"Need any help?"

"No, I'll bring Shawn, my installer—more brawn than brain—but what he does, he does well."

"How will you hang them?"

"With carpet tack-strips. Do you mind if we make it around five o'clock?"

Fran always made business calls to Qwilleran's residence in the late afternoon, obligating him to offer a cocktail, which led to a dinner invitation. How did VanBrook get away with a cup of tea? . . . Not that Qwilleran objected to dining with his interior designer. She was good company. But Polly disapproved.

Fran dropped him at Scottie's, where he was fitted for a dark blue suit. He was to be a pallbearer at Dennis's funeral, and it occurred to him—too late—that he should have opted for a dark blue suit instead of a dinner jacket for the steeplechase party. He wondered if Scottie would take it back. It irked him to buy two of anything if one would do. Still, he decided not to suggest it. During the fitting, Scottie wanted to talk about the suicide, but Qwilleran turned him off with frowns and curt responses.

His next stop was the *Moose County Something,* and when he walked into Arch Riker's office, the publisher jumped to his feet. "Qwill! Where've you been? I heard it on the air last night and tried to reach you. Why didn't you call back? Today we're running a 'Died Suddenly,' but no one at the police department would talk to us. What happened?"

"I don't know," Qwilleran said.

"Does this mean the VanBrook case is wrapped up?"

"No, it doesn't. That's definite."

"What makes you so sure? Are you getting vibrations from Koko?" Riker asked in an attempt at banter.

"The police have evidence to that effect. That's all I can say, and don't ask me how I know. But I'd like to make a suggestion, Arch."

"Let's hear it."

"I think you should run that editorial I suggested: A crime is a crime! Offer a reward of $50,000 for information regarding the shooting. It'll squelch the rumor that Dennis was a suspect, and it may help Brodie. The K Fund will cover it."

"Do we identify the benefactor?"

"No. Keep it anonymous. How soon can you run it?"

"Friday."

"Good. I won't be here. I'm going to Lockmaster for a steeplechase weekend."

"You lucky dog! I hear it's a gas!"

It was too early for Qwilleran to go home; Mrs. Fulgrove would still be there, furiously mopping and cleaning and polishing. He went instead to the library—to tell Polly about his plans for the weekend. He had neither seen her nor talked with her for two days, not since the unexplained phone call that made her cheeks redden and her eyes sparkle.

In the vestibule of the library the daily quotation was: *The evil that men do lives after them; the good is oft interred with their bones.* The greetings from the clerks were appropriately solemn. As he headed for the stairs to the mezzanine, one of them called out, "She's not in, Mr. Q."

"She's having her hair done," the other explained.

"I'm just going up to read the papers," he said.

On the table in the reading room was a copy of the *Lockmaster Logger*, a publication established during lumbering days, more than a century before. Circulation: 11,500. Editor: Kipling MacDiarmid.

The first page of the *Logger* was devoted to steeplechase news: Five races with a combined purse of $75,000, preceded by the Trial of Hounds, the parade of carriages, and a concert by the Lockmaster High School band. A few parking spaces overlooking the course were still available for $100, but that would admit as many persons as could fit into the vehicle. There were sidebars listing the horses, owners, trainers, and riders who would participate in the event, and there were instructive features on what to wear to the races and what to pack in the picnic basket.

When Qwilleran heard Polly's sensible library shoes on the stairs, he put down his newspaper, and their eyes met. She was looking well-groomed but not as girlishly radiant as she had been on the day following the long brunch at the Palomino Paddock.

She walked immediately to his table. "Qwill, I'm so sorry about Dennis," she said softly. "You must be grieving."

"A lot of people are grieving, Polly."

"I suppose we can assume that Dennis . . . that the VanBrook case is closed now," she said, sitting down at the table.

"I don't assume anything, but I know that Moose County has lost a good builder and a talented actor."

"To some persons in Pickax the principal was such a villain that Dennis is now a candidate for a folk hero . . . Is that the *Lockmaster Logger* you're reading? What do you think of it?" Her face lighted up when she spoke the name of the town.

"It's more conservative than the *Something* in makeup, but it has a friendly slant. I hear Lockmaster is a friendly town. Did you find it *friendly?*" He gazed at her pointedly as he repeated the word.

Polly's eyes wavered for a fraction of a second. "I found everyone very cordial and hospitable." Then she added brightly, "Would you like to do something exciting this weekend? Would you like to go birdwatching in the wetlands near Purple Point?"

This was Qwilleran's moment. "I'd like to, but I'll be horse watching in Lockmaster. That's what I came to tell you. The Bushlands have invited me for the races. I'll be gone for three days."

"Oh, really?" she said with half-concealed disappointment. "You never told me you were interested in horses."

"Chiefly I'm interested in horse *people*. I may find some stuff for the 'Qwill Pen' column."

"Shall I feed Koko and Yum Yum while you're away?"

"Their royal highnesses are invited to go along—and have their portraits taken by a master photographer."

"How grand!" she said archly. "When do you leave?"

"Friday. After the funeral."

"Why don't you come over for dinner tomorrow night? I could prepare chicken divan."

"I wish I could, but Fran is hanging the new tapestries at five o'clock, and I don't know how long the operation will take or how many problems we'll encounter."

Polly straightened her shoulders and drew a deep breath as she always did when confronted by her personal demon: Jealousy. She stood up. "Then I'll see you when you return."

Qwilleran walked slowly back to the apple barn. The events of the morning had fired his determination to write a biography of the Mystery Man of Moose County. It would require prodigious research. First he would want to see Lyle Compton's file on the late principal. Teachers and parents in Pickax and Lockmaster would be glad to cooperate. VanBrook's attorney would no doubt grant an interview, and there would be Fiona Stucker, of course, whose connection with VanBrook might be a story in itself. The colleges that granted the man's degrees and the Equity records in New York would have to be researched. Qwilleran relished the challenge. He had a propensity for snooping and a talent for drawing information from shy or reluctant subjects.

He recalled the letter from Fiona Stucker. If VanBrook would chisel a few hundred dollars from the Theatre Club, he might have a history of other misdeeds, great or small: a fling at embezzlement, a witty financial fraud, some successful tax evasion. He had the nerve and the brains to carry off such schemes. The smuggling of Oriental treasures would appeal to him, both intellectually and esthetically. What was in those hundreds of cartons on the second floor of his strangely furnished house?

As Qwilleran approached the barn he could hear the cats' yowling welcome, and that brought to mind another question: On the night of the party, when Koko stared so intently at VanBrook's head, was the cat sensing a questionable operator? A felonious mentality? Farfetched as the idea might seem, it was not beyond the capabilities of that remarkable animal.

On the other hand, Qwilleran had to admit, Koko might have been staring at hair that he recognized as false.

CHAPTER 7

On Thursday morning Qwilleran emerged sleepily from his bedroom on the balcony and heard a familiar whistle: *who-it? who-it? who-it?* "Good question," he mumbled as he groped his way down the circular staircase to the computerized coffeemaker. "How about giving us a few answers?" He pressed a button and heard the grinding of the coffee beans, a reassuring sound. It was one of his constant fears that he might stumble down to the kitchen some bleak morning and find the machine out of order.

A feline imperative could be heard, drifting down from the upper reaches of the barn, and he went up the ramp to the top balcony to release the Siamese from their loft apartment. Yum Yum emerged sedately, like the princess that she knew herself to be, but Koko scampered down the ramp to the lower balcony, then flew through space, landing in the cushions of a lounge chair on the main floor. From there he rushed to the window-wall to greet his new-found friend. For a while he sat transfixed, fluttering the tip of his tail as the cardinal turned his head sideways to make eye contact. Shortly, the dump truck arrived to spread crushed stone on the trail, and the cardinal departed for more congenial surroundings.

Qwilleran thawed a Danish for his breakfast, fed the Siamese their roast beef from the deli with a garnish of Roquefort cheese, threw some clothing and towels into the washer, and finally showered and shaved in time to greet Susan Exbridge, who arrived in her long, sleek, top-of-the-line wagon.

"Oh, Qwill! I'm positively destroyed!" she said as she entered the barn and dropped into the nearest chair. "Dennis was such a darling! How could he throw it all away? What was his *motive?*"

Qwilleran said, "There's more to the story than meets the eye. Would you like a cup of coffee?"

"Could you add a touch of something *comforting?*"

"Like . . . rum?"

She nodded gratefully.

"Okay, Susan, tell me how you're going to handle the crowds on Saturday."

After taking a few sips she opened her briefcase and ticked off the arrangements. "The tickets instruct people to use the Main Street parking lots belonging to the theatre, courthouse, and church. We've cleared it with all of them."

"Suppose someone elects to drive up Trevelyan Trail to avoid the traffic jam?"

"The Trail is reserved for guides, and the entrance will be blockaded. Signs will direct visitors through the woods and to the front door of the barn. Indoors there will be plastic runners to protect the floors. Roped stanchions will keep visitors off the rugs. Only a certain number will be admitted at one time."

"Will they go up to the balconies? I wouldn't care to have them snooping in my bedroom."

"Definitely not. The ramps will be roped off. Visitors will

simply circle the main floor and exit through the kitchen door. The guides will keep the line moving. No picture taking permitted."

"And for this they're paying five dollars?" he asked in amazement.

"The tickets are sold out, and we could have sold more. There was a sudden demand, you know, after . . . after Tuesday night. The library will realize twenty-five hundred dollars. Polly is simply *ecstatic!*"

Qwilleran knew that the chief librarian was never ecstatic. Pleased, or quietly happy, or even mildly overjoyed, but never ecstatic. Susan's mocking emphasis on *ecstatic* was a subtle reminder that the two women were library associates but not friends.

"You're very well organized, Susan," he complimented her. "Here are the keys for the front and back doors. Hang onto them after the tour, and I'll pick them up at your shop next week."

A handsome and interesting woman, he reflected as she drove away—more fashionable than Polly—but too aggressive and theatrical for his taste, and she never sat down and read a book.

Another woman visitor arrived in the afternoon while he was regaling the Siamese with the devious exploits of Sir Edmund Backhouse. Lulled by his mellifluous voice, they were lounging dreamily in relaxed postures when a sound inaudible to human ears suddenly alerted them. Ears perked, heads lifted, necks craned, bodies raised on forelegs, hindquarters prepared to spring, they raced to the front door as if to greet a shipment of fresh lobster. Moments later, Qwilleran heard what they heard: the rumble of a car that had not recently had a tune-up.

It was Lori Bamba's vintage vehicle—Lori, his part-time secretary and adviser on all matters pertaining to cats. She had long golden hair, which she braided and tied with ribbons, and these tempting appendages held a hypnotic fascination for the Siamese, who greeted her with enthusiastic prowling and ankle rubbing.

"A pleasant surprise, Lori," said Qwilleran as he admitted her to the barn. Her husband usually delivered her finished work and picked up the week's correspondence.

"Nick told me what miracles you've done with the barn, so I had to come and see for myself. I'll bet the cats love those ramps and balconies."

"May I show you around? The five-dollar tour on Saturday limits visitors to the main floor; as an intimate of Koko and Yum Yum you're entitled to go up on the catwalks and visit their loft."

"First let me give you your correspondence. There are forty-seven letters for you to sign. On the less personal ones, I forged your signature. The crank letters were chucked into the wastebasket."

Qwilleran and Lori walked up the ramps, followed by the Siamese with erect tails, then down again. As soon as she sat down, both cats piled into her lap.

Qwilleran said, "I wish I could get Yum Yum to walk on a leash. With Koko it's no problem; he walks me on a leash."

"Just let her wear her harness around the house until she gets used to the feel of it," she suggested. "And do you realize, Qwill, that you have a perfect setup here for blowing bubbles?"

"Bubbles?" he asked dubiously.

"Soap bubbles. Stand on the balcony and let them float down to the cats below. They'll have a wonderful time— jumping and trying to catch them."

"Hmmm," he said, stroking his moustache. He could imagine the town gossips peeking in the window and carrying the news back to the coffee shops: "Mr. Q has started blowing bubbles!"

"The best thing for blowing bubbles," Lori advised, "is the old-fashioned clay pipe. They have them at the hardware store in Wildcat."

At that moment Koko leaped from her lap and bounded to the window, and they all heard the clear-toned *who-it? who-it? who-it?*

"That's a cardinal," Lori said.

"He's Koko's buddy."

"They're a couple of aristocrats," she said.

"Yes, they act like two potentates at a summit meeting. The orchard is full of other species, but somehow Koko is attracted to the cardinal. I don't know whether he appreciates the bird's regal demeanor or just likes red."

"I've read conflicting opinions about a cat's ability to see color. I'm inclined to believe they *feel color.* They get different sensations from different hues."

"I'll buy that," he said. "Koko is equipped with a lot more senses than the basic five. He's an especially gifted animal."

Lori said, "Let me tell you something interesting. I have an elderly aunt who lost her sight totally a few years ago, but she still recognizes red. She claims she can *feel it!* And she likes to wear red. She says it restores her energy."

"I'd like to meet her. It would make an interesting topic for my column . . . Would you like a glass of cider, Lori?"

"No, thanks, Qwill. Just give me the week's mail. I've got to dash. I've got a baby-sitter."

Later, he was signing the forty-seven letters when a black van with gold lettering on the panels pulled into the barnyard, and a young blond giant leaped out. He opened the rear doors and hoisted to his shoulders—with apparent ease—a large paper-wrapped cylinder, eight feet in length and about a yard in diameter. Fran Brodie was with him, and she directed him to the back door.

"This is Shawn, our world-class installer," she said to Qwilleran.

"Hi!" said the giant with an amiable smile.

She guided him through the kitchen to the great hall, four stories high, and told him to put the tapestry on the floor at the foot of the ramp. Going down on one knee, like Atlas with the world on his shoulders, Shawn dropped the cylinder on the floor with a thud. Then he stood up and gazed at the balconies, the triangular windows, and the fireplace cube with its three stacks.

"How much did this job cost?" he said in awe. "It's sure different! . . . Is this where the guy hung himself?"

"Shawn!" Fran said sharply. "Bring in the toolbox, the tackstrips, and the rope." To Qwilleran she said, "I want to unroll the tapestries down here for inspection. This is the moment of truth!"

The wrapping was carefully removed, and the eight-by-tenfoot wall hanging was spread out on the floor.

"Beautiful!" said Qwilleran.

"Gorgeous!" Fran said.

Shawn shook his head and said, "Crazy!"

The design was a stylized tree dotted with a dozen bright red apples the size of basketballs. Tufting gave them dimension.

"They look real enough for plucking," Qwilleran observed.

"Don't you think," Fran remarked, "that the artist actually captured their juiciness?"

"You guys must be nuts," said the installer. "All I know—it weighs a ton."

The Siamese, watching from the top of the fireplace cube, had no comment.

"Now, this tapestry," the designer explained, "will hang from the railing of the highest catwalk, Qwill, making an exciting focal point that draws the eye upward into that *delicious* galaxy of radiating beams and triangular windows. Also, it will add warmth and color to an interior with *lots* of wood and *lots* of open space. Don't you agree?"

"Yow!" said Koko.

"Okay, Shawn," she said, "roll it up again and carry it to the top level."

"No elevator?"

"You don't need an elevator."

The tack-strips were installed on the top surface of the catwalk railing; the top edge of the tapestry was pressed down securely on the tacks; and then it was slowly unrolled as the ropes were played out.

"Hope it doesn't drop and kill a cat," said the installer with a grin.

"If it does," Qwilleran said, "I'll be after you with a shotgun."

"The other tapestry will be easy," Fran assured Shawn. "We'll hang it on the blank wall of the fireplace cube, facing the foyer, and it's a little smaller."

"Why'n't ya put the heavy one down here?" he asked.

Again the wrappings were removed, and the tapestry was unrolled on the floor—a galaxy of birds and green foliage.

"Yow!" came a comment from the fireplace cube, and Koko jumped to the floor. Birds native to Moose County were flitting among weeds, grazing on the ground, sipping nectar from flowers, warbling from tree branches, and swaying on tall grasses. He walked purposefully across the tapestry and sniffed the red bird with black face patch and red crest.

"Amazing!" Qwilleran said.

The bird extravaganza was hung and admired, and then Fran glanced at her watch. "I can't hang around," she said. "This is my mother's birthday, and Dad and I are taking her out to dinner. When are you leaving for Lockmaster, Qwill?"

"After the funeral."

"Have a good time at the races. Don't lose all your money."

Qwilleran was glad to avoid socializing. He wanted to stay home and plan his trip and learn how to pack his new luggage. It was the last word in nylon with leather bindings and straps and more pockets and compartments than he needed. It replaced his two old suitcases lost in a disaster Down Below. Imitation leather, scuffed and battered, they had traveled with him from city to city during his lean years. Polly said they were a disgrace. He said they were easy to pack. "Just throw everything in."

After dinner, when he opened his new luggage on the bed to consider its complexities, Koko moved into the two-suiter and Yum Yum took possession of the carry-on. He left them sleeping there and settled down with the Thursday edition of the *Lockmaster Logger*.

The race course, he learned, was a little over two miles—in a natural setting surrounded by gentle hills from which viewing was convenient. For first-time race goers there were instructions for reading the race chart: the name of the horse and the weight he was carrying; the names of owner, trainer, and rider; the color of the racing silks; the horse's color, sex, and age; the names of sire and dam. Such details were more than Qwilleran cared to know.

There was only one entry that aroused his interest: Robin Stucker would be riding in a race that permitted amateurs. He asked himself: Wasn't Stucker the name of the woman who played Queen Katharine? Didn't her note to VanBrook mention that she had to buy boots for Robbie? The horse, according to the chart, was owned by W. Chase Amberton. The trainer was S. W. O'Hare. The name of the horse—and this was what caused Qwilleran to smooth his moustache in speculation— was Son of Cardinal.

CHAPTER 8

The funeral on Friday morning was a doubly somber affair attended by a few members of the Theatre Club— doubly somber because many of the mourners thought they were saying farewell to a murderer as well as a suicide. No one mentioned it, but glances were exchanged as the pastor of Larry Lanspeak's church spoke his ambiguous platitudes. Only the Lanspeaks and Fran Brodie believed stubbornly that the rumor was false. Only Qwilleran, Hixie Rice, and Chief Brodie knew the truth. Brodie was there—not in uniform but in kilt and tam-o'-shanter—playing a dirge on the bagpipe at Qwilleran's suggestion.

"It will allay suspicions without formally denying them," he told the chief.

Hixie drew Qwilleran aside and said in a low but emotional voice, "It's frustrating, isn't it? Why don't the police come up with a suspect? Why don't *you* do something about it, Qwill?"

He said, "It happened only a week ago, Hixie. The police

have information not available to me. What's more, they have computers."

"But you solved the Fitch murders when the police were stymied. And you identified the killer at the museum before anyone knew there was a murder!"

Qwilleran massaged his moustache thoughtfully: He was reluctant to reveal that it was Koko's inquisitive sniffing and catly instincts that had turned up the clues. Only his closest friends and a few journalists Down Below knew about the cat's aptitudes, and it was better to leave it that way. "I'll think about it," he told Hixie.

He thought about it as he packed his binoculars and dinner jacket for the weekend at the races. Getting away from Pickax, he hoped, would restore his perspective. For the cats he packed some canned delicacies and vitamin drops, their favorite plate and water dish, the turkey roaster that served as their commode, and a supply of kitty gravel. This was to be their first experience as house guests. Qwilleran was nervous about the prospect, but Koko hopped into the travel coop eagerly—a good omen—and scolded Yum Yum until she followed suit.

When they pulled away from the barn, the route took them south past the potato farms and sheep ranches—and the usual dead skunk on the highway, which caused a flurry of complaints from the backseat. As they neared the county line, Qwilleran began to notice the name Cuttlebrink on rural mailboxes and then suddenly a roadside sign:

WELCOME TO WILDCAT
POP. 95

A few hundred feet beyond, another sign suggested that the Cuttlebrinks had a sense of humor:

YOU JUST PASSED WILDCAT

Qwilleran eased on the brakes and made a U turn slowly and carefully. Any sudden stop or start, or any turn in excess of twelve degrees, upset Yum Yum's gastrointestinal apparatus and caused a shrill protest—or worse. Returning to the crossroads that constituted downtown Wildcat, he counted a total of four structures: a dilapidated bar, an abandoned gas station, the remains of an old barn, and a weathered wood building with a faded sign:

CUTTLEBRINK'S HDWE. & GENL. MDSE.
ESTAB. 1862

The windows, he guessed, had last been cleaned for the centenary of the store in 1962. The frame building itself had last been painted at the turn of the century. As for the items faintly visible through the dirty glass (dusty horse harness, fan belts, rusty cans of roof cement), they had evidently been dropped there at some point in history, and no one had ever happened to buy them.

The interior was dimly lighted by low-watt lightbulbs hanging from the stamped metal ceiling, and the floorboards—rough and gray with age—were worn down into shallow concavities in front of the cash register and the tobacco case. In the shadows a man could be seen sitting on a barrel—a man with a bush of yellowish-white whiskers and strands of matching hair protruding beneath his feed cap.

"Nice day," he said in a high-pitched, reedy voice.

"Indeed it is," said Qwilleran. "We're having beautiful weather for September, although the weatherman says we can expect rain in a couple of days." He had learned that discussion of the weather was one of the social niceties in Moose County.

"Won't rain," the old man declared.

While speaking, Qwilleran had been perusing the merchandise on shelves, counters, and floor: kerosene lanterns, farm buckets, fish scalers, flashlights, rolls of wire fencing, light bulbs, milk filters, corncob pipes . . . but no clay pipes.

"He'p ya?" asked the old man without moving.

"Just looking around, thank you."

"No law 'gainst that!"

"You have a remarkable assortment of merchandise."

"Yep."

There were nails by the pound, chains by the foot, rat traps, wooden matches, wire coat hangers, some things called hog rings, button hooks, work gloves, and alarm clocks. "I've seen some interesting stores, but this tops them all," said Qwilleran sociably. "How long has it been here?"

"Longer'n me!"

"Are you a Cuttlebrink?"

"All of us be Cuttlebrinks."

Qwilleran continued his search, trying to appear like a casual browser. He found rubber boots, steel springs, plungers, tarpaulins, more fan belts, fifty-pound salt blocks, gnaw bones for rabbits, dill pickles, ammunition . . . but still no bubble pipes. Examining a cellulose sponge—which, according to the label, would clean, sanitize, and remove manure—he asked, "Is this a good sponge?"

"You got a cow?" Cuttlebrink asked. "That be an udder sponge."

"It would be good for washing the car," Qwilleran said, although he intended it for cleaning and sanitizing the cats' turkey roaster.

The old man shrugged and wagged his head at the eccentricity of cityfolk. "You from Pickax?"

"I've lived there for a while."

"Thought so."

Paint thinner. Goat feed. Fuses. Axle grease. Razor blades. Red bandannas. Pitch forks. Swine dust. Another kind of work glove.

"You seem to have just about everything," Qwilleran remarked.

"Yep. What folks want. No fancy stuff."

"Do you happen to have any clay bubble pipes? I'd like to get some for my young ones."

The storekeeper hoisted himself off the barrel and hobbled to the rear of the store, where he climbed a shaky ladder, one unsure step at a time. On the top shelf he found a cardboard box in the last stages of decay and brought it down, one unsure step at a time.

"You amaze me," Qwilleran said with admiration. "How do you manage to find things?"

"They ain't lost."

The box held half a dozen clay pipes that had once been white but were now gray with dust.

"Good! I believe I'll take them all."

"Won't be none left to sell," Cuttlebrink objected.

"How about five?"

"Sell ya four."

Qwilleran paid for the four pipes, the sponge, and a dill pickle, and the sale was rung up on an old brass cash register on which was taped a crayoned sign: BROWNING GUNS WANTED. The storekeeper hobbled back to his barrel, and the three travelers went on their way.

At the county line the terrain changed from rocky pastureland to rolling green hills. This was Lockmaster's famous hunting country, where miles of fences dipped and curved across the landscape, and here and there an opulent farmhouse with barns and stables crowned a hill. Then came the restaurant known as the Palomino Paddock, with luxury cars in the parking lot, after which the highway became Main Street.

In the nineteenth century wealthy shipbuilders and lumber barons chose to build their residences fronting on the chief thoroughfare, to be admired and envied by all. With affluent families striving to outdo each other, houses as large as resort hotels were lavished with turrets, balconies, verandahs, bowed windows, bracketed roofs, decorative gables, and stained glass.

Zoning had changed with the times, however. Now they were upscale rooming houses, gourmet bed-and-breakfast establishments, law offices, insurance agencies. One imposing structure was a funeral home, another a museum, another the Bushlands' photographic studio. Having inherited it from Vicki's side of the family, they combined business with living quarters. It was a massive three-story frame building with a circular tower bulging from the southwest corner.

Qwilleran drove under the porte cochere that sheltered the side door, saying to his passengers, "We're here! I expect you to be on your best behavior for the next forty-eight hours. If you cooperate, you may wind up on the cover of a slick magazine." There was no reply. Were they asleep? He turned to see two pairs of blue eyes staring at him with inscrutable intensity as if they knew something that he did not know.

Leaving the Siamese and their gear in the car, Qwilleran lugged his own traveling bag to the carriage door and rang the bell. He was greeted by Vicki in a chef's apron.

"Excuse me for arriving early," he said. "I thought I might explore the town."

"Good idea!" exclaimed his hostess. "Come on in. Bushy's in his darkroom and can't be disturbed, and I'm wrestling with pie crust, but your room's ready and you can go straight up. We're giving you our really grand guestroom in the southwest corner. You can put the cats in the connecting room; I know they're used to having their own pad."

"Truthfully I'd prefer to have them with me," he said. "In a new environment I like to keep a fatherly eye on them."

"Whatever makes you comfortable, Qwill. Make yourself at home."

He walked slowly and wonderingly across the broad foyer and up the wide staircase, observing the carved woodwork, gaslight fixtures converted for electricity, velvety walls hung with ancestral portraits in oval frames, and the jewel-like stained glass in the windows. The choice guestroom was in he front of the house, a large, square space ballooning into a circular bay—actually the base of the tower. Furnished with canopy bed, writing desk, chaise, wingback chairs, dresser, highboy, blanket chest, and scattering of ruby-red Oriental rugs, it was homey enough for a week's stay. Nothing matched, but family heirlooms gave it a hospitable togetherness. In the circular bay, rimmed with window seats, there was a round table holding a bowl of polished apples, a dish of jelly beans, and magazines devoted to photography and equestrian arts. There was also a four-page newsletter titled *Stablechat*—a collection of steeplechase news and horsey gossip listing S. W. O'Hare as publisher and Lisa Amberton as editor.

Qwilleran sampled a red jelly bean, the only color he considered worth eating, and went downstairs for the cats' accoutrements. When at last he brought the carrier into the room, its occupants emerged cautiously and slithered under the bed, where they remained.

"For your future reference," he said, addressing the bed, "your cushion's on the chaise; your water dish and commode are in the bathroom; and I'm going for a walk."

He went down to the kitchen in search of Vicki, who was cutting Z-shaped vents in the crusts of two apple pies. "May I ask you the significance of the Z?" he asked. "Or is it a horizontal N?"

"I don't know," she said. "My mother always did it that way, so I do it that way. How's everything upstairs?"

"Everything's fine. The room looks very comfortable. You have quite a collection of antiques."

"It's all been handed down in the family, with each generation adding its own touch, for better or worse. My great-great-grandfather Inglehart built the house. Grandmother Inglehart lives on the third floor. We call her Grummy. Are you going to drive around town?"

"I prefer to walk. Which way shall I go?"

"Well, you might go down the hill to the courthouse and turn right on Fourth Street. That's where all the stores are. It ends at the river. Originally both banks of the river were crammed with sawmills and shipyards. Now there's Inglehart Park on one side and condos on the other."

"Do you have a bookstore?"

"Two doors beyond the city hall. It's a cast-iron storefront where Bushy's grandfather used to have his watch-the-birdie photo studio before World War I."

Qwilleran enjoyed walking and sightseeing, and as he strode down the hill he was amazed at the huge houses, masterpieces of architectural gingerbread, their details accentuated with two or even three colors of paint. They looked festive compared to the stolid stone mansions of Pickax! He found the store with the cast-iron front and bought a book on horsemanship. In the basement there were used books, but *City of Brotherly Crime* was not among them. At an antique shop he found a collection of printshop mementos and bought a small engraving of a whale.

Many of the stores capitalized on the horseyness of Lockmaster. Equus was a men's store. The Tacky Tack Shop displayed gaudy sweatshirts, T-shirts, and posters with a steeplechase theme. In the Foxtrottery everything from paper napkins to fireplace andirons had a horse or fox motif, but nothing appealed to Qwilleran. And then he spotted the public library!

It was obviously built from the same set of Greek temple blueprints that produced the Pickax library—with the same classical columns, the same seven steps, the same pair of ornamental lampposts. He entered, expecting a Shakespeare quotation on a chalkboard in the vestibule, but there was only a bulletin board announcing new video releases. He asked for the chief librarian whom he knew only as Polly's friend, Shirley.

"Mrs. Corcoran is in her office on the mezzanine," said the clerk.

The stairway was the same design as in Pickax; the glass-enclosed office occupied the same location; and the woman sitting behind the desk could have been Polly's sister. She had the graying hair, pleasant face, conservative suit, and size sixteen figure.

He introduced himself. "Mrs. Corcoran, I'm Bootsie's godfather."

"Oh, you must be Jim Qwilleran," she cried. "Polly has talked about you so much. Do sit down. How is Bootsie?"

Qwilleran pulled up a chair, characteristically of varnished oak and hard-seated.

"He's a handsome cat with an insatiable appetite. In another few years, I estimate, he'll be the size of a small pony."

"His mother and siblings are the same way, and yet they never put on weight. I wish I knew their secret. Are you down for the 'chase?"

"Yes, it's my first venture. I'm staying with the Bushlands."

"That should be pleasant. Bushy was the official photographer at my son's wedding. You should have come down with Polly. Everyone had a wonderful time. I've just received the album of wedding pictures. Would you like to see them?"

"Yes, I would," he said with convincing sincerity, although wedding pictures were second only to weddings on his list of things to avoid.

Mrs. Corcoran opened the album to a portrait of the happy couple at the altar, after the vows. "These are the kids, Donald and Heidi. Doesn't he look handsome? He's just out of law school and he has a position with Summers, Bent & Frickle. Heidi is a lovely girl, a dietician. Her father is a stockbroker and her mother is a psychiatrist. They go to our church.... And here they are with both sets of proud parents... And here are the attendants. The maid of honor caught the bouquet..."

Qwilleran murmured appropriate remarks as he politely viewed the candid shots of wedding guests. "Here's someone I know," he said, pointing to a man with ashen hair. "He's a reporter at the *Moose County Something*."

"Yes. Dave Landrum. One of Donald's golfing friends," she said.

And then Qwilleran caught a glimpse of Polly. She was wearing an electric blue dress he had never seen before, and she was dancing with a man who wore a red beard. She was looking entirely too happy. She had probably been imbibing champagne instead of her usual thimbleful of sherry. As the pages of the album turned, he watched with more interest. There she was again! This time she was sitting at a table with the same bearded man and having an animated conversation. He was wearing a green plaid sports coat that seemed inappropriate at a wedding reception.

"Who is the fellow with the beard?" Qwilleran asked casually, adding untruthfully, "He looks familiar."

"Oh, he's one of Donald's horsey friends," the librarian said. "I can't remember them all. Perhaps you noticed the beautiful horse farms on your way down here."

"Did the wedding festivities continue at the Palomino Paddock Sunday noon?" Qwilleran asked innocently.

"Heavens, no! We were all exhausted. The kids left on their honeymoon at nine o'clock, and the rest of us carried on like blithering fools until the bar closed. I'm glad I have no more offspring to marry off!"

Qwilleran said, "As a quiet change of pace perhaps you and Mr. Corcoran would drive up to Pickax and have dinner with Polly and me—some weekend when the autumn color is at its height."

"We'd be delighted! Polly has told us about your apple barn, and I'd love to see how my little Bootsie has grown. Do you think he'll remember me?"

Qwilleran walked back up the hill without noticing the architectural splendors of Main Street. He was thinking about the man with the red beard and plaid coat. Had he also taken Polly to Sunday brunch at the Paddock? Was he the mysterious Monday morning caller who phoned her office and gave her a guilty thrill? It was not that Qwilleran felt any jealousy; he was merely curious. Polly had conservative tastes, and here was the type she would keep at arm's length: bearded, flashily dressed, and . . . *horsey!*

Arriving at the Bushland house he met the photographer coming out of his darkroom.

"What d'you think of our town?" Bushy asked.

"Looks like a thriving community."

"It's extra busy today—everybody getting ready for the 'chase."

"How much time do I have to clean up? I stopped at Cuttlebrink's on the way down, and I feel as if the dust of ages has settled on my person."

"I know what you mean. No hurry. People aren't coming till six, and you don't have to dress up. We've asked Kip and Moira MacDiarmid—he's editor of the *Logger*—and Vicki invited Fiona Stucker, the one who went up to Pickax to act in your play."

Qwilleran's moustache bristled with interest. "She did an excellent job," he said, "and I'll look forward to telling her so."

As he walked up the wide staircase to the second floor, he wondered what surprises the Siamese had devised for him. He was sure of one thing: They would have found their blue cushion on the chaise and would be taking their ease like visiting royalty.

That proved to be not quite true. They had come out of hiding, and their attitude was regal and aloof, but they were lounging in the middle of the canopy bed. It was remarkable how they always took possession of the best chair, the softest cushion, the warmest lap, and the exact center of a bed. Lori Bamba had told him that a person or object has an aura or field of energy, some more and some less. A cat, detecting the difference, moves in to take advantage of the vibrations. Lori had an explanation for everything.

As Qwilleran walked to the closet, stripping off his sweater, he stepped on something small and hard. Not completely hard. In fact, slightly squashy. He hesitated to look down, fearing what might be under his foot—a reaction based on past experience. Much to his relief it proved to be a jelly bean—a red one. There were fang marks in it. He should have known better than to leave the candy dish uncovered. Koko liked to sink his fangs in anything gummy or chewy. Checking the candy dish Qwilleran found that all the red jelly beans had been eliminated, and he found them scattered about the floor, camouflaged by the red Orientals. Something was at work in Koko's mind, although his intention was not clear. The Siamese watched from the bed as the man crawled about the room on his hands and knees. They watched the performance as if it were a freak show.

"You're the freaks in this family!" he scolded them. "I should have left you at home."

After hiding the candy in the top drawer of the highboy, he showered and dressed and spent some time with his new book on horsemanship. Always thirsty for knowledge on any subject, he learned for the first time in his life the location of a horse's withers. He discovered that a horse has no collarbone, and a "stud" is an establishment where horses are bred. He looked at pictures of the Arabian, the Morgan, the Andalusian, the Pinto, and his favorite, the Clydesdale. Finally, at six o'clock he opened a can of crabmeat for the Siamese and walked downstairs to the foyer that was ablaze with jewel-toned sunlight pouring through stained-glass windows.

The front parlor with its marble fireplace and sumptuous Victorian furnishings was stiffly formal. Bushy used it as a studio for posing brides and family groups in quaint settings. Now the photographer was in the back parlor preparing to mix drinks, and Vicki was in the adjoining dining room, putting finishing touches on the table.

"I'd like to ask one question," Qwilleran asked. "Why did the founding fathers build such large houses?"

"For one thing," Bushy said, "lumber was plentiful and labor was cheap."

"And they had lots of kids," Vicki added. "Usually there was at least one unmarried sister or widowed aunt or destitute cousin living with them. Also, when guests came for a visit, they stayed at least a month, because it took a week to get here by stagecoach and sailing ship. There were plenty of servants in those days."

"How are the cats doing?" Bushy asked.

"They've commandeered the bed, and I may have to spend the night on the window seat."

Vicki said, "Grummy is looking forward so much to meeting you, Qwill. She's a sweet old lady, just turned eighty-eight. When my parents retired to Arizona for Dad's health, Grummy deeded this house to Bushy and me, with no strings attached."

"How do you take care of such a big place?"

"I have part-time help. Once upon a time they had a housekeeper, cook, two maids, houseman, gardener, and a driver to take care of the horses and drive the family to church in the carriage."

"They didn't have any riding mowers or leaf-vacuums in those days," Bushy put in.

"And no microwaves or food processors," Vicki added. "Would you like to bring the cats down now, Qwill?"

"I think they should make their formal debut tomorrow morning," he said, "when there are no strangers around. You remember their behavior the last time we were here. I don't want to be embarrassed again."

"Whatever you think best. By the way, Grummy won't join us for cocktails. She'll come down for dinner at seven and won't stay long. She tires easily. We installed an elevator for her—velvet walls and a needlepoint bench—tiny, but she loves it."

Bushy interrupted. "Vicki, did I tell you that Fiona called?"

"No. What's happened *this time?*" she said with exasperation.

"She and Steve will be a little late. He got tied up at the track."

"Well, I'm serving exactly at seven, regardless. We can't keep Grummy waiting. It seems to me that Steve is always getting tied up. He's probably sleeping one off."

"Give him a break!" her husband said. "All kinds of emergencies come up before a race."

At that point the doorbell rang, and the editor and his wife arrived. They were introduced as Kip and Moira MacDiarmid.

"Spelled M-a-c-capital D-i-a-r-m-i-d," said Moira.

"I know how to spell a good Scottish name like that. My mother was a Mackintosh. The question is: Do you know how to spell Qwilleran?"

"With a *QW!*" they said in unison.

"We always read you in the *Something*," the editor explained. "Don't tell your publisher I said so, but your column's the best thing in the whole paper! I wish you were writing for us."

"Make me an offer," Qwilleran said genially.

"I'm sure we couldn't afford you."

"Aren't you the collector of old typefaces? I picked up a few items at the Goodwinter sale this spring."

"So did I. Do you go in for book type or jobbing faces?"

"Mostly I'm interested in small mounted cuts of animals that will fit into a typecase, but I have a modest assortment of fat-face caps, like Ultra Bodoni. What's your specialty?"

"Book faces. I just acquired some 1923 Erasmus, the most beautiful typeface ever designed. I'd like to show you my collection some day."

"Be happy to see it."

Moira said to Qwilleran, "Bushy tells us you've converted a barn."

"Yes, an octagonal apple barn, more than a hundred years old. The orchard is defunct, but the barn is in good shape."

"We ran a couple of pieces on the Orchard Incident," said Kip. "What's happening to the investigation? We have a morbid interest in the victim, you know. All the time VanBrook was principal here he was a thorn in everyone's side."

"That's a delicate way of putting it," said Moira with a smirk.

Kip explained, "My wife was president of the PTA during his reign of terror. Actually, though, he did great things for the school system. He was some kind of genius, but an odd duck."

Qwilleran agreed. "I'd like to write a biography of that guy, if I could unearth some of his secrets. The Mystery Man of Moose County, I'd call it."

"If you do, come down here and we'll tell you some tales that will make your blood boil."

At that moment the doorbell rang, and the couple who entered gave Qwilleran a mild shock. First to walk into the foyer was Fiona Stucker, who had played the role of Queen Katharine with such regal poise and forceful emotion. She was small; she was mousy; she extended a limp hand and smiled shyly. She had large eyes, but they were filled with anxiety. He remembered her eyes; with stage makeup they had been her most compelling feature.

Behind her was a man introduced as Steve O'Hare. Qwilleran took one look at him and thought, It's Redbeard! And he's still wearing the green plaid coat! So this was the "horsey friend" who had attached himself to Polly at the wedding festivities!

"Glad to meetcha," said the man with a hearty handgrip.

It was too hearty, Qwilleran thought. He disliked him on sight. Nevertheless he said politely, "I hear you're involved in the 'chase tomorrow. What's your responsibility?"

"I'm just a stable bum," Redbeard replied with a grin.

"On the contrary," Bushy said, "Steve's a very good trainer."

Fiona piped up in her small voice, "He trained the horse Robbie's riding tomorrow. Robbie's my son."

"I understand he's riding Son of Cardinal," Qwilleran said,

glad that he'd done his homework. "Does he have a chance to win?"

"Absolutely!" said the trainer, and he turned away to sneeze.

Someone said, "If you sneeze on it, it's true."

Turning to Fiona Qwilleran said, "Let me compliment you, Ms. Stucker, on your dynamic performance in *Henry VIII*."

"Ummm . . . thank you," she said, somewhat flustered. "I guess you saw the play."

"I saw it twice, and I was greatly impressed by your voice quality and the depth of your emotion, especially in your scene with Cardinal Wolsey . . . Did you see the play, Steve?"

"Naw, I'm not much for that kind of entertainment."

"Did your son see it?" Qwilleran asked Fiona.

"Ummm . . . No, he was working. He . . . uh . . . works with Steve. At the stables, you know. Amberton Farm."

"We have twenty horses," the trainer said. "We're up at five in the morning—feeding, watering, grooming, mucking, and exercising the nags. And that's seven days a week! Plus training sessions. No end to it! But I wouldn't want to do anything else." He sneezed again, and Fiona handed him a tissue.

Bushy announced, "Last call for a quickie from the bar. We're calling Grummy in a few minutes."

"Shall I go up and get her?" Moira volunteered.

"Better not. She likes to feel independent, and she likes to make a grand entrance."

"She descends in her electronic chariot like a goddess from Olympus," said the editor.

"That's right!" said Vicki as she moved toward the intercom. "Some old folks resent new technology, but not Grummy! . . . Fiona, would you help me a bit in the kitchen?" She spoke to the box on the wall. "Grummy, dear, dinner is served."

The party swallowed their drinks quickly and sauntered to the far end of the foyer where the elevator was located. A light on the touch plate indicated that the car was in operation. It descended slowly. The door opened sedately. Qwilleran found himself holding his breath in anticipation.

Chapter 9

Qwilleran stood in the foyer of the grand old Inglehart house and waited—along with the other guests—for the elevator door to open. Never having known his own grandparents, he felt drawn to anyone over seventy-five years of age, and in this northern region, where many lived to be a hundred, he had met many memorable oldsters.

The elevator door opened sedately, and a distinguished-looking, white-haired woman in a floor-length hostess gown of wine red velvet stepped from the car, leaning on two ivory-headed canes yellow with age. She moved slowly, but her posture was erect. Seeing the waiting audience, she inclined her head graciously toward each one until she caught sight of Qwilleran in the background.

"And this is Mr. Qwilleran!" she exclaimed in a cultivated voice that had become tremulous with the years. She had a handsome face for a woman nearing ninety, like fine-lined porcelain, with kind, blue eyes and thin lips accustomed to smiling. No eyeglasses, Qwilleran noted. He guessed that Grummy would have the latest in contact lenses.

As he stepped forward she tucked one cane under the other arm in order to extend a hand. "My pleasure, Mrs. Inglehart," he murmured, bowing gallantly over her trembling hand. It was a courtly gesture he reserved for women of a certain age.

"I'm thrilled to meet you at last," she said. "I used to read your column when you were writing for newspapers Down Below. But now you are living among us! How fortunate we are! I not only admire your writing talent, Mr. Qwilleran, and what you have to say, but . . ." she added with a coy smile, "I adore your moustache!"

Fleetingly he wondered if the Inglehart library might contain a copy of *City of Brotherly Crime*.

"Shall we go into dinner, Grummy?" asked Bushy, offering his arm. The others followed them into the dining room and waited until the elderly woman was seated on her granddaughter's left. Qwilleran was motioned to sit opposite, next to Moira, and the party waited for Grummy to raise her soup spoon.

Glancing brightly around the table she said, "For what we are about to receive, we give thanks."

Redbeard, sitting at the other end of the table, next to the host, sneezed loudly.

Fiona said apologetically, "He's allergic."

"To everything," said the man who was blowing his nose. "Including horses."

"Is that true?" Kip asked.

"Absolutely."

"You should give up horses and go in for newspapering. You're doing a good job with *Stablechat*."

"Nothing to it," said Steve. "I've got a bunch of kids digging up the stuff, and Mrs. Amberton puts it together."

"What's your circulation now?"

"Almost a thousand."

"Another ten thousand," said the editor of the *Logger*, "and we'll start to worry."

Grummy leaned toward Qwilleran. "Victoria tells me you've brought your cats. I do hope they don't kill birds."

"Have no fear," he replied. "They're indoor cats, and their interest in birds is purely academic. Koko has a friend who's a cardinal, and they stare at each other through the window glass and communicate telepathically."

Steve said, "Take the glass away and it'd be a different story. Cats are cats."

Vicki said quickly, "Grummy has a feeding station outside her window in the tower, and she records the migration of different species in a notebook ... Don't forget your soup, Grummy dear." With her spoon poised above the soup plate Mrs. Inglehart was gazing at Qwilleran like a starstruck young girl.

Moira said, "One year I decided to feed the birds, but all I attracted were starlings. They came from three counties to my backyard—millions of noisy, messy invaders. That was the end of birding for me!"

"My problem," Qwilleran said, "is blackbirds. When I bike on country roads, they rise up out of the ditch in a great cloud and dive-bomb me and my bike, screaming *chuck chuck chuck*."

"That's in nesting season," said Grummy. "They're protecting their young."

"Whatever their motive, they're very unfriendly, and when I talk back to them, they're really burned up."

"What do you say to an unfriendly blackbird?" Moira asked.

"*Chuck chuck chuck.* But the biggest mystery is the behavior of seagulls when a farmer plows a field. Within five minutes after he starts, a hundred seagulls flock in from the lake, thirty miles away, and circle the field like vultures."

Kip said, "Seagulls have an intelligence network that puts the CIA to shame."

Vicki removed the soup plates, and Fiona helped serve the main course: pasta shells (easy for Grummy to fork with her trembling hand) with a sauce of finely chopped vegetables in meat juices, plus meatballs for the guests.

As the Parmesan cheese was being passed, Grummy returned to her favorite subject. "When I came to live in this house as a bride, I instructed the gardener to plant everything that would attract birds, and I've kept a birdbook for seventy years. Teddy Roosevelt had a birdbook, and he recorded the birds he saw on the White House lawn."

Occasionally there would be a sneeze from Redbeard; Bushy would ask if anyone wanted more wine; Fiona would cast surreptitious stares in Qwilleran's direction; Kip would mention the forthcoming millage vote. But always Grummy would bring the conversation back to birds.

The editor said, "One of the fillers that we ran recently stated that a hummingbird has a pulse rate of 615 beats a minute. I hope it wasn't a typo."

"Not at all," said the old lady. "The hummingbird is one of nature's small miracles."

Qwilleran confessed, "I can't tell one bird from another. They don't stand still long enough for me to look in the field guide."

"When I had my bird garden," Grummy said, "I could entice wild birds to eat out of my hand, and once I raised a family of baby robins after their mother was killed by a boy with a gun."

Steve sneezed again.

"Grummy dear," said Vicki quietly and gently, "don't forget to eat your pasta."

Mrs. Inglehart was having a wonderful time, but when the salad was served she seemed tired and asked to be excused. Bushy escorted her to the elevator.

After the apple pie and coffee, Steve said he had to get back to the farm and be up at five in the morning, and Fiona said she had to go home and make sure Robbie went to bed early on the eve of his first race. As she left she said to Qwilleran in her small voice, "I . . . uh . . . wanted to talk to you . . . about Mr. Van-Brook, you know, but I didn't . . . uh . . . get a chance."

"Did you know him well?"

She nodded. "Maybe . . . tomorrow? Vicki invited me to the 'chase."

"We'll have a talk then," Qwilleran promised. "It's been a pleasure meeting you."

She left, giving him a backward glance. He was watching her go. Despite her self-effacing manner, there was something fascinating about the woman—her large and sorrowful eyes, perfect eyes for Queen Katharine.

Then the MacDiarmids said good night because they had hired a baby-sitter who wanted to be home by ten o'clock. "See you at the 'chase," they said, explaining to Qwilleran, "Our parking slot is next to Bushy's, so we do a little friendly betting."

The host and hostess kicked off their shoes and poured another drink. Qwilleran accepted his third cup of coffee. "Pleasant evening," he said. "Grummy is a treasure, and I liked Kip and Moira. Fiona came as a surprise; she was so different on stage. This fellow Steve . . . what's their relationship?"

The Bushlands exchanged glances, and Vicki spoke first. "Well, he's Robin's mentor in horsemanship, and Fiona's very ambitious for her son to succeed at *something*. He dropped out of high school, and his only interest is horses."

"He's not alone, I understand. What's our schedule tomorrow morning?"

"After breakfast," Vicki said, "you'll have time to take the cats up to visit Grummy. She'll be thrilled."

Her husband said, "We'll leave about eleven and pick up Fiona, and that will give us time to fight the traffic and get in place for a tailgate picnic before post time, which is two o'clock."

"Kip mentioned betting. How does that work?"

"It's more fun if you have a few bucks on a horse, so we usually have a five-dollar pool going with the MacDiarmid crowd."

"Breakfast at eight-thirty," Vicki said. "What do you like?"

"Coffee and whatever. And now I think I'll amble upstairs and see if the cats have adjusted."

"Would they like a meatball? We have some left over."

Qwilleran followed her into the kitchen. "How long have you known Fiona?" he asked.

"Ever since junior high. My family used to include her in our picnics and vacation trips because she had no decent homelife of her own. It was the old story: absent father, alcoholic mother. I liked her. She was so eager and appreciative, and she had those heart-breaking eyes!"

"That's what I remember most about her portrayal of Katharine. What kind of life has she had since schooldays?"

"Rough," Vicki said. "Her only dream was to have a home and family of her own, so she married right after high school. It was so ironic! Her husband deserted her right after Robin was born."

"How has she managed financially?"

"She does housekeeping. She helps me two days a week. With some kind of training she could do better, but she lacks confidence. If everything works out, I'd like to start a catering service with Fiona as assistant. We'd specialize in hunt breakfasts. They're all the rage in Lockmaster."

"What was her connection with VanBrook?"

Vicki shrugged mysteriously. "Better ask Fiona about that."

Qwilleran said good night to the Bushlands and started for the second floor. Halfway up the stairs he could hear exultant cries coming from the best guestroom. The Siamese knew he was approaching and bearing meatballs. They met him at the door, Koko prancing and Yum Yum snaking between his ankles. Putting the plate on the bathroom floor, he then gave the bedroom a quick inspection for evidence of mischief. Everything was in order except for shredded paper in the circular window bay, but it was only the copy of *Stablechat*; they frequently reacted to fresh ink.

After their treat, the two satisfied animals found their blue cushion on the chaise, where they washed up and settled down. Qwilleran read for a while before sinking into his own bed and reviewing his day. He had buried Dennis Hough, bought bubble pipes for the cats, discovered Polly's strange Lockmaster connection, and met a charming octagenarian. And tomorrow he might learn something about VanBrook from a woman who wanted to talk about him. He turned off the bedlamp, and in a few moments two warm bodies came stealing into the bed, nosing under the blanket, Yum Yum on his left and Koko on his right, snuggling closer and closer until he felt confined in a strait jacket.

"This is ridiculous!" he said aloud. Jumping out of bed he transferred their blue cushion to the bathroom floor, placed them on it with a firm hand, and closed the door. Immediately the yowling and shrieking began, until he feared they would disturb Grummy on the third floor and the Bushlands in the master bedroom below.

He opened the bathroom door, hopped back into bed and

waited anxiously in the dark. For a while nothing happened. Then the first body landed lightly on the bed, followed by a second. He turned his back, and they snuggled down behind him. There they stayed for the night, peacefully sleeping, gradually pressing closer as he inched away. By morning he was clinging to the edge of the mattress, and the Siamese were sprawled crosswise over the whole bed.

"How did you guys sleep?" Bushy asked the next morning when the aroma of bacon lured the three of them to the kitchen.

"Fine," Qwilleran said. "Good bed! They didn't let me have much of it, but what I had was comfortable."

"How do you like your eggs?" Vicki asked.

"Over easy." He looked around the kitchen. "Do I smell coffee?"

"Help yourself, Qwill."

Nursing a cup of it he trailed after the Siamese as they explored the house, reveling in patches of tinted sunlight thrown on the carpet by the stained-glass windows. He himself checked the library, but there was no sign of *City of Brotherly Crime*.

By the time breakfast was ready, the two cats were chasing each other gleefully up and down the broad staircase. "They're making themselves right at home," he said to the photographer. "You shouldn't have any trouble getting pictures tomorrow."

"I have a couple of poses in mind," Bushy said, "but mostly I'll let them find their own way. When I took Grummy's tray upstairs this morning, she said to remind you she's expecting them after breakfast."

When the time came for the visit, Vicki called upstairs on the intercom, and Qwilleran collected the Siamese, climbing the stairs to the third floor with one under each arm. Grummy greeted them graciously, wearing a long flowered housecoat and leaning on her two elegant canes.

"Welcome to my eyrie," she said in a shaky voice. "And these are the two aristocrats I've heard about!"

They regarded her with blank stares and wriggled to escape Qwilleran's clutches. They were acting disappointingly catlike.

"I've made some blueberry leaf tea," she said to him, "and if you'll carry the tray we'll sit in the tower alcove."

The suite of rooms was furnished with heirlooms in profusion, and on every surface there were framed photographs, including one of Theodore Roosevelt, signed. Glass cabinets displayed a valuable collection of porcelain birds, causing Koko to sit up on his haunches and paw the air. One of them was a cardinal. Even Qwilleran knew a cardinal when he saw one.

As Mrs. Inglehart, veteran of thousands of formal teas, poured with graceful gestures, she said, "So this is your first steeplechase, Mr. Qwilleran! Do you know the origin of the name?"

"I'm afraid not."

She spoke in the precise, carefully worded style of one who has presided at thousands of club meetings. "In early days, horses and their riders raced through the countryside, taking fences and hedges and brooks, racing to the church steeple in the next village. In Lockmaster the sport of riding was unknown until my father-in-law introduced it. Until then there were only workhorses, pulling wagons, and tired old nags used for transportation. Then riding became fashionable. We all took lessons in equitation. I loved the hunt and the music of the hounds. I had my own hunter, of course. His name was Timothy."

"You have good posture, Mrs. Inglehart. I imagine you looked splendid in the saddle."

Yum Yum was now in Grummy's lap, being stroked. "Yes, everyone said I had a good seat and excellent balance and control. To control twelve hundred pounds of animal with one's hands, legs, voice, and body weight is a thrilling challenge . . . But I am doing all the talking. Forgive me."

"It's a pleasure to listen to someone so well-spoken. What provoked your interest in birds?"

"Well, now . . . let me think . . . After I married Mr. Inglehart, I avoided the needlework clubs and boring book clubs that young matrons were expected to join, and I started the Ladies' Tuesday Afternoon Bird Club. Oh, how the townfolk ridiculed us—for studying birds instead of shooting them! They wrote letters to the newspaper, referring to our idle minds and idle hands."

"Do you mean it was customary to shoot songbirds?"

"Yes, indeed! A young lad would come home with a string of tiny birds over his shoulder and sell them to the butcher. They were in demand for dinner parties! I'm sorry to say we still have a few sharpshooters who think of a bird as a target. Of course, it all started when the government put a bounty on birds because they were thought to destroy crops. Then scientists discovered that birds protect fields from rodents, insect pests, and even destructive weeds ... Now, I'm afraid, the farmers rely on those spraying machines and all kinds of chemicals."

Koko could be heard chattering at the birds in the feeding station outside the east window as he stood on his hind legs with forepaws on the sill. Yum Yum was purring and kneading Grummy's lap with her paws.

"I believe she likes me," said the old lady.

"What kind of birds come to your feeder?" Qwilleran asked.

"Innumerable species! My favorites are the chickadees. They're so sociable and entertaining, and they stay all winter. Koko will have his friend all winter, too. Cardinals are non-migratory, and don't they look beautiful against the snow?"

"One wonders how birds survive in this climate."

"They wear their winter underwear—a nice coat of fat under their feathers," she explained. "Oh, I could talk forever about my bird friends, but you'll be leaving soon for the 'chase."

"I'm in no hurry," he said. "You must have a wealth of memories, Mrs. Inglehart, in addition to riding and bird watching."

"May I tell you a secret?" she asked with a conspiratorial smile. "You have honest eyes, and I know you won't tell on me. Promise you won't tell Victoria?"

"I promise," he said with the sincerity that had won confidences throughout his career in journalism.

"Well!" she began with great relish. "When everyone leaves the house, I go downstairs in my elevator—I call it my magic time capsule—and I walk from room to room, reliving my life! I sit at the head of the dining table where I used to pour tea for the Bird Club, and I imagine it laid with Madeira linen and flowers in a cut-glass bowl and silver trays of dainties—and all the ladies wearing hats! ... Does that sound as if I've lost my senses?"

"Not at all. It sounds charming."

"Then I go into the front parlor and sit at the rosewood piano and play a few chords, and I can almost hear my husband's beautiful tenor voice singing, 'When you come to the end of a perfect day.' I can almost see the sheet music with pink roses on the cover. How happy we were! . . . I go into other rooms, too, and give the housekeeper her orders for the day and take a basket of cut flowers from the gardener . . . Sometimes—but not always—I walk into the reception hall and remember reading the telegram about my son in Korea." She turned to gaze out the window. "After that, nothing was quite the same."

"Where are you?" called a voice from the head of the stairs. "Oh, there you are!" Vicki walked toward the alcove with a covered tray.

"Not a word to Victoria," Grummy cautioned Qwilleran in a whisper.

"Grummy dear, it's time for us to leave for the 'chase, and I'm putting your lunch in the refrigerator. Just warm up the soup, and there's a muffin and a nice little cup custard."

"Thank you, Victoria," said the old lady. "Have a lovely time. I'll be with you in memory."

Vicki gave her grandmother a hug. "We'll see you after the fifth race."

"Thank you for your hospitality, Mrs. Inglehart," said Qwilleran, bowing over her trembling hand and returning her confidential wink.

"Please leave the little ones with me," she said. "I'll enjoy their company."

Vicki said to Qwilleran as they walked downstairs, "She refuses to have a sitter when we go out, but she has a hot line to the hospital. In case of emergency, she only has to press the red button."

Bushy had removed the photographic gear from the van, and they packed it with food baskets and coolers, folding chairs, and snack tables. Vicki, wearing a flamboyant creation from the Tacky Tack Shop, said, "How do you like my sweatshirt? Fiona gave it to me for my birthday."

When they picked up Fiona at her apartment over a drug store, she too was wearing a shirt stenciled in the rah-rah spirit of the steeplechase—quite unlike her drab attire of the night before. En route, she sat quietly, biting her thumbnail.

"I suppose you've attended many of these events," Qwilleran remarked.

"Ummm . . . yes . . . but I'm kind of nervous. It's Robbie's first race."

The stream of traffic heading for the race course included cars and vans packed to the roof with passengers, the younger ones boisterous with anticipation. South of town the route lay through hunting country, finally turning into a gravel road where race officials in Hunt Club blazers checked tickets and sold souvenir programs of the seventy-fifth annual Lockmaster Steeplechase Race Meeting. After one more hill and a small bridge and a clump of woods, the steeplechase course burst into view—a vast, grassy bowl, a natural stadium, its slopes overlooking the race course, which was defined by portable fencing.

Bushy backed into the parking slot designated G-12, with the tail of the van down-slope. Chairs and snack tables were set up on the downside, and he went about mixing drinks. "Bloody Mary okay for everybody?" he asked.

"You know how I want mine," Qwilleran said.

"Right. Extra hot, two stalks of celery, and no vodka."

Already the hillsides were dotted with hundreds of vehicles and swarming with thousands of fans. Race officials in pink riding coats, mounted on thoroughbreds, patrolled the grassy course, controlling the crowd that crossed over to the refreshment tents in the infield. Near G-12, there was a judges' tower overlooking the finish line. Across the field a stand of evergreens concealed the backstretch. Three ambulances and a veterinary wagon were lined up in conspicuous readiness.

An amplified voice from the judges' tower announced the Trial of Hounds, and soon the baying and trumpeting of the pack could be heard as they came down the slope from the backstretch.

Bushy said, "That sound is music if you're a fox hunter."

Or blood curdling, Qwilleran thought, if you're a fox.

Then the MacDiarmid camper pulled into G-11. The door opened, and a stream of young people poured out. Qwilleran counted three, six, eight, eleven—emerging with exuberance and rushing off to the refreshment tents. Kip and Moira and four other adults stepped out of the camper in their wake.

Qwilleran asked the editor, "How many of these kids are yours?"

"Only four, thank God. Did we miss the hounds? We got lost. They sent us to the wrong gate." He introduced his guests, all connected with the newspaper, and the women busied themselves with the food. Joining with the Bushlands they set up a tailgate spread of ham, potato salad, baked beans, coleslaw, olives, dill pickles, pumpkin tarts, and chocolate cake.

Again the voice from the tower reverberated around the hillsides, announcing the parade of carriages, and a dozen turn-outs came around the bend: plain and fancy carriages drawn by high-steppers, the drivers and passengers in period costumes.

There was still a half hour before post time. The high school band was blasting away, with drums and trumpets almost drowned out by the hubbub of the race crowd, all of whom were wildly excited. They were circulating, greeting friends, showing off their festive garb, sharing food and drink, shouting, laughing, screaming. Qwilleran observed them in amazement; they were getting a high-voltage charge from the occasion that totally escaped him.

"Would you like to stroll around?" he asked Fiona, who had been quiet and introspective.

She responded eagerly, and as they circled the rim of the bowl she ventured to say, "It's quite a sight!" Long folding tables were laid with fringed cloths, floral centerpieces, champagne buckets, and whole turkeys on silver platters.

"I'm sorry I didn't meet you during the run of the play," he said, "but you always disappeared right after the curtain."

"I had a long drive home," she explained, "and then . . . ummm . . . I have to keep an eye on Robbie."

"Altogether, with rehearsals and performances, you had to do a lot of driving. I hope VanBrook appreciated that."

"Oh, yes," she said. "He sent me money out of his own pocket to pay for my gas."

Qwilleran huffed silently into his moustache. "Very thoughtful of him. How did you two meet? In the theatre?"

"Oh, no! I was . . . uh . . . working in a restaurant . . . and this man used to come in to eat all the time. He was . . . well, not very good-looking, and the other waitresses made fun of him. I liked him, though. He was, you know, *different.* Then one day he asked me—right out of nowhere—if I'd like a job. He needed a live-in housekeeper. Robbie was eight then, and we both went to live with him. It was, well, like a gift from heaven!" As Fiona talked, the wonder of it overcame her shyness.

"Was he hard to get along with?" Qwilleran asked. "People in Pickax found him rather crotchety."

"Well, he was strange in some ways, but I got used to it. He kept saying I should *educate* myself, and he gave me books to read. They weren't . . . uh . . . very interesting."

"How did you get involved in *Henry VIII?*"

"Well, he was going to do the play—here in Lockmaster, you know—and he said he wanted me to be in it. I almost fell over! I'd never been in a play. He said he'd coach me. I was good at memorizing, and I just did everything the way he told me to."

"Would you like to be in another play?"

"Ummm . . . it would be nice, but I couldn't do it without him."

"How did he and Robin get along?" Qwilleran asked.

"He treated Robbie like a son—always getting after him to study and get better grades. After he moved to Pickax, he came down to see us once a month. He was always offering to put Robbie through college if he'd study *Japanese!* He said the future belongs to people who know Japanese." Fiona uttered a whimsical little laugh. "Robbie thought he was crazy. So did I."

The high school band stopped playing, and Qwilleran's watch told him it was almost post time. "We'll talk some more at the party tonight," he promised. They hurried back to G-12 and arrived just as Kip MacDiarmid was passing a hat.

"Five dollars, please, if you want to get in the pool," he said.

Qwilleran drew Number Five, a four-year-old chestnut gelding named Quantum Leap, according to the program. Following an announcement from the tower, the band played the national anthem. There was a fanfare of trumpets, and a mounted colorguard came around the bend in the course, followed by Hunt Club officials on horseback. The field for the first race was in the paddock, with the riders in their colorful silks. Number Five wore blue and white. Then the officials led the racers to the starting line, and before Qwilleran could focus his binoculars, they were off and taking the first hurdle.

They disappeared around the bend and behind the trees. In a moment, they came around again. The crowd was cheering. Qwilleran couldn't even find Quantum Leap. Horses and riders disappeared again and reappeared at the far end of the course, and in a few moments it was all over. Number Five had finished sixth, and one of Kip's guests won the fifty-dollar kitty. Qwilleran felt cheated—not because of losing but because it had all happened so fast.

Vicki said, "You're supposed to cheer your horse on, Qwill. No wonder he came in sixth!"

By nature Qwilleran was not demonstrative, and the fleeting glimpses of his horse in the next three races failed to arouse him to any vocal enthusiasm. He could wax more excited about a ballgame, and even in the ballpark he seldom shouted.

Fiona won the pool in the second race, and everyone was pleased. In the third race, Qwilleran's horse went down on the fourth hurdle, according to an announcement from the tower, and immediately the veterinary wagon and one of the ambulances started for the backstretch.

One of the MacDiarmid youngsters soon came racing back to the camper. "Hey, Dad, they had to shoot the horse!" he shouted.

"How about the rider?"

"I dunno. They took him in the ambulance. Can you let me have five bucks against my allowance?"

"You'll have to clear it with your mother."

There were only five entries in the last race, in which amateur riders were acceptable, and Kip as official bookmaker suggested going partners on the bets.

Fiona said, "I can't bet. I'm rooting for Robbie."

"So am I," said Qwilleran.

"We will, too," said the Bushlands.

The pool was called off, and the Bushland and MacDiarmid crowd swarmed down the hill to the infield fence, the better to cheer for Son of Cardinal. As the horses were led from the paddock, Robin Stucker looked pathetically young and thin in his red and gold silks.

"Oh, God! Oh, God! Let him win!" Fiona was saying softly.

They were off! And for the first time Qwilleran felt moved to cheer. They took the first hurdle and thundered up the slope, disappearing behind the distant trees. Before they came into view again, there was a shout of alarm from the spectators on the backstretch.

"Oh, no!" Fiona whimpered. "Oh, no! Somebody's down!"

The emergency vehicles rushed to the scene, and a crackling announcement came from the tower: "Number Four down on the third hurdle!"

Qwilleran's group groaned with relief. Robin was Number Three.

As the four horses finished the first lap, Robin's rooters were in full voice, cheering him over the next hurdle and up the slope to the hidden backstretch. When the field came into view again, Son of Cardinal was running a close second.

Other fans were yelling, "Go, Spunky!" or, "Go, Midnight!" But the crew from G-12 and G-11 was howling, "Go, Robbie! . . . Ride 'im, Rob! . . . Keep it up! You're gaining!" Son of Cardinal took the hurdle smoothly and pelted up the slope. "Attaboy, Rob! Three to go!" There were moments of suspense as the horses covered the backstretch. "Here they come! He's ahead! . . . Go, Robbie! . . . He's in! He's in! . . . A winner!"

Fiona burst into tears. Vicki hugged her, and the others clustered around with congratulations.

"Let's have a drink to celebrate!" Bushy announced. "And it'll give the traffic time to thin out."

"If you don't mind," Fiona said, "I'll just walk over to the stables to see Robbie. Steve can drive me back to town."

"Okay," Vicki said, "but be all dressed and ready to go at seven-thirty. We'll pick you up."

The MacDiarmids collected their horde of youngsters and said goodbye. "When are you coming down again, Qwill?" asked Kip. "I'd like to show you my type collection."

On the way home in the van Qwilleran asked, "Does Robin's win have any importance other than the $5,000 purse?"

"It should increase the value of the horse and give Robin a boost up the ladder," Bushy said. "Also it should sweeten the deal for the Ambertons when they sell the farm."

"Are they selling? Why are they selling?"

"The way I hear it, Amberton wants to move to a warmer climate. He's pushing sixty and has arthritis pretty bad. His wife doesn't want to sell. She's the one who edits the *Stablechat* newsletter."

"Lisa is quite a bit younger than her husband," Vicki put in, "and she's interested in Steve O'Hare as well as the newsletter."

"That's unfounded gossip, Vicki," her husband reproved her.

"Steve is a womanizer," she explained to Qwilleran. "I hate that word, but that's what he is."

When they reached the turreted mansion on Main Street, Qwilleran could hear Koko howling.

Bushy said, "I hear the welcoming committee."

Qwilleran pounded his moustache with a fist. "That's not Koko's usual cry! Something's wrong!"

The three of them jumped out of the van, Bushy and Qwilleran dashing up the steps and into the foyer, with Vicki close behind. Koko was in the foyer, howling in that frenzied tone that ended in a falsetto shriek. Yum Yum was not in sight.

Bushy started up the stairs three at a time. Vicki ran to the intercom. "Grummy!" she shouted. "Are you all right? We're coming up!" Then she, too, bolted up the stairs.

Koko bounded to the elevator at the rear of the foyer, and Qwilleran followed. Touching the signal panel, he could hear a mechanical door closing. Then the car started to descend, activating a red light on the panel. Koko was quiet now, watching the elevator door.

The Bushlands had reached the third floor, and their voices echoed down the open stairwell. "She's not here!" Vicki screamed in panic.

Slowly the car descended, and slowly the door opened on the main floor. There they were—both of them: Grummy slumped on the needlepoint bench, and Yum Yum crouched at her feet, looking worried.

CHAPTER 10

Vicki was hysterical. Bushy was yelling into two phones at once. Qwilleran quietly picked up both cats and carried them upstairs. From the window he could see the paramedics arriving, then the doctor's car, and finally the black wagon from the funeral home. When all was quiet, he went downstairs.

"Is there anything I can do?" he asked.

Vicki was walking back and forth and moaning. "Poor Grummy! The excitement was too much for her."

"She lived a long life, enjoying it to the very end," Qwilleran said, "and she went quickly. That's a blessing."

"Why was she on the elevator? Upstairs she could have pressed the emergency button. They might have saved her. She had no need to come downstairs."

Qwilleran knew the answer, but he kept her secret. He suspected she had already been downstairs, reliving her life, and was on her way up again. The memory of the telegram from the war department may have triggered the attack.

Bushy said, "You'll have to go to the club without us, Qwill. You can take the tickets and pick up Fiona."

"No . . . no!" Qwilleran protested. "Not under the circumstances. I'd better pack up and drive back to Pickax. You'll be busy for the next few days."

"The funeral will probably be Tuesday."

Vicki said to her husband, "Would you call Fiona and break the news? I can't talk to anyone about it—yet. Ask her if she wants to use the tickets."

Qwilleran went upstairs and packed the dinner jacket he had never worn and the blue cushion the cats had not used. Then he said a somber farewell to his stunned and saddened hosts. "We'll talk about this another time," he said, "after the shock has worn off. She was a grand and glorious Grummy."

Bushy said forlornly, "Bring the cats again some weekend, Qwill. We'll give it another try."

Qwilleran drove away—up the avenue of giant gingerbread houses—thinking about the last twenty-four hours. The Siamese, knowing they were on the way home, snoozed peacefully in their carrier, leaving him free to think about many things. He had explored a new city, experienced his first steeplechase, met a fellow journalist, witnessed the swan song of a gallant old lady, and discovered the bearded man who had evidently captivated Polly. He stroked his moustache in wonderment as he drove. She had always disliked beards and avoided anyone from the sporting world. It also puzzled him how she had managed to buy that bright blue dress without his knowledge; she usually consulted him on the rare occasions when she went shopping for something to wear.

Yet, the most amazing discovery of the weekend was the diffident little woman who had been transformed into the regal Katharine on stage. VanBrook had endowed her with a completely new persona for the duration of the play. She moved like a queen; she projected her voice; she actually looked taller. Offstage she reverted to nervous mannerisms, anxious glances, and shy conversation, but for a few hours she had been VanBrook's creation. His failure to fashion Robin in his own image must have been a vexing disappointment.

There were other questions Qwilleran wanted to ask Fiona:

Did VanBrook ever talk about his past Down Below or in Asia? Was his Lockmaster house furnished in the Japanese style? Did he cultivate an indoor garden, and if so, what did he grow? Why did he wear turtlenecks all the time? Was he hiding something? A scar perhaps. Did he ever unpack all his books? After four years in Pickax the majority were still in cartons. And there were other questions of a more personal nature that might be asked.

When Qwilleran reached the Moose County line, his watch said seven o'clock. The Living Barn Tour would be over. He hoped the interior would not look like a bus terminal on Sunday morning. Undoubtedly his answering machine would be jammed with messages, which he would ignore until Monday; there was no reason to explain his premature return to the world at large. His only call would be to Polly. He would tell her about the death in the family, and then he would say, "I stopped in the library and met your friend Shirley. She inquired about Bootsie and showed me the wedding pictures. There were a couple of candids of you in a blue dress that I've never seen." And then he would say, "I met some interesting individuals down there. One was a horse trainer—an amiable fellow with a red beard. His name was Steve something or other." After a moment's pause her reaction would be a nonchalant, "Oh, really?"

This entertaining scenario occupied his attention until he arrived at Trevelyan Trail. Mr. O'Dell had installed a new mailbox. The driveway was graded and graveled. In the orchard the debris left from the storm had been removed. Inside the barn there was no indication that half of Pickax had tramped through the place, but the Siamese knew that five hundred strangers had been there. With inquisitive noses they inspected every inch of the main floor.

Meanwhile, Qwilleran phoned Polly and received no answer. She might be having dinner with her widowed sister-in-law. He called back at nine o'clock and again at eleven. No answer. Most unusual! Polly never stayed out late when she was driving alone. Weary after his eventful visit to Lockmaster, he retired early but was slow in falling asleep. Polly's absence worried him.

On Sunday morning he called her number again. It was the hour when she would be feeding Bootsie and preparing poached eggs for her own breakfast. The phone rang twelve times before he hung up. This was disturbing. He began to fear she had arranged a date with Redbeard. The trainer could have left Lockmaster after the fifth race and reached Pickax in an hour. Qwilleran put on a jacket and went for a brisk walk on the pretext of picking up the Sunday papers. Detouring down Goodwinter Boulevard, he noted that Polly's car was not parked in its accustomed place; she might have driven to meet the man at some out-of-the-way rendezvous.

Polly and Qwilleran had been close friends for two years, sharing confidences, giving each other priority, consulting on every question that arose. And now she had bought a dress of strikingly different style and color without mentioning it. There was a possibility that her good friend Shirley had arranged to pair her with Redbeard at the wedding reception. There was no knowing what those two women talked about when they were together! It seemed significant that Shirley, when asked about the fellow photographed with Polly, *had forgotten his name!*

Systematically, Qwilleran reviewed the evidence: Polly canceled a dinner date at Tipsy's the day after the wedding, claiming to be tired. She was secretive about the mysterious phone call that came to her office. She had been to the hairdresser twice in less than a week—after a lifetime of washing and setting her own hair. Everything pointed to a rift in their intimate relationship. True, the last two years had seen ups and downs, tiffs and misunderstandings, but only because Polly was inclined to be jealous of the women he met in the course of everyday life.

Feeling frustrated and perhaps a trifle lonely, Qwilleran called Susan Exbridge to inquire about the barn tour.

"Darling, it was magnificent!" she cried. "Everyone loved everything!"

"I called to compliment you on leaving the place in perfect condition, but can you explain why I smelled apple pie when I walked in?"

"Did you like it? We simmered apples and cinnamon on the range all day. The Mayfus Orchard donated seven bushels of apples, and every guest was invited to take one. How was your weekend?"

"Pretty good. Were there any momentous local happenings while I was away?"

"Only an editorial in the *Something*, offering a huge reward for information on the VanBrook murder. I hope something develops to exonerate Dennis soon. You know, Qwill, I spent a lot of time and pulled a lot of strings in order to introduce that boy to Moose County's finest families—hoping to get him some jobs—and it will reflect on me if he turns out to be a murderer."

His next call was to Arch Riker at the publisher's apartment in Indian Village. "I hear you ran the editorial and offered the reward, Arch. Get any response?"

"Two, only. The city desk got a call from a crackpot who's always calling the paper. They know her voice. They call her Dear Heart. First she accused Lyle Compton. Her second choice was Larry Lanspeak. Take your pick . . . Then there was a tip that involved a member of our own staff."

"Who?" Qwilleran's mind raced through the roster of employees.

"Dave Landrum."

"Dave! He was in Lockmaster at a wedding Saturday night, I happen to know. That's why Roger took the night shift. How did they try to connect Dave with the case?"

"Well, this is a roundabout explanation. Are you ready? A year ago there was a fatal accident at the humpback bridge. Remember?"

The humpback bridge over Black Creek was notorious as an accident site. By speeding across it, young drivers could get a roller-coaster thrill, and if they traveled fast enough they were airborne for a second or two.

Qwilleran said, "As I recall, two kids were killed at the bridge, but it turned out to be a double suicide. Right?"

"That's the one—a lovers' pact. It happened September tenth—exactly one year before VanBrook got his. The person who called us seemed to think that was noteworthy."

"Do you know who called?"

"He declined to identify himself, but we gave him a code name so he can collect his fifty grand if the tip checks out."

"How was Dave supposed to be involved?"

"He's the father of one of the kids."

"I don't get it," Qwilleran said.

"Neither did I, until we checked our files. Dave's daughter was valedictorian of the June class at Pickax High, and her boyfriend was a football player. We ran a 'Died Suddenly' obit when it happened, and then the usual letters came in from irate readers demanding that the humpback bridge should be flattened out. Nothing was ever done about the bridge, of course, but Roger, who gets around to the coffeeshops a lot, came up with the scuttlebutt. The young couple had hoped to attend a state college where they could live in a coed dorm. Unfortunately, the boy's grades were borderline, and VanBrook refused to graduate him."

"Nothing wrong with that, is there?"

"Except that it was considered an act of vengeance on the principal's part. His regime had been opposed by Concerned Parents of Pickax for a couple of years, and the football player's father was the most outspoken of the whole pack. After the suicides, he went to VanBrook's office and staged a violent scene in front of witnesses. He may have made threats."

"What's his name? Do I know him?"

"Possibly. He has a soft-drink distributorship—Marv Spencer."

"Are we supposed to assume that the two fathers collaborated on revenge—on the anniversary of the suicides?"

"That was the general idea. We turned the information over to the police."

"They'll listen, but they won't buy it," Qwilleran said, although he later recalled that Dave Landrum had been rehearsing for the Duke of Suffolk in *Henry VIII* until insulting treatment from the director caused him to walk off the set in anger.

Riker asked, "How was the steeplechase?"

"I'm writing a column on it for Tuesday. You'll have it at noon tomorrow. Frankly, it would be a better show with more horses and fewer people."

At six o'clock Qwilleran tried once more to reach Polly—and again at eight o'clock. Worried, he phoned her sister-in-law and expressed his fears.

"She went away for the weekend," said the woman. "She didn't say where, Mr. Q, but the invitation came up suddenly, and she asked me to feed Bootsie. She'll be home later this evening."

"Thank you," he said. "Now I can stop worrying." Truthfully, the news only exacerbated his unease.

He wrote his Tuesday column, presenting Lockmaster and the steeplechase from a Moose County point of view: factual, descriptive, politely complimentary, and not overly enthusiastic. He hand-delivered it to the city desk Monday morning and then headed for the public library.

Passing the Toodle Market (Toodle was an old family name in Moose County) he stopped in to buy powdered soap for bubble blowing—a brand recommended by Lori Bamba. He also purchased some deli turkey breast for the Siamese. That was when he noticed a sign behind the butcher counter: YES, WE HAVE RABBITS.

"How do you sell the rabbits?" he asked the butcher.

"Frozen," said the man, with the expressionless face of one who has spent too much time at ten degrees Fahrenheit.

"I'll take one," Qwilleran said, thinking he could keep it in his freezer while scouting for someone to cook it for the Siamese.

The butcher disappeared into the walk-in cold vault and returned clutching something that was almost the size and shape of a baseball bat, but red and raw.

"Is that a rabbit?" Qwilleran asked with a queazy gulp.

"That's what you asked for."

"Will it stay frozen till I get it home?"

"If you don't live south of the equator." For emphasis he raised the rabbit and slammed it down on the butcher block, neither of which suffered from the blow.

"Wrap it well, please," said Qwilleran. "I'm walking."

The package he received resembled a concealed shotgun, and he shouldered it for the walk to the library, covering the four blocks more briskly than usual. In the foyer the Shakespeare quotation on the chalkboard was *Silence is the perfect herald of joy*. He huffed into his moustache. What was that supposed to mean? Dodging the friendly clerks he headed for the stairs to the mezzanine.

There she was, in her glass-enclosed office, like a sea captain in the pilot house, wearing her usual gray suit but with a blouse that was brighter and silkier than usual.

"Good-looking shirt," he said, dropping into a chair with a loud thump; he had forgotten the hard oak seats.

"Thank you," she said. He waited for her to say where she had bought it—and why—but she merely smiled pleasantly. And cryptically, he thought. Had it been a gift from Redbeard? he wondered.

"I tried to reach you this weekend," he said. "You should train Bootsie to answer the phone."

"Perhaps I should invest in an answering machine," she said.

Polly had always resisted the idea, and he found her sudden change of attitude suspect. "Did you have a good weekend?" he asked.

"Very enjoyable. Irma Hasselrich invited me to her family's cottage near Purple Point. We went birding in the wetlands and saw hundreds of Canada geese getting ready to migrate."

Qwilleran drew a deep breath of relief. "I didn't know Irma was a birder."

"One of the best! Her lifelist puts mine to shame. Last year she sighted a Kirtland's warbler while she was traveling in Michigan. How did you enjoy the steeplechase?"

"I ate too much and lost twenty bucks, and somehow the sight of ten thousand people screaming and jumping up and down like puppets fails to stir my blood, but I explored Lockmaster, and when I found the library I went in and met your friend."

"How did you like Shirley?"

"She's as friendly as an old shoe. In fact, I suggested that she and her husband come up here and have dinner with us some weekend. She showed me the wedding pictures, including a couple of shots of you. You seemed to be having an unusually good time. I hardly recognized you in that bright blue dress."

"Do you like it? Now that my hair is turning gray, I think I should start wearing brighter colors. Did you have brunch at the Palomino Paddock?"

"No, but the Bushlands gave a dinner party, and I met the editor of the *Lockmaster Logger*—also a fellow who trains horses and publishes a newsletter called *Stablechat.*" Qwilleran was observing her reactions closely. "He said he'd met you at the wedding. Perhaps you remember a stocky man with a reddish beard and receding hair."

"I don't recall," said Polly, although he thought her cheeks became suddenly hollow. "There were so many guests—about three hundred at the reception. Would you like some tea?"

"No, thanks."

"Coffee?"

"No, thanks. In the snapshots you were dancing with this fellow. His name is Steve, as I recall."

"I think perhaps I do remember him," she admitted uncertainly.

"I also met the woman who played Katharine in *Henry VIII*. We should invite her and Steve up here some weekend. We could have drinks at the barn and then dinner at the Mill."

Polly turned pale, and he relented. He had taunted her long enough; it pained him to see her squirm. Charitably, he asked if she might be free for dinner.

"I have a dinner meeting with the library board," she said with obvious regret. "Tomorrow night . . . perhaps?"

"There's a funeral in Lockmaster tomorrow, so I'd better not count on dinner. The editor down there has a type collection he wants me to see."

"How about Wednesday?"

"That's the judging of the Tipsy contest. But we'll get together soon." He stood up. "I've got to get this thing home before it starts leaking."

"What is it?"

"A frozen rabbit from Toodle's. For the Siamese."

"Really? Are they eating wild game now?"

"Well, they like venison and pheasant, and when they started knocking the rabbit out of my typecase, I assumed they were trying to tell me something."

"Perhaps they want you to read *Watership Down*," she said, and it was not clear whether she was teasing or being helpful.

After two years of intimacy, during which Qwilleran had confided in Polly about Koko's uncanny modes of communication, he was still unsure whether she really believed. He sometimes suspected she humored him—going along with the gag, so to speak. Nevertheless, he took her suggestion and checked out *Watership Down* from the library's fiction room. He had read it before, and it merited being read aloud.

At the apple barn he was greeted vociferously by his housemates, who showed no interest in the package from the butcher but plenty of interest in the library book. Either they knew it was all about rabbits, or they knew it had been previously borrowed by subscribers who lived with pets. He tossed the frozen rabbit into the freezer and invited the Siamese to join him for a read in the library area. Here were deep-cushioned lounge chairs in pale taupe leather, arranged around one wall of the fireplace cube. White lacquered shelves were loaded with old books. Over the white lacquered desk hung the printer's typecase, its eighty-nine compartments half-filled with old typeblocks.

"Is everyone comfortable?" Qwilleran asked as he opened the book. His feet were on the ottoman, Yum Yum was on his lap, and Koko made a comfortable bundle at his elbow. No sooner had he read the first sentence, which consisted of only four words, than the telephone rang. Grumbling mildly, he disturbed his listeners and went to the desk to take the call.

"Hello . . . Is this . . . uh, Mr. Qwilleran?" asked a wavering voice.

"Yes."

"This is Fiona in Lockmaster—Fiona Stucker."

"Of course. I recognized your voice," he said. "I'm sorry about Saturday night, but we were all upset about Mrs. Inglehart, and it was hardly an occasion for celebration."

"Ummm . . . yes, it's too bad. She was a nice old lady."

"Are you going to the funeral tomorrow?"

"I don't think so. I have to work."

There was an awkward pause during which Qwilleran heard voices in the background. He said, "How does Robin feel about being a winner?"

"He's all excited. He's only seventeen, you know."

There was another pause, and Qwilleran filled in with the usual pleasantry. "How's the weather down there? It's a beautiful day in Pickax."

"It's nice here, too."

Employing his professional escape clause he said, "I'm sorry our conversation will have to be brief, but I have a newspaper deadline."

"Oh. I'm sorry," she said. "Steve wanted me to call you about something."

"In connection with what?"

"Ummm . . . would you like to . . . buy a horse farm?"

"A horse farm!"

"There's one for sale. He says it's a good bet."

"I'm afraid that's not my kind of venture, Fiona."

"It's the Amberton farm. Steve is stablemaster, you know, and Robbie works there."

"I know, but—"

"He gave me a list of things to tell you. Want me to read them?"

"Go ahead."

Koko was on the desk, standing on his hind legs and reaching for the typecase. Qwilleran pushed him away, at the same time listening attentively as Fiona read:

"Sixty-eight acres, one-third wooded. All pastures fenced. Eight horses, including Son of Cardinal. Stables for twenty. Twelve horses now being boarded. Restored seventy-year-old farmhouse with all improvements, worth four hundred thousand. Swimming pool. Guest house. Historic barn on property."

Somewhat awed by this recital, Qwilleran failed to notice Koko's stealthy return to the desk until a typeblock was spirited out of its niche, landing on the telephone book and bouncing to the floor. Mention of the historic barn prompted him to ask, "Is the farm a going business or just a hobby for the owners?"

"Steve says it makes money. They breed horses and train them, and board horses for people, and give riding lessons."

Wild fantasies were racing through Qwilleran's head. "Is it on the market yet? Is it listed with a broker?"

"Not yet. Mr. Amberton wants to try selling it first. Steve says he has a couple of leads."

"I'd like to speak with Amberton."

"He's in Arizona. Steve drove him to the airport yesterday, but he has all the information—Steve, I mean—if you want to talk to him."

"Is he there? Let me speak with him."

"He's . . . no, he's at the farm, but—uh—he'd be glad to come up and see you. Wednesday is his day off."

"Okay. Wednesday afternoon," Qwilleran said. "Tell him to come equipped with facts and figures."

"Ummm . . . could I come with him and bring Robbie? I'd like you to meet Robbie."

"All right. Make it about one-thirty."

Qwilleran hung up the phone slowly and thoughtfully, telling himself, This is insane! And yet . . . he had lived in Pickax for four years, and he was becoming restless. As a journalist Down Below he had lived the life of a gypsy, switching newspapers, moving from city to city, seeking challenges, accepting new assignments. His present circumstances required him to live in Moose County for five years or forfeit the Klingenschoen inheritance. He had one more year to go . . .

"What do you think about this, Koko?" he asked the cat, who was sitting nearby with his ears cocked and his tail flat out on the floor.

"Yow!" said Koko.

Absentmindedly, automatically, Qwilleran picked up the scattered typeblocks. There were now three on the floor. One was the rabbit. One was a skunk. The other was a horse's head.

Chapter 11

Driving south to Lockmaster for Grummy's funeral on Tuesday morning, Qwilleran crossed the county line into horse country with its hilly pastureland, picturesque fences, and well-kept stables. Horses were being exercised. Riders were practicing jumps. A large recreation vehicle was pulling away from a posh farmhouse, drawing a horse trailer. One could adapt to that kind of life, he thought: horse shows, equitation events, steeplechasing, show jumping, carriage driving.

The funeral services were held in an impressive brick church overlooking Inglehart Park on the riverbank, after which Qwilleran drove to the cemetery with the MacDiarmids.

"Grummy was the last Inglehart around here," said Kip. "The others are scattered all over the country. We seem to have a big population turnover—old families moving out, new ones moving in. The equestrian environment attracts them."

"Do you consider Lockmaster a good place to live?" Qwilleran asked.

"Are you thinking of moving down here?" the editor countered. "If so, we've got a place for you at the paper. We'll put your column on page one."

The cemetery was an old one located on a wooded hill, and Grummy was laid to rest in a large family plot dominated by an Inglehart monument befitting a founder of the town. At the instant of interment her Bird Club associates released flights of doves, and the mourners raised their heads and watched them disappear into the sky.

"I'm sorry I knew her such a short time," Qwilleran said. "She might have converted me to birding. No one else has succeeded."

On the way back to town, Kip pointed out big-name horse farms, the Riding and Hunt Club, kennels of the Lockmaster Hounds, the Foxhunters' Club, and other points of interest related to the local passion. Moira sat quietly alongside him in a pensive mood.

From the backseat Qwilleran asked, "Is a horse farm a good investment?"

"I doubt it. The average one around here is a status symbol or a private obsession, to my way of thinking," Kip said. "Do you like horses? Do you ride?"

"The horse is an animal I admire greatly. They're beautiful beasts, but I've never had any particular desire to sit on one. I might enjoy living among them, though, if I didn't have to do any of the work."

"The Ambertons are selling their farm, and they have good stock and the best of everything in facilities."

"Horse breeding is a high-risk venture, you know," Moira put in quietly.

"What do you know about their stablemaster?"

"Steve? He hasn't been here long," Kip replied, "but people say he's an excellent trainer. You saw how Son of Cardinal came through on Saturday. From what I hear, he knows the business inside out."

"Where did he come from?"

"Various places—New York State, Kentucky, Tennessee, I believe."

"Why is he working in Lockmaster?" Qwilleran asked.

The driver changed his grip on the wheel and looked out the side window before answering. "I suppose he liked the environment . . . and the opportunity to move around. The Ambertons travel around the country, eventing."

Moira spoke up sharply. "Why don't you tell the truth, Kip?"

She turned to face Qwilleran. "He got into trouble Down Below, doping racehorses."

Her husband said, "I'm sure he's clean now."

The car was slowing, and she was unbuckling her seatbelt. "Maybe so," she said, "but most owners are afraid of him." She hopped out in front of the insurance agency where she worked. "Next time we see you, Qwill," she said with a wave of the hand, "let's hope it's a happier occasion."

They drove on, and Kip said, "Why don't you stick around and have dinner with us tonight?"

Suddenly Qwilleran wanted to return to Pickax. "Thanks, but I'm due home at five o'clock."

"Okay. Next time. By the way, that's a very generous reward Pickax is offering in the VanBrook case. We picked it up and ran a short piece in yesterday's paper."

"I hope it gets results," Qwilleran said absently. He was pondering Moira's statements.

"Where do you want to be dropped off?"

"My car's parked at the church . . . Moira seems to have reservations about Steve, doesn't she?"

"Well, he's not a bad guy . . . but we were all at a party at the Hunt Club on New Year's Eve—a boozy affair, you know—and Steve got out of line, rather crudely. Moira took umbrage, to put it mildly. She's still miffed. It wasn't anything serious. He was drunk. He likes his liquor, and he likes women."

Qwilleran picked up his car and stopped at a phone booth to call Polly at the Pickax library. "Correction," he said. "I can be home in time for dinner. If you're free, we could go to the Mill." She accepted, and he found himself driving back to Pickax faster than usual.

At the barn Koko greeted him with the excited chasing that meant a message on the answering machine. He checked it out and immediately put in a call to Susan Exbridge, suspecting an auspicious development in the Dennis Hough situation that had been bothering her.

"Darling! I have exciting news!" she exclaimed. "Hilary's attorney in Lockmaster called me about liquidating the estate, and he came up here today to discuss it. He's Torry Bent of Summers, Bent & Frickle, and he's the personal representative for the estate."

"Did you go through Hilary's house?"

"Yes, he had a key, which he turned over to me after he decided I had credentials and an honest face. It's a strange place, and I do mean *strange!* The upstairs rooms are filled to the ceiling with boxes of books, and one room is full of dead plants!"

"What will you do with all those books?"

"God knows! Secondhand books are an absolute *glut* on the market, but we'll open all the boxes—what a job!—and hope to find something rare and valuable. Edd Smith will be able to advise us on that."

"I'll be glad to help you open boxes," Qwilleran said with alacrity. "I'm very good at sorting books, and after tomorrow night I have nothing scheduled."

"Qwill, you're a darling! How about Thursday morning? I'll take you to lunch. I took Torry to lunch at the Mill, and he was *quite* impressed!"

"By the restaurant or the liquidator?"

"Both, if I'm tuned in to the right channel, and I might add that he's a charmer! Also, he's *divorced*—tra la!"

On this salubrious note the conversation ended, and Qwilleran marked Thursday for Susan in his datebook—something he would avoid mentioning to the chief librarian.

When he called for Polly at her carriage house, she was wearing a vibrant pink blouse with her gray suit—her *other* gray suit, reserved for social occasions.

"That color is becoming to you," he said. "What do you call it?"

"Fuchsia. You don't think it's too intense?"

"Not at all."

It was a short drive to the Old Stone Mill on the outskirts of town, and they filled the time with comments on the weather: the highs and lows, humidity and visibility, yesterday and today. At the restaurant they were shown to Qwilleran's favorite table, and he ordered the usual dry sherry for Polly and the usual

Squunk water for himself. When the drinks arrived, they both raised their glasses and said "Cheers!"

There was a lull before Polly ventured, "Whose funeral did you attend?"

"Vicki Bushland's grandmother. A splendid woman, eighty-eight years old and an enthusiastic birder. You would have liked her."

"You seem to be gravitating toward Lockmaster lately."

"It's very pleasant country down there," he said, "and there's a horse farm coming up for sale that might be an investment for the K Fund. I believe I could get interested in horses without trying too hard."

"You wouldn't live down there, would you?"

"Not right away, but it's a beautiful setup." He then gave a glowing description of the Amberton farm. "A delegation is coming up tomorrow for a conference."

"It sounds as if you're serious."

"It's tempting! I have one reservation, however. The stablemaster is highly competent, but he has an unsavory past. Besides having a reputation as a heavy drinker and a womanizer, he was chased out of jobs Down Below for illegal use of drugs in connection with racehorses. Too bad. I believe I mentioned him before. His name is Steve O'Hare."

Polly put down her glass abruptly and turned pale.

"Do you feel all right?" he asked.

"A little dizzy, that's all. I skipped lunch—trying to lose a few pounds," she said with a pathetic smile. "The sherry—"

"We'll have the soup served right away." He signaled the waitress. "Eat a roll. I'll butter it for you. And don't worry about losing weight, Polly. I like you best just the way you are." When the chicken gumbo was served and she had revived, he went on. "Do you realize this is our first dinner together in ten days? And we've missed two weekends! That's no kind of track record for you and me."

"I know," she said ruefully. "We belong together. The last two years have been the best years of my life, dearest."

"I could say the same . . . What are we going to do about it?"

"What do you want to do about it?"

The halibut steaks arrived, with broccoli spears and squash soufflé, and the answer was deferred.

Polly said, while dealing with a small bone in the fish, "Is there . . . anything new . . . at the barn?"

"You won't recognize the orchard. It was damaged by last week's storm, but the debris has been cleared up and some of the worst trees removed. The number of prowlers has increased since the barn tour. Those who objected to paying five dollars are now trying to get a free peek. I've ordered mini-blinds, but it takes three weeks."

"Have the tapestries arrived?"

"Yes, and they've been hung. I think you'll like them. The largest hangs from the railing of the topmost catwalk, and I only hope it's secure. It's hooked onto tack-strips, and in our household we're subject to Yum Yum's law: *If anything can be unhooked, untied, unbuckled, or unlatched, DO IT!* She started with shoelaces and advanced to desk drawers. Tapestries may be next on her list, so I'm monitoring the situation closely. Her voice is changing, too. After all, she's about five years old—a mature female. Frequently she delivers a very assertive contralto yowl that sounds suspiciously like NOW!"

"What does Koko think about all of this?" Polly asked.

"He has his own pursuits. Lately he's been chummy with a cardinal in the orchard. They commune through the window glass, and here's the astonishing thing: Last Saturday a horse named Son of Cardinal won the fifth race at the steeplechase. Is that a coincidence or not? Suppose Koko could pick winners! He'd be a very valuable animal . . . Did I tell you I met the woman who played in *Henry VIII?* She's a retiring, insecure little creature that VanBrook reshaped in the image of Queen Katharine—a Pygmalion act that must have bolstered his ego."

Qwilleran was unusually talkative, rambling from one subject to another—evidence that he had missed Polly's company more than he realized. She, on the other hand, was unusually quiet, simply asking questions.

At one point she asked, "Did you read the letter that an

eleven-year-old girl wrote to the editor of the *Something* last week?"

"I never read anything written by eleven-year-old girls," he stated in his mock-curmudgeon style.

"There were several replies in Friday's paper. I knew you were out of town, so I photocopied them for you. It's about the Tipsy problem."

"Problem? What kind of problem?"

"Read the original letter, and you'll see what I mean."

The communication from one Debbie Watts of Kennebeck had been printed with all the juvenile errors that made Qwilleran wince.

I am 11 years old in 5th grade. My gramma told me to rite. We have a famly ablum. It has a pitcher of my gramma when she was a girl. She worked at Tipsy's. They took a pitcher of her and Tipsy out in front. She says Tipsy had white feet. Her feet are white in the pitcher.

"Hmmm," Qwilleran said, considering the significance of this revelation. "The portrait in the restaurant has black feet."

"Exactly! If the prize goes to a Tipsy look-alike, does that mean black feet or white feet? Now read the replies."

The first was signed by a Mrs. G. Wilson Goodwinter of West Middle Hummock. That was an old family name of distinction, and the suburb was an affluent one.

Little Debbie Watts is correct. My housekeeper's daughter works in a nursing home Down Below, and one of her patients is an old sailor who knew Tipsy when she lived at Gus's Timberline Bar on the waterfront. Gus was from Moose County, and during the Depression he came back here and opened a restaurant, bringing Tipsy with him and naming the establishment in her honor. The patient describes Tipsy as having white feet. He is quite definite about it.

Qwilleran said, "This looks bad for Hixie Rice and her bright idea."

"Read on," Polly instructed him.

Next was a letter from Margaret DeRoche of Sawdust City:

My husband's cousin was the artist who painted the portrait of Tipsy in the 1930s. He was an artist of great integrity and would never paint black feet on a subject if that were not the case. I write because he is not here to defend himself, having passed away three years ago. His name was Boyd Smithers, and he signed the canvas with his initials.

"The plot thickens," Qwilleran said. "Here's one from the Kennebeck Chamber of Commerce. I'll bet they're in favor of black feet. This is getting to be a political issue."

For fifty years or more Tipsy with black boots has been the image we connect with the restaurant and the town of Kennebeck. Two generations of Moose County residents have raised cats with black boots and named them after Tipsy. Why rock the boat now?

Polly said, "Read the one from Samantha Campbell. She's the registrar of the Historical Society."

In reference to the Tipsy debate I wish to note that the Historical Society archives contain a Tipsy file of clippings from the late lamented Pickax Picayune. In 1939 a brief article referred to Tipsy as being "all white with a black hat." An item in the same paper in 1948 refers to Tipsy's "black boots." I mention this to emphasize the necessity of accuracy in the public press, since newspaper accounts go into historical records. Thank you.

"And thank *you*, Ms. Campbell," Qwilleran said. "I should take Koko to the restaurant and let him give the portrait the Siamese Sniff Test. He knows right from wrong."

Polly said, "You're not taking this seriously, Qwill. Read the last one." It was written by Betty Bee Warr of Purple Point.

My grandmother, who is in the Senior Care Facility with arthritis real bad in her hands, remembers that a man named Gus brought Tipsy to

Kennebeck in the Depression and had an artist paint her picture. When Gus sold his place in the 1940s the new owners paid my grandmother, who did a little painting as a hobby, to touch up the feet with black. They said it would give the picture "more oomph." Now she realizes she did wrong to paint over it, but she needed the money.

Qwilleran said, "This is the stickiest mess since the flypaper controversy in the city council meeting, but Hixie and the chamber of commerce will have to cope with it. I'm only a judge, and I have other things on my mind."

"Is the mystery of VanBrook's murder bothering you?" Polly asked, knowing he could be tormented by unanswered questions.

"No. The mystery of his identity. Was he what he claimed to be or was he a phony? I suspect the latter. Koko knew there was something not quite genuine about him from the beginning. That cat knows a fake when he sniffs it, whether it's a hairpiece or imitation turkey."

Polly sighed. "Do you think Bootsie will ever be as smart as Koko?"

"Not with a moniker like that! It lacks dignity. Koko's name is Kao K'o Kung, as you know . . . Will you have dessert?"

"No, thank you. I'd better not."

"Coffee?"

Polly hesitated, then said sweetly, "Shall we go to my place for coffee?"

Later that evening, when they were saying good night at her carriage house, Polly mentioned casually, "This weekend may be the last chance to go birding in the wetlands. Shall we?"

"Sure," said Qwilleran, after concealing a gulp. "Or we could fly down to Chicago with the Lanspeaks for a ballgame."

"That would be nice," she said.

He arrived home elated and charged with energy, but it was midnight, and his housemates wanted only their bedtime snack and lights-out. Qwilleran retired to his studio to continue reading the biography of Sir Edmund Backhouse. What a difference: The British sinologist had a winning personality and a deferential manner; VanBrook was all contempt and ego.

The next day being Wednesday, he rose early to avoid the garrulous and censorious Mrs. Fulgrove. He avoided her by writing his Friday column at the newspaper office, visiting the bookstore to chat with Edd Smith, and buying a pair of cashmere gloves for Polly at the Lanspeak store—gray to go with her gray winter coat.

While cashing a check, he met Hixie at the bank. He said, "Are you concerned about the controversy over Tipsy's feet?"

She tossed her pageboy defiantly. "No problem, Qwill. It's simply creating more publicity. We'll award two prizes—one for the popular Tipsy with black boots and one for the authentic look-alike. Don't forget, we're expecting you as our dinner guest before the judging . . . Want to have lunch?"

"Can't," he said. "I'm expecting company at the barn."

Promptly at one-thirty a van made its way up Trevelyan Trail, and the delegation from the Amberton Farm emerged: Fiona carrying a tissue box and wearing non-descript garments that flapped about her thin frame, then the red-bearded stablemaster, walking with a broad-shouldered swagger, and finally the boy, short and thin like his mother, ambling with the loose gait of his generation, his thumbs hooked in his back pockets. The two men wore dark jeans and navy blue nylon jackets with the Amberton insigne—a red cardinal— embroidered on the breast pocket.

Qwilleran greeted them at the door and invited them into the foyer. They entered slowly, swinging their heads from side to side and up and down in astonishment.

"Oh! I've never seen anything like it!" Fiona cried.

"Hey," said Steve, nudging Robbie, "how about this, kid?"

Robbie nodded, and a half-smile passed between them, which Qwilleran interpreted as: *We've got our pigeon; he's loaded; this setup cost a coupla million, easy.* Three or four years ago the thought would have annoyed him, but now he was accustomed to the imaginary dollar sign tattooed on his forehead.

Fiona said, "Mr. Qwilleran, this is—uh—my son Robbie."

"Congratulations, young man. I saw you ride on Saturday. Good show!"

The boy nodded, looking pleased.

Qwilleran ushered them into the lounge area with its luxurious oatmeal-colored seating pieces. "Won't you sit down?"

Robbie looked at the pale upholstery and then at his mother.

"It's all right," she said. "Your pants are clean. I just washed them."

Qwilleran thought, Her son's a mute! No one had ever mentioned that he couldn't speak. "Would anyone like a glass of cider?" he asked.

"Do you happen to have a beer?" Steve replied.

"Robbie and I will have cider," said Fiona. Mother and son were sitting close together on one sofa; Steve sprawled comfortably on the other and had thrown his jacket on the rug.

The Siamese were observing the strangers from the railing of the first balcony, and Steve caught sight of them. "Are those *cats?*"

"Siamese," Qwilleran said.

"Why are they staring at me?"

"They're not staring; they're just nearsighted."

The trainer jerked his thumb toward the remains of the orchard. "What happened to your trees?"

"They suffered a blight some years ago," Qwilleran explained, "and the storm last week raised havoc, so I thought the time had come to get rid of the dead wood."

"It'd make a good pasture if you wanted to board a couple of horses."

"Unfortunately there's a city ordinance: No horses, cattle, pigs, chickens, or goats within the city limits."

While they drank their refreshments, the visitors ogled the fireplace cube, the loft ladders, the catwalks and massive beams. Steve said, "I read in the *Logger* that some guy hung himself up there."

"What's the ladder for?" Robbie asked.

He can speak! Qwilleran thought. "Sort of a fire escape," he replied. "Did you bring the information about the farm, Steve?"

"Absolutely!" He fished an envelope from his jacket pocket and handed it over. "I got these figures from Amberton. He'd like to meet you and show you around when he gets back from Arizona."

"Where does the operation derive its income?"

"Breeding horses. Selling horses. Winning races. Boarding and training horses. Giving riding lessons. There's a lot of wealthy families in Lockmaster, wanting their kids to take lessons and win ribbons."

"Would you manage the operation?"

"Absolutely! That's what I do."

"Do you have a résumé?" When the stablemaster hesitated, Qwilleran added, "I must explain that I have no money of my own to invest. All business ventures are handled by the Klingenschoen Memorial Fund, and I'll have to discuss the proposition with the trustees. They'll want to know your background, where and for whom you've worked, and for how long. Also why you left each employ, and so forth."

Steve sneezed, and Fiona got up and handed him the tissue box, saying, "I could write it out for you, Steve."

He mopped his brow. "Whew! It's hot in here."

"It's his allergy," Fiona explained. "He gets hot and cold flashes."

Qwilleran turned to Robbie. "And what is your job on the farm?"

"I help Steve," said the youth, with a glance at his mother.

"He's very good with horses," she said with maternal pride. "He's going to ride some big winners when he gets older, isn't he, Steve?"

The trainer sneezed again.

"You should get shots for that allergy," Qwilleran suggested.

"That's what I told him," said Fiona.

At that moment there was a slight commotion on the balcony—some rumbling and a little yipping, after which both cats took off as if shot from a cannon: up the ramps and across the catwalks, circling up to the roof and then racing down again until they reached the first balcony. From there they swooped down like dive-bombers, Koko landing on the back of the sofa behind Steve and Yum Yum landing virtually in his lap. He flinched and Fiona squealed.

"Jeez! What's happening here?" he demanded.

"Sorry. You've just attended the seventeenth Weekly Pickax Steeplechase Race Meeting," Qwilleran said.

Koko was still on the sofa back exactly as he had come to rest: legs stiff, back arched, tail crooked like a horseshoe. Then he sneezed: *chfff.* As sneezes go, it was only a whisper, but a fine spray of vapor was discernible in the sunlight slanting in from the triangular windows.

The trainer mopped his neck with a tissue. "Guess we'd better be getting back to the farm."

"Thanks for bringing this information," said Qwilleran, waving the sheet of paper. "If you'll send us that résumé, we'll go to work on it and hope that the trustees are interested."

"Come on, Robbie," said his mother. "Say thank you for the cider."

The three visitors stood up, and as Steve put on his jacket he noticed something on the floor. He picked it up. "What's this?" It was a small metal engraving of a horse's head, mounted on a wooden block.

"That's an old printing block," said Qwilleran. "The cats have been batting it around."

"I could use that on the front page of *Stablechat.*"

"Take it. You're welcome to it."

"Oh! That's very nice of you," said Fiona.

"Don't forget your tissue box."

"Here's the latest issue of *Stablechat,*" Steve said, tossing it on the coffee table. "It has all the race results from the 'chase."

Qwilleran accompanied the delegation out to their van, making the requisite remarks about the temperature and the possibility of rain. When he returned, Yum Yum was wriggling flatly out from under the sofa, and Koko was busy tearing up the last issue of *Stablechat.* Holding it down with his forepaws, he grabbed a corner with his fangs and jerked his head. Qwilleran watched the systematic destruction, admiring the cat's efficiency. Was there something about the smell of the ink or the quality of the paper that gave him a thrill? This was the second time he had shredded the horsey newsletter.

Abruptly, Koko dropped his task. His head rose on a stretched neck and swiveled like a periscope in the direction of the entrance. The tableau lasted for only a second before he dashed to the window adjoining the door.

At the same moment, Qwilleran heard a gunshot, followed by a triumphant laugh. He made a dash for the door. The van was starting down the lane, and on the ground near the berry bushes lay a small red body.

"My God!" he gasped. "That stupid kid shot the cardinal!"

Chapter 12

Qwilleran dug a hole near the berry bushes and buried the lordly cardinal in a coffee can to keep marauding animals from desecrating the remains. Raccoons and roving dogs sometimes appeared from nowhere in violation of city ordinance. From a window Koko watched the interment with his ears askew, and when Qwilleran returned indoors he was yowling and pacing the floor.

"Okay, we'll go out and pay our respects to the deceased," Qwilleran said calmly, although his teeth were clenched in anger.

He harnessed both cats. Yum Yum rolled over in a leaden lump of uncooperative fur, but Koko was eager to go. As soon as he was outside the door, he walked directly to the spot on the earth where the cardinal had fallen, then sniffed the burial place. Eventually he was persuaded to explore the perimeter of the barn, and after ten minutes—when the telephone summoned them indoors—he had had enough. He toppled over and lay on his side to lick his paws.

The call was from Mildred Hanstable, one of the judges in the Tipsy contest. "You sound angry," she said after Qwilleran had barked into the mouthpiece.

"Someone shot a cardinal in my barnyard! I'm not angry; I'm mad as hell!"

"Do you know who did it?"

"Yes, and he's going to get a tongue lashing that he won't forget! What's on your mind? Is the contest called off?"

"No, you'll be sorry to hear. We're due at Tipsy's for dinner around six o'clock. I have a hair appointment this afternoon, and then I'll have some time to kill, in case you want to invite me over. I could use a fortifying drink before having dinner with my boss. Lyle is such a sourpuss!"

"It's all an act," Qwilleran reassured her. "Lyle Compton is a pussycat masquerading as an English bull."

"Anyway, I'm dying to see the barn without five hundred paying guests bumping into me. I was one of the guides, you know."

"You're invited," he said with curt hospitality.

Koko was still licking his paws, and Yum Yum was still in a simulated coma, although she revived promptly as soon as the harness was removed. Qwilleran glanced at his watch. The delegation would have had time to return to Lockmaster, unless Steve stopped on the way for a drink.

He phoned the Bushland house. "This is Qwill. How do I reach Fiona?"

"You sound upset. Is anything wrong?" Vicki asked in alarm. "She was due at your place with Steve and Robbie a couple of hours ago."

"They were here and they left, and that brat shot a bird in my barnyard—a cardinal! I want to have a few words with his mother before I light into him."

"I'm so sorry, Qwill. I'll have her call you," Vicki said. "She's due here to help me with a hunt breakfast for tomorrow."

"Do that. Not later than five o'clock."

The arrival of Mildred Hanstable was therapy for Qwilleran's bruised sensibilities. A healthy, happy, outgoing, buxom woman of his own age, she had an aura of generosity that attracted man and beast. The Siamese greeted her with exuberance, sensing there was a packet of homemade crunchies for them in her voluminous handbag.

Seating herself on a sofa, Mildred arranged the folds of the ample garment that camouflaged her avoirdupois. She had given up the battle to lose weight and now concentrated on disguising the excess. "I'm happier," she confessed to Qwilleran, "now that I've decided Nature intended me to be rotund. I'm the prototypical Earth Mother. Why fight it? . . . And, to answer the question you haven't asked: Yes, I'd like a Scotch. . . . Tell me, Qwill, how does it feel to be wallowing in space?" She waved an arm to indicate the vast interior of the barn.

"Wide open spaces are fine," he said, "but I'm used to four walls and a door. Instead of rooms I have areas: a foyer area, a library area, a dining area. You're sitting in the main lounge area. I'm going to do the honors in the bar area adjoining the snack area. It's all too vague." He served drinks and a bowl of nuts on a small pewter tray, a barn-warming gift from his designer.

"Your kitchen area is scrumptious," she said. "Are you going to learn to cook? Or are you thinking of getting married?" she asked mischievously. Mildred taught home economics in the Pickax schools and had offered to give him lessons in egg boiling.

"Neither could be further from my mind," he said as he picked up a few dark blocks scattered on the pale Moroccan rug.

"What are those things, Qwill?"

"I've started collecting antique typeblocks, and the cats keep stealing them out of the typecase that hangs in the library area."

"Why don't you move it to an area they can't reach?"

"There's no such thing as a place Siamese can't reach. They'll swing from a chandelier if necessary." He showed her a small metal plate mounted on wood. "This is their favorite block, which I take to mean that they'd like an occasional dish of hasenpfeffer. Do you know how to cook rabbit?"

"Of course! It's just like chicken. When we were first married, Stan did a lot of rabbit hunting, and I made Belgian stew every weekend."

"Would you be good enough to cook a batch for the cats? I bought a frozen rabbit from Toodle's."

"You know I'd be happy to. And may I ask a favor? Now that

you've moved out of your garage, Qwill, would you allow the hospital auxiliary to use it for a gift shop? We need a central location."

"I'll put you on the list," he said, "but the Arts Council wants it for a gallery, and the Historical Society wants it for an antique shop. Actually, I hesitate to let it go until I've spent one winter in this barn. The cost of heating and snow removal may be prohibitive."

"If you can afford to feed the Siamese lobster tail, you can afford a big heating bill," she said. As if they understood "lobster tail," Koko and Yum Yum immediately presented themselves, and Mildred went on: "The father of one of my students runs the animal shelter, and he told me that one mating pair of cats can produce twelve cats in a year and sixty-three in two years. In ten years there will be *eighty million* direct descendents!"

"Tipsy lived fifty years ago," Qwilleran said. "No wonder there are so many black-and-white cats around."

"The animal shelter is swamped with unwanted cats and kittens. Also, hundreds of homeless cats roam the countryside—having litters, starving, freezing, and getting run over."

"What are you trying to tell me, Mildred?" He knew she was a zealous crusader for causes.

"I think the Klingenschoen Fund should underwrite a campaign for free spaying and neutering. I'll be glad to present a proposal to the trustees. Hixie Rice could organize it. We'll need publicity, programs in schools, rescue teams—" She was interrupted by the telephone.

"Excuse me," Qwilleran said. He took the call in the library area.

"Oh, Mr. Qwilleran!" cried a shaken voice on the line. "I feel terrible about the bird! Robbie didn't do it. He wanted to use Steve's gun, but I wouldn't let him. Steve likes to—uh—take pot shots at—uh—targets, you know."

"I appreciate your calling," he said stiffly. "Sorry I accused your son. I'll have plenty to say to Steve about this thoughtless act!"

When he returned to the lounge area, Mildred was struggling

to get out of the deep-cushioned sofa. "I guess it's time we got on the road," she said.

"Before we leave, Mildred, I'd like your opinion on a domestic problem—in the laundry area." He led her to a partitioned alcove where racks were hung with yellow towels, yellow shirts, and yellow undershorts.

"My favorite color!" she said.

"But not mine."

"Did you leave something in a pocket when you put it in the washer? What was it? Do you know?"

"It was a sprig of green leaves with a purple flower."

"Where did you get it? And why was it in your pocket? Or am I being too nosy?"

"It's a long story," he said evasively.

She buried her nose in a towel. "It could be saffron. I used to put it in boiled rice, and it turned it a lovely color. Do you know what saffron costs today? Twelve dollars for a measly *pinch!* The stores up here don't even carry it any more."

"Why so expensive?"

"Well, it comes from the inside of a tiny flower. That's all I know. Have you tried bleach?"

They drove to Kennebeck in Qwilleran's car, and while Mildred chattered about roadside litter and the high cost of art supplies, he was pondering VanBrook's indoor garden. If the man had been raising saffron, he had a $20,000 crop in one small room. He would have to export it, of course—to gourmet centers around the country. By using lights he might grow five crops a year—a lucrative hobby for a rural principal ... And then Qwilleran thought, Did VanBrook know of another use for saffron? Did he learn something in the Orient? Perhaps it could be smoked! In that case, the crop was worth millions! And then he wondered, as he had done earlier, What was in those hundreds of boxes—besides books?

Before he could formulate a satisfying guess, they arrived at Tipsy's restaurant. Hixie Rice greeted them and conducted them to a table, the one beneath the fraudulent black-booted Tipsy. Lyle Compton was already there, sipping a martini.

Hixie said, "I'll brief you and then leave you while I marshal the contestants in the lodge hall across the street." She produced two stacks of snapshots. "These are the finalists in both categories, a total of fifty. Run through them while you're having your drinks and choose the likeliest candidates, based on markings. Later, when you judge them live, your final selection will be based on the sweetest and funniest . . . See you shortly. The crowd is already lining up on the sidewalk, and the doors don't open for another hour." She bounced out of the dining room with the supreme confidence that was her trademark.

"I'm having another drink," Compton announced, bestowing his grouchy grimace on the other two judges.

Mildred said, "I'm not sure I approve of a duplicate prize based on a forgery. What kind of values are we presenting to our young people?"

Qwilleran said, "No one ever told me what the prize is going to be."

"Don't you read your own newspaper?" she scolded. "It's a case of catfood, fifty pounds of kitty gravel, and an all-expense weekend for two in Minneapolis."

"Let's go through this bunch of fakes first," said the superintendent, picking up the black-booted entries. He was accustomed to taking charge of a meeting. "The definitive marking, as we all know, is the so-called hat—the black patch over one ear and eye. That'll eliminate most of them."

Qwilleran said, "I see black collars, black earmuffs, black moustaches, black sunglasses, black epaulets, and black cummerbunds, but no hats."

Mildred spotted a hat with a chin-strap.

"Hang onto it. You may have a winner," said Compton.

"Are all these finalists going to be present in person?" Qwilleran asked.

"That's the idea. With fifty live cats in one room, there won't be much sweetness of expression," the superintendent predicted.

The white-footed entries were in the minority, and there were only three with hats, as opposed to seven hatted contestants in the other category.

"Having any luck?" asked Hixie when she breezed back into the dining room.

"Here's the best we can do." Mildred spread the ten snapshots on the table.

"Good! Turn them over, and you'll see a code number on the back: W-2, B-6, B-12, and so forth. Okay? When the cats parade in front of you, each will be accompanied by a chaperon wearing the assigned code number. When you spot the ten preselected numbers, direct them to the runner up platform. Then put your heads together and make the final decision. Take your time. Delay will add to the suspense ... Now, is everything clear? I'll be back to get you in an hour. Enjoy your dinner. Be sure to have the bread pudding for dessert; it's super! ... And wait till you see the enthusiastic crowd! This is the greatest thing that ever happened to Kennebeck! By the way, we have sweeter-and-funnier T-shirts for you if you care to wear them."

"Are you kidding?" Mildred asked.

The judges watched Hixie stride from the dining room. Every time the restaurant door opened, the hubbub across the street could be heard, and Compton said, "Sounds more like a riot to me!" They ordered steaks, and he turned to Qwilleran. "My wife says your barn tour was a big success."

"So I hear. I was glad to be out of town."

"It's true," said Mildred. "The visitors loved it, and they were simply *floored* by the apple tree tapestry. They objected to the zoological prints, though. Why do people have such an antipathy to bats? They're such cute little things, and they eat tons of mosquitoes."

"They're disgusting," Compton said.

"Not so!" Mildred was always ready to defend the underdog. "When I was in the second grade at Black Creek Elementary, our teacher had a bat in a cage, and we fed him bits of our lunch on the point of a pencil."

"They're filthy little monsters."

She flashed an indignant rebuttal at her boss. "We called him Boppo. He was very clean—always washing himself like a cat. I remember his bright eyes and perky ears, and he had a little pink mouth with sharp little teeth—"

"—which can start a rabies epidemic."

Mildred ignored the remark. "He'd hang upside down from his little hooks, and then he'd walk on his elbows. Such a clown! And I'm sure that both of you educated gentlemen know that a bat's wing structure is a lesson in aerodynamic design."

"I only know," Compton said with a scowl, "that there are other topics I'd rather discuss with my steak."

They talked about the steeplechase, the questionable merits of tourism, the success of *Henry VIII*, and the VanBrook case. After coffee, when Mildred excused herself briefly, the superintendent hunched his shoulders and leaned across the table toward Qwilleran.

"While she's out of hearing," he said, "I have something confidential to report. You questioned Hilary's credentials the other day, so I did a little checking on the three colleges that supposedly granted his degrees. One institution doesn't exist and never did, and the other two have no record of the guy—by either of his names."

Qwilleran said in a low voice, "There's evidence that he was deceitful in petty ways, so I'm not surprised."

"This is off the record, of course. I see no need of announcing it, now that he's gone. He did a helluva good job for us, even though he was a miserable tyrant."

"The amazing thing is that he had such a fund of erudition, or so it seemed. Did you check Equity?"

"Yes, and I drew another blank—no evidence that he'd ever been a professional actor. But he wasn't all bad." Compton glanced around. "Here she comes. There's more to the story. I'll tell you later."

Mildred announced, "The crowd is fighting to get into the lodge hall. I hope they can control them during the judging."

At that moment Hixie arrived, flushed and breathless. "We have more people than we expected," she said. "A troop of Cub

Scouts came just to see the show, and the first three rows are filled with seniors from the retirement village. Every cat has from five to a dozen supporters. We didn't count on that. The fire department may stop people from entering the building. All the chairs are taken, and yet most of those outside are contestants. We can't start until they're all in the hall, and we can't throw the first-comers out."

"Turn on the fire hose," Compton grumbled.

"Is there anything we can do?" Mildred asked.

"Just put on your judges' badges and take your places on the platform. I'll take you in the back door."

"Do I have to wear a badge?" Qwilleran asked. "I'd rather be anonymous when the shooting starts."

Hixie smuggled them into the lodge hall, and their appearance on the platform was greeted by cheers and whistles. They seated themselves at a long table covered with black felt, on which was a bushel basket of catnip toys thoughtfully provided by the promoters—one toy for each contestant whether a winner or not.

The rows of folding chairs were already filled, and an overflow crowd was standing in the aisles. At the rear of the hall, members of the chamber of commerce, wearing sweeter-and-funnier T-shirts, were trying to reason with the horde that demanded admittance. Those carrying feline finalists were loudly vocal in their indignation. Overpowering the official attendants, they pressed into the hall, and soon the room was filled with squabbling families and caterwauling cats. Some were in arms and some were in carrying coops, but all were black-and-white and all were unhappy.

"Something tells me," Compton said dryly, "that this whole thing is not going to work."

In an effort to restore order and explain the unexpected situation, the president of the chamber of commerce appeared on the platform. He was greeted by a round of booing and catcalls. Raising his hand and shouting into the microphone, he tried to get the attention of the noisy audience, but the public address system was useless. Nothing could be heard above the din, and the feedback added ear-shattering electronic screeches to the pandemonium. Cat chaperons were shaking their fists at the stage. Mothers shrieked that their children were being trampled. Two black-and-white cats-in-arms flew at each other and engaged in a bloody battle. At the height of the confusion, a giant black-and-white tomcat broke away from his chaperon and bounded to the platform and the basket of catnip toys. Instantly, every cat who could break loose followed the leader, leaping across the white heads of screaming seniors in the front rows, until the judges' table was alive with fighting animals and the air was thick with flying fur. The judges ducked under the table just as the police appeared on the platform with bullhorns nd, mysteriously, the sprinkler system went into operation.

Under the table Compton yelled, "For God's sake, let's get out of here!" The three of them crawled backstage on hands and knees and escaped out the back door. For a moment they stood and looked at each other as they caught their breath.

Mildred was the first to speak. "I move that we go back to Tipsy's for a drink."

"I second the motion," said her boss.

"Too bad there's no TV coverage in Moose County," Qwilleran observed. "The crews would have a field day with this one. It has everything: kids, cats, old folks, even blood!"

Main Street was choked with police cars and emergency vehicles, their red and blue lights flashing, as sheriff's deputies and state police tried to control the mob. Ambulances were standing by, and fire trucks were primed for action. The only prudent way for the judges to reach the restaurant was to circle the block and enter through the kitchen door.

In the relative quiet of Tipsy's bar they collapsed into chairs. They saw no more of Hixie that evening, and as soon as it was deemed safe, they were glad to leave.

Qwilleran pulled Lyle Compton aside. "What else were you going to tell me about VanBrook? You said there was more to the story."

"It hasn't been officially announced," the superintendent said in confidential tones, "and I haven't even told the school board yet, but his attorney notified me today that VanBrook left his entire estate to the Pickax school system. I believe we've earned it, to be perfectly frank."

Qwilleran heard the news with skepticism. "What's the catch? Do you have to rename it VanBrook High School?"

"Nothing like that, although we might name the library after him. His book collection is supposed to number ninety thousand volumes."

Later that evening Qwilleran made a call to Susan Exbridge. "What time tomorrow are we unpacking books?"

"How about nine o'clock? It's a big job—and probably a dirty job. Wear old clothes," she advised.

"Would you object if I brought Koko along? He has a nose like a bloodhound when it comes to sniffing out rare books."

"Darling . . . do *whatever* makes you happy."

Qwilleran was exhilarated, the VanBrook revelation having canceled out the Tipsy fiasco. He said to the Siamese, "How would you guys like a little sport? Something new!" He produced a bubble pipe and whipped up a bowl of suds in the kitchen, watched by two bemused cats who were baffled by a bowl of anything that was inedible and unpotable.

"You stay down here," he said as he carried the equipment to the first balcony. They followed him up the ramp.

He dipped the pipe in the suds and put it to his lips, making one mistake. His pipe-smoking days had accustomed him to drawing on a pipe; bubble blowing was different. He spat it out and tried again. This time he produced one beautiful bubble—iridescent in the barn's galaxy of uplights and downlights—until it burst in his face. He tried again, gradually mastering the technique.

"Okay. Go downstairs," he commanded the cats, adding a tap on the rump. "Down! Down!" They wanted to go up! It was past their bedtime. They stayed on the balcony.

To tantalize them he blew a series of bubbles and bubble clusters and bubbles within bubbles, wafting them into space, watching them float lazily in the air currents until they spontaneously disappeared. The Siamese were unimpressed. They watched this absurd specimen of homo sapiens blowing a pipe, waving his arm, and peering over the railing. Bored, they ambled up the ramp to their loft.

"*Cats-s-s!*" Qwilleran hissed.

Chapter 13

Thursday, September 22, would be one of the most memorable days in Qwilleran's four-year residency in Pickax. It started routinely enough. He fed the cats, thawed a roll for his own breakfast, and harnessed Koko for the trip to Goodwinter Boulevard. He also buckled up Yum Yum for the sake of practice, hoping she might eventually accept the idea. This time, instead of falling over, she stood in the awkward crazy-leg posture that resulted from the buckling process. Koko, on the other hand, strutted on his slender brown legs, dragging his leash, eager for action. For two minutes and seven seconds, according to Qwilleran's watch, Yum Yum remained in her unlovely pose as if cast in stone, with an air of martyrdom, until he removed the harness. Then she walked away with the exasperatingly graceful step of a female Siamese who has succeeded in making her point.

Moments later, Susan Exbridge arrived in her wagon, and Qwilleran placed Koko's carrier on the backseat. As they set out for VanBrook's house he asked, "Have you had a chance to spend any time at Hilary's place?"

"A couple of mornings," she said. "I have to keep my shop open in the afternoon, you know. But I'm getting an overview of his collection, and in the evening I check my art books. It's really fascinating!"

"Have you found anything valuable?"

"Definitely! There's a Japanese screen with horses in color

and gold that the horsey set in Lockmaster will *swoon* over! And there's a magnificent cloisonné vase, two feet high, that I'd love to have myself. Then—hidden away in lacquered cabinets—are small objects like inro and netsuke and fans. It's all very exciting! Hilary had a *staggering* collection of fans."

"Fans?" Qwilleran echoed, doubting that he'd heard correctly.

"Folding fans, you know, with ivory sticks and hand-painted leaves, most of them *signed!* To research these I may have to fly to Chicago . . . Want to come along?" she added playfully.

"How about the stuff on the second floor?"

"Oh, *that junk!* I threw out a roomful of dead plants, but there were a lot of growing lights that will be salable."

It occurred to Qwilleran that she might have thrown out a $20,000 crop of whatever VanBrook was cultivating in the back room.

"I haven't touched the books," she was saying. "Most of the cartons are sealed, so I brought a craft knife for you to use and a legal pad in case you want to make notes, or lists, or whatever. I don't know how to tell you to sort them. You can decide that when you see what's there."

"I wonder if Hilary catalogued his books. There should be a catalogue."

"If there is, you'll probably find it in his study upstairs. It's really good of you, Qwill, to do this for me."

"Glad to help," he murmured.

"Yow!" came a comment from the backseat.

Koko entered the spacious high-ceilinged house in grand style, seated regally in his carrier as if in a palanquin. He was conducted around the main floor on a leash to avoid accidental collision with a two-foot cloisonné vase. He was tugging, however, toward the staircase, a fact that Qwilleran considered significant. The cat liked books, no doubt about it. He enjoyed sniffing the spines of fine bindings, probably detecting glue made from animal hides, and occasionally he found cause to knock a pertinent title off the bookshelf. (To discourage this uncivilized practice, Qwilleran had installed a shelf in the cats' apartment, stocked with nickel-and-dime books that Koko could knock about to his heart's content, although it was characteristic of feline perversity that he ignored them.)

"Where shall we start?" Qwilleran asked as the cat pulled him up the stairs.

For answer, Koko tugged toward VanBrook's study with its four walls of bookshelves. There he prowled and sniffed and jumped effortlessly onto shelves eight feet above the floor, while Qwilleran made a superficial search for a catalogue of the 90,000 books. Ninety thousand? He found it difficult to believe. Unfortunately the desk drawers were locked and the Oriental box had been removed from the desktop, no doubt by the attorney. Either place would be the logical spot for a catalogue.

"No luck," Qwilleran said to his assistant. "Let's go next door and start unpacking." There were several large rooms on the second floor, originally bedrooms but now storerooms for book cartons. He chose to begin with the room nearest the staircase. Like the others, it contained nothing but casual stacks of corrugated cartons, formerly used for shipping canned soup, chili sauce, whiskey, and other commodities. Now, according to the adhesive labels, they contained Toynbee, Emerson, Goethe, Gide and the like, as well as classifications such as Russian Drama, Restoration Comedy, and Cyprian History. Each sticker carried a number in addition to identification of the contents.

"There's got to be a catalogue," Qwilleran muttered, for the benefit of any listening ear.

There was no reply from Koko. The cat was surveying the irregular stacks of boxes like a mountain goat contemplating Mount Rushmore, and soon he bounded up from ledge to ledge until he reached the summit and posed haughtily on a carton of Western Thought. Meanwhile, Qwilleran closed the door and went to work with his craft knife, slitting open a box of Dickens, labeled A-74.

It was no idle choice, Dickens being a writer he admired greatly. It was no treasure trove either; the volumes were inexpensive editions. He took time, however, to look up his favorite passages: the opening paragraph of *A Tale of Two Cities*; the description of the coachman's coat in *The Pickwick Papers*; and a scene from *A Christmas Carol* that he knew virtually by heart. Every Christmas Eve, he remembered, his mother had read aloud the account of the Cratchits' modest Christmas dinner, beginning with that mouth-filling line: "Then up rose Mrs. Cratchit, Cratchit's wife, dressed out but poorly in a twice-turned gown, but brave in ribbons, which are cheap and make a goodly show for sixpence." A wave of nostalgia tingled his spine. The room was quiet except for an occasional murmur or grunt from Koko as he explored his private mountain, and Qwilleran read greedily from *The Pickwick Papers* until alerted by the unmistakable sound of claws on corrugated cardboard. The thinking man's cat was diligently scratching a box on the fifth tier, labeled "Macaulay A-106." Qwilleran immediately pulled it down, slit the flaps, and found the famous three-volume *History of England*, plus essays, biographies, and the questionably titled collection of poems, *Lays of Ancient Rome*. He huffed into his moustache as he realized that the Macaulay box had originally contained a shipment of canned salmon. Koko was no fool.

Nevertheless, Qwilleran had always wanted to check out a statement made by a typesetter of the old school—a claim that Macaulay used more consonants in his writing, while Dickens used more vowels. Sitting cross-legged on the floor with a pad of paper, he started counting consonants and vowels, selecting random excerpts from each author. It was a brain-numbing, eye-torturing task, and he was disappointed with the result. While racking up 390 consonants, Dickens used 250 vowels and Macaulay actually used more—a total of 258. The typesetter was either misinformed or a practical joker, but there was nothing he could do about it; the man had died two years before.

There was a tap on the door, and Susan called out to him, "Coffee's ready downstairs."

Qwilleran confined Koko to the room with the Dickens and Macaulay and joined her in the kitchen.

"Making good progress?" she inquired.

"I haven't found anything of value as yet," he replied, truthfully.

"I've found a green dragon dish documented as fourteenth century!"

He wondered: *Yes, but are the documents forged?*

"I have a feeling," she said, "that a lot of these things should go to New York for auction. They'll bring a *fortune* on the east coast."

If they're genuine, Qwilleran thought.

After coffee he returned upstairs, and as he opened the door Koko shot out of the room and made a skidding U-turn into the study where the books were on shelves instead of in boxes. Qwilleran followed, but the cat was already on one of the top shelves, looking down impudently at his pursuer.

"Get down here!" Qwilleran demanded at his sternest.

Koko rubbed his jaw against a large volume—teasing, knowing he was just beyond reach.

Qwilleran climbed on a chair and made a grab for him.

With infuriating impertinence Koko slinked behind a row of books with only the tip of his brown tail giving a clue to his whereabouts.

"I'll get you, young man, if I have to strip this whole bookcase!" Shifting the chair a few feet, he started removing books from the top shelf, piling them in his left arm, until the cat was revealed, crouched mischievously in his hiding place.

"You devil!" Qwilleran clutched him with his free hand, stepped off the chair, dumped his armful of books on the desk, and deposited the cat in the other room, slamming the door as a rebuke. Then he returned to the study to replace the dislodged books, which appeared to be a collection of eighteenth-century erotica. Squelching his curiosity he lined the books up on the high shelf. That was when he noticed a volume that had been concealed behind the others, either purposely or accidentally. *Memoirs of a Merry Milkmaid* was the title tooled in gold on good cowhide. He put it under his arm and stepped off the chair. As he did so, the book rattled in a muffled way. He shook it, and it rattled again. Enjoying the excitement of discovery he returned to the Dickens-Macaulay room, closed the door, and opened the book. It was all cover and no pages!

There in the hollow volume—a secret filing place—was a small notebook, alphabetized. He turned to the letter D and found "Dickens A-74." Under M there was listed "Macaulay A-106" as well as Mencken, Melodrama, Milton, Morality Plays and others. This was the catalogue he knew must exist. Though inadequate for finding titles, it was apparently useful for Van-Brook's purposes, whatever they might be. If he had anything to hide, this was not a bad system.

There were other documents and scraps of paper in the hollow book, but for the moment the catalogue was all that mattered. Entries were grouped from A to F, evidently referring to the six rooms in which boxes were stored. It was while leafing through its pages that he spotted a small red dot alongside certain items: "Latin A-92," for instance.

Koko was sitting quietly on A-106 in his sphinx pose, guarding the salmon carton. "We've got to find A-92," Qwilleran said impatiently as he began slinging boxes around. They were stacked in no particular order, and the noise of heavy boxes being shifted soon brought a tap on the door.

"Come in," he yelled without stopping his frenzied search.

"Are you onto something?" Susan asked.

"I think so . . . I found the catalogue . . . Boxes, not titles," he said between heavy breathing. "Some have a special mark . . . A red dot . . . I'm looking for A-92."

He found it at the bottom of a stack, behind two other stacks—a vodka carton filled with textbooks, grammars, ponies, a Latin-English dictionary, and the works of Cicero and Virgil.

"They're Latin books, all right," he announced with disappointment. "Nothing but books."

"Well, let's work another half hour and then go to lunch," Susan suggested.

"If you don't mind," he said, "I'll take a raincheck, since I have Koko with me and I'm not dressed for lunch at the Mill. But if you want to pick us up again, I'll be glad to help any day you say."

He repacked A-92, shoving Koko away as the cat tried to climb into the vodka carton. Then, working fast during the next half hour, he opened other boxes that warranted a red dot. He found only books in an eclectic assortment of subjects: Nordic Mythology, Indian Authors, Chaucer, Japanese Architecture. One box contained Famous Frauds—accounts of imposters, swindlers, and other white-collar crooks. In the stacking of boxes a slight pattern emerged; the red dots were all found to the left of the door as one entered the room, concealed behind other book-boxes. Qwilleran counted the red dots in the catalogue, and there were fifty-two, distributed equally among rooms *A* to *F*.

When they pulled away from the house in Susan's wagon, Qwilleran had three books tucked under his arm. He said, "I hope no one objects if I borrow something to read. I found a couple of good titles."

"Keep them," she said. "No one will ever know or care."

Sandwiched between novels of Sir Walter Scott, which came from a red-dot carton, was *Memoirs of a Merry Milkmaid*.

When Susan dropped her passengers off at the apple barn, Koko was greeted by his mate as if he had returned from an alien planet, contaminated by radioactive gasses. Belly to the floor, Yum Yum crept toward him cautiously, caught a whiff of something evil, and skulked away with lowered head and bushy tail. Unconcerned, he walked to the kitchen area and stared pointedly at an empty plate on the floor until a piece of turkey appeared on it miraculously.

Qwilleran had dropped his three books on a table in the foyer area. After his exertions at the VanBrook house he was tremendously hungry. He thawed a carton of chili, a small pizza, and two corn muffins, and while sitting down to this lunch in the snack area he heard a loud *plop!* It was followed by another loud *plop!* He recognized the sound, that of a book falling on an uncarpeted floor. Leaving his lunch, he investigated the main floor and found two volumes of Sir Walter Scott on the earthen tiles of the foyer. Koko was pushing *Ivanhoe* around with his nose, but it was not the spine he was sniffing; he was nosing the fore-edges.

Qwilleran retrieved it—a book in flexible leather binding with gold tooling and gilt edges—published in 1909 with end papers and frontispiece in Art Nouveau style. It was a better edition than the set of Dickens but damaged by dryness. He riffled the pages—and gasped! They were interleaved with money! With ten-dollar bills! The other book, he soon discovered, was the same. The "bookmarks" in *The Bride of Lammermoor* were twenties! Both books had come from a red-dot carton. He tried a little computation: fifty-two red-dot boxes . . . approximately twenty books per carton . . . twenty or thirty bills in each book . . . And yet, considering the rate of inflation and opportunities for investment, who would hide this amount of money in the house? Unless . . .

Hurrying to the telephone he called Exbridge & Cobb Antiques. "Susan," he said, "I've discovered something remarkable about the red dots, and I think you should get the attorney up here in a hurry before we open any more cartons . . . No, I can't tell you on the phone . . . Yes, I'm willing to meet with him—any time."

Qwilleran had forgotten his chili, and he knew the pizza would be cold, but they could be reheated. There was little left to reheat, however. The cheese and pepperoni had disappeared, and the chili was reduced to beans, while two cats washed up assiduously. No matter; food was no longer on Qwilleran's mind. He carried the two volumes of Scott and *Memoirs of a Merry Milkmaid* to his studio, followed by two well-fed Siamese.

There were other personal papers in the hollow book, in addition to the catalogue: unidentified phone numbers onscraps of paper, legal documents in Summers, Bent & Frickle envelopes, columns of figures in five digits or more, cryptic memos that the late principal had written to himself, onion-skin copies of old business agreements signed "William Brooks." Little of it seeped into Qwilleran's comprehension, but Koko, who was sitting on the desk watching every move, occasionally extended a tentative paw. Yum Yum was on her hindlegs searching the wastebasket for crumpled paper, which had an irresistible attraction for her.

She searched, however, in vain. Qwilleran had learned never to crumple discarded paper if he expected it to stay in the round file for more than three minutes.

Among the items that tempted Koko's paw was an envelope labeled "Copies." The originals, according to the notation, were in the files of Summers, Bent & Frickle. One of them, titled "Last Will and Testament of William Smurple," was dated recently, September 8, and it bequeathed the principal's entire estate to the Pickax School District, exactly as Lyle Compton had confided to Qwilleran.

The other document caused a tingling in Qwilleran's upper lip that made him reach for the phone. He asked directory assistance for a number in Lockmaster, and when he called it, a woman's musical voice said, "Amberton Farm."

"This is Jim Qwilleran, calling from Pickax," he said. Soothed by her pleasant voice he spoke less brusquely than he had intended. "Is this the right number for Steve O'Hare?"

"No, Mr. Qwilleran, this is the farmhouse. His office in the stables has its own phone—"

"I'm sorry."

"That's perfectly all right. I'm Lisa Amberton, and I understand you're interested in our farm. I'd like to show you around if you'd care to drive down."

"I'll take you up on that later, but right now I need to talk to Mr. O'Hare."

She gave him the number, and he called the trainer. "Okay, Steve, I'm ready to talk," he announced. "How soon can you come up to Pickax?"

"Jeez, that's sooner than I expected, but I can come any time. I'd like to bring Mrs. Amberton, okay? She says she wants to meet you."

"Not this time. I want you to come alone for some private discussion—just a deal between you and me."

"Sure. I understand," Steve said genially. "How about at five o'clock? I get through at three, and I'll have to clean up. I didn't line up that information you wanted, though." He sneezed loudly.

"The résumé? Forget it for now. See you at five."

Qwilleran massaged his moustache with satisfaction and tripped jauntily down the spiral staircase to the kitchen, where he pressed the button on the coffeemaker.

While he was waiting for the beverage to brew, the telephone rang, and he took the call in the library area. It was Vicki Bushland's anxious voice. "Qwill, there's been an accident down here!" she said. "Fiona's son is in the hospital. We're very much upset. I thought you'd want to know."

"What kind of accident?"

"He was taking jumps, and the horse went down. Robbie's hurt seriously. He wasn't wearing his hard hat. I don't mind telling you, Fiona's almost out of her mind."

"When did this happen?"

"A couple of hours ago. Isn't it tragic? So soon after winning his first race! Fiona's afraid he'll never walk again—let alone ride. I think it's his spine."

"Terrible news," Qwilleran murmured. Then he added, "I was talking to Steve just a moment ago. To Mrs. Amberton, also. They never said a word about an accident."

"They're very cool—that Amberton crew," Vicki said with a sign of bitterness. "The way they think, stableboys are a dime a dozen. Twenty more are begging to take Robbie's place! It would have been a different story if the horse had been Son of Cardinal. They had to destroy it."

Qwilleran was silent.

"Fiona says you're interested in buying the farm, Qwill."

"Let's put it this way: They're interested in selling it ... What's Fiona's number? I'll call her."

"Try to give her some hope. She's terribly down. If she isn't home, try the hospital." Vicki gave him two numbers.

Phoning the hospital he learned only that the patient was in surgery; no report on his condition had been issued.

"Could you locate Fiona Stucker, his mother?"

"I'll connect you with the ICU lounge," the operator said.

The volunteer who presided over the lounge said Ms. Stucker had just stepped out. "Will you leave a message?"

"No, thanks. I'll call back."

As he hung up he heard Yum Yum mumbling to herself in the adjacent lounge area, intent on some personal project. Here was a situation he always investigated; she had a hobby of stealing wrist watches and gold pens and stashing them away under the furniture. As he suspected, she was lying on her side near one of the sofas, reaching underneath it to fish out a hidden treasure. It was a piece of crumpled paper. To her consternation he confiscated it, knowing she would swallow pieces of it—the predatory instinct.

"N-n-NOW!" she demanded.

"No!" Qwilleran insisted.

It was a yellow slip of paper he had not seen before, and when he smoothed it out, it proved to be a salescheck from the Tacky Tack Shop, Lockmaster, for the purchase of two sweatshirts. The date of the transaction was September 9. The customer's name was not recorded, but it appeared that Fiona had dropped it when she visited on the day before. Penciled scribbling on the back looked like directions for reaching the Qwilleran barn. Yum Yum had found it, hiding it under the sofa for future reference.

A sudden movement from the cats alerted him, and he caught a glimpse of activity in the woods. Someone was approaching from the direction of Main Street—on foot. That alone was unusual. Although the gate was left open during daylight hours, most visitors arrived on wheels. Very few persons in Pickax chose to use their legs. This caller was walking timidly, and he was carrying a book.

Putting the salescheck in his pocket, Qwilleran went out to meet Eddington Smith.

"I found something for you," said the elderly bookseller.

"Why didn't you phone me? I could have picked it up."

"Dr. Hal told me to start taking walks. It wasn't far. Only a few blocks." He was breathing hard. "It's a nice day. I think this will be the last warm weekend we have."

Qwilleran reached for the book. Like most of the stock in Eddington's shop it had lost its dust jacket, and the cover suggested years of storage in a damp basement. Then he looked at the spine. "*City of Brotherly Crime!* It's my book!" he yelped. "You found it! This is worth a lot to me, Edd."

"You don't owe me anything, Mr. Q. I want you to have it. You're a good customer."

Qwilleran clapped the frail man on the back. "Come in and have a drink of cider. Let me show you around the barn. Say hello to the cats."

"I was here the night Mr. VanBrook was shot, but I didn't see much of the barn. Too many people."

Qwilleran served cider with a magnanimous flourish and explained the design of the building: the fireplace cube, the triangular windows, the ramps and catwalks, and the use of tapestries.

"That's quite an apple tree," said Eddington, looking up at the textile hanging overhead. He was chiefly impressed, however, by the presence of books on every level. Even in the loft apartment the cats had their own library: *Beginning Algebra*, *Learning to Drive*, Xenophon's *Anabasis*, and other titles from the ten-cent table at his shop.

After climbing the ramps—slowly, for the old man's sake—they reached the topmost catwalk and could look down on the dramatic view of the main floor.

"I've never been this high up, where I could look down," the bookseller said in wonder.

Yum Yum, who had followed them on the tour, jumped to the catwalk railing, now conveniently cushioned by the top edge of the tapestry, and arranged herself in fiddle position: haunches up, body elongated, and forelegs stretched forward like the neck of a violin.

"Siamese like a high altitude," Qwilleran explained. "It's their ancient heritage. They used to be watch-cats on the walls of temples and palaces."

"That's interesting," said Eddington. "I never knew that before."

"Yes, so they say, at any rate. But Yum Yum's developed a bad habit of pulling everything apart with her paw . . . NO!"

he scolded, tapping the corner of the tapestry back on the tack-strip.

She gazed into space, afflicted by sudden deafness, a common disorder in felines.

"Someone's coming," said the bookseller. "I'd better get back to the store." A van winding up the Trevelyan Trail was visible through the high triangular windows.

"That's my five o'clock appointment," Qwilleran mumbled. He combed his moustache with his fingertips. "I'd appreciate it, Edd, if you'd stay a little longer."

"It's getting late."

"I'll drive you home."

"I shouldn't put you to the trouble, Mr. Q."

"No trouble."

"Won't I be in the way?"

"You'll be doing me a favor, Edd. Just stay up here—and listen." Qwilleran started down the ramp. "And keep out of sight," he called over his shoulder.

The bookseller opened his mouth to speak, but no words came. What could he say? It was a strange request from a good customer.

In the barnyard Qwilleran greeted Redbeard as he jumped out of his van. "Nice day," he said.

"Yeah, this is the last warm weekend coming up. It's gonna rain, though, sometime. I can always tell by the way the horses act."

"I envy someone like you who's an expert on horseflesh," Qwilleran said, indulging in gross flattery. He himself was an expert in uttering complimentary untruths.

"Spent my whole life with the buggers," said Steve. "Ought to know something by this time."

"Come on in and have a drink ... How long does it take you to drive up here?" Qwilleran asked as they entered the barn.

"Fifty minutes. Sometimes less. I like to drive fast."

"One thing you don't have to worry about is red lights."

"Yeah. Only problem is the old geezers driving trucks and

tractors down the middle of the road like they owned it." Steve was eyeing the pale tweed sofas with uncertainty.

"Let's sit over there," Qwilleran suggested, motioning toward the library area. "It's closer to the bar."

"Man, I'm all for that! It's been a hard day. I could use a drink." He dropped his jacket on the floor and sank into a big leather chair with a sigh that was almost a groan. "Shot and a beer, if you've got it."

Koko had taken up a position on the fireplace cube where he could keep the visitor under surveillance, his haunches coiled, his tail lying flat in a horseshoe curve.

Without ceremony Qwilleran put a shot glass and a can of beer on a table at Steve's elbow. His own drink of Squunk water was in a martini glass, straight up, with a twist. "I hear you had an accident at the farm today," he said casually.

The trainer tossed off the whiskey. "Where'd you hear that?"

"On the radio." Not true, of course.

"Yeah. Too bad. He was a good horse—great promise—but we hadda put him down."

"What about the rider? Did he get up and walk away?"

"Damn that Robbie! It was his own fault—pushing too hard, taking chances! You know how kids are today—no discipline! Serves him right if he has to quit riding. There'll be other riders and other horses, I always say. You can't let yourself get upset about things like that."

"You're remarkably philosophical."

"You hafta be in this business. But we got some good news. Wanna hear some good news?"

"By all means."

"Mrs. Amberton is staying on at the farm after it's sold. She's a helluva good instructor, and it'd be a crime to lose her. Plus, she has an idea for a tack shop—setting it up right on the farmgrounds. Only top-grade gear—everything from boots and saddles to hats and stock-ties. It'll be a big investment, but it'll pay off. The kids around here have a lotta dough to spend, and Lisa—Mrs. Amberton, that is—insists they've gotta have the best turnout if they ride under her colors. A good tack shop will be a money-maker!"

"Who are these kids you talk about?"

"Local kids, crazy about riding—some talented, some not—but they're all hell-bent on winning ribbons and working their way up to Madison Square Garden! Lisa—Mrs. Amberton—has as many as fifty in some of her classes. If you like young chicks, we've got 'em in all shapes and sizes."

"How often do they compete?"

"Coupla times a month. Lessons three times a week. Costs them plenty, but they've got it to spend. There's all kinds of money in Lockmaster."

Qwilleran stood up and headed for the bar. "Do it again?"

"Sounds good," said Steve.

"Same way?"

The trainer made an okay sign with his fingers.

Koko was still staring at the visitor. Qwilleran kept the man talking and drinking, and eventually he began to fidget in his chair. "Well, whaddaya think about the farm? How does it sound, price and all?"

"Sounds tempting," Qwilleran said, "but first I wanted to ask you a question."

"Shoot."

"Why did you land in Lockmaster?"

"Tried everywhere else. Nice country up here. Good working conditions. Healthy climate. Everybody'll tell ya that."

"Is it true you got into trouble Down Below?" Qwilleran asked the question in an easy conversational tone.

"Whaddaya mean?"

"I heard some scuttlebutt about . . . illegal drugs at the racetrack."

Steve shrugged. "Everybody was doin' it. I just got caught."

"I have a bone to pick with you," Qwilleran said in a casual way.

"Yeah? What is it?"

"When you were here yesterday, you shot a bird on the way out."

"So? Something wrong with that?"

"We don't shoot birds around here."

"Hell! You got millions more. One'll never be missed. I can't say no to a redbird."

"You seem pretty handy with a gun."

"Yeah, I'm a good shot, drunk or sober." He looked up at Koko on the fireplace cube. "Sittin' right here I could get that cat between the eyes." He cocked a finger at Koko, who jumped to the floor with a grunt and went up the vertical loft ladder in a blur of fur—straight up to the top catwalk, ending on the railing forty feet above Steve's head. "What's with him?" the trainer asked.

Qwilleran could envision an aerial attack, and he launched an attack of his own. He said calmly, "Were you drunk or sober when you killed VanBrook?"

"What! Are you nuts?"

"Just kidding," Qwilleran said. "The police can't come up with a suspect, and I thought you were here that night."

"Hell, no! I was at a wedding in Lockmaster."

"The party was over at midnight. You can drive up here in fifty minutes. VanBrook was killed at 3 A.M."

"I don't know what the hell you're talkin' about."

"How about another drink?" Qwilleran said amiably, standing up and ambling to the bar area. He made bartending noises with bottles and glasses as he went on talking. "You knew Van-Brook was going to be here, didn't you? You found out somehow."

"Me? I never knew the guy!" Now Steve was standing up and facing the bar.

"You also knew there'd be a lot of other people here to provide a cover-up." Qwilleran pulled a yellow slip of paper from his pocket. "Does this look familiar? It came out of your pocket, and it has directions for finding this place."

"You lie! I was never here before yesterday! I didn't know the guy you're talkin' about."

"You don't need a formal introduction when you've got a good motive for murder. And I happen to know your motive.

I've also got a dead bird in a coffee can, waiting for the crime lab."

Hearing that, Steve pulled a gun, and Qwilleran ducked behind the bar.

"Don't shoot! I've got three witnesses upstairs!"

There was a motionless moment as a befuddled brain wrestled with the options.

Then came a muffled *whoosh* overhead. The man looked up—too late. The apple tree was dropping on him. Steve pulled the trigger, but the bullet went wild as he went down under the weighty tapestry.

Groans came from beneath the eight-by-ten-foot textile, and a hunched body squirmed to get free. Qwilleran, rushing to the kitchen, grabbed a long, blunt object from the freezer. He gave it a mighty swing above his head and brought it down on the struggling mass. It stopped struggling.

"Call the police!" he shouted to Eddington on the catwalk. "Call the police! Use the phone in my studio!"

As Qwilleran guarded the silent mound under the tapestry, the bookseller trotted feebly down the ramps to the second balcony and leaned over the railing to ask in a barely audible voice, "What shall I tell them?"

Qwilleran enjoyed excellent police protection in Pickax. If anything were to happen to the Klingenschoen heir, his fortune would go to alternate heirs on the east coast and be lost forever to Moose County. In a matter of three minutes, therefore, two Pickax police cars and the state troopers were on the scene, and Chief Brodie himself was the first to arrive.

Brodie said to Qwilleran, "Funny thing! Just half an hour ago an informant called us and fingered this guy. We didn't expect to have him delivered to us . . . at least, not so soon."

"Who tipped you off?"

"Anonymous caller. We gave them a code name so they can collect the reward. What was he doing here, anyway?"

"Trying to sell me a horse farm. I might have killed him with my club if one of those apples hadn't cushioned the blow."

"Club? Where is it?"

"I put it back in the freezer."

Brodie grunted and gave Qwilleran the same incredulous look he bestowed on fireplaces with white smokestacks.

"Excuse me," said Eddington Smith. "Is it all right if I go now?"

Qwilleran said, "Stick around for a while, Edd, and if Andy doesn't drive you home, I will. What made you think of releasing the tapestry?"

"The cats were pulling the corners up off the tacks, so I helped them a bit," said the bookseller. "Did I do right?"

"I would say you created a successful diversion."

Koko was back on top of the fireplace cube, hunched in his hungry pose, gazing down disapprovingly at the strangers in uniform, and probably wondering, Where's the red salmon? Yum Yum was absent from the scene, although the two of them usually presented a united front at mealtime. In fact, it was the female—with her new assertiveness—who had recently assumed the role of breadwinner, ordering dinner with a loud "n-n-NOW!"

As the police scoured the barn for the bullet that went wild, a chill swept over Qwilleran. *Where was Yum Yum?*

"My other cat's missing!" he yelled. "You guys look around down here! I'll try the balconies!"

Chapter 14

After searching the upper reaches of the barn, calling Yum Yum's name and hearing no answer, Qwilleran finally spotted her on one of the radiating beams just below the roof. The gunshot had frightened her, and she was hiding in one of the angles where all eight beams met, her ears flattened like the wings of an aircraft. No amount of coaxing or endearments would convince her to come forth.

"What can we do?" Qwilleran asked Koko, who was trotting back and forth on the beam between the cat and the man. They had to leave her huddled in her secluded corner.

After a while the bullet was discovered in the typecase, lodged between a mouse and an owl. Only when Qwilleran boiled a frozen lobster tail did the prima donna make an appearance, ambling down the ramp with a relaxed gait as if she had spent a week at a spa.

"Cats!" he muttered.

He was watching them devour the lobster when the phone rang and he heard an exultant voice. "Qwill, Robbie's going to be all right! With therapy he'll be able to walk!"

"That's extremely good news, Vicki. Fiona must be greatly relieved. I was unable to reach her at the hospital."

"She's here now, and she wants to talk to you."

"Good! Put her on."

"Mr. Qwilleran," came a faltering voice, "you don't know

what I've just been through. I still can't believe the doctors could save him."

"We were all pulling for him, Fiona."

"I don't care if he'll ever . . . ride in competition any more, but he's promised to go back to school."

"That's a plus," Qwilleran said, adding lightly, "He may switch his interest from horses to Japanese."

"Mr. Qwilleran," she said hesitantly, and it was clear she had not noticed his quip, "I have something terrible to tell you, and I . . . uh . . . don't know how to begin."

"Start at the beginning."

"Well, it's something Robbie told me before he went into surgery. The poor boy thought . . . he thought he was going to die . . ." She stopped to stifle a few whimpering sobs. "He told me he knew about . . . Mr. VanBrook's murder . . ." Her voice trailed off.

"Go on, Fiona. I think I know what you're going to say."

"I can't . . . I can't . . ."

"Then let me say it for you. VanBrook had written a will making Robin his heir. Is that right?"

"Yes."

"And when Robin dropped out of school, VanBrook threatened to cut him off entirely."

"How did you know that?"

Qwilleran passed over her question. This part of the scenario he had only deduced, but he had been right. He went on. "Robin had the bright idea of killing VanBrook before he had a chance to rewrite his will."

"No! No! It wasn't Robbie's idea!" she cried. "But they talked about it—him and Steve. They thought they could use the money and buy the farm . . . O-h-h-h!" she wailed. "They didn't tell me! I could have stopped it!"

"When did you find out?"

"Not till Robbie was . . . Not till they were wheeling him into the operating room. 'Mommy, am I gonna die?' he kept saying."

"Was Steve the shooter?"

"Yes."

"Did Robin ride along in the van?"

"Oh, no! He was in bed when I got back from the theatre that night. I told him I wouldn't go to the party. I got home about one o'clock."

"Are you sure Robin didn't sneak out after you returned home?"

There was a gasp followed by a breathless silence.

"The police have Steve in custody, Fiona."

She groaned. "I turned him in. Robbie begged me to. He said there was a big reward. He thought he was going to die . . ." Her voice dissolved in a torrent of sobs.

Vicki returned to the line. "What will happen now?"

"Robin is an accessory, but he can turn state's evidence," Qwilleran told her.

Soon afterward, Arch Riker called the apple barn in high spirit. "It worked! It worked!" he said. "The reward brought in a tip to the police, and they've arrested the suspect. He'll be charged with murder. And Dennis is off the hook. Tell Koko he can stop working on the case."

"Good," was Qwilleran's quiet reply.

"It was someone from Lockmaster, just as you said from the beginning. It'll be in the paper tomorrow. For once, something big happened on our deadline . . . You seem remarkably cool. What's the matter?"

"I know the story behind the story, Arch, but it's not for publication."

"You rat!"

Fran Brodie was the next to call. "Dennis is cleared!" she exclaimed. "Isn't that wonderful? . . . But I hear the apple tree came down! Shawn will rehang it tomorrow."

As far as Qwilleran was concerned, the VanBrook case was closed, but the Mystery Man of Moose County would remain a puzzle forever. He spent Friday with Susan and the attorney at the house on Goodwinter Boulevard, slitting red-dot boxes and shaking out the leaves of almost a thousand books.

On Saturday he wanted Polly to fly to Chicago for a ballgame;

she wanted to go birding in the wetlands. They compromised on a picnic lunch—with binoculars—on the banks of the Ittibittiwassee River. When he called for her at her carriage house shortly before noon, he was in a less than amiable mood—after an abortive bubble-blowing session with two unresponsive and ungrateful Siamese, followed by a hair-raising incident involving Yum Yum and her harness.

On arrival, he handed Polly four clay pipes and a family-size box of soap flakes. "Now you can blow bubbles for Bootsie," he said grumpily. "Lori Bamba says cats like to chase bubbles."

"Well . . . thank you," she said dubiously. "Do yours chase bubbles?"

"No. They don't think they're cats . . . What do we have to pack in the car?"

"You take the folding table and chairs, and I'll carry the picnic basket. Did you remember to bring your binoculars?"

There was a maudlin scene as Polly said goodbye to Bootsie, causing Qwilleran to grumble into his moustache. Then they headed for the Ittibittiwassee—past the spot where he had fallen from his bicycle three years before, and past the ditch where his car had landed upside down the previous year.

As they unfolded the table and chairs on a flat, grassy bank at a picturesque bend in the river, Polly said, "Look! There's a cedar waxwing!"

"Where?" he asked, picking up the binoculars.

"Across the river."

"I don't see it. I don't see anything."

"Take the lens covers off, dear. It's in that big bush."

"There are lots of big bushes."

"Too late. It flew away." She was unpacking a paper tablecover and napkins. "It's breezier than I anticipated. We may have trouble anchoring these . . . Do you like deviled eggs?"

"With or without mashed eggshells?"

"*Really*, Qwill! You're slightly impossible today. By the way," she added with raised eyebrows, "I hear you spent the day at the VanBrook house with Susan Exbridge yesterday."

"Has Dear Heart been prowling with her telescope?"

"Quick! There's a male goldfinch!"

"Where?" He reached for the glasses again.

"On that wild cherry branch. He has a lovely song, almost like a canary."

"I don't hear it."

"He's stopped singing." Polly poured tomato juice into paper cups. "What were you doing at VanBrook's house?" she persisted. "Or shouldn't I ask?"

"I was helping Susan *and the attorney from Lockmaster* to open sealed boxes said to contain books. She's been commissioned to liquidate the estate."

"And what did you find in the boxes?"

"Books . . . but there's also some valuable Oriental art."

"We were all delighted to read in the paper that he bequeathed everything to the Pickax schools . . . Help yourself to sandwiches, Qwill."

He loaded a limp paper plate with moist tuna sandwiches and hard-cooked eggs with moist stuffing, neither of which was compatible with an oversized moustache. "VanBrook was a complex character," he said. "I'd like to delve into his past and write a book."

"I hear his credentials were falsified."

"Where did you hear that?"

Polly shrugged. "The story is going around."

"I suspect he was a self-educated genius," said Qwilleran. "He had a couple of aliases, and that's probably why he avoided personal publicity in my column. He was in hiding—or in trouble . . . Hey!" A sudden gust of wind caught his paper plate and conveyed it across the river like a flying carpet, carrying part of a stuffed egg. "VanBrook spoke Japanese and was familiar with Asia. He might have tricked Americans into investing in fictitious enterprises in Japan."

"Isn't that rather a bizarre venture for a school principal?"

"Not for VanBrook." Qwilleran was thinking of some flimsy business agreements he had found in *Memoirs of a Merry Milkmaid*. He was thinking of the secret of the red dot. He had no intention, however, of telling Polly that books in fifty-two cartons were leaved with paper money—*counterfeit* paper money.

"Listen to that blue jay," she said.

"Now there's a bird with decent visibility and audibility!" he said. "I'm for blue jays and cardinals. Face it, Polly. I can identify a split infinitive or dangling participle or hyphenated neologism, but I'm not equipped to spot a tufted titmouse or yellow-bellied sapsucker."

"Are you ready for coffee?" she asked, uncorking a Thermos bottle. "And I made chocolate brownies."

After several brownies Qwilleran was feeling more agreeable. In a mellow mood he murmured, "This is supposed to be our last warm weekend."

"I've enjoyed our picnic," she said. "I've enjoyed every minute of it."

"So have I. We belong together, Polly."

"I'm happiest when I'm with you, Qwill."

"Say something from Shakespeare."

"*My bounty is as boundless as the sea, my love as deep. The more I give to thee, the more I have, for both are infinite.*"

Qwilleran reached across the table and grasped her hand—the one with the birthstone ring he had given her. With brooding eyes intent on her face he said, "I want to ask a question, Polly."

There was a breathy pause as she smiled and waited for the question.

"What did you and Steve talk about at the wedding?"

Up to that moment there had been no reference to Polly's brief fling with the trainer, nor had the subject of his arrest been mentioned.

Taking a moment to collect herself and rearrange her facial expression, she said, "We talked about horses, and my interest in books, and the *Stablechat*, and his allergy, but mostly horses. Shirley had told him about you, and I elaborated on the generous things you and the K Fund have done for Moose County. When I heard about his arrest, I wondered if he had been using me for an alibi on the night of the murder."

"No, the timing was off. More likely he was trying to establish a financial connection. The Amberton Farm is looking for an angel."

"When did you first suspect him, Qwill?"

"When he came to the barn to talk about the farm last Wednesday. He asked what happened to my trees in the orchard. If he hadn't been there before, how would he have known the orchard had been cleaned out? Also, it looked as if some work had been done on the righthand side of his van, at the approximate height of my mailbox, but I couldn't be sure. Nothing really clicked until Koko found a file of VanBrook's personal papers. There were two wills: one dated recently, naming Pickax as the beneficiary, and a prior will naming Steve's stableboy as the sole heir."

Polly frowned. "Stableboy?"

Qwilleran helped himself to another brownie and described the principal's curious relationship with his housekeeper and her son. "It was Steve's idea to eliminate VanBrook before he could change his will, but it was too late. When I saw those two wills, I had a hunch that the gun used to kill Koko's cardinal had also killed Cardinal Wolsey." He patted his moustache.

"Look!" cried Polly. "I believe that's a female black-throated green warbler!"

"If you say so, I believe it . . . Would you like to come up and see my tapestries?" he asked as they started packing the picnic things.

Polly said she would be delighted.

"Just don't sit under the apple tree," he warned her.

On the way to the apple barn he apologized for his bad humor before lunch. "I'd had a hair-raising experience with Yum Yum," he explained. "She won't walk on a leash, the way Koko does. The first time I buckled her harness, she played dead. The second time, she froze. This morning she galloped up the ramp and disappeared. We found her on one of the radiating beams that meet in the center of the barn. She'd been up there before, but this time her harness snagged on a bolt. She couldn't get loose. I had to go after her."

"Heavens, Qwill! It's forty feet above the floor!"

"Yes, Polly, that thought occurred to me. And the beam was only twelve inches wide. I had to crawl out there and dislodge her and then back up all the way to the catwalk, clutching her in one hand. It seemed like half a city block! She enjoyed it! She was purring her head off all the way."

"And what was Koko doing?"

"Trying to help—by crouching on my back. He thought it was a steeplechase! . . . Why did I ever get involved with *cats?*"

They had a seven o'clock reservation at the Old Stone Mill, and Qwilleran took Polly home to feed Bootsie, take a nap, and dress for dinner. Back at the apple barn Koko was on the desk, sitting on *Watership Down.*

"Okay, we have time for one chapter," Qwilleran said, sinking into his favorite leather chair. Yum Yum settled down on his lap slowly and softly like a hot-air balloon deflating, ending in a flat mound of virtually weightless fur. Koko perched on the arm of the chair, sitting tall with ears alert, whiskers bristling with anticipation, and eyes bright with intelligence.

Qwilleran shook his head in wonder. "I never know what's going on in that transistorized brain of yours. Did you know VanBrook was going to get it in the back of the head? Did you know Redbeard was the murderer? Did you know something vital was hidden behind the books in VanBrook's office?"

Koko shifted his feet impatiently and waited for the reading to begin. Qwilleran had to answer his own questions. No, he thought; it's all coincidence, plus my imagination. He's only a cat . . . But why did he keep twisting his tail like a horseshoe? Why did he twice tear up *Stablechat?* Why did he sink his fangs in every one of the red jelly beans?

"Don't just sit there; say something!" he said to Koko. "Read my mind!"

"Yow!" Koko said, a yowl that ended in a cavernous yawn.

Qwilleran opened the book to page eight. "Chapter two. This

is about the Chief Rabbit . . ." He closed the book again. "One more question: Was your sudden interest in rabbits supposed to put the finger on Mr. O'Hare?"

Koko stiffened, turned his head, swiveled his ears, leaped impulsively from the arm of the chair, and bounded to the front windows. And from the berry bushes came a whistle, loud and clear: *who-it? who-it? who-it?*